Cryptid Kids

THE BAWK-NESS MONSTER

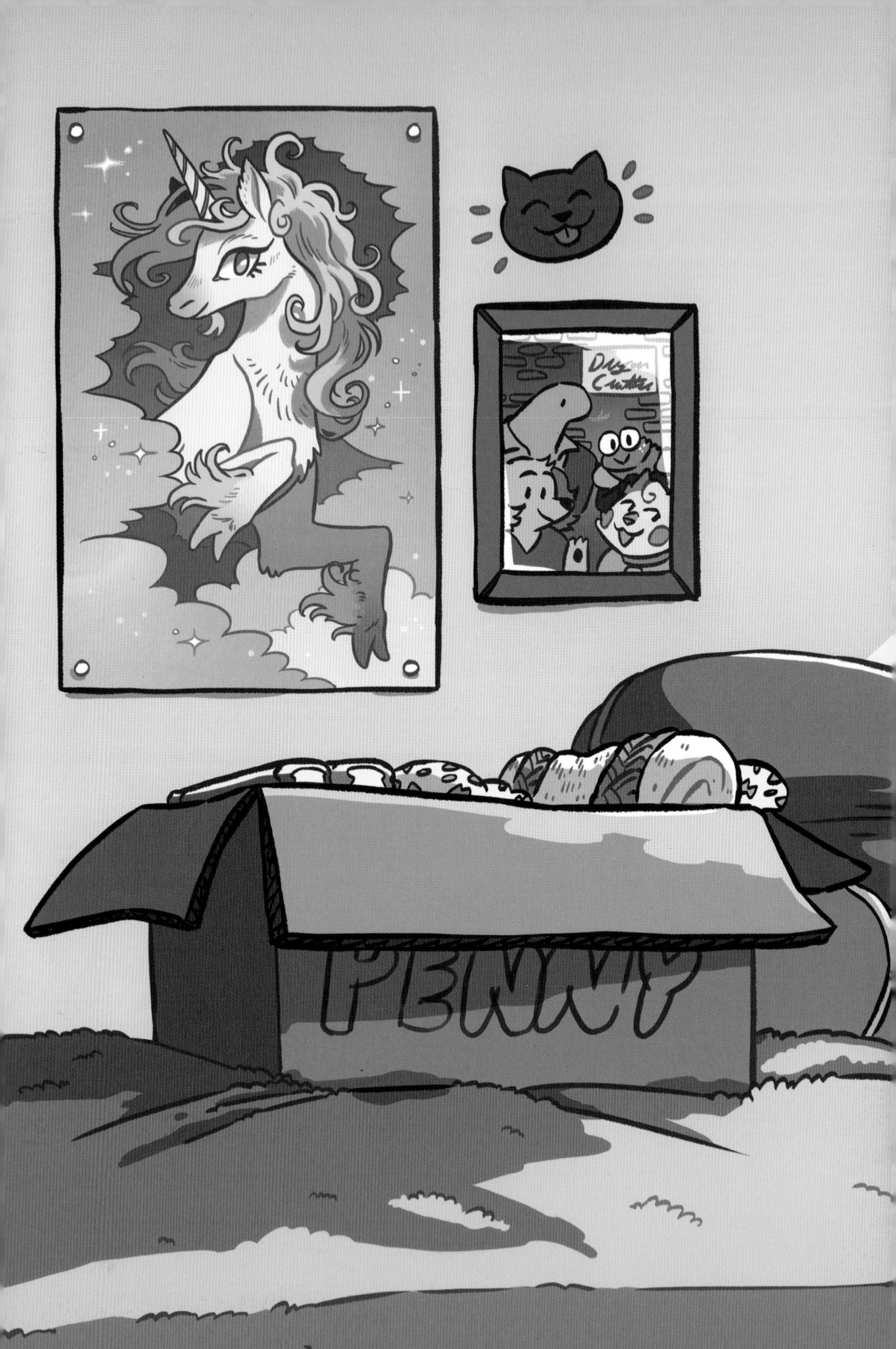
PENNY

Cryptid Kids

THE BAWK-NESS MONSTER

SARA GOETTER & NATALIE RIESS

:01

First Second

NEW YORK

:01

First Second

Published by First Second
First Second is an imprint of Roaring Brook Press,
a division of Holtzbrinck Publishing Holdings Limited Partnership
120 Broadway, New York, NY 10271
firstsecondbooks.com
mackids.com

Library of Congress Cataloging-in-Publication Data is available.

Our books may be purchased in bulk for promotional, educational, or
business use. Please contact your local bookseller or the Macmillan
Corporate and Premium Sales Department at (800) 221-7945 ext. 5442
or by email at MacmillanSpecialMarkets@macmillan.com.

FIRST
EDITION

First edition, 2023
Edited by Calista Brill and Benjamin A. Wilgus
Cover and interior book design by Molly Johanson
Production editing by Avia Perez

Character art was penciled with Pilot Color Eno light blue lead and inked
with a combination of a Kuretake Brush Pen, Pentel Futayaku Double-Sided
Brush Pen, and Kuretake Bimoji Brush Pen. Lettering was done with a
Zebra Disposable Brush Pen. Corrections were done in Photoshop.

Printed in China by 1010 Printing International Limited, North Point, Hong Kong

ISBN 978-1-250-83466-9 (paperback)
1 3 5 7 9 10 8 6 4 2

ISBN 978-1-250-83467-6 (hardcover)
1 3 5 7 9 10 8 6 4 2

Don't miss your next favorite book from First Second!
For the latest updates go to firstsecondnewsletter.com and sign up
for our enewsletter.

BY ART
WE LIVE

We dedicate this book to LGBTQ+
kids and the adults who stand up and
fight for them.

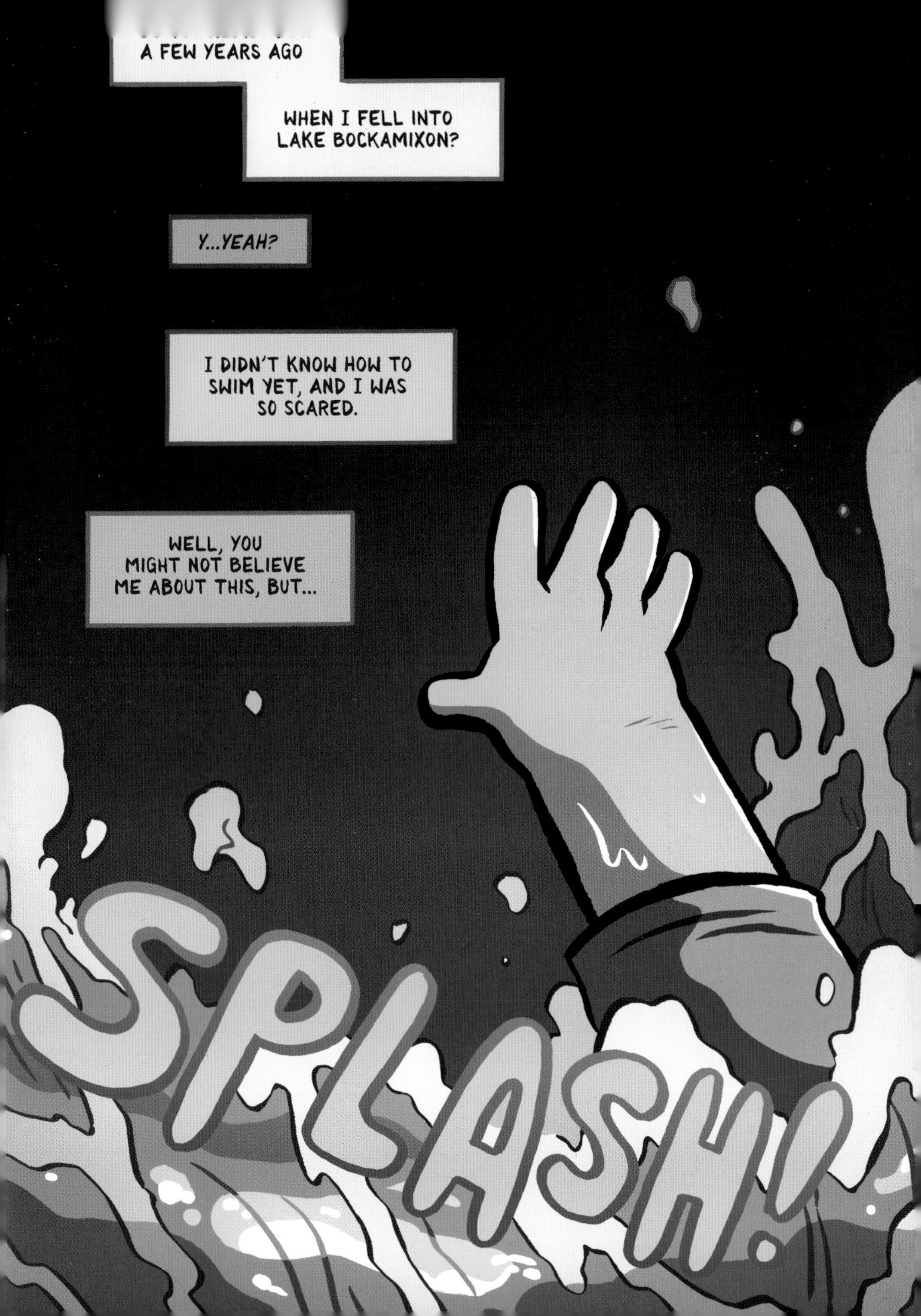

A FEW YEARS AGO
WHEN I FELL INTO LAKE BOCKAMIXON?
Y...YEAH?
I DIDN'T KNOW HOW TO SWIM YET, AND I WAS SO SCARED.
WELL, YOU MIGHT NOT BELIEVE ME ABOUT THIS, BUT...
SPLASH!

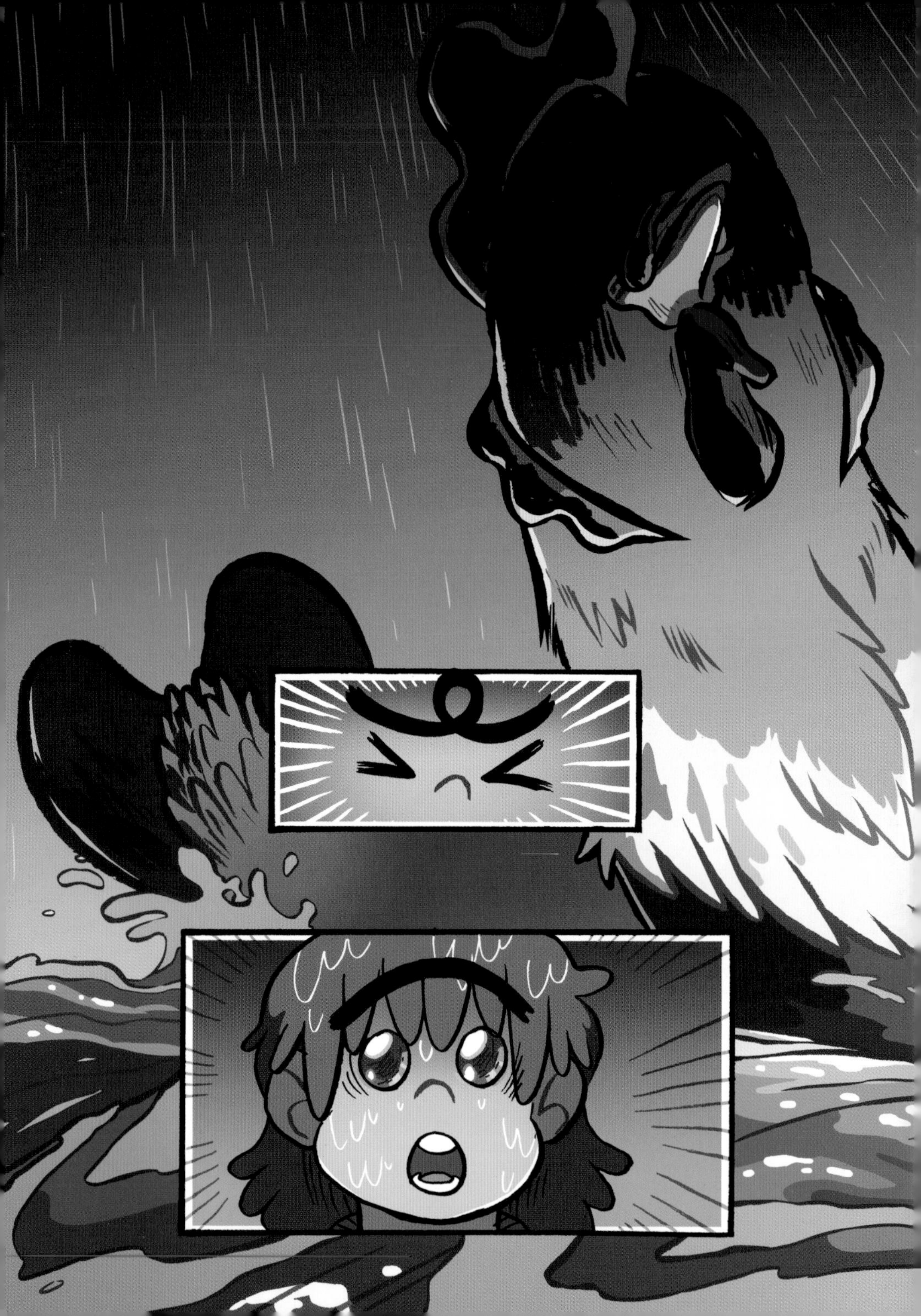

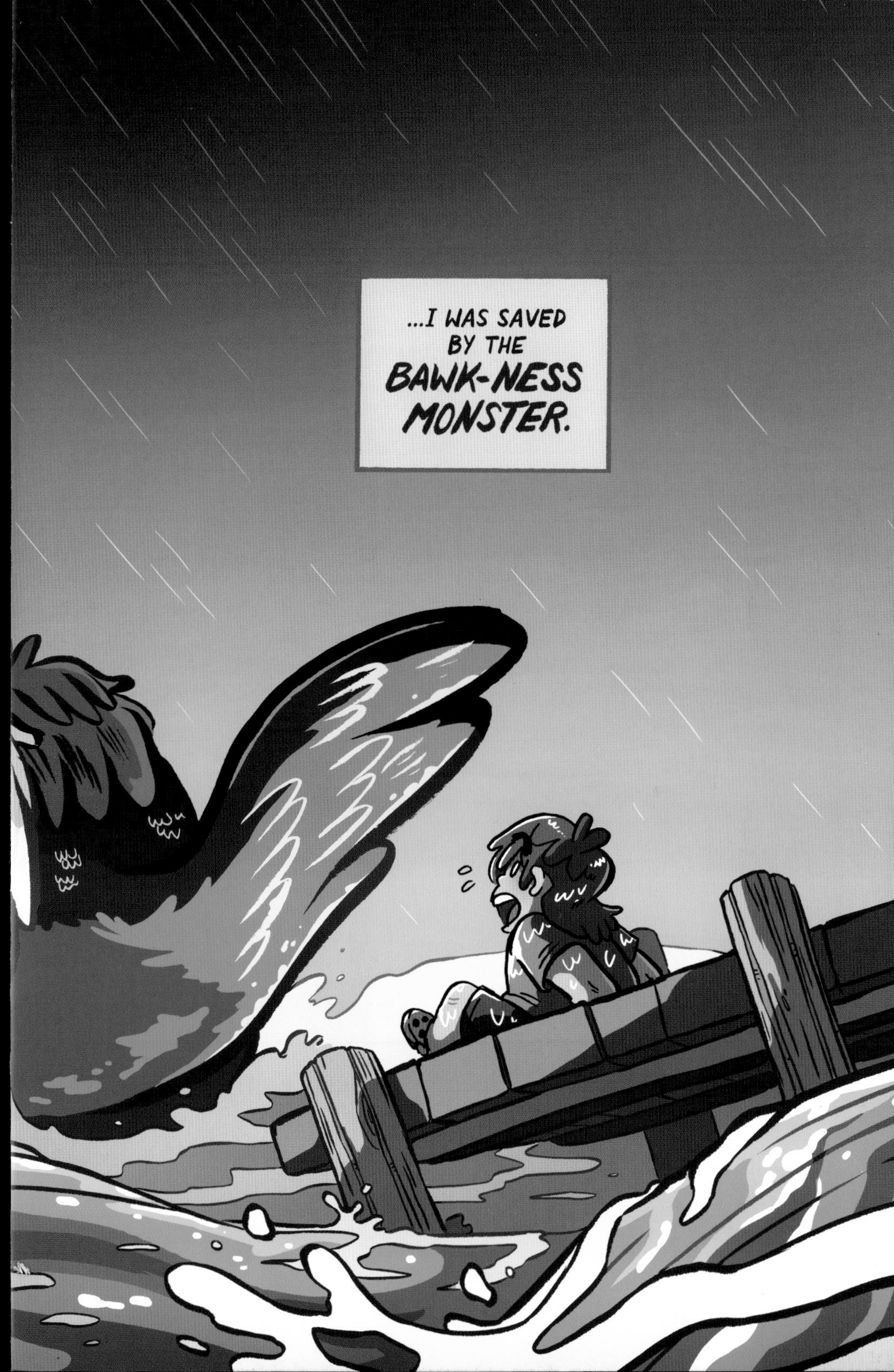
...I WAS SAVED BY THE BAWK-NESS MONSTER.

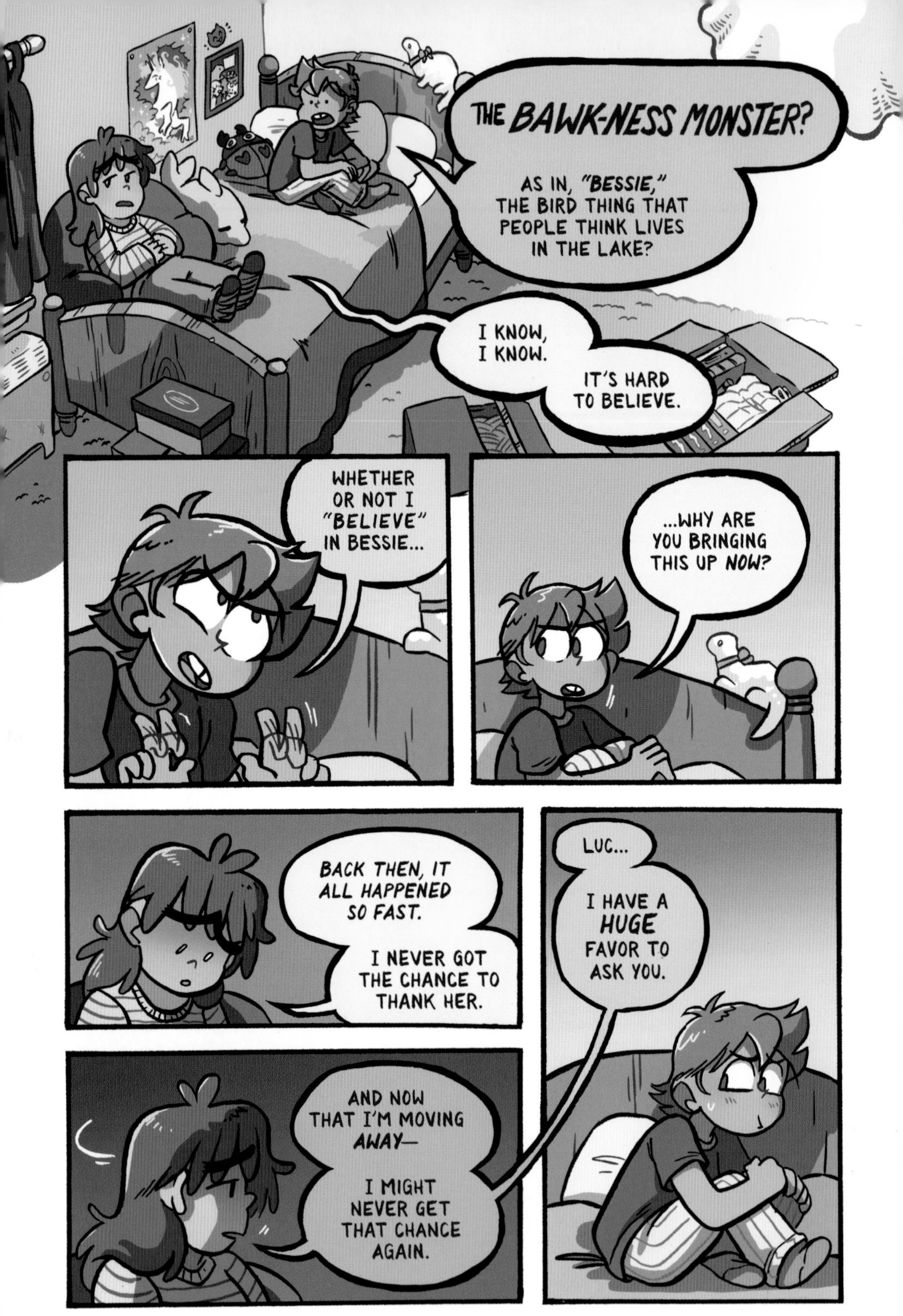
THE BAWK-NESS MONSTER?
AS IN, "BESSIE," THE BIRD THING THAT PEOPLE THINK LIVES IN THE LAKE?
I KNOW, I KNOW.
IT'S HARD TO BELIEVE.
WHETHER OR NOT I "BELIEVE" IN BESSIE...
...WHY ARE YOU BRINGING THIS UP NOW?
BACK THEN, IT ALL HAPPENED SO FAST.
I NEVER GOT THE CHANCE TO THANK HER.
AND NOW THAT I'M MOVING AWAY—
I MIGHT NEVER GET THAT CHANCE AGAIN.
LUC...
I HAVE A HUGE FAVOR TO ASK YOU.

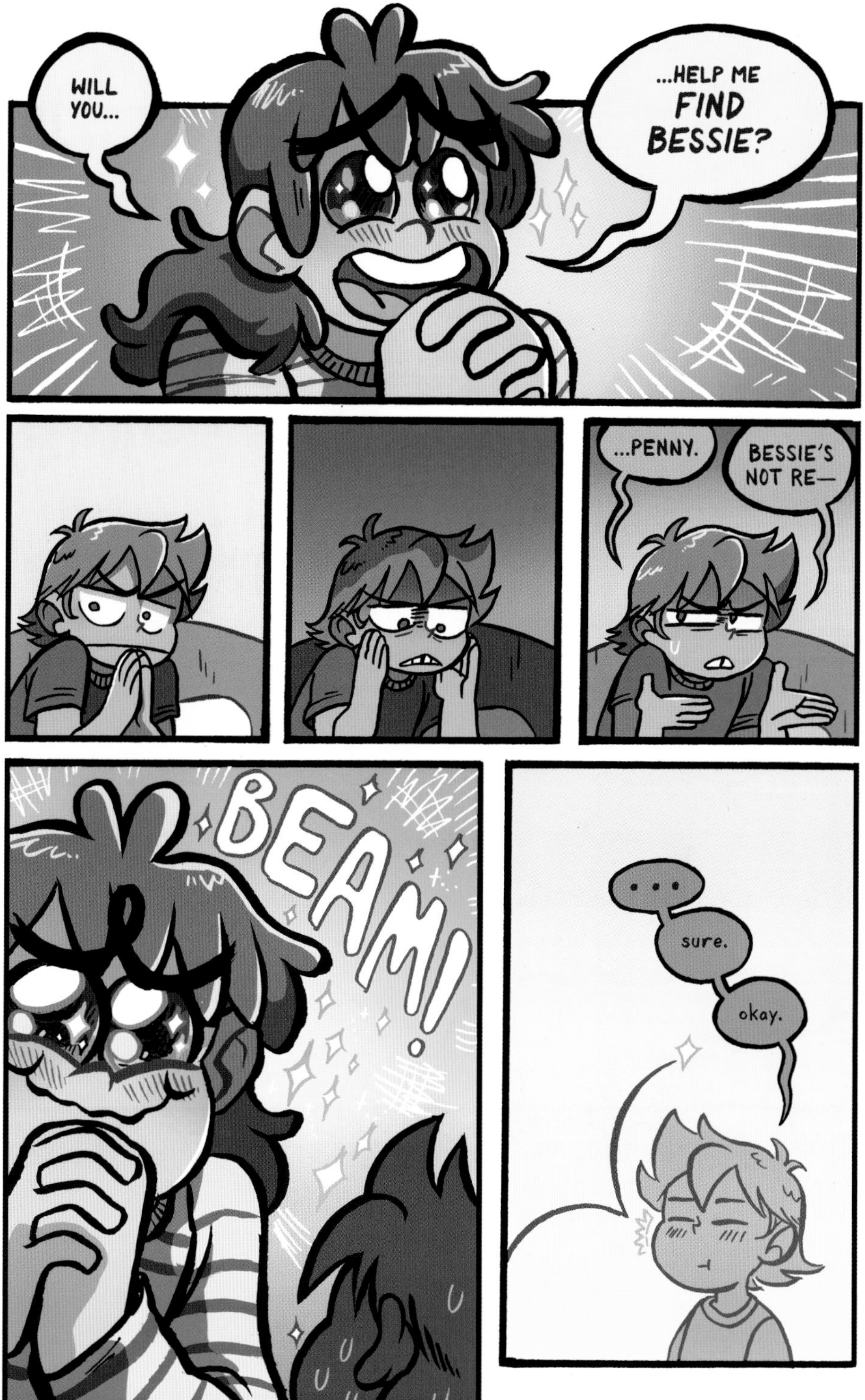
WILL YOU...
...HELP ME FIND BESSIE?
...PENNY.
BESSIE'S NOT RE—
BEAM!
...
sure.
okay.

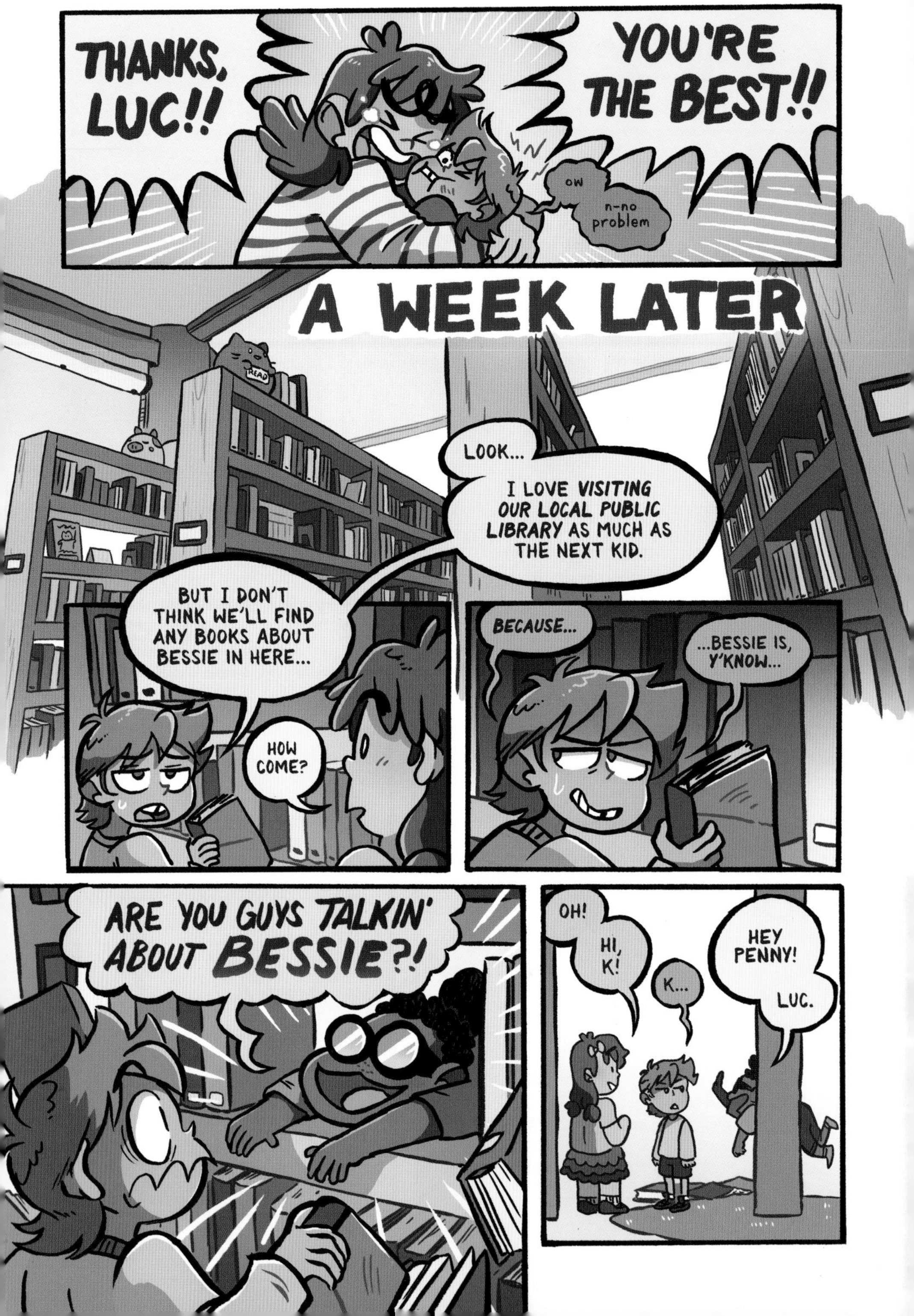
THANKS, LUC!!
YOU'RE THE BEST!!
ow
n-no problem
A WEEK LATER
READ
LOOK...
I LOVE VISITING OUR LOCAL PUBLIC LIBRARY AS MUCH AS THE NEXT KID.
BUT I DON'T THINK WE'LL FIND ANY BOOKS ABOUT BESSIE IN HERE...
HOW COME?
BECAUSE...
...BESSIE IS, Y'KNOW...
ARE YOU GUYS TALKIN' ABOUT BESSIE?!
OH!
HI, K!
K...
HEY PENNY!
LUC.

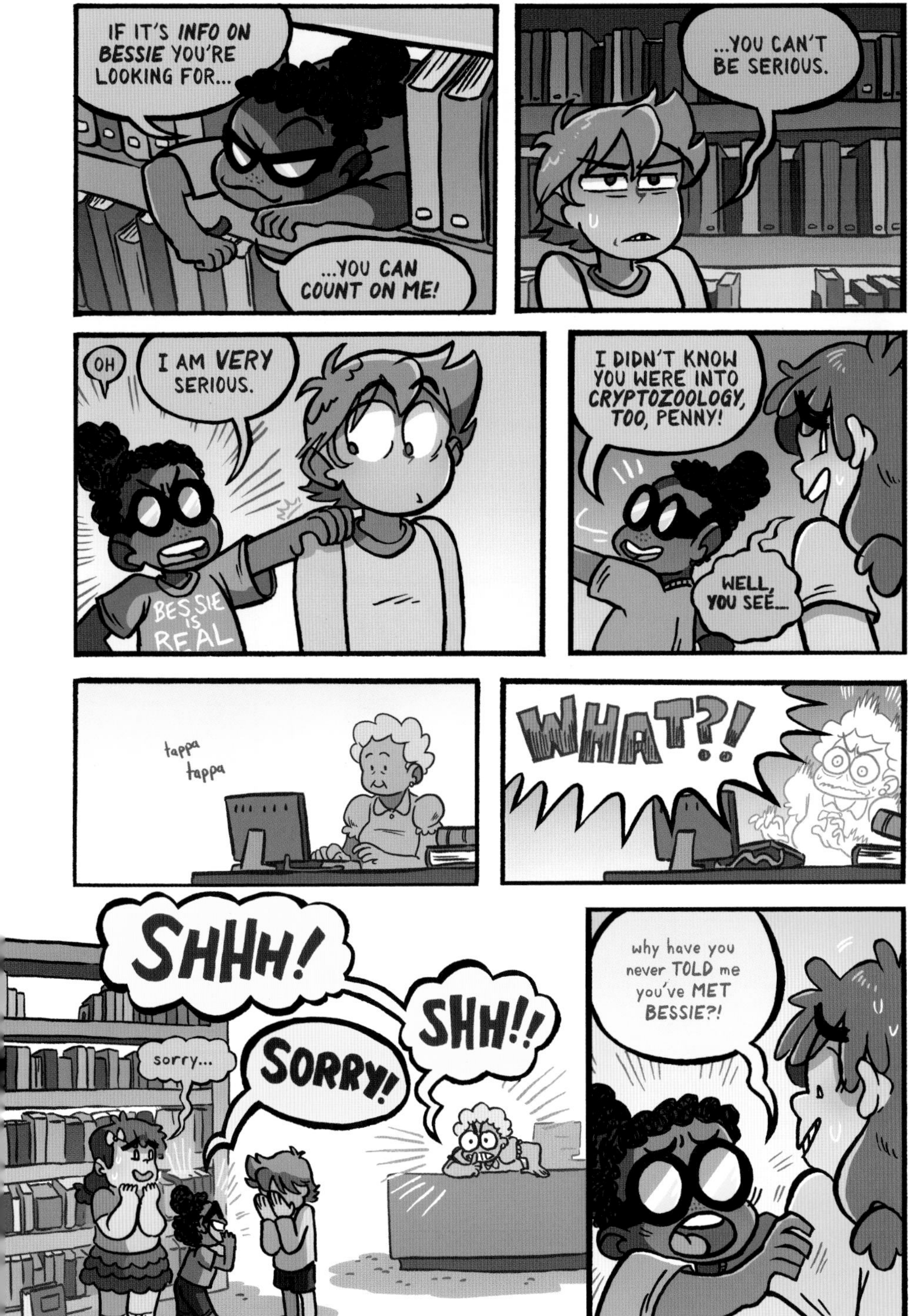
IF IT'S INFO ON BESSIE YOU'RE LOOKING FOR...
...YOU CAN COUNT ON ME!
...YOU CAN'T BE SERIOUS.
OH
I AM VERY SERIOUS.
BESSIE IS REAL
I DIDN'T KNOW YOU WERE INTO CRYPTOZOOLOGY, TOO, PENNY!
WELL, YOU SEE...
tappa tappa
WHAT?!
SHHH!
SHH!!
SORRY!
sorry...
why have you never TOLD me you've MET BESSIE?!

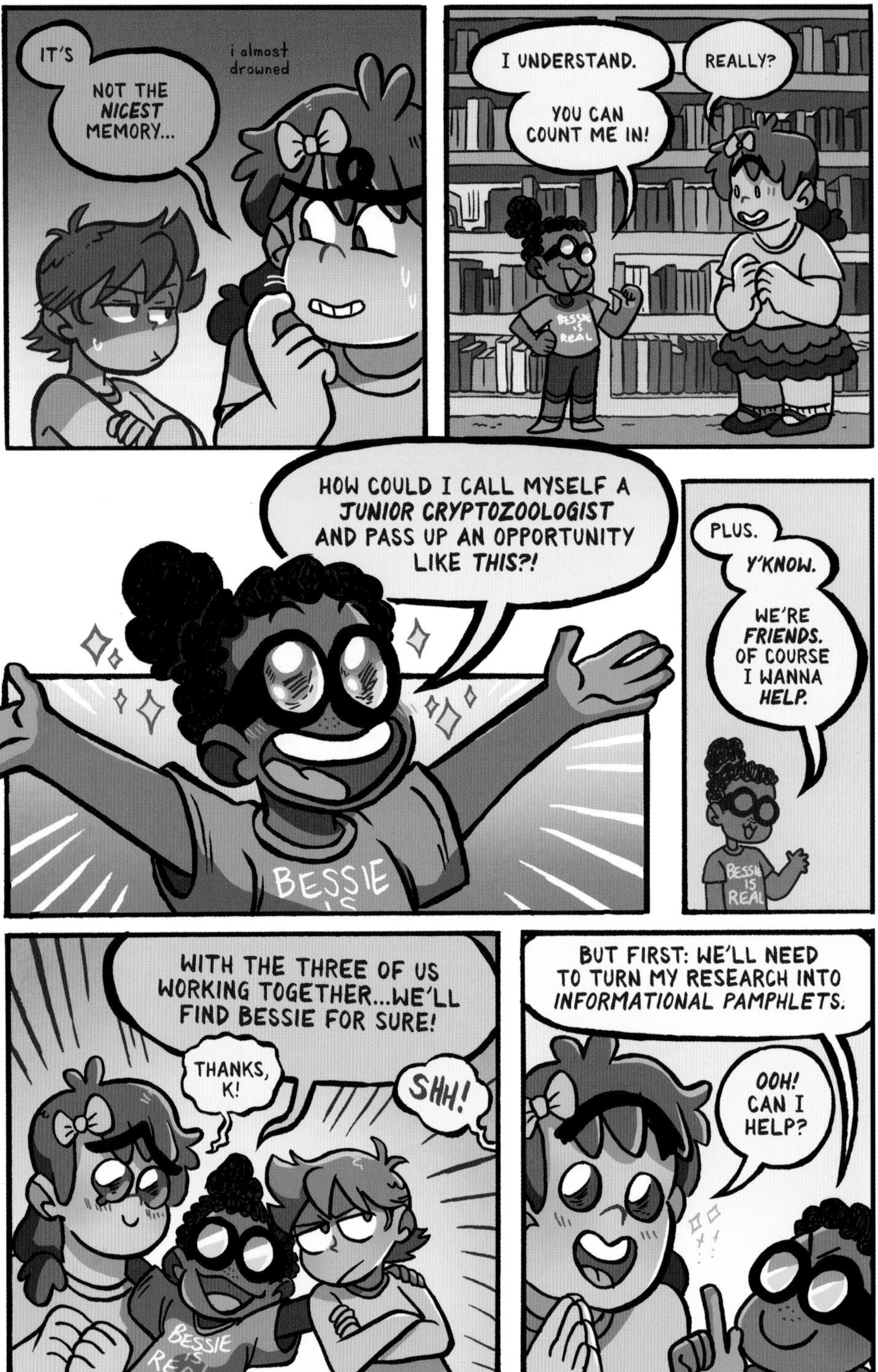
IT'S
NOT THE NICEST MEMORY...
i almost drowned
I UNDERSTAND.
YOU CAN COUNT ME IN!
REALLY?
BESSIE IS REAL
HOW COULD I CALL MYSELF A JUNIOR CRYPTOZOOLOGIST AND PASS UP AN OPPORTUNITY LIKE THIS?!
BESSIE
PLUS.
Y'KNOW.
WE'RE FRIENDS. OF COURSE I WANNA HELP.
BESSIE IS REAL
WITH THE THREE OF US WORKING TOGETHER...WE'LL FIND BESSIE FOR SURE!
THANKS, K!
SHH!
BESSIE IS REAL
BUT FIRST: WE'LL NEED TO TURN MY RESEARCH INTO INFORMATIONAL PAMPHLETS.
OOH! CAN I HELP?

MY *NEW* JOB STARTS NEXT MONTH.

I KNOW!

IT'S SUDDEN, BUT IT'LL BE A *HUGE* STEP UP.

TOTALLY WORTH IT.

THE MOVE?

YEAH, IT'S GOING GREAT.

WE'LL BE LOADING UP THE TRUCK ON MONDAY.

Ha Ha

YEAH. YEAH.

HIKEY LIKEY

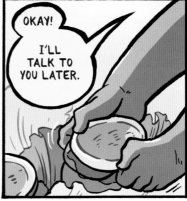

OKAY!

I'LL TALK TO YOU LATER.

OH, HEY, PUM'KIN.

HAD FUN AT THE LIBRARY?

HI, MOM

YEP

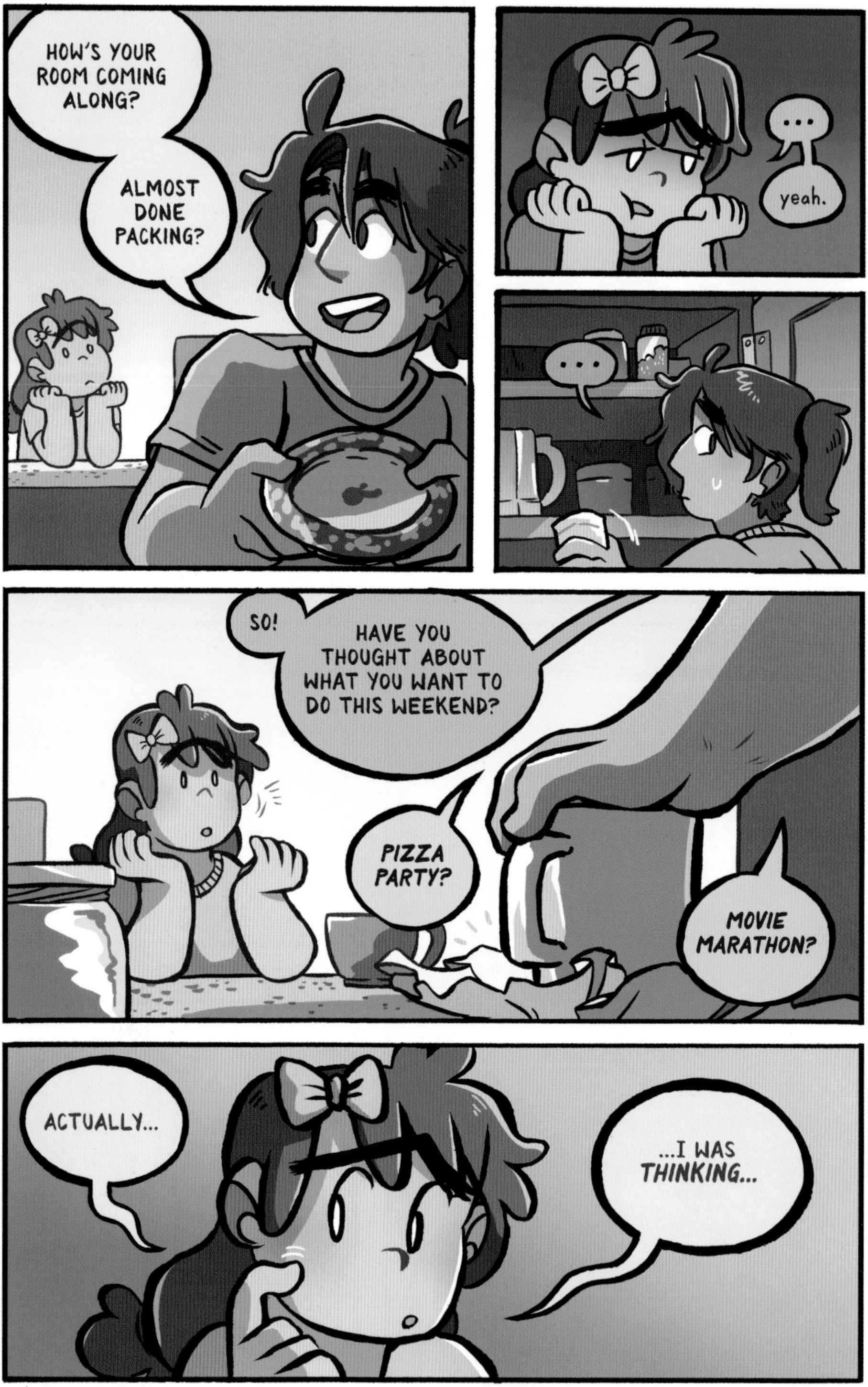
HOW'S YOUR ROOM COMING ALONG?
ALMOST DONE PACKING?
...
yeah.
...
SO!
HAVE YOU THOUGHT ABOUT WHAT YOU WANT TO DO THIS WEEKEND?
PIZZA PARTY?
MOVIE MARATHON?
ACTUALLY...
...I WAS THINKING...

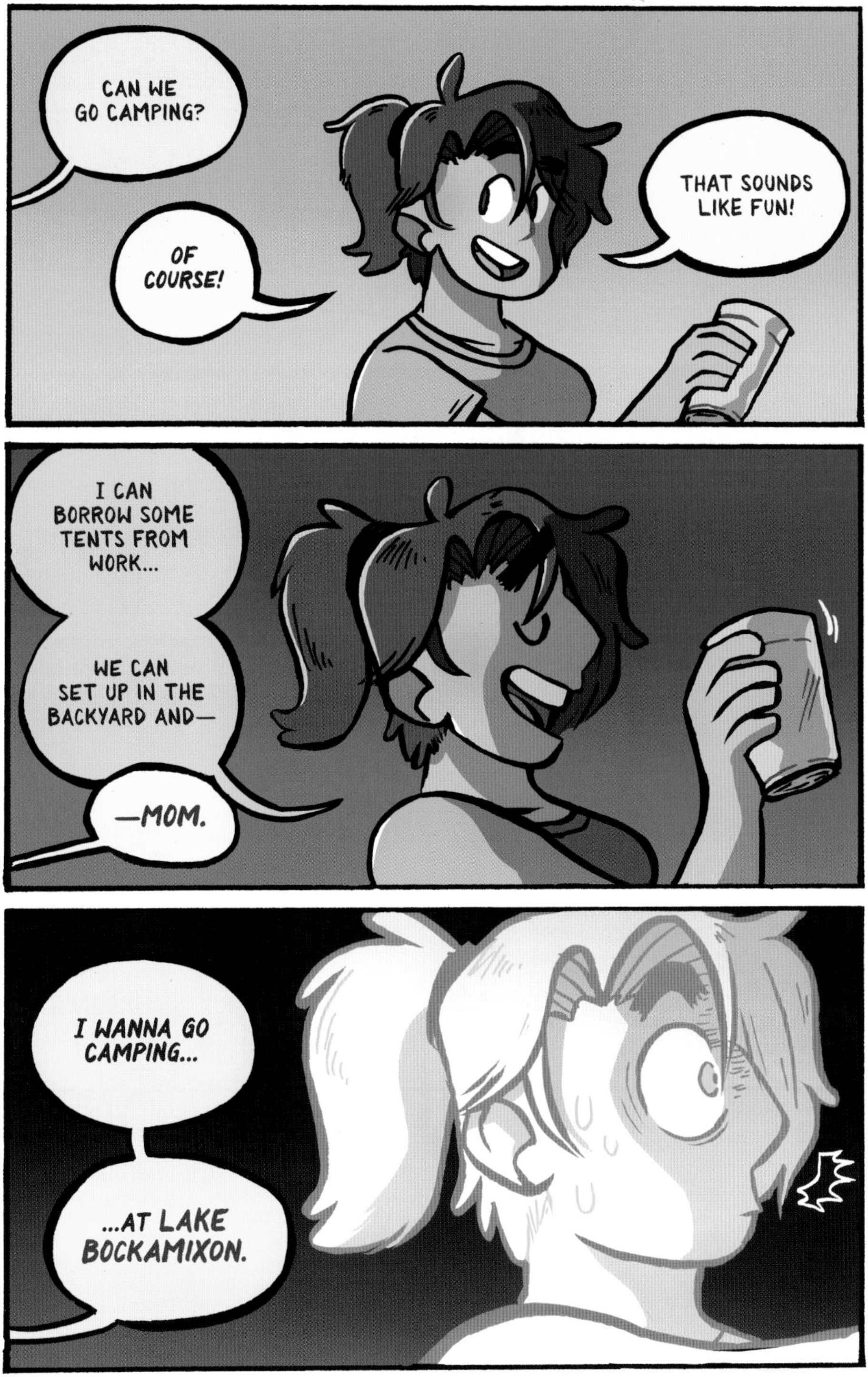
CAN WE GO CAMPING?
OF COURSE!
THAT SOUNDS LIKE FUN!
I CAN BORROW SOME TENTS FROM WORK...
WE CAN SET UP IN THE BACKYARD AND—
—MOM.
I WANNA GO CAMPING...
...AT LAKE BOCKAMIXON.

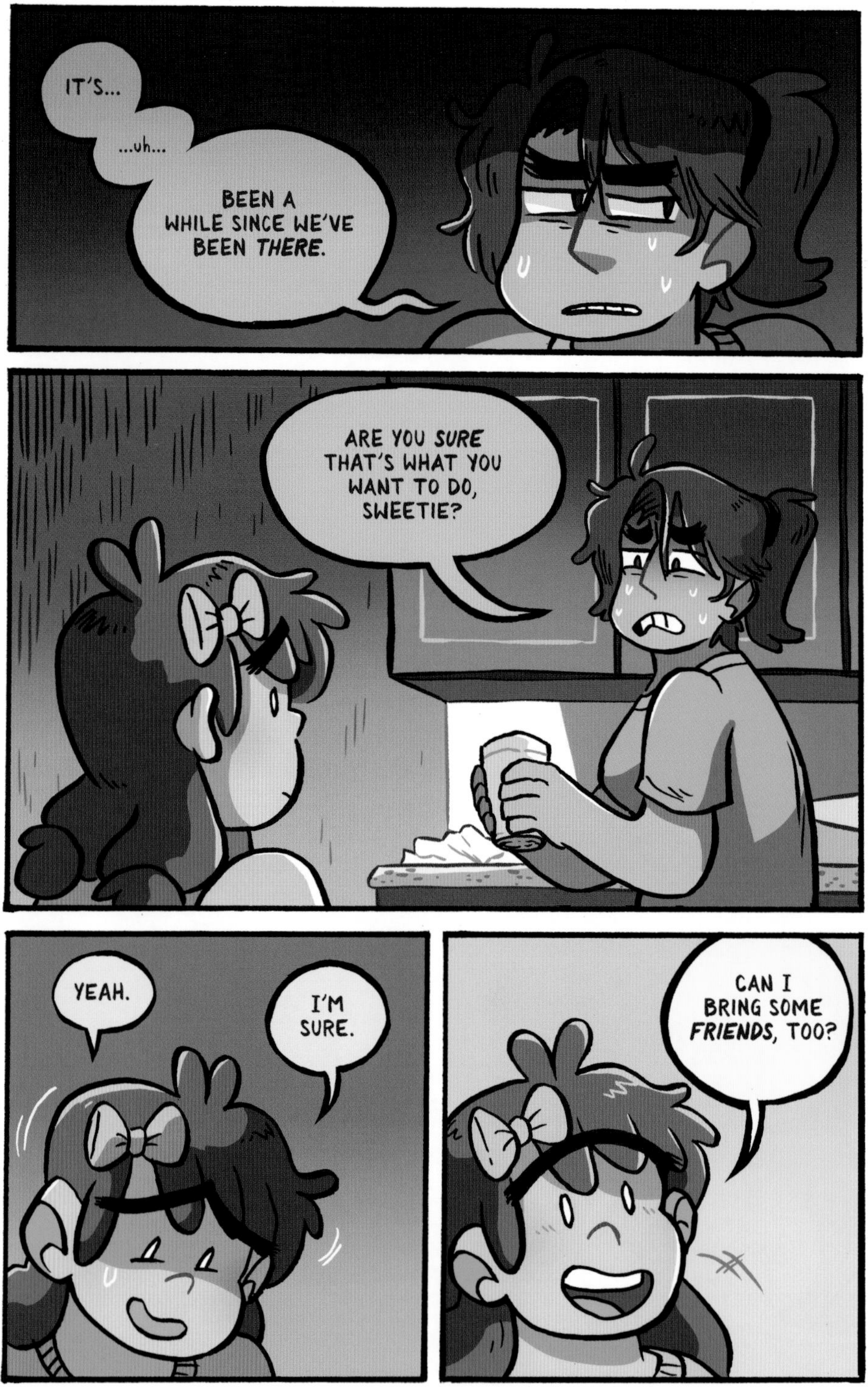
IT'S...
...uh...
BEEN A WHILE SINCE WE'VE BEEN *THERE*.
ARE YOU *SURE* THAT'S WHAT YOU WANT TO DO, SWEETIE?
YEAH.
I'M SURE.
CAN I BRING SOME *FRIENDS*, TOO?

THAT WEEKEND

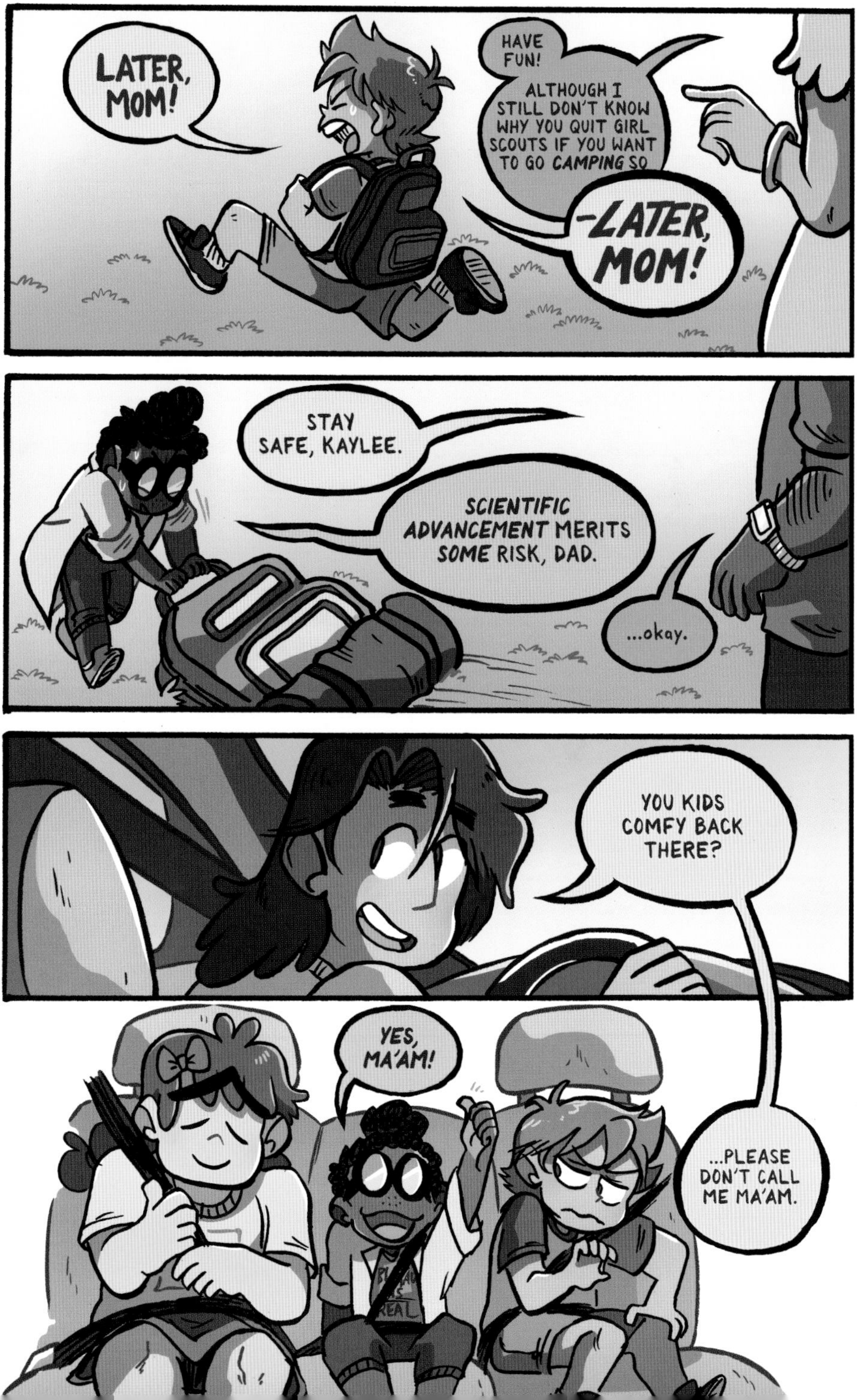

LATER, MOM!
HAVE FUN!
ALTHOUGH I STILL DON'T KNOW WHY YOU QUIT GIRL SCOUTS IF YOU WANT TO GO *CAMPING* SO
–LATER, MOM!
STAY SAFE, KAYLEE.
SCIENTIFIC *ADVANCEMENT* MERITS SOME RISK, DAD.
...okay.
YOU KIDS COMFY BACK THERE?
YES, MA'AM!
...PLEASE DON'T CALL ME MA'AM.

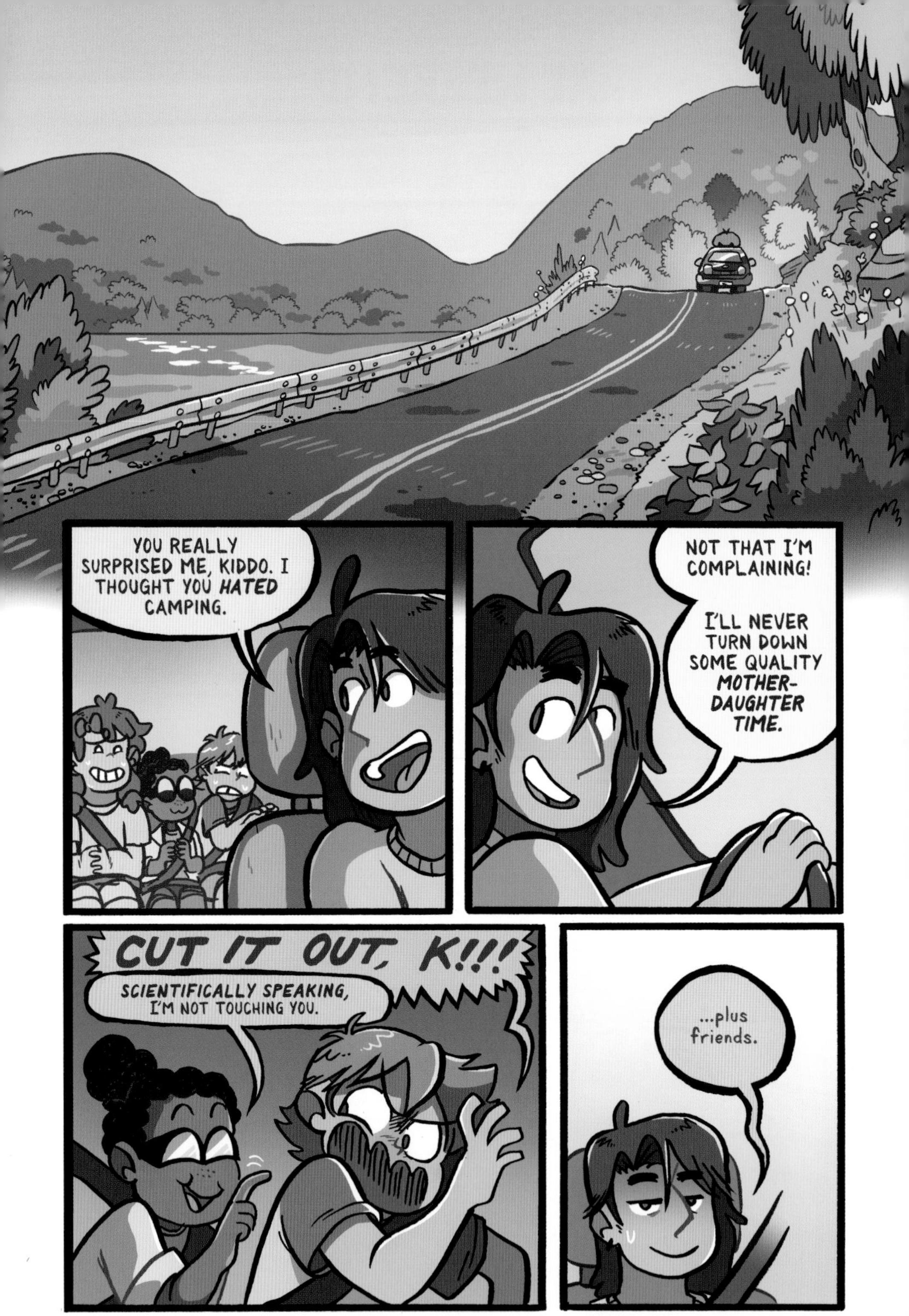
YOU REALLY SURPRISED ME, KIDDO. I THOUGHT YOU *HATED* CAMPING.
NOT THAT I'M COMPLAINING!
I'LL NEVER TURN DOWN SOME QUALITY *MOTHER-DAUGHTER TIME.*
CUT IT OUT, K!!!
SCIENTIFICALLY SPEAKING, I'M NOT TOUCHING YOU.
...plus friends.

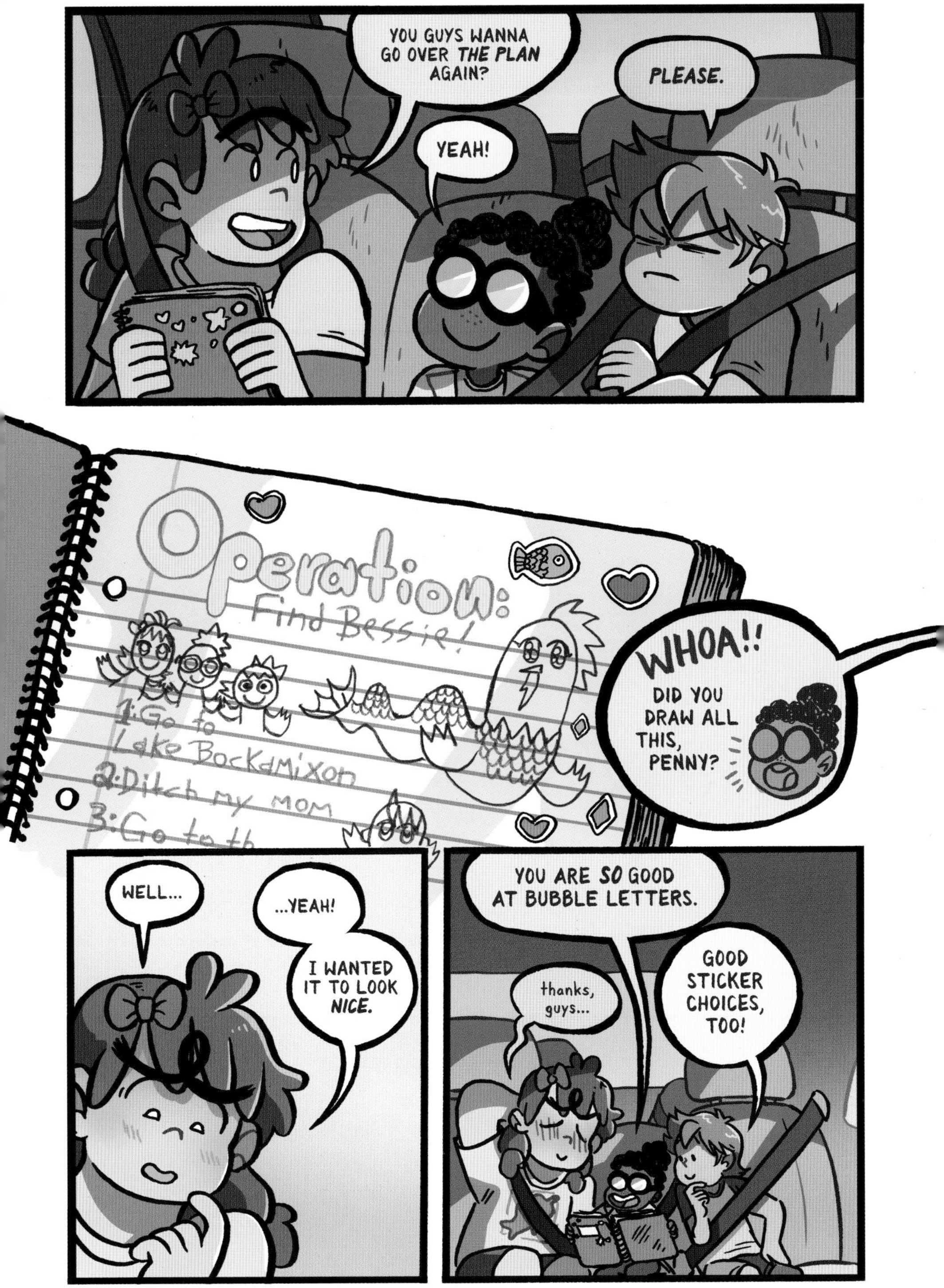

YOU GUYS WANNA GO OVER THE PLAN AGAIN?
PLEASE.
YEAH!
Operation: Find Bessie!
1: Go to Lake BockaMixon
2: Ditch my MOM
3: Go to th
WHOA!!
DID YOU DRAW ALL THIS, PENNY?
WELL...
...YEAH!
I WANTED IT TO LOOK NICE.
YOU ARE SO GOOD AT BUBBLE LETTERS.
thanks, guys...
GOOD STICKER CHOICES, TOO!

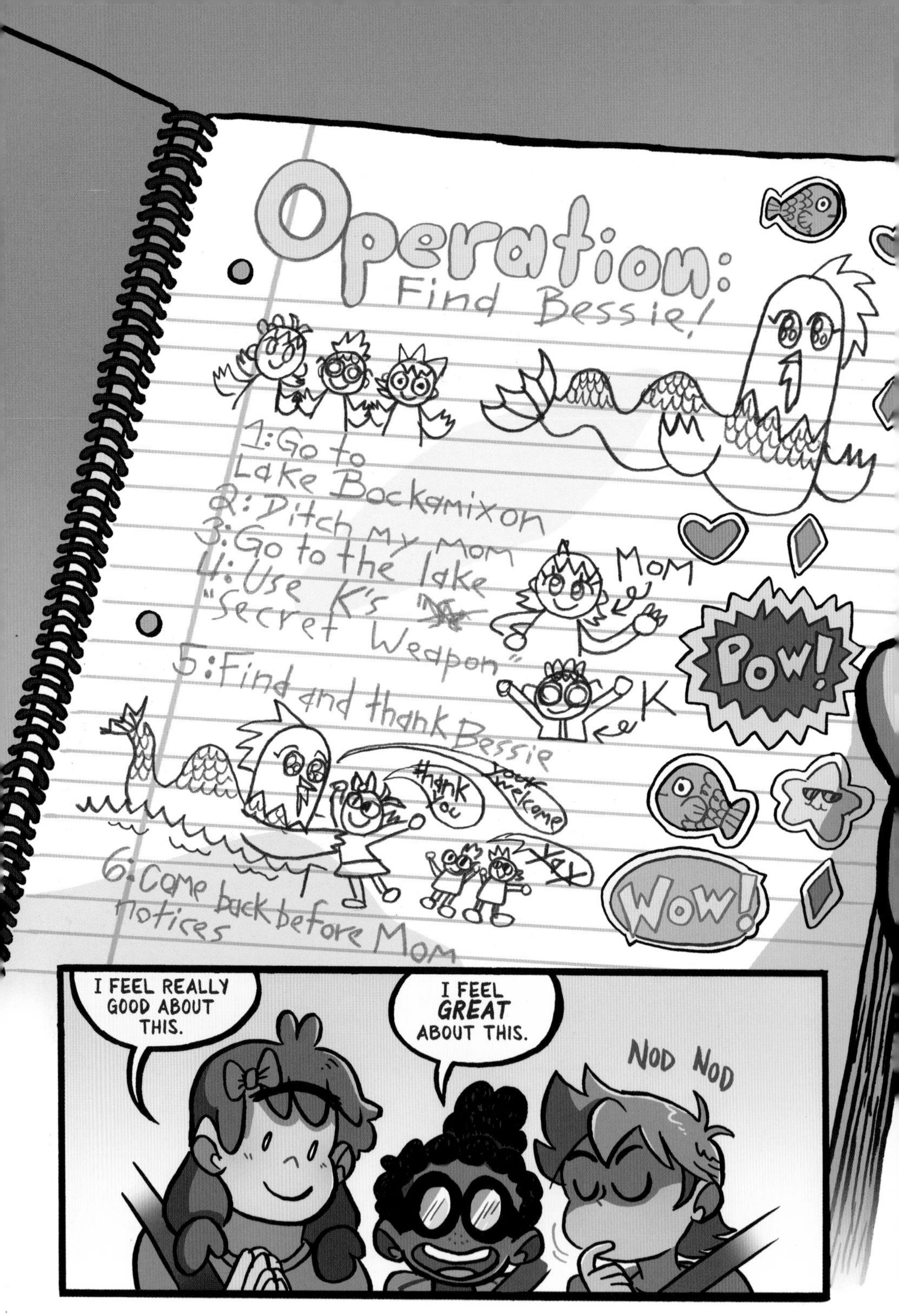
Operation: Find Bessie!
1: Go to Lake Bockamixon
2: Ditch my Mom
3: Go to the lake
4: Use K's "Secret Weapon"
5: Find and thank Bessie
6: Come back before Mom notices
Mom
K
POW!
thank you
welcome
WOW!
I FEEL REALLY GOOD ABOUT THIS.
I FEEL GREAT ABOUT THIS.
NOD NOD

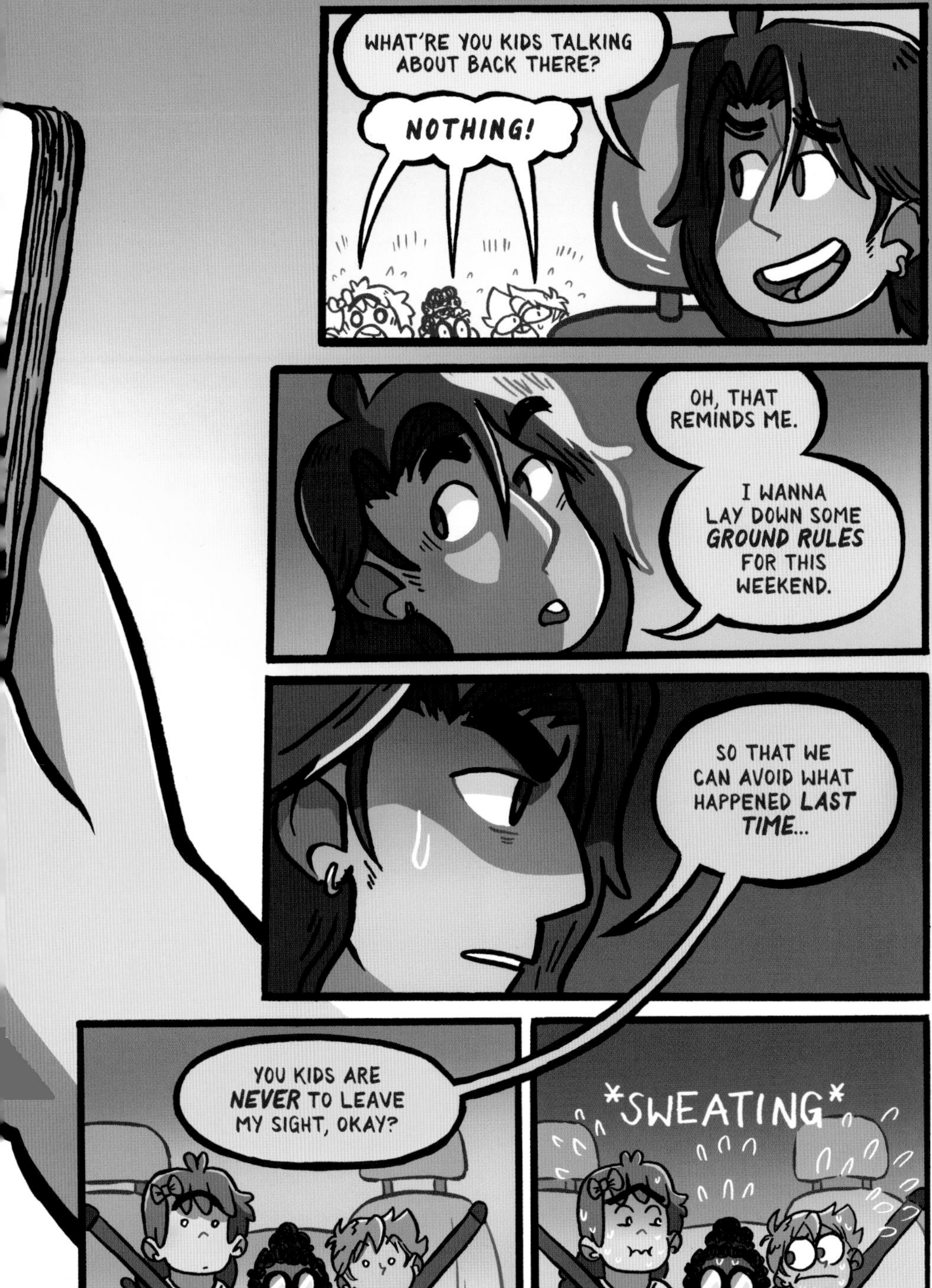
WHAT'RE YOU KIDS TALKING ABOUT BACK THERE?
NOTHING!
OH, THAT REMINDS ME.
I WANNA LAY DOWN SOME GROUND RULES FOR THIS WEEKEND.
SO THAT WE CAN AVOID WHAT HAPPENED LAST TIME...
YOU KIDS ARE NEVER TO LEAVE MY SIGHT, OKAY?
SWEATING

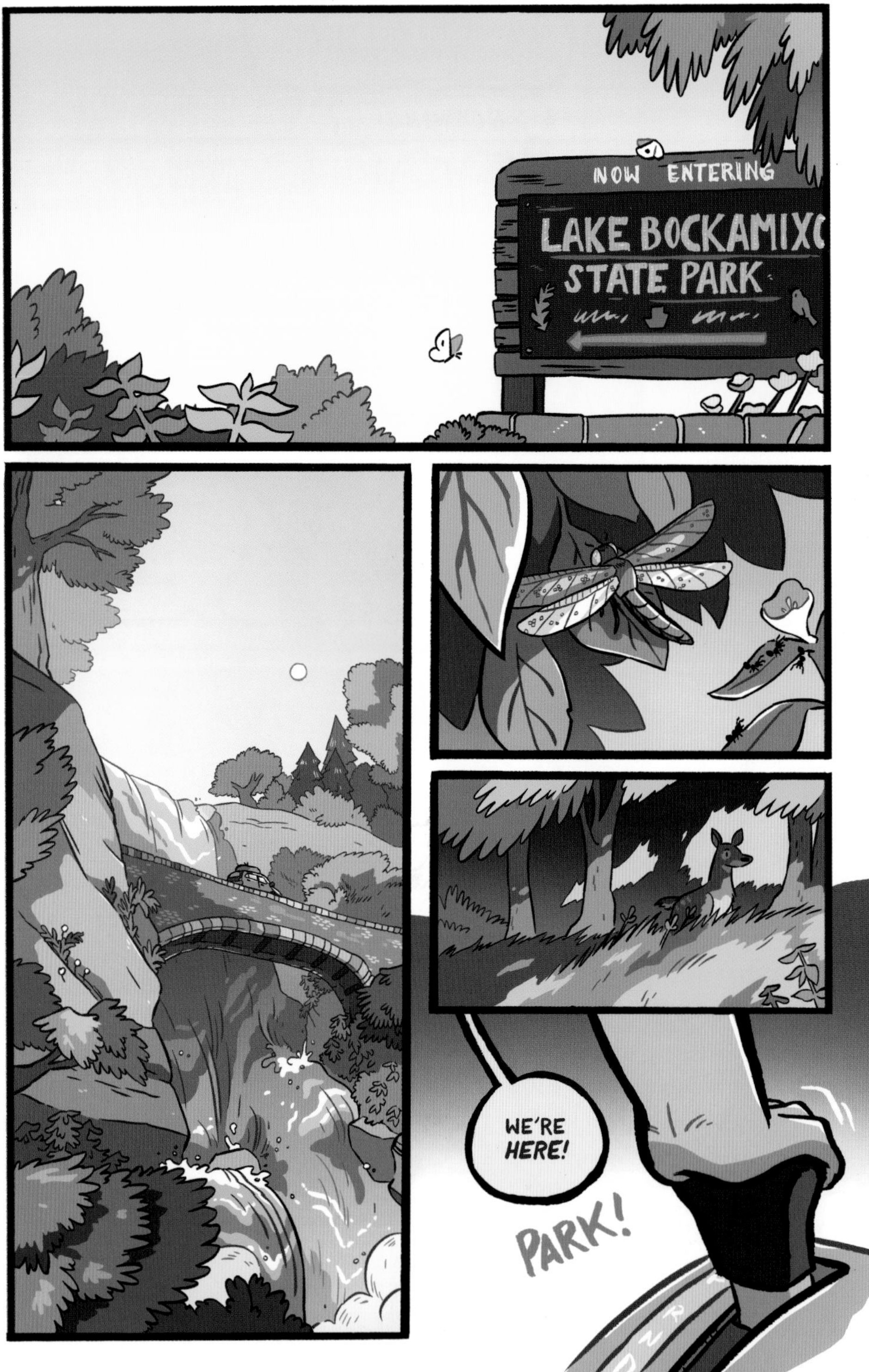
NOW ENTERING
LAKE BOCKAMIX
STATE PARK
WE'RE HERE!
PARK!

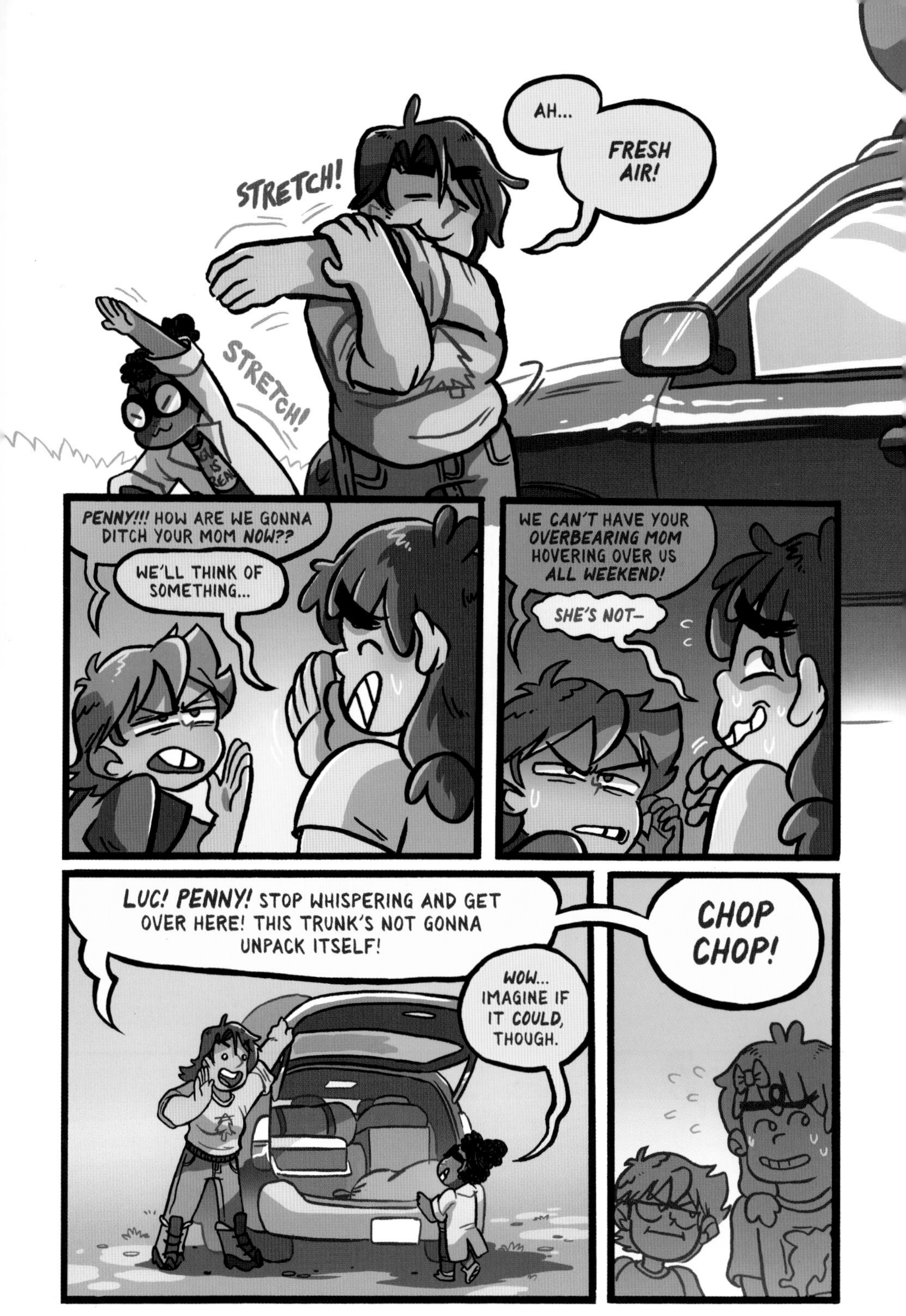
AH...
FRESH AIR!
STRETCH!
STRETCH!
PENNY!!! HOW ARE WE GONNA DITCH YOUR MOM NOW??
WE'LL THINK OF SOMETHING...
WE CAN'T HAVE YOUR OVERBEARING MOM HOVERING OVER US ALL WEEKEND!
SHE'S NOT—
LUC! PENNY! STOP WHISPERING AND GET OVER HERE! THIS TRUNK'S NOT GONNA UNPACK ITSELF!
WOW... IMAGINE IF IT COULD, THOUGH.
CHOP CHOP!

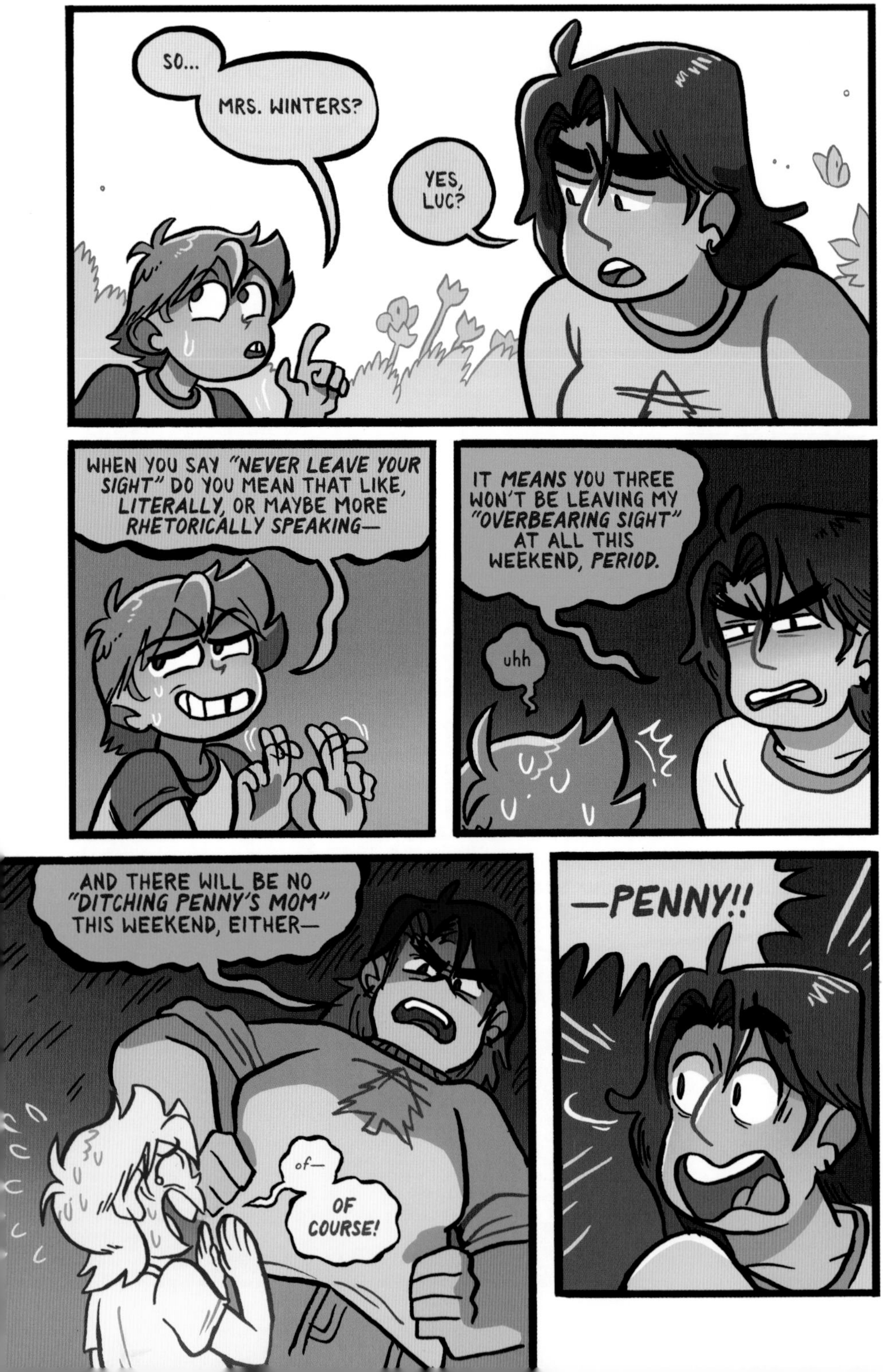
SO...
MRS. WINTERS?
YES, LUC?
WHEN YOU SAY *"NEVER LEAVE YOUR SIGHT"* DO YOU MEAN THAT LIKE, *LITERALLY*, OR MAYBE MORE *RHETORICALLY SPEAKING*—
IT *MEANS* YOU THREE WON'T BE LEAVING MY *"OVERBEARING SIGHT"* AT ALL THIS WEEKEND, *PERIOD.*
uhh
AND THERE WILL BE NO *"DITCHING PENNY'S MOM"* THIS WEEKEND, EITHER—
of—
OF COURSE!
—PENNY!!

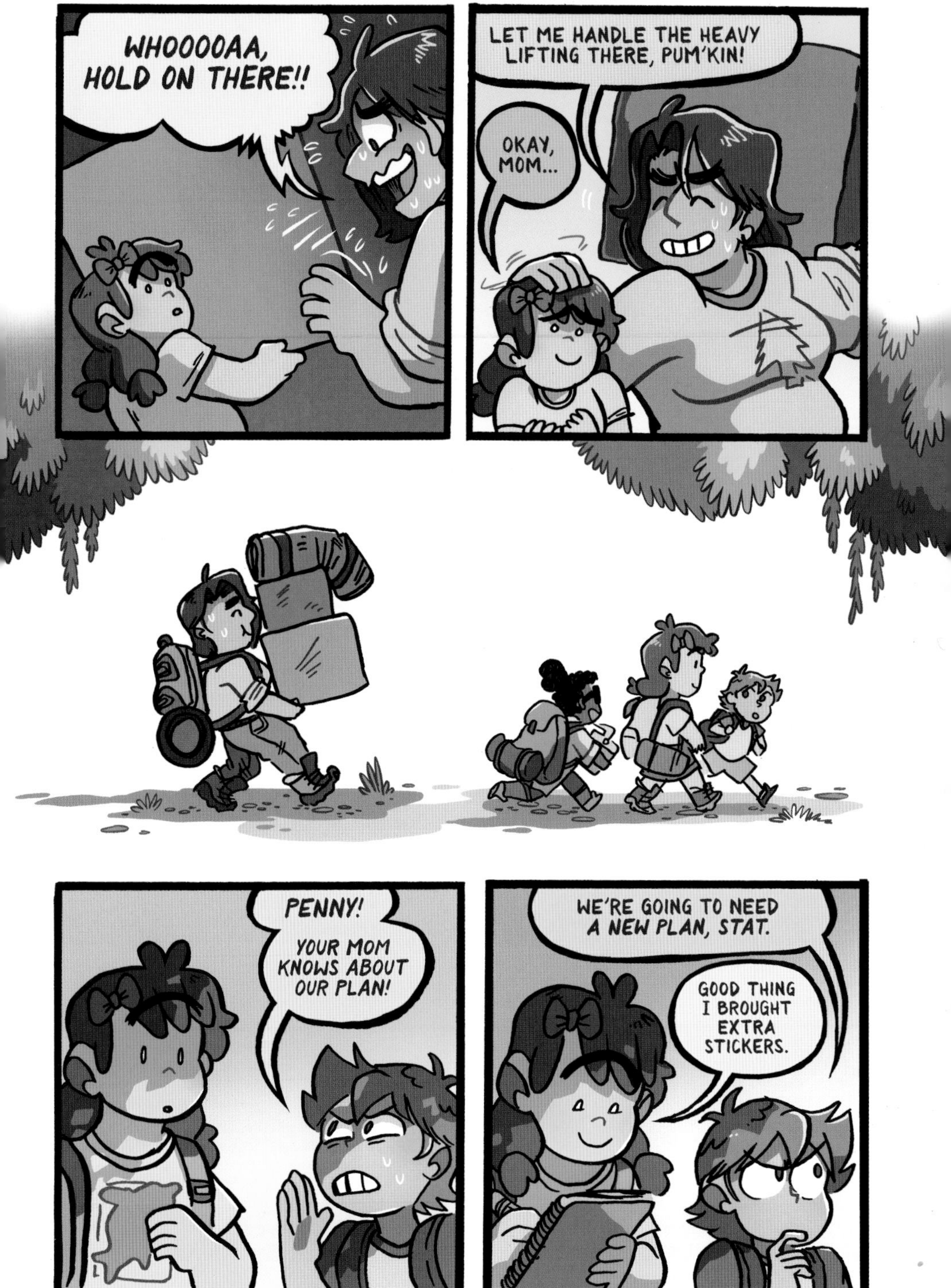
WHOOOOAA, HOLD ON THERE!!
LET ME HANDLE THE HEAVY LIFTING THERE, PUM'KIN!
OKAY, MOM...
PENNY!
YOUR MOM KNOWS ABOUT OUR PLAN!
WE'RE GOING TO NEED A NEW PLAN, STAT.
GOOD THING I BROUGHT EXTRA STICKERS.

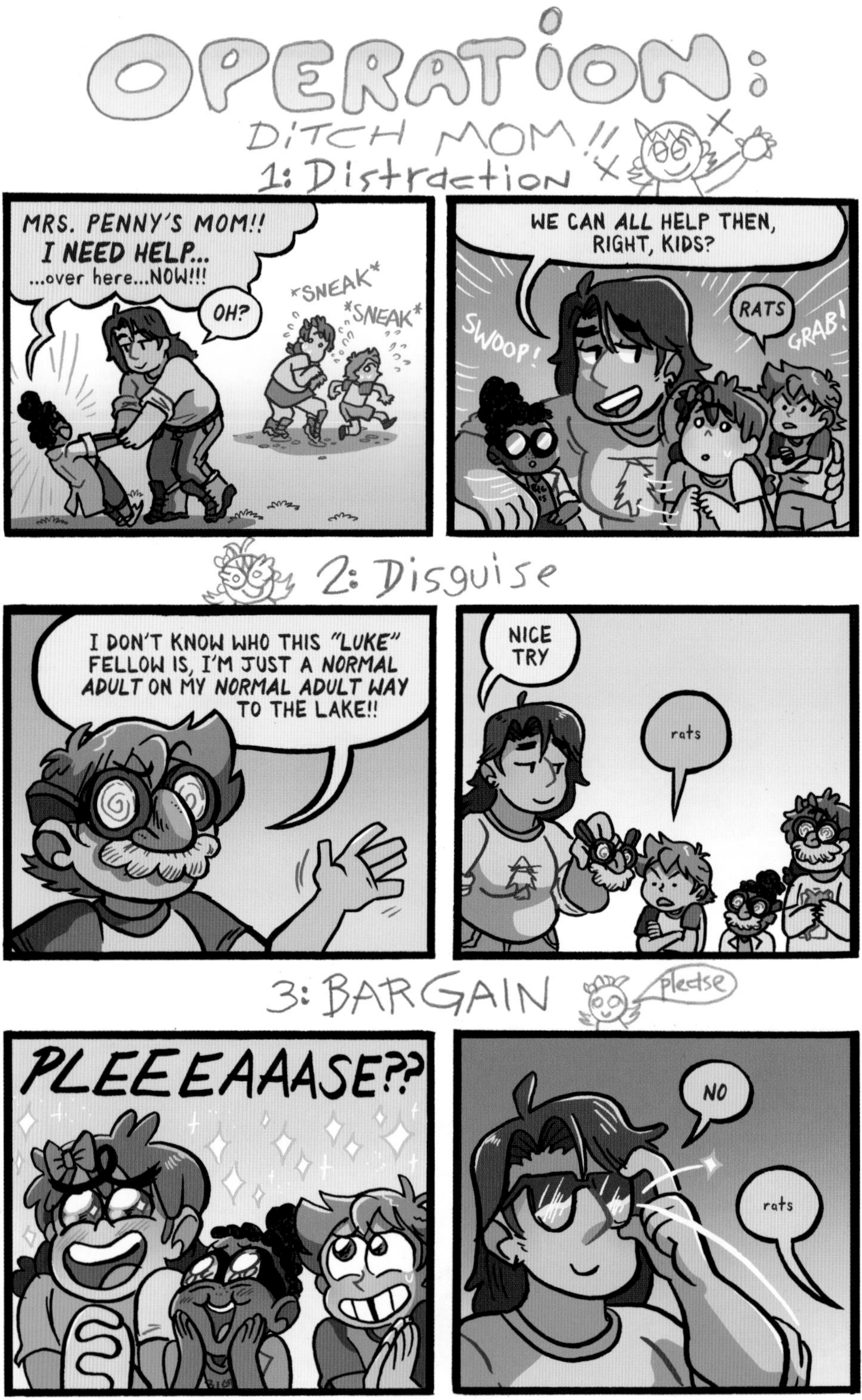
OPERATION:
DITCH MOM!!
1: Distraction
MRS. PENNY'S MOM!! I NEED HELP... ...over here...NOW!!!
OH?
SNEAK
SNEAK
WE CAN ALL HELP THEN, RIGHT, KIDS?
SWOOP!
RATS
GRAB!
2: Disguise
I DON'T KNOW WHO THIS "LUKE" FELLOW IS, I'M JUST A NORMAL ADULT ON MY NORMAL ADULT WAY TO THE LAKE!!
NICE TRY
rats
3: BARGAIN
please
PLEEEAAAASE??
NO
rats

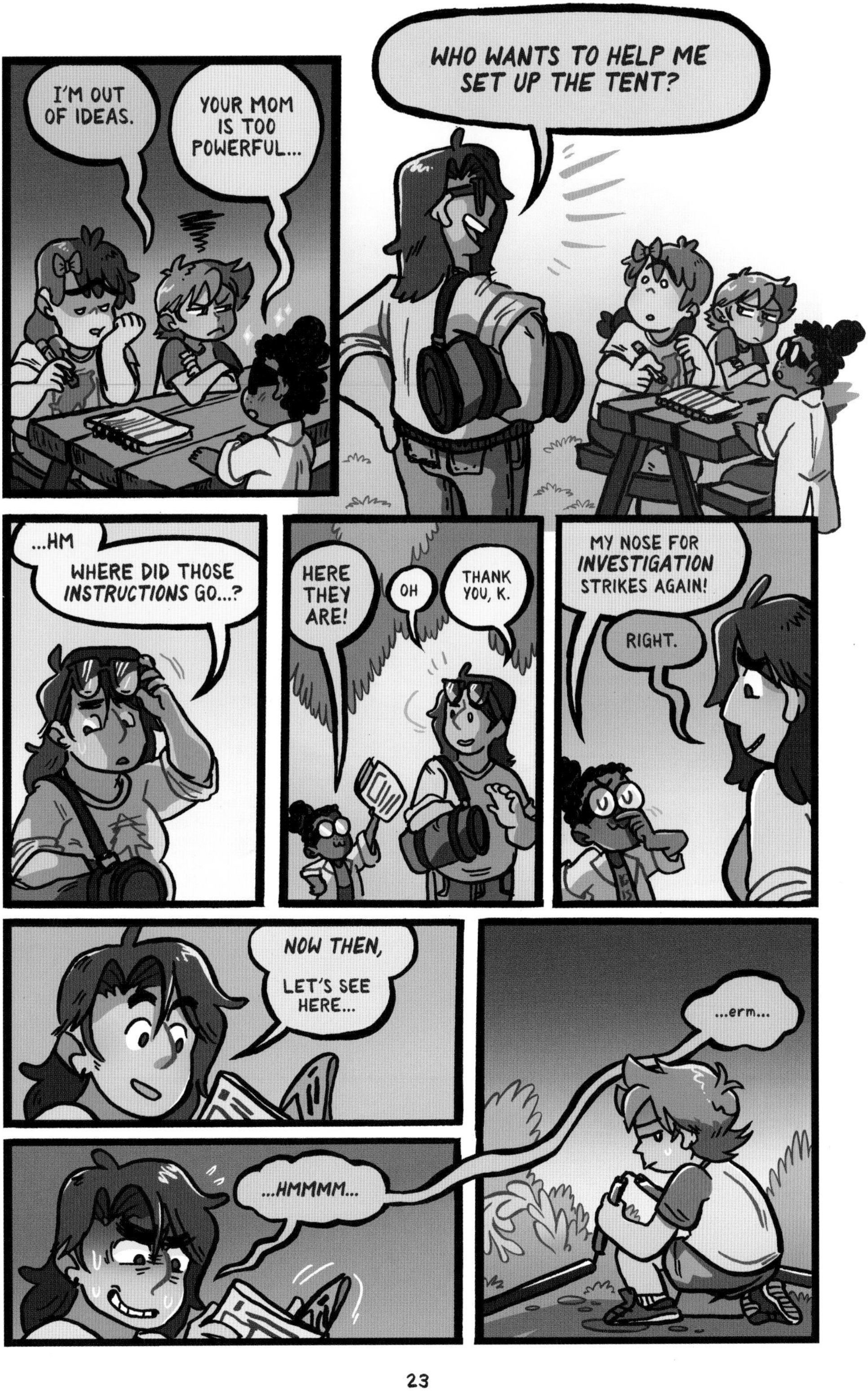
I'M OUT OF IDEAS.
YOUR MOM IS TOO POWERFUL...
WHO WANTS TO HELP ME SET UP THE TENT?
...HM
WHERE DID THOSE *INSTRUCTIONS* GO...?
HERE THEY ARE!
OH
THANK YOU, K.
MY NOSE FOR *INVESTIGATION* STRIKES AGAIN!
RIGHT.
NOW THEN,
LET'S SEE HERE...
...HMMMM...
...erm...

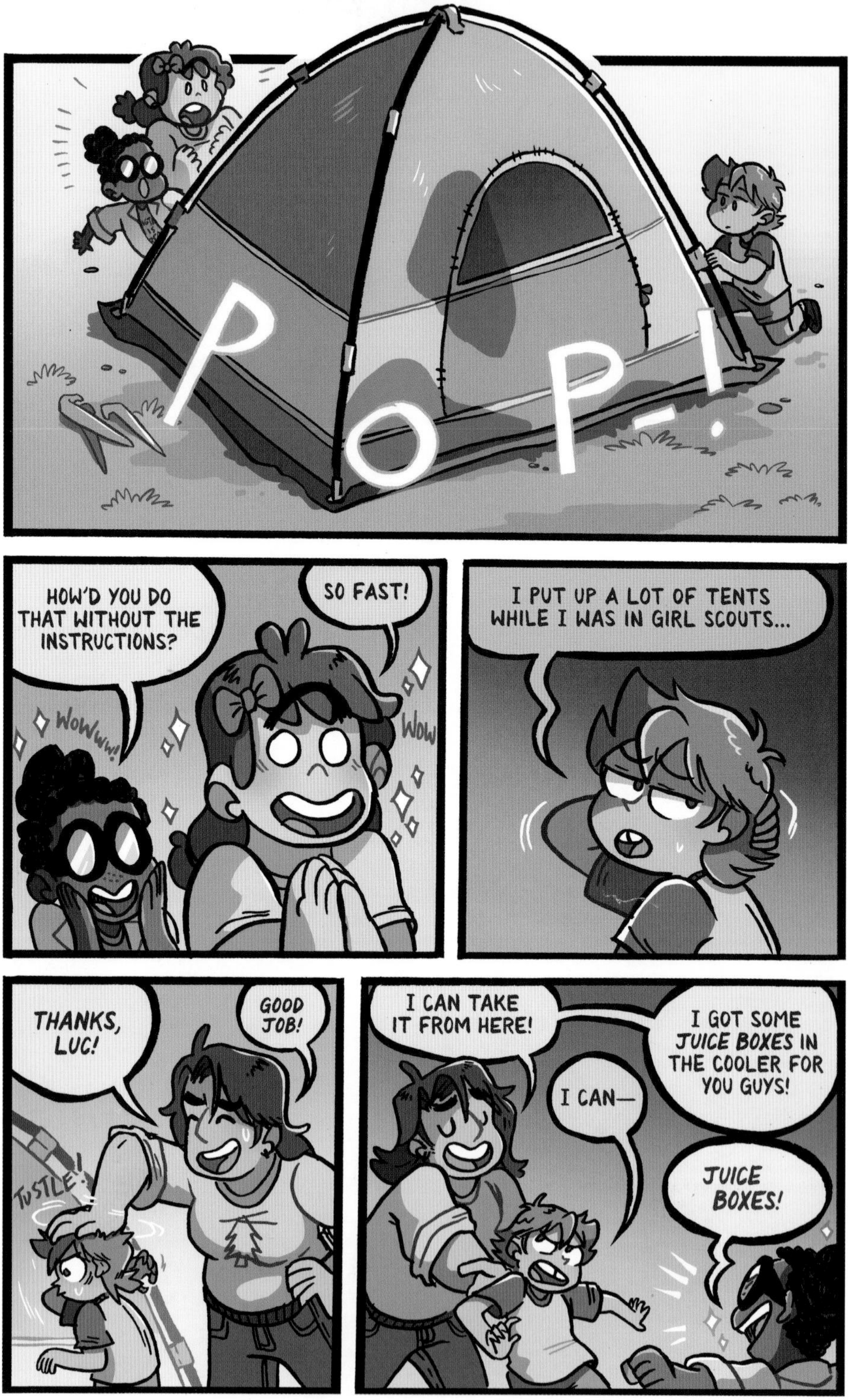
POP!
HOW'D YOU DO THAT WITHOUT THE INSTRUCTIONS?
SO FAST!
WOWWW!
WOW
I PUT UP A LOT OF TENTS WHILE I WAS IN GIRL SCOUTS...
THANKS, LUC!
GOOD JOB!
TUSTLE!
I CAN TAKE IT FROM HERE!
I CAN—
I GOT SOME JUICE BOXES IN THE COOLER FOR YOU GUYS!
JUICE BOXES!

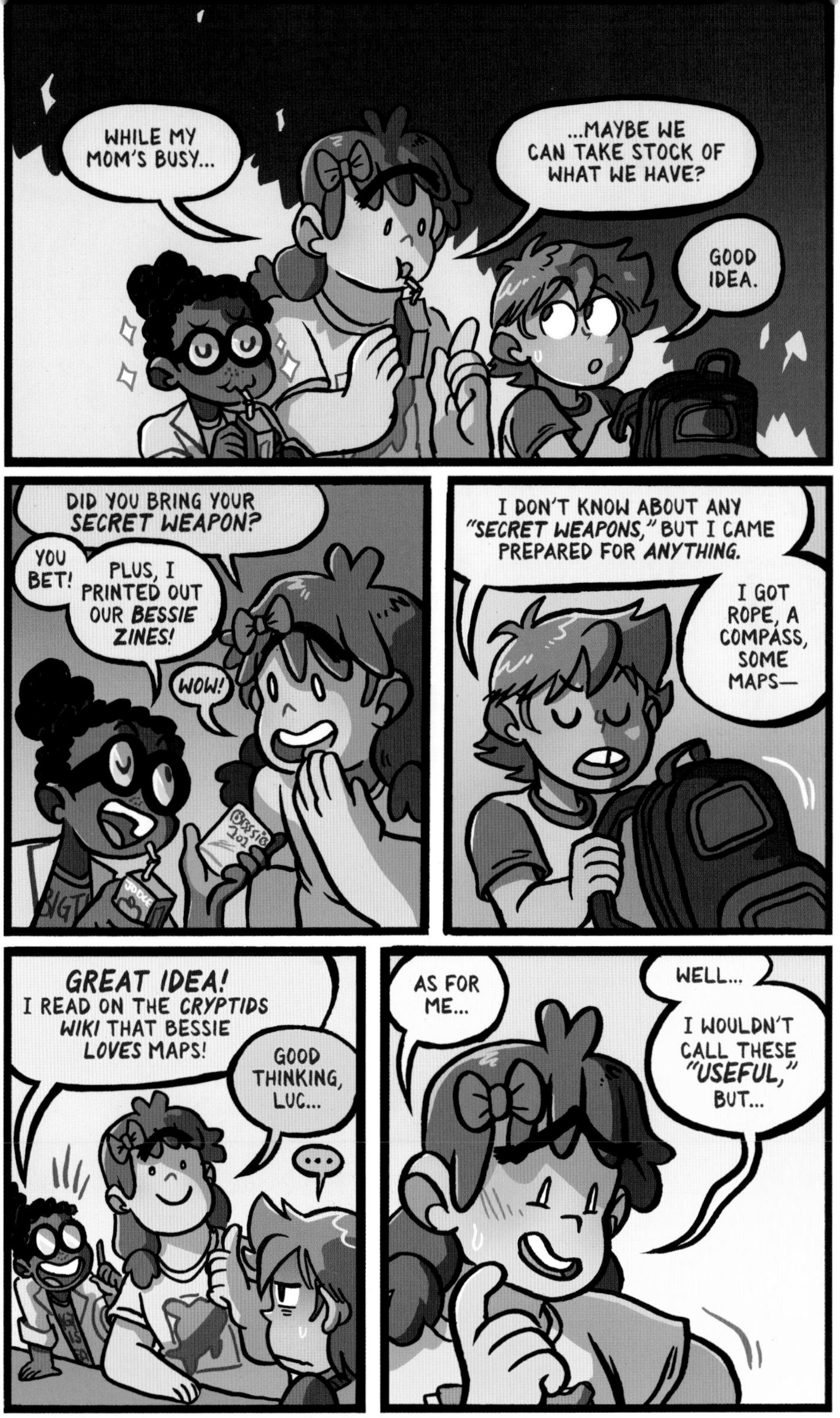
WHILE MY MOM'S BUSY...
...MAYBE WE CAN TAKE STOCK OF WHAT WE HAVE?
GOOD IDEA.
DID YOU BRING YOUR *SECRET WEAPON?*
YOU BET!
PLUS, I PRINTED OUT OUR *BESSIE ZINES!*
WOW!
I DON'T KNOW ABOUT ANY *"SECRET WEAPONS,"* BUT I CAME PREPARED FOR *ANYTHING.*
I GOT ROPE, A COMPASS, SOME MAPS—
GREAT IDEA! I READ ON THE *CRYPTIDS WIKI* THAT BESSIE *LOVES* MAPS!
GOOD THINKING, LUC...
...
AS FOR ME...
WELL...
I WOULDN'T CALL THESE *"USEFUL,"* BUT...

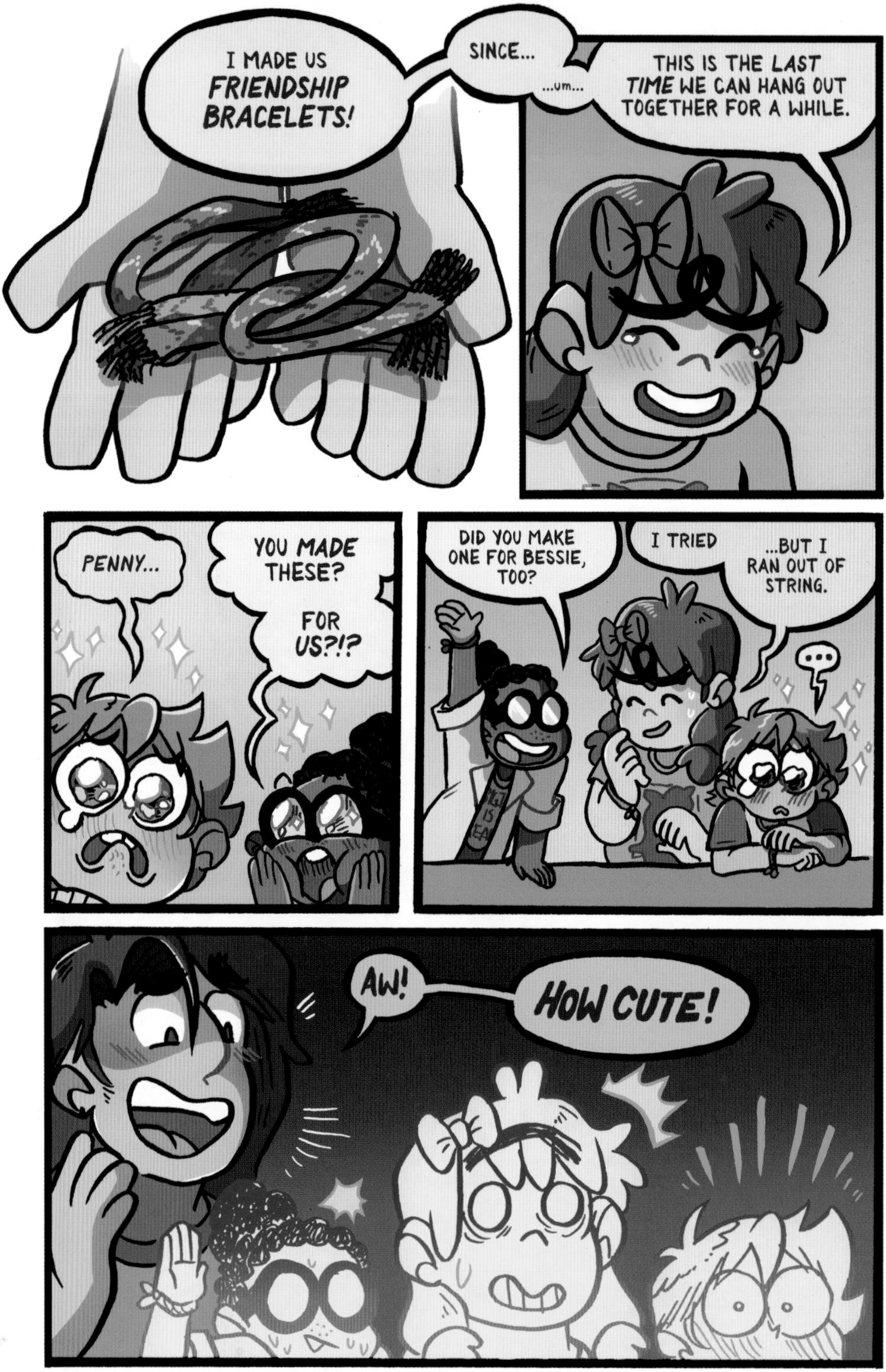
I MADE US FRIENDSHIP BRACELETS!
SINCE...
...um...
THIS IS THE LAST TIME WE CAN HANG OUT TOGETHER FOR A WHILE.
PENNY...
YOU MADE THESE?
FOR US?!?
DID YOU MAKE ONE FOR BESSIE, TOO?
I TRIED
...BUT I RAN OUT OF STRING.
...
AW!
HOW CUTE!

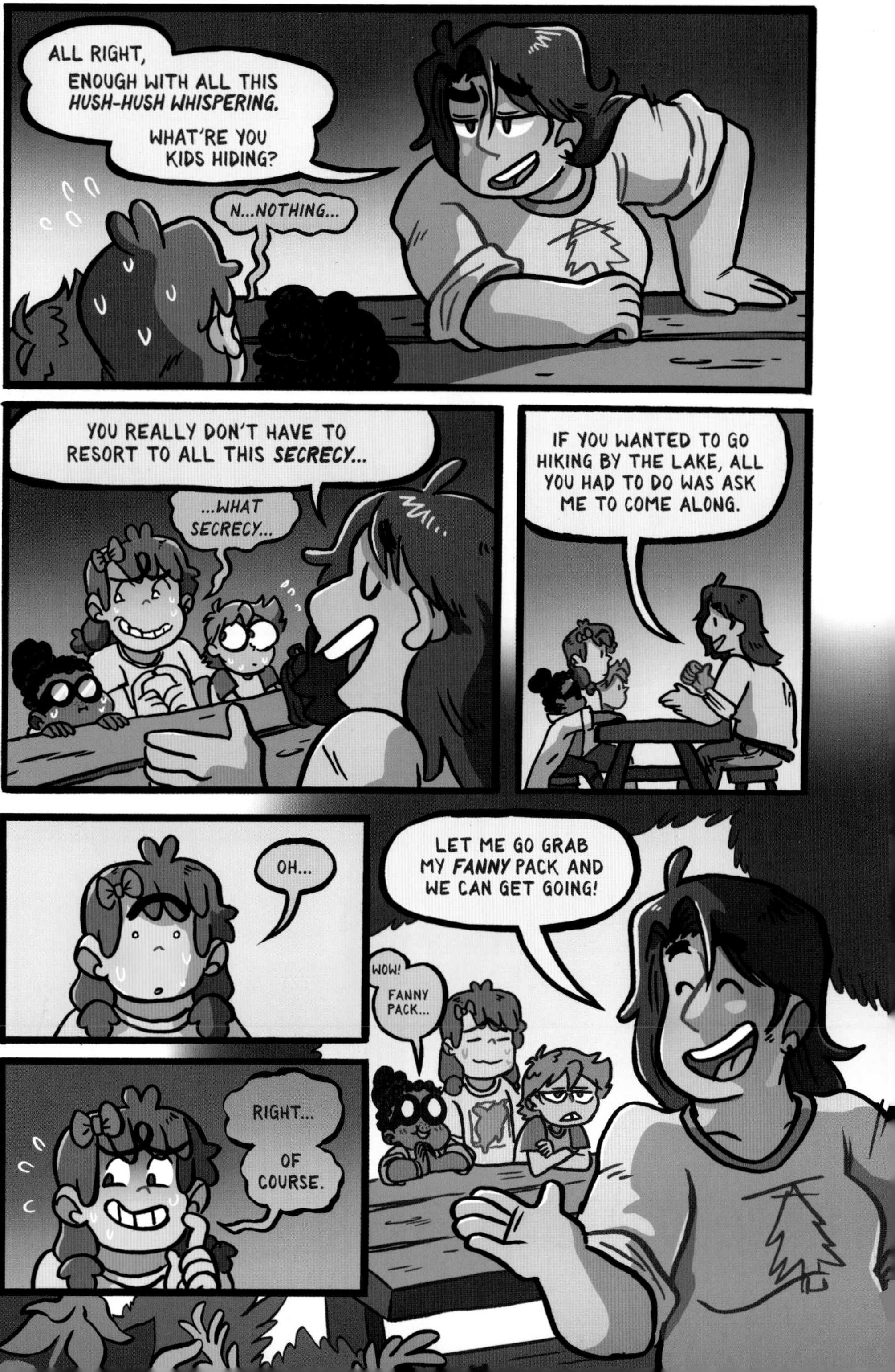
ALL RIGHT,
ENOUGH WITH ALL THIS *HUSH-HUSH WHISPERING.*
WHAT'RE YOU KIDS HIDING?
N...NOTHING...
YOU REALLY DON'T HAVE TO RESORT TO ALL THIS *SECRECY...*
...WHAT SECRECY...
IF YOU WANTED TO GO HIKING BY THE LAKE, ALL YOU HAD TO DO WAS ASK ME TO COME ALONG.
OH...
RIGHT...
OF COURSE.
LET ME GO GRAB MY *FANNY* PACK AND WE CAN GET GOING!
WOW!
FANNY PACK...

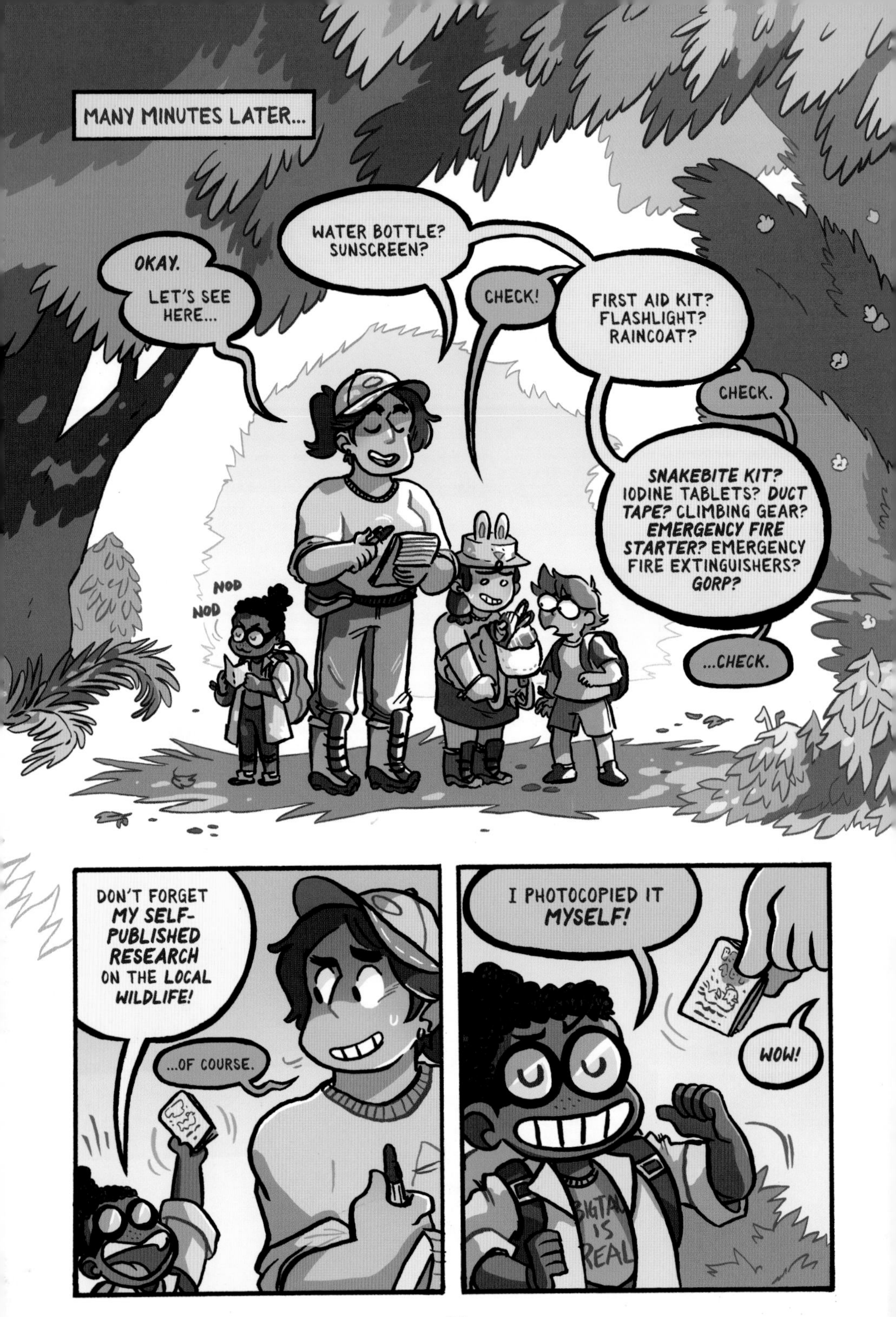
MANY MINUTES LATER...
OKAY.
LET'S SEE HERE...
WATER BOTTLE? SUNSCREEN?
CHECK!
FIRST AID KIT? FLASHLIGHT? RAINCOAT?
CHECK.
SNAKEBITE KIT? IODINE TABLETS? DUCT TAPE? CLIMBING GEAR? EMERGENCY FIRE STARTER? EMERGENCY FIRE EXTINGUISHERS? GORP?
NOD
NOD
...CHECK.
DON'T FORGET MY SELF-PUBLISHED RESEARCH ON THE LOCAL WILDLIFE!
...OF COURSE.
I PHOTOCOPIED IT MYSELF!
WOW!
BIGTAIL IS REAL

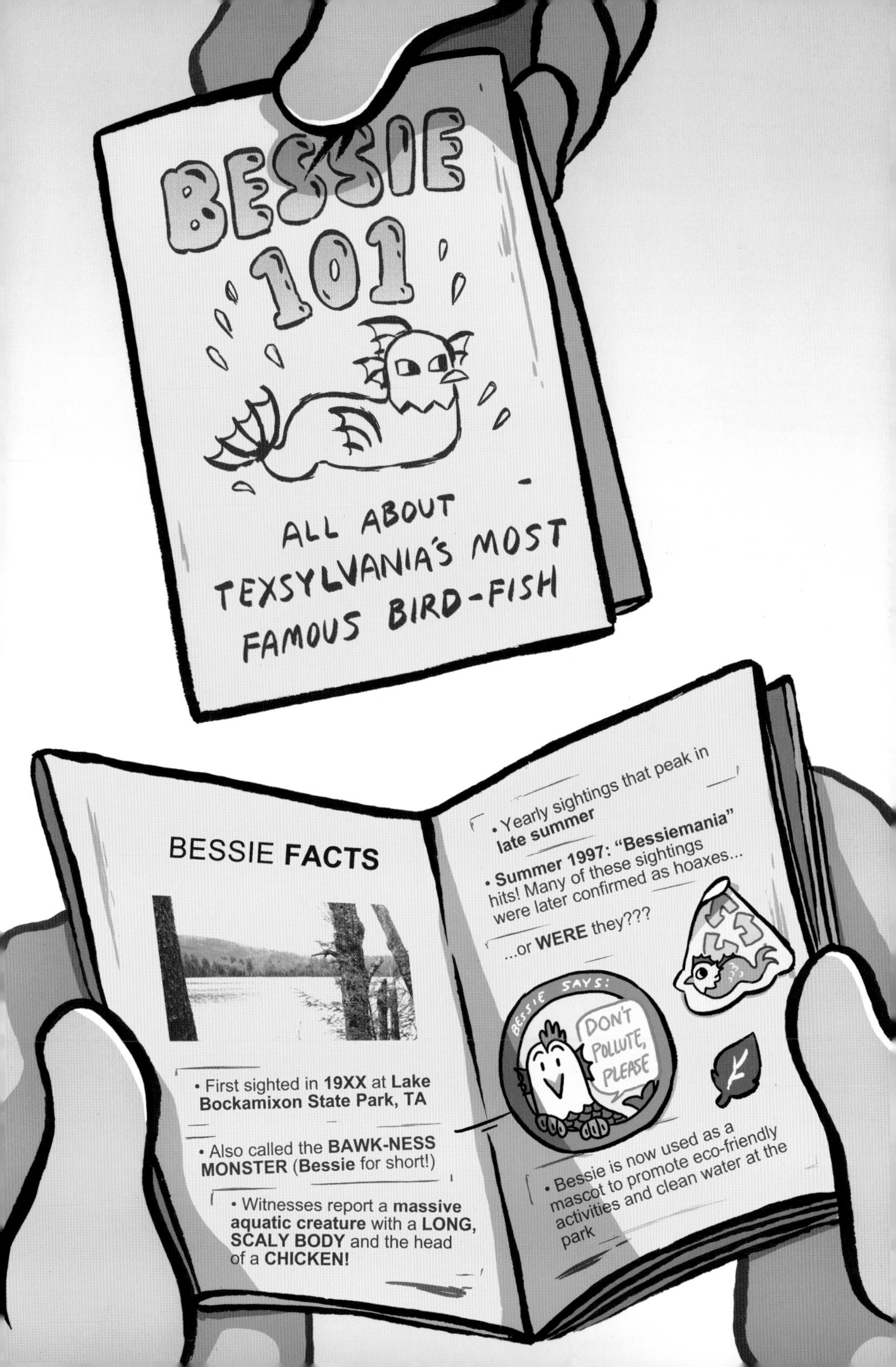

BESSIE 101
ALL ABOUT TEXSYLVANIA'S MOST FAMOUS BIRD-FISH
BESSIE FACTS
• First sighted in 19XX at Lake Bockamixon State Park, TA
• Also called the BAWK-NESS MONSTER (Bessie for short!)
• Witnesses report a massive aquatic creature with a LONG, SCALY BODY and the head of a CHICKEN!
• Yearly sightings that peak in late summer
• Summer 1997: "Bessiemania" hits! Many of these sightings were later confirmed as hoaxes...
...or WERE they???
BESSIE SAYS:
DON'T POLLUTE, PLEASE
• Bessie is now used as a mascot to promote eco-friendly activities and clean water at the park

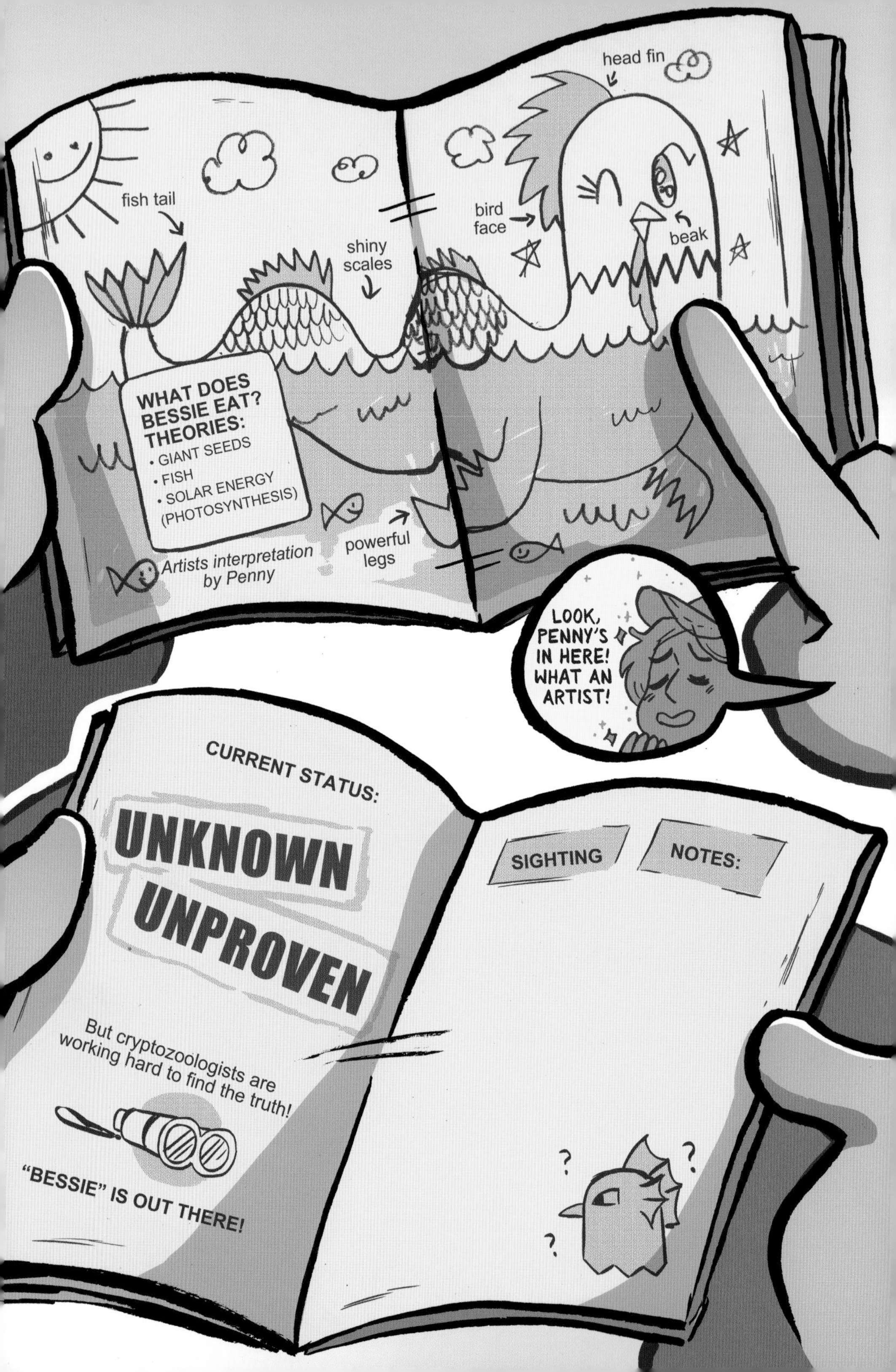
head fin
fish tail
bird face
beak
shiny scales
WHAT DOES BESSIE EAT? THEORIES:
• GIANT SEEDS
• FISH
• SOLAR ENERGY (PHOTOSYNTHESIS)
powerful legs
Artists interpretation by Penny
LOOK, PENNY'S IN HERE! WHAT AN ARTIST!
CURRENT STATUS:
UNKNOWN
UNPROVEN
But cryptozoologists are working hard to find the truth!
"BESSIE" IS OUT THERE!
SIGHTING
NOTES:
?
?
?

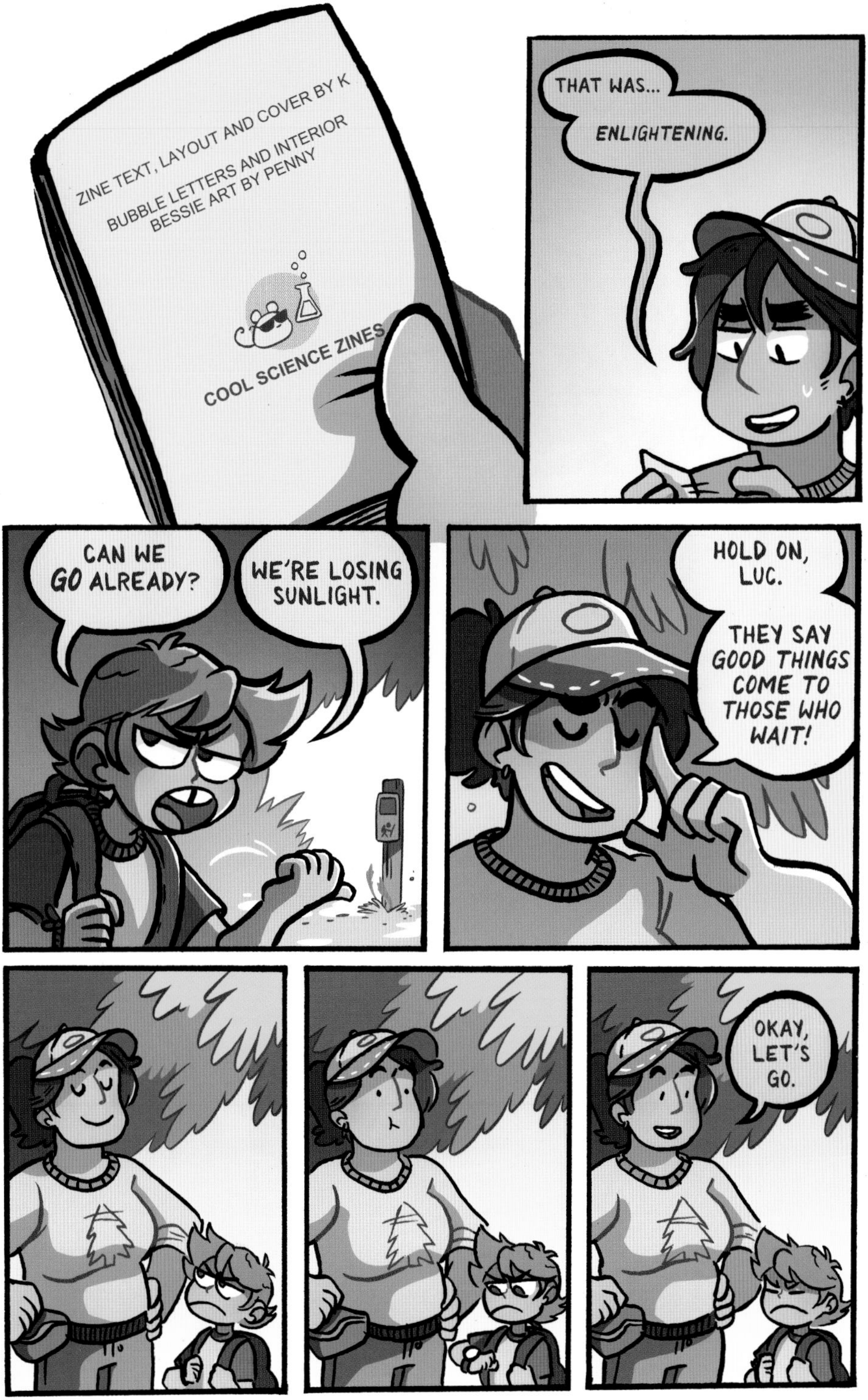
ZINE TEXT, LAYOUT AND COVER BY K
BUBBLE LETTERS AND INTERIOR BESSIE ART BY PENNY
COOL SCIENCE ZINES
THAT WAS...
ENLIGHTENING.
CAN WE GO ALREADY?
WE'RE LOSING SUNLIGHT.
HOLD ON, LUC.
THEY SAY GOOD THINGS COME TO THOSE WHO WAIT!
OKAY, LET'S GO.

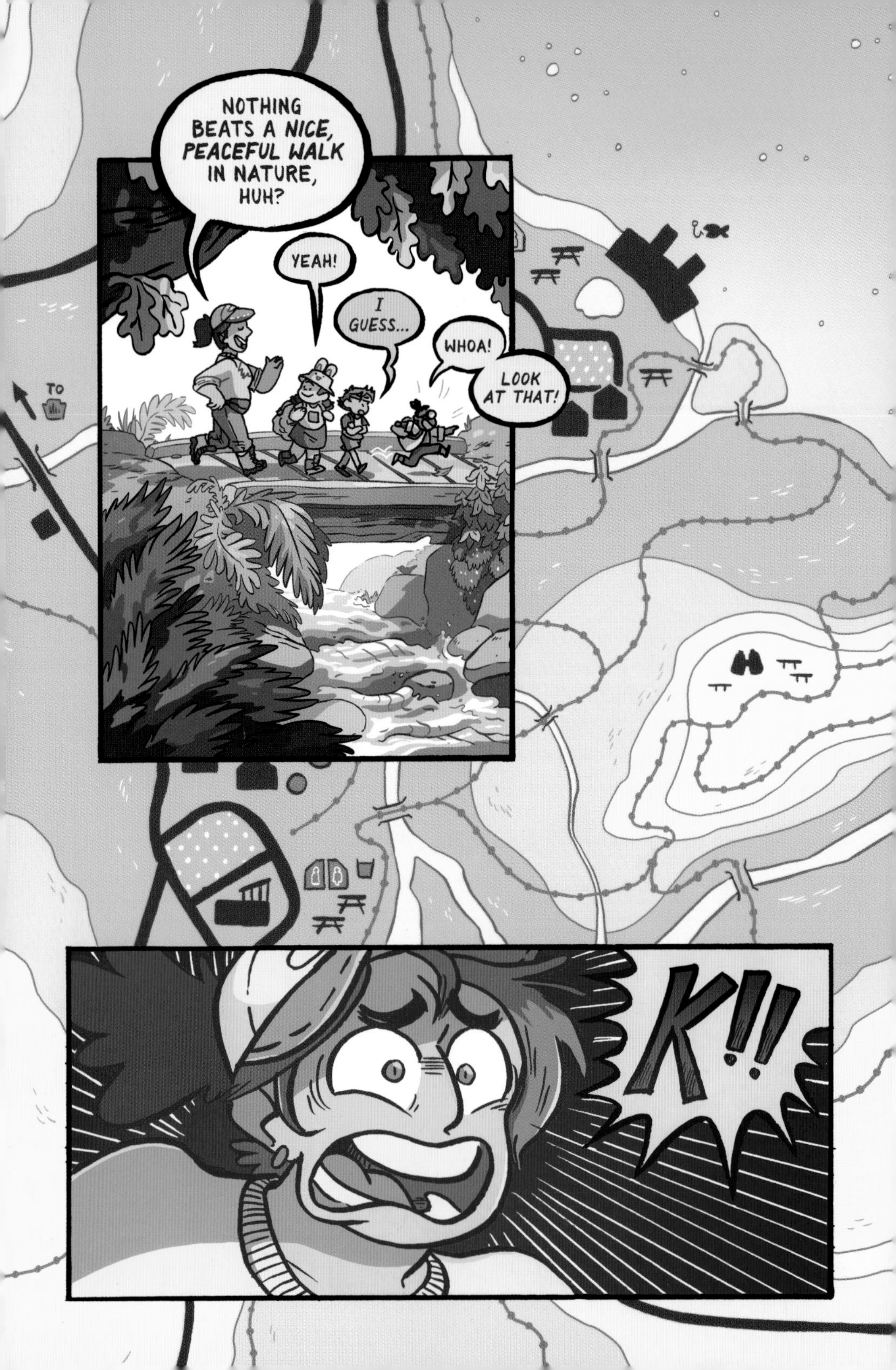
NOTHING BEATS A NICE, PEACEFUL WALK IN NATURE, HUH?
YEAH!
I GUESS...
WHOA!
LOOK AT THAT!
TO
K!!

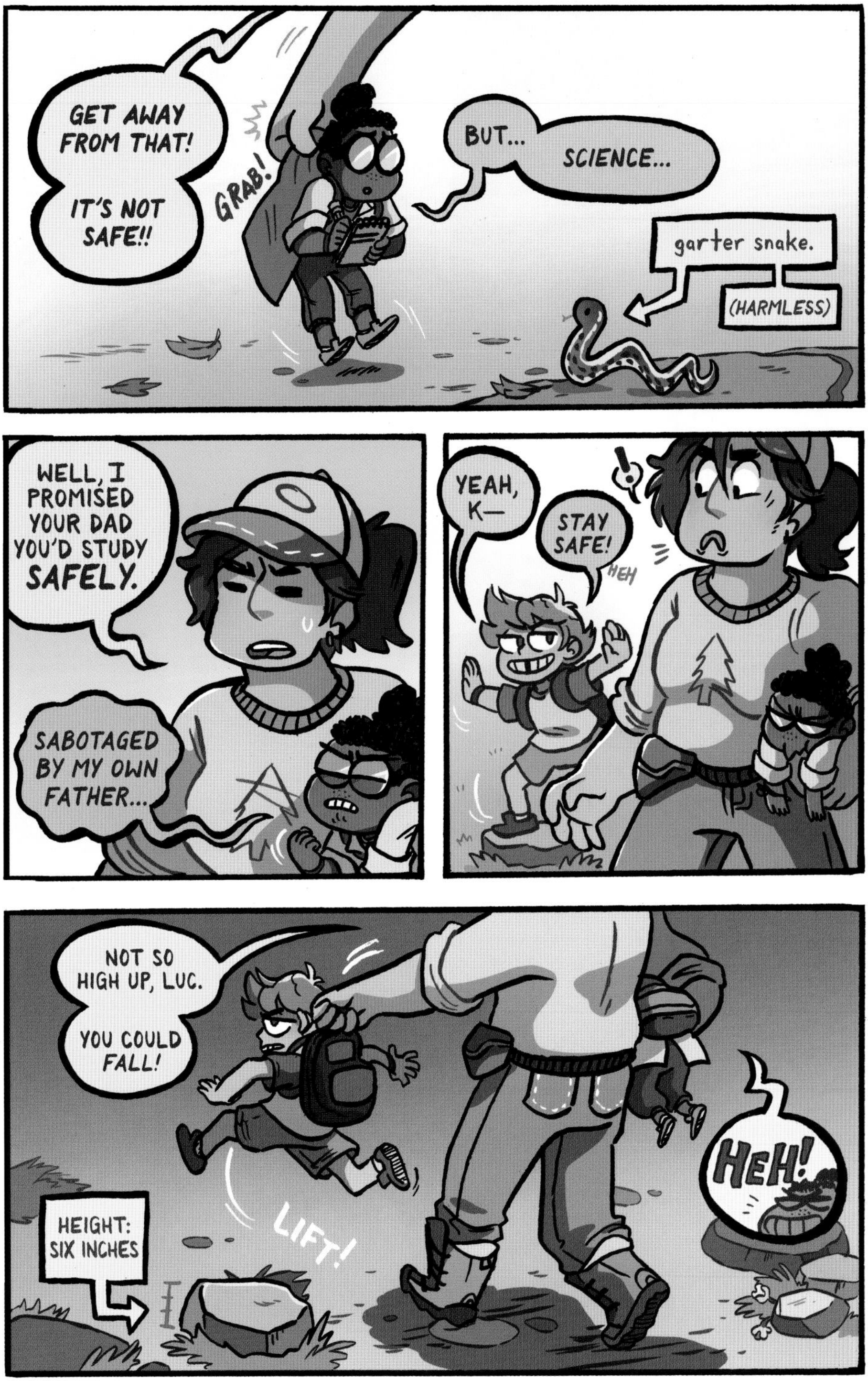
GET AWAY FROM THAT!
IT'S NOT SAFE!!
GRAB!
BUT...
SCIENCE...
garter snake.
(HARMLESS)
WELL, I PROMISED YOUR DAD YOU'D STUDY SAFELY.
SABOTAGED BY MY OWN FATHER...
YEAH, K—
STAY SAFE!
HEH
!
NOT SO HIGH UP, LUC.
YOU COULD FALL!
LIFT!
HEH!
HEIGHT: SIX INCHES

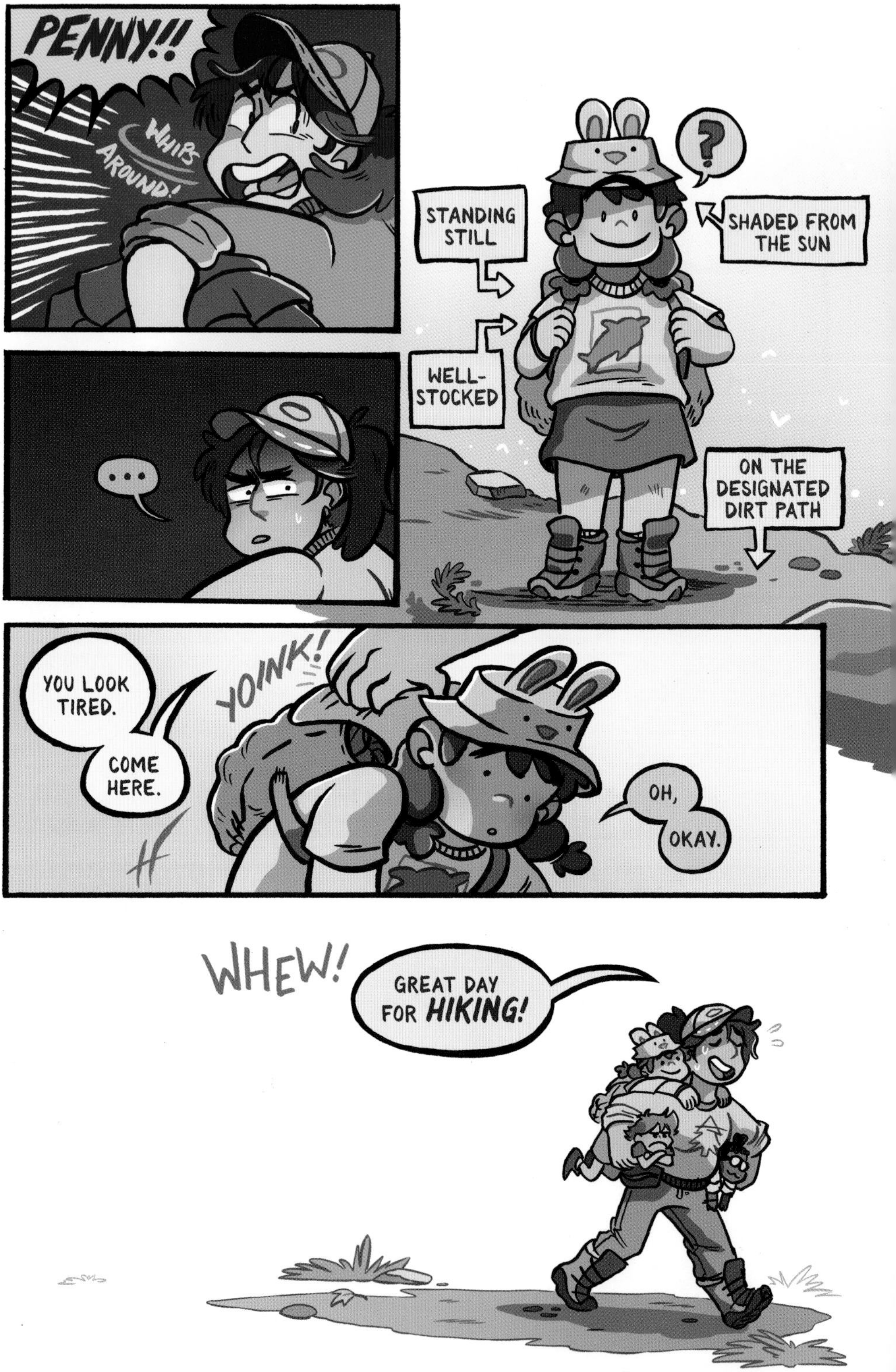
PENNY!!
WHIPS AROUND!
?
STANDING STILL
WELL-STOCKED
SHADED FROM THE SUN
ON THE DESIGNATED DIRT PATH
...
YOINK!
YOU LOOK TIRED.
COME HERE.
OH,
OKAY.
WHEW!
GREAT DAY FOR HIKING!

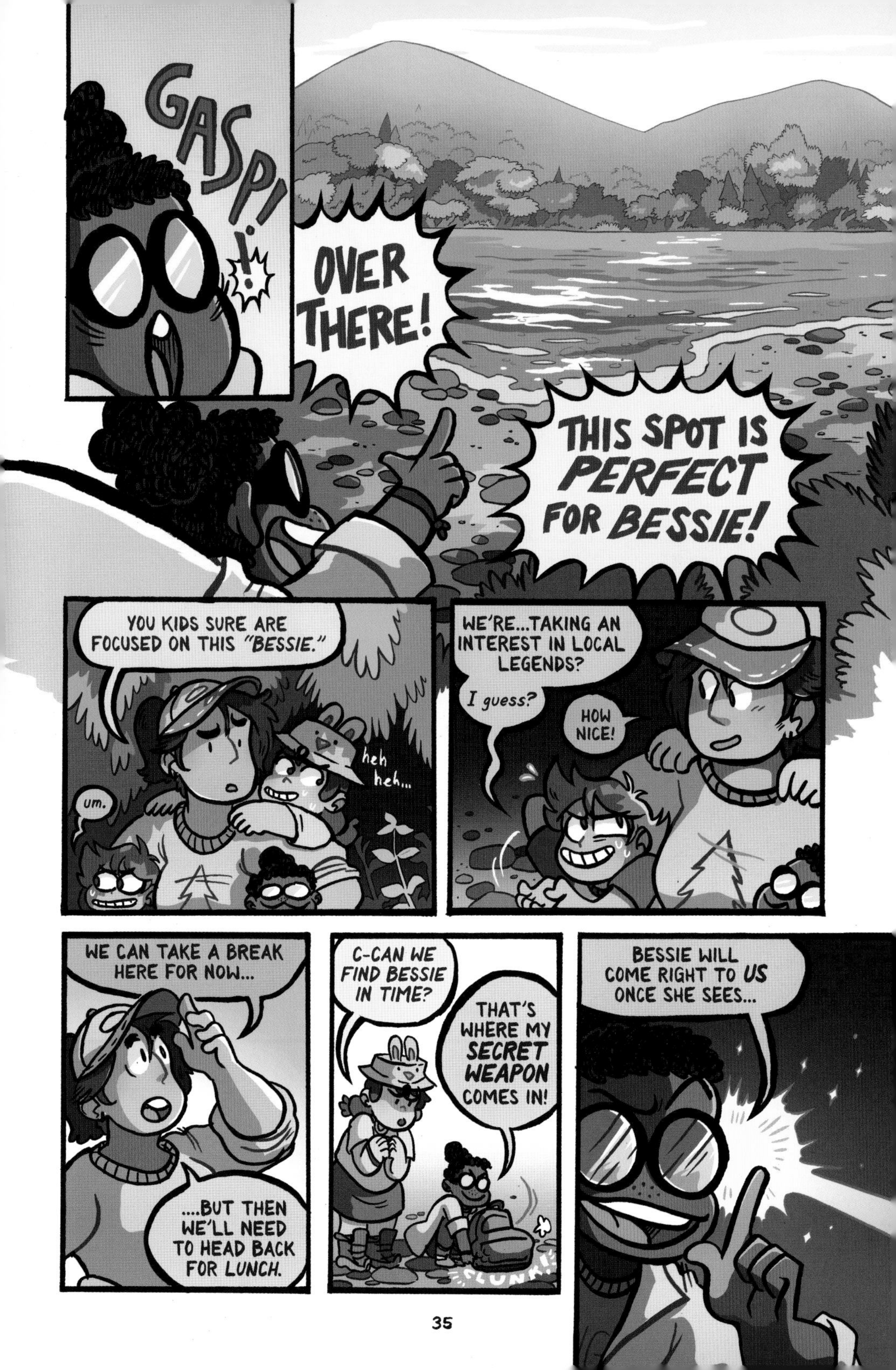
GASP!
OVER THERE!
THIS SPOT IS PERFECT FOR BESSIE!
YOU KIDS SURE ARE FOCUSED ON THIS "BESSIE."
heh heh...
um.
WE'RE...TAKING AN INTEREST IN LOCAL LEGENDS?
I guess?
HOW NICE!
WE CAN TAKE A BREAK HERE FOR NOW...
....BUT THEN WE'LL NEED TO HEAD BACK FOR LUNCH.
C-CAN WE FIND BESSIE IN TIME?
THAT'S WHERE MY SECRET WEAPON COMES IN!
CLUNK!
BESSIE WILL COME RIGHT TO US ONCE SHE SEES...

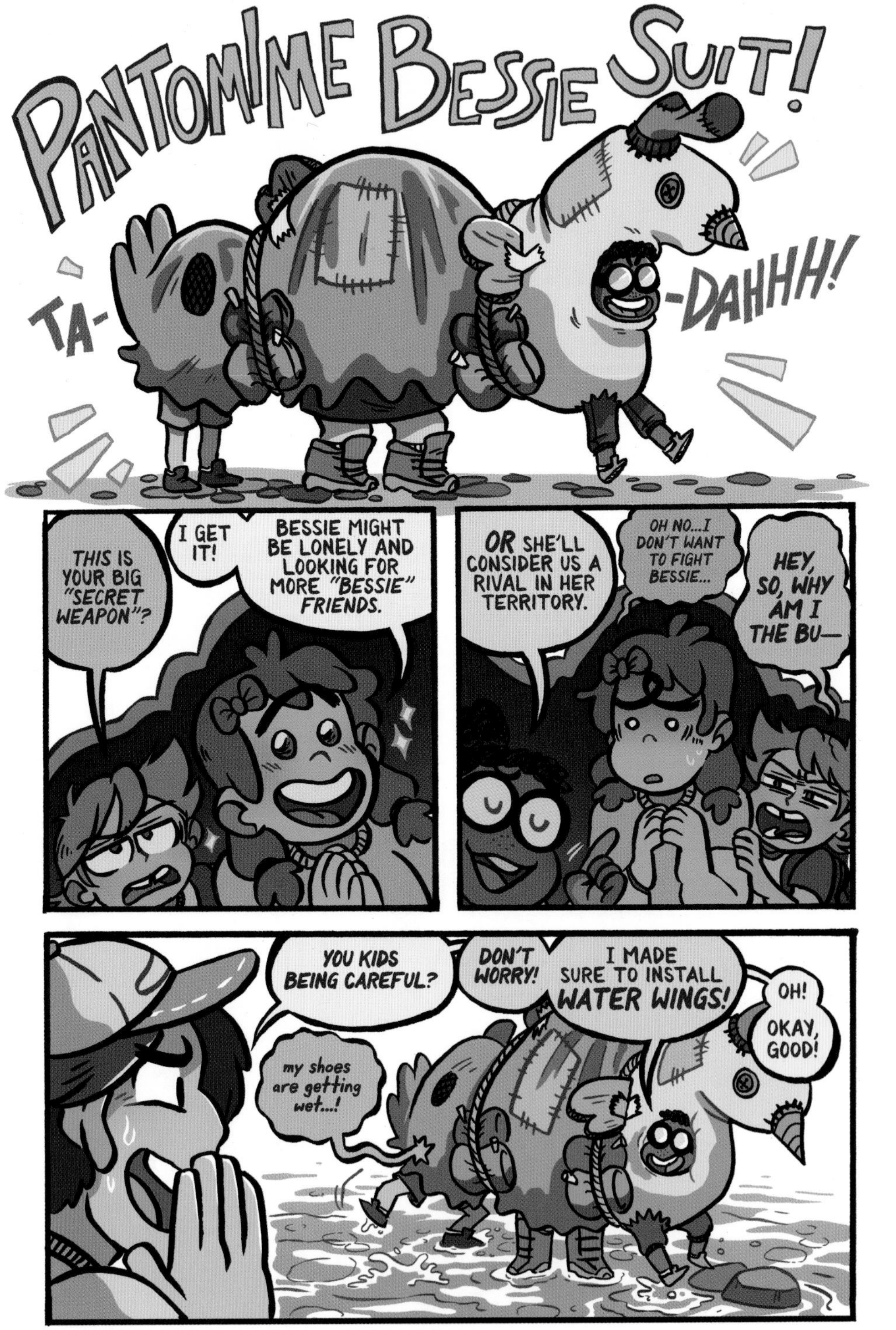
PANTOMIME BESSIE SUIT!
TA-
-DAHHH!
THIS IS YOUR BIG "SECRET WEAPON"?
I GET IT!
BESSIE MIGHT BE LONELY AND LOOKING FOR MORE "BESSIE" FRIENDS.
OR SHE'LL CONSIDER US A RIVAL IN HER TERRITORY.
OH NO...I DON'T WANT TO FIGHT BESSIE...
HEY, SO, WHY AM I THE BU—
YOU KIDS BEING CAREFUL?
my shoes are getting wet...!
DON'T WORRY!
I MADE SURE TO INSTALL WATER WINGS!
OH!
OKAY, GOOD!

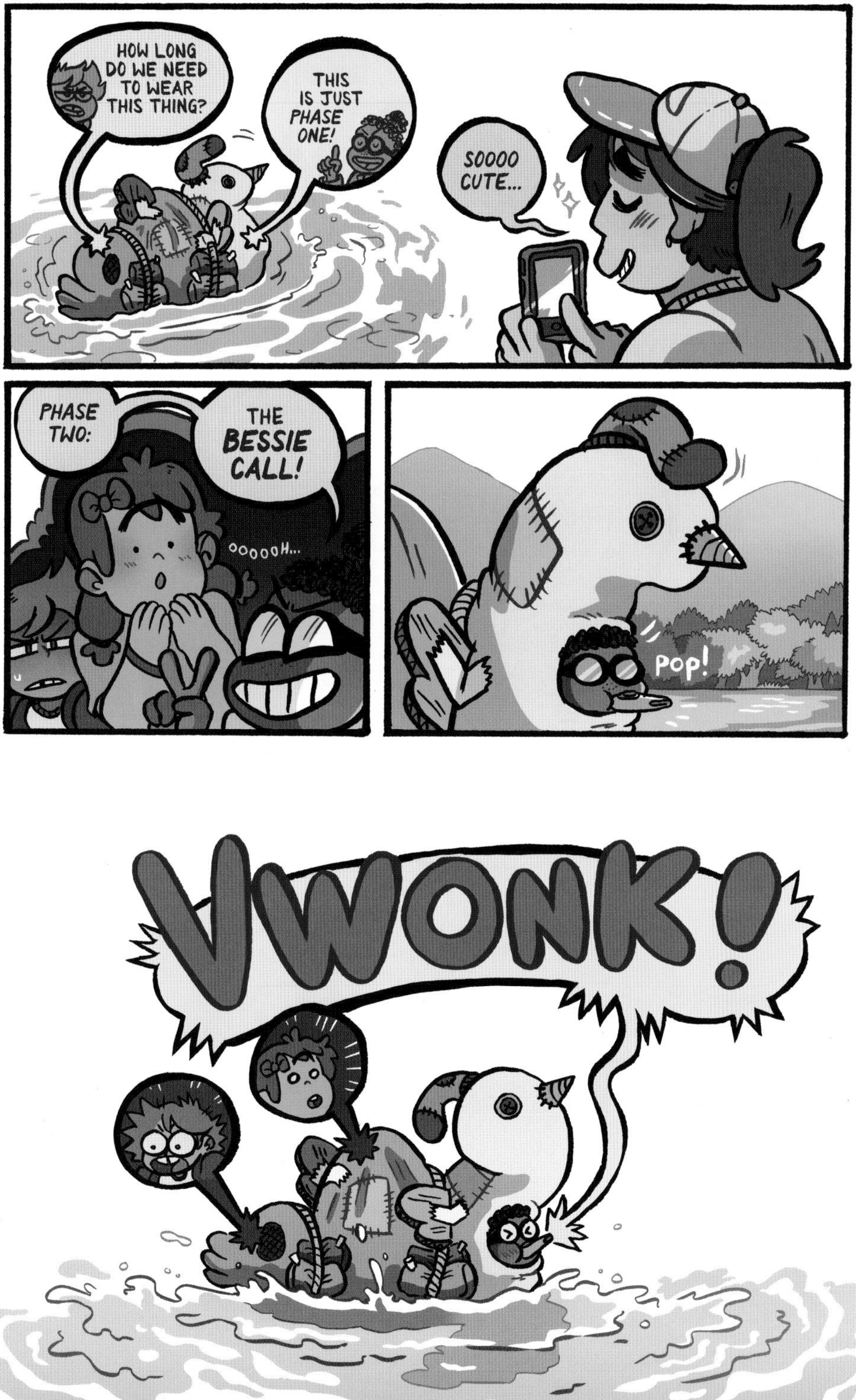
HOW LONG DO WE NEED TO WEAR THIS THING?
THIS IS JUST PHASE ONE!
SOOOO CUTE...
PHASE TWO:
THE BESSIE CALL!
OOOOOH...
POP!
VWONK!

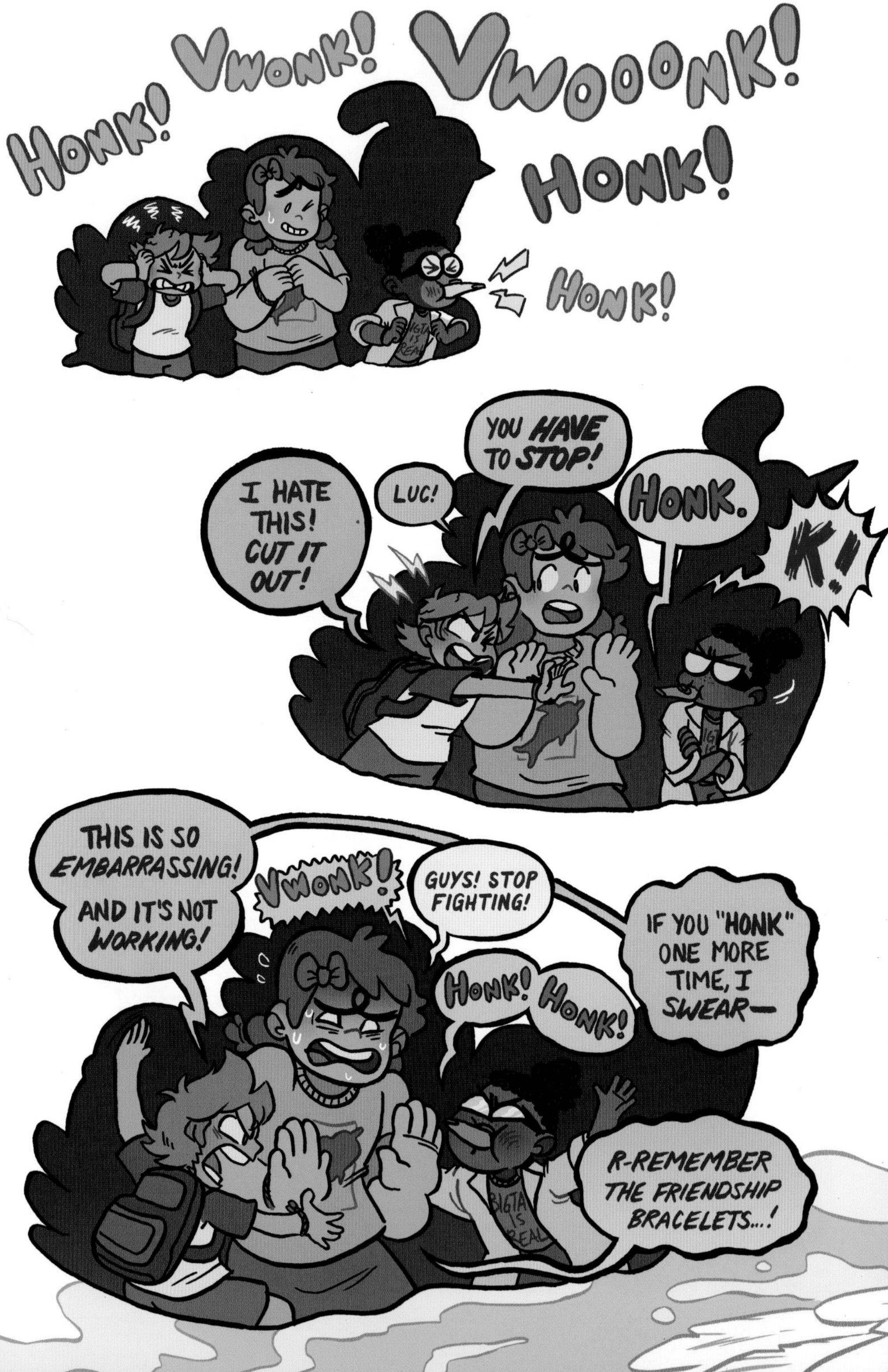
HONK! VWONK! VWOOONK! HONK!
HONK!
I HATE THIS! CUT IT OUT!
LUC!
YOU HAVE TO STOP!
HONK.
K!
THIS IS SO EMBARRASSING! AND IT'S NOT WORKING!
VWONK!
GUYS! STOP FIGHTING!
HONK! HONK!
IF YOU "HONK" ONE MORE TIME, I SWEAR—
R-REMEMBER THE FRIENDSHIP BRACELETS...!

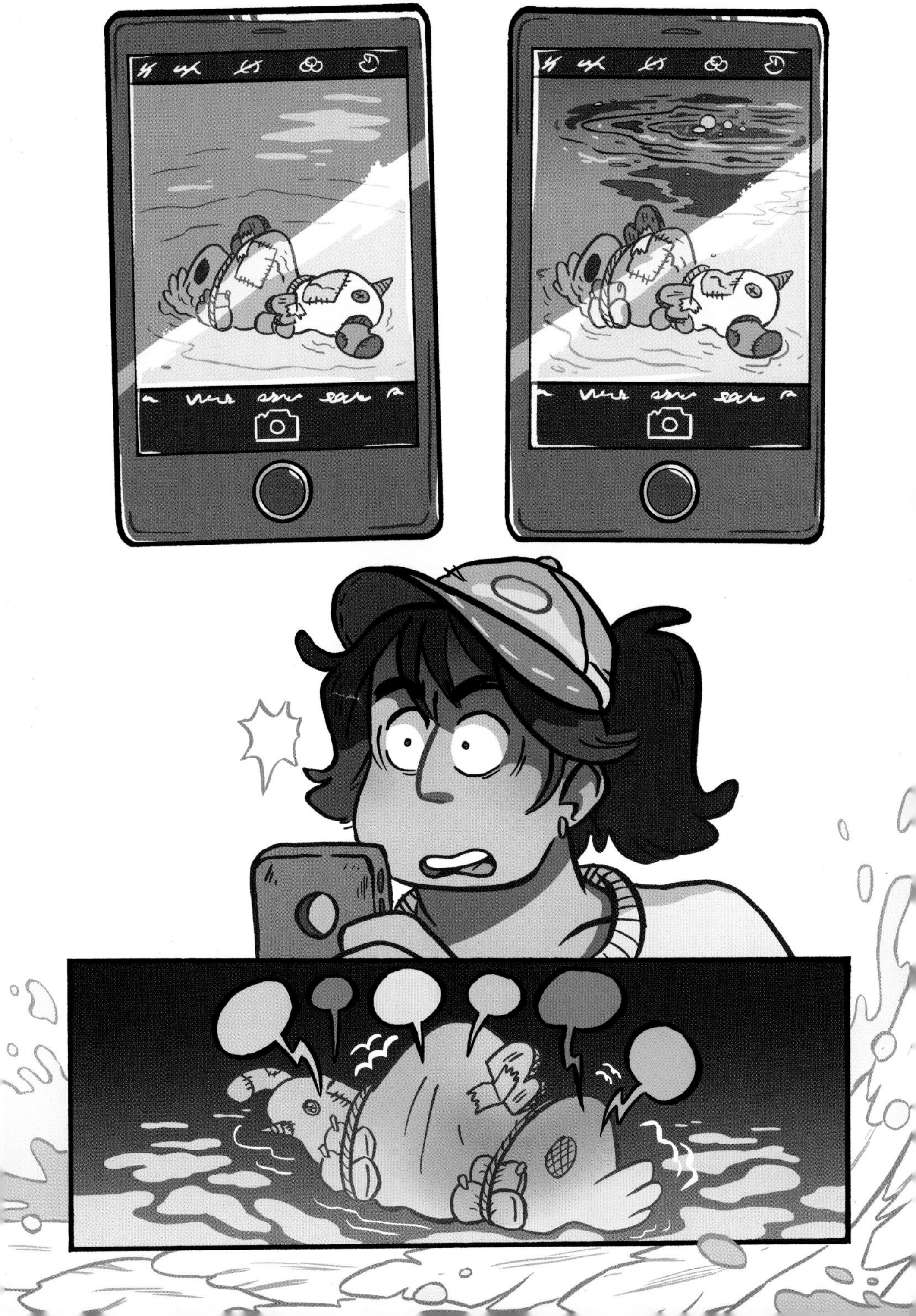

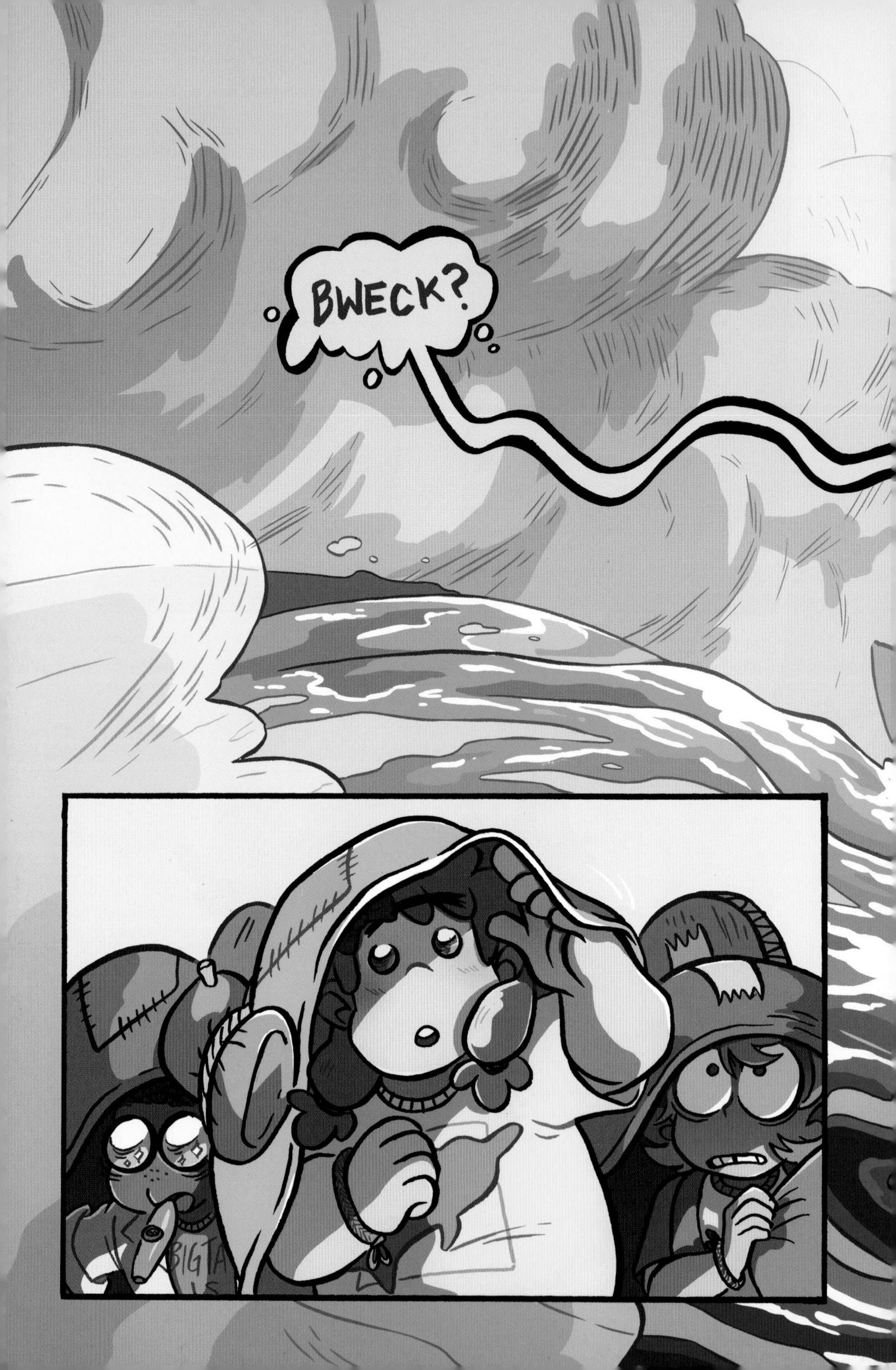
BWECK?

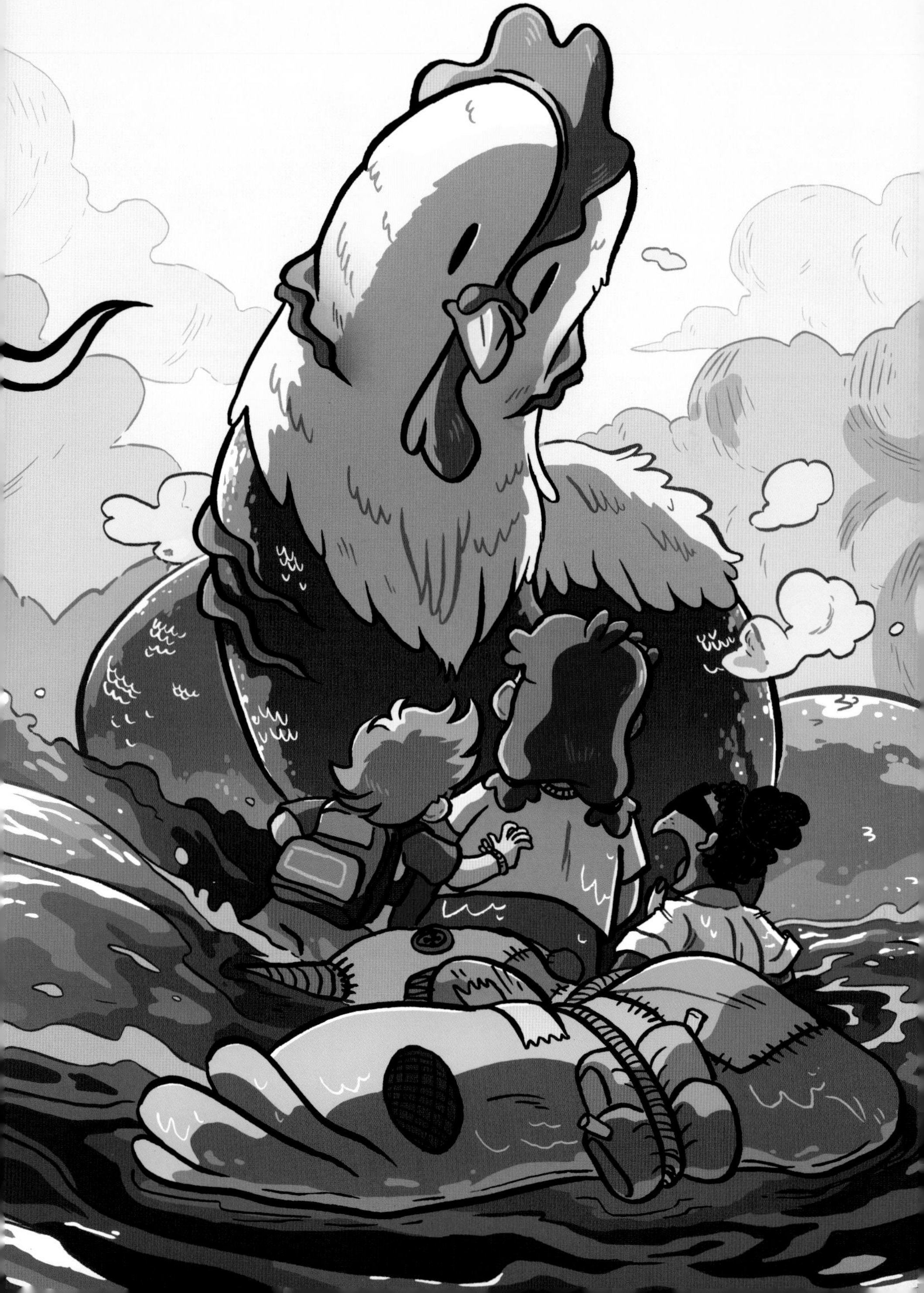

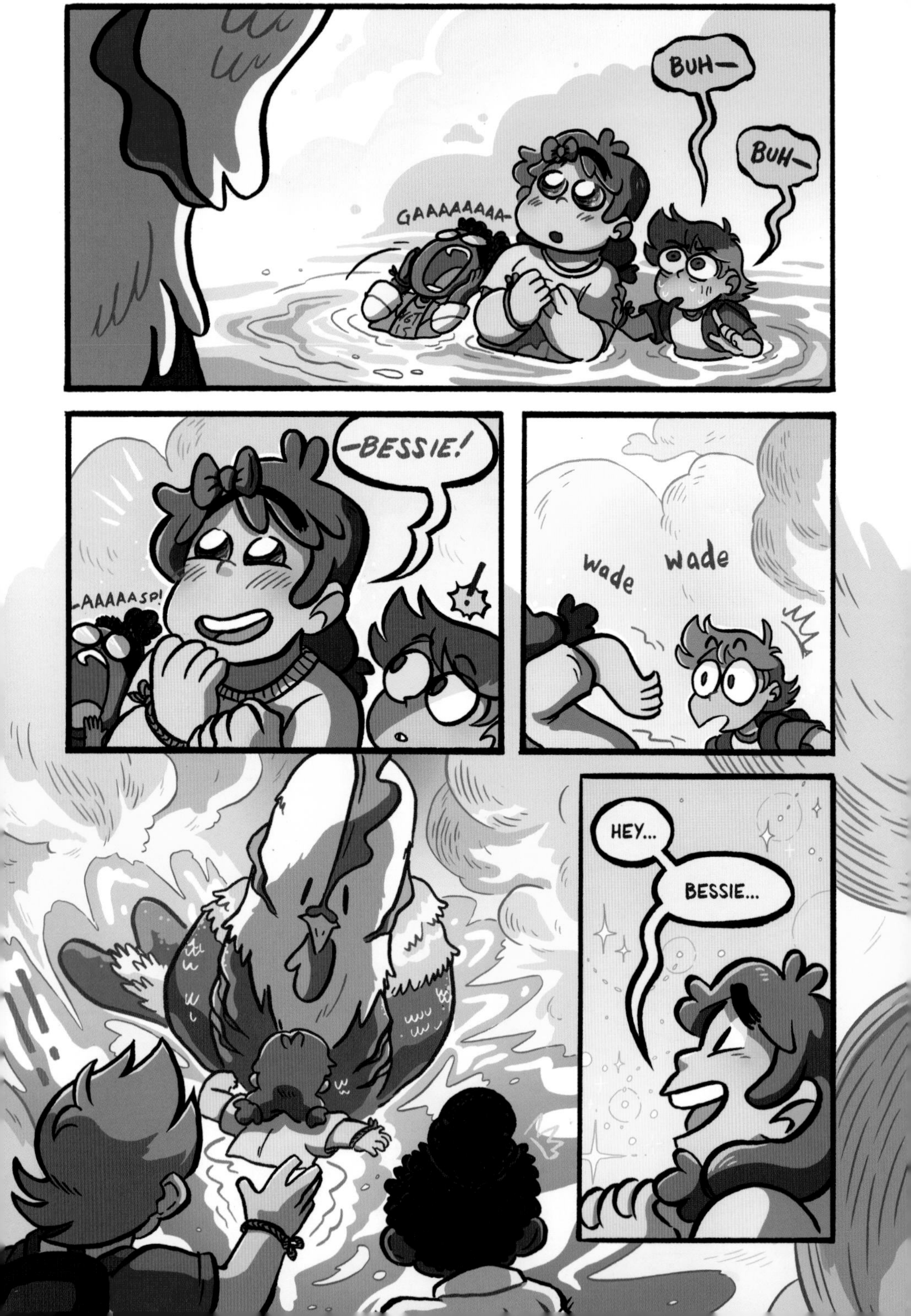
BUH—
BUH—
GAAAAAAAA-
—BESSIE!
-AAAAASP!
wade
wade
HEY...
BESSIE...

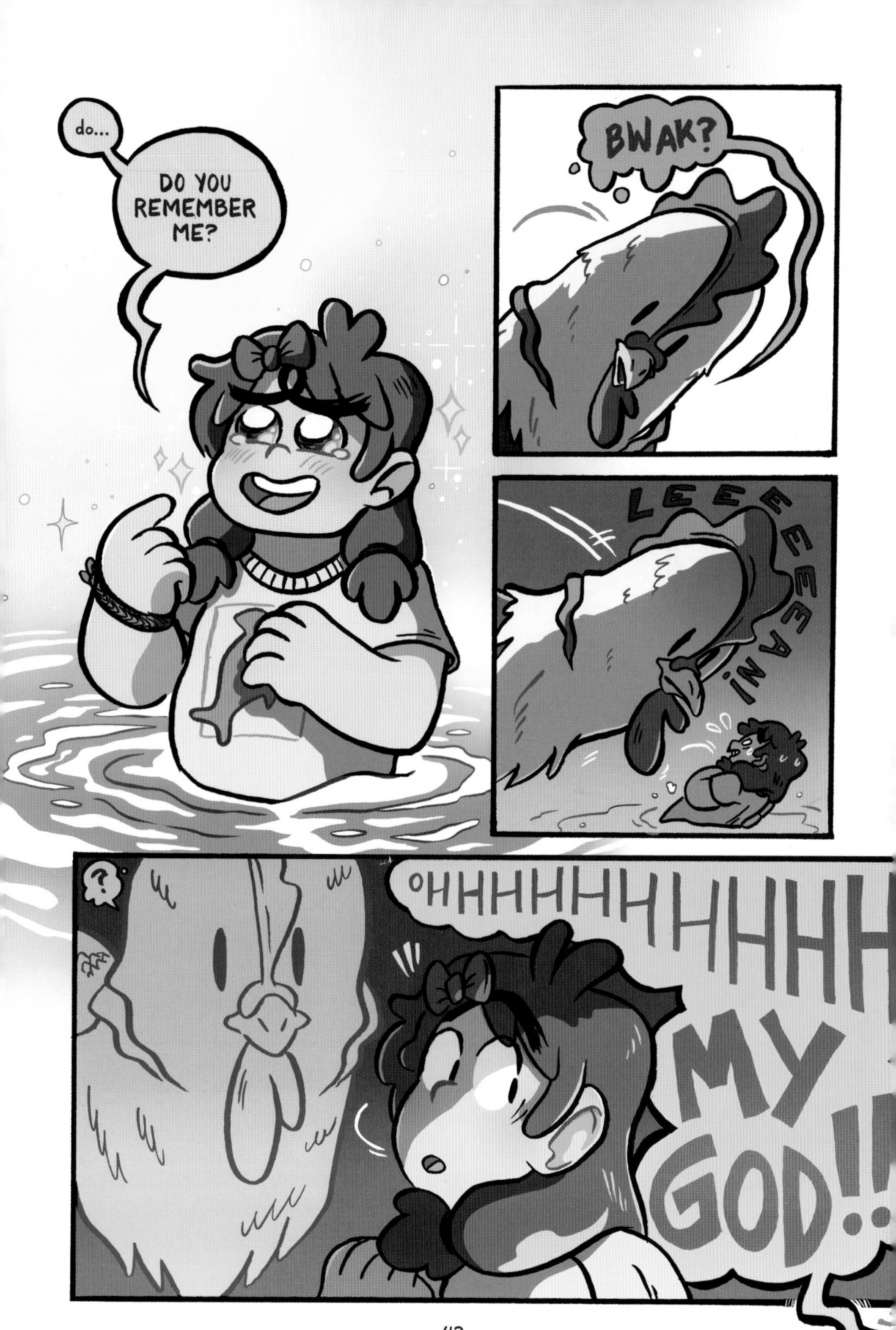
do...
DO YOU REMEMBER ME?
BWAK?
LEEEEEEEAN!
?
OHHHHHHHHHH
MY GOD!!

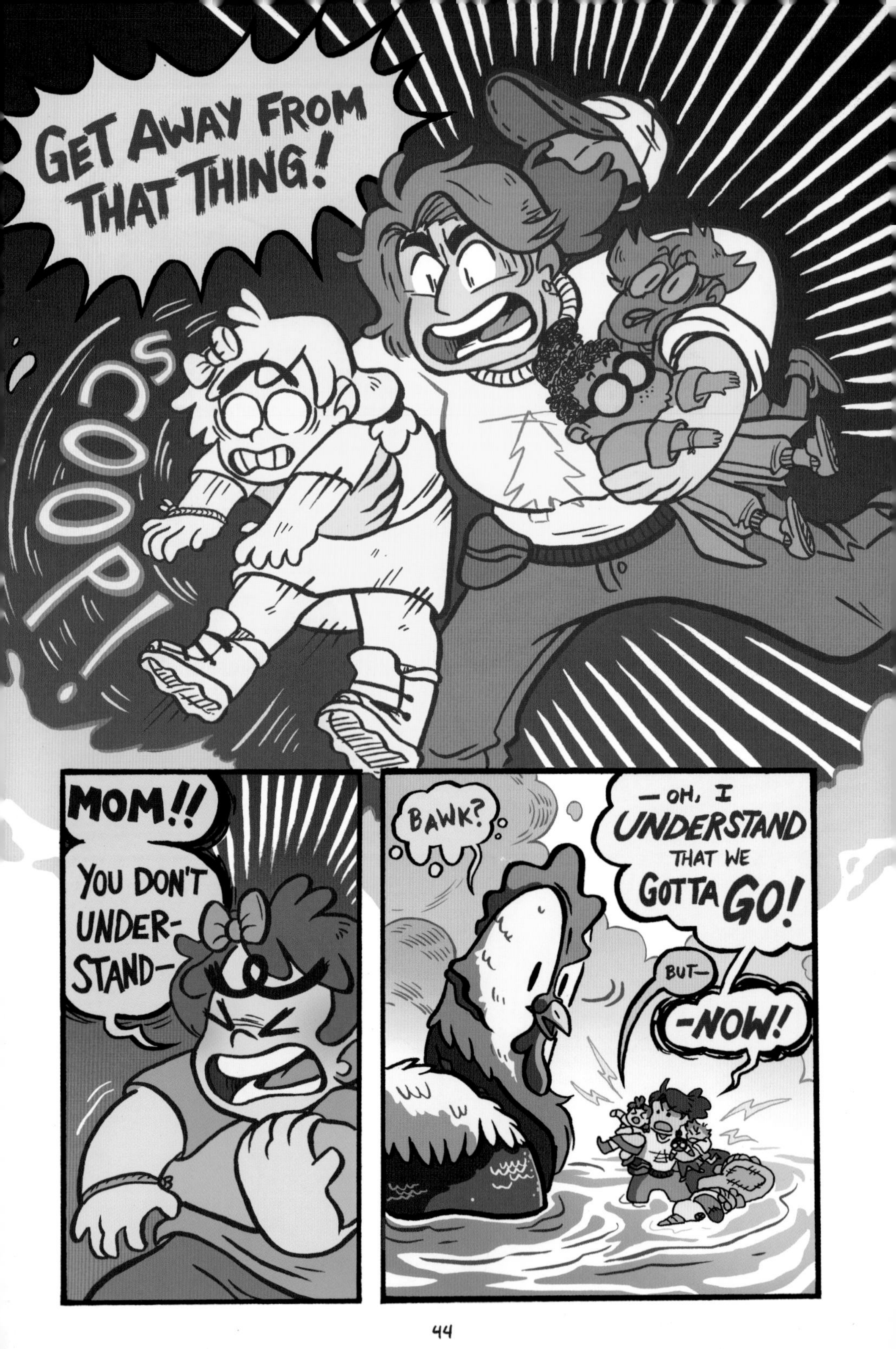
GET AWAY FROM THAT THING!
SCOOOP!
MOM!!
YOU DON'T UNDER-STAND-
BAWK?
—OH, I UNDERSTAND THAT WE GOTTA GO!
BUT—
-NOW!

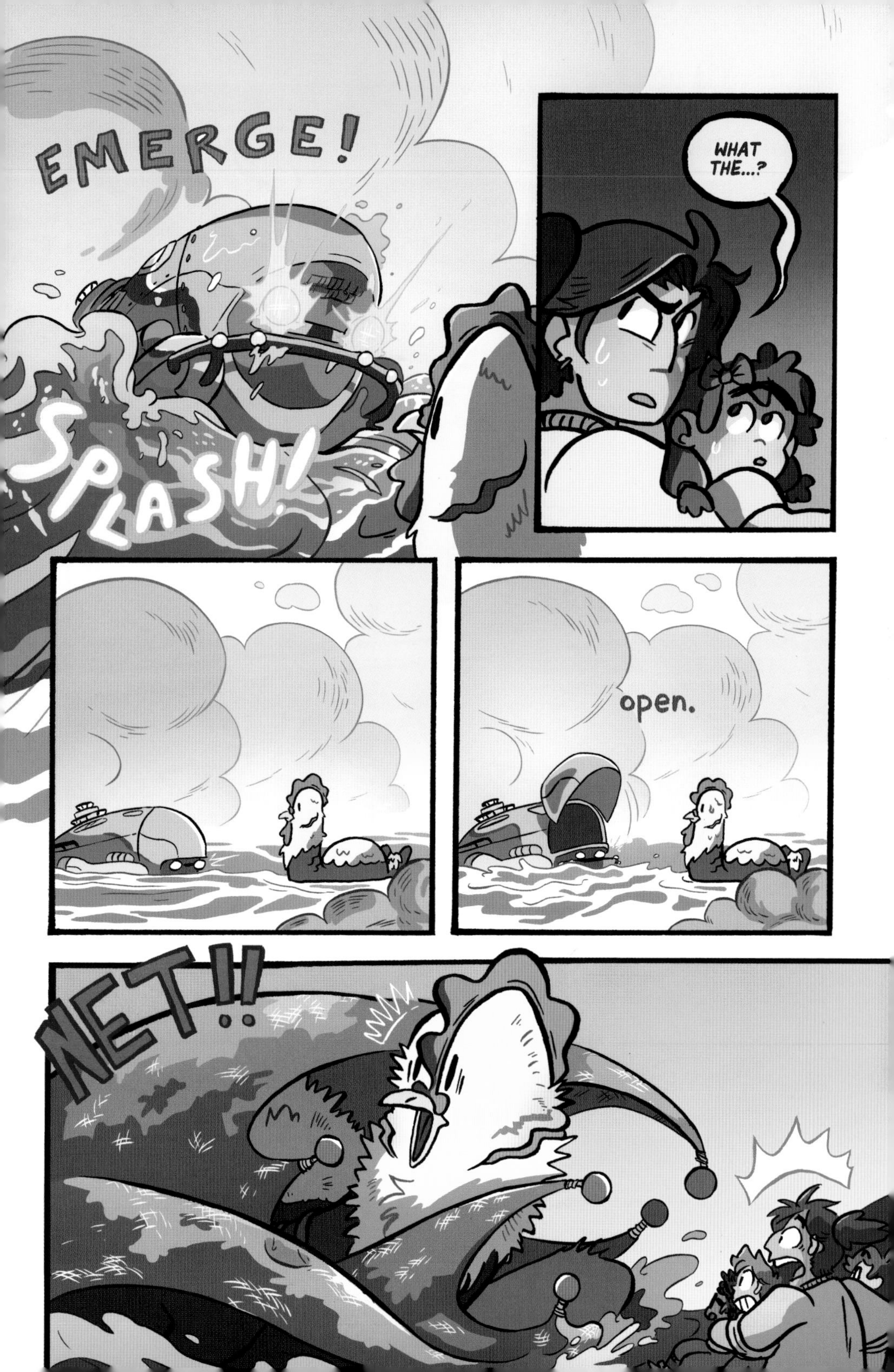
EMERGE!
SPLASH!
WHAT THE...?
open.
NET!!

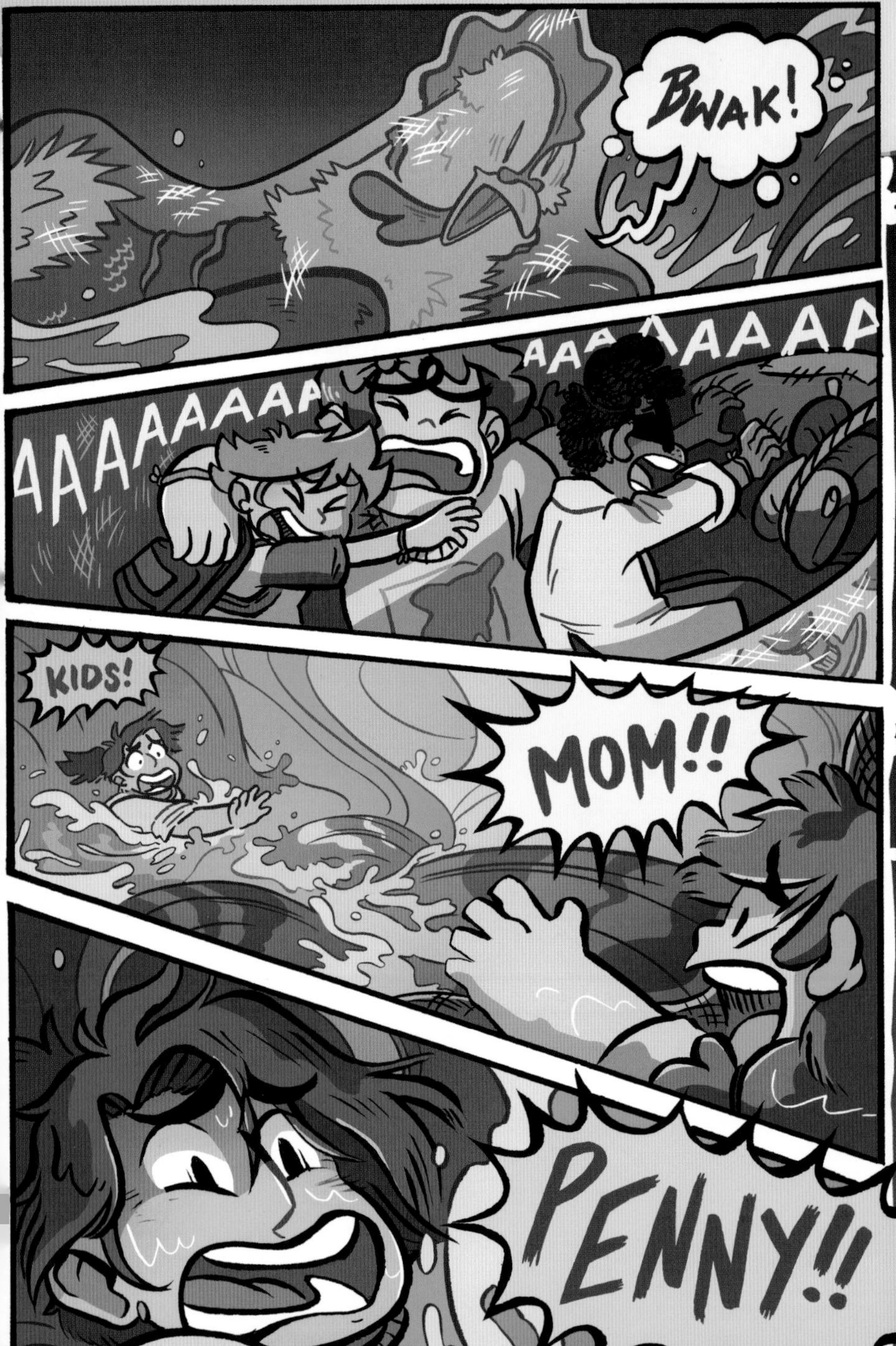
BWAK!
AAAAAAAAAAAAAAAAAAA
KIDS!
MOM!!
PENNY!!

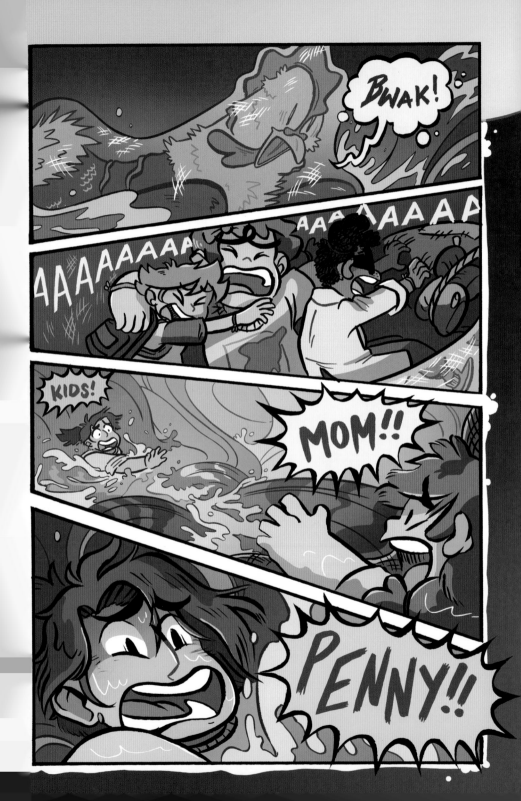

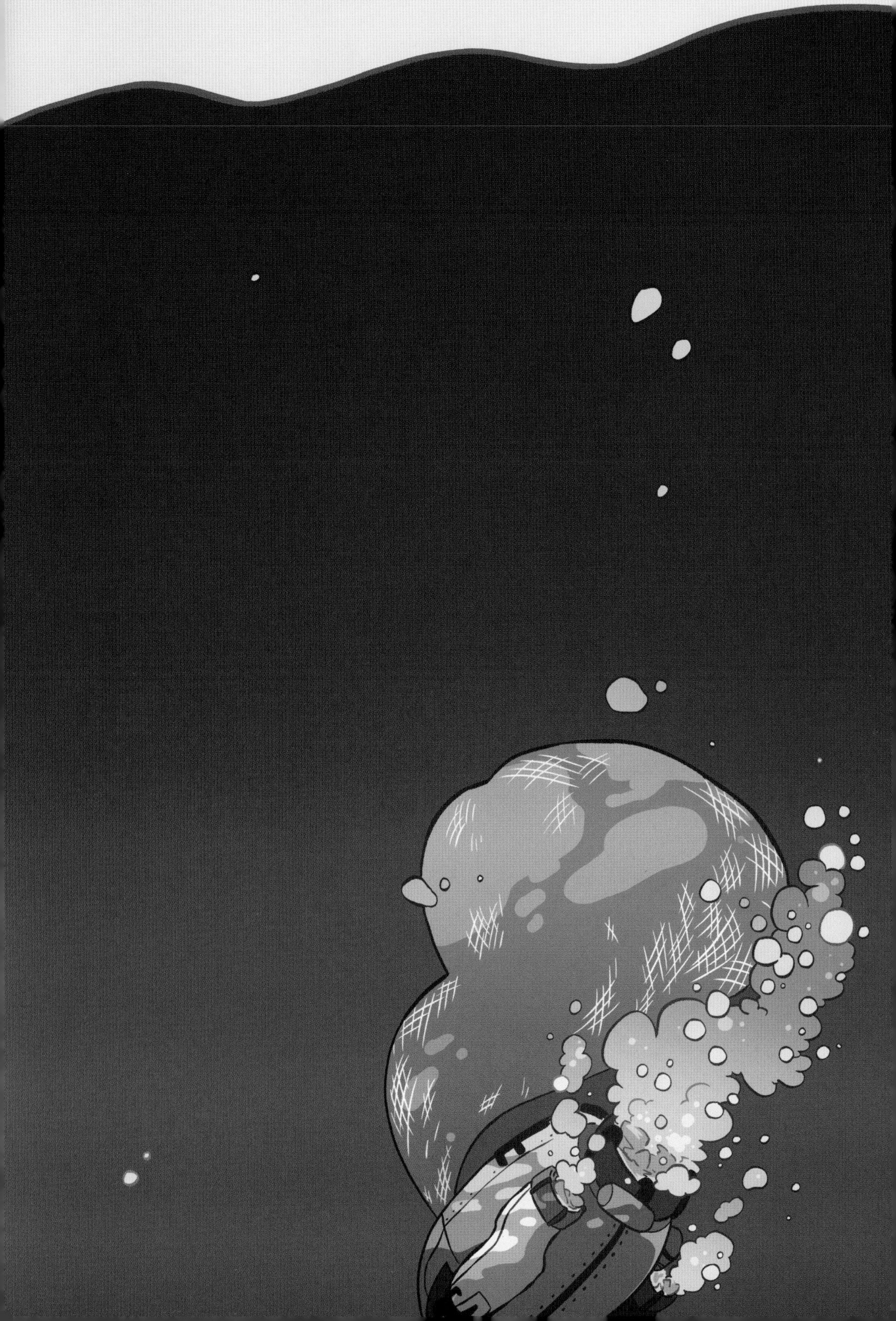

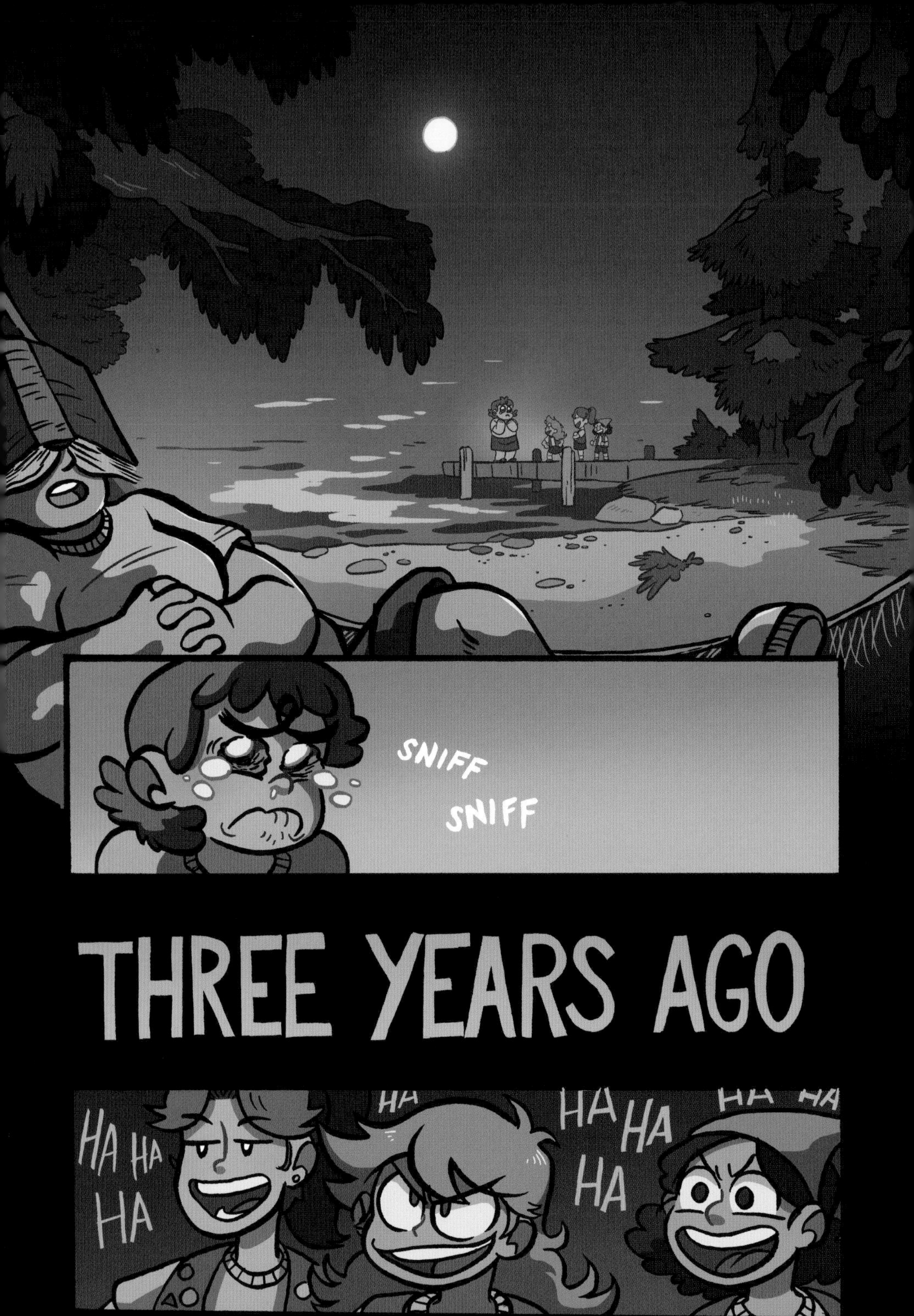
SNIFF
SNIFF
THREE YEARS AGO
HA HA HA
HA
HA HA HA
HA HA

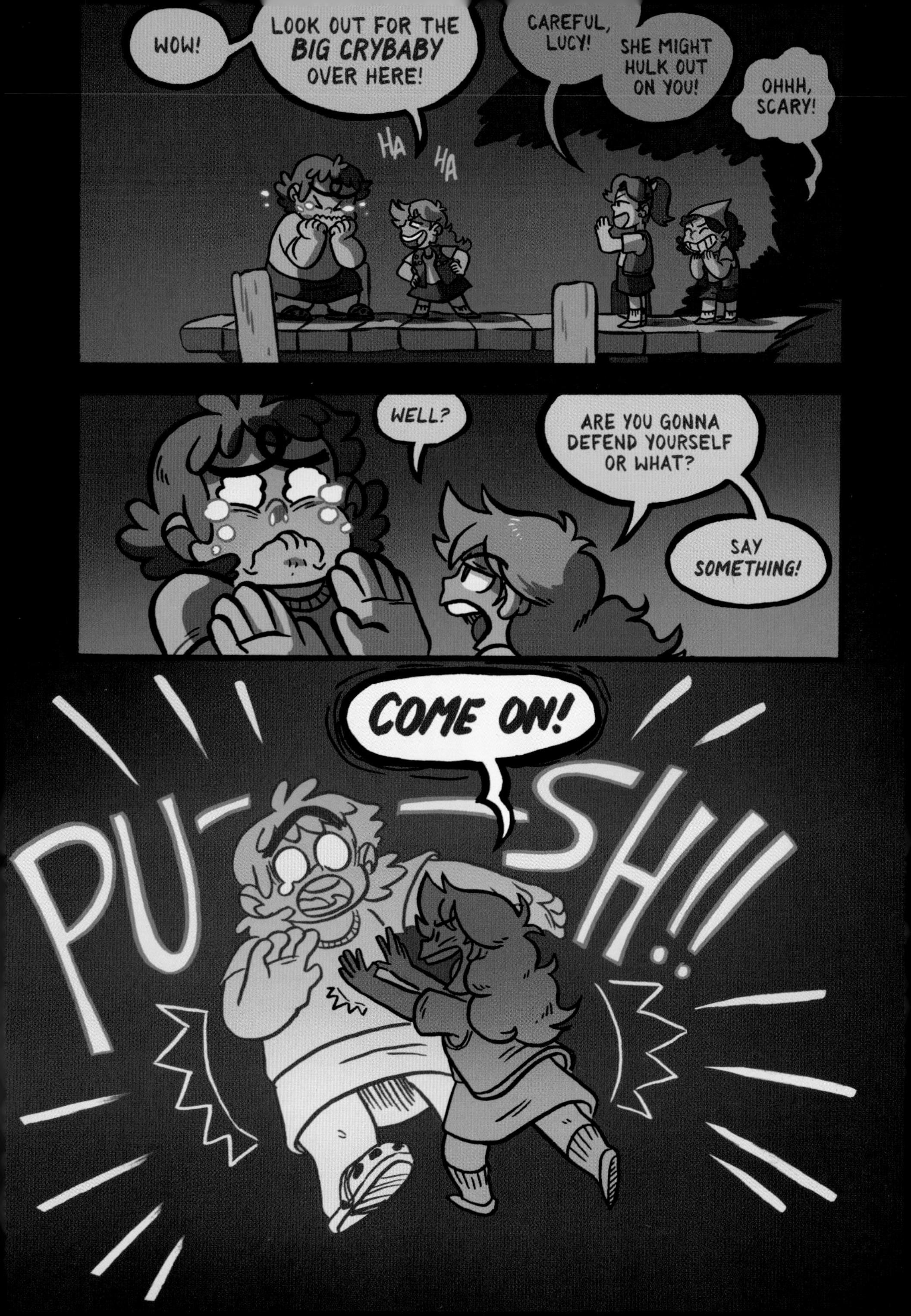
WOW!
LOOK OUT FOR THE BIG CRYBABY OVER HERE!
CAREFUL, LUCY!
SHE MIGHT HULK OUT ON YOU!
OHHH, SCARY!
HA HA
WELL?
ARE YOU GONNA DEFEND YOURSELF OR WHAT?
SAY SOMETHING!
COME ON!
PU--SH!!

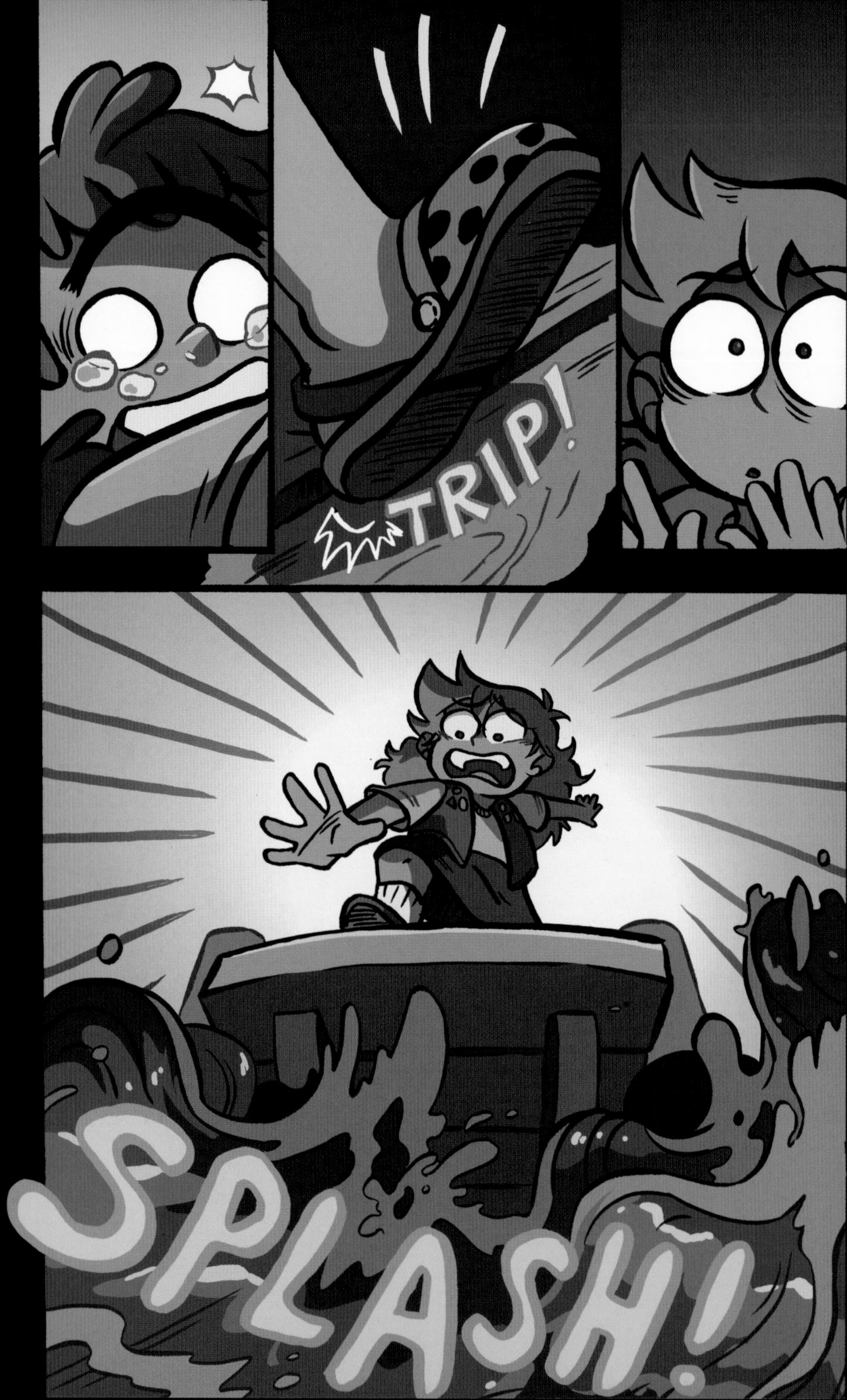
TRIP!
SPLASH!

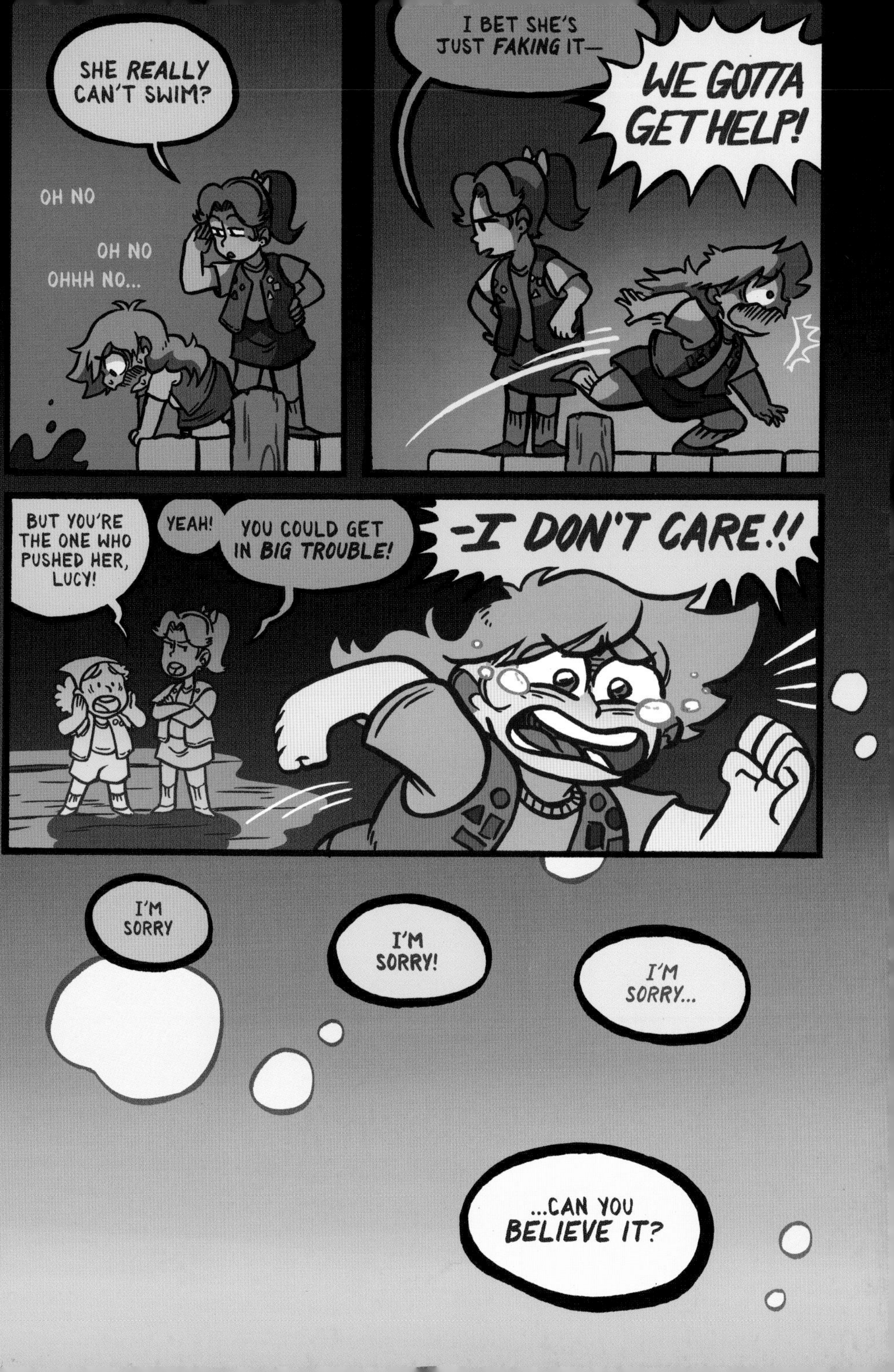
SHE REALLY CAN'T SWIM?
OH NO
OH NO
OHHH NO...
I BET SHE'S JUST FAKING IT—
WE GOTTA GET HELP!
BUT YOU'RE THE ONE WHO PUSHED HER, LUCY!
YEAH!
YOU COULD GET IN BIG TROUBLE!
—I DON'T CARE!!
I'M SORRY
I'M SORRY!
I'M SORRY...
...CAN YOU BELIEVE IT?

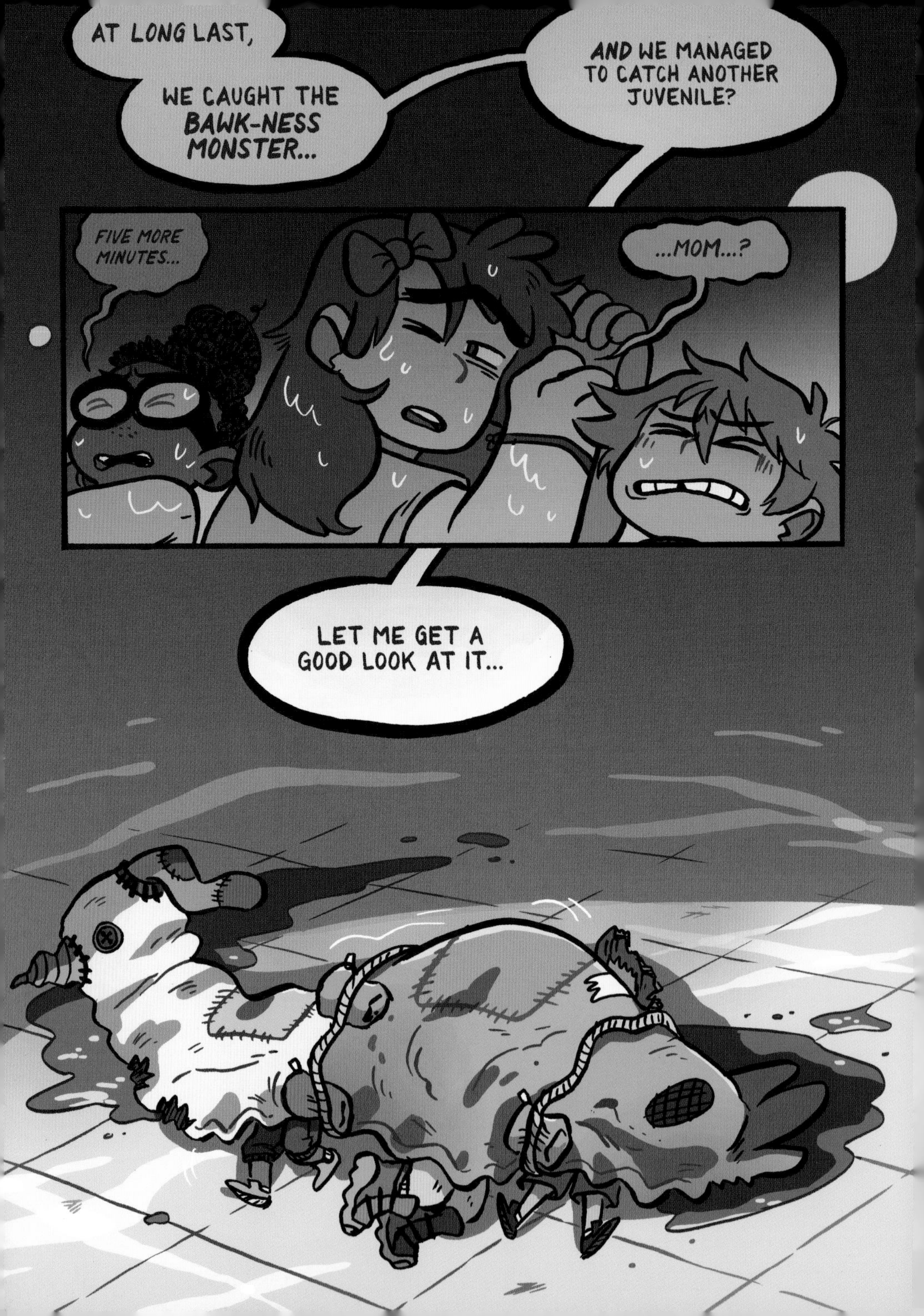
AT LONG LAST,
WE CAUGHT THE BAWK-NESS MONSTER...
AND WE MANAGED TO CATCH ANOTHER JUVENILE?
FIVE MORE MINUTES...
...MOM...?
LET ME GET A GOOD LOOK AT IT...

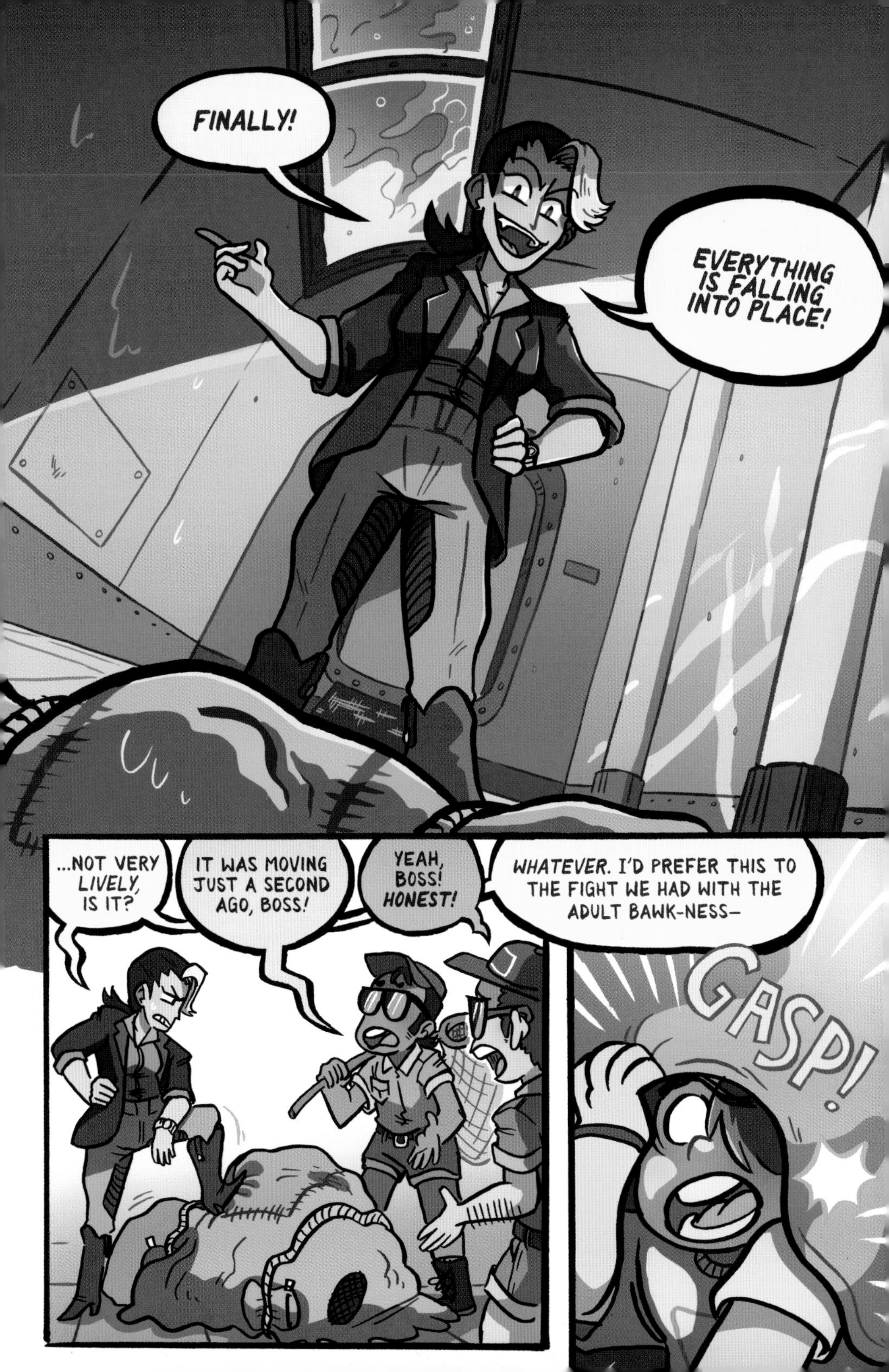

FINALLY!
EVERYTHING IS FALLING INTO PLACE!
...NOT VERY LIVELY, IS IT?
IT WAS MOVING JUST A SECOND AGO, BOSS!
YEAH, BOSS! HONEST!
WHATEVER. I'D PREFER THIS TO THE FIGHT WE HAD WITH THE ADULT BAWK-NESS—
GASP!

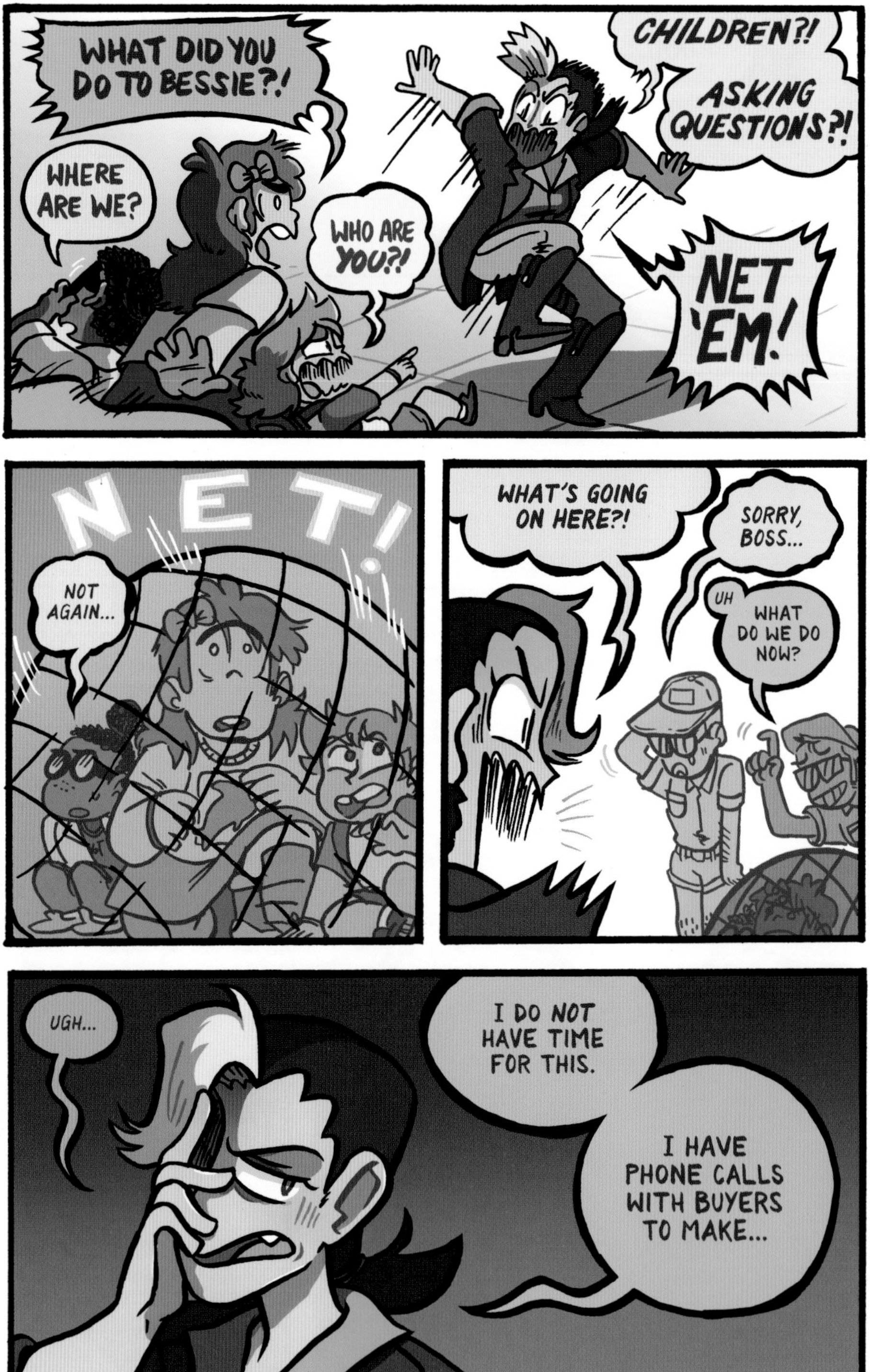
WHAT DID YOU DO TO BESSIE?!
WHERE ARE WE?
WHO ARE YOU?!
CHILDREN?!
ASKING QUESTIONS?!
NET 'EM!
NET!
NOT AGAIN...
WHAT'S GOING ON HERE?!
SORRY, BOSS...
UH
WHAT DO WE DO NOW?
UGH...
I DO NOT HAVE TIME FOR THIS.
I HAVE PHONE CALLS WITH BUYERS TO MAKE...

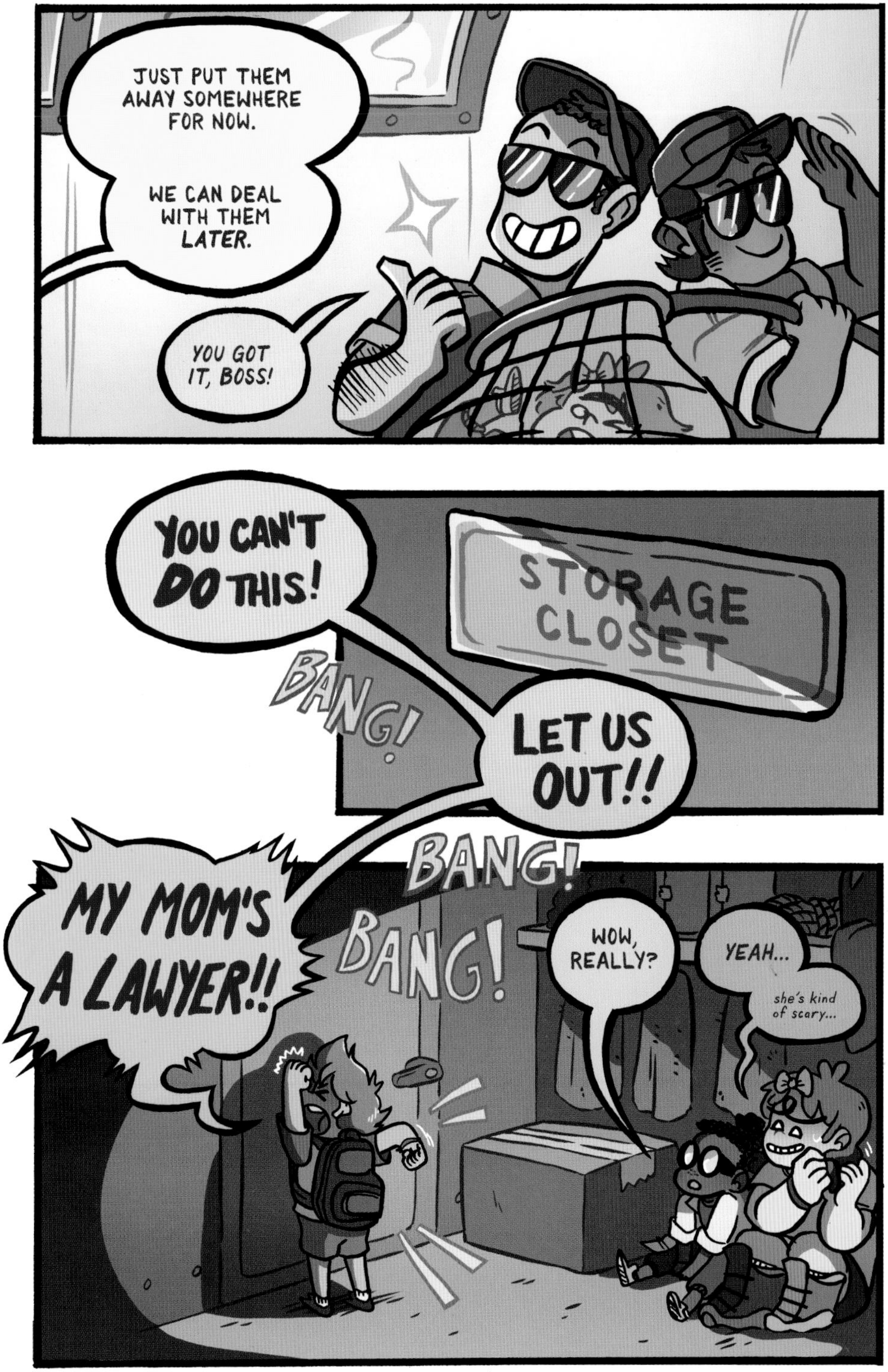
JUST PUT THEM AWAY SOMEWHERE FOR NOW.
WE CAN DEAL WITH THEM LATER.
YOU GOT IT, BOSS!
STORAGE CLOSET
YOU CAN'T DO THIS!
BANG!
LET US OUT!!
BANG!
MY MOM'S A LAWYER!!
BANG!
WOW, REALLY?
YEAH...
she's kind of scary...

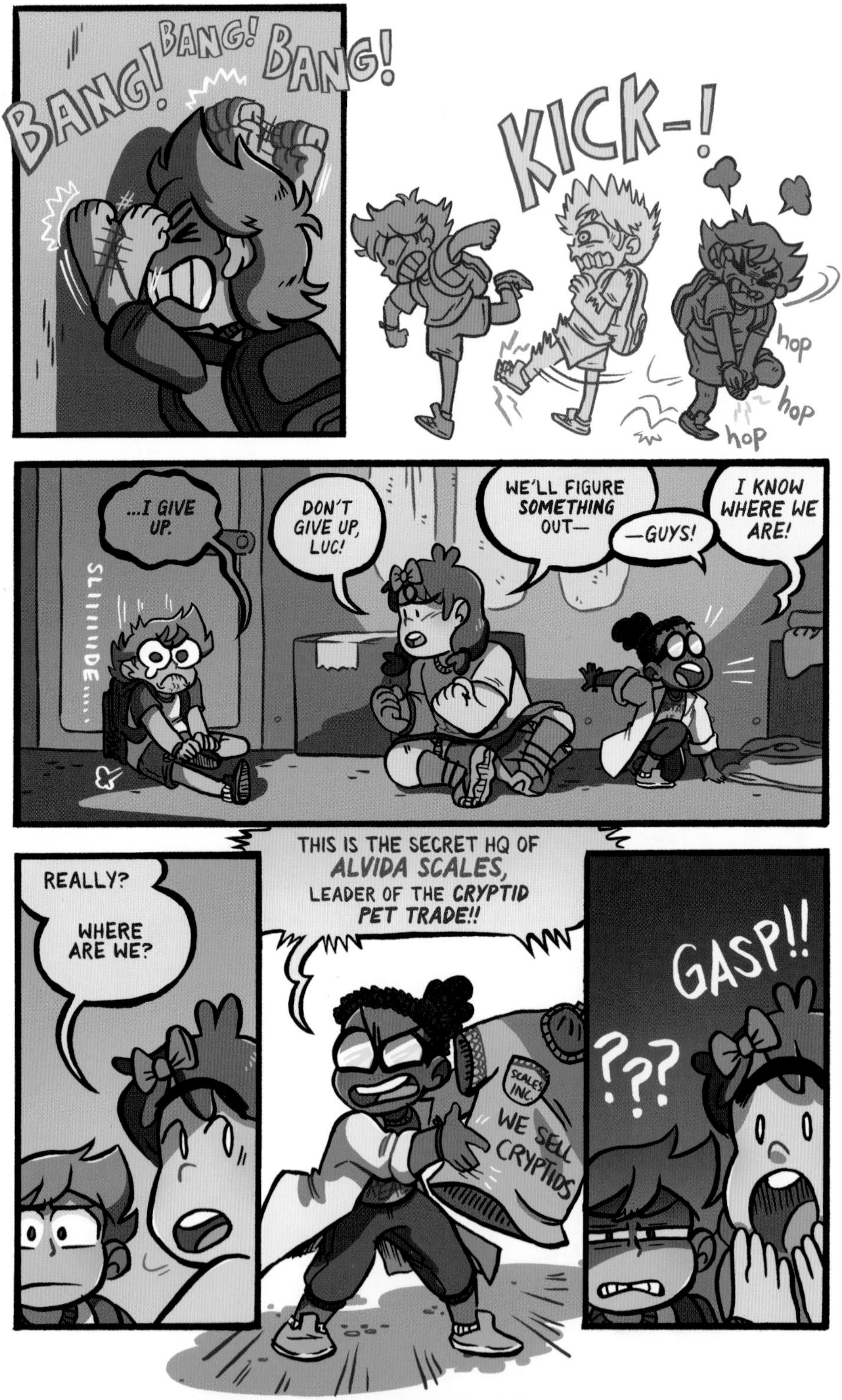
BANG! BANG! BANG!
KICK-!
hop
hop
hop
...I GIVE UP.
SLIIIIIIDE....
DON'T GIVE UP, LUC!
WE'LL FIGURE SOMETHING OUT—
—GUYS!
I KNOW WHERE WE ARE!
REALLY?
WHERE ARE WE?
THIS IS THE SECRET HQ OF ALVIDA SCALES, LEADER OF THE CRYPTID PET TRADE!!
SCALES INC.
WE SELL CRYPTIDS
GASP!!
???

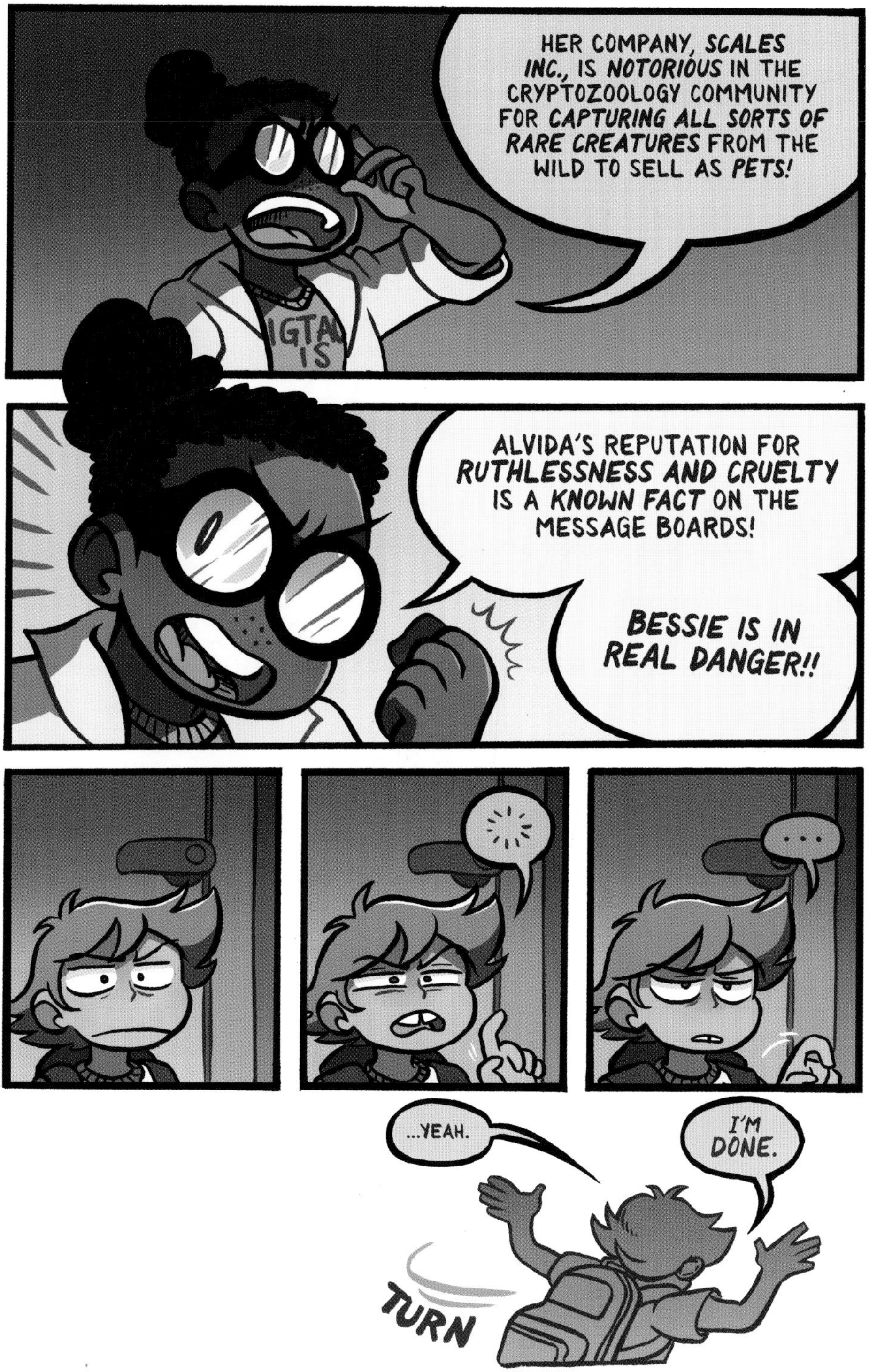
HER COMPANY, SCALES INC., IS NOTORIOUS IN THE CRYPTOZOOLOGY COMMUNITY FOR CAPTURING ALL SORTS OF RARE CREATURES FROM THE WILD TO SELL AS PETS!
ALVIDA'S REPUTATION FOR RUTHLESSNESS AND CRUELTY IS A KNOWN FACT ON THE MESSAGE BOARDS!
BESSIE IS IN REAL DANGER!!
...
...YEAH.
I'M DONE.
TURN

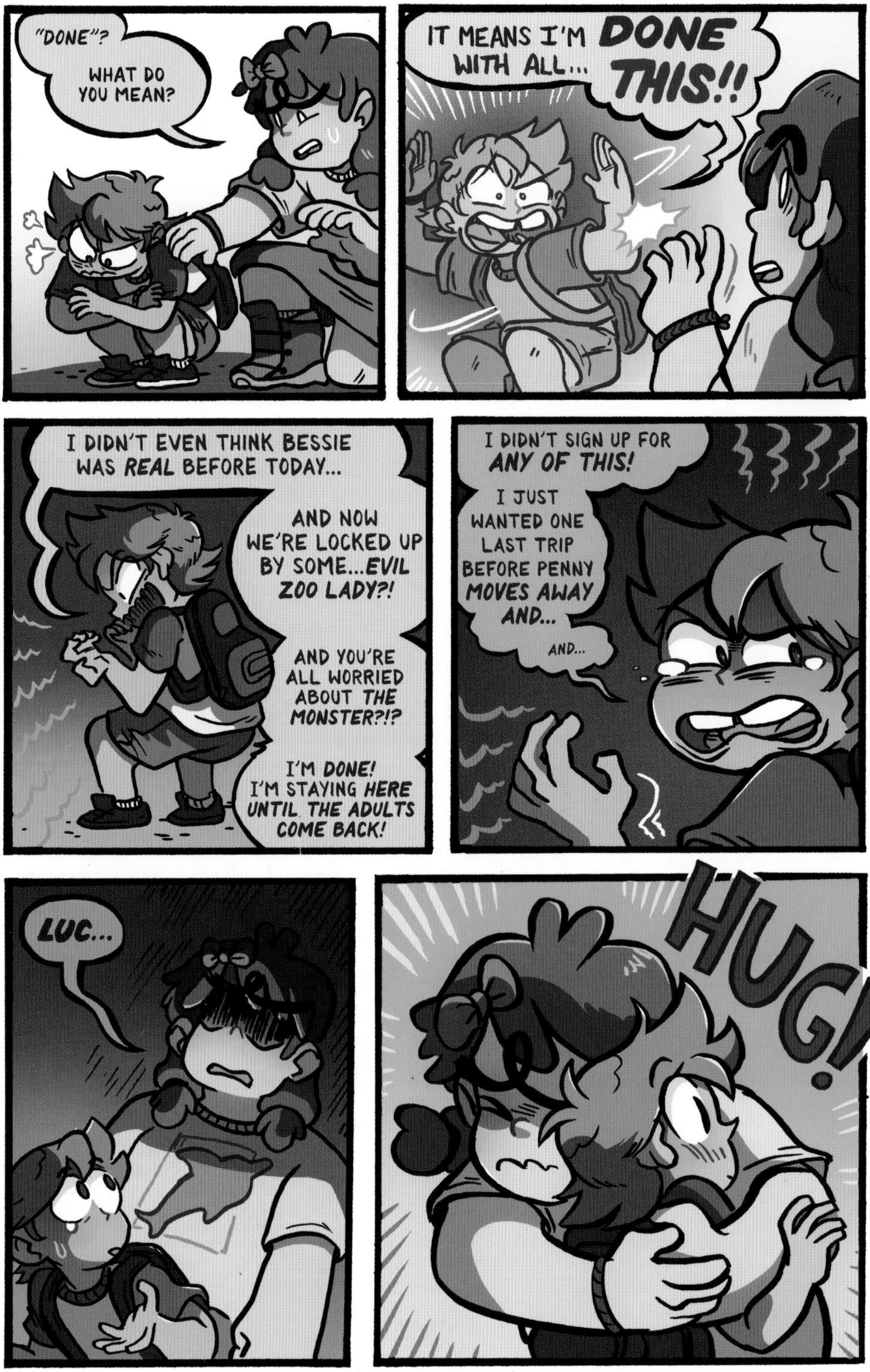
"DONE"?
WHAT DO YOU MEAN?
IT MEANS I'M DONE WITH ALL... THIS!!
I DIDN'T EVEN THINK BESSIE WAS REAL BEFORE TODAY...
AND NOW WE'RE LOCKED UP BY SOME...EVIL ZOO LADY?!
AND YOU'RE ALL WORRIED ABOUT THE MONSTER?!?
I'M DONE! I'M STAYING HERE UNTIL THE ADULTS COME BACK!
I DIDN'T SIGN UP FOR ANY OF THIS!
I JUST WANTED ONE LAST TRIP BEFORE PENNY MOVES AWAY AND...
AND...
LUC...
HUG!

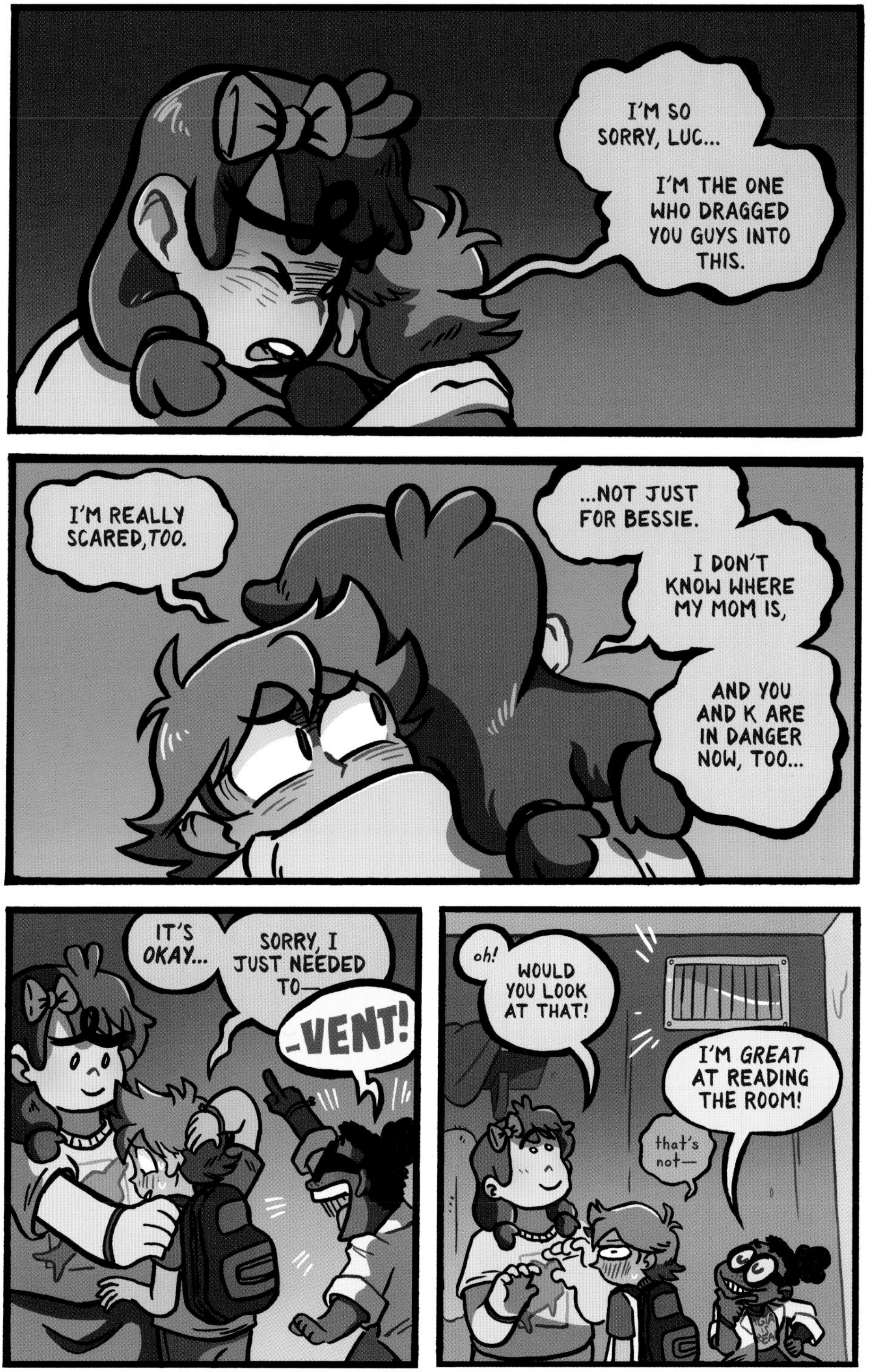
I'M SO SORRY, LUC...
I'M THE ONE WHO DRAGGED YOU GUYS INTO THIS.
I'M REALLY SCARED, TOO.
...NOT JUST FOR BESSIE.
I DON'T KNOW WHERE MY MOM IS,
AND YOU AND K ARE IN DANGER NOW, TOO...
IT'S OKAY...
SORRY, I JUST NEEDED TO—
—VENT!
oh!
WOULD YOU LOOK AT THAT!
I'M GREAT AT READING THE ROOM!
that's not—

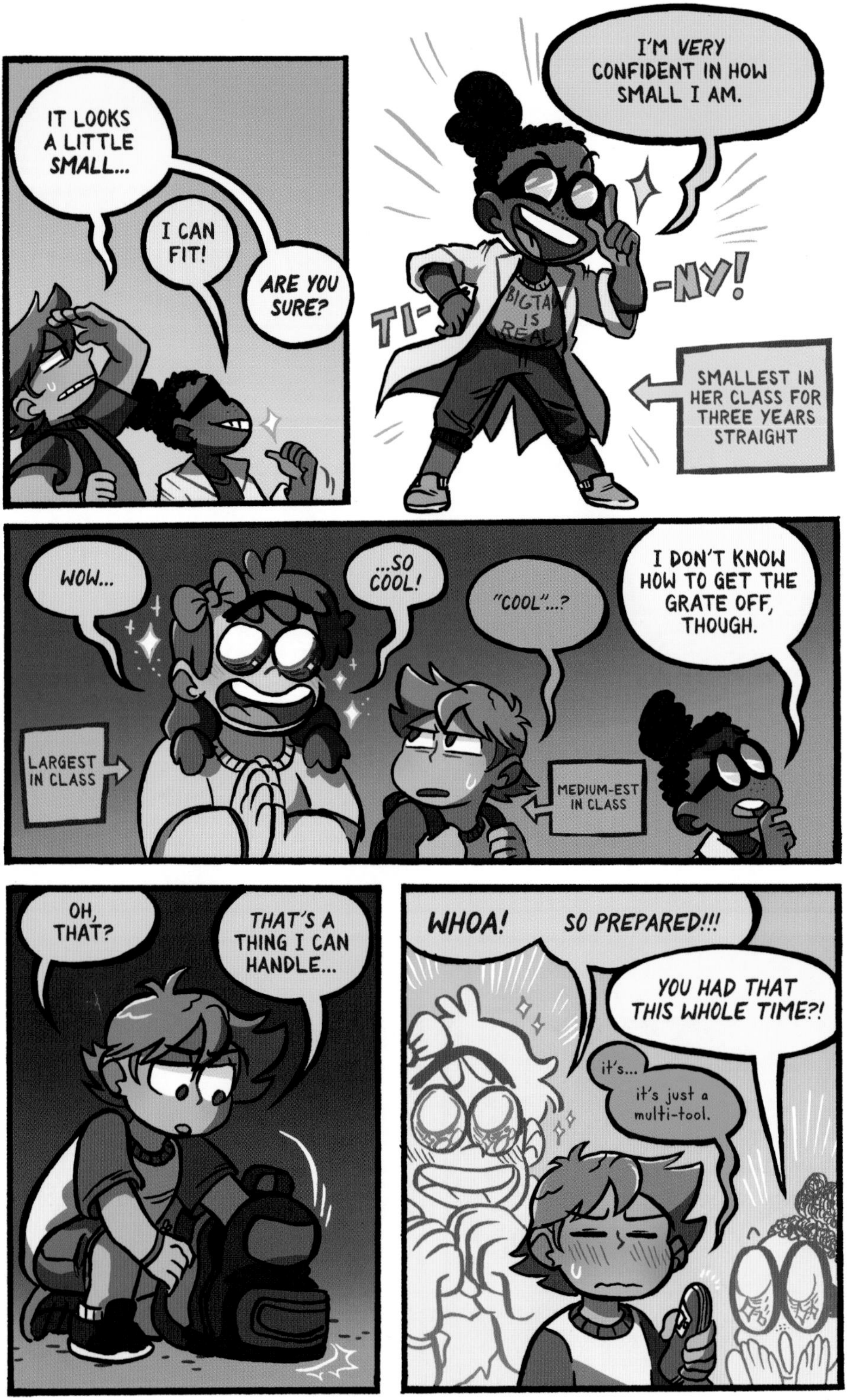
IT LOOKS A LITTLE SMALL...
I CAN FIT!
ARE YOU SURE?
I'M VERY CONFIDENT IN HOW SMALL I AM.
TI- -NY!
BIGTAU IS REAL
SMALLEST IN HER CLASS FOR THREE YEARS STRAIGHT
WOW...
...SO COOL!
"COOL"...?
I DON'T KNOW HOW TO GET THE GRATE OFF, THOUGH.
LARGEST IN CLASS
MEDIUM-EST IN CLASS
OH, THAT?
THAT'S A THING I CAN HANDLE...
WHOA!
SO PREPARED!!!
YOU HAD THAT THIS WHOLE TIME?!
it's...
it's just a multi-tool.

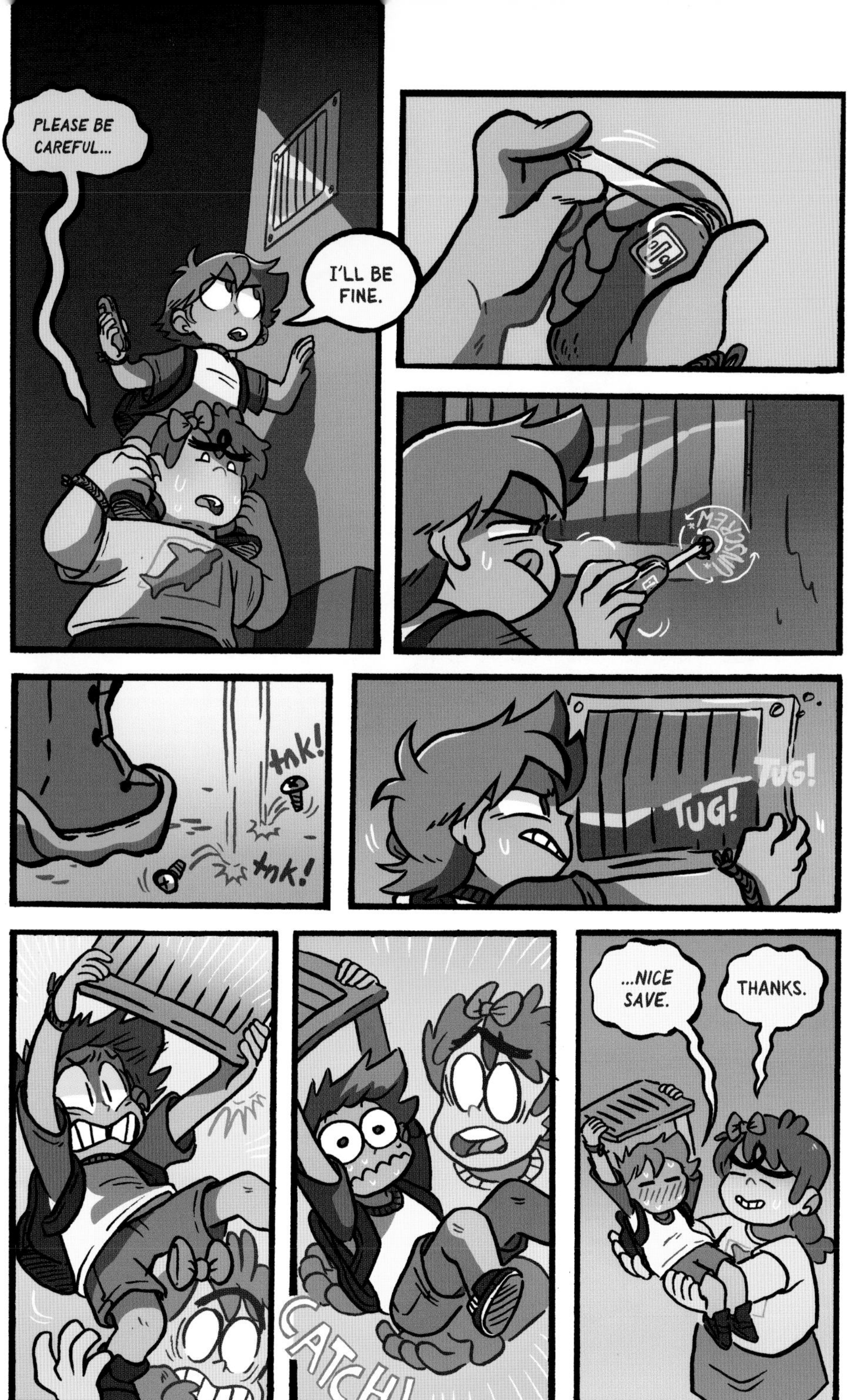
PLEASE BE CAREFUL...
I'LL BE FINE.
UNSCREW
tnk!
tnk!
TUG!
TUG!
CATCH!
...NICE SAVE.
THANKS.

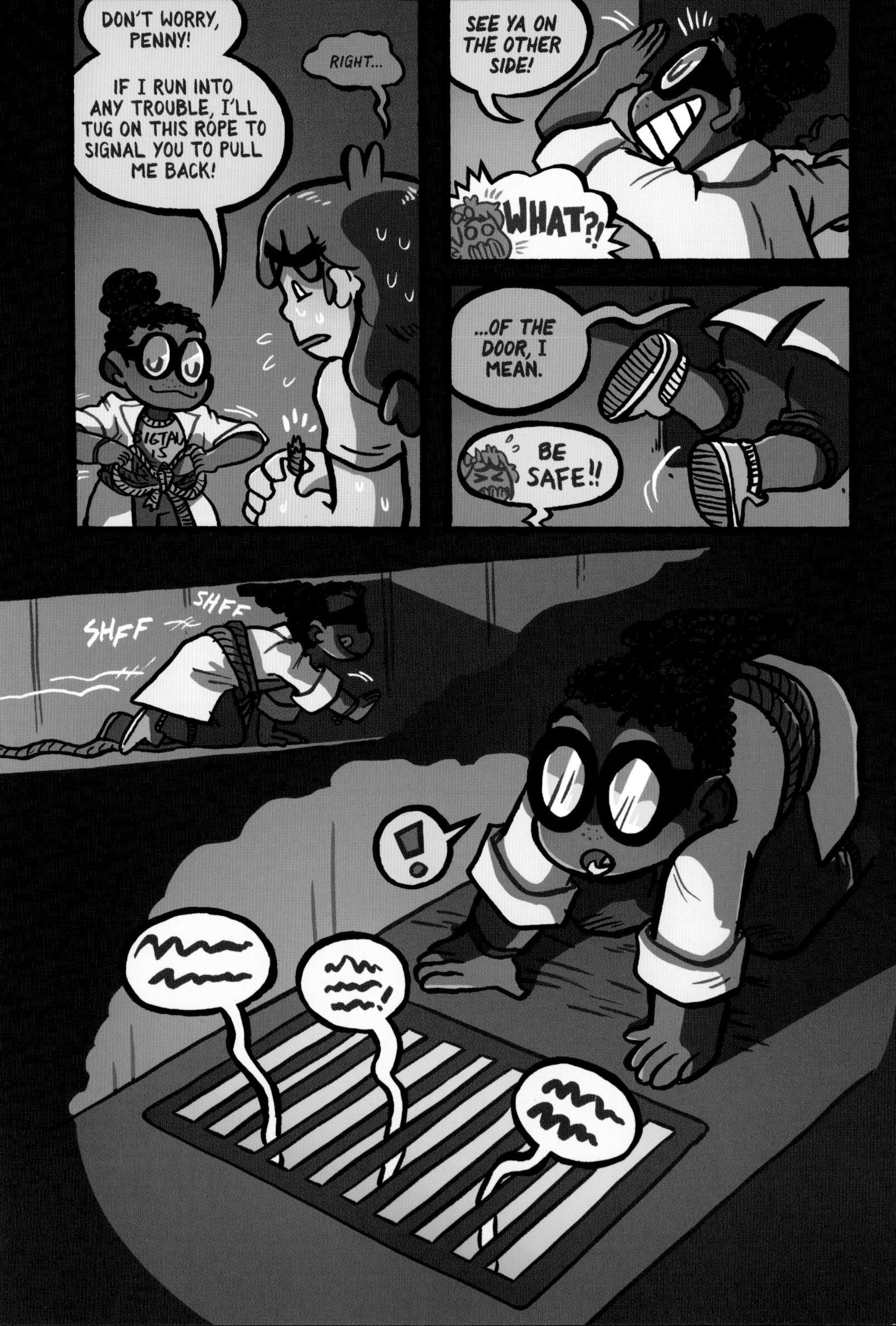
DON'T WORRY, PENNY!
IF I RUN INTO ANY TROUBLE, I'LL TUG ON THIS ROPE TO SIGNAL YOU TO PULL ME BACK!
RIGHT...
SEE YA ON THE OTHER SIDE!
WHAT?!
...OF THE DOOR, I MEAN.
BE SAFE!!
SHFF
SHFF
!

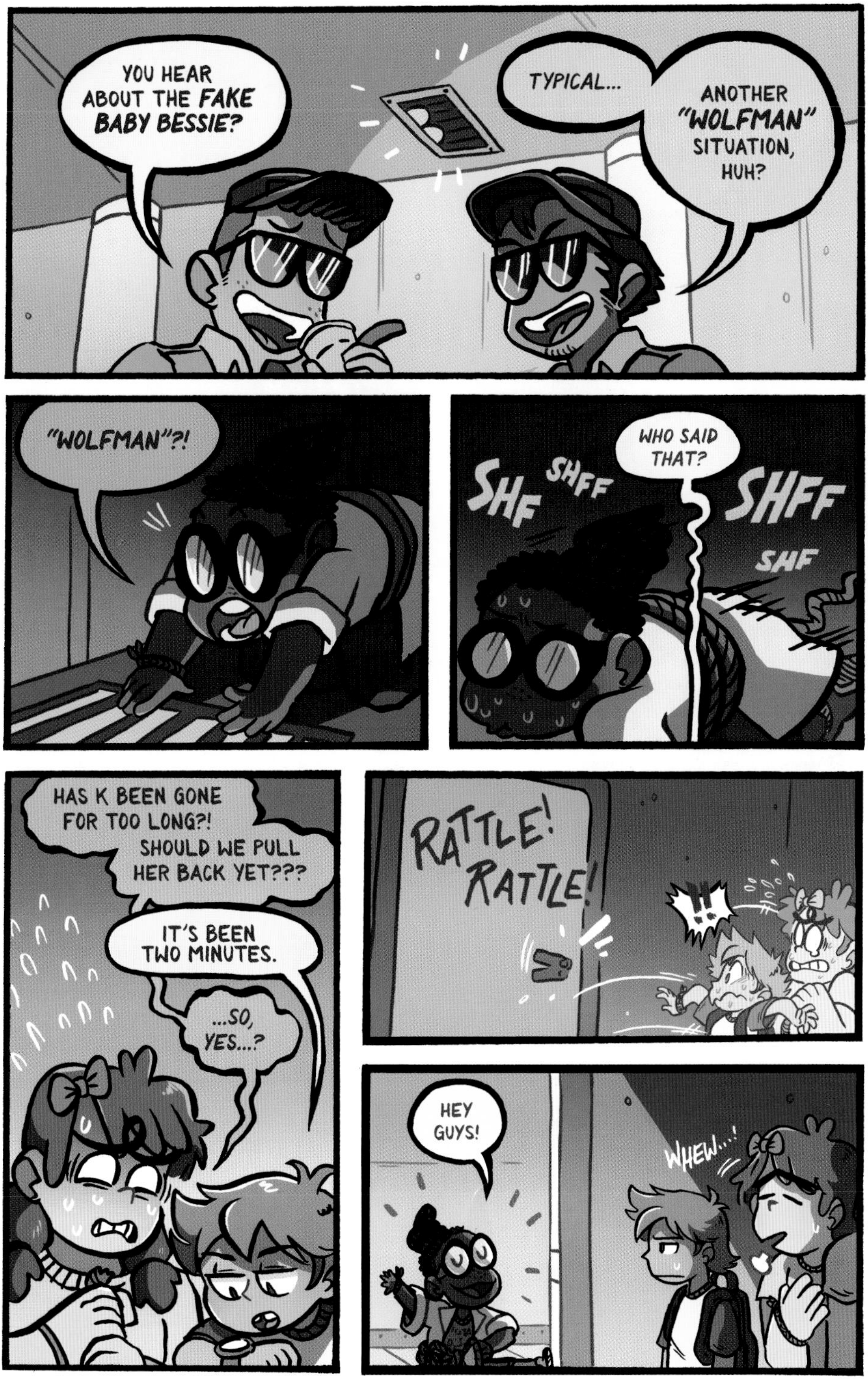
YOU HEAR ABOUT THE FAKE BABY BESSIE?
TYPICAL...
ANOTHER "WOLFMAN" SITUATION, HUH?
"WOLFMAN"?!
SHF
SHFF
WHO SAID THAT?
SHFF
SHF
HAS K BEEN GONE FOR TOO LONG?!
SHOULD WE PULL HER BACK YET???
IT'S BEEN TWO MINUTES.
...SO, YES...?
RATTLE! RATTLE!
HEY GUYS!
WHEW...!

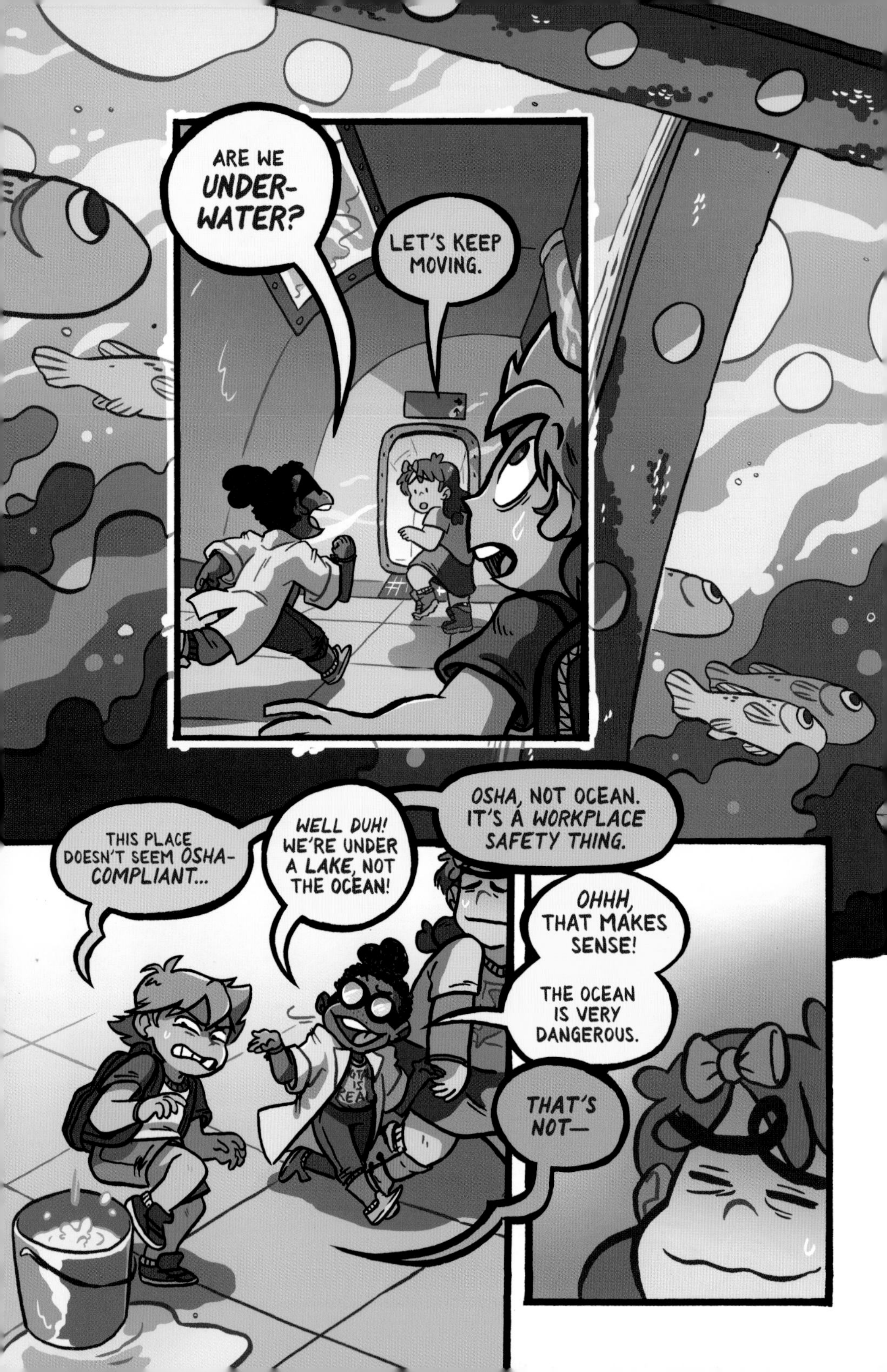
ARE WE UNDER-WATER?
LET'S KEEP MOVING.
THIS PLACE DOESN'T SEEM OSHA-COMPLIANT...
WELL DUH! WE'RE UNDER A LAKE, NOT THE OCEAN!
OSHA, NOT OCEAN. IT'S A WORKPLACE SAFETY THING.
OHHH, THAT MAKES SENSE!
THE OCEAN IS VERY DANGEROUS.
THAT'S NOT—

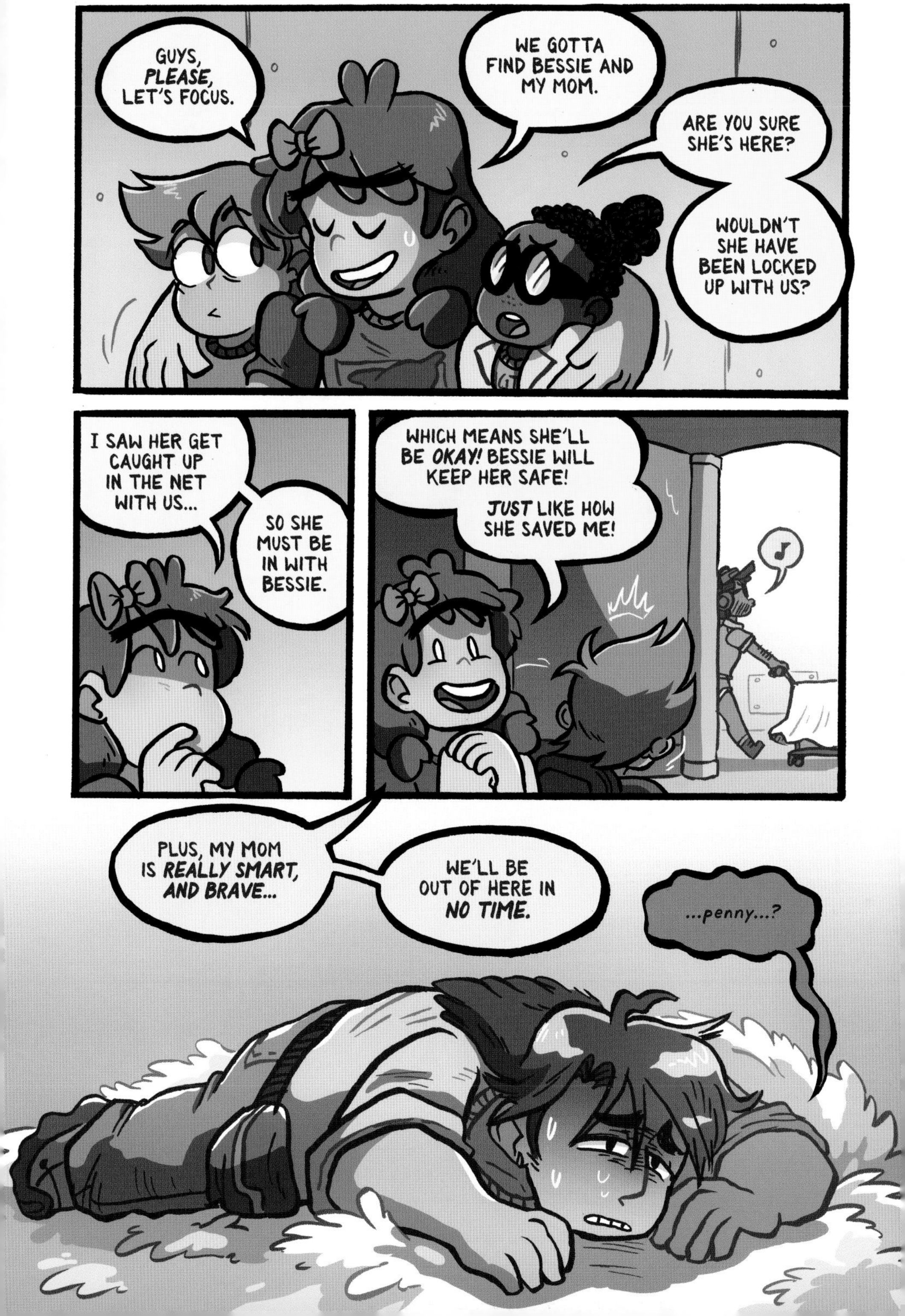
GUYS, *PLEASE,* LET'S FOCUS.
WE GOTTA FIND BESSIE AND MY MOM.
ARE YOU SURE SHE'S HERE?
WOULDN'T SHE HAVE BEEN LOCKED UP WITH US?
I SAW HER GET CAUGHT UP IN THE NET WITH US...
SO SHE MUST BE IN WITH BESSIE.
WHICH MEANS SHE'LL BE *OKAY!* BESSIE WILL KEEP HER SAFE!
JUST LIKE HOW SHE SAVED ME!
♪
PLUS, MY MOM IS *REALLY SMART, AND BRAVE...*
WE'LL BE OUT OF HERE IN *NO TIME.*
...penny...?

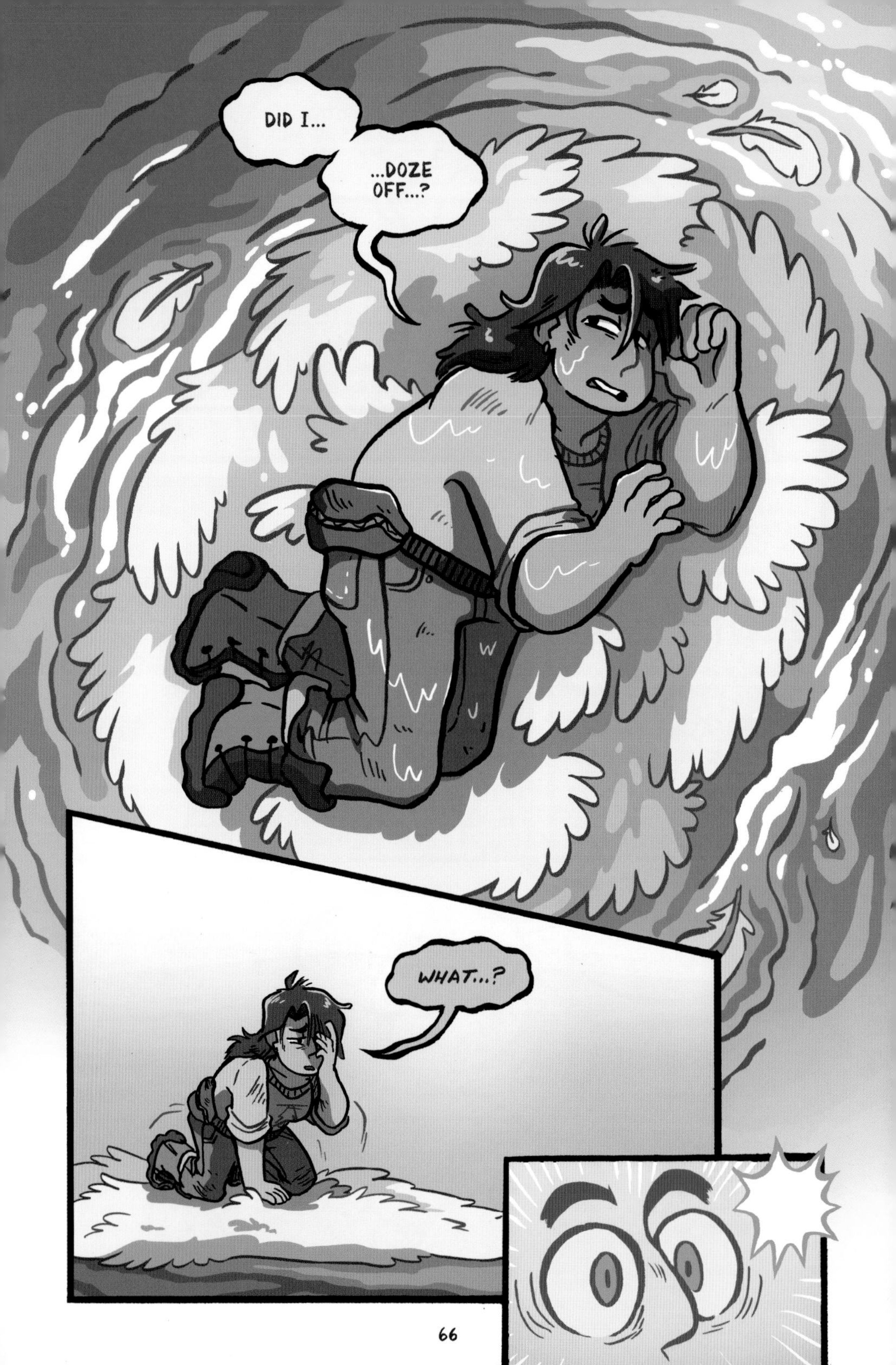
DID I...
...DOZE OFF...?
WHAT...?

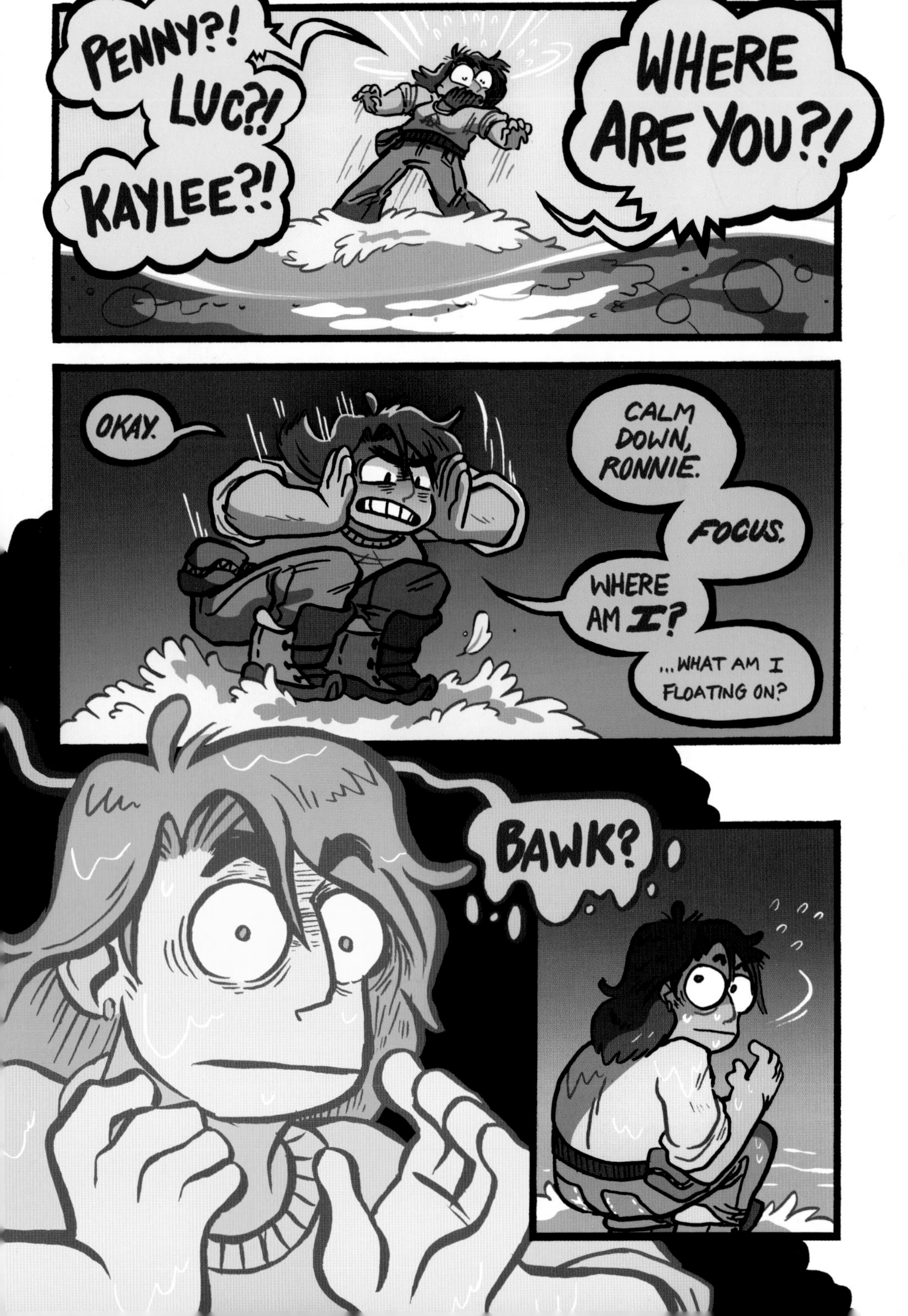
PENNY?! LUC?!
KAYLEE?!
WHERE ARE YOU?!
OKAY.
CALM DOWN, RONNIE.
FOCUS.
WHERE AM I?
...WHAT AM I FLOATING ON?
BAWK?

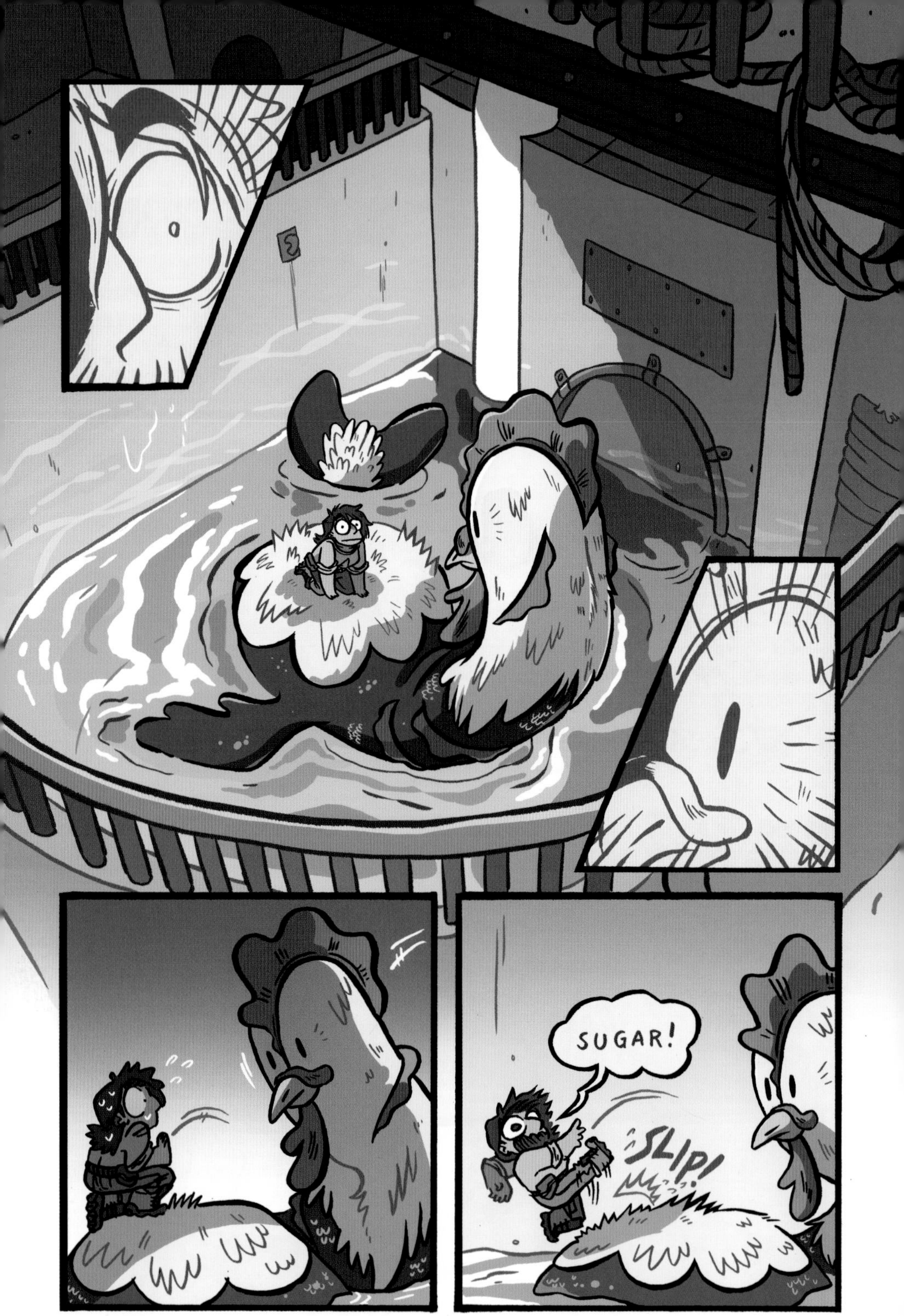
SUGAR!
SLIP!

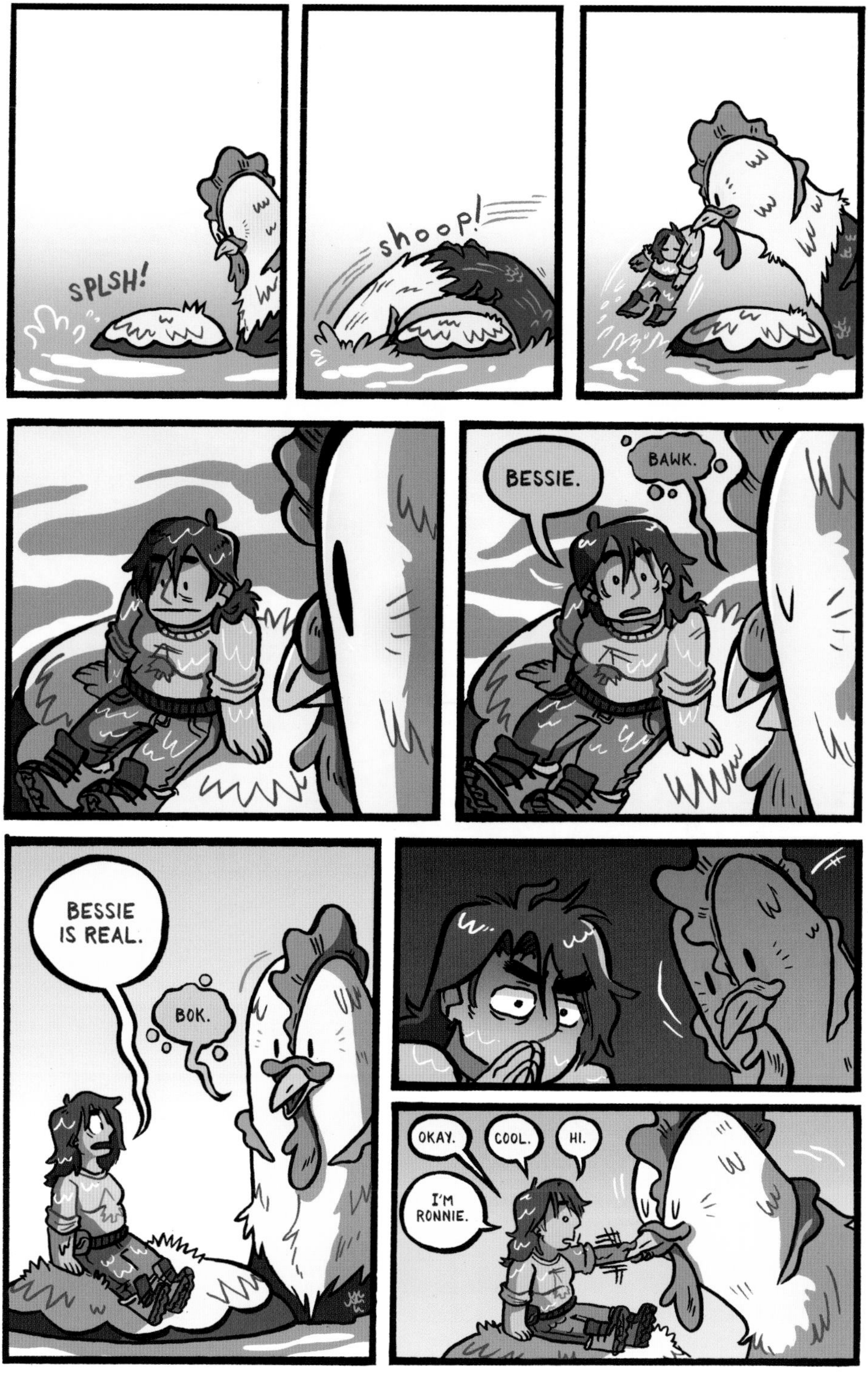
SPLSH!
shoop!
BESSIE.
BAWK.
BESSIE IS REAL.
BOK.
OKAY.
COOL.
HI.
I'M RONNIE.

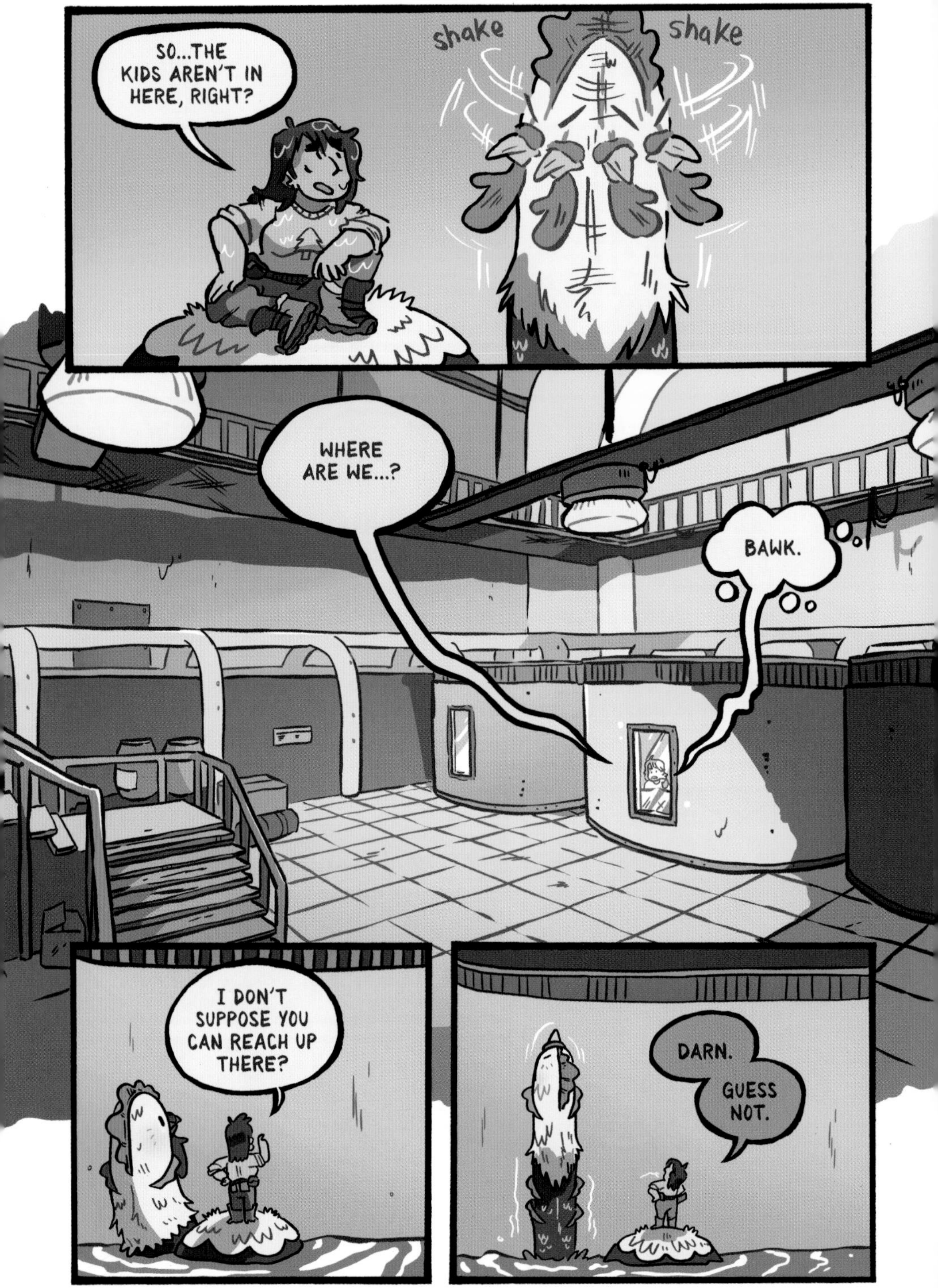
SO...THE KIDS AREN'T IN HERE, RIGHT?
shake
shake
WHERE ARE WE...?
BAWK.
I DON'T SUPPOSE YOU CAN REACH UP THERE?
DARN.
GUESS NOT.

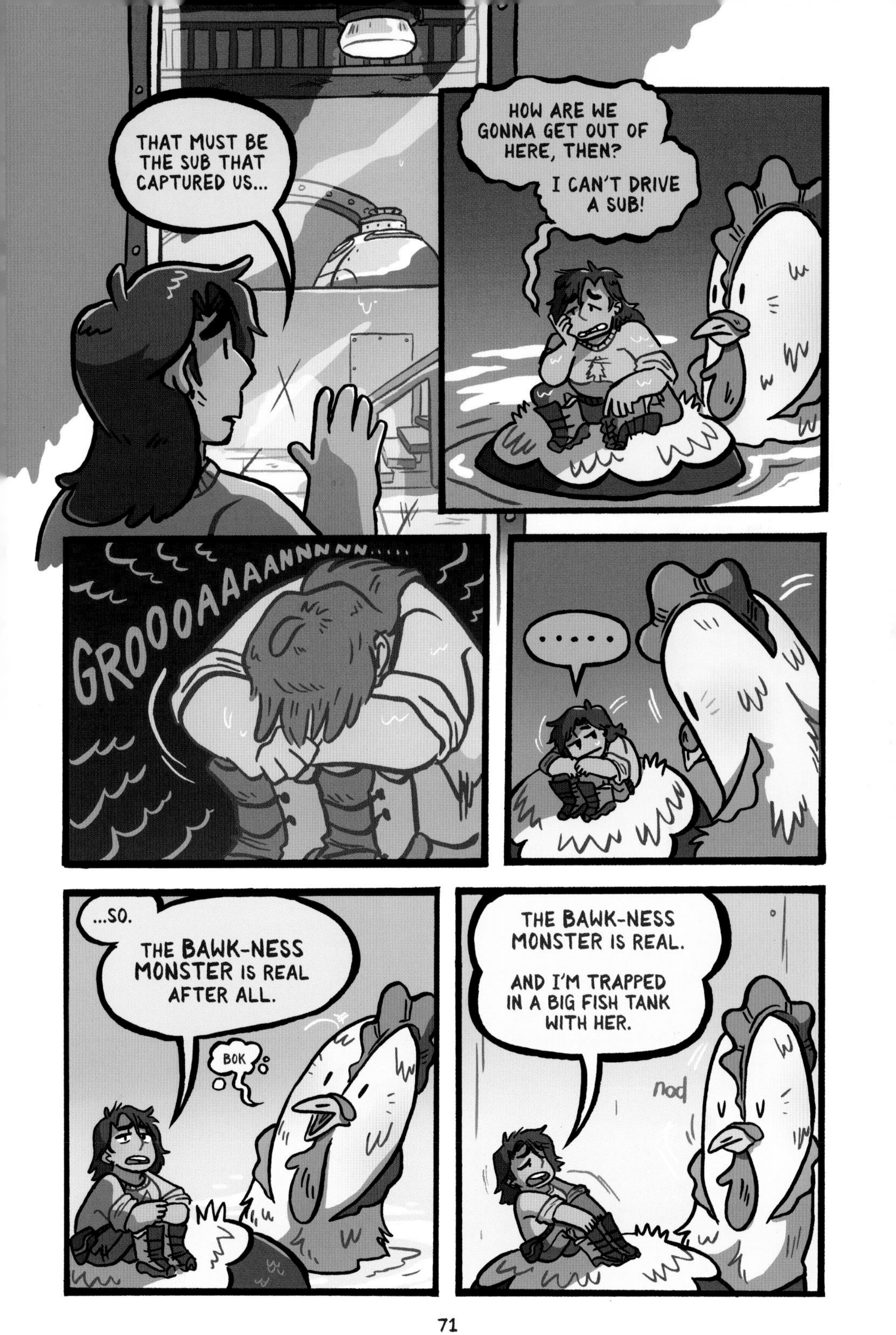
THAT MUST BE THE SUB THAT CAPTURED US...
HOW ARE WE GONNA GET OUT OF HERE, THEN?
I CAN'T DRIVE A SUB!
GROOOAAAANNNNNN.....
.....
...SO.
THE BAWK-NESS MONSTER IS REAL AFTER ALL.
BOK
THE BAWK-NESS MONSTER IS REAL.
AND I'M TRAPPED IN A BIG FISH TANK WITH HER.
nod

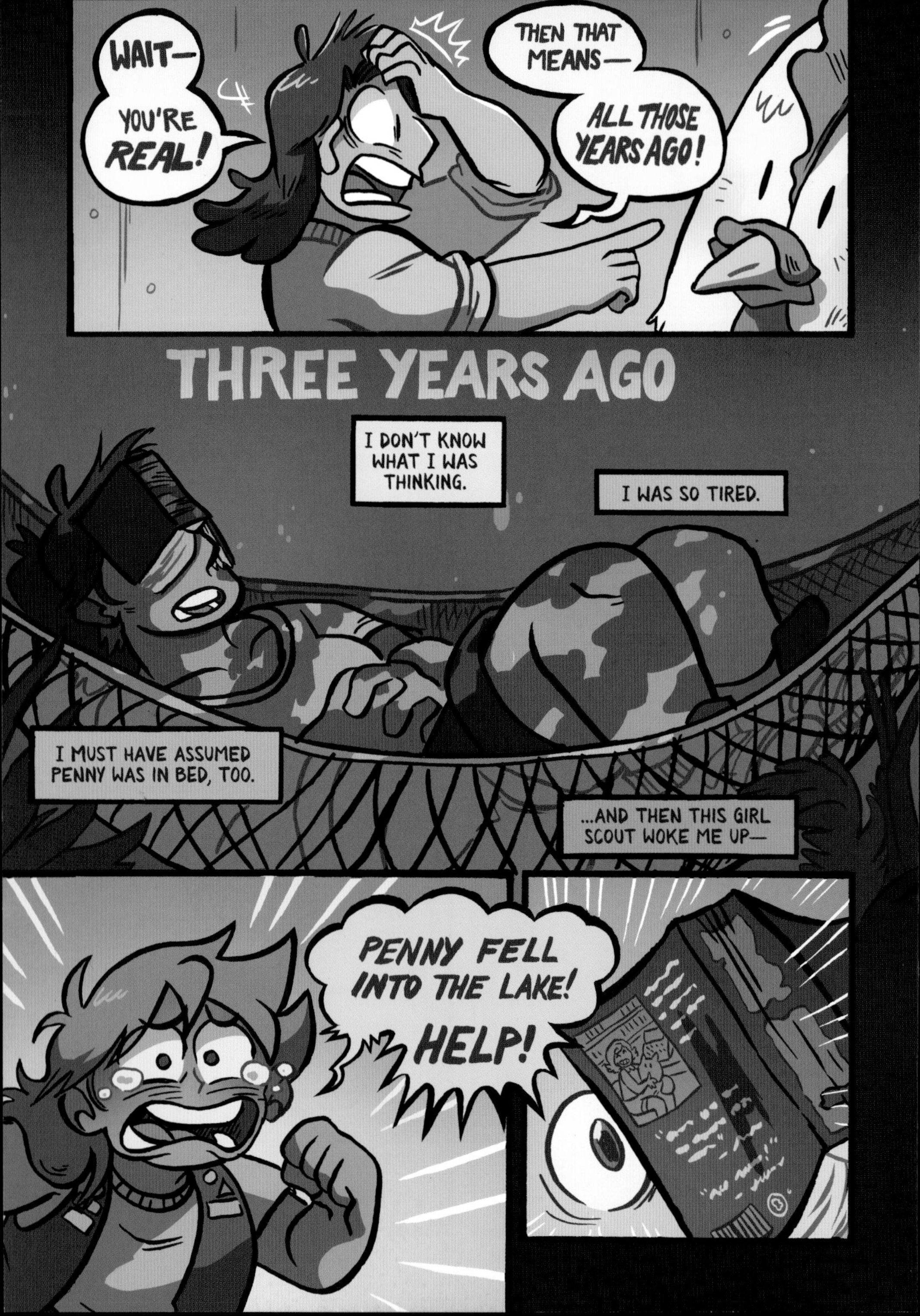
WAIT—
YOU'RE REAL!
THEN THAT MEANS—
ALL THOSE YEARS AGO!
THREE YEARS AGO
I DON'T KNOW WHAT I WAS THINKING.
I WAS SO TIRED.
I MUST HAVE ASSUMED PENNY WAS IN BED, TOO.
...AND THEN THIS GIRL SCOUT WOKE ME UP—
PENNY FELL INTO THE LAKE! HELP!

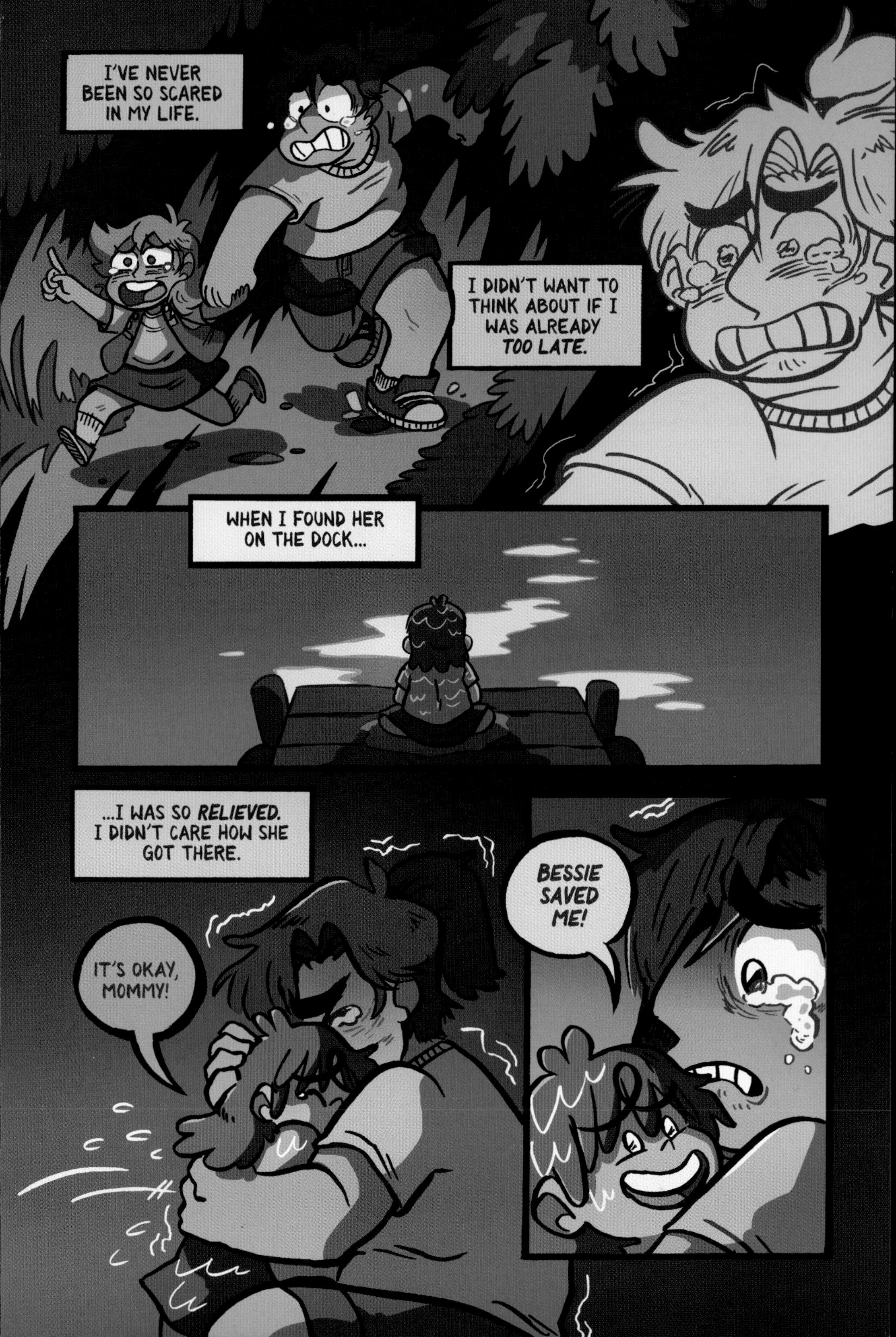
I'VE NEVER BEEN SO SCARED IN MY LIFE.
I DIDN'T WANT TO THINK ABOUT IF I WAS ALREADY *TOO LATE.*
WHEN I FOUND HER ON THE DOCK...
...I WAS SO *RELIEVED.* I DIDN'T CARE HOW SHE GOT THERE.
IT'S OKAY, MOMMY!
BESSIE SAVED ME!

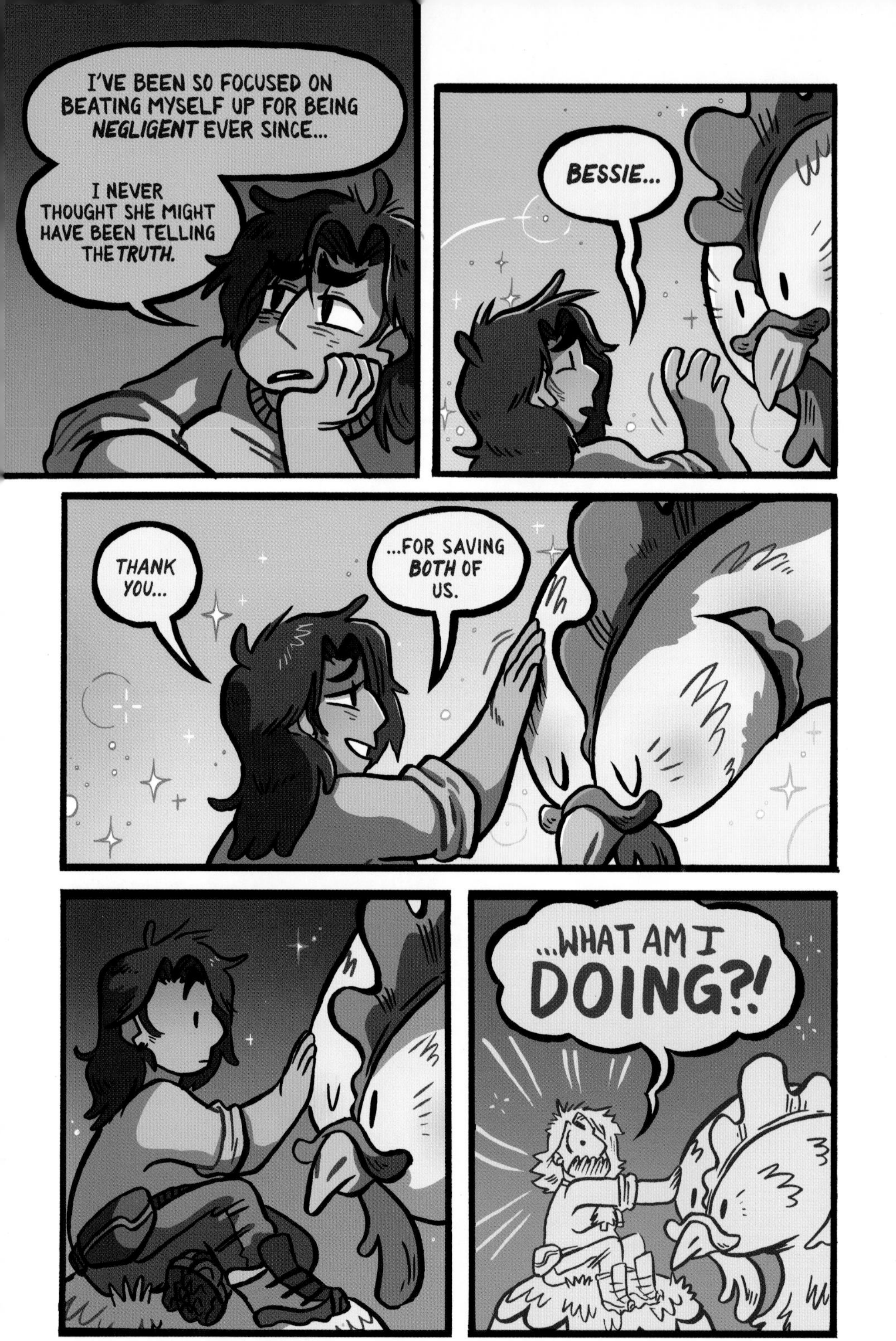
I'VE BEEN SO FOCUSED ON BEATING MYSELF UP FOR BEING NEGLIGENT EVER SINCE...
I NEVER THOUGHT SHE MIGHT HAVE BEEN TELLING THE TRUTH.
BESSIE...
THANK YOU...
...FOR SAVING BOTH OF US.
...WHAT AM I DOING?!

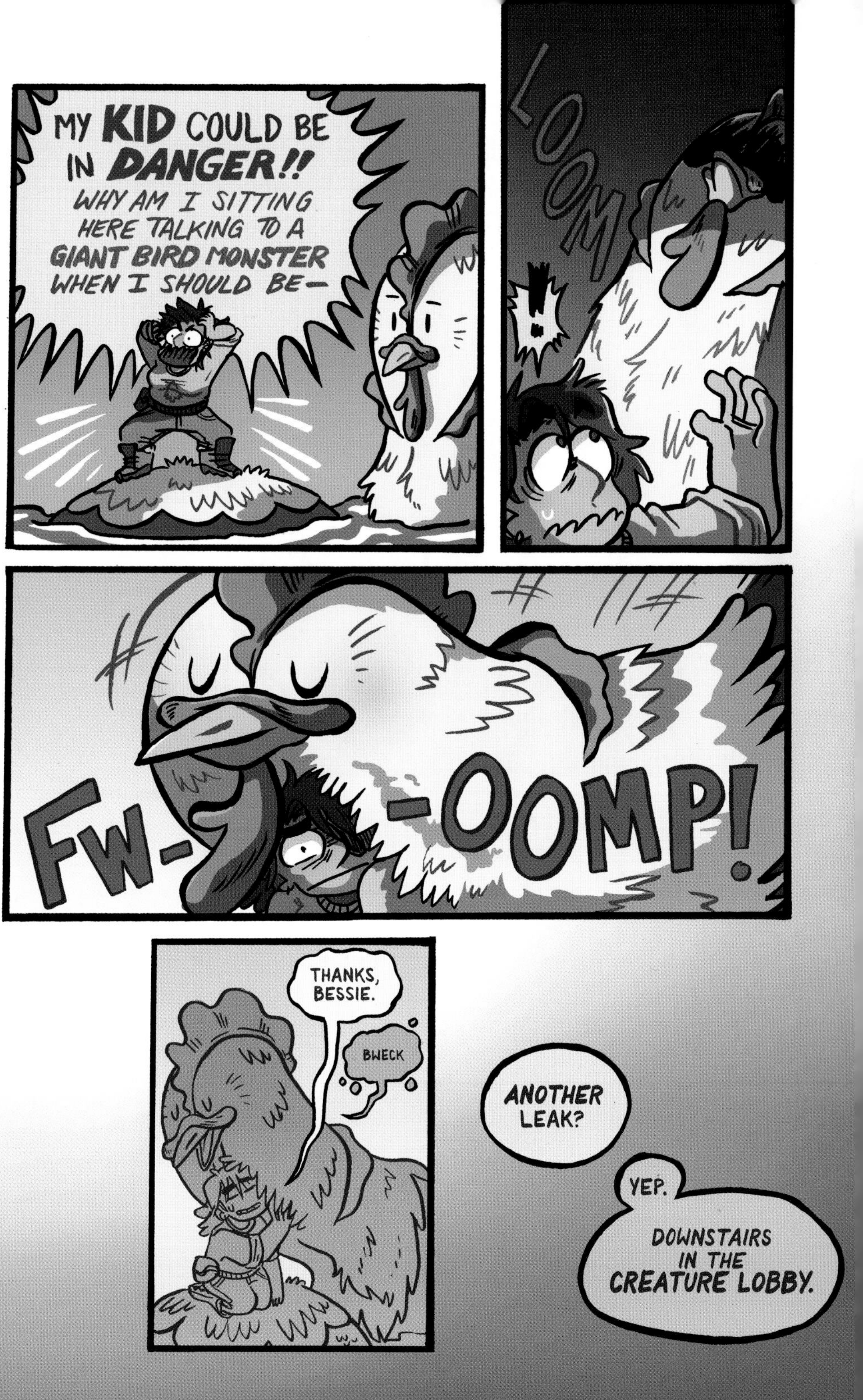
MY KID COULD BE IN DANGER!! WHY AM I SITTING HERE TALKING TO A GIANT BIRD MONSTER WHEN I SHOULD BE—
LOOOM
!
FW- -OOMP!
THANKS, BESSIE.
BWECK
ANOTHER LEAK?
YEP.
DOWNSTAIRS IN THE CREATURE LOBBY.

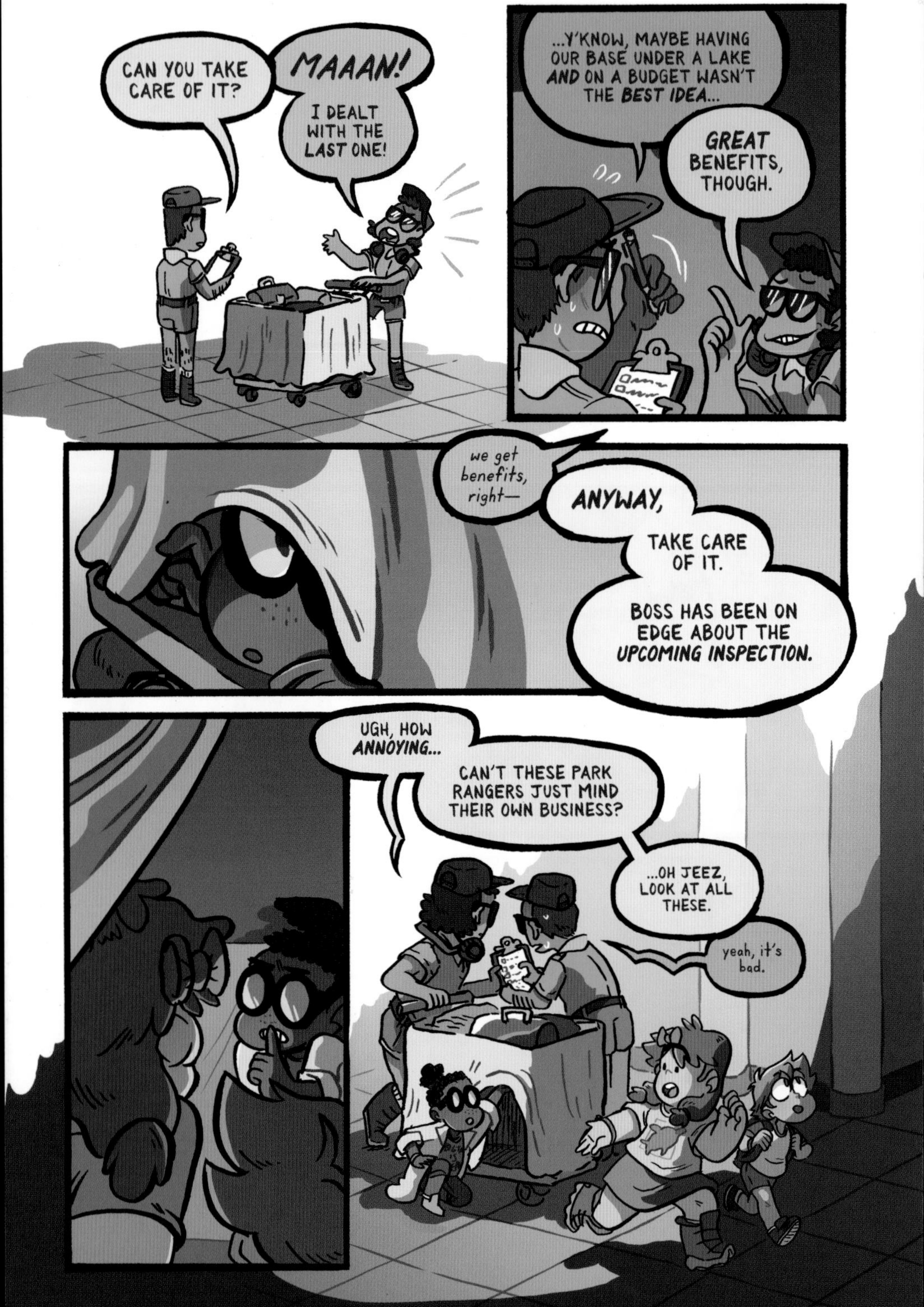
CAN YOU TAKE CARE OF IT?
MAAAN!
I DEALT WITH THE LAST ONE!
...Y'KNOW, MAYBE HAVING OUR BASE UNDER A LAKE AND ON A BUDGET WASN'T THE BEST IDEA...
GREAT BENEFITS, THOUGH.
we get benefits, right—
ANYWAY,
TAKE CARE OF IT.
BOSS HAS BEEN ON EDGE ABOUT THE UPCOMING INSPECTION.
UGH, HOW ANNOYING...
CAN'T THESE PARK RANGERS JUST MIND THEIR OWN BUSINESS?
...OH JEEZ, LOOK AT ALL THESE.
yeah, it's bad.

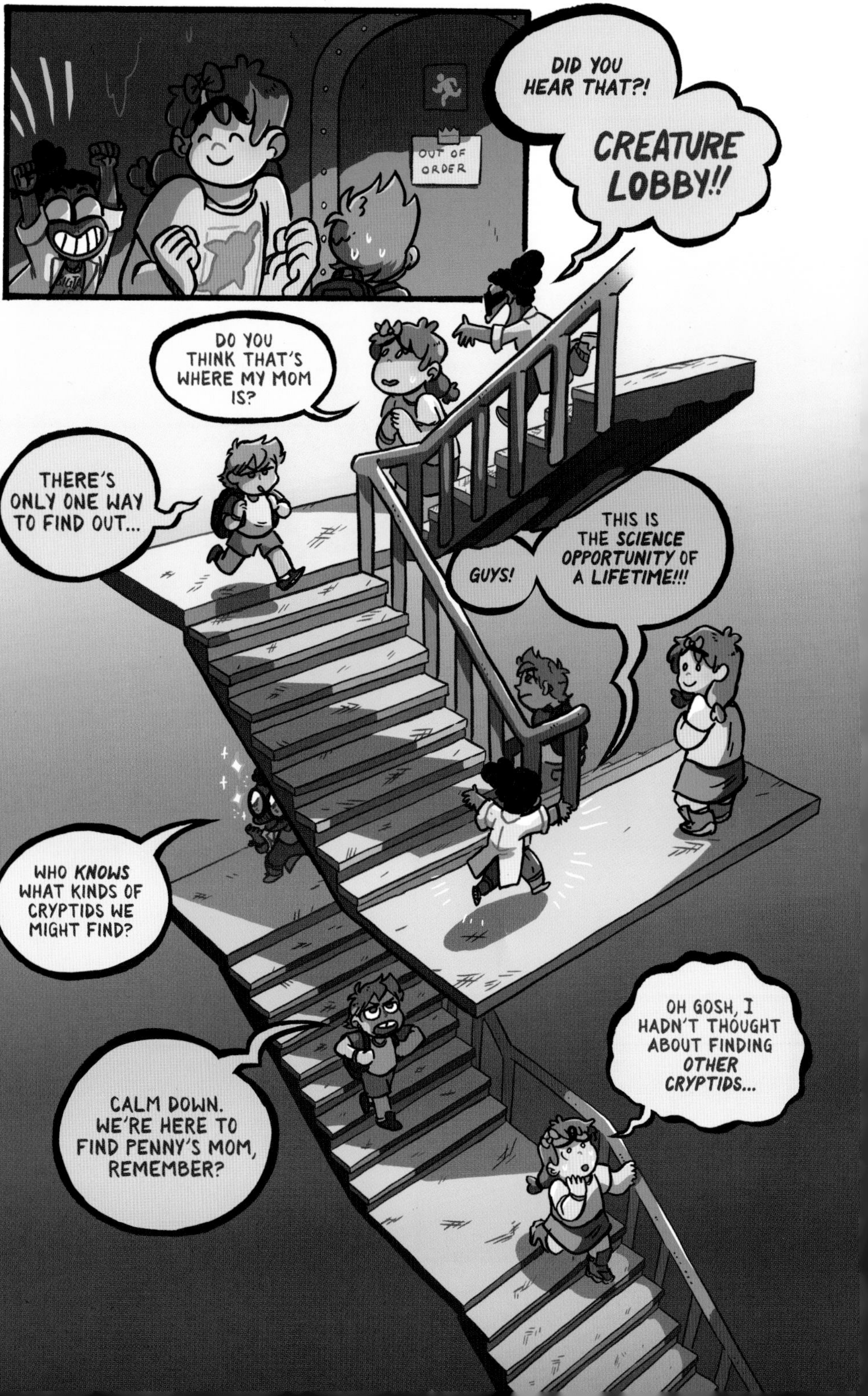
OUT OF ORDER
DID YOU HEAR THAT?!
CREATURE LOBBY!!
DO YOU THINK THAT'S WHERE MY MOM IS?
THERE'S ONLY ONE WAY TO FIND OUT...
GUYS!
THIS IS THE SCIENCE OPPORTUNITY OF A LIFETIME!!!
WHO KNOWS WHAT KINDS OF CRYPTIDS WE MIGHT FIND?
OH GOSH, I HADN'T THOUGHT ABOUT FINDING OTHER CRYPTIDS...
CALM DOWN. WE'RE HERE TO FIND PENNY'S MOM, REMEMBER?

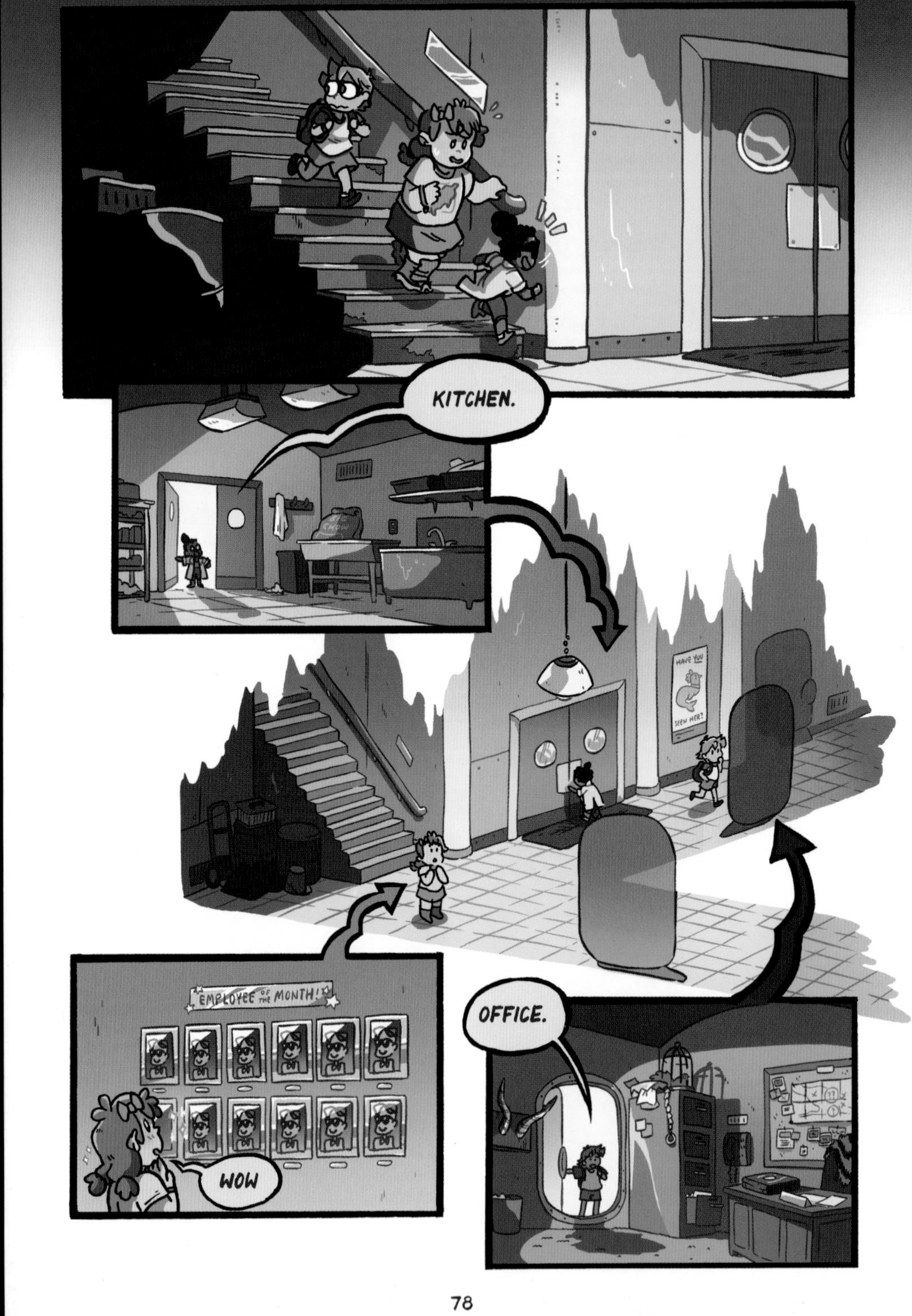

KITCHEN.
HAVE YOU SEEN HER?
EMPLOYEE OF THE MONTH!
WOW
OFFICE.

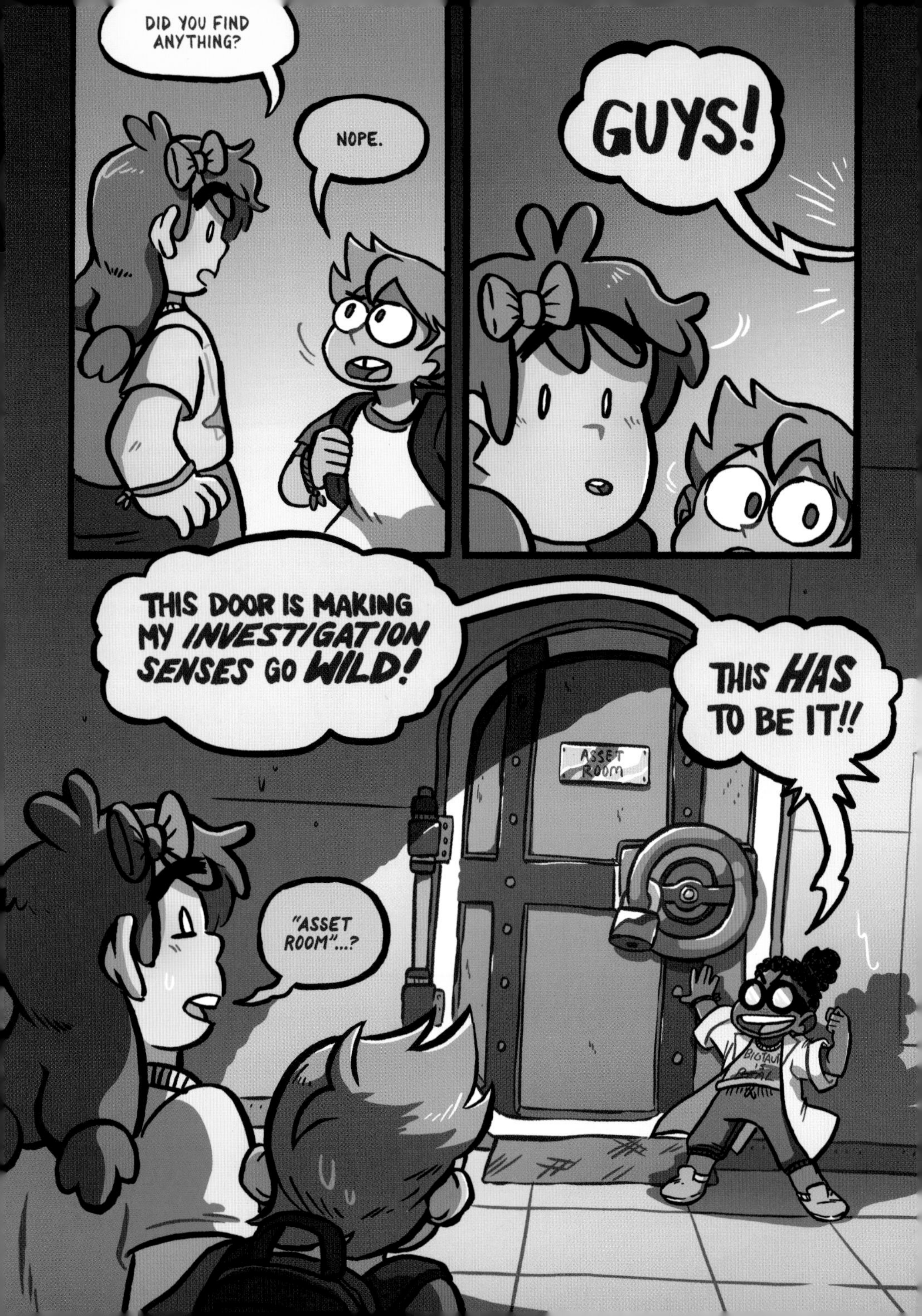
DID YOU FIND ANYTHING?
NOPE.
GUYS!
THIS DOOR IS MAKING MY *INVESTIGATION SENSES* GO *WILD!*
THIS *HAS* TO BE IT!!
ASSET ROOM
"ASSET ROOM"...?

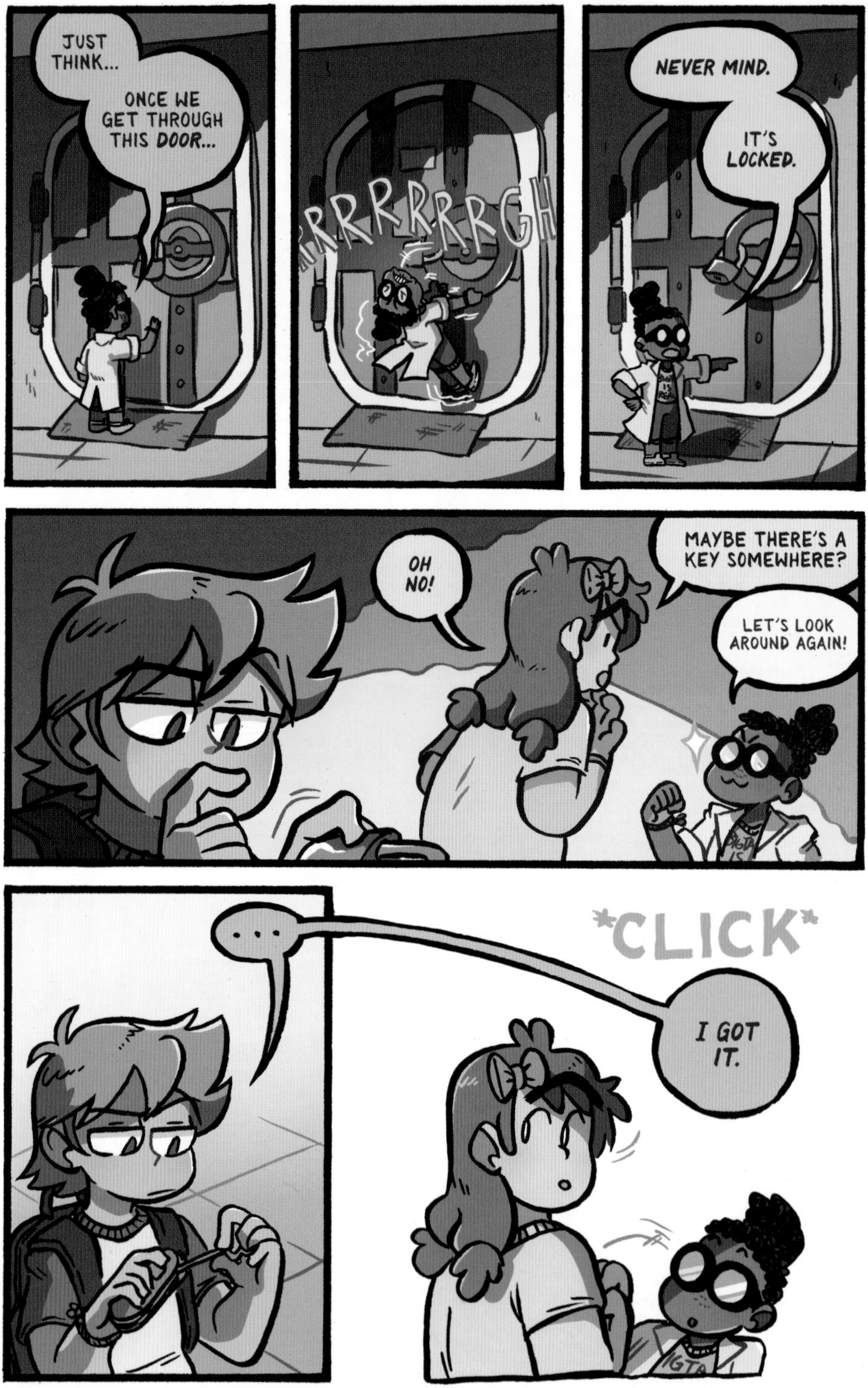

JUST THINK...
ONCE WE GET THROUGH THIS DOOR...
RRRRRRRRGH
NEVER MIND.
IT'S LOCKED.
OH NO!
MAYBE THERE'S A KEY SOMEWHERE?
LET'S LOOK AROUND AGAIN!
...
CLICK
I GOT IT.

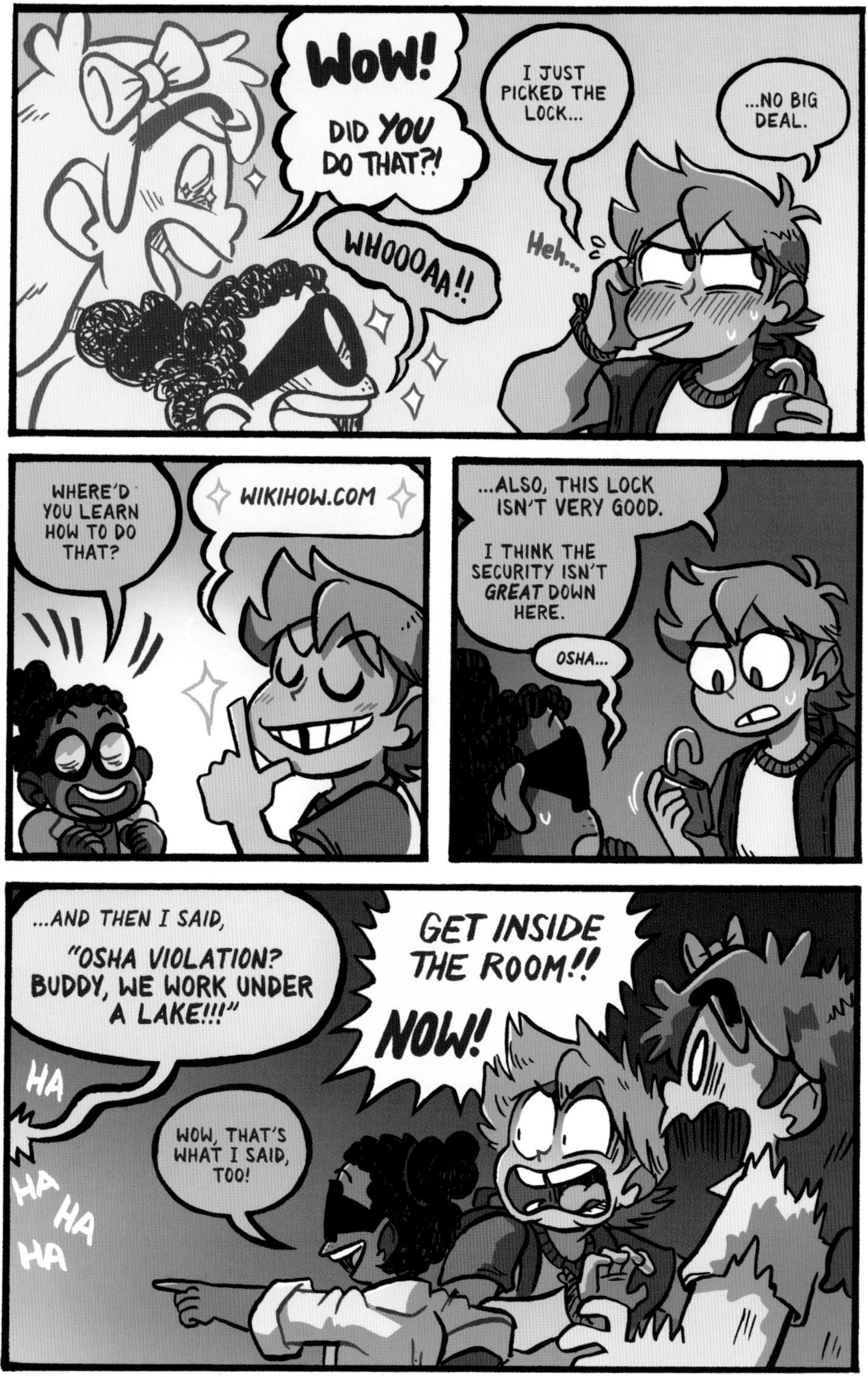
WOW!
DID YOU DO THAT?!
WHOOOAA!!
I JUST PICKED THE LOCK...
Heh...
...NO BIG DEAL.
WHERE'D YOU LEARN HOW TO DO THAT?
WIKIHOW.COM
...ALSO, THIS LOCK ISN'T VERY GOOD.
I THINK THE SECURITY ISN'T GREAT DOWN HERE.
OSHA...
...AND THEN I SAID, "OSHA VIOLATION? BUDDY, WE WORK UNDER A LAKE!!!"
HA
HA HA HA
WOW, THAT'S WHAT I SAID, TOO!
GET INSIDE THE ROOM!!
NOW!

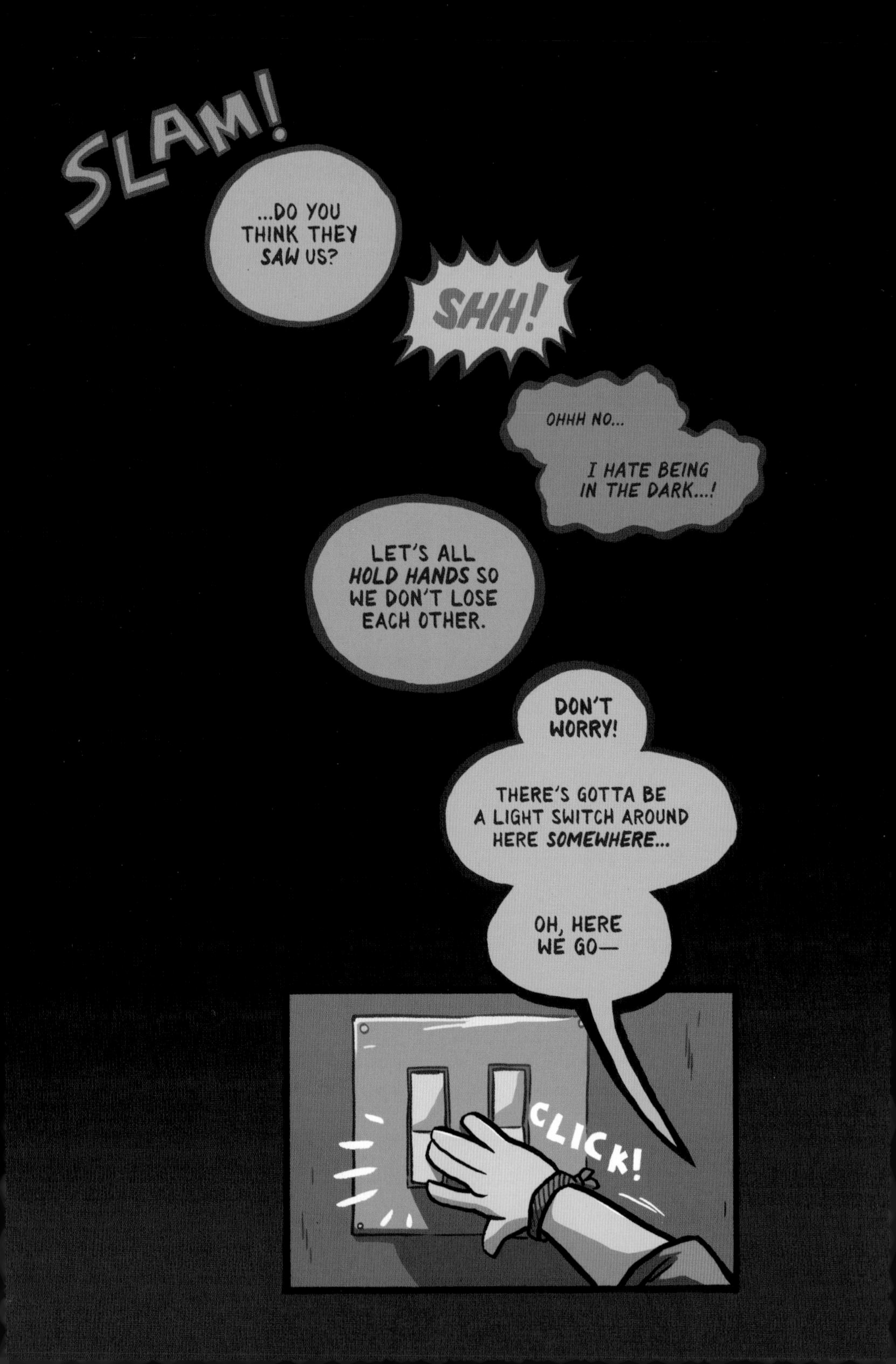
SLAM!
...DO YOU THINK THEY SAW US?
SHH!
OHHH NO...
I HATE BEING IN THE DARK...!
LET'S ALL HOLD HANDS SO WE DON'T LOSE EACH OTHER.
DON'T WORRY!
THERE'S GOTTA BE A LIGHT SWITCH AROUND HERE SOMEWHERE...
OH, HERE WE GO—
CLICK!

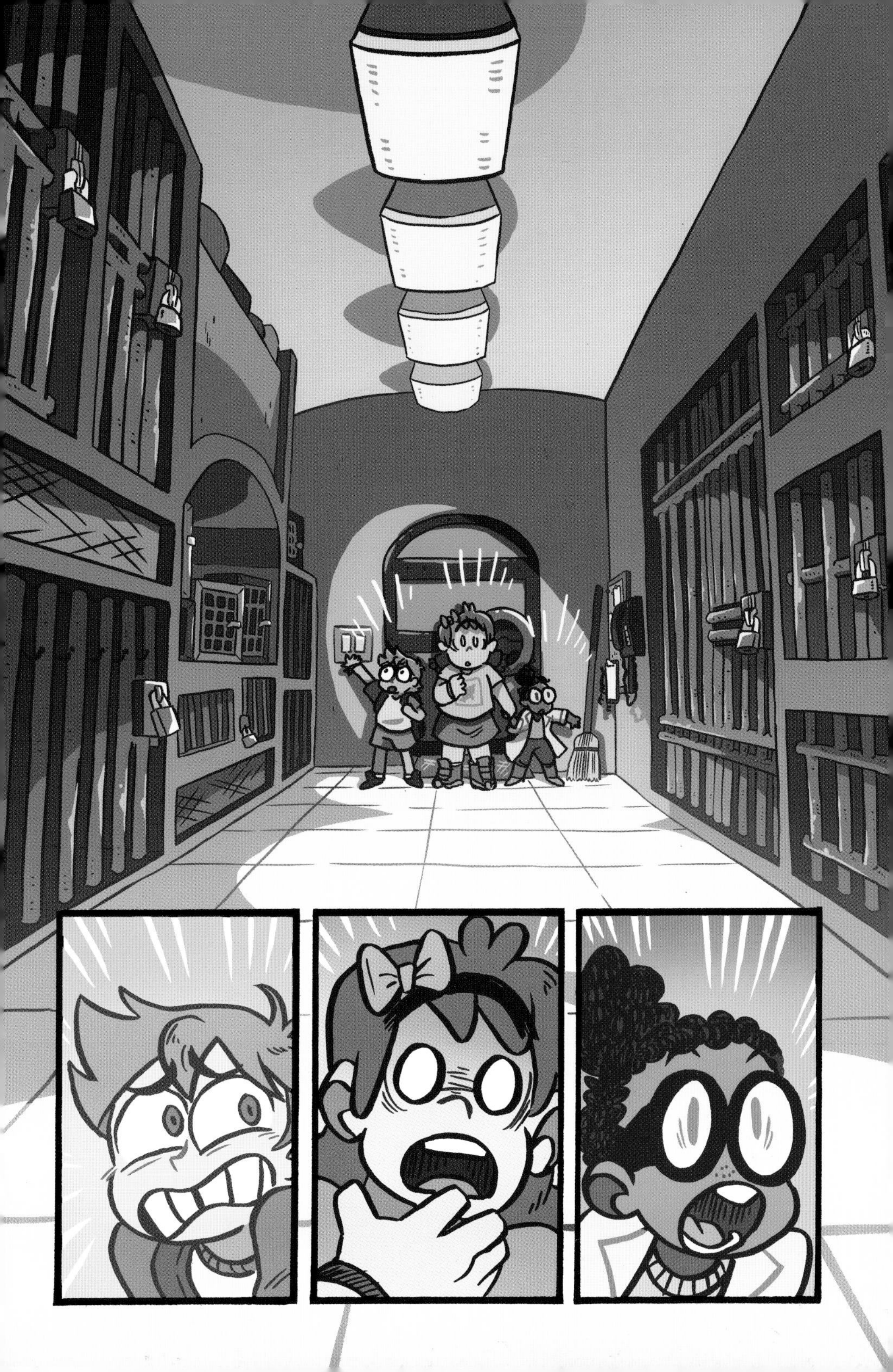

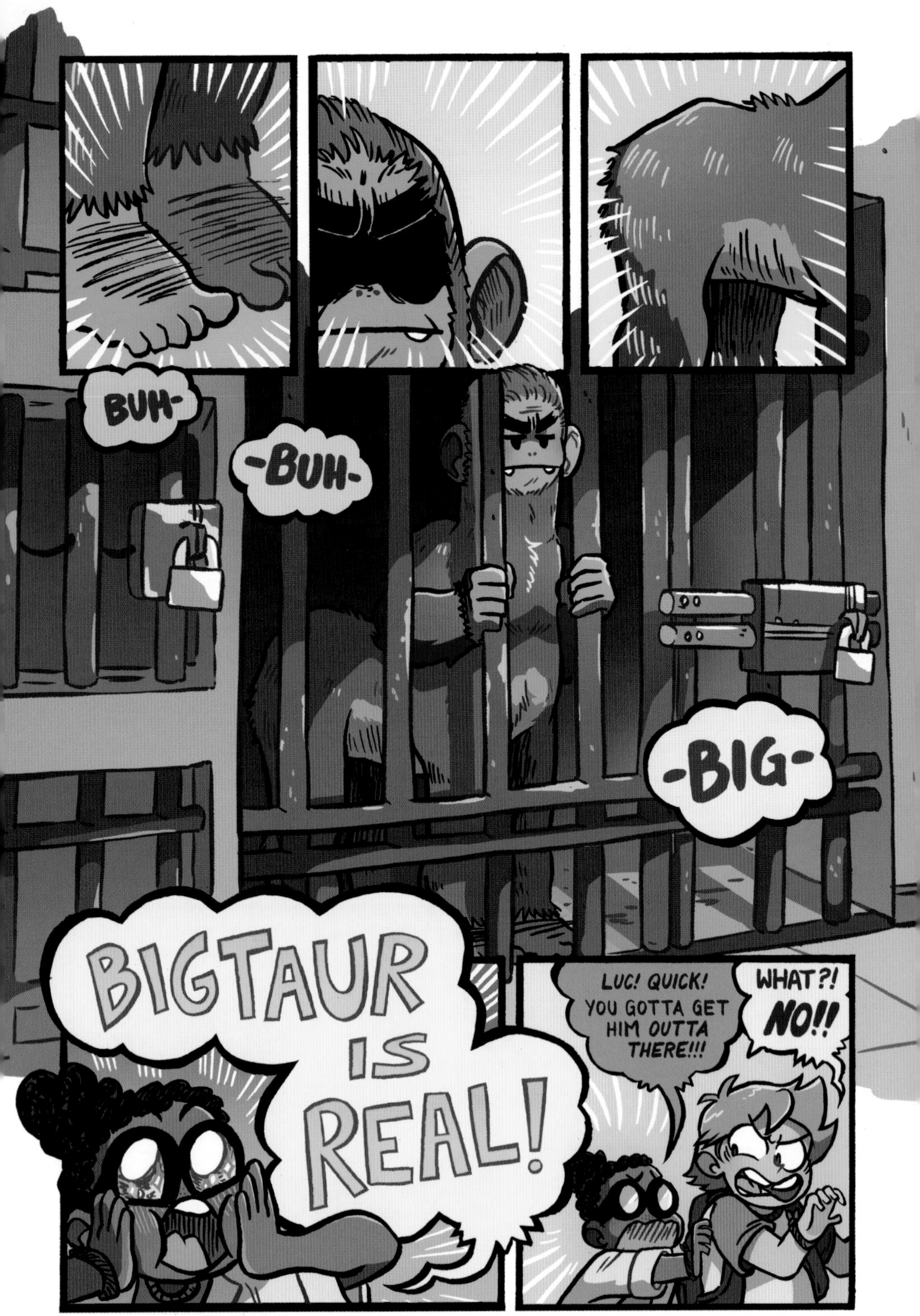
BUH-
-BUH-
-BIG-
BIGTAUR IS REAL!
LUC! QUICK! YOU GOTTA GET HIM OUTTA THERE!!!
WHAT?! NO!!

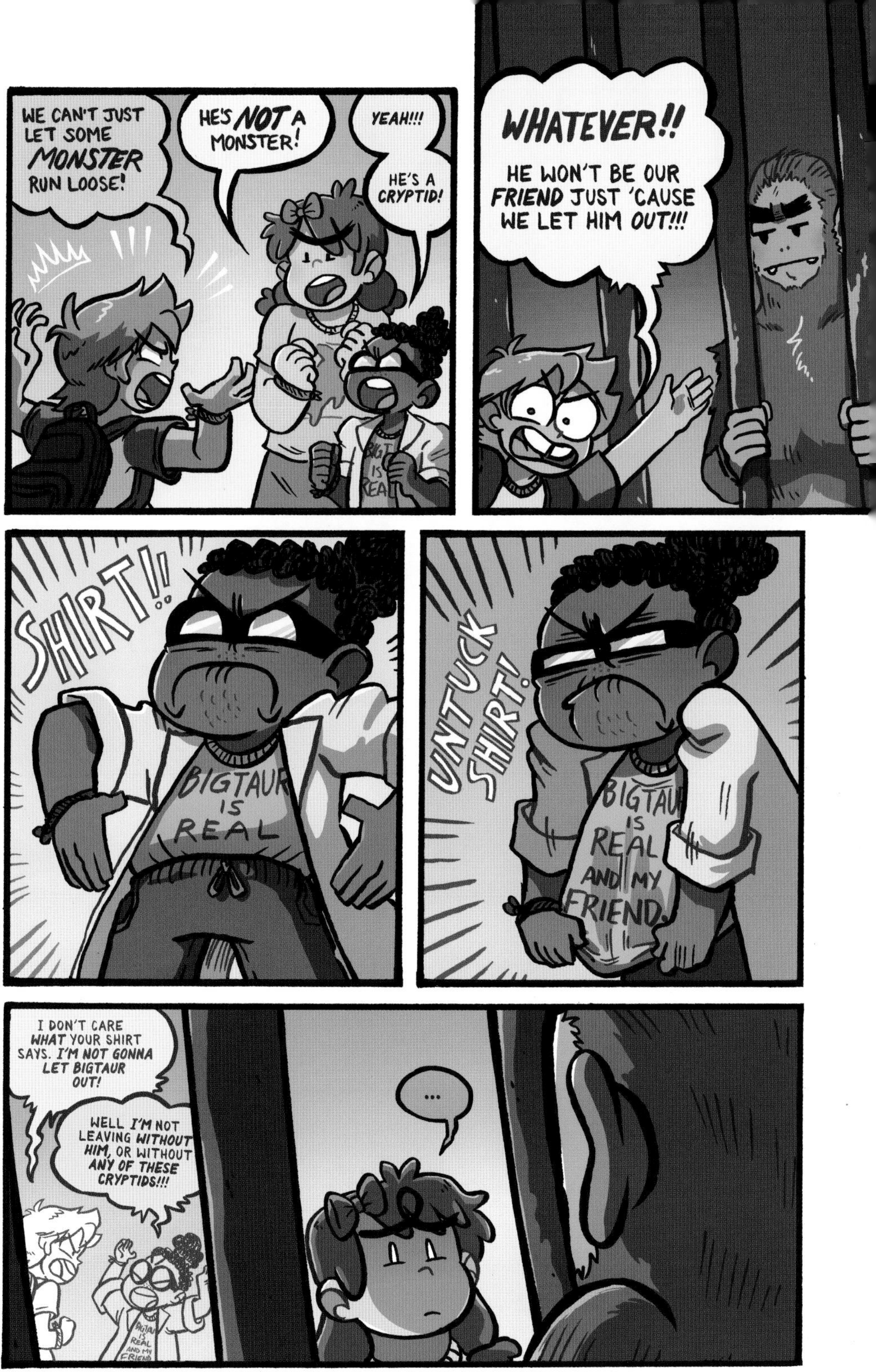
WE CAN'T JUST LET SOME MONSTER RUN LOOSE!
HE'S NOT A MONSTER!
YEAH!!!
HE'S A CRYPTID!
BIGT IS REAL
WHATEVER!!
HE WON'T BE OUR FRIEND JUST 'CAUSE WE LET HIM OUT!!!
SHIRT!!
BIGTAUR IS REAL
UNTUCK SHIRT!
BIGTAUR IS REAL AND MY FRIEND.
I DON'T CARE WHAT YOUR SHIRT SAYS. I'M NOT GONNA LET BIGTAUR OUT!
WELL I'M NOT LEAVING WITHOUT HIM, OR WITHOUT ANY OF THESE CRYPTIDS!!!
...
BIGTAU IS REAL AND MY FRIEND

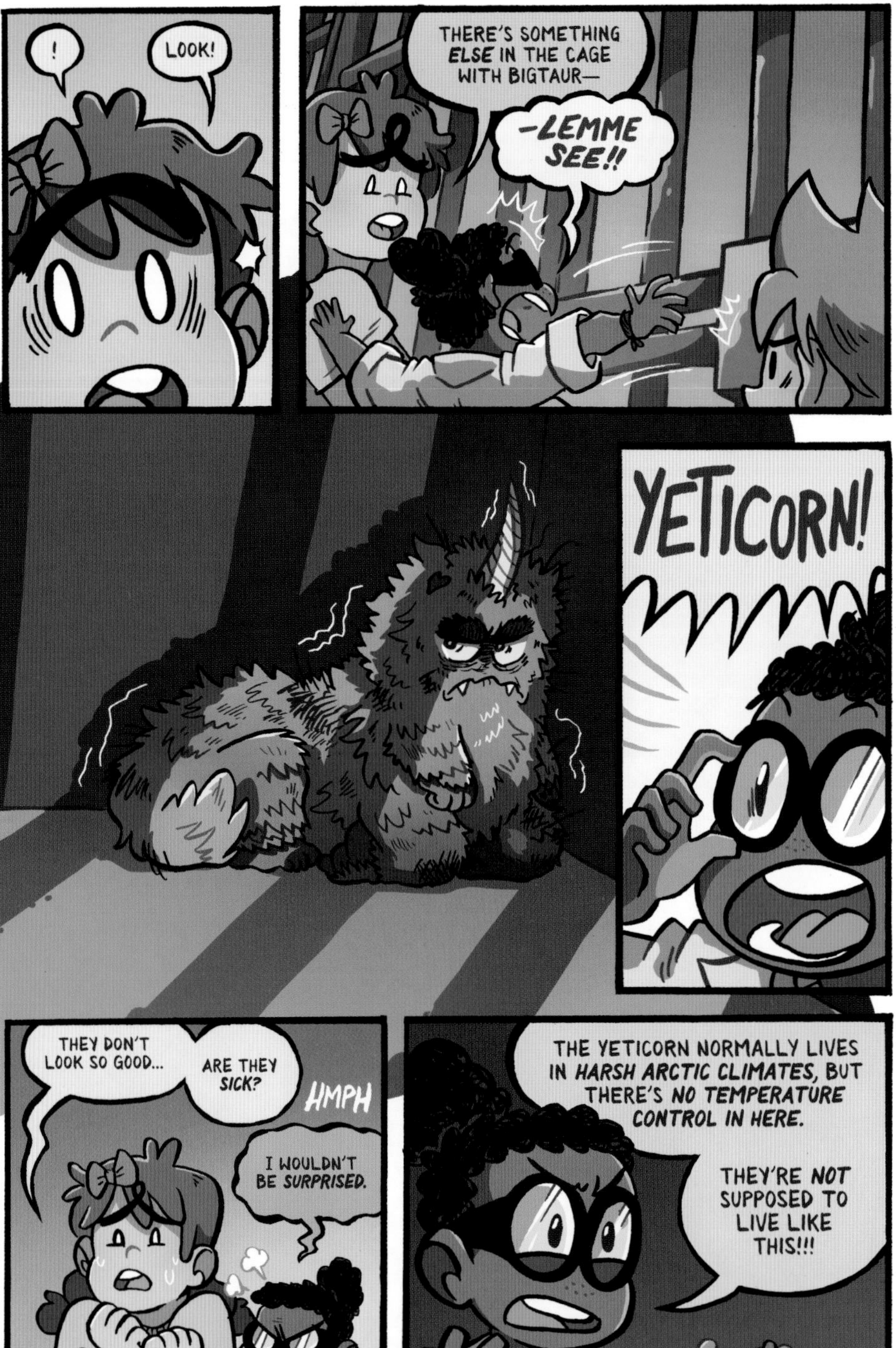
!
LOOK!
THERE'S SOMETHING ELSE IN THE CAGE WITH BIGTAUR—
—LEMME SEE!!
YETICORN!
THEY DON'T LOOK SO GOOD...
ARE THEY SICK?
HMPH
I WOULDN'T BE SURPRISED.
THE YETICORN NORMALLY LIVES IN HARSH ARCTIC CLIMATES, BUT THERE'S NO TEMPERATURE CONTROL IN HERE.
THEY'RE NOT SUPPOSED TO LIVE LIKE THIS!!!

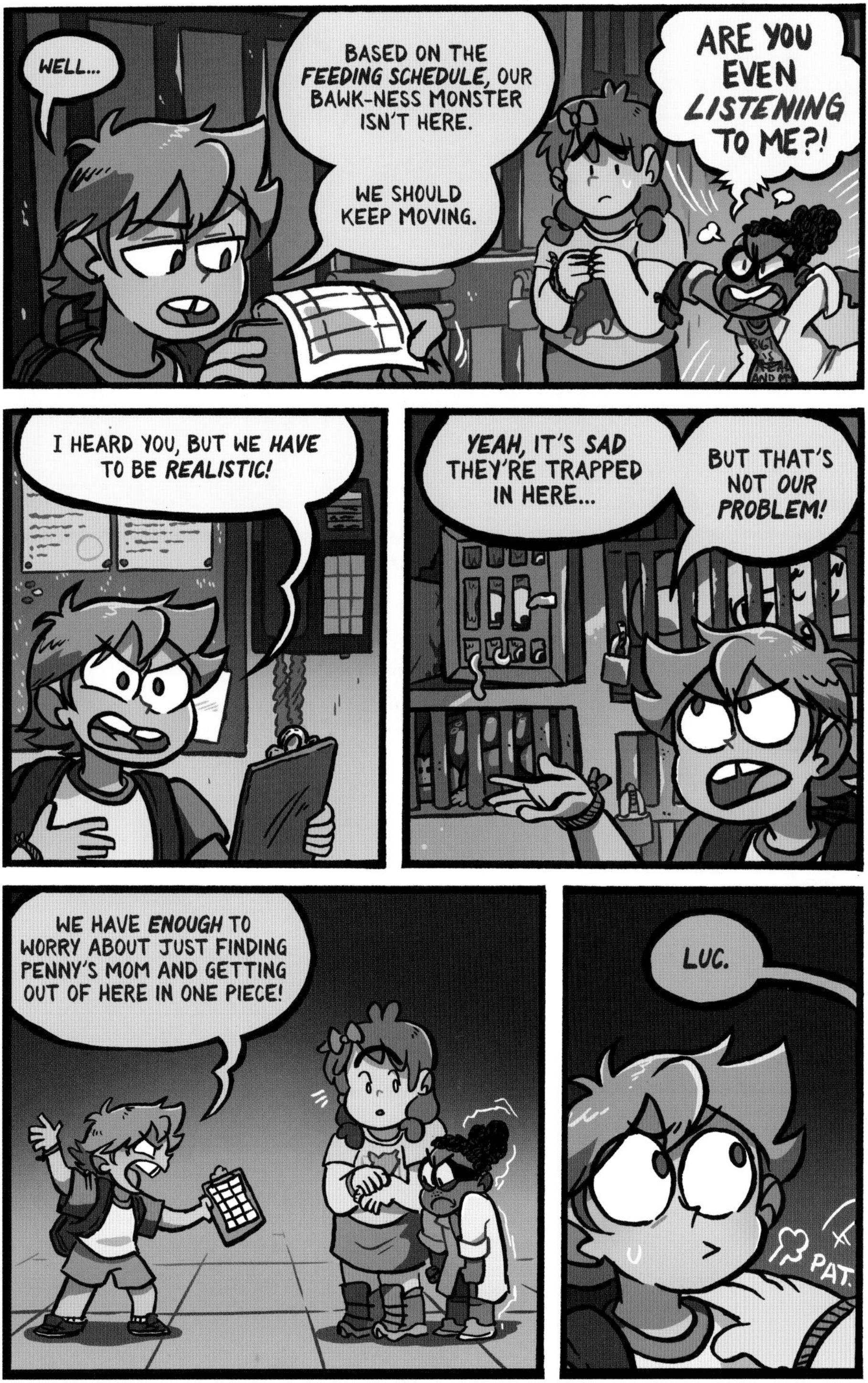
WELL...
BASED ON THE FEEDING SCHEDULE, OUR BAWK-NESS MONSTER ISN'T HERE.
WE SHOULD KEEP MOVING.
ARE YOU EVEN LISTENING TO ME?!
I HEARD YOU, BUT WE HAVE TO BE REALISTIC!
YEAH, IT'S SAD THEY'RE TRAPPED IN HERE...
BUT THAT'S NOT OUR PROBLEM!
WE HAVE ENOUGH TO WORRY ABOUT JUST FINDING PENNY'S MOM AND GETTING OUT OF HERE IN ONE PIECE!
LUC.
PAT.

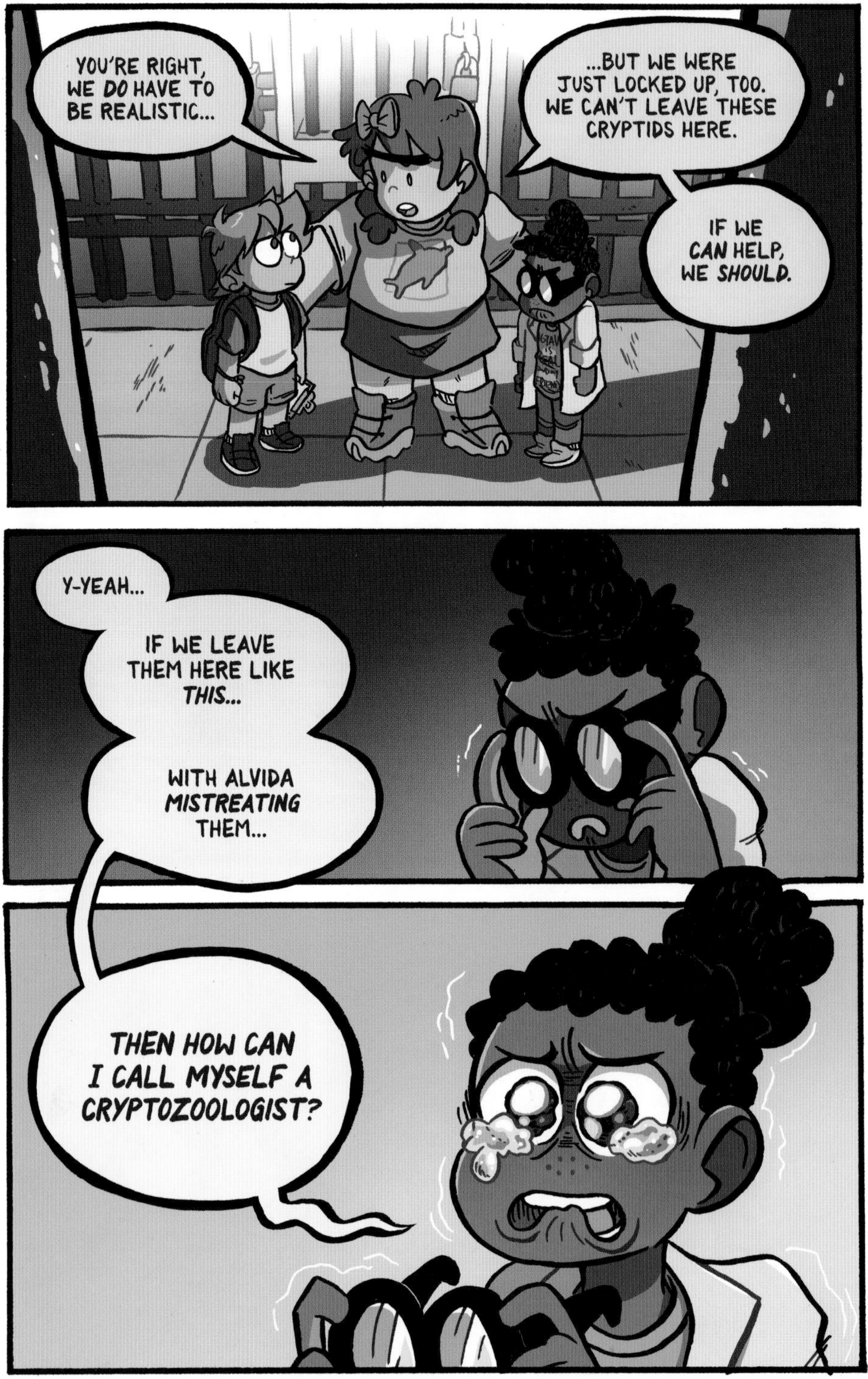
YOU'RE RIGHT, WE DO HAVE TO BE REALISTIC...
...BUT WE WERE JUST LOCKED UP, TOO. WE CAN'T LEAVE THESE CRYPTIDS HERE.
IF WE CAN HELP, WE SHOULD.
Y-YEAH...
IF WE LEAVE THEM HERE LIKE THIS...
WITH ALVIDA MISTREATING THEM...
THEN HOW CAN I CALL MYSELF A CRYPTOZOOLOGIST?

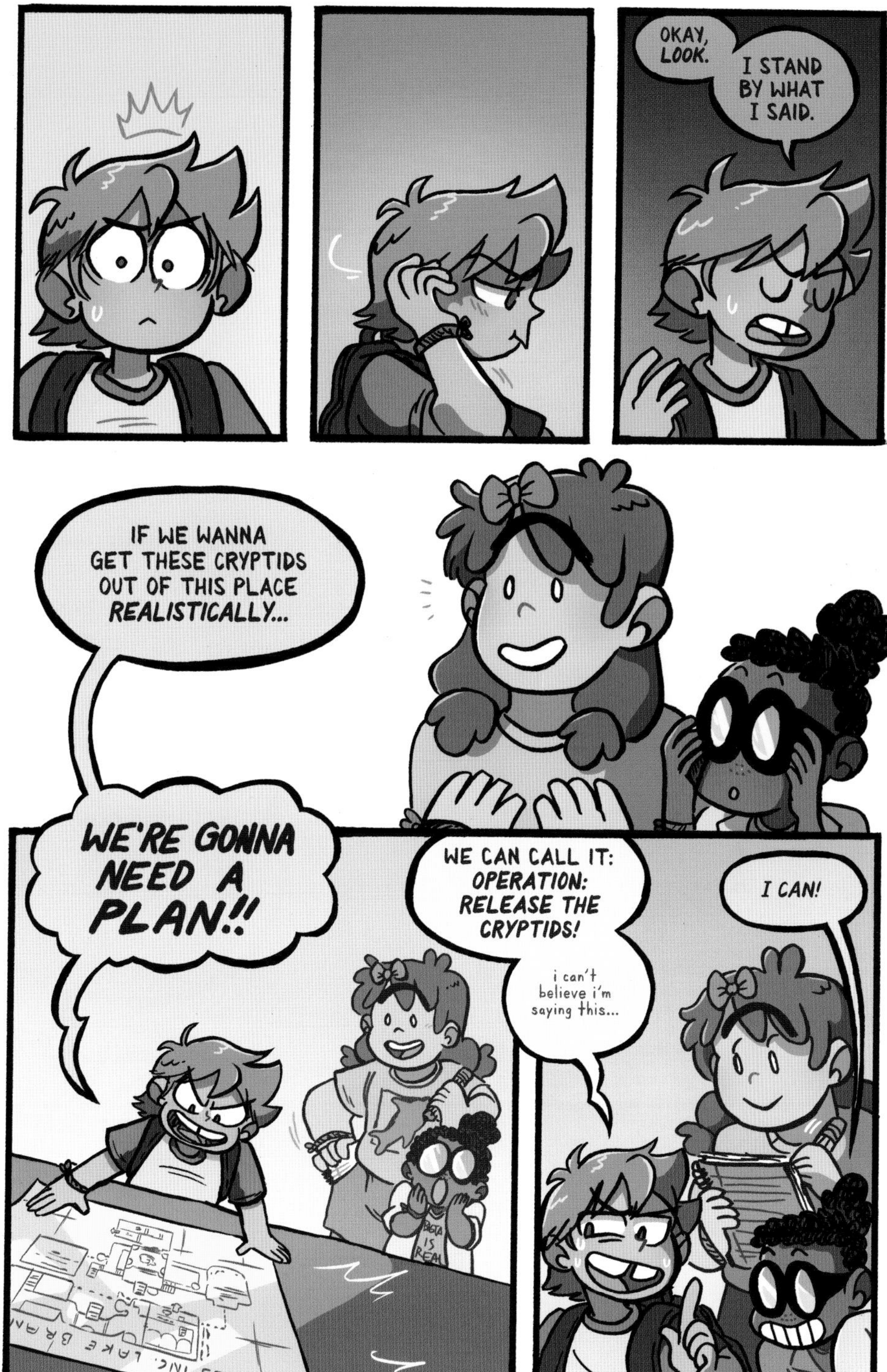
OKAY, LOOK.
I STAND BY WHAT I SAID.
IF WE WANNA GET THESE CRYPTIDS OUT OF THIS PLACE *REALISTICALLY...*
WE'RE GONNA NEED A PLAN!!
WE CAN CALL IT: ***OPERATION: RELEASE THE CRYPTIDS!***
i can't believe i'm saying this...
I CAN!

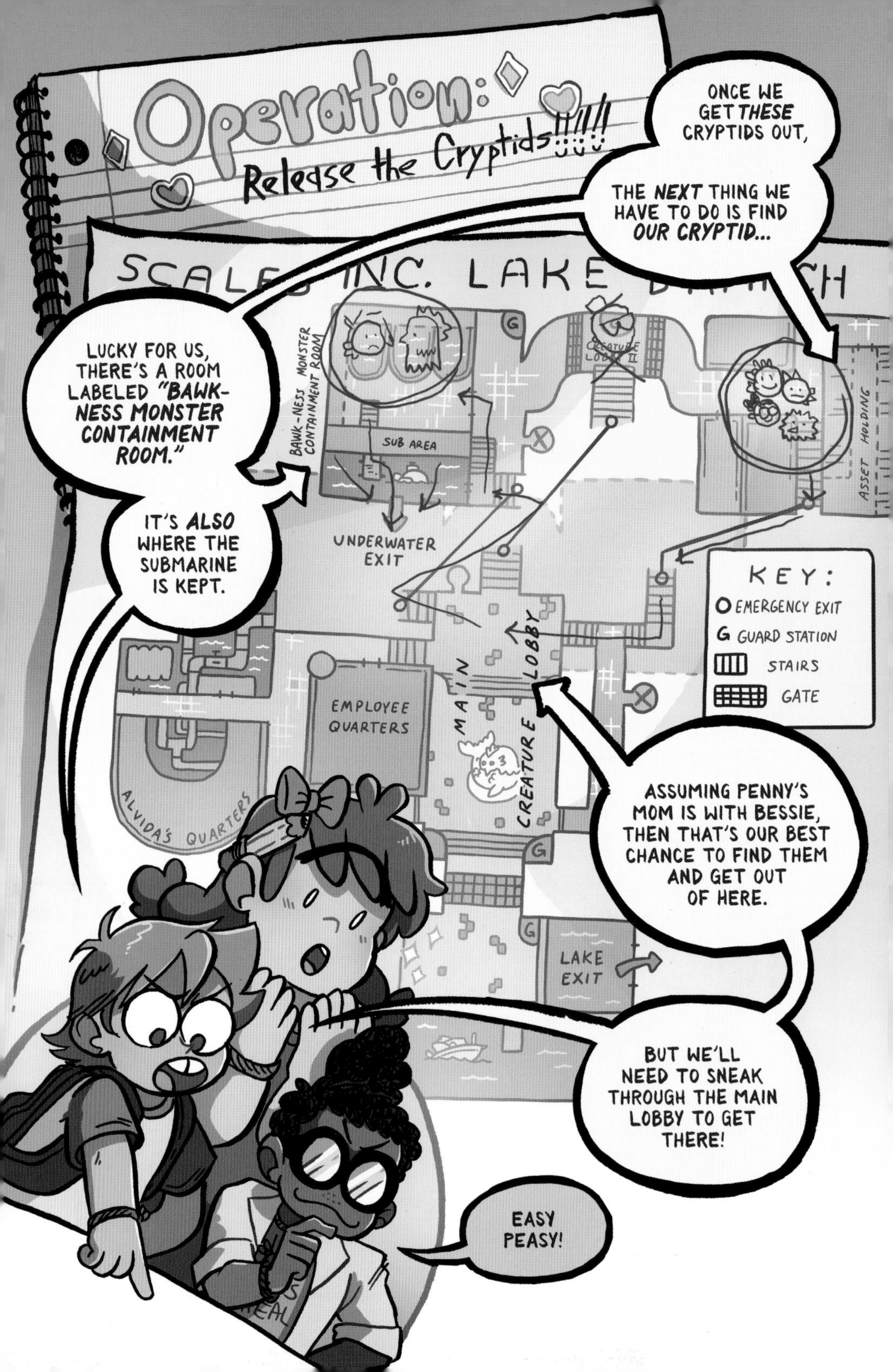

Operation: Release the Cryptids!!!!!!
SCALES INC. LAKE BRANCH
ONCE WE GET THESE CRYPTIDS OUT,
THE NEXT THING WE HAVE TO DO IS FIND OUR CRYPTID...
LUCKY FOR US, THERE'S A ROOM LABELED "BAWK-NESS MONSTER CONTAINMENT ROOM."
IT'S ALSO WHERE THE SUBMARINE IS KEPT.
BAWK-NESS MONSTER CONTAINMENT ROOM
SUB AREA
UNDERWATER EXIT
CREATURE LOBBY II
ASSET HOLDING
KEY:
EMERGENCY EXIT
G GUARD STATION
STAIRS
GATE
MAIN CREATURE LOBBY
EMPLOYEE QUARTERS
ALVIDA'S QUARTERS
LAKE EXIT
ASSUMING PENNY'S MOM IS WITH BESSIE, THEN THAT'S OUR BEST CHANCE TO FIND THEM AND GET OUT OF HERE.
BUT WE'LL NEED TO SNEAK THROUGH THE MAIN LOBBY TO GET THERE!
EASY PEASY!

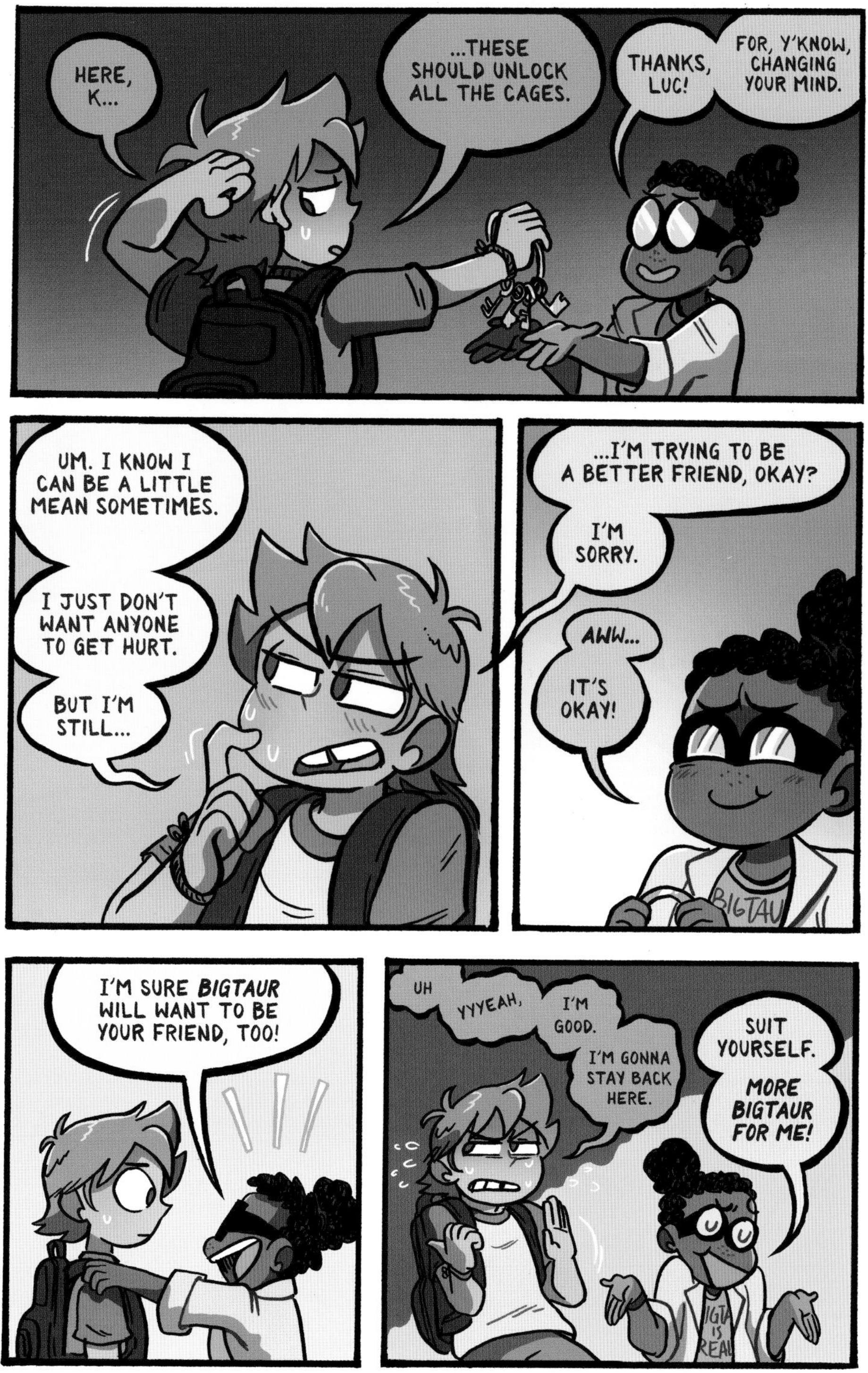
HERE, K...
...THESE SHOULD UNLOCK ALL THE CAGES.
THANKS, LUC!
FOR, Y'KNOW, CHANGING YOUR MIND.
UM. I KNOW I CAN BE A LITTLE MEAN SOMETIMES.
I JUST DON'T WANT ANYONE TO GET HURT.
BUT I'M STILL...
...I'M TRYING TO BE A BETTER FRIEND, OKAY?
I'M SORRY.
AWW...
IT'S OKAY!
BIGTAU
I'M SURE BIGTAUR WILL WANT TO BE YOUR FRIEND, TOO!
UH
YYYEAH,
I'M GOOD.
I'M GONNA STAY BACK HERE.
SUIT YOURSELF.
MORE BIGTAUR FOR ME!

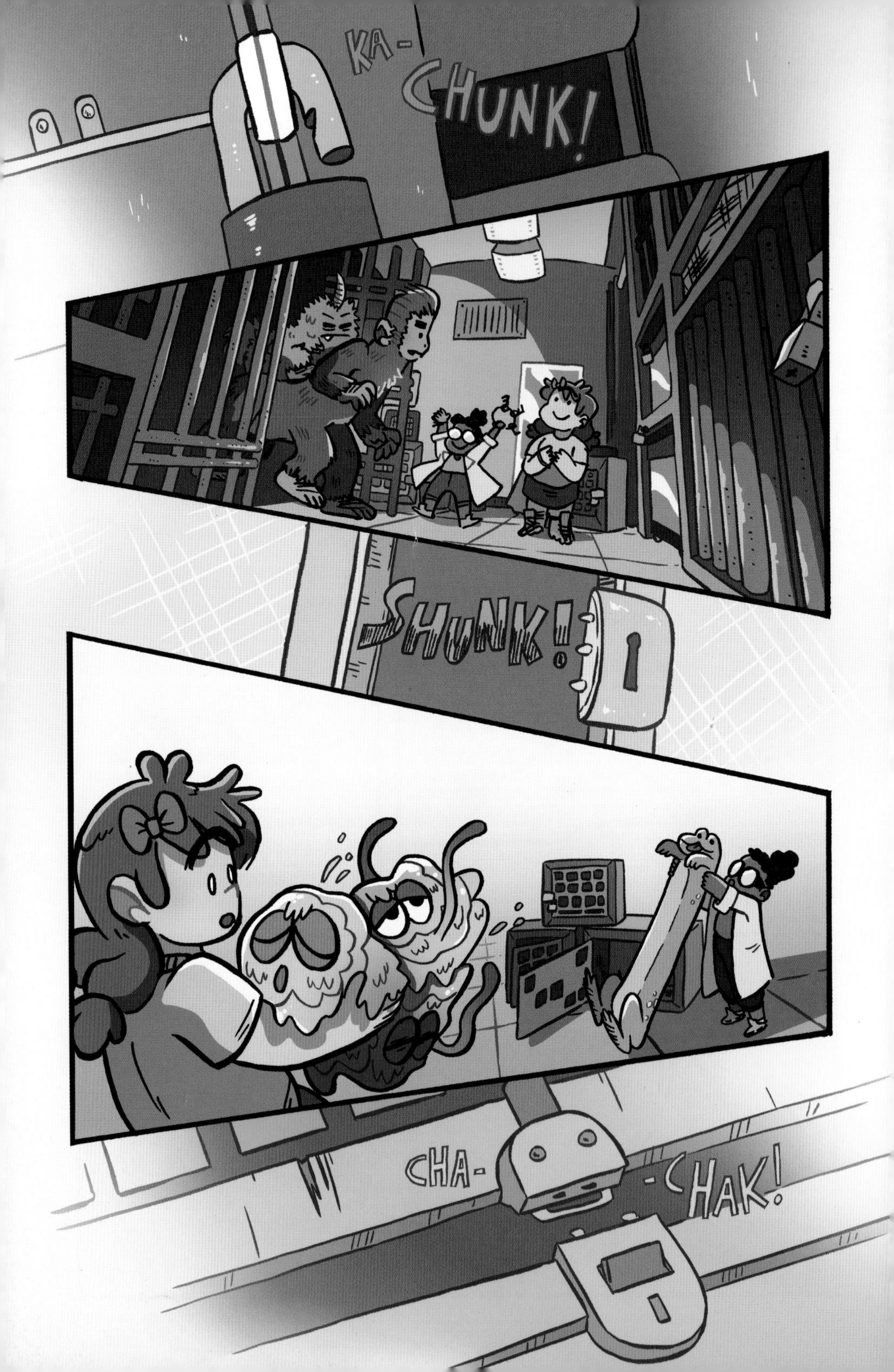
KA-CHUNK!
SHUNK!
CHA-
-CHAK!

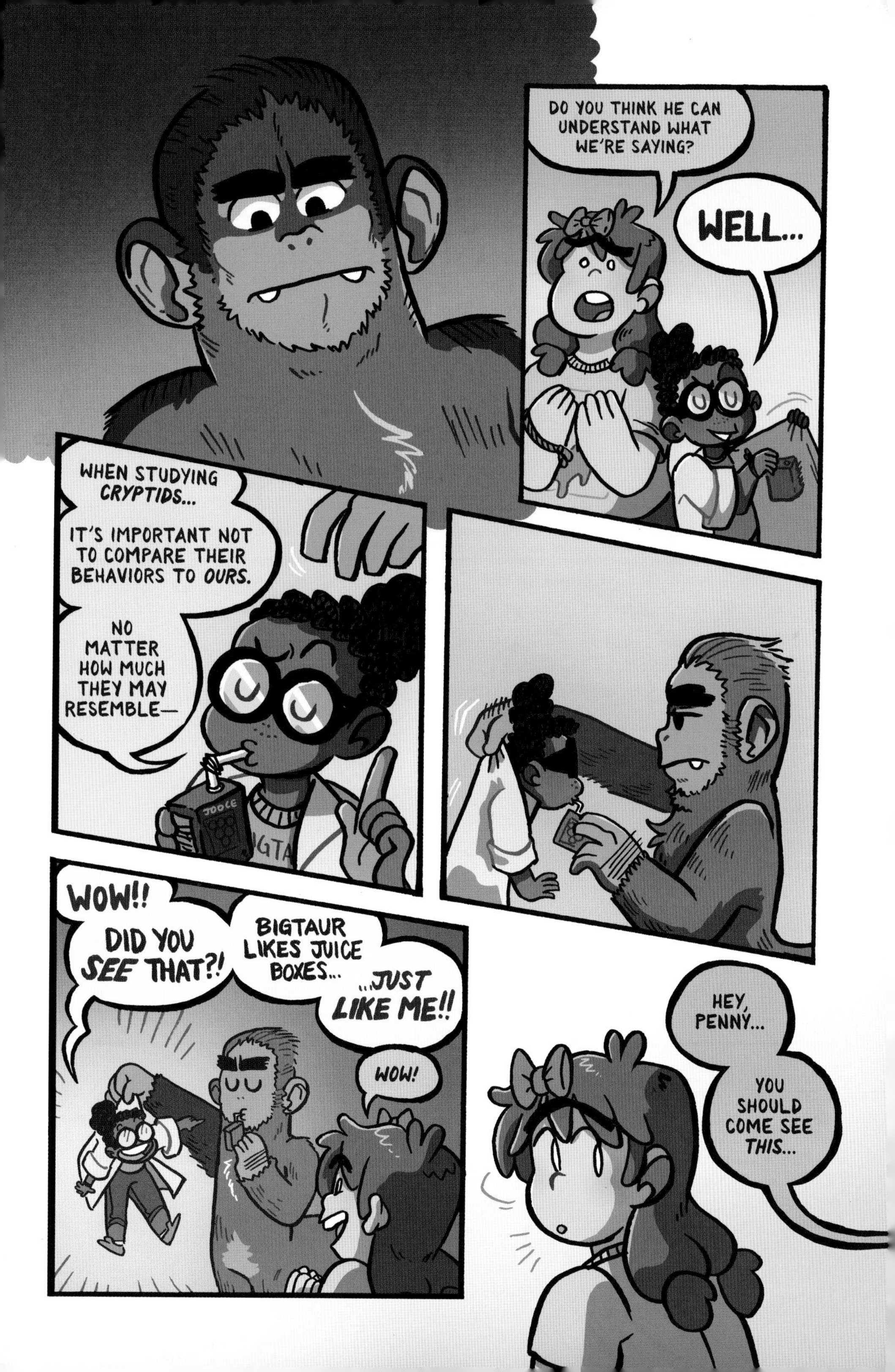

DO YOU THINK HE CAN UNDERSTAND WHAT WE'RE SAYING?
WELL...
WHEN STUDYING CRYPTIDS...
IT'S IMPORTANT NOT TO COMPARE THEIR BEHAVIORS TO OURS.
NO MATTER HOW MUCH THEY MAY RESEMBLE—
JOOCE
WOW!!
DID YOU SEE THAT?!
BIGTAUR LIKES JUICE BOXES...
...JUST LIKE ME!!
WOW!
HEY, PENNY...
YOU SHOULD COME SEE THIS...

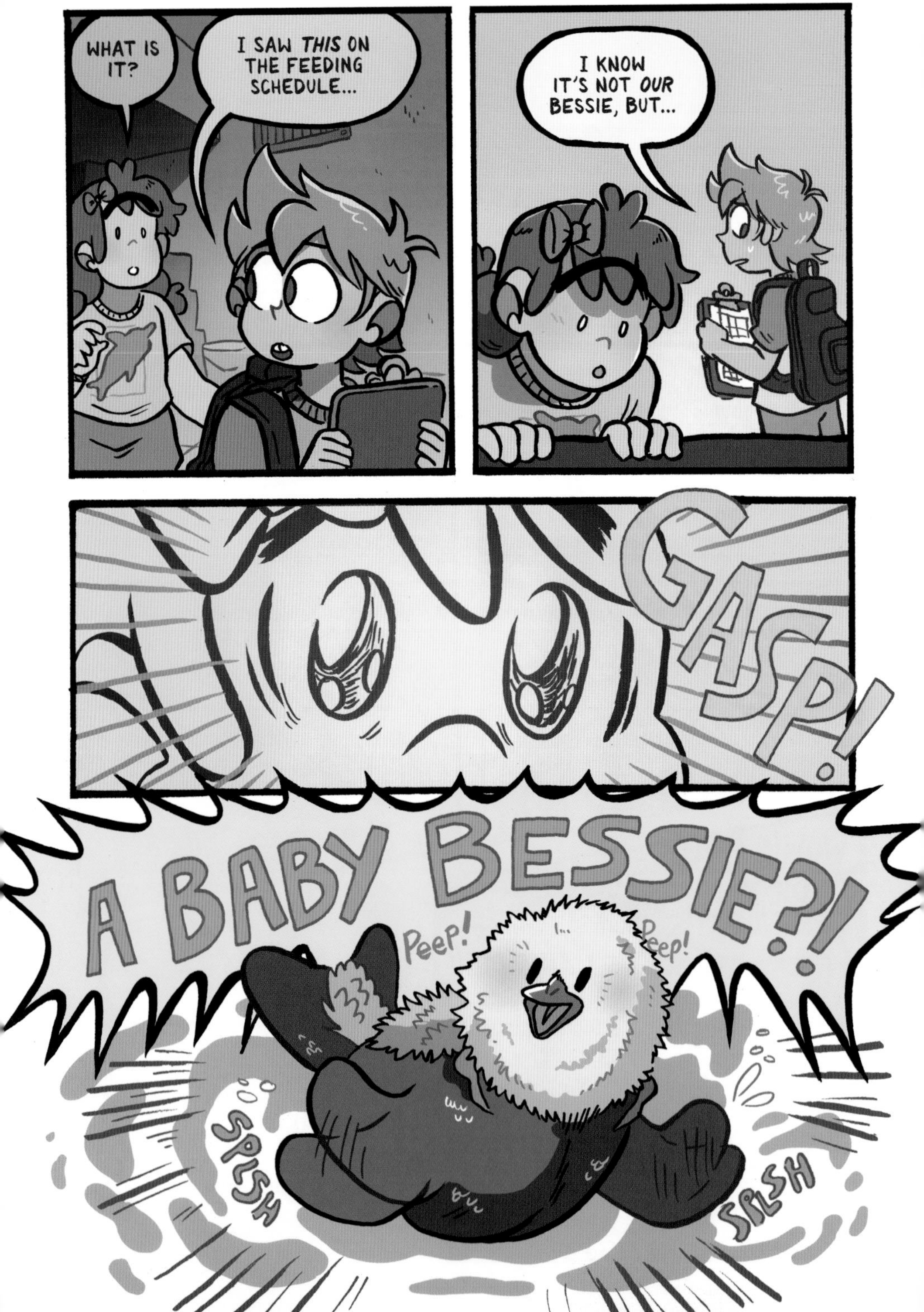
WHAT IS IT?
I SAW THIS ON THE FEEDING SCHEDULE...
I KNOW IT'S NOT OUR BESSIE, BUT...
GASP!
A BABY BESSIE?!
Peep!
Peep!
SPLSH
SPLSH

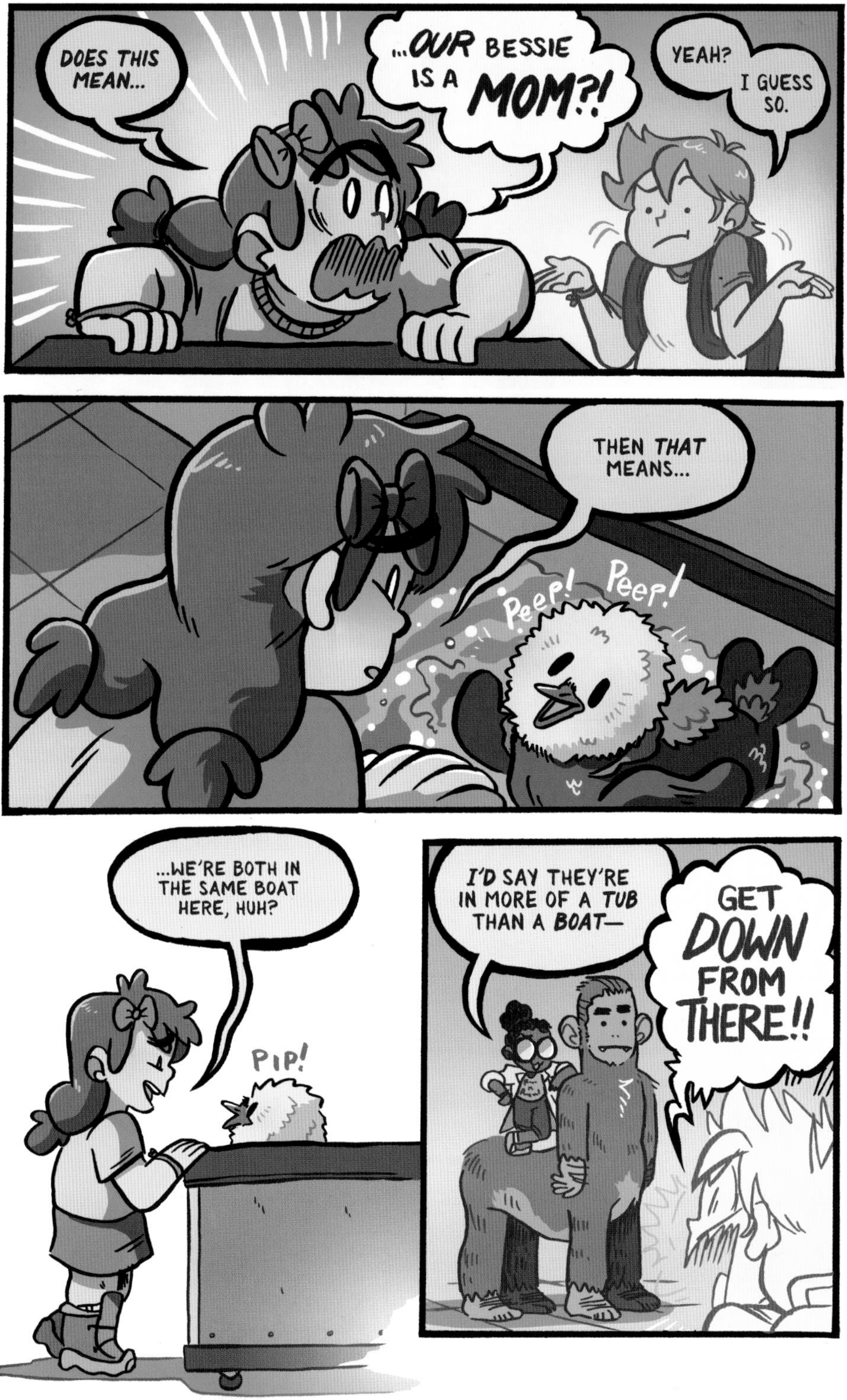
DOES THIS MEAN...
...OUR BESSIE IS A MOM?!
YEAH? I GUESS SO.
THEN THAT MEANS...
Peep! Peep!
...WE'RE BOTH IN THE SAME BOAT HERE, HUH?
PIP!
I'D SAY THEY'RE IN MORE OF A TUB THAN A BOAT—
GET DOWN FROM THERE!!

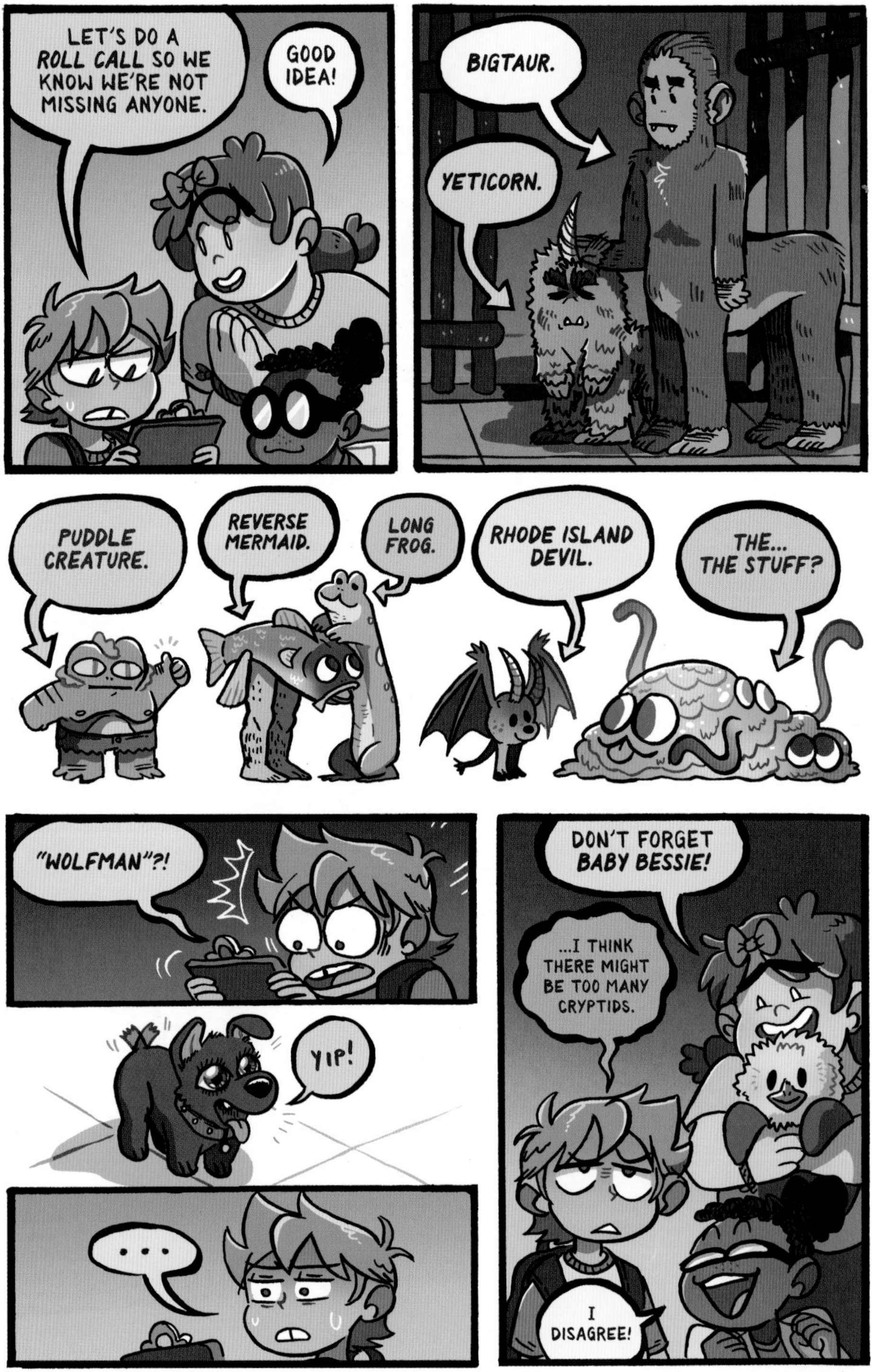
LET'S DO A ROLL CALL SO WE KNOW WE'RE NOT MISSING ANYONE.
GOOD IDEA!
BIGTAUR.
YETICORN.
PUDDLE CREATURE.
REVERSE MERMAID.
LONG FROG.
RHODE ISLAND DEVIL.
THE... THE STUFF?
"WOLFMAN"?!
YIP!
...
DON'T FORGET BABY BESSIE!
...I THINK THERE MIGHT BE TOO MANY CRYPTIDS.
I DISAGREE!

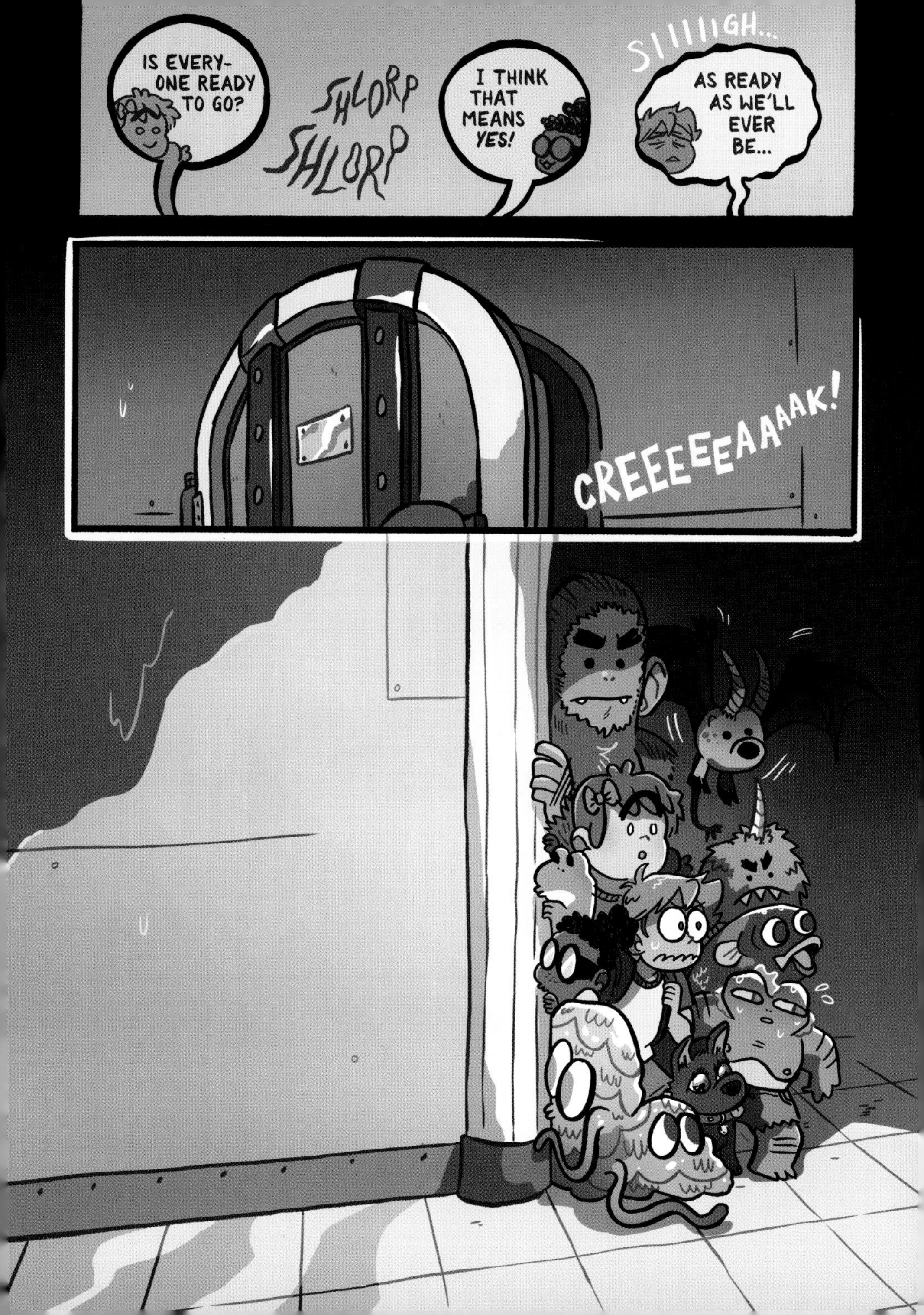

IS EVERY-ONE READY TO GO?
SHLORP SHLORP
I THINK THAT MEANS YES!
SIIIIIGH...
AS READY AS WE'LL EVER BE...
CREEEEEAAAAAK!

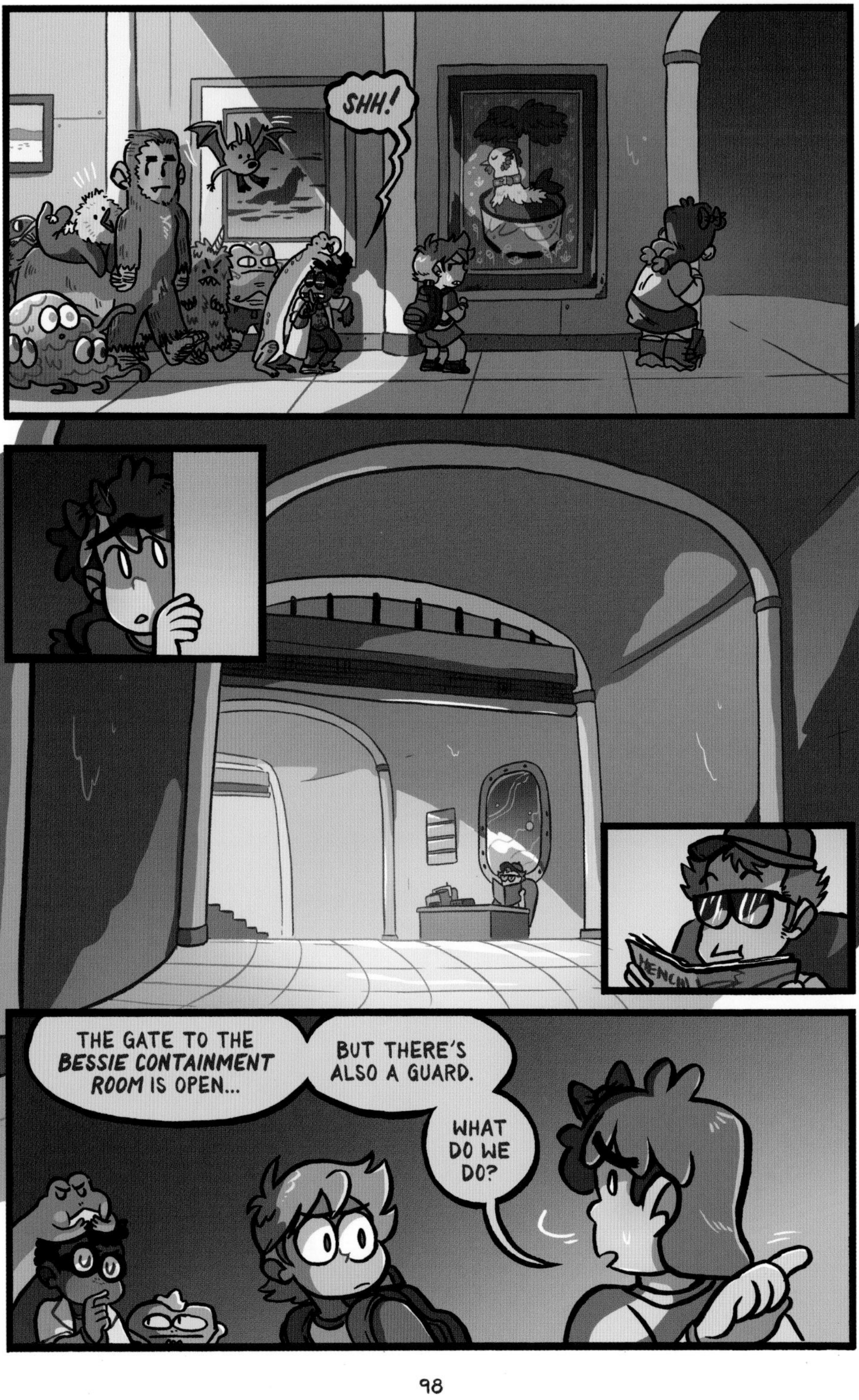
SHH!
THE GATE TO THE BESSIE CONTAINMENT ROOM IS OPEN...
BUT THERE'S ALSO A GUARD.
WHAT DO WE DO?

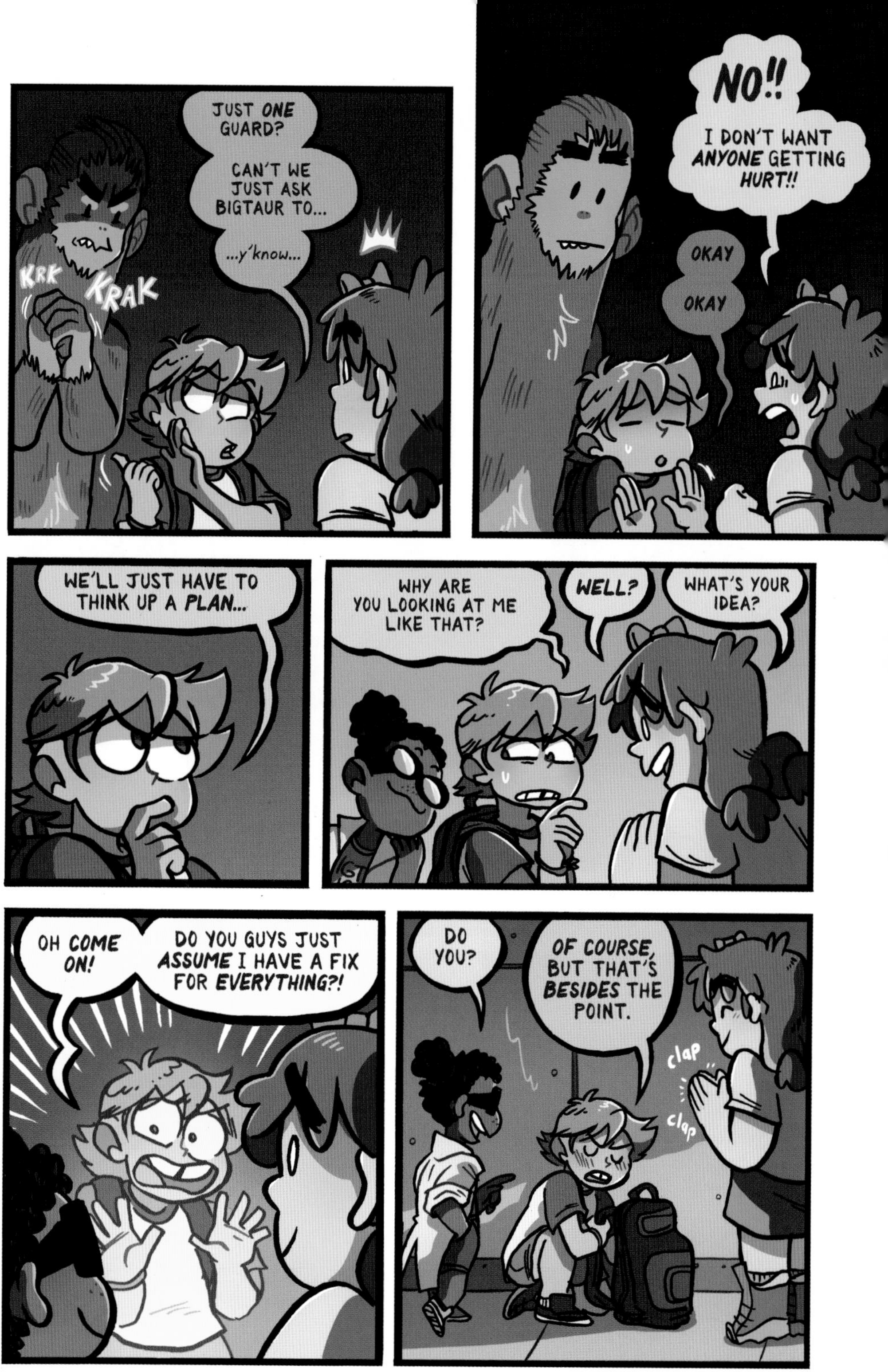

JUST ONE GUARD?
CAN'T WE JUST ASK BIGTAUR TO...
...y'know...
KRK KRAK
NO!!
I DON'T WANT ANYONE GETTING HURT!!
OKAY
OKAY
WE'LL JUST HAVE TO THINK UP A PLAN...
WHY ARE YOU LOOKING AT ME LIKE THAT?
WELL?
WHAT'S YOUR IDEA?
OH COME ON!
DO YOU GUYS JUST ASSUME I HAVE A FIX FOR EVERYTHING?!
DO YOU?
OF COURSE, BUT THAT'S BESIDES THE POINT.
clap
clap

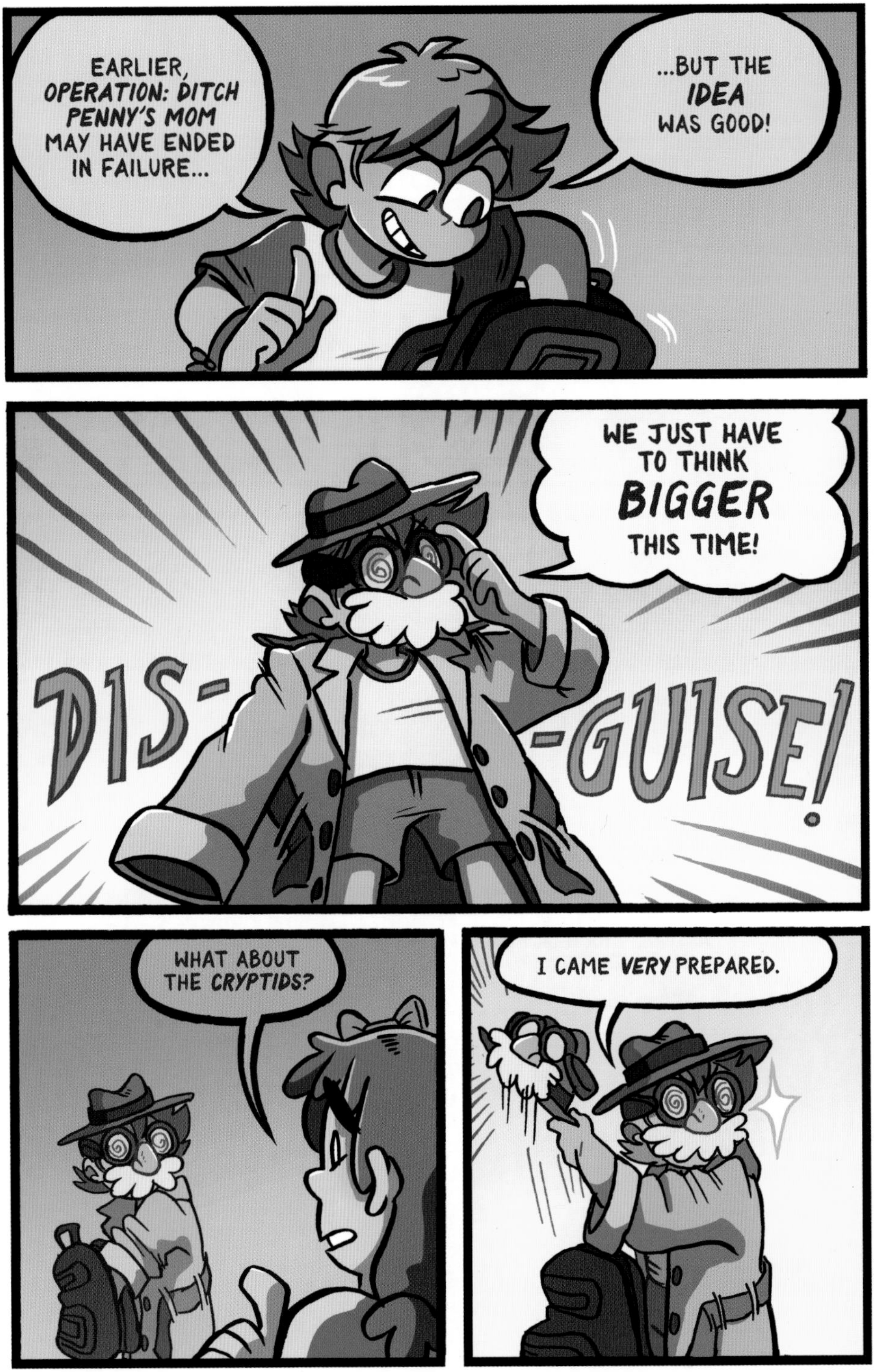
EARLIER, *OPERATION: DITCH PENNY'S MOM* MAY HAVE ENDED IN FAILURE...
...BUT THE *IDEA* WAS GOOD!
WE JUST HAVE TO THINK **BIGGER** THIS TIME!
DIS-
-GUISE!
WHAT ABOUT THE *CRYPTIDS?*
I CAME *VERY* PREPARED.

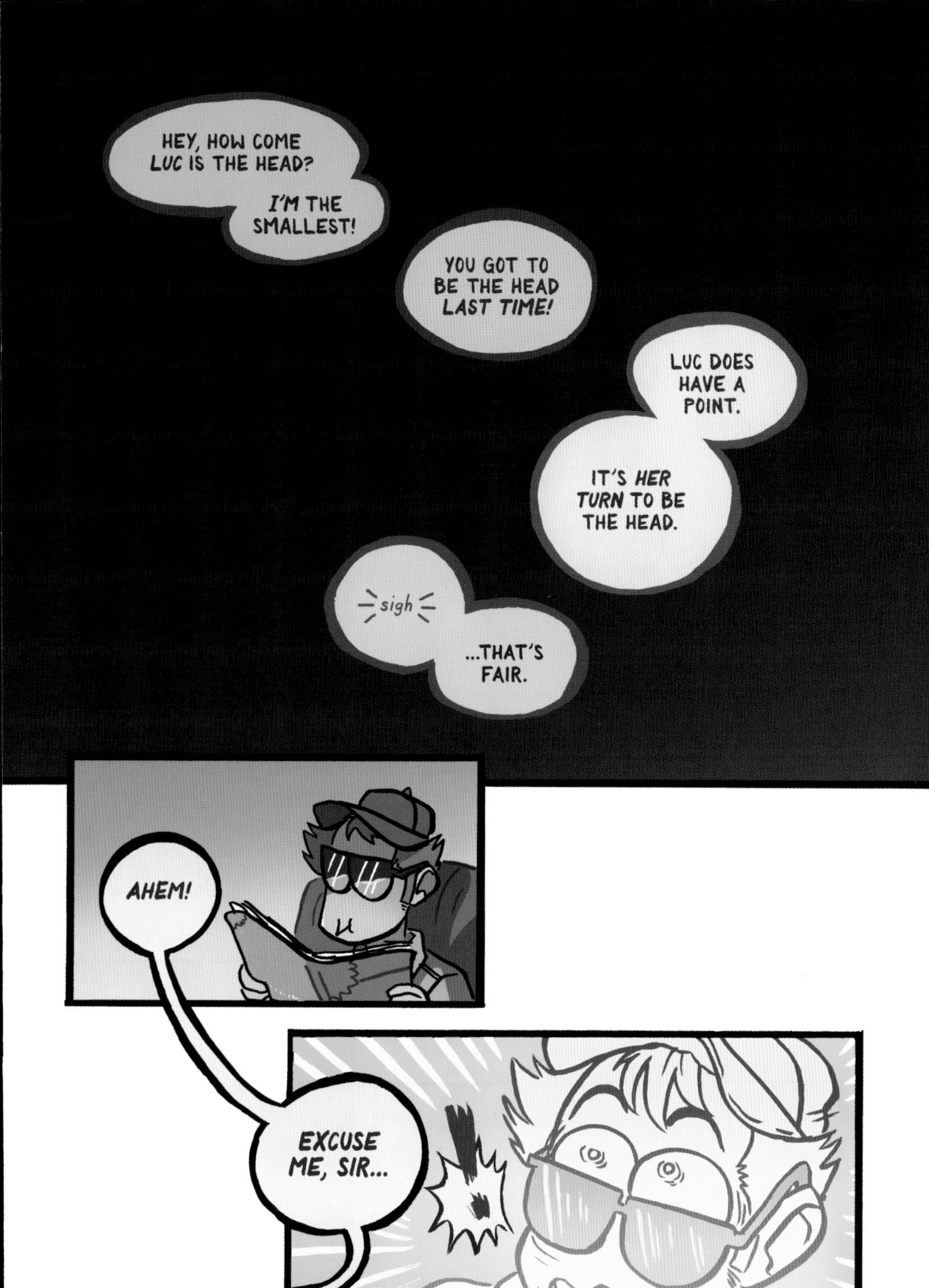
HEY, HOW COME LUC IS THE HEAD?
I'M THE SMALLEST!
YOU GOT TO BE THE HEAD LAST TIME!
LUC DOES HAVE A POINT.
IT'S HER TURN TO BE THE HEAD.
sigh
...THAT'S FAIR.
AHEM!
EXCUSE ME, SIR...

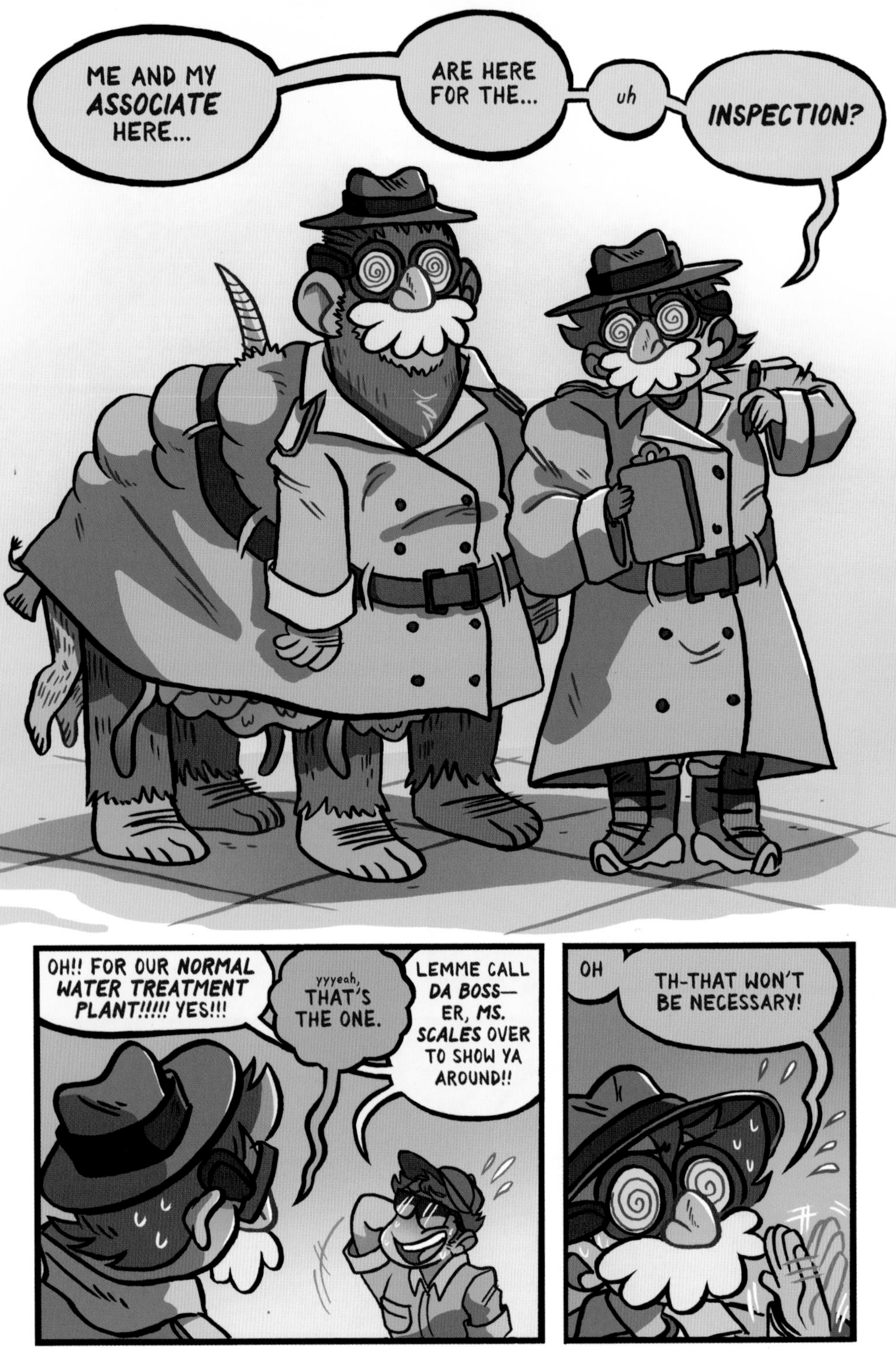
ME AND MY ASSOCIATE HERE...
ARE HERE FOR THE...
uh
INSPECTION?
OH!! FOR OUR NORMAL WATER TREATMENT PLANT!!!!! YES!!!
yyyeah, THAT'S THE ONE.
LEMME CALL DA BOSS— ER, MS. SCALES OVER TO SHOW YA AROUND!!
OH
TH-THAT WON'T BE NECESSARY!

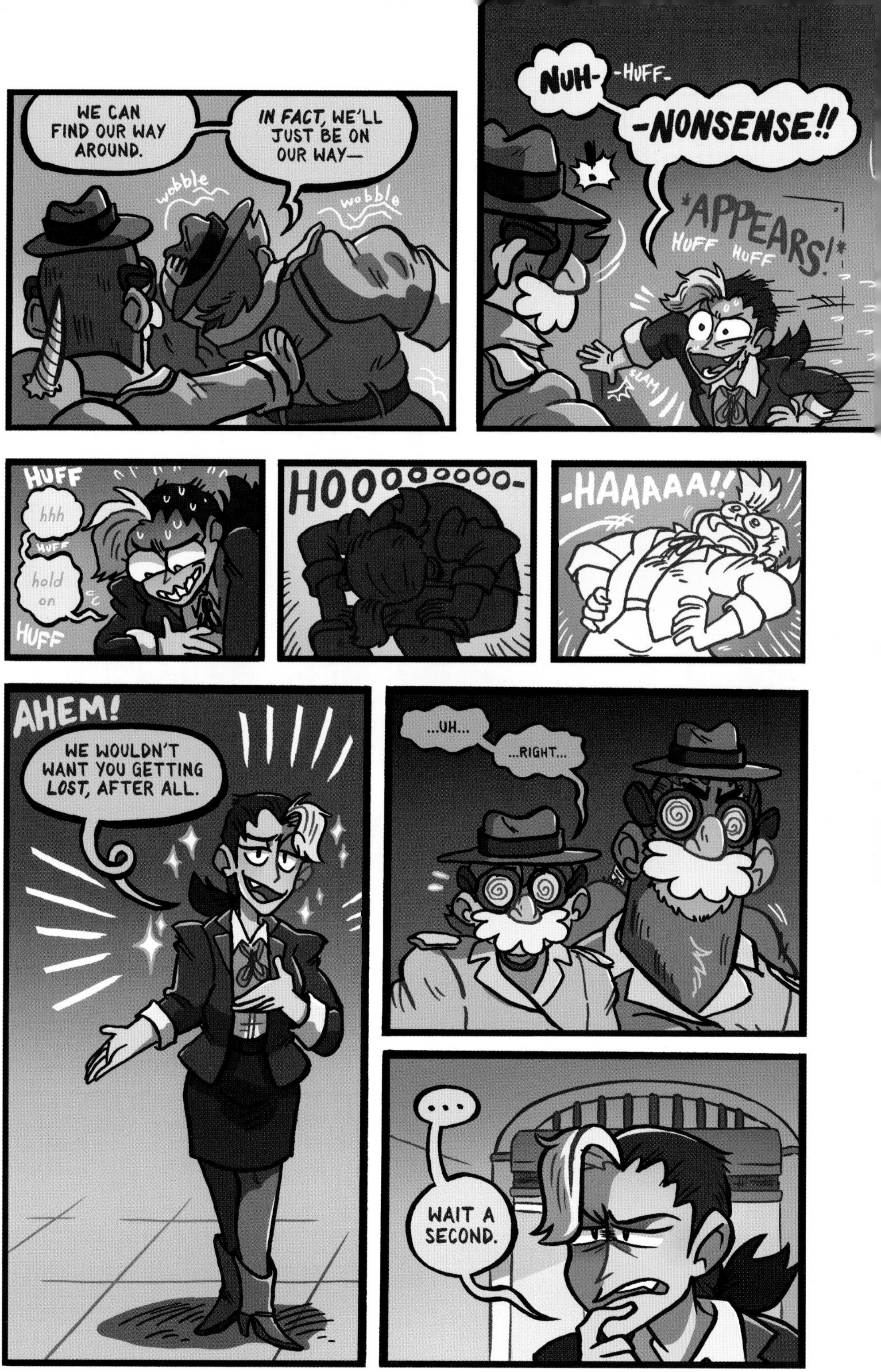
WE CAN FIND OUR WAY AROUND.
IN FACT, WE'LL JUST BE ON OUR WAY—
wobble
wobble
NUH-
-HUFF-
-NONSENSE!!
APPEARS!
HUFF HUFF
SLAM
HUFF
hhh
HUFF
hold on
HUFF
HOOOOOOOO-
-HAAAAA!!
AHEM!
WE WOULDN'T WANT YOU GETTING LOST, AFTER ALL.
...UH...
...RIGHT...
...
WAIT A SECOND.

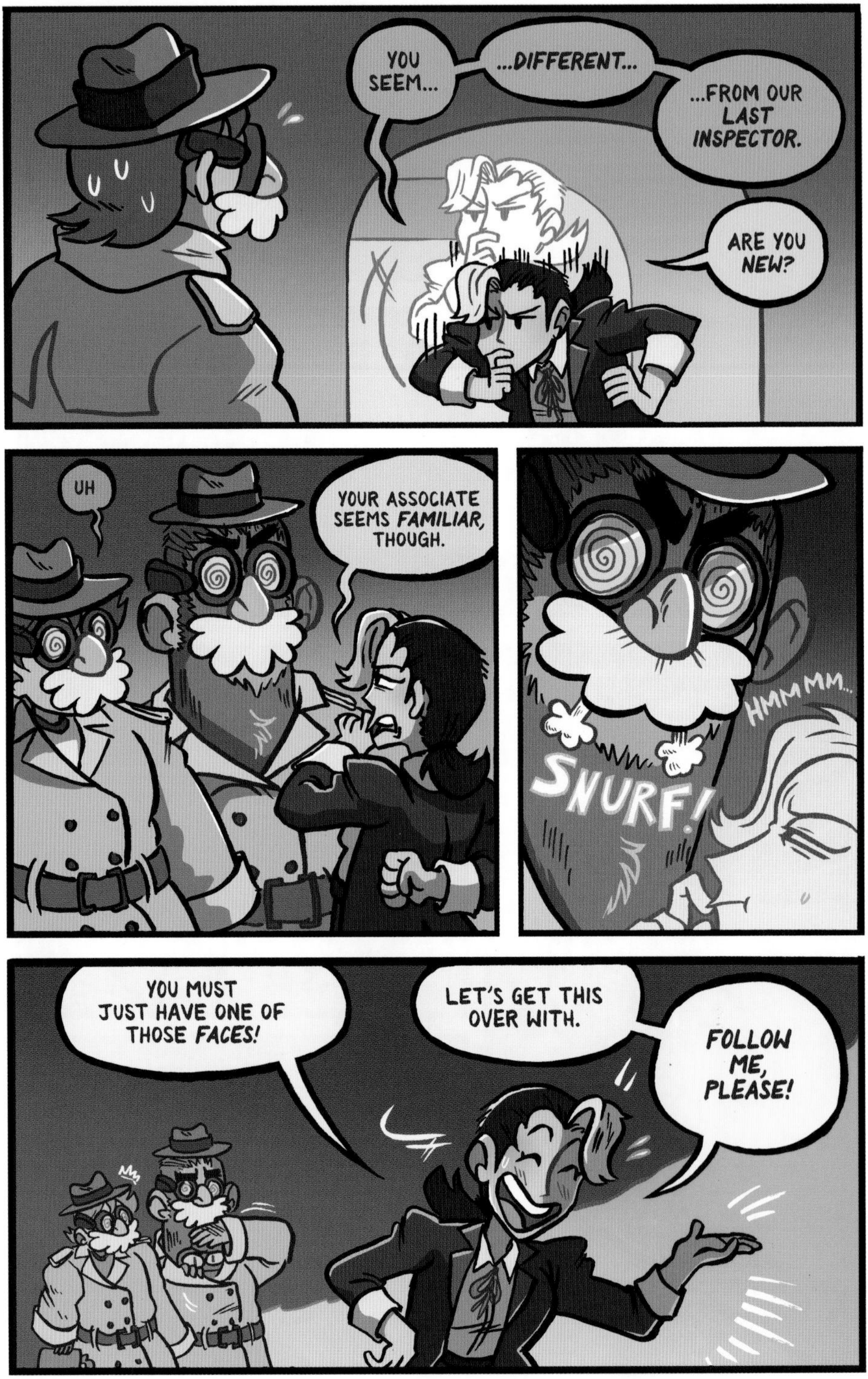
YOU SEEM...
...DIFFERENT...
...FROM OUR LAST INSPECTOR.
ARE YOU NEW?
UH
YOUR ASSOCIATE SEEMS FAMILIAR, THOUGH.
HMMMM...
SNURF!
YOU MUST JUST HAVE ONE OF THOSE FACES!
LET'S GET THIS OVER WITH.
FOLLOW ME, PLEASE!

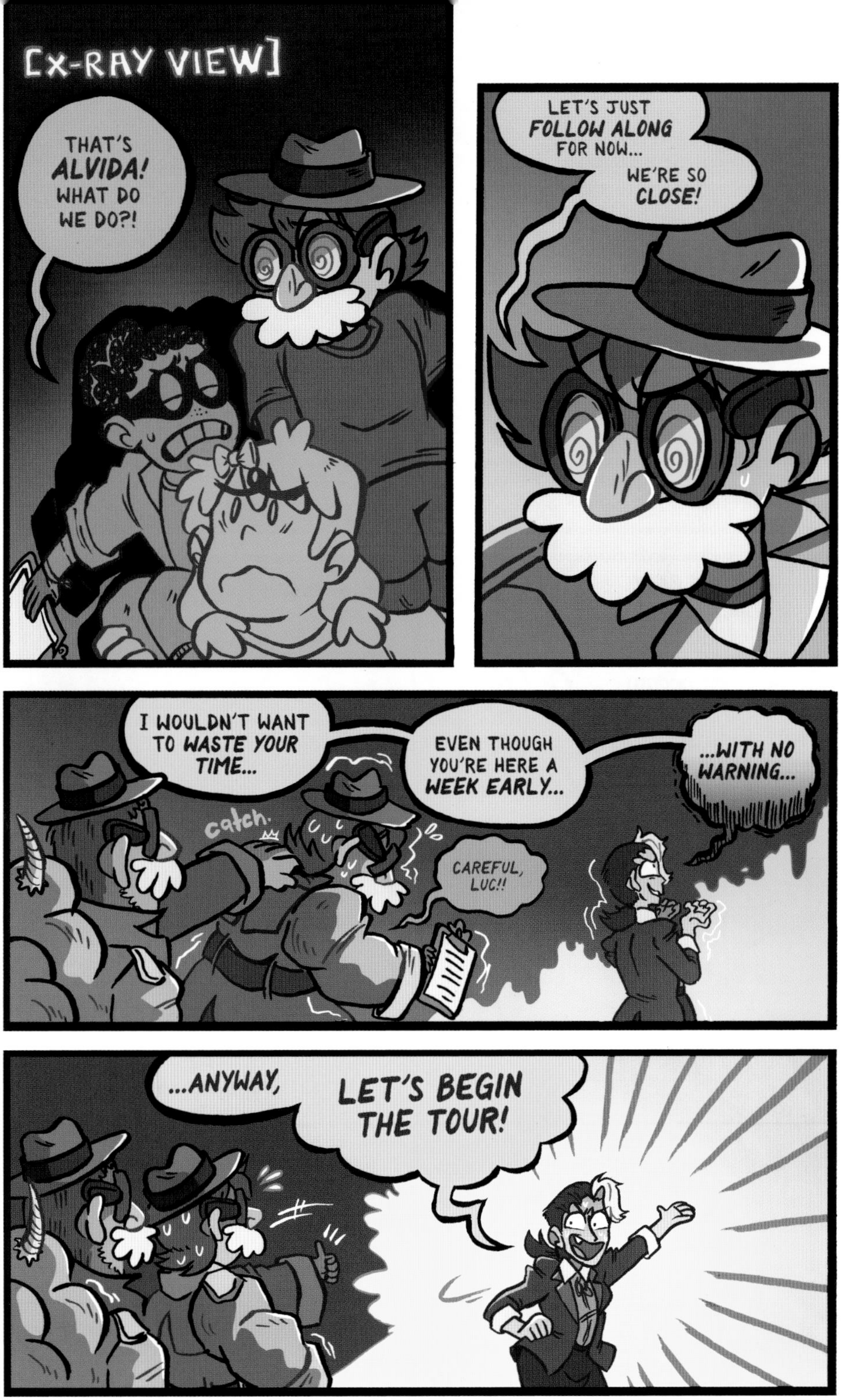
[X-RAY VIEW]
THAT'S ALVIDA! WHAT DO WE DO?!
LET'S JUST FOLLOW ALONG FOR NOW...
WE'RE SO CLOSE!
I WOULDN'T WANT TO WASTE YOUR TIME...
EVEN THOUGH YOU'RE HERE A WEEK EARLY...
...WITH NO WARNING...
catch.
CAREFUL, LUC!!
...ANYWAY,
LET'S BEGIN THE TOUR!

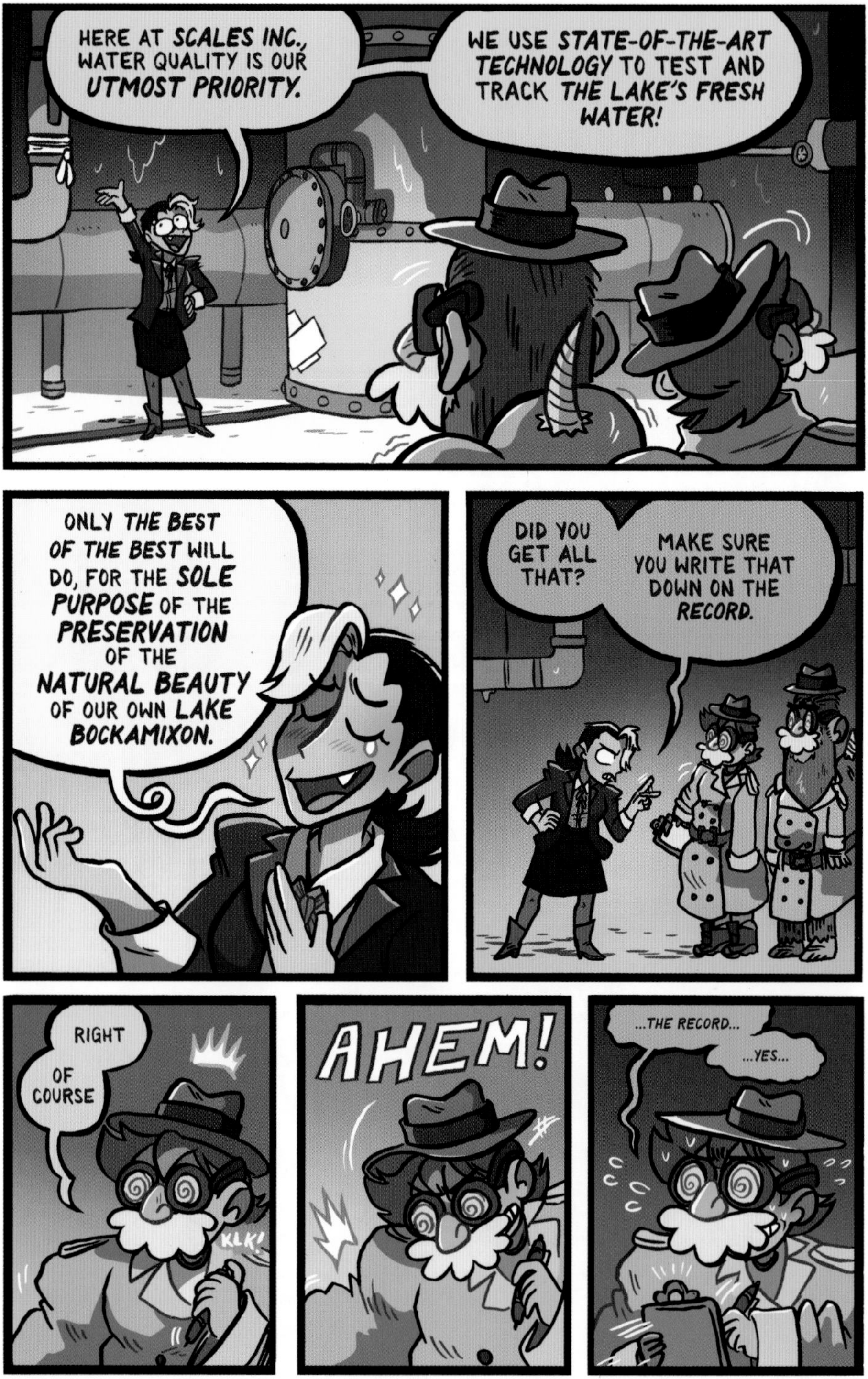
HERE AT SCALES INC., WATER QUALITY IS OUR UTMOST PRIORITY.
WE USE STATE-OF-THE-ART TECHNOLOGY TO TEST AND TRACK THE LAKE'S FRESH WATER!
ONLY THE BEST OF THE BEST WILL DO, FOR THE SOLE PURPOSE OF THE PRESERVATION OF THE NATURAL BEAUTY OF OUR OWN LAKE BOCKAMIXON.
DID YOU GET ALL THAT?
MAKE SURE YOU WRITE THAT DOWN ON THE RECORD.
RIGHT
OF COURSE
KLK!
AHEM!
...THE RECORD...
...YES...

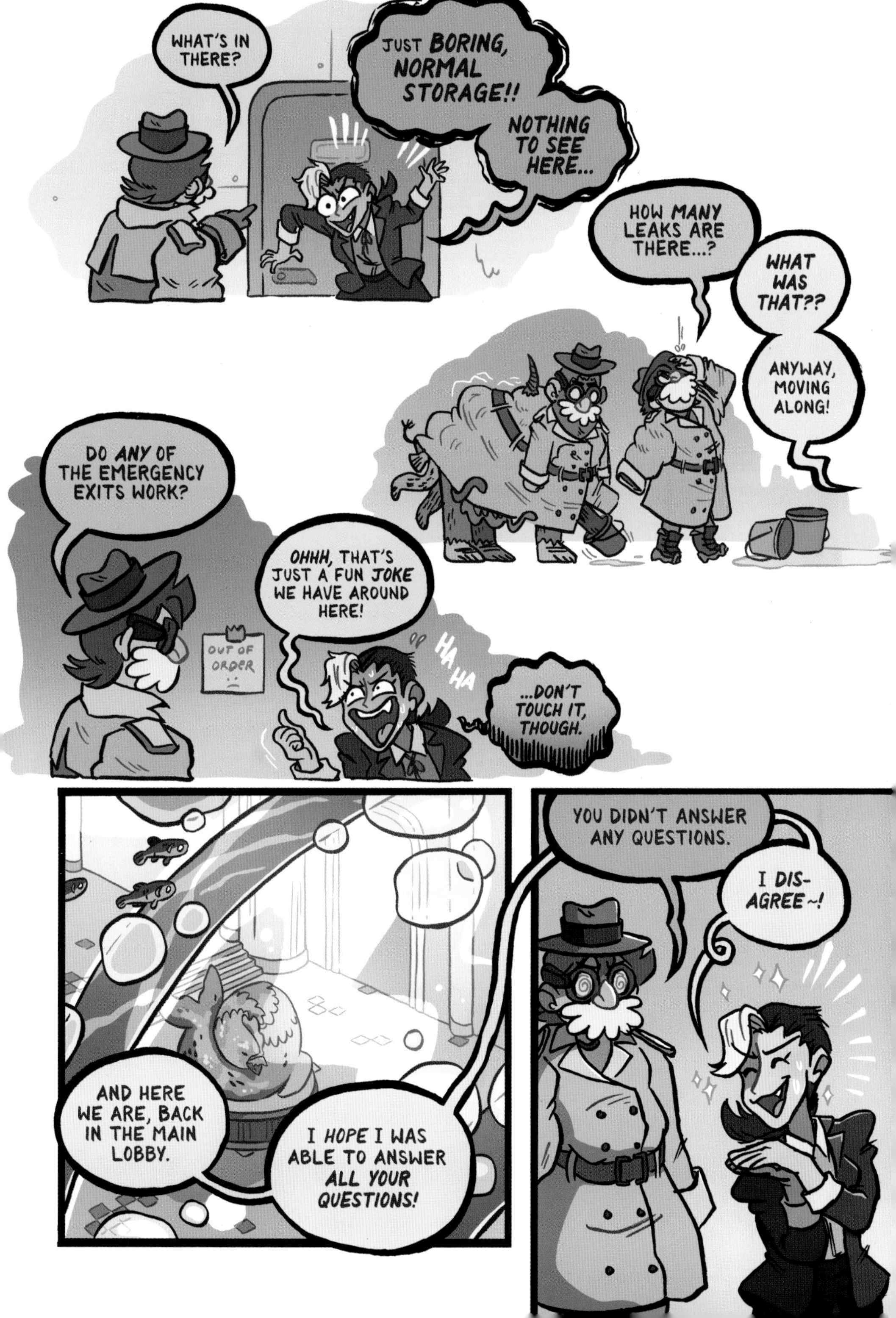
WHAT'S IN THERE?
JUST BORING, NORMAL STORAGE!!
NOTHING TO SEE HERE...
HOW MANY LEAKS ARE THERE...?
WHAT WAS THAT??
ANYWAY, MOVING ALONG!
DO ANY OF THE EMERGENCY EXITS WORK?
OUT OF ORDER
OHHH, THAT'S JUST A FUN JOKE WE HAVE AROUND HERE!
HA HA
...DON'T TOUCH IT, THOUGH.
AND HERE WE ARE, BACK IN THE MAIN LOBBY.
I HOPE I WAS ABLE TO ANSWER ALL YOUR QUESTIONS!
YOU DIDN'T ANSWER ANY QUESTIONS.
I DIS-AGREE~!

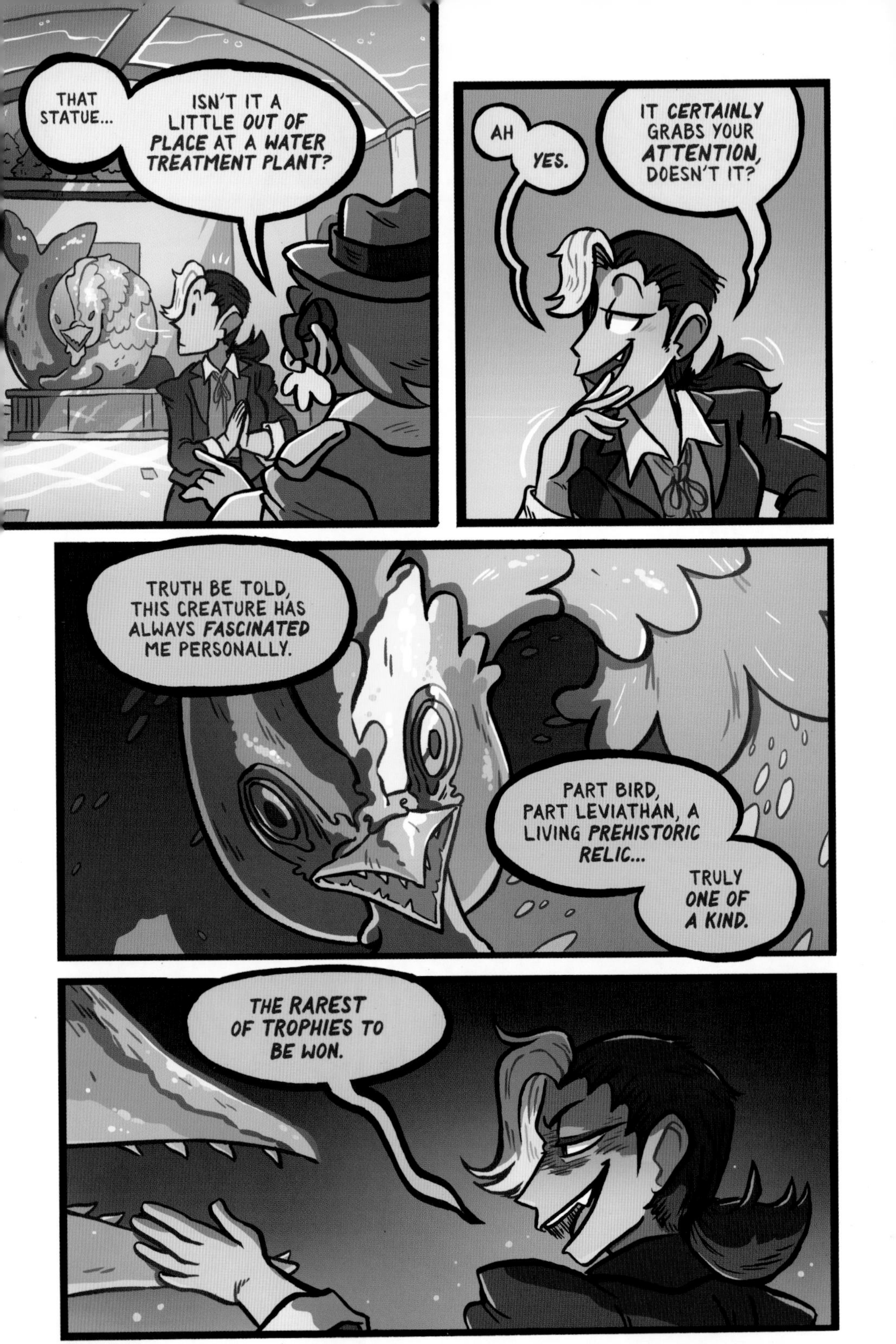
THAT STATUE...
ISN'T IT A LITTLE OUT OF PLACE AT A WATER TREATMENT PLANT?
AH
YES.
IT CERTAINLY GRABS YOUR ATTENTION, DOESN'T IT?
TRUTH BE TOLD, THIS CREATURE HAS ALWAYS FASCINATED ME PERSONALLY.
PART BIRD, PART LEVIATHAN, A LIVING PREHISTORIC RELIC...
TRULY ONE OF A KIND.
THE RAREST OF TROPHIES TO BE WON.

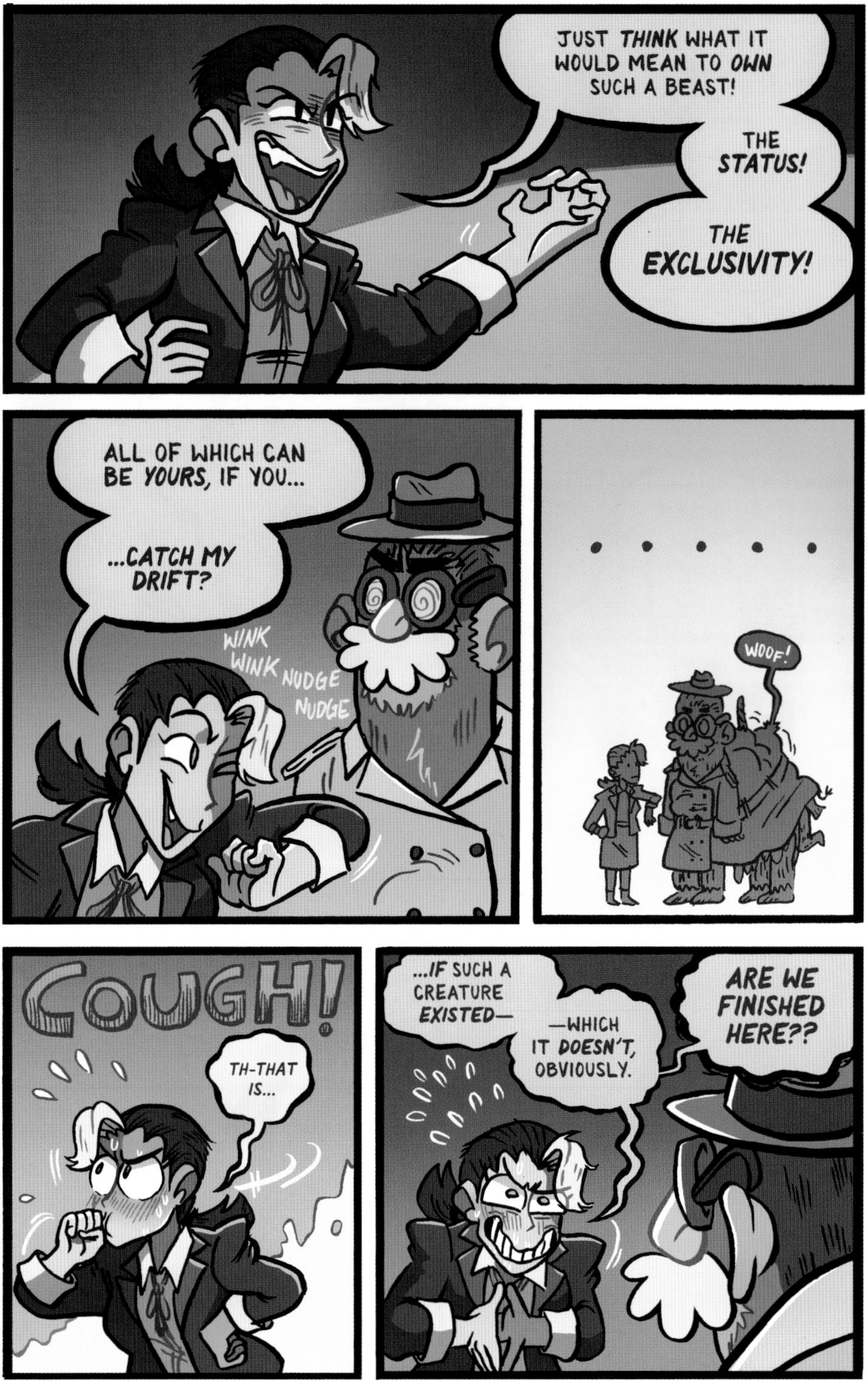
JUST *THINK* WHAT IT WOULD MEAN TO *OWN* SUCH A BEAST!
THE *STATUS!*
THE **EXCLUSIVITY!**
ALL OF WHICH CAN BE *YOURS,* IF YOU...
...CATCH MY DRIFT?
WINK WINK NUDGE NUDGE
. . . . .
WOOF!
COUGH!
TH-THAT IS...
...*IF* SUCH A CREATURE *EXISTED*—
—WHICH IT *DOESN'T,* OBVIOUSLY.
ARE WE FINISHED HERE??

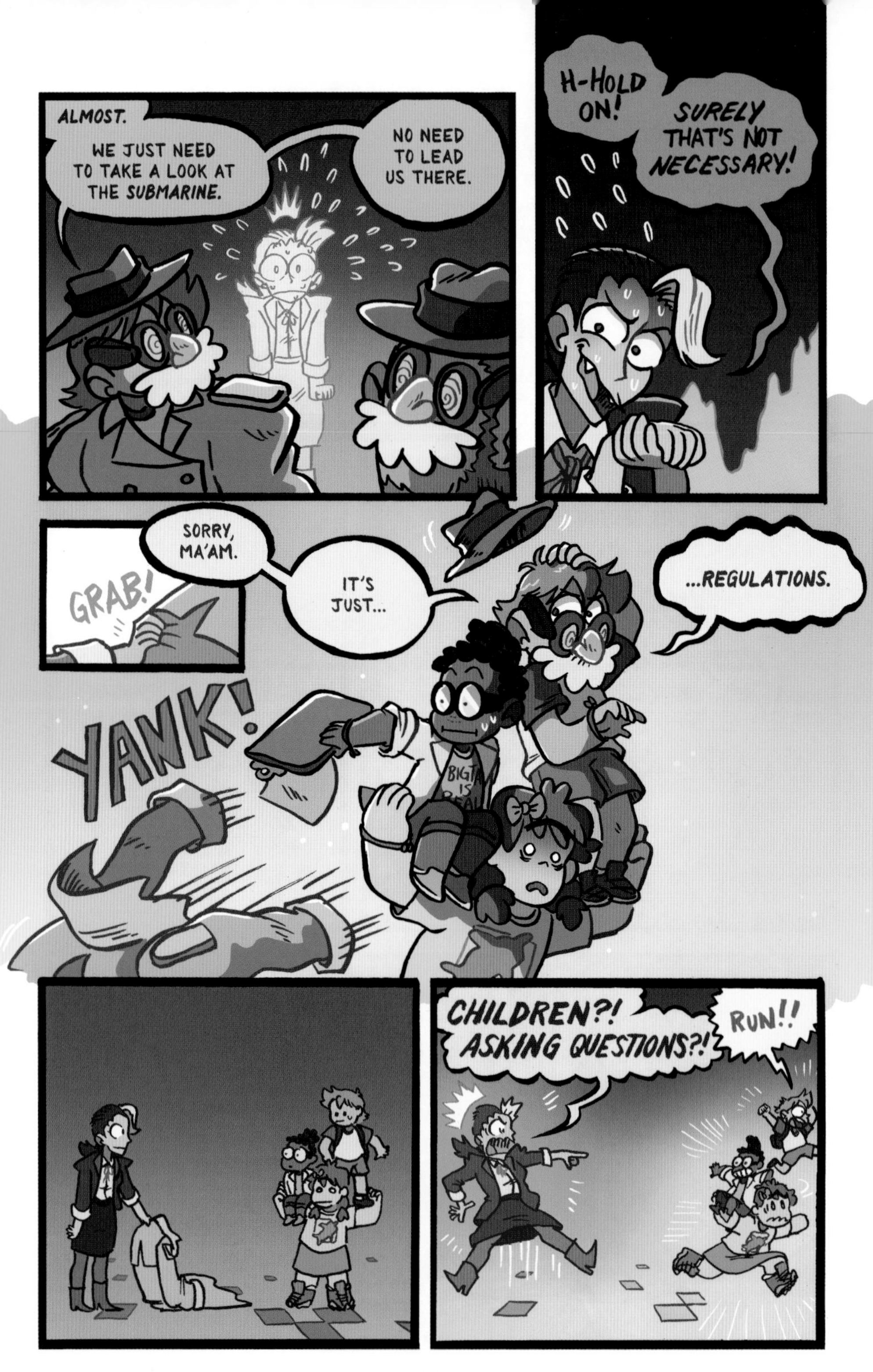
ALMOST.
WE JUST NEED TO TAKE A LOOK AT THE SUBMARINE.
NO NEED TO LEAD US THERE.
H-HOLD ON!
SURELY THAT'S NOT NECESSARY!
SORRY, MA'AM.
GRAB!
IT'S JUST...
...REGULATIONS.
YANK!
CHILDREN?! ASKING QUESTIONS?!
RUN!!

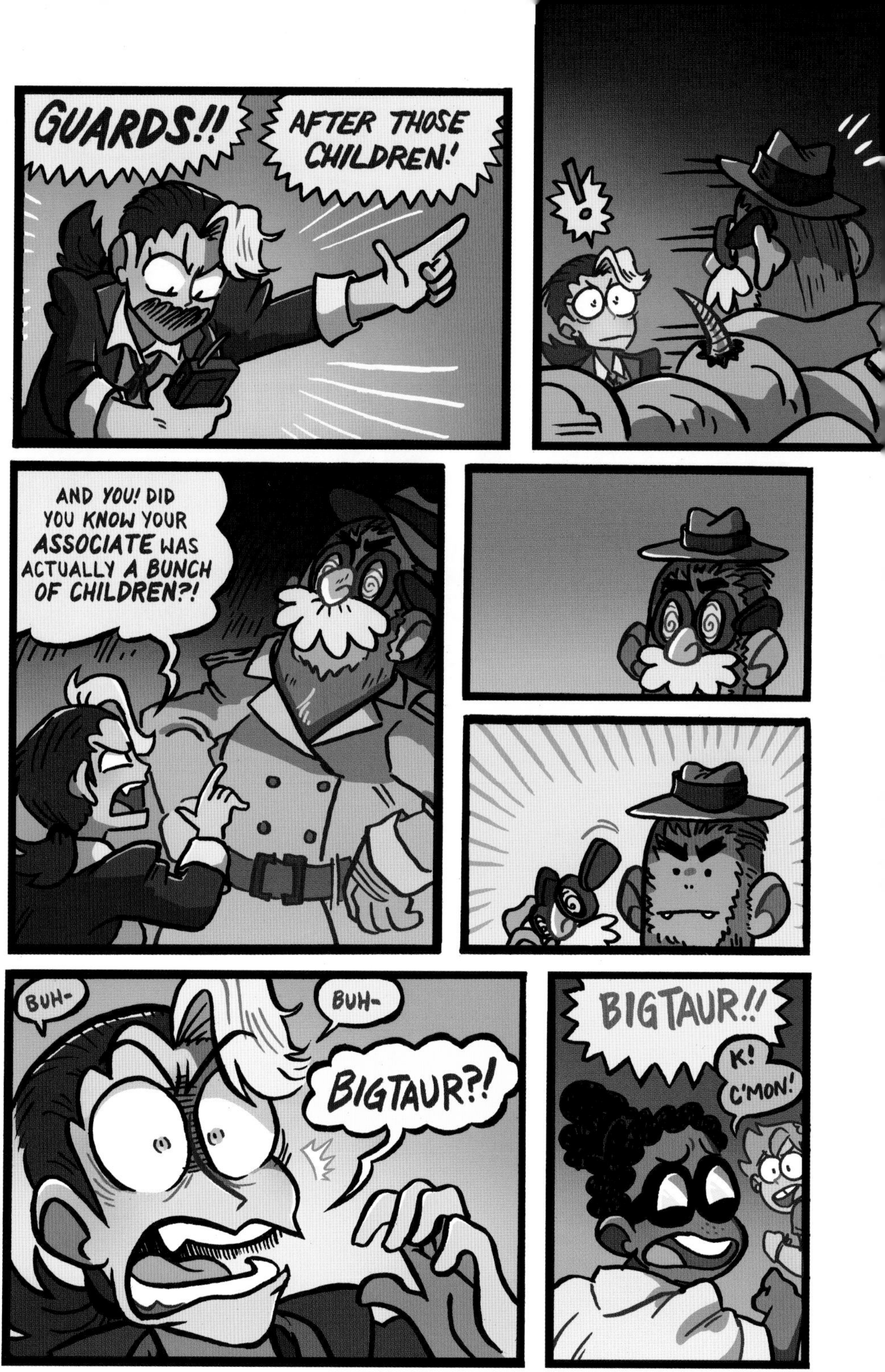
GUARDS!!
AFTER THOSE CHILDREN!
!
AND YOU! DID YOU KNOW YOUR ASSOCIATE WAS ACTUALLY A BUNCH OF CHILDREN?!
BUH-
BUH-
BIGTAUR?!
BIGTAUR!!
K! C'MON!

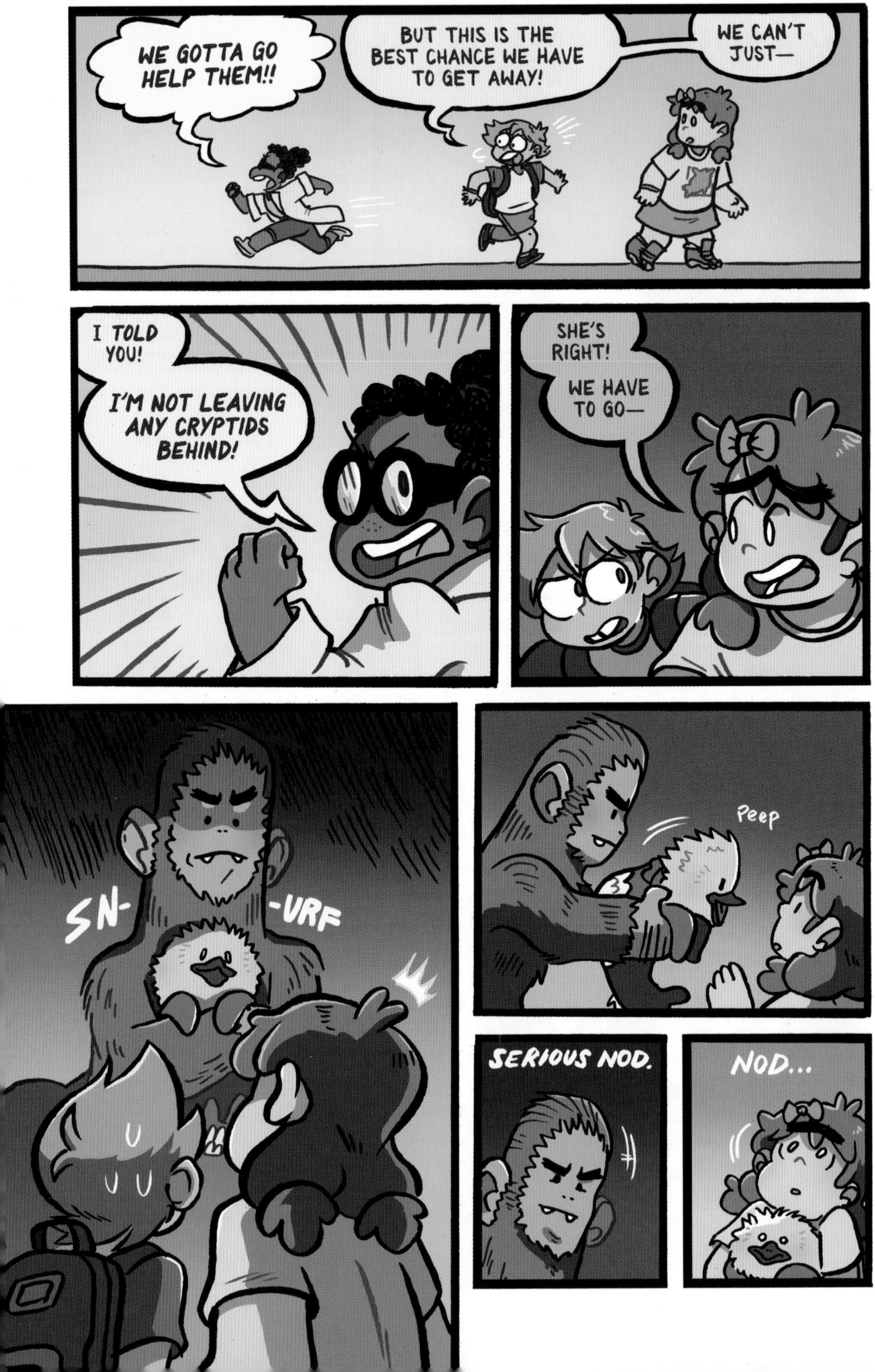
WE GOTTA GO HELP THEM!!
BUT THIS IS THE BEST CHANCE WE HAVE TO GET AWAY!
WE CAN'T JUST—
I TOLD YOU!
I'M NOT LEAVING ANY CRYPTIDS BEHIND!
SHE'S RIGHT!
WE HAVE TO GO—
SN-
-URF
Peep
SERIOUS NOD.
NOD...

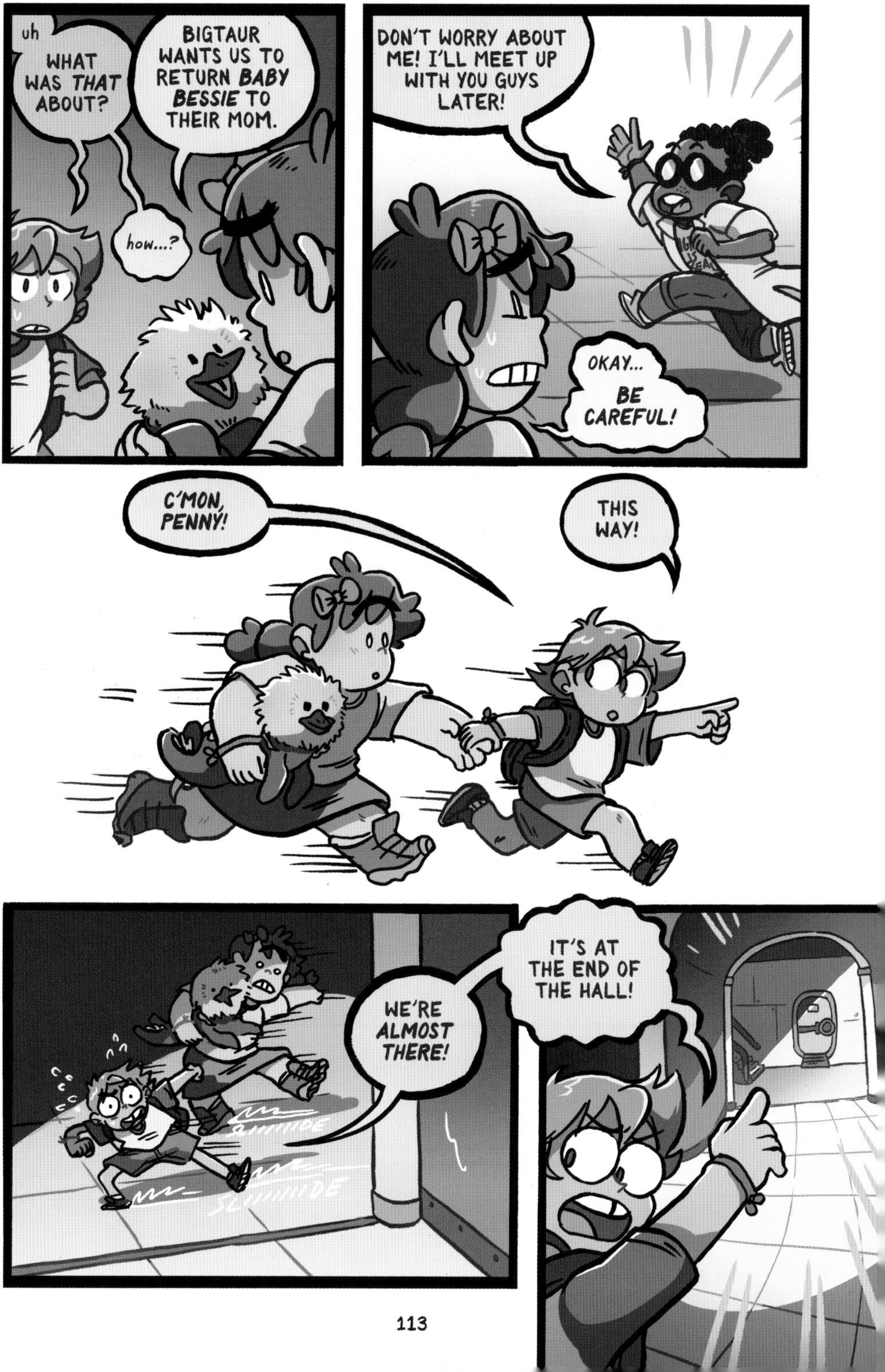
uh
WHAT WAS THAT ABOUT?
BIGTAUR WANTS US TO RETURN BABY BESSIE TO THEIR MOM.
how...?
DON'T WORRY ABOUT ME! I'LL MEET UP WITH YOU GUYS LATER!
OKAY... BE CAREFUL!
C'MON, PENNY!
THIS WAY!
SLIIIIIDE
SLIIIIIDE
WE'RE ALMOST THERE!
IT'S AT THE END OF THE HALL!

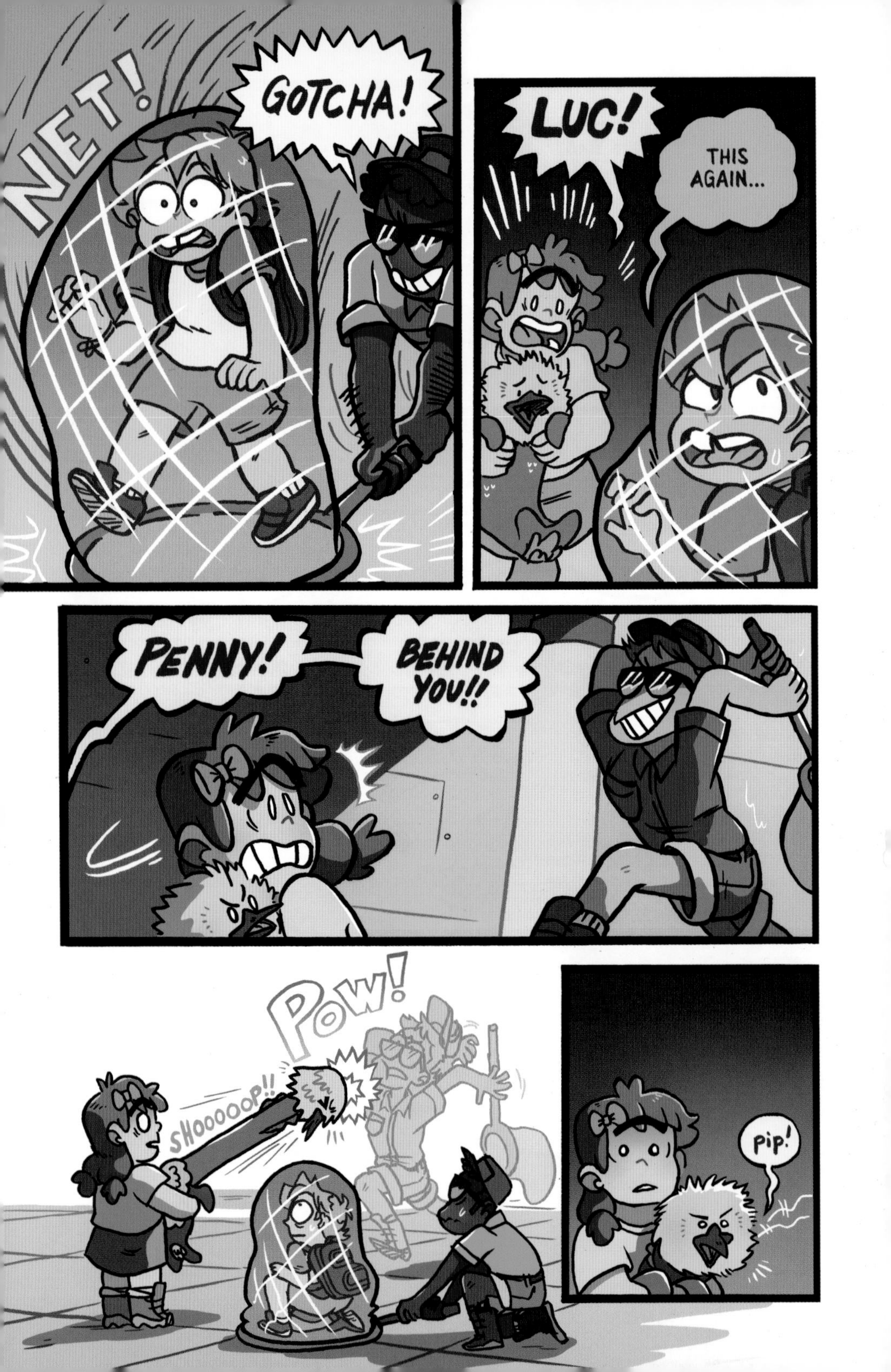
NET!
GOTCHA!
LUC!
THIS AGAIN...
PENNY!
BEHIND YOU!!
POW!
SHOOOOOP!!
pip!

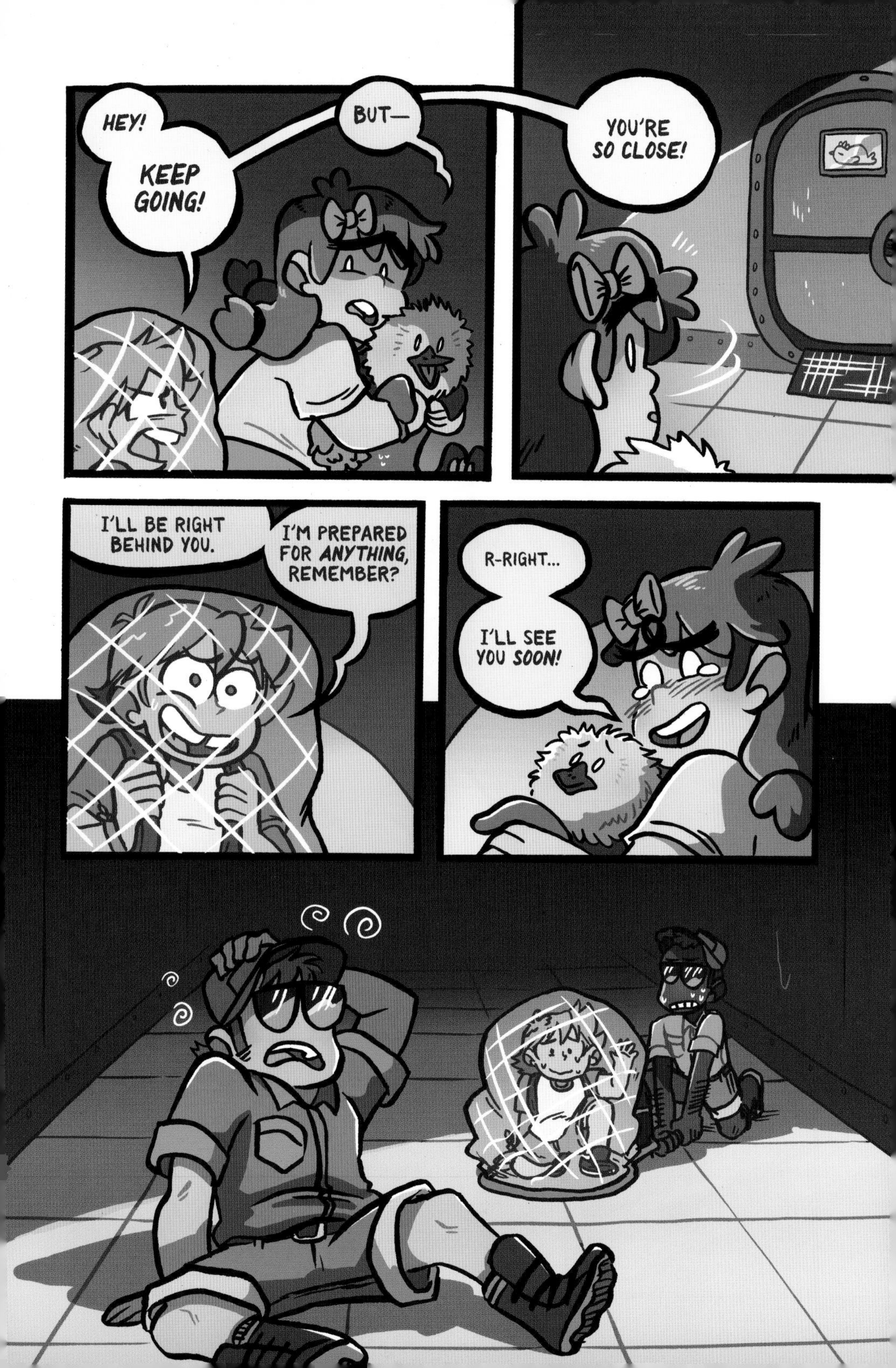
HEY!
KEEP GOING!
BUT—
YOU'RE SO CLOSE!
I'LL BE RIGHT BEHIND YOU.
I'M PREPARED FOR *ANYTHING*, REMEMBER?
R-RIGHT...
I'LL SEE YOU *SOON*!

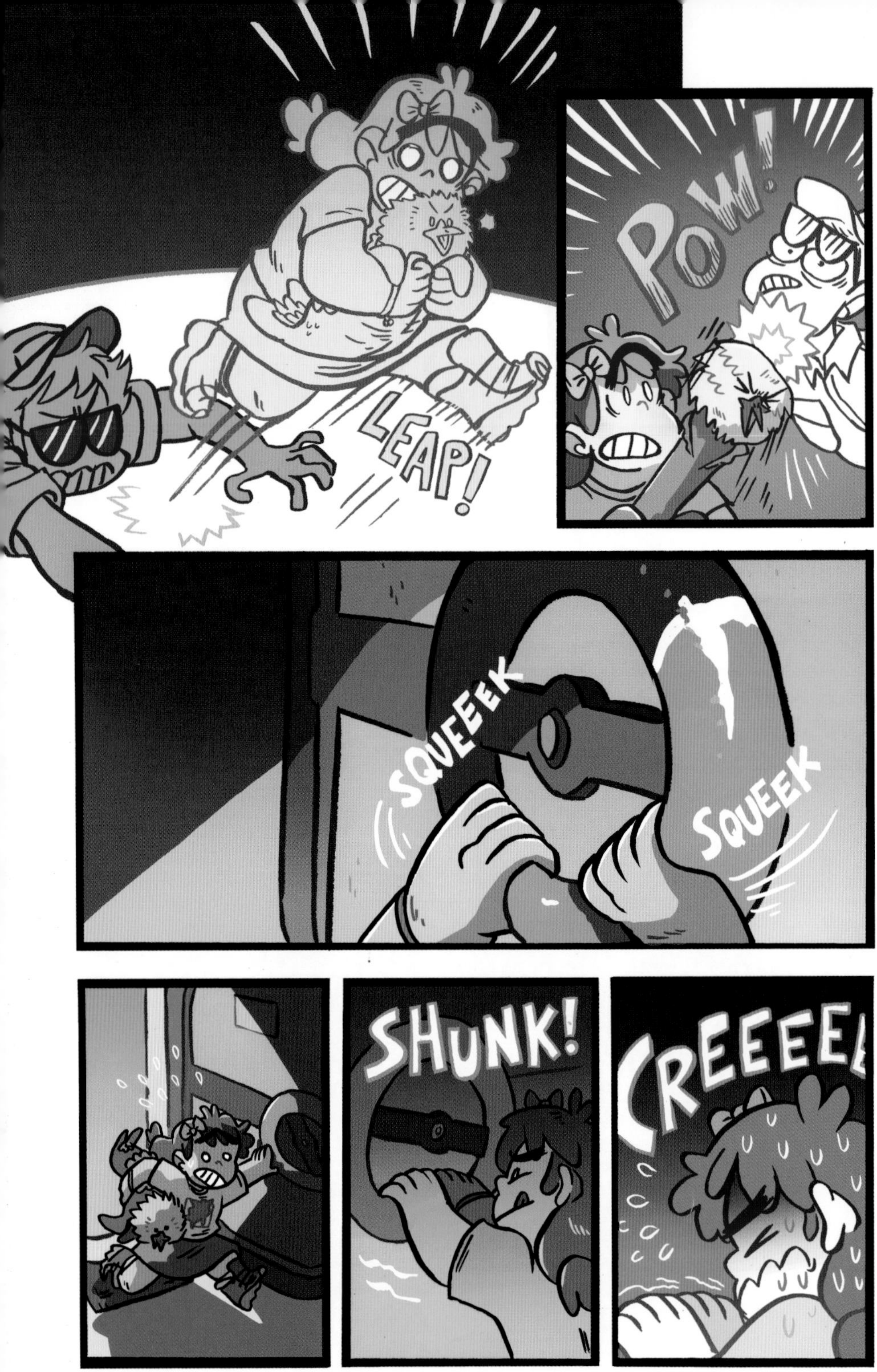
LEAP!
POW!
SQUEEEK
SQUEEK
SHUNK!
CREEEEE

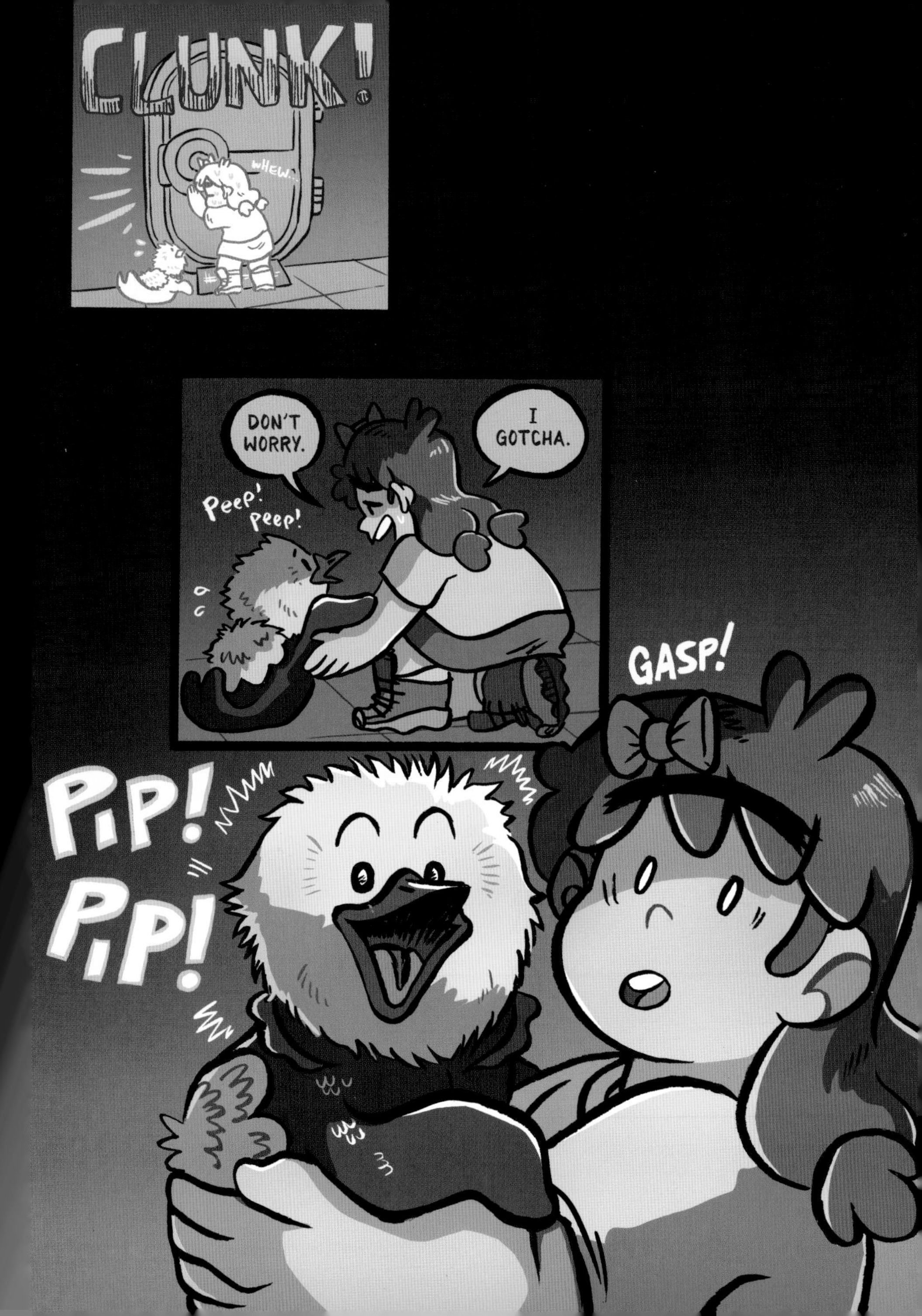
CLUNK!
WHEW...
DON'T WORRY.
I GOTCHA.
Peep! peep!
GASP!
P,P! P,P!

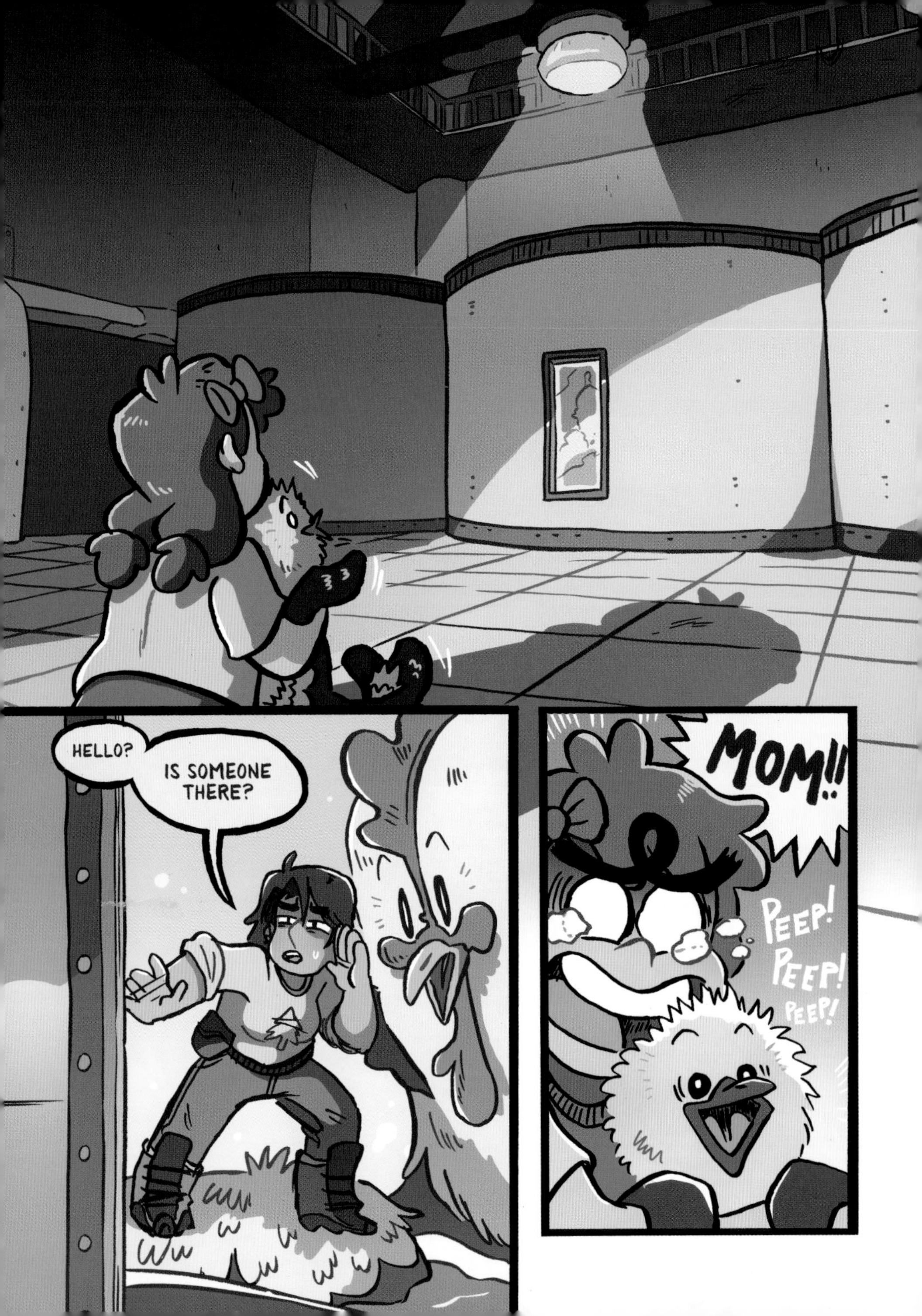
HELLO?
IS SOMEONE THERE?
MOM!!
PEEP!
PEEP!
PEEP!

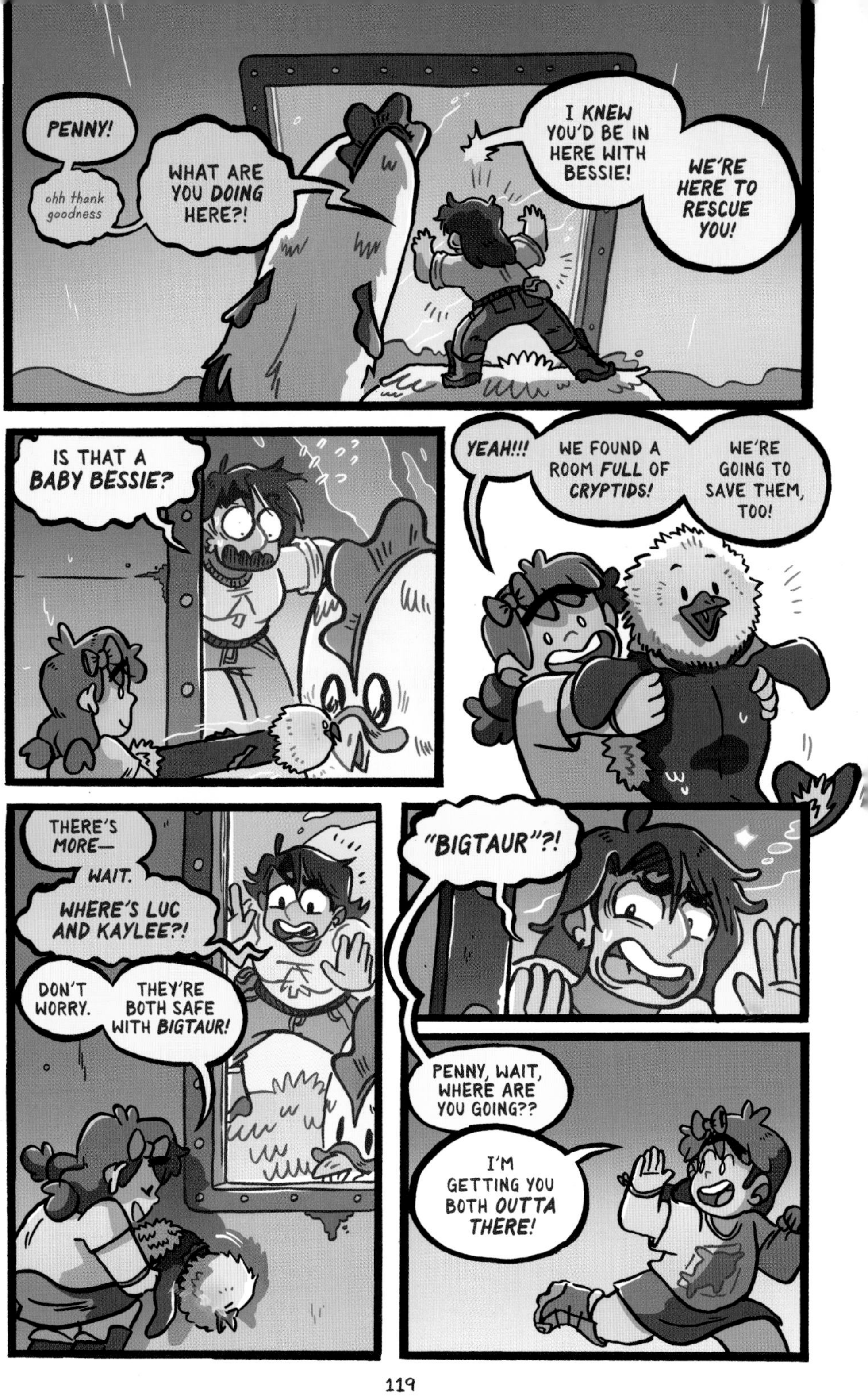
PENNY!
ohh thank goodness
WHAT ARE YOU DOING HERE?!
I KNEW YOU'D BE IN HERE WITH BESSIE!
WE'RE HERE TO RESCUE YOU!
IS THAT A BABY BESSIE?
YEAH!!!
WE FOUND A ROOM FULL OF CRYPTIDS!
WE'RE GOING TO SAVE THEM, TOO!
THERE'S MORE—
WAIT.
WHERE'S LUC AND KAYLEE?!
DON'T WORRY.
THEY'RE BOTH SAFE WITH BIGTAUR!
"BIGTAUR"?!
PENNY, WAIT, WHERE ARE YOU GOING??
I'M GETTING YOU BOTH OUTTA THERE!

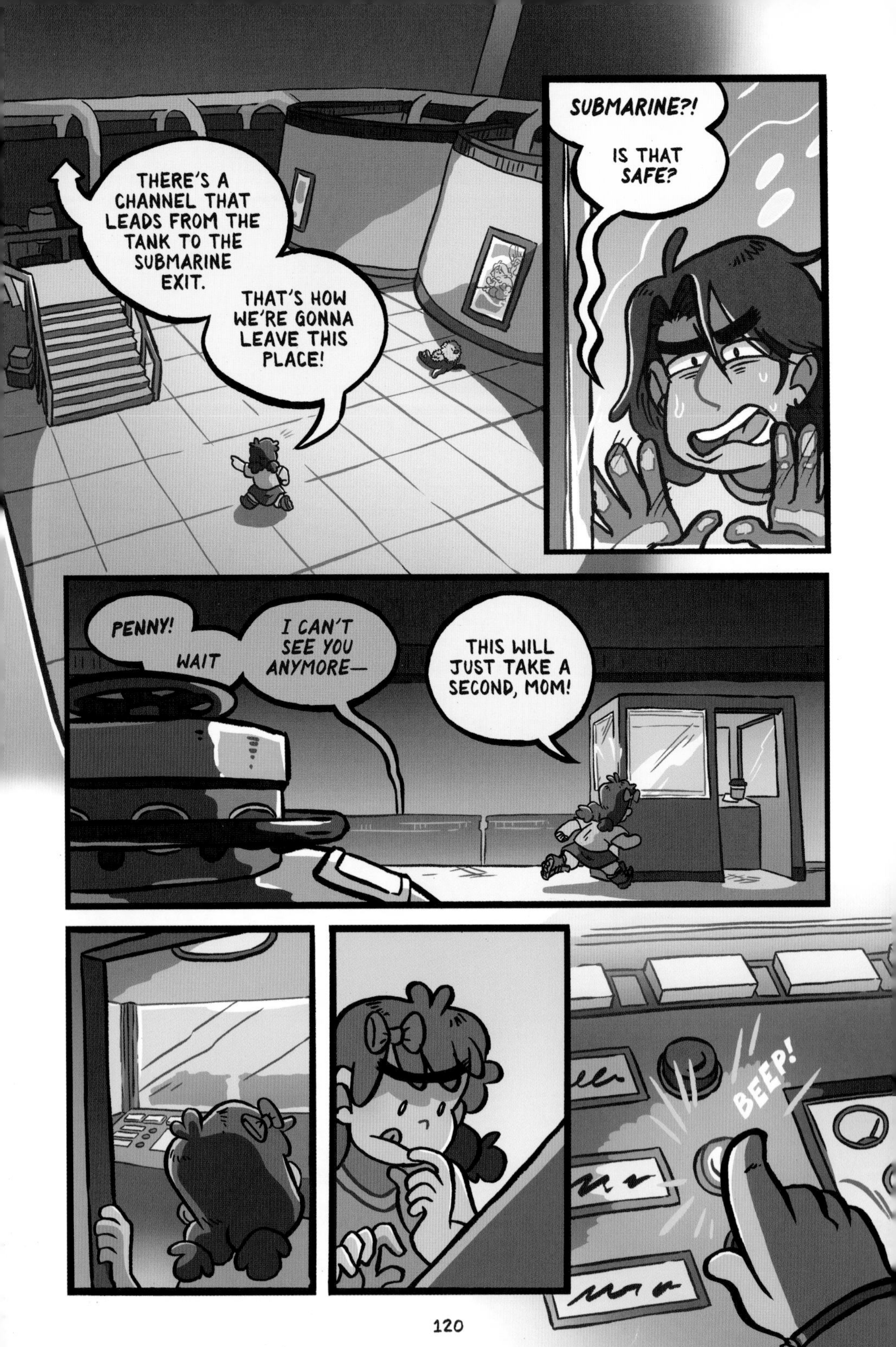
THERE'S A CHANNEL THAT LEADS FROM THE TANK TO THE SUBMARINE EXIT.
THAT'S HOW WE'RE GONNA LEAVE THIS PLACE!
SUBMARINE?!
IS THAT SAFE?
PENNY!
WAIT
I CAN'T SEE YOU ANYMORE—
THIS WILL JUST TAKE A SECOND, MOM!
BEEP!

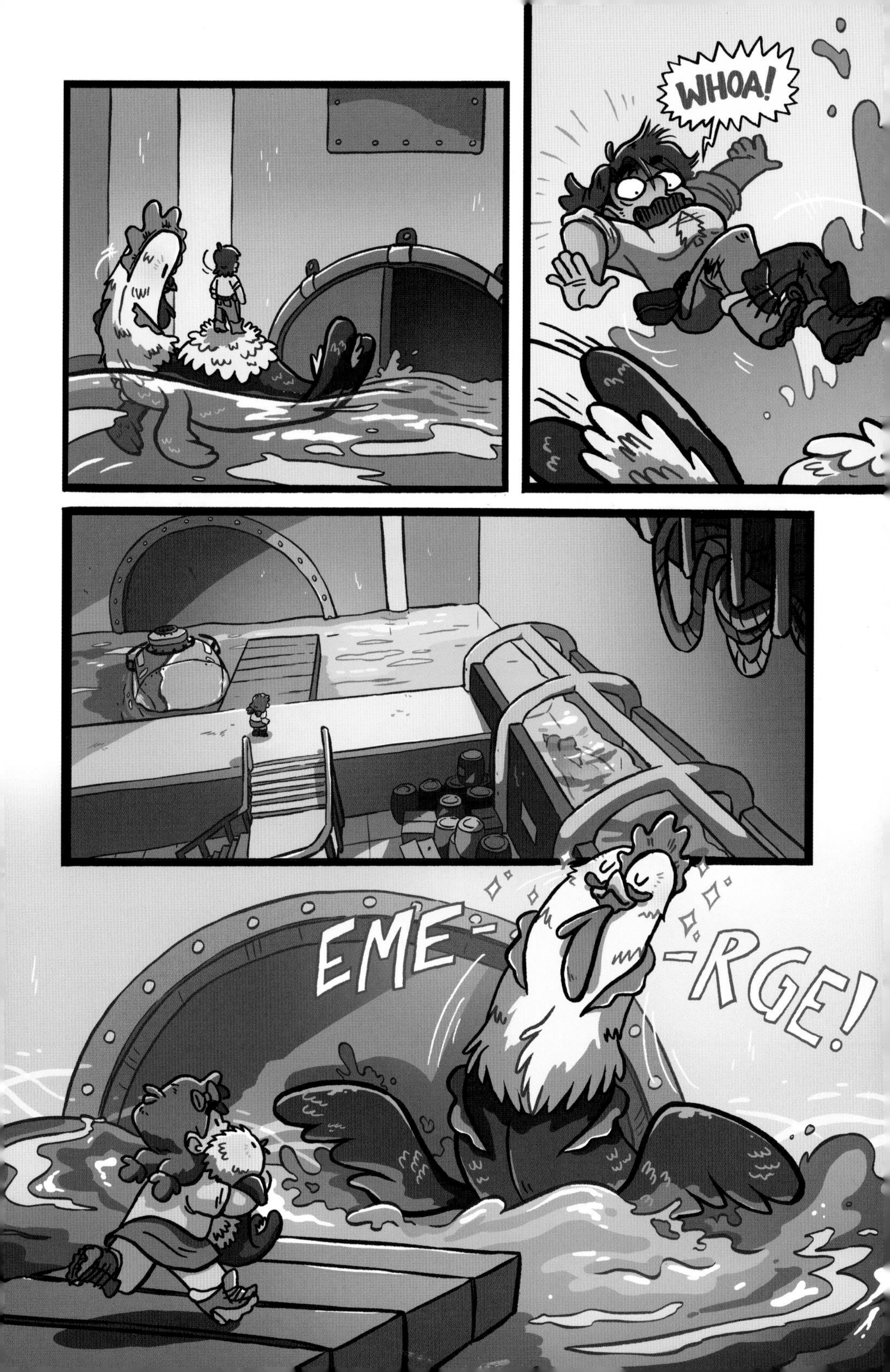
WHOA!
EME-
-RGE!

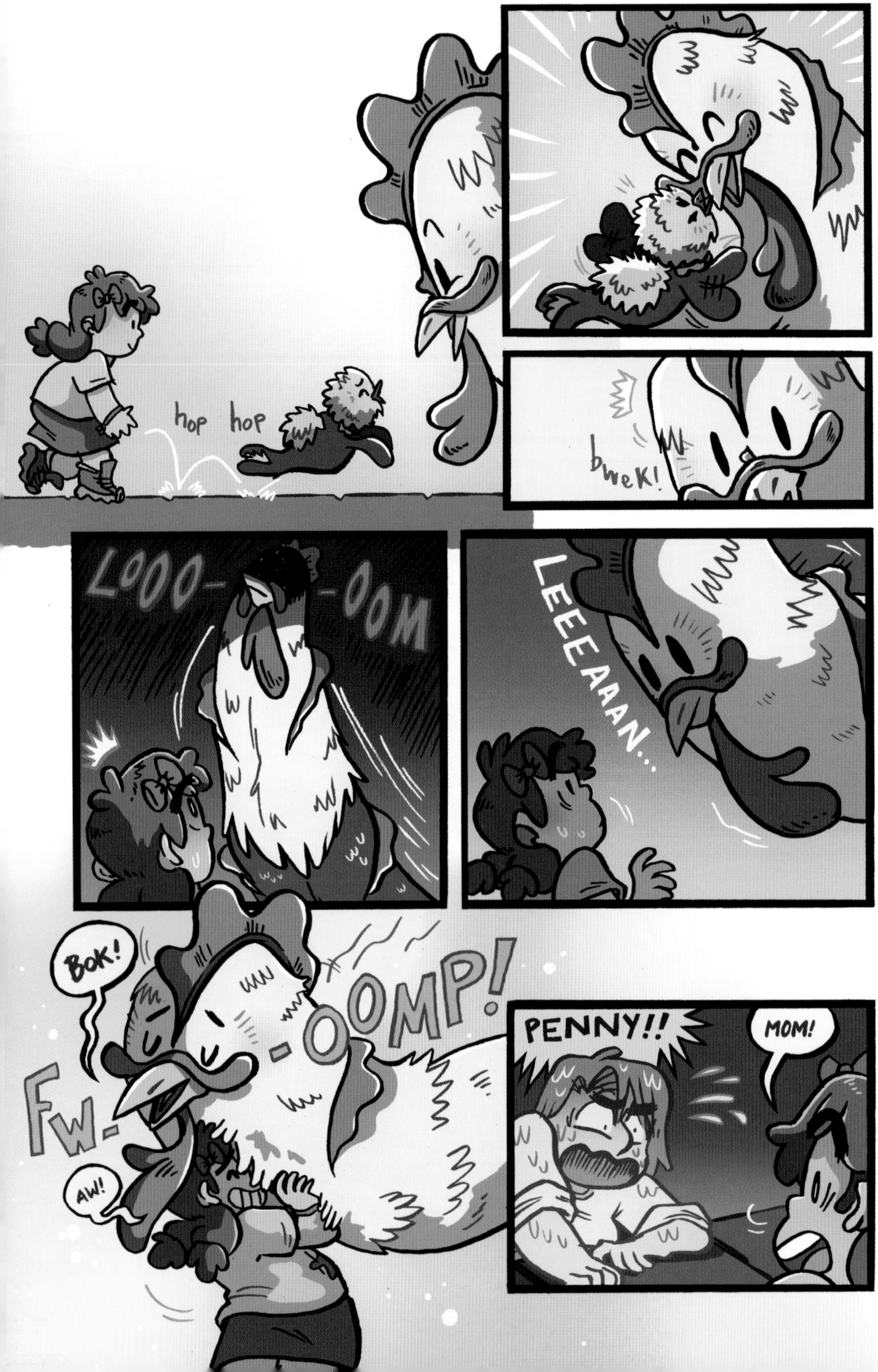
hop hop
bwek!
LOOO-
-OOM
LEEEAAAN...
BOK!
FW-
-OOMP!
AW!
PENNY!!
MOM!

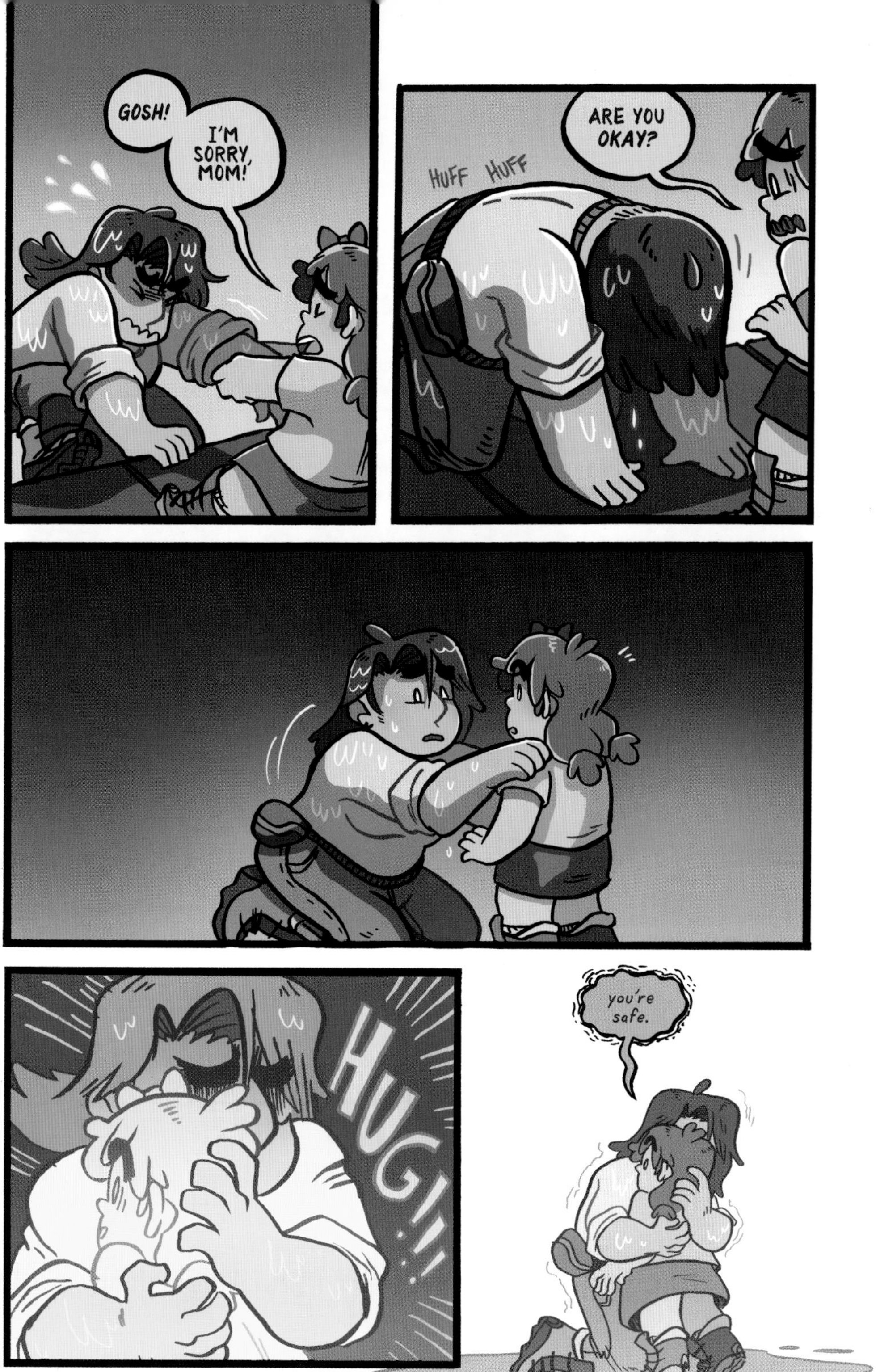
GOSH!
I'M SORRY, MOM!
HUFF HUFF
ARE YOU OKAY?
HUG!!!
you're safe.

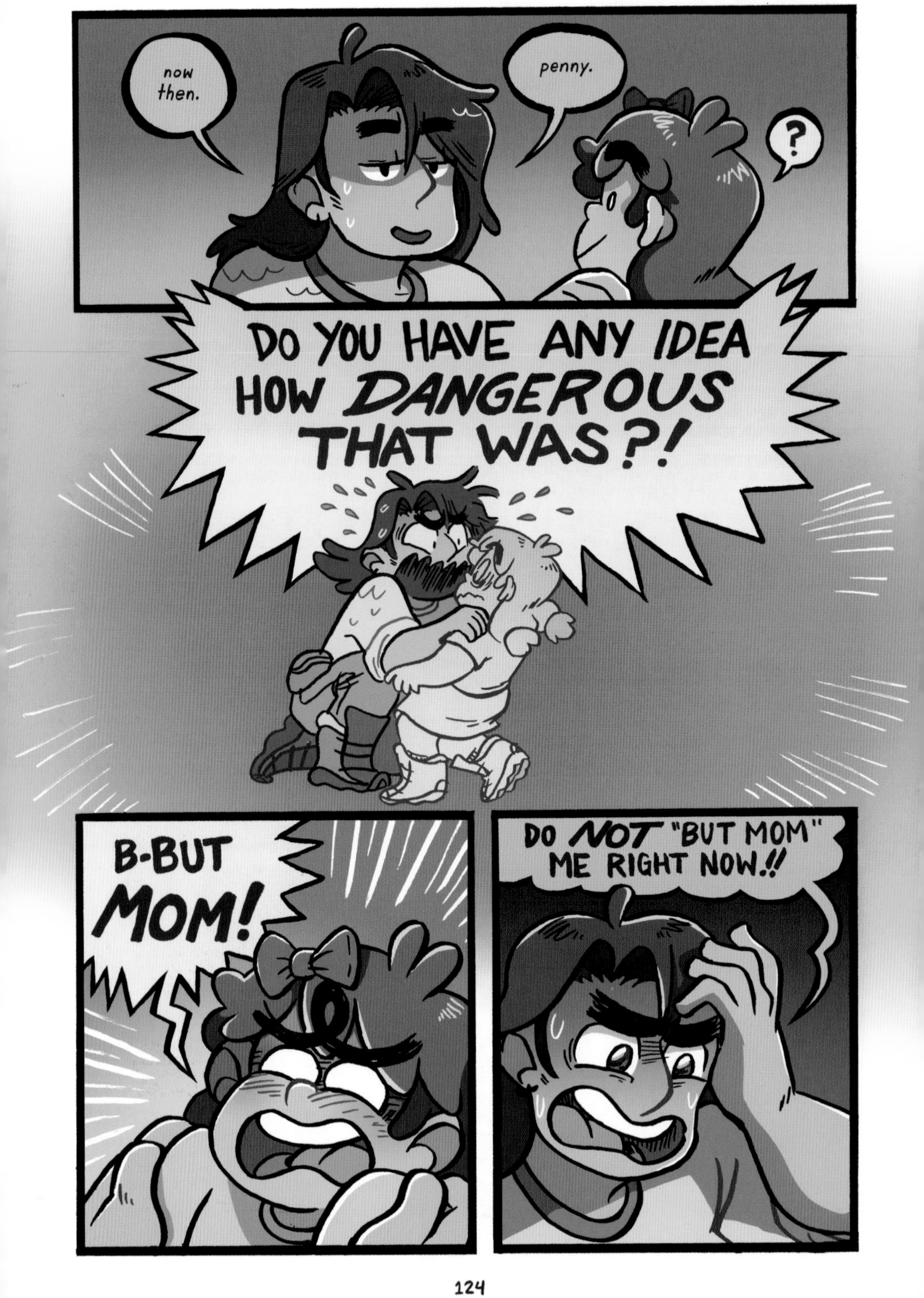
now then.
penny.
?
DO YOU HAVE ANY IDEA HOW DANGEROUS THAT WAS?!
B-BUT MOM!
DO NOT "BUT MOM" ME RIGHT NOW.!!

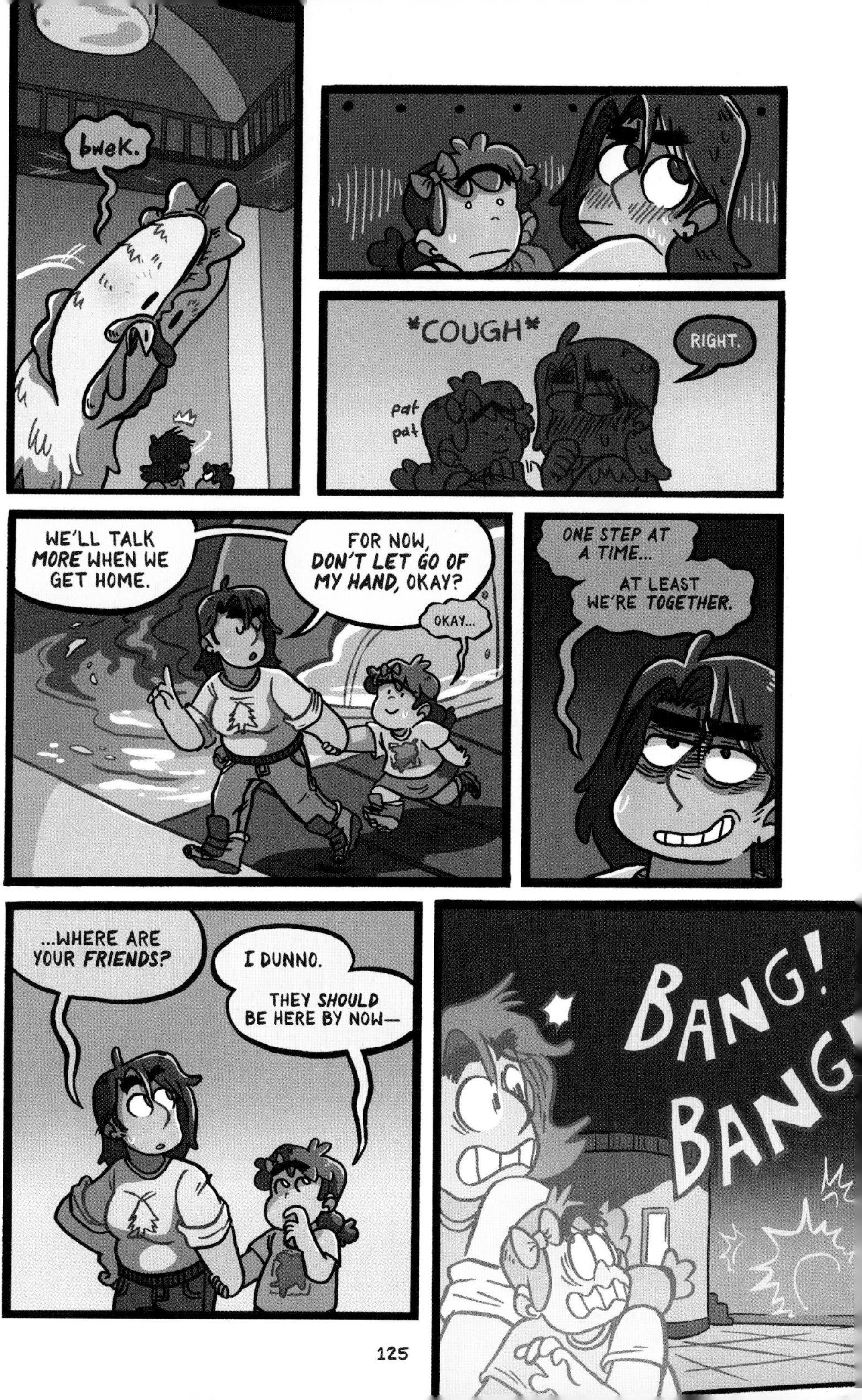

bwek.
COUGH
pat pat
RIGHT.
WE'LL TALK MORE WHEN WE GET HOME.
FOR NOW, DON'T LET GO OF MY HAND, OKAY?
OKAY...
ONE STEP AT A TIME...
AT LEAST WE'RE TOGETHER.
...WHERE ARE YOUR FRIENDS?
I DUNNO.
THEY SHOULD BE HERE BY NOW—
BANG! BANG!

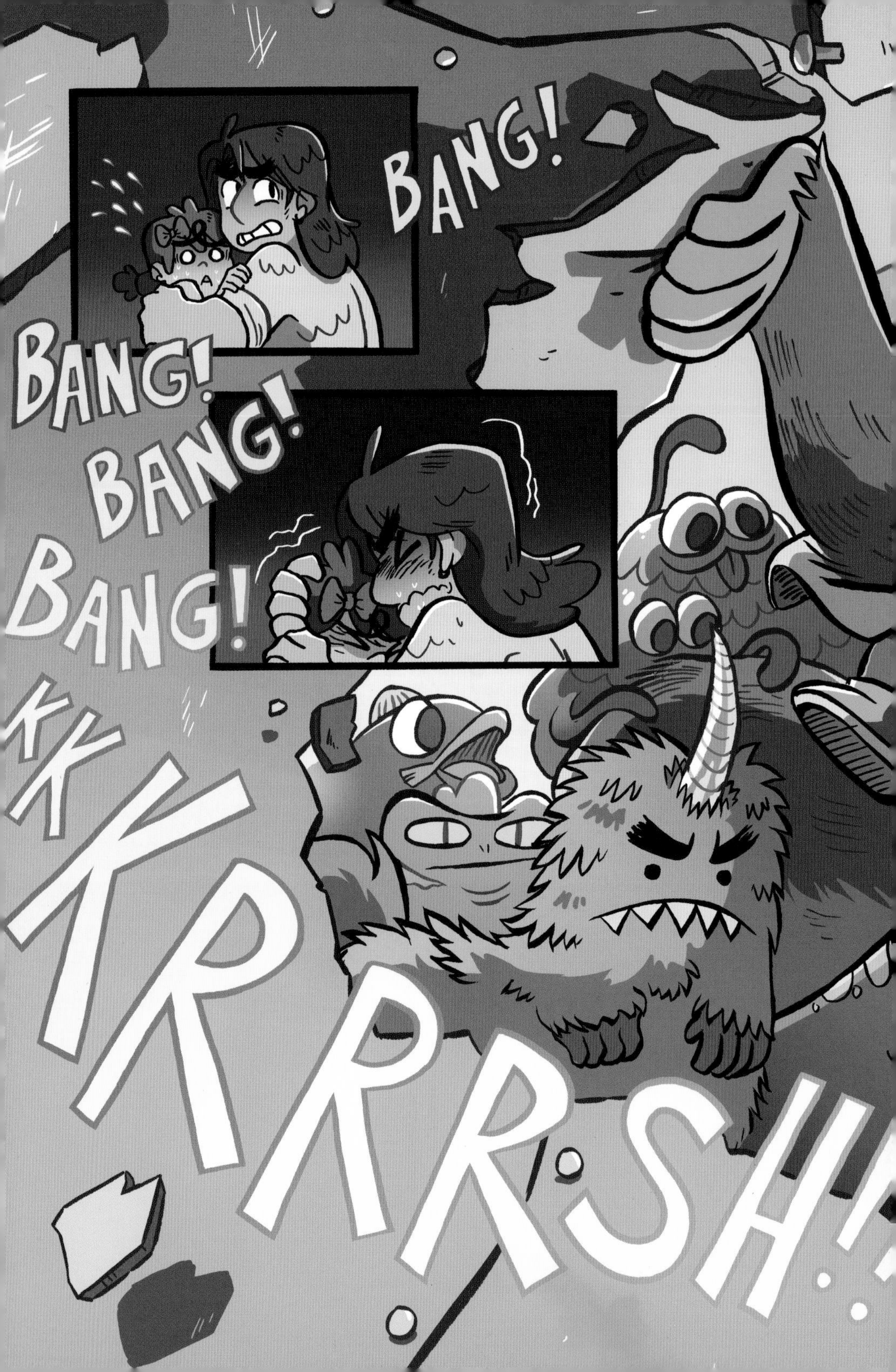
BANG!
BANG!
BANG!
BANG!
KK
KRRRSH!!

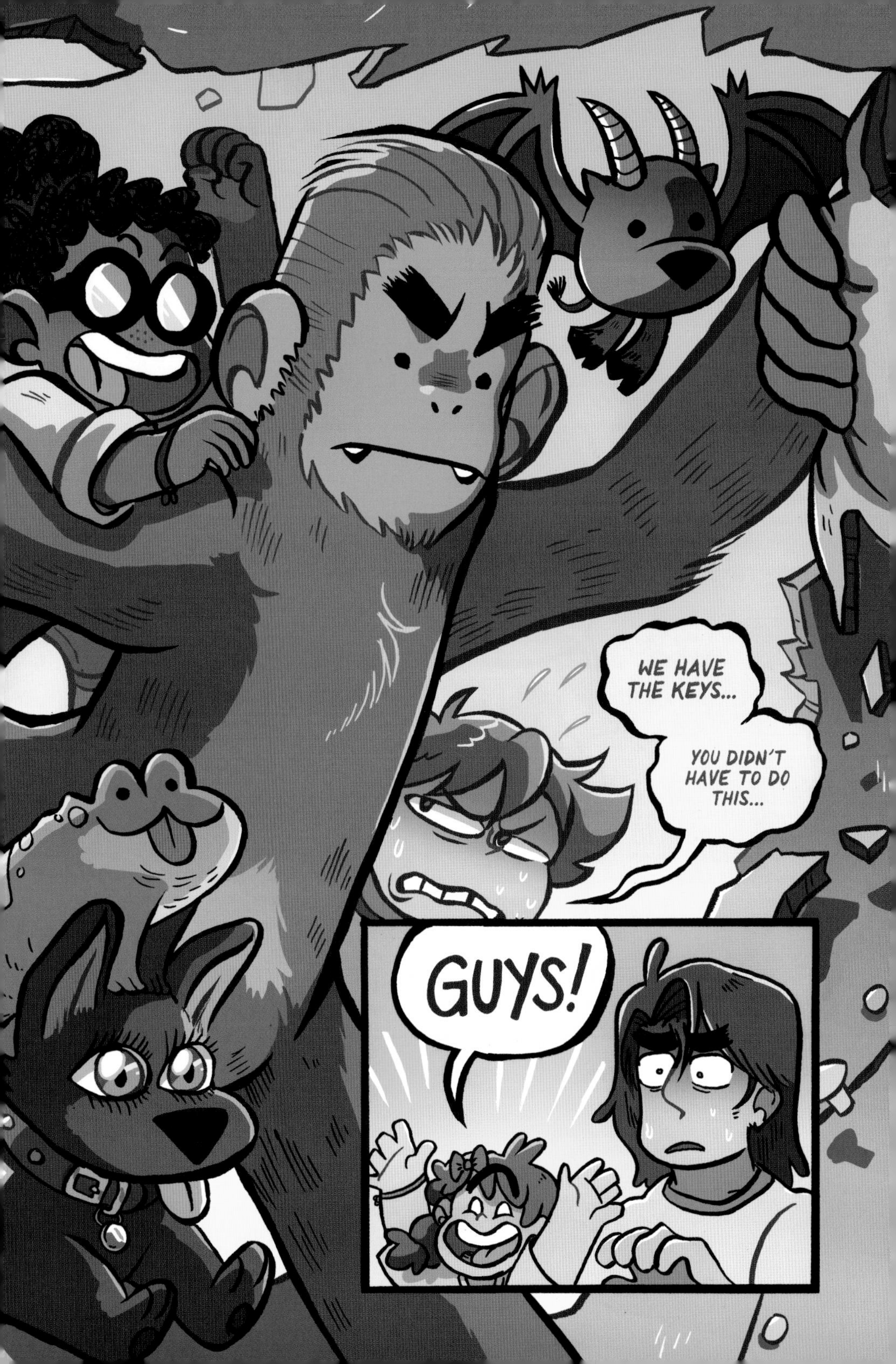
WE HAVE THE KEYS...
YOU DIDN'T HAVE TO DO THIS...
GUYS!

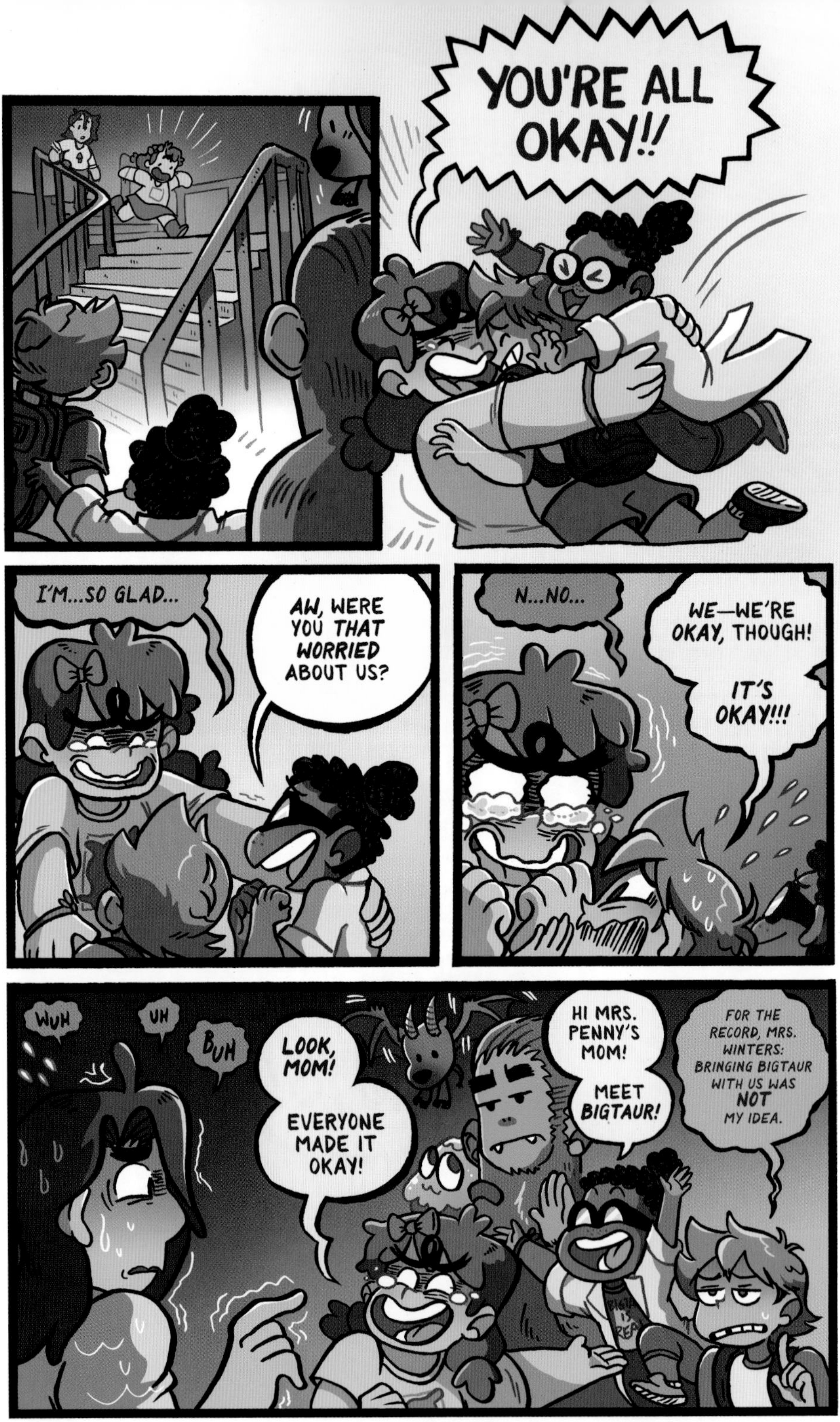
YOU'RE ALL OKAY!!
I'M...SO GLAD...
AW, WERE YOU THAT WORRIED ABOUT US?
N...NO...
WE—WE'RE OKAY, THOUGH!
IT'S OKAY!!!
WUH
UH
BUH
LOOK, MOM!
EVERYONE MADE IT OKAY!
HI MRS. PENNY'S MOM!
MEET BIGTAUR!
FOR THE RECORD, MRS. WINTERS: BRINGING BIGTAUR WITH US WAS NOT MY IDEA.

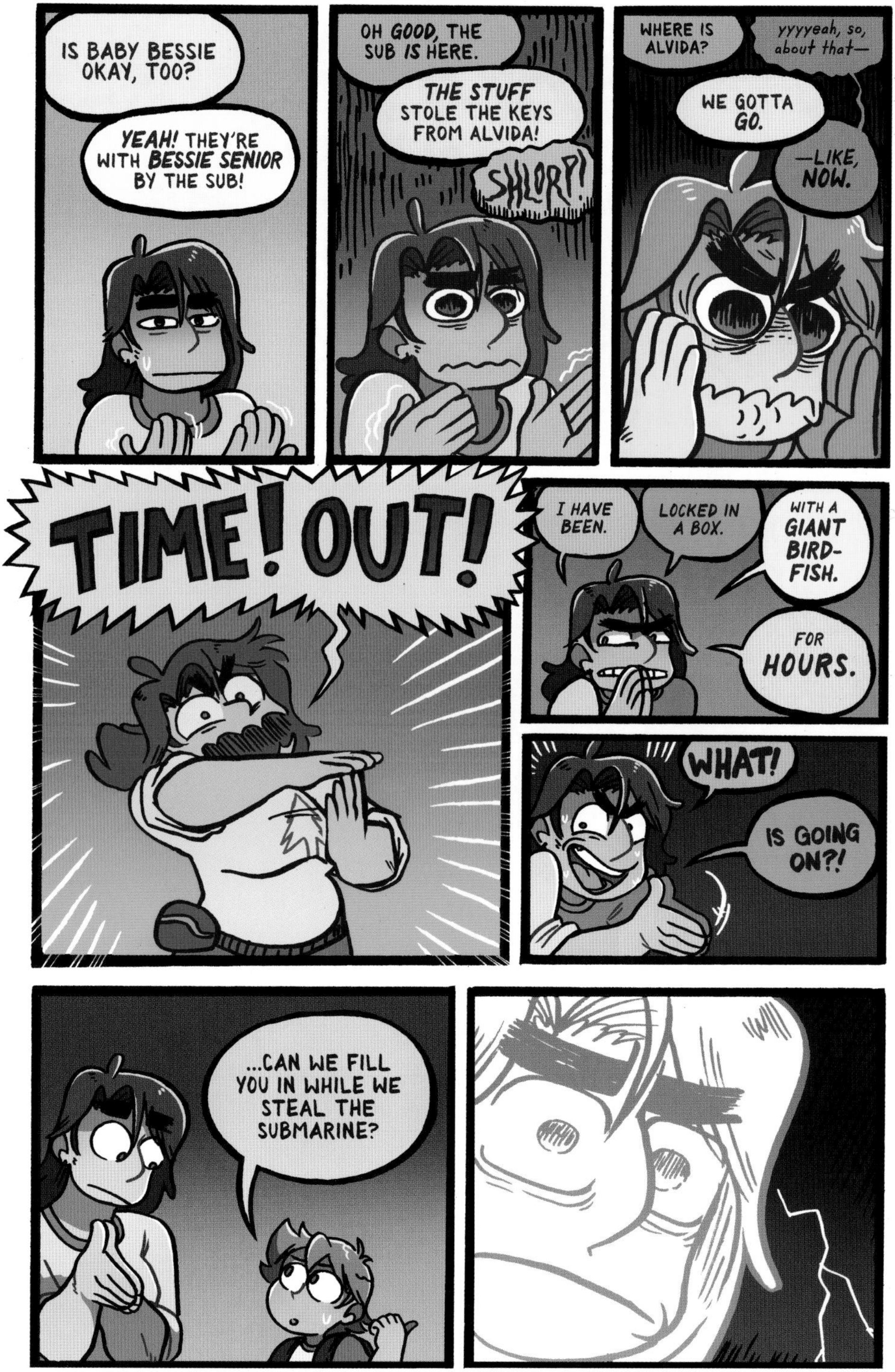

IS BABY BESSIE OKAY, TOO?
YEAH! THEY'RE WITH BESSIE SENIOR BY THE SUB!
OH GOOD, THE SUB IS HERE.
THE STUFF STOLE THE KEYS FROM ALVIDA!
SHLORP!
WHERE IS ALVIDA?
yyyyeah, so, about that—
WE GOTTA GO.
—LIKE, NOW.
TIME! OUT!
I HAVE BEEN.
LOCKED IN A BOX.
WITH A GIANT BIRD-FISH.
FOR HOURS.
WHAT!
IS GOING ON?!
...CAN WE FILL YOU IN WHILE WE STEAL THE SUBMARINE?

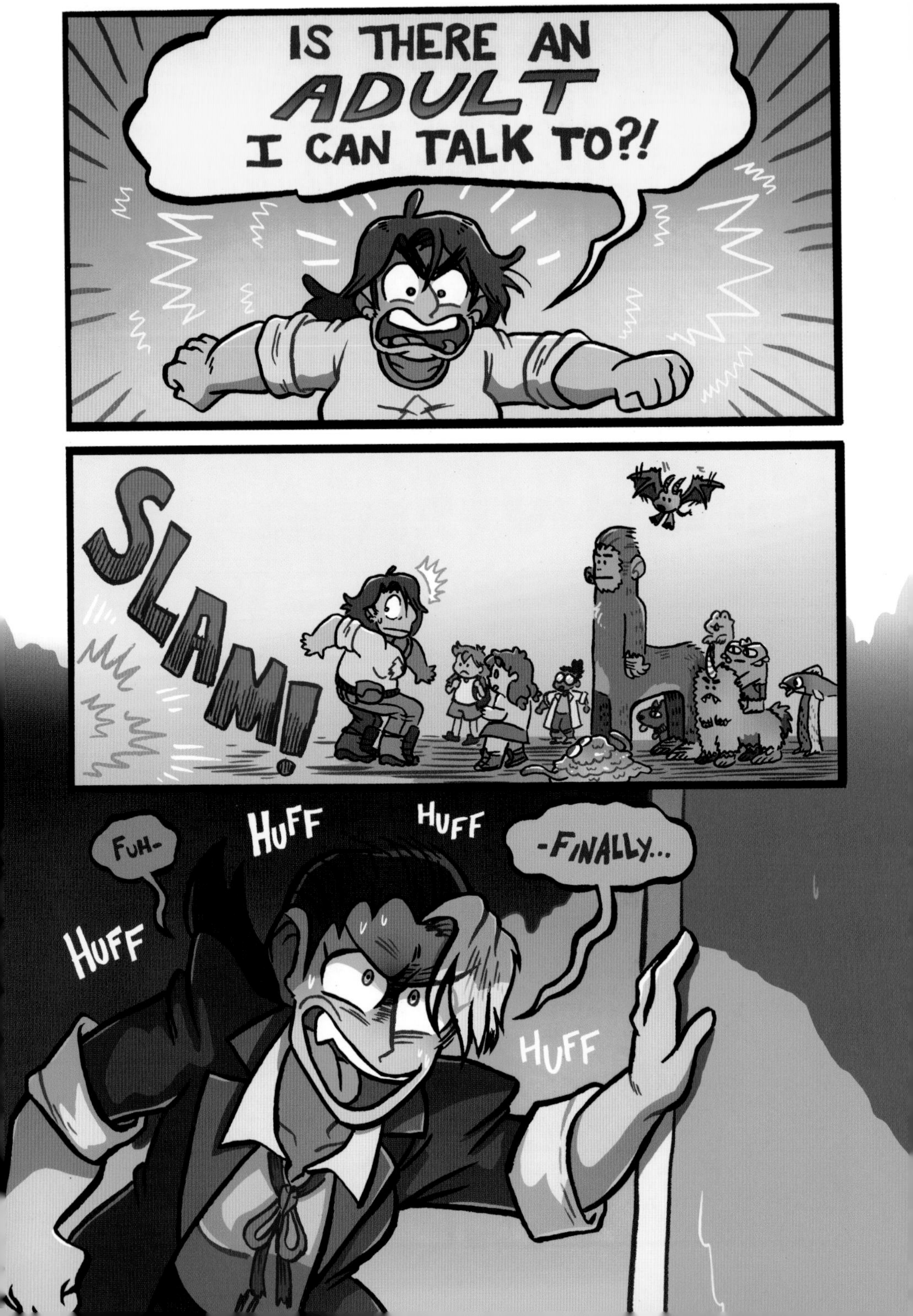
IS THERE AN ADULT I CAN TALK TO?!
SLAM!
FUH-
HUFF
HUFF
HUFF
-FINALLY...
HUFF

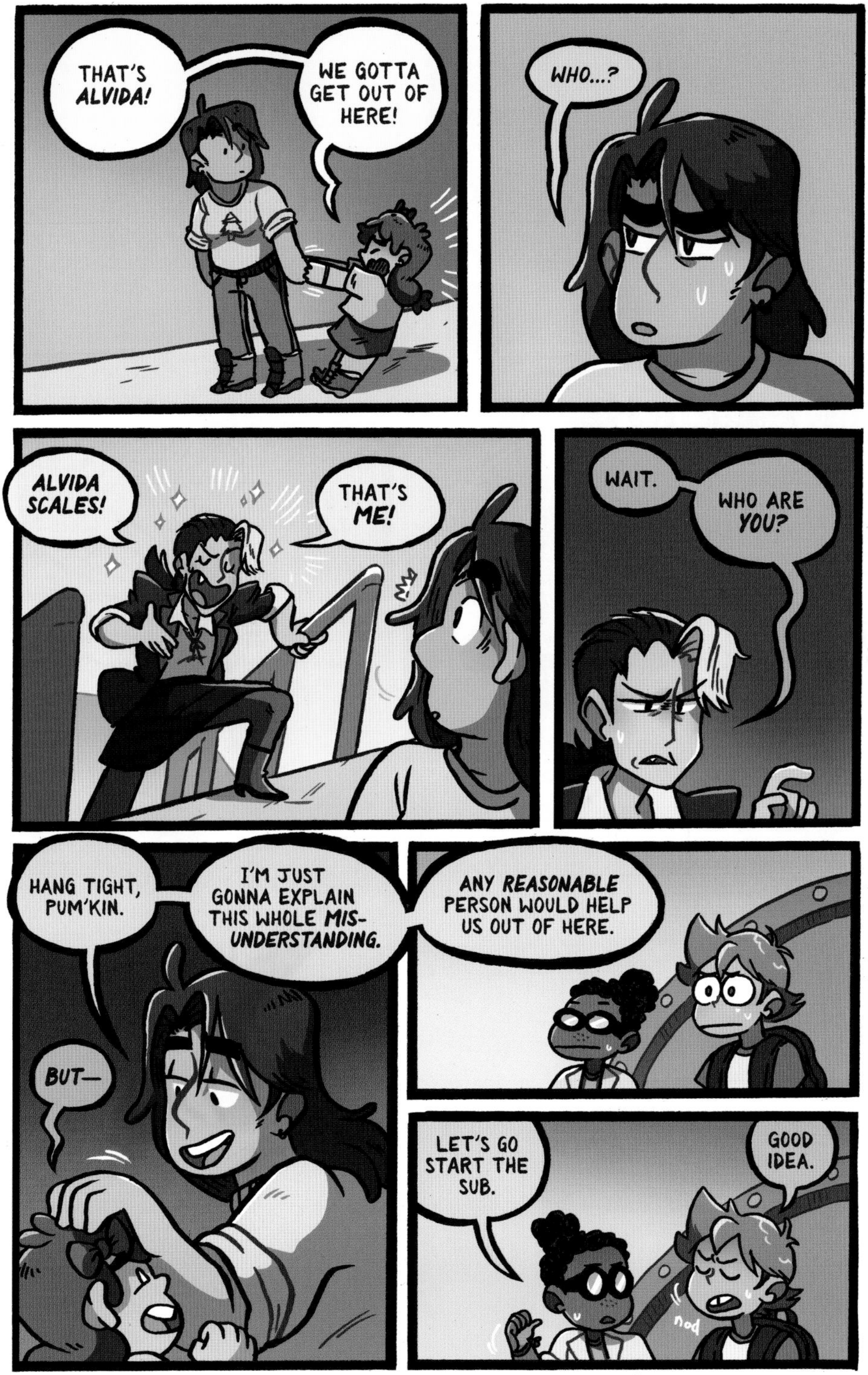
THAT'S ALVIDA!
WE GOTTA GET OUT OF HERE!
WHO...?
ALVIDA SCALES!
THAT'S ME!
WAIT.
WHO ARE YOU?
HANG TIGHT, PUM'KIN.
I'M JUST GONNA EXPLAIN THIS WHOLE MIS-UNDERSTANDING.
BUT—
ANY REASONABLE PERSON WOULD HELP US OUT OF HERE.
LET'S GO START THE SUB.
GOOD IDEA.
nod

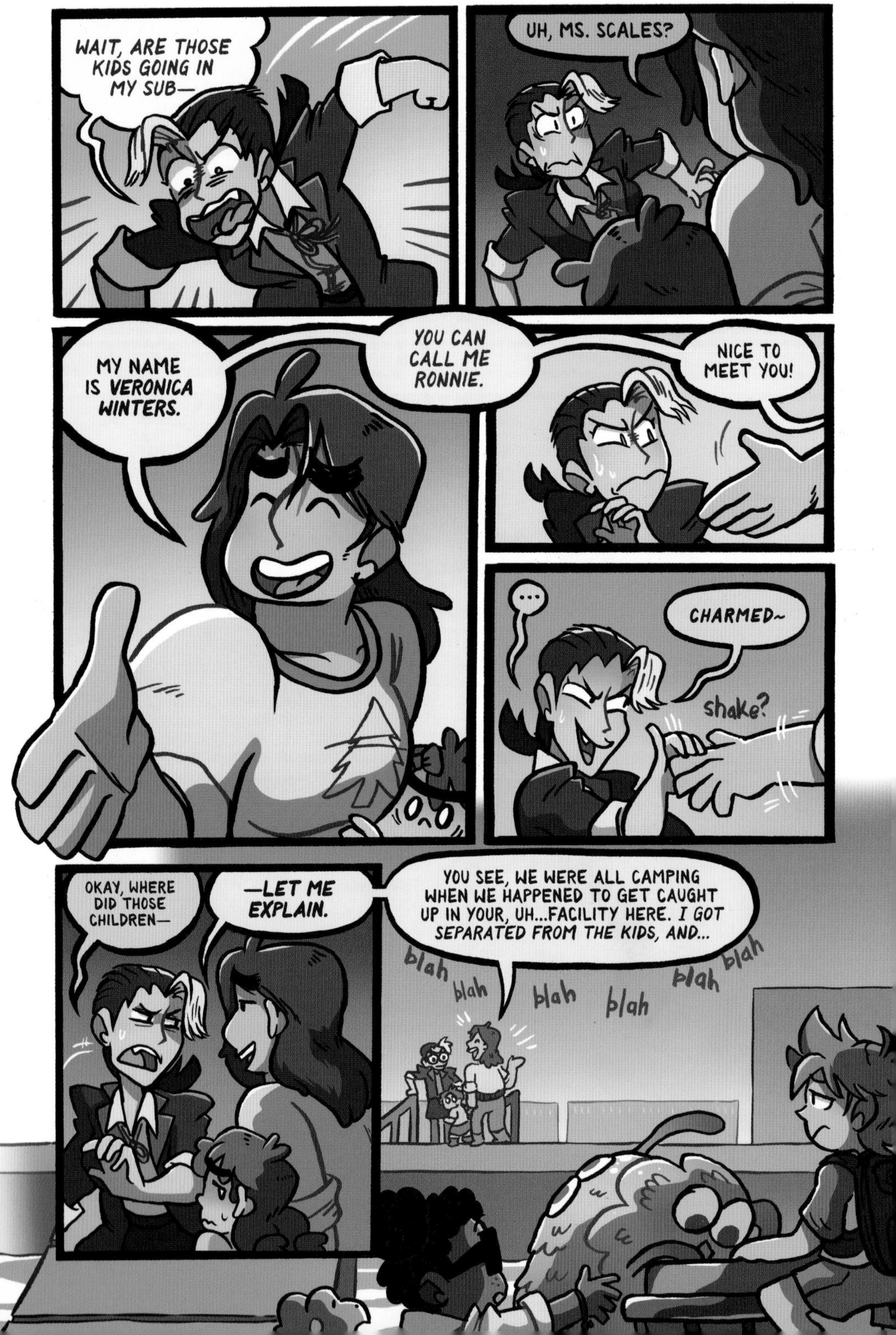
WAIT, ARE THOSE KIDS GOING IN MY SUB—
UH, MS. SCALES?
MY NAME IS VERONICA WINTERS.
YOU CAN CALL ME RONNIE.
NICE TO MEET YOU!
...
CHARMED~
shake?
OKAY, WHERE DID THOSE CHILDREN—
—LET ME EXPLAIN.
YOU SEE, WE WERE ALL CAMPING WHEN WE HAPPENED TO GET CAUGHT UP IN YOUR, UH...FACILITY HERE. I GOT SEPARATED FROM THE KIDS, AND...
blah
blah
blah
blah
blah
blah

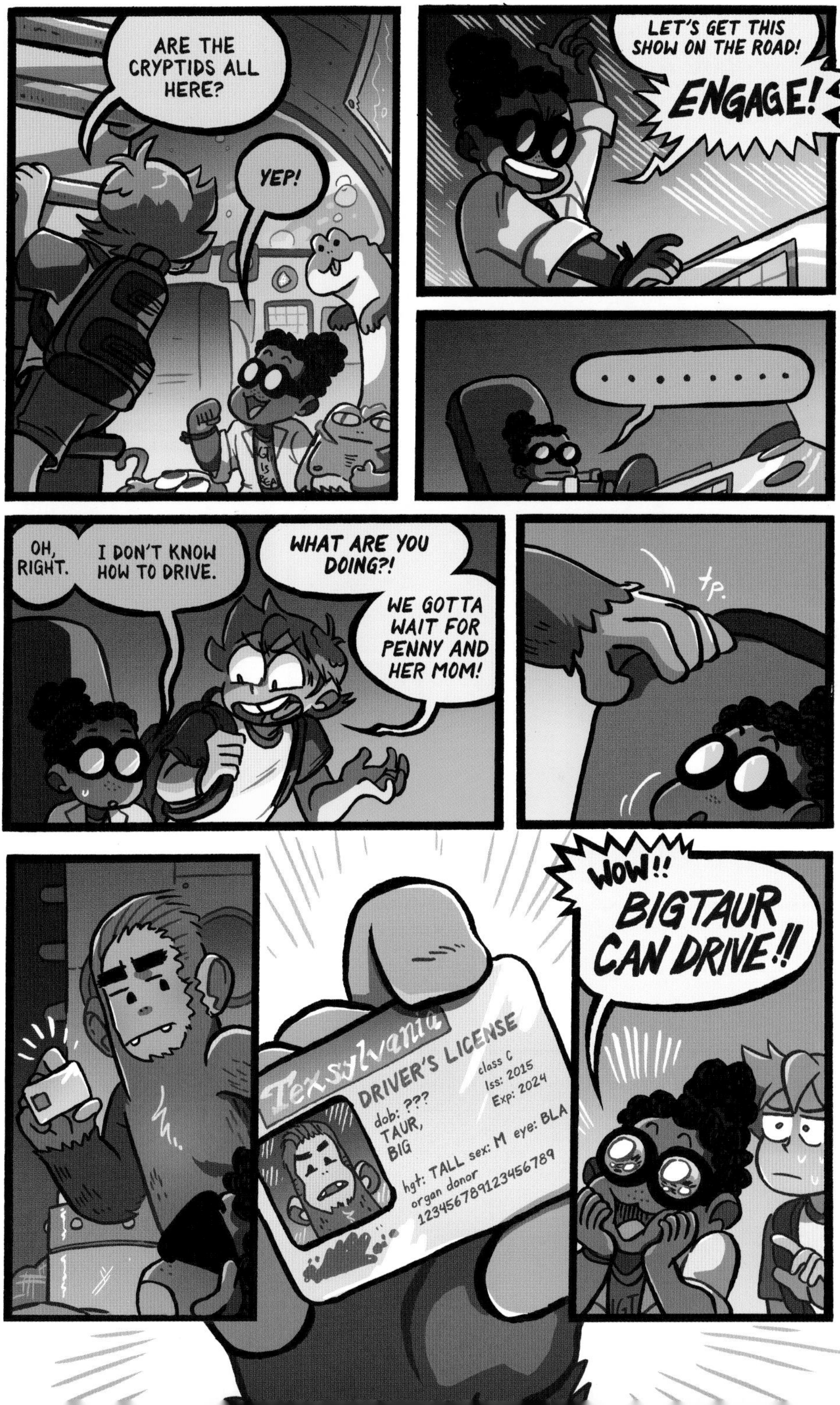
ARE THE CRYPTIDS ALL HERE?
YEP!
LET'S GET THIS SHOW ON THE ROAD!
ENGAGE!
. . . .
OH, RIGHT.
I DON'T KNOW HOW TO DRIVE.
WHAT ARE YOU DOING?!
WE GOTTA WAIT FOR PENNY AND HER MOM!
TP.
WOW!!
BIGTAUR CAN DRIVE!!
Texsylvania
DRIVER'S LICENSE
class C
Iss: 2015
Exp: 2024
dob: ???
TAUR, BIG
hgt: TALL sex: M eye: BLA
organ donor
123456789123456789

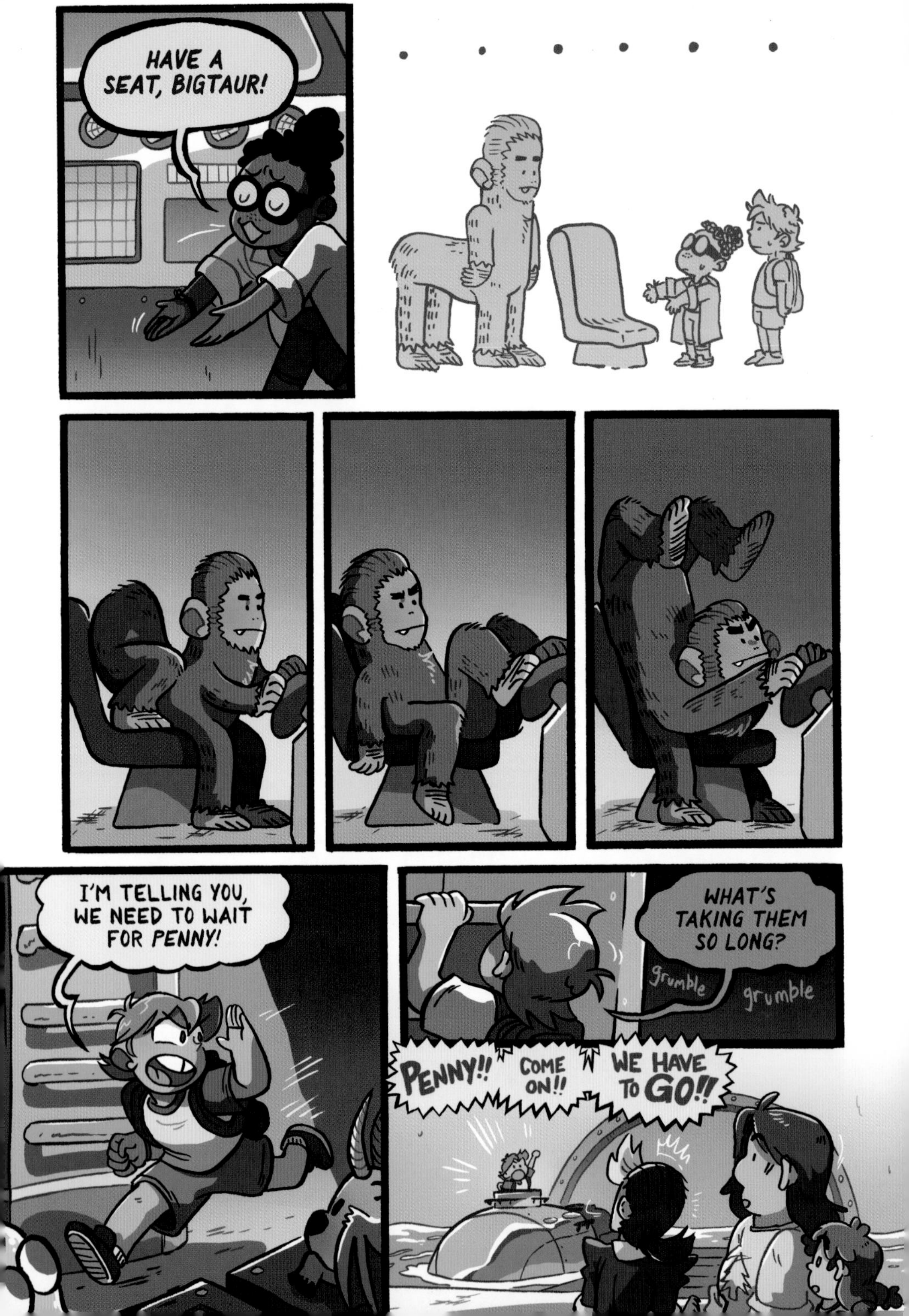
HAVE A SEAT, BIGTAUR!
I'M TELLING YOU, WE NEED TO WAIT FOR PENNY!
WHAT'S TAKING THEM SO LONG?
grumble
grumble
PENNY!!
COME ON!!
WE HAVE TO GO!!

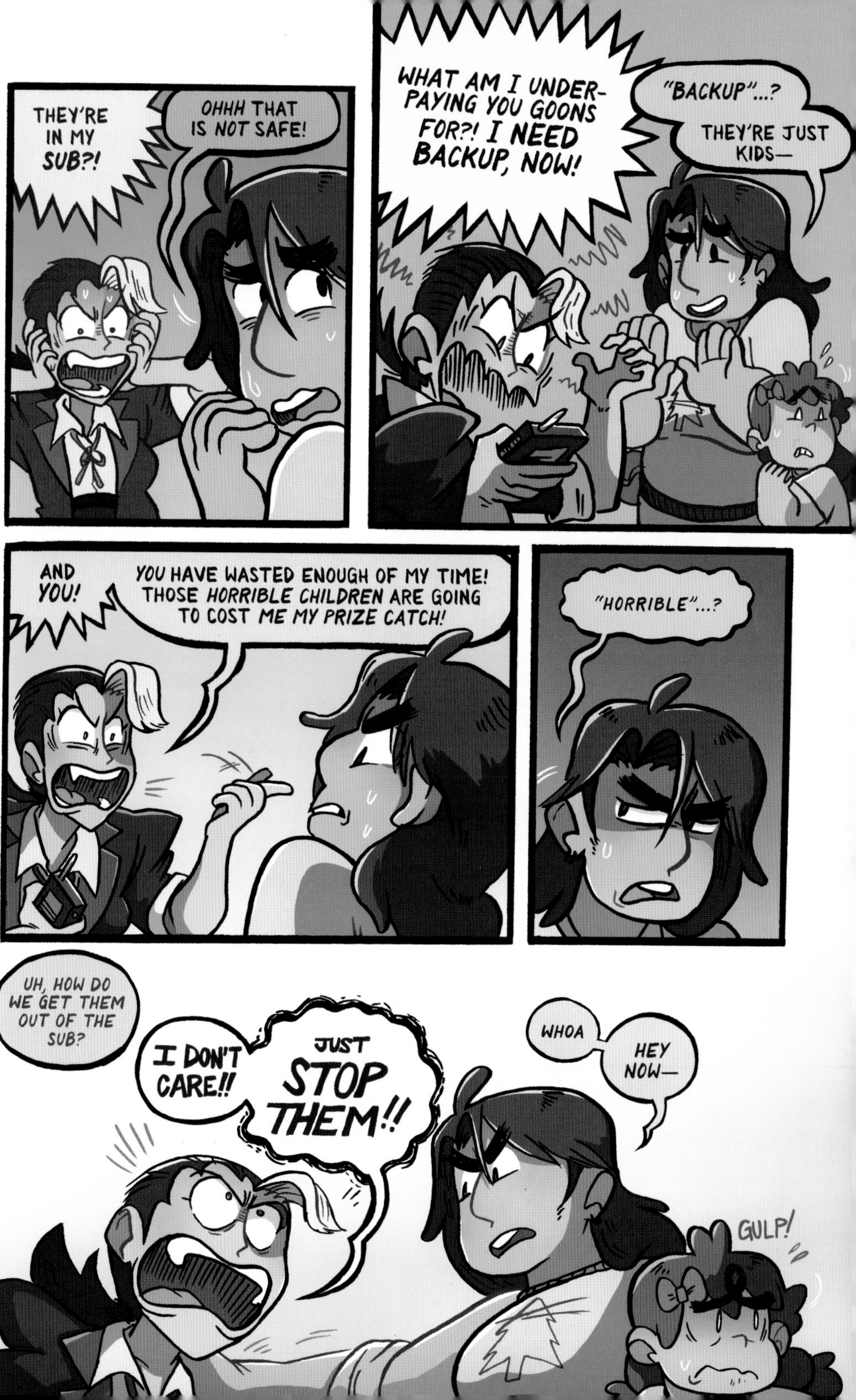
THEY'RE IN MY SUB?!
OHHH THAT IS NOT SAFE!
WHAT AM I UNDER-PAYING YOU GOONS FOR?! I NEED BACKUP, NOW!
"BACKUP"...?
THEY'RE JUST KIDS—
AND YOU!
YOU HAVE WASTED ENOUGH OF MY TIME! THOSE HORRIBLE CHILDREN ARE GOING TO COST ME MY PRIZE CATCH!
"HORRIBLE"...?
UH, HOW DO WE GET THEM OUT OF THE SUB?
I DON'T CARE!!
JUST STOP THEM!!
WHOA
HEY NOW—
GULP!

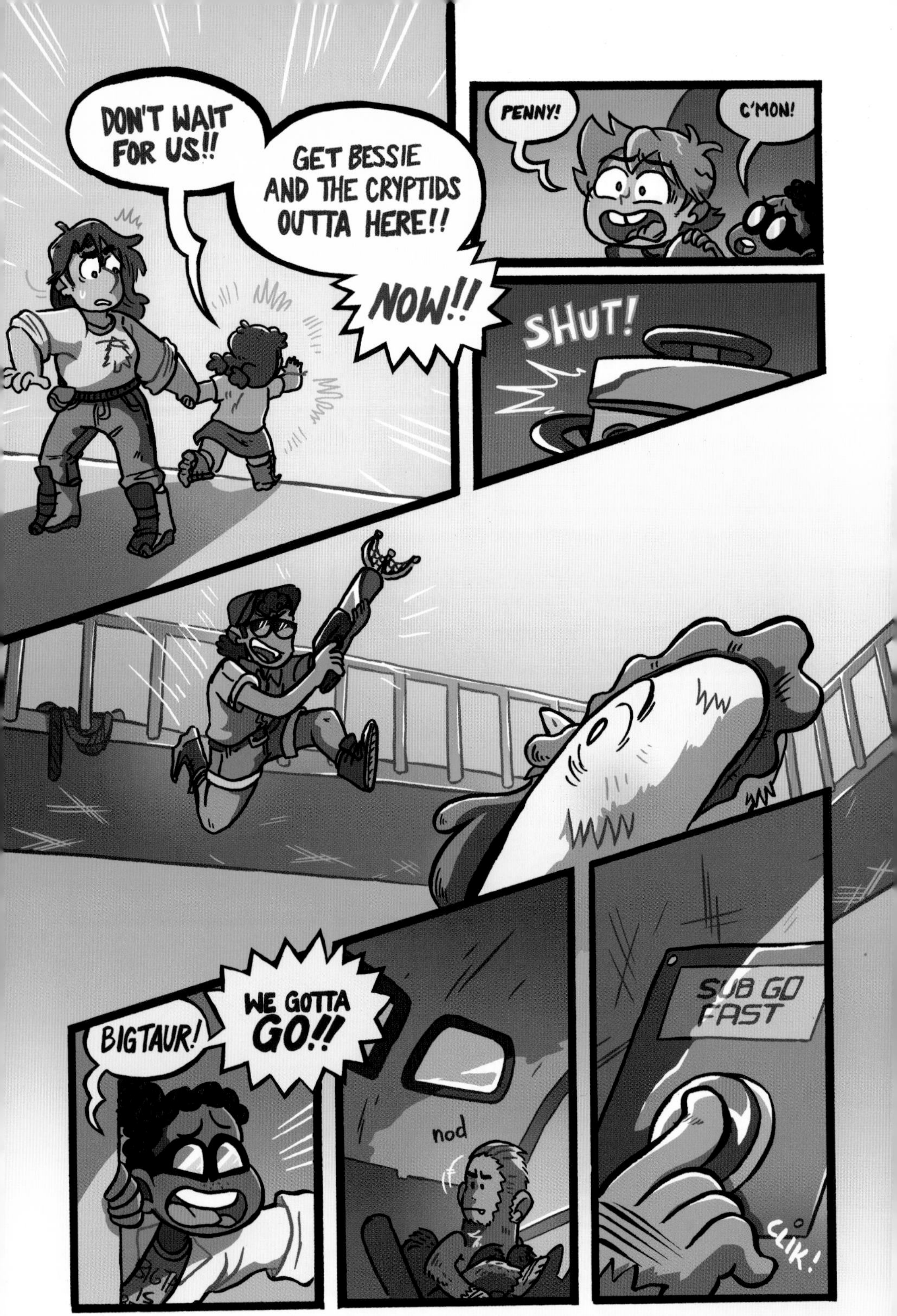
DON'T WAIT FOR US!!
GET BESSIE AND THE CRYPTIDS OUTTA HERE!!
NOW!!
PENNY!
C'MON!
SHUT!
BIGTAUR!
WE GOTTA GO!!
nod
SUB GO FAST
CLIK!

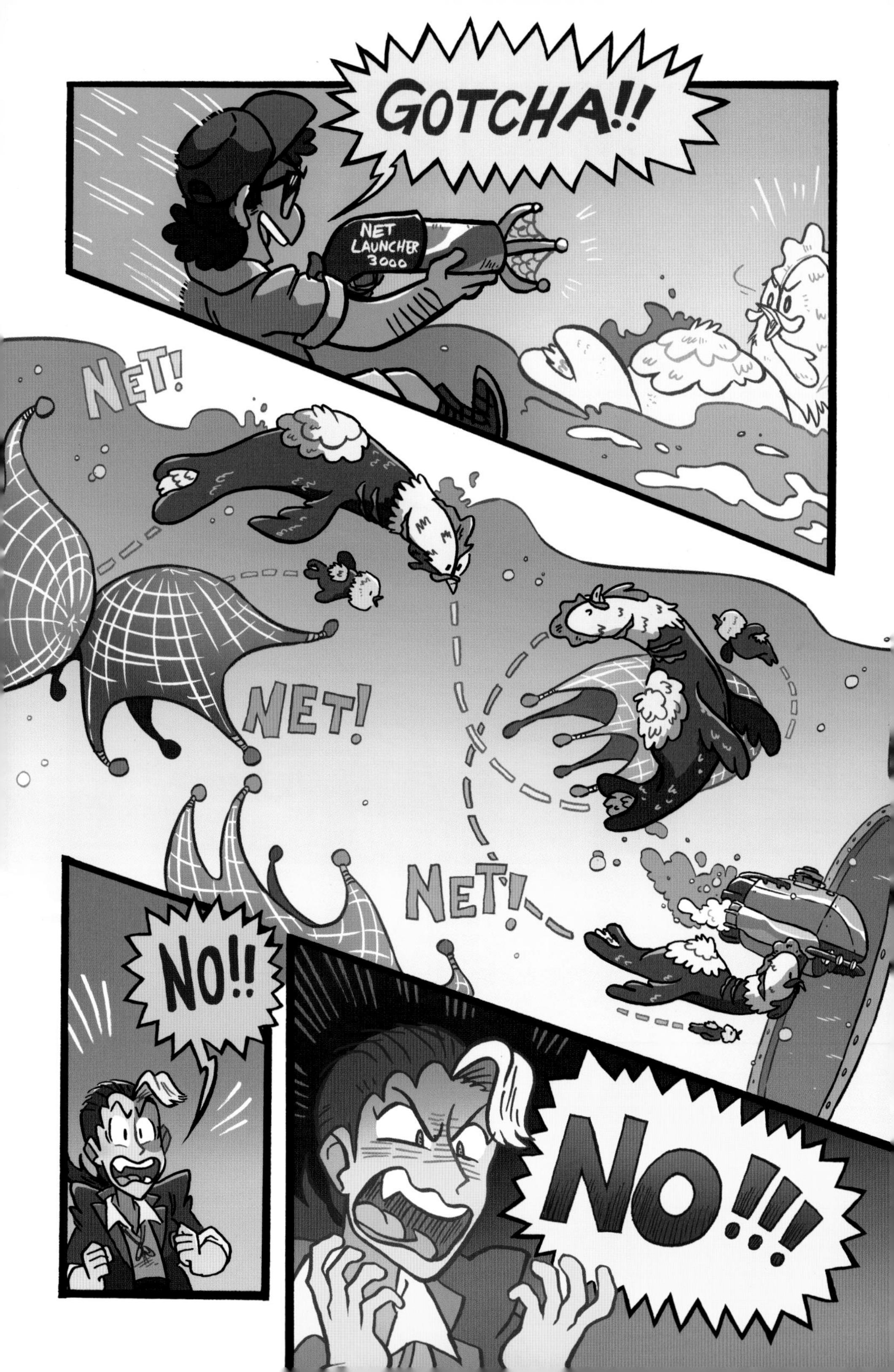
GOTCHA!!
NET LAUNCHER 3000
NET!
NET!
NET!
NO!!
NO!!!

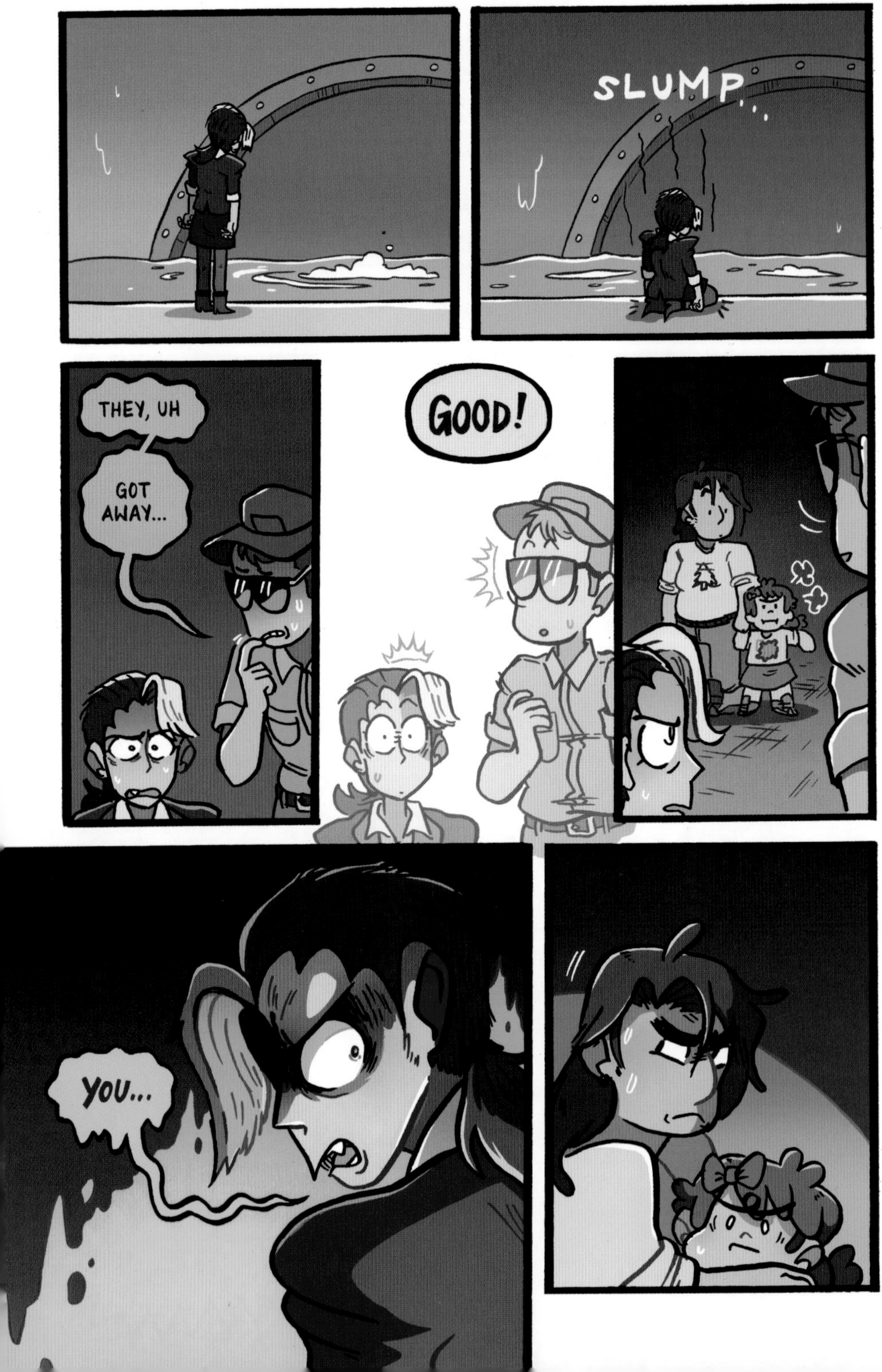
SLUMP...
THEY, UH
GOT AWAY...
GOOD!
YOU...

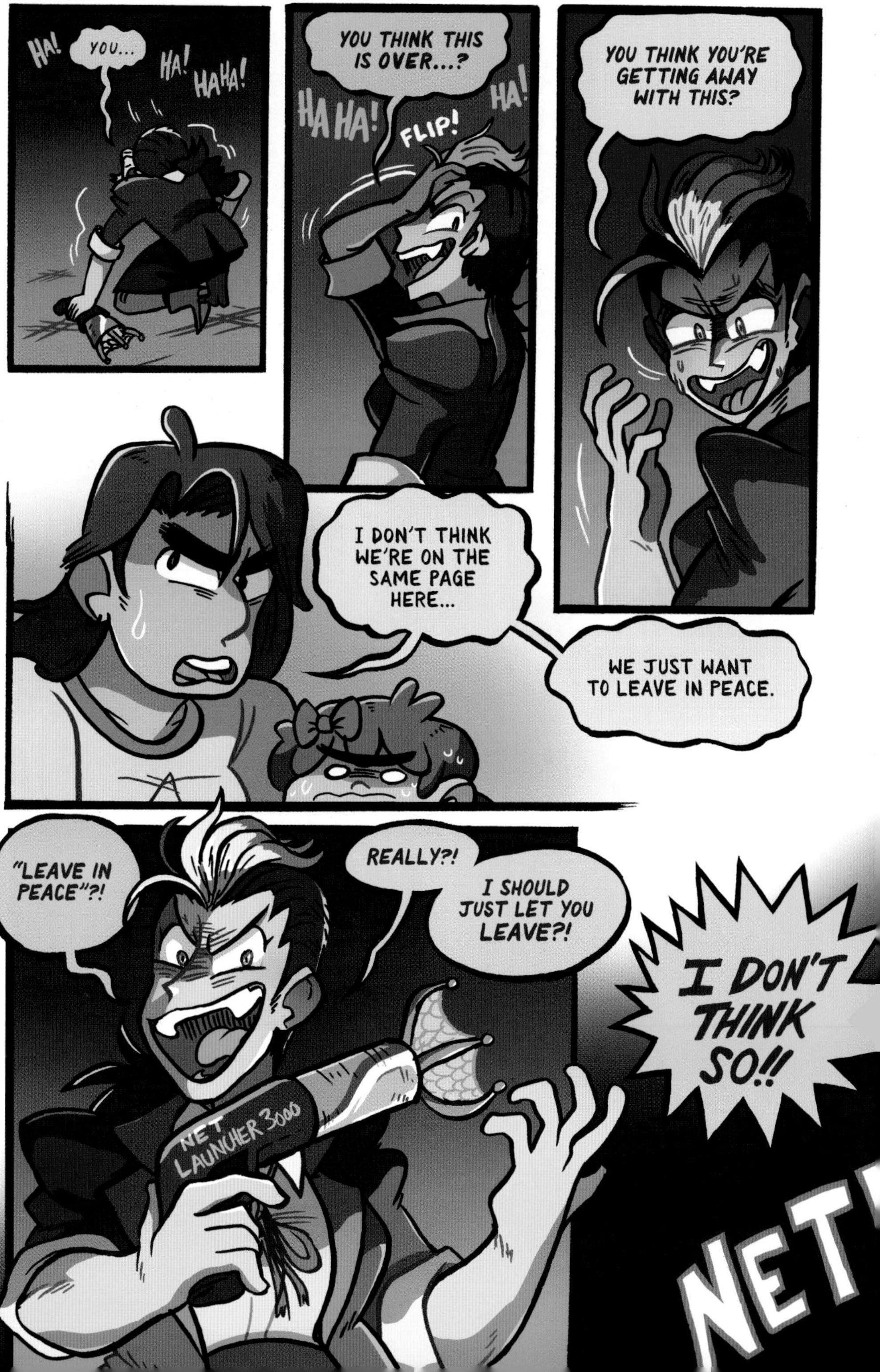
HA!
YOU...
HA!
HAHA!
YOU THINK THIS IS OVER...?
HA HA!
FLIP!
HA!
YOU THINK YOU'RE GETTING AWAY WITH THIS?
I DON'T THINK WE'RE ON THE SAME PAGE HERE...
WE JUST WANT TO LEAVE IN PEACE.
"LEAVE IN PEACE"?!
REALLY?!
I SHOULD JUST LET YOU LEAVE?!
NET LAUNCHER 3000
I DON'T THINK SO!!
NET

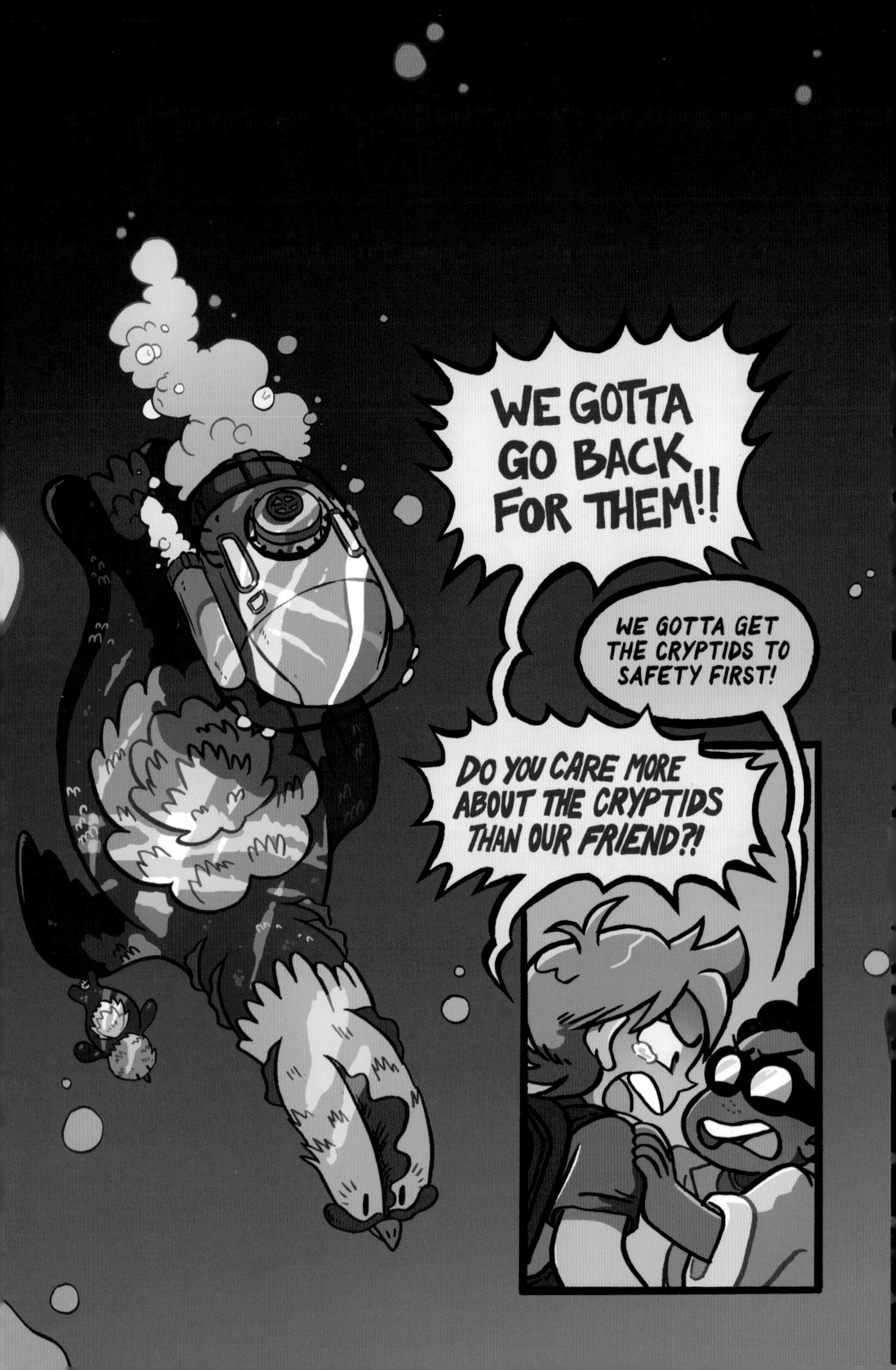
WE GOTTA GO BACK FOR THEM!!
WE GOTTA GET THE CRYPTIDS TO SAFETY FIRST!
DO YOU CARE MORE ABOUT THE CRYPTIDS THAN OUR *FRIEND*?!

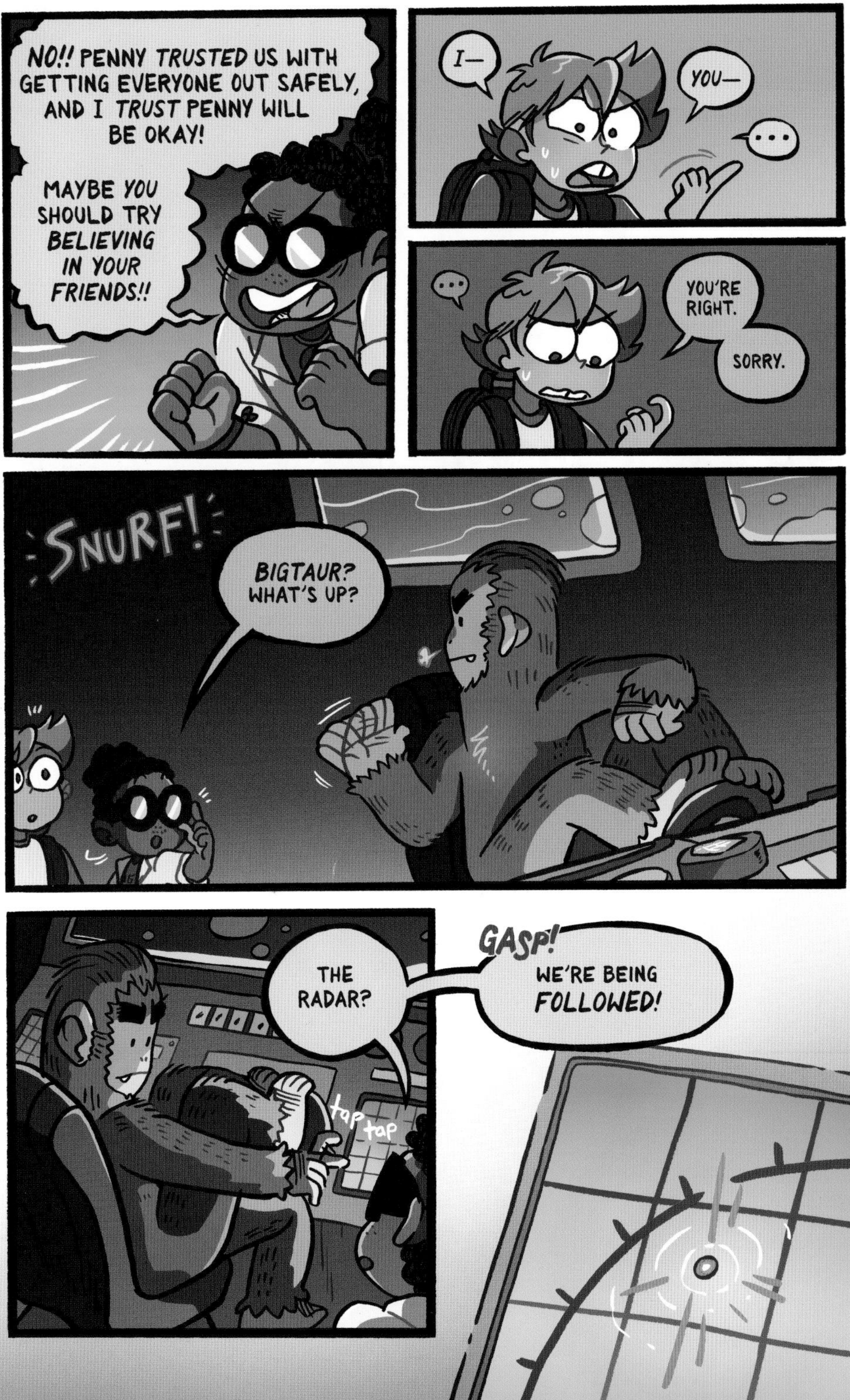
NO!! PENNY TRUSTED US WITH GETTING EVERYONE OUT SAFELY, AND I TRUST PENNY WILL BE OKAY!
MAYBE YOU SHOULD TRY BELIEVING IN YOUR FRIENDS!!
I—
YOU—
...
...
YOU'RE RIGHT.
SORRY.
SNURF!
BIGTAUR? WHAT'S UP?
THE RADAR?
tap tap
GASP!
WE'RE BEING FOLLOWED!

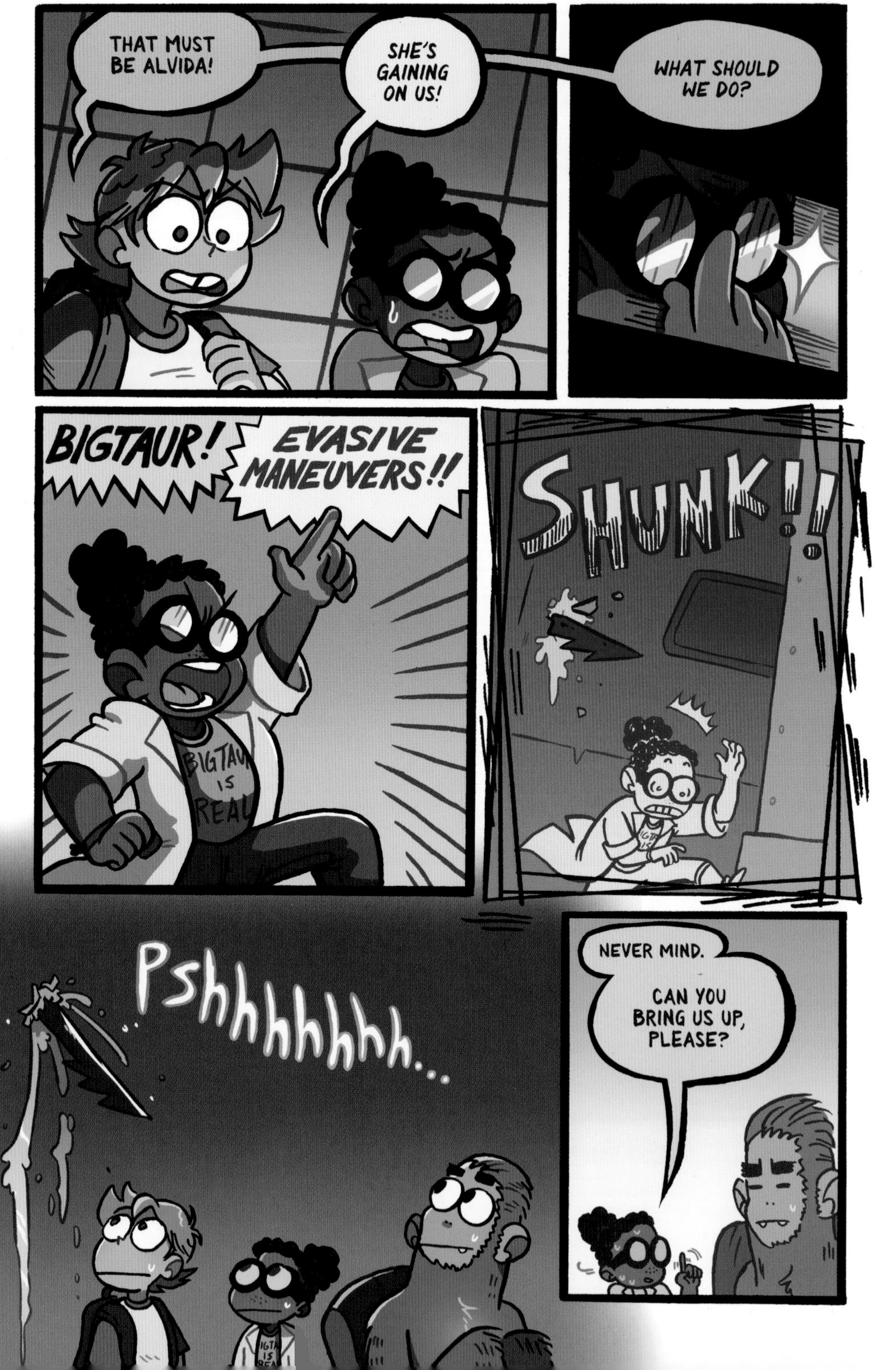
THAT MUST BE ALVIDA!
SHE'S GAINING ON US!
WHAT SHOULD WE DO?
BIGTAUR!
EVASIVE MANEUVERS!!
BIGTAUR IS REAL
SHUNK!!
Pshhhhhhhh...
NEVER MIND.
CAN YOU BRING US UP, PLEASE?

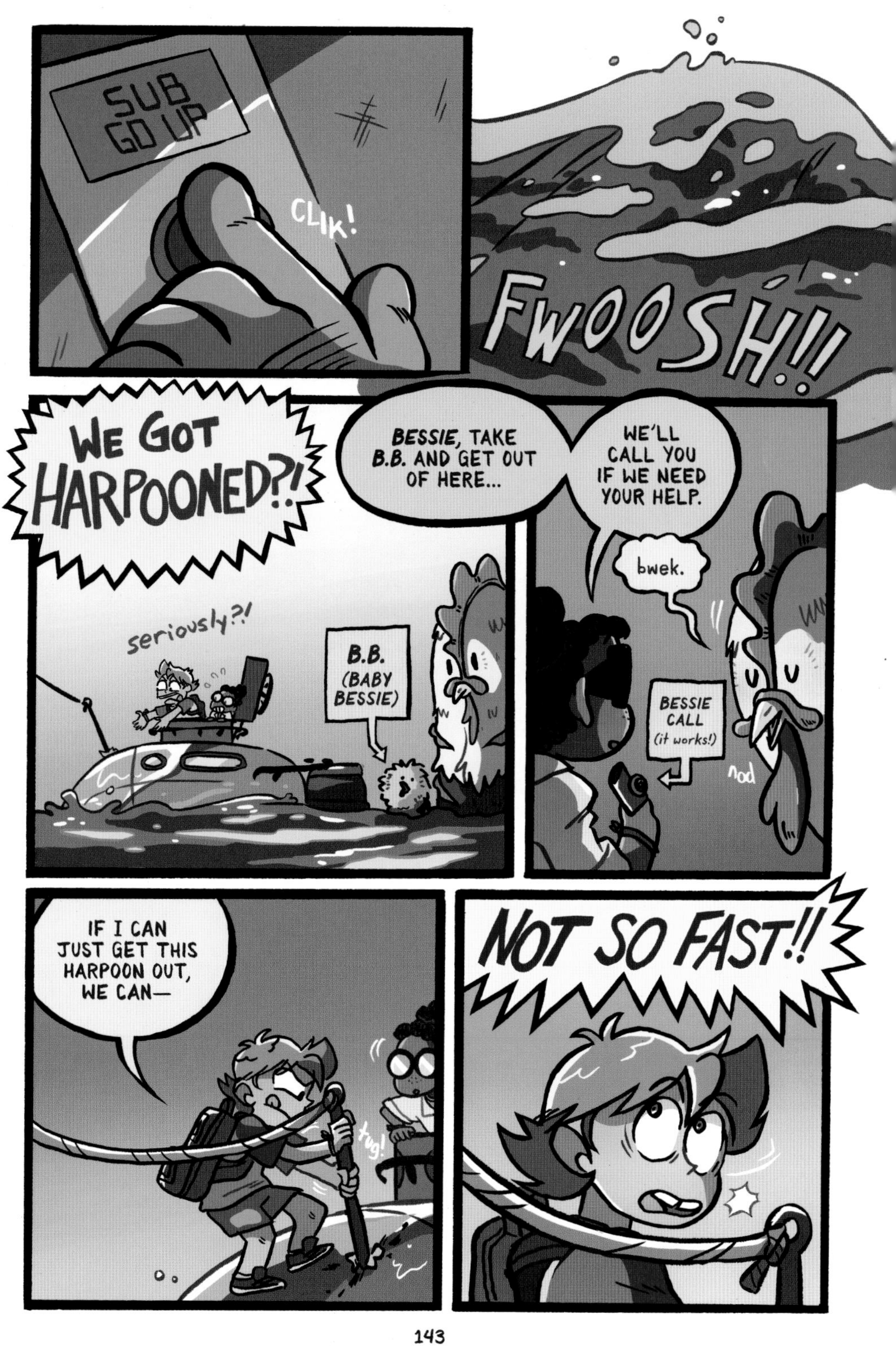
SUB GO UP
CLIK!
FWOOSH!!
WE GOT HARPOONED?!
seriously?!
BESSIE, TAKE B.B. AND GET OUT OF HERE...
B.B. (BABY BESSIE)
WE'LL CALL YOU IF WE NEED YOUR HELP.
bwek.
BESSIE CALL (it works!)
nod
IF I CAN JUST GET THIS HARPOON OUT, WE CAN—
tug!
NOT SO FAST!!

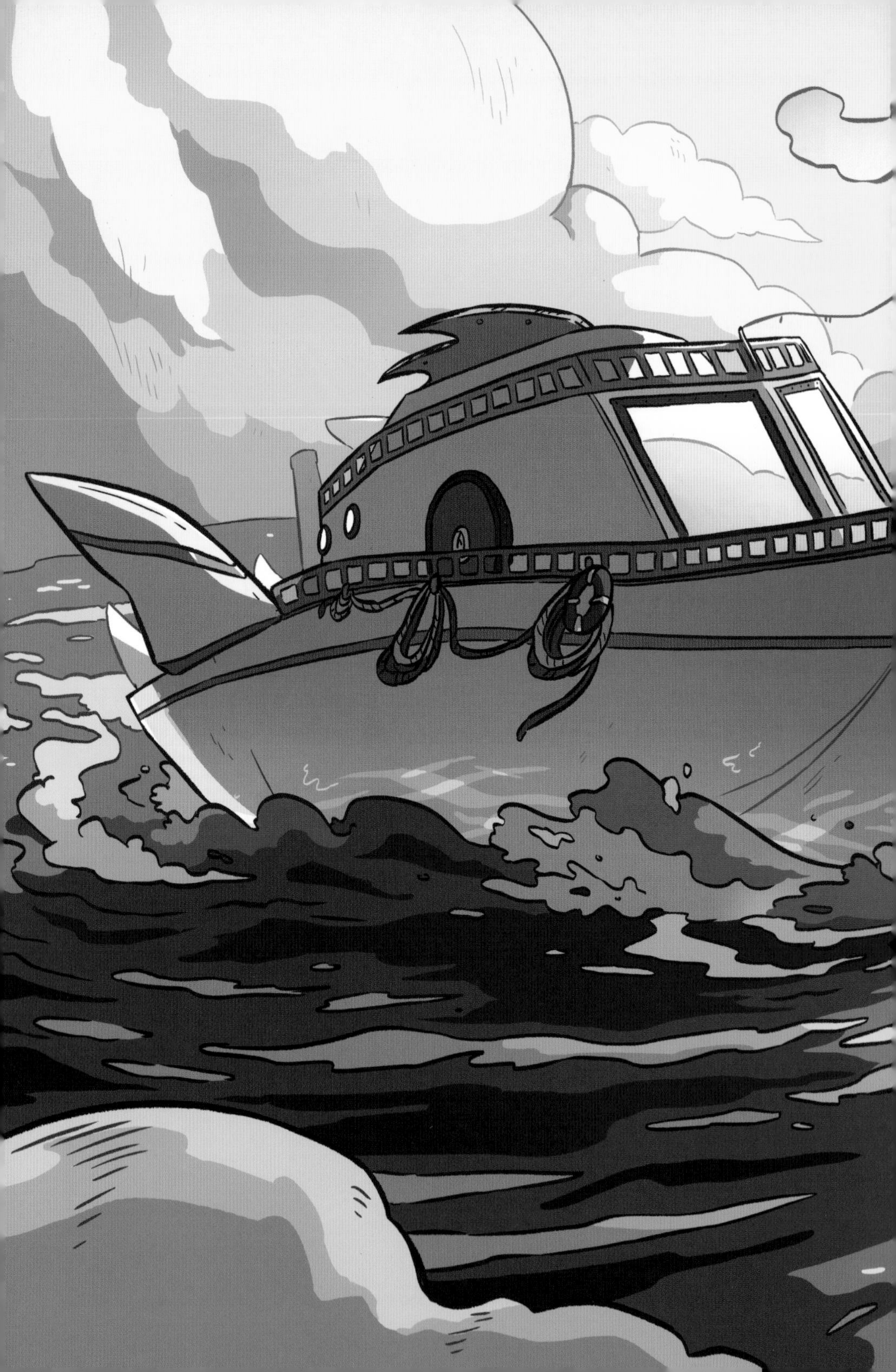

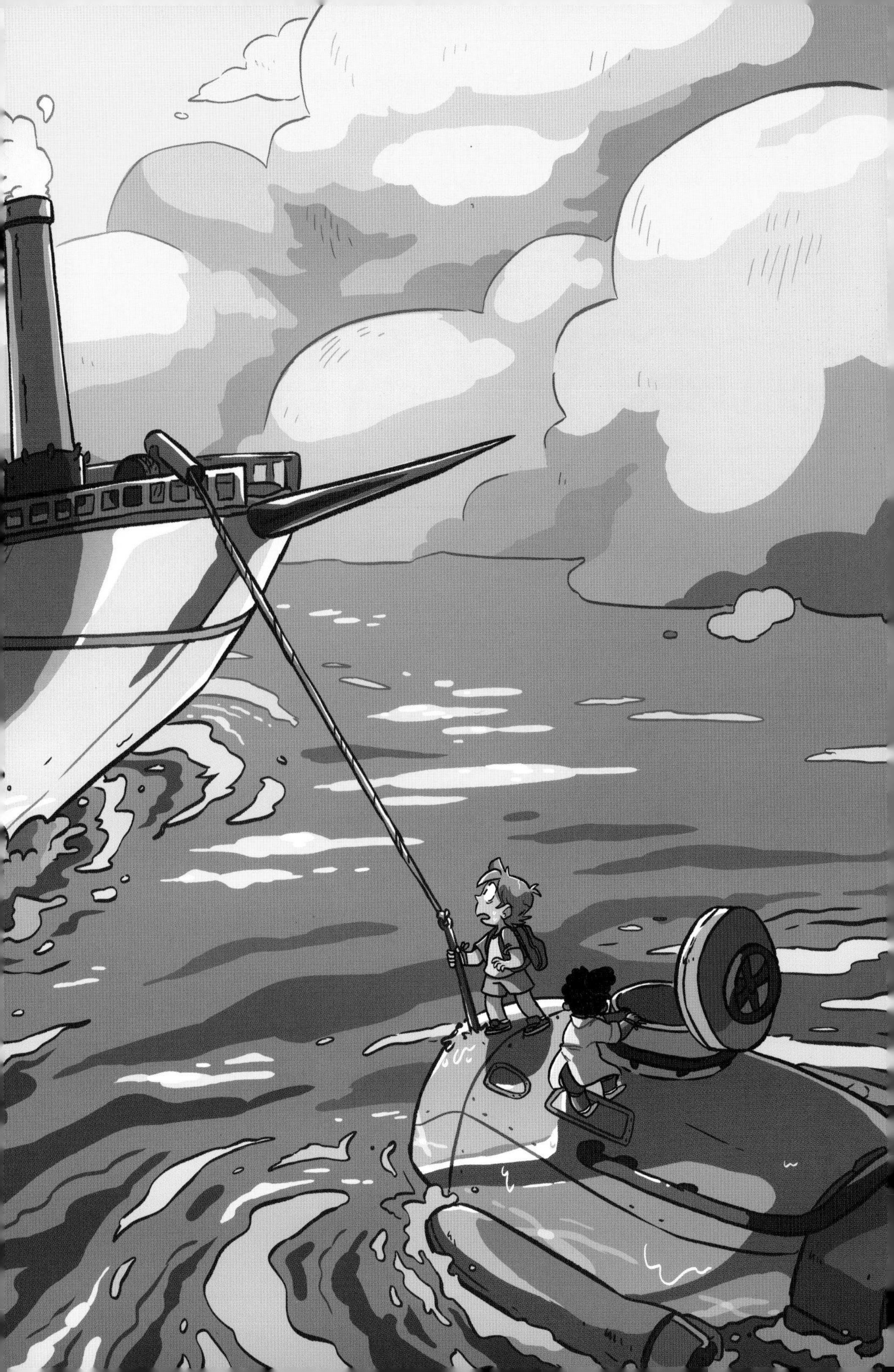

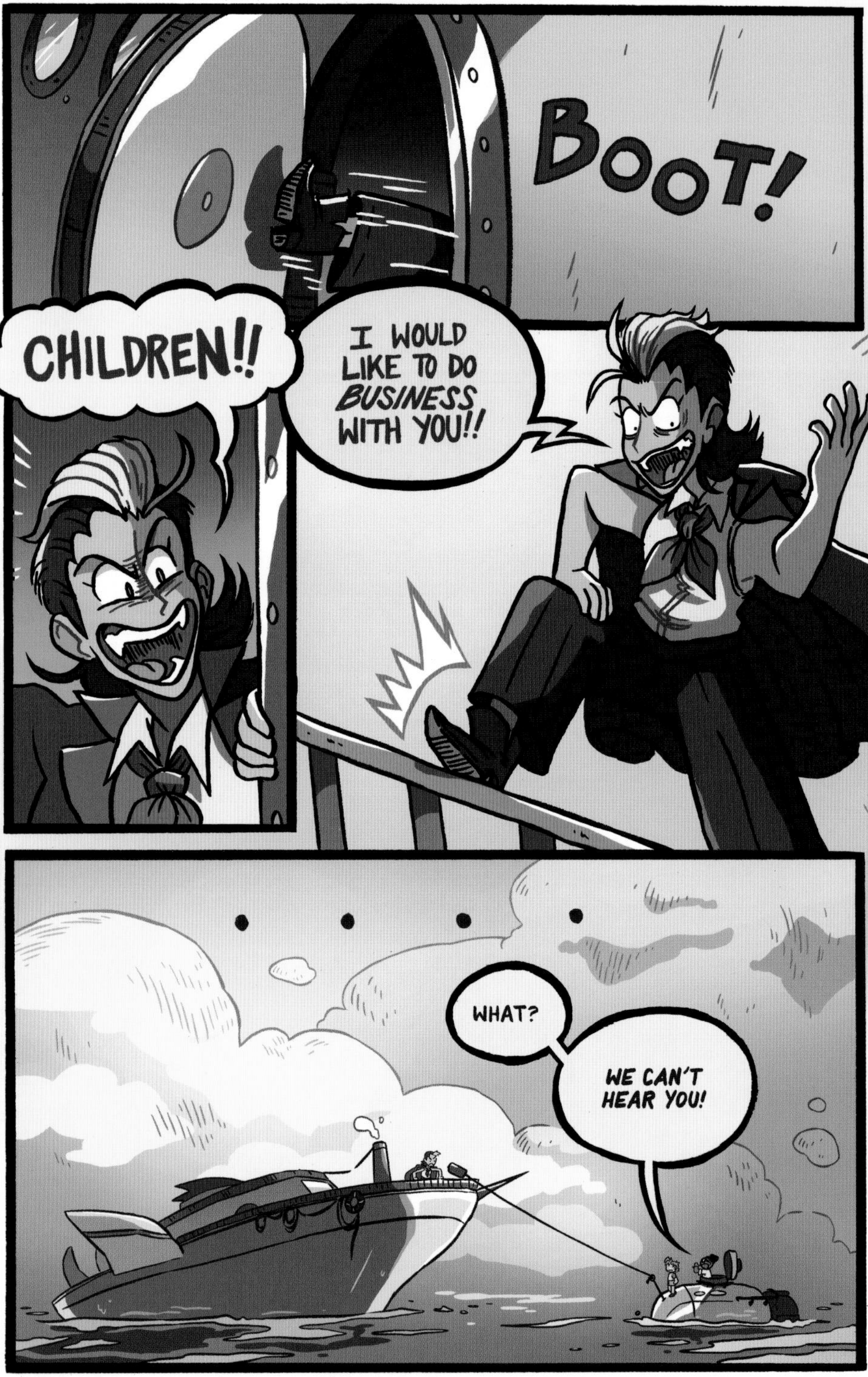
BOOT!
CHILDREN!!
I WOULD LIKE TO DO BUSINESS WITH YOU!!
• • • •
WHAT?
WE CAN'T HEAR YOU!

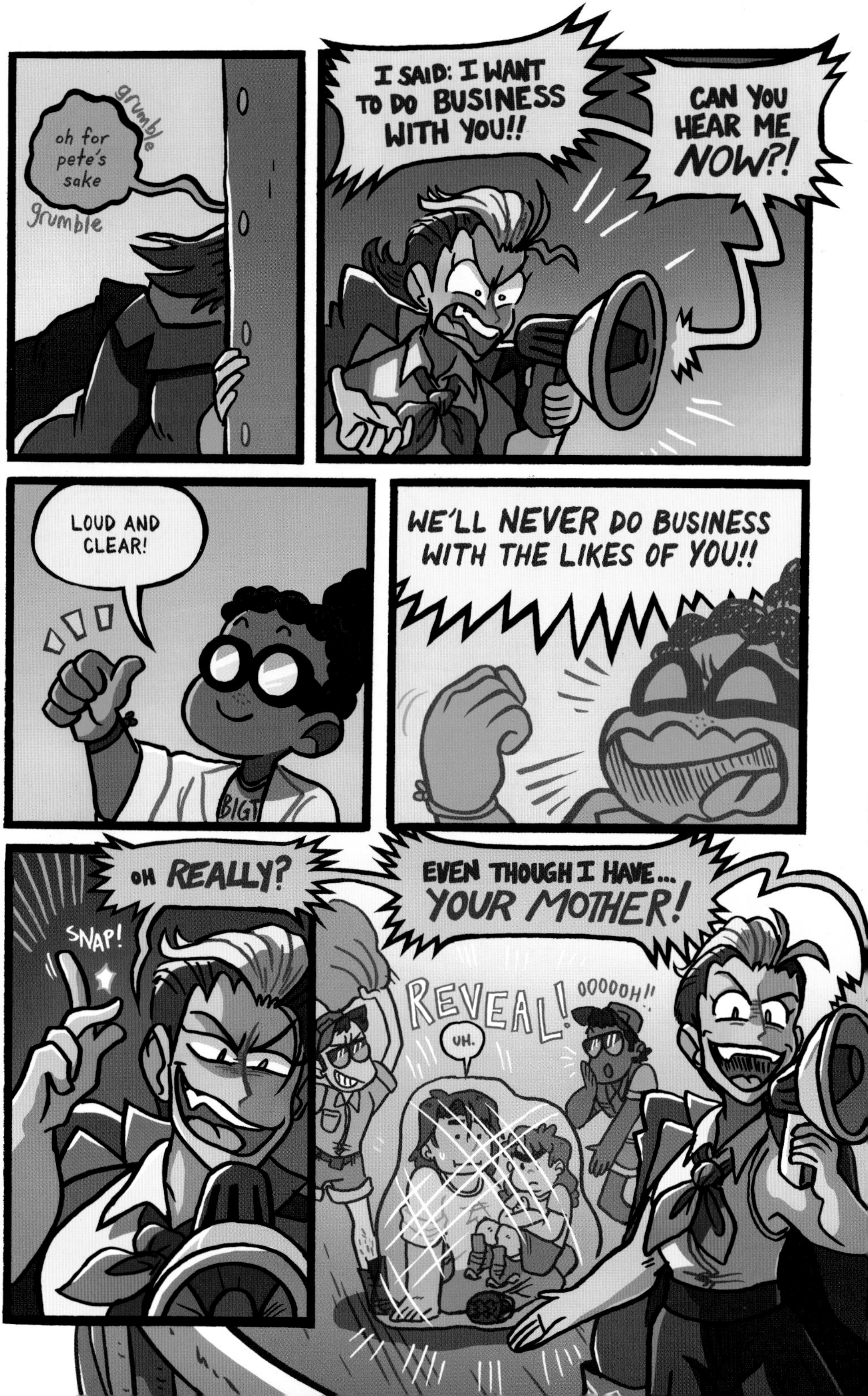
oh for pete's sake
grumble
grumble
I SAID: I WANT TO DO BUSINESS WITH YOU!!
CAN YOU HEAR ME NOW?!
LOUD AND CLEAR!
WE'LL NEVER DO BUSINESS WITH THE LIKES OF YOU!!
SNAP!
OH REALLY?
EVEN THOUGH I HAVE... YOUR MOTHER!
REVEAL!
OOOOOH!!
UH.
BIGT

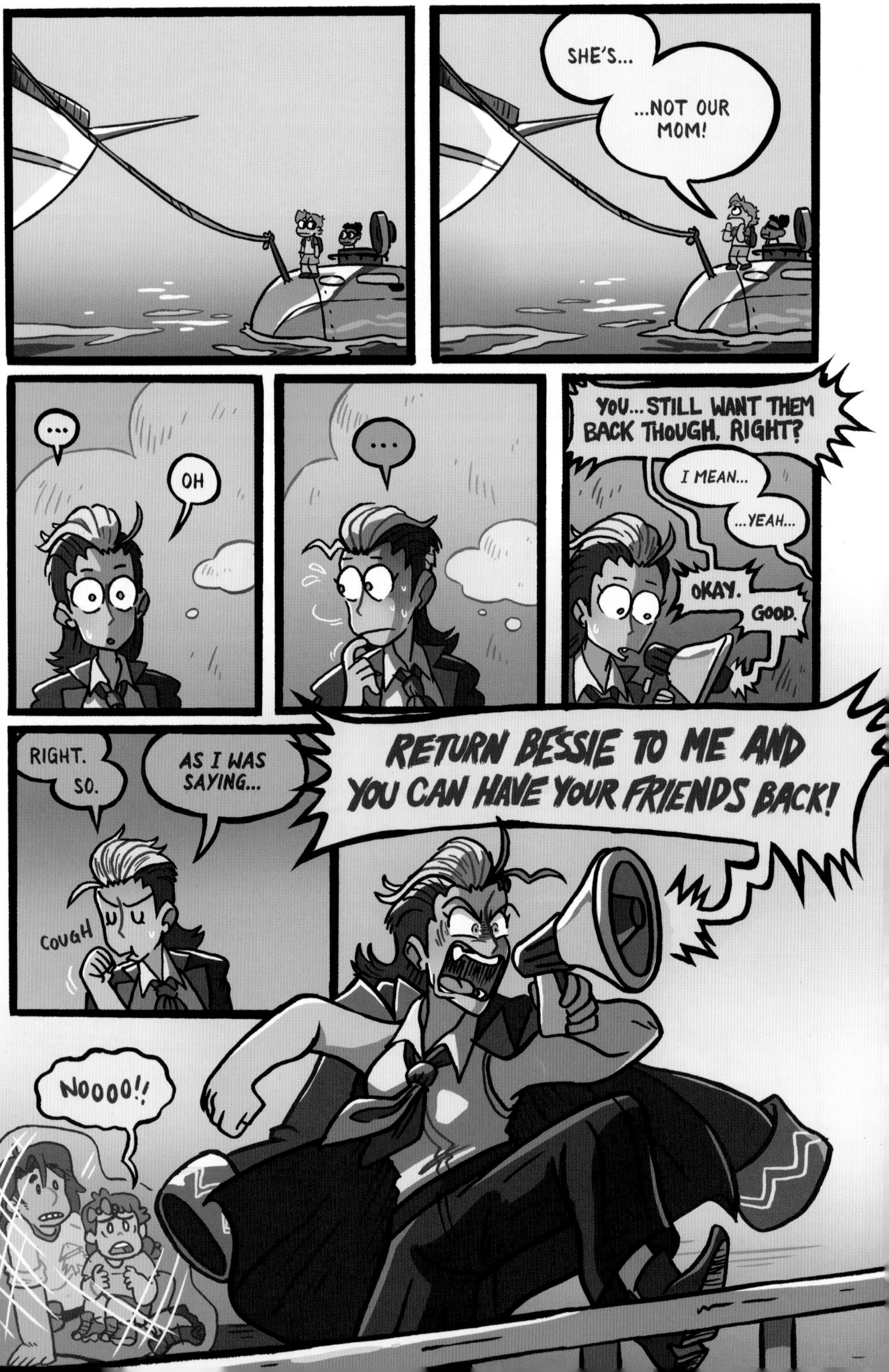
SHE'S...
...NOT OUR MOM!
...
OH
...
YOU... STILL WANT THEM BACK THOUGH, RIGHT?
I MEAN...
...YEAH...
OKAY.
GOOD.
RIGHT.
SO.
AS I WAS SAYING...
COUGH
RETURN BESSIE TO ME AND YOU CAN HAVE YOUR FRIENDS BACK!
NOOOO!!

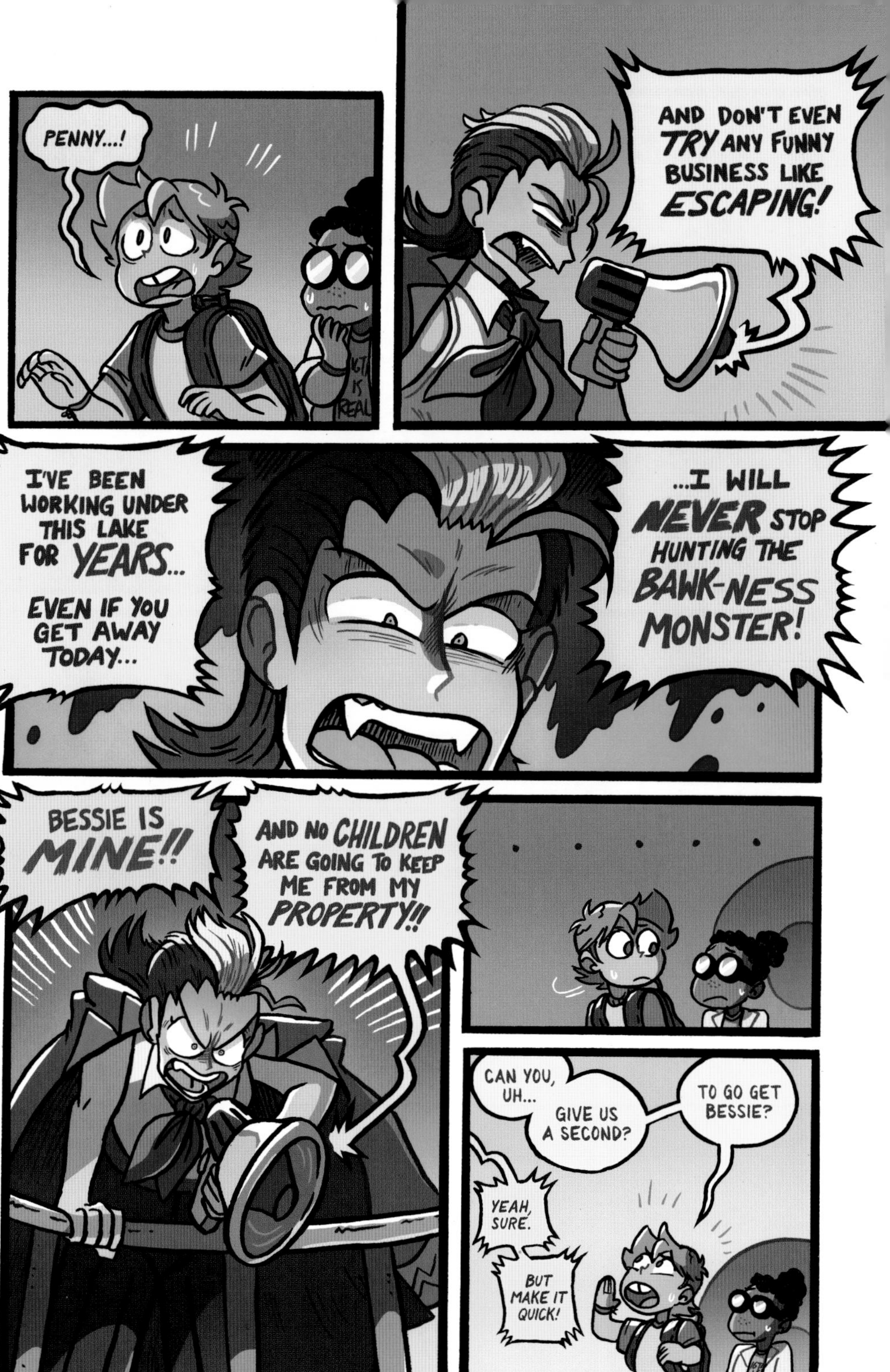
PENNY...!
AND DON'T EVEN TRY ANY FUNNY BUSINESS LIKE ESCAPING!
I'VE BEEN WORKING UNDER THIS LAKE FOR YEARS...
EVEN IF YOU GET AWAY TODAY...
...I WILL NEVER STOP HUNTING THE BAWK-NESS MONSTER!
BESSIE IS MINE!!
AND NO CHILDREN ARE GOING TO KEEP ME FROM MY PROPERTY!!
. . . . .
CAN YOU, UH...
GIVE US A SECOND?
TO GO GET BESSIE?
YEAH, SURE.
BUT MAKE IT QUICK!

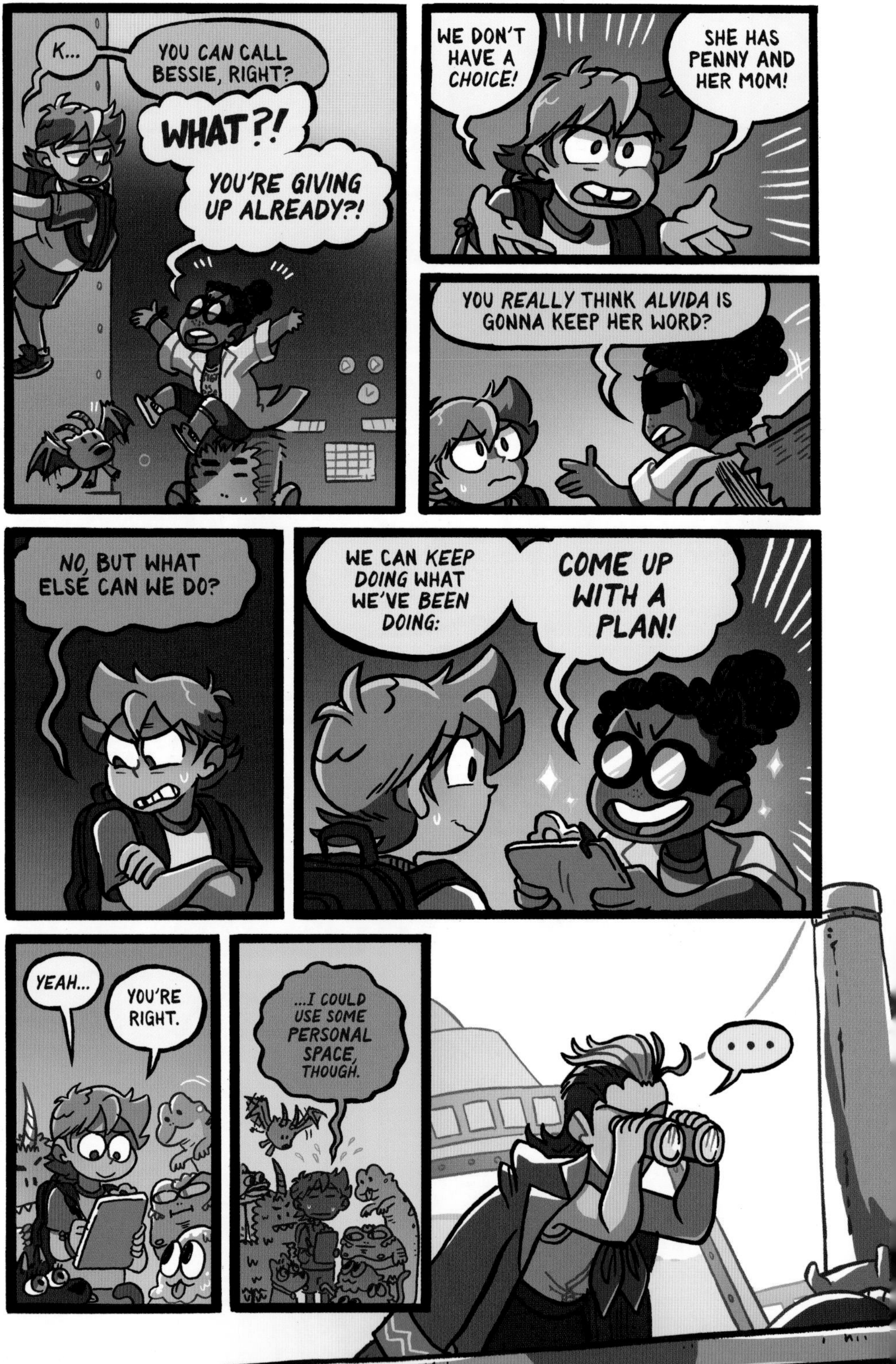
K...
YOU CAN CALL BESSIE, RIGHT?
WHAT?!
YOU'RE GIVING UP ALREADY?!
WE DON'T HAVE A CHOICE!
SHE HAS PENNY AND HER MOM!
YOU REALLY THINK ALVIDA IS GONNA KEEP HER WORD?
NO, BUT WHAT ELSE CAN WE DO?
WE CAN KEEP DOING WHAT WE'VE BEEN DOING:
COME UP WITH A PLAN!
YEAH...
YOU'RE RIGHT.
...I COULD USE SOME PERSONAL SPACE, THOUGH.
• • •

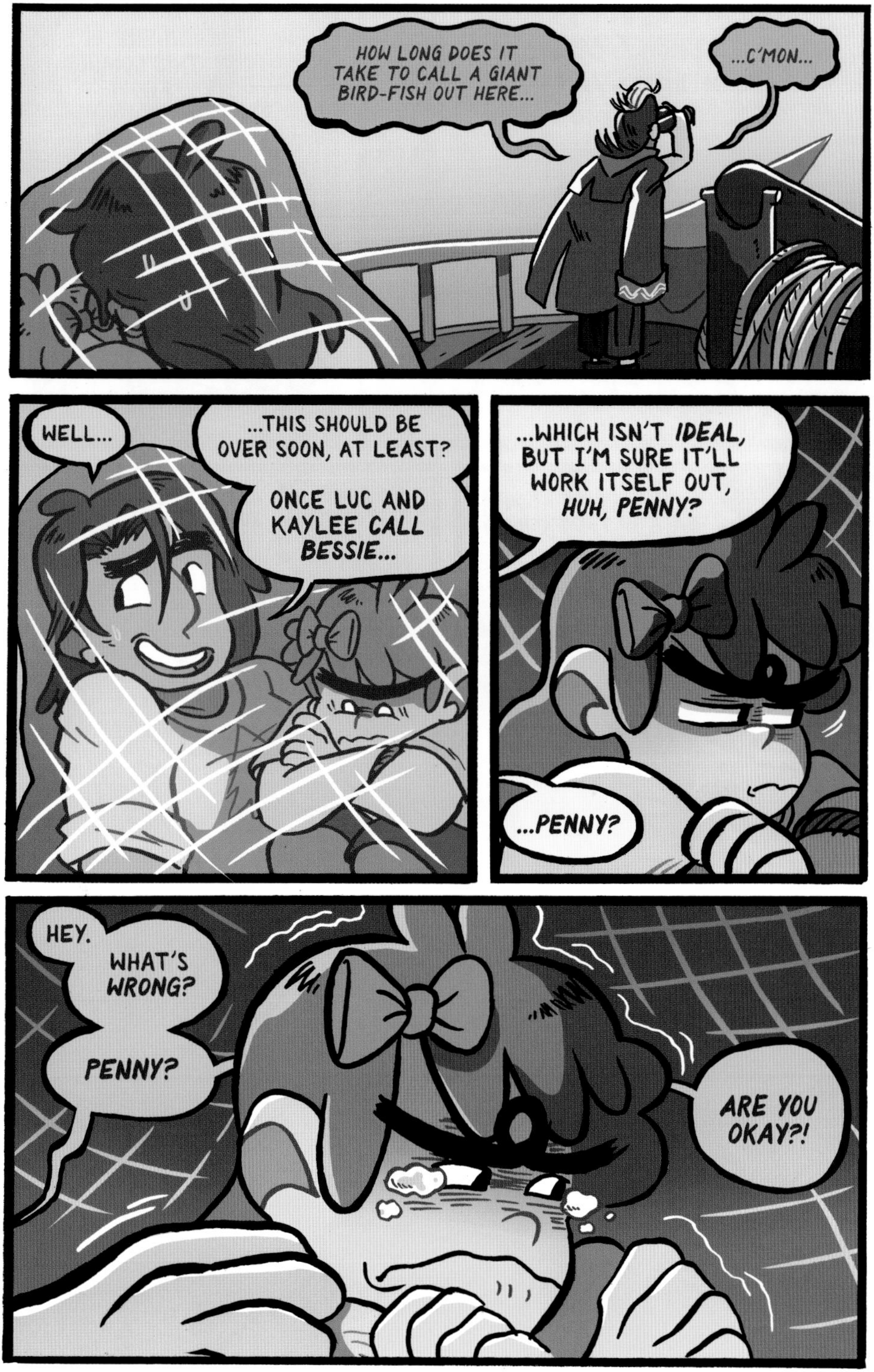
HOW LONG DOES IT TAKE TO CALL A GIANT BIRD-FISH OUT HERE...
...C'MON...
WELL...
...THIS SHOULD BE OVER SOON, AT LEAST?
ONCE LUC AND KAYLEE CALL BESSIE...
...WHICH ISN'T IDEAL, BUT I'M SURE IT'LL WORK ITSELF OUT, HUH, PENNY?
...PENNY?
HEY.
WHAT'S WRONG?
PENNY?
ARE YOU OKAY?!

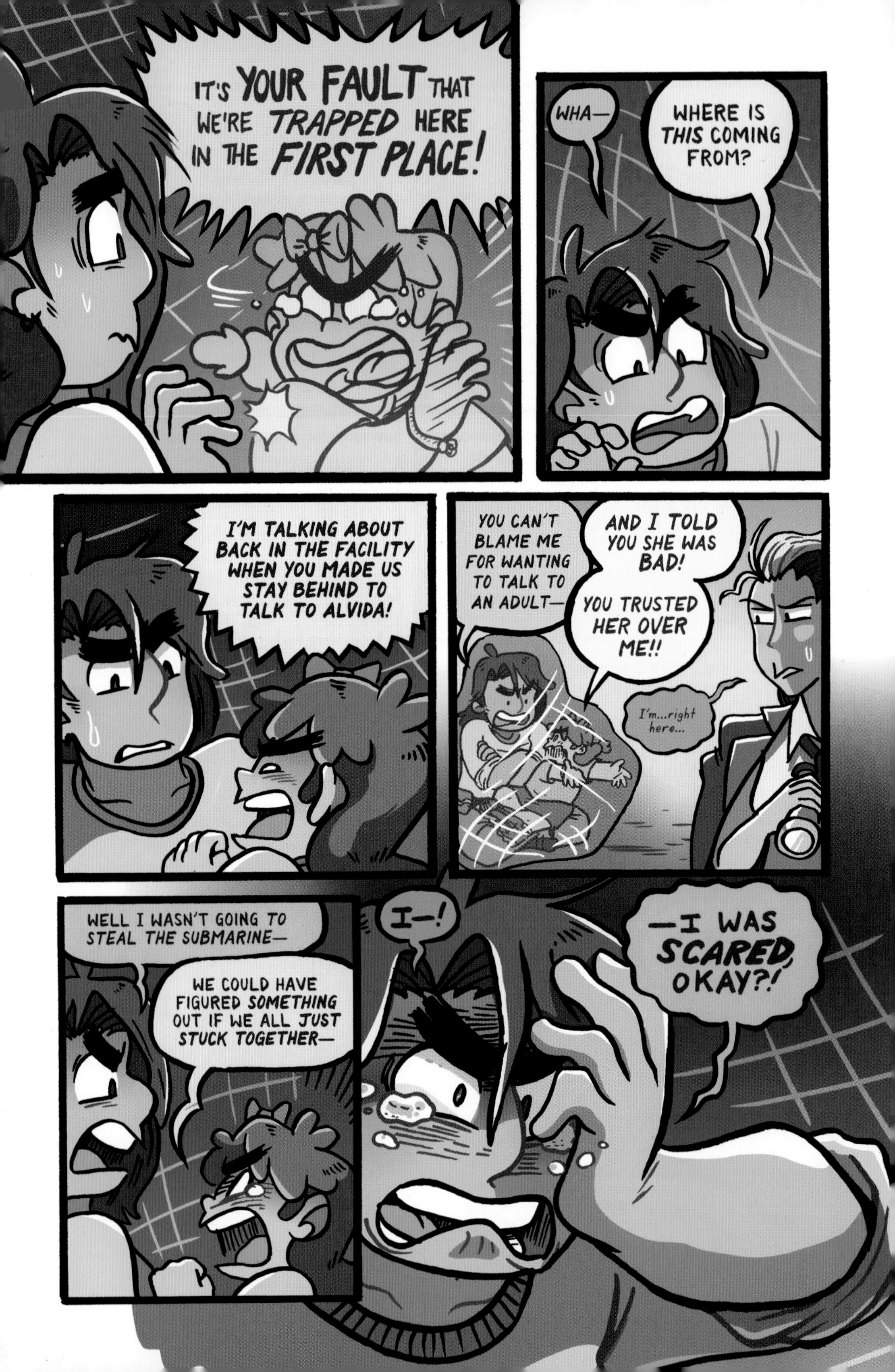
IT'S YOUR FAULT THAT WE'RE TRAPPED HERE IN THE FIRST PLACE!
WHA—
WHERE IS THIS COMING FROM?
I'M TALKING ABOUT BACK IN THE FACILITY WHEN YOU MADE US STAY BEHIND TO TALK TO ALVIDA!
YOU CAN'T BLAME ME FOR WANTING TO TALK TO AN ADULT—
AND I TOLD YOU SHE WAS BAD!
YOU TRUSTED HER OVER ME!!
I'm...right here...
WELL I WASN'T GOING TO STEAL THE SUBMARINE—
WE COULD HAVE FIGURED SOMETHING OUT IF WE ALL JUST STUCK TOGETHER—
I—!
—I WAS SCARED, OKAY?!

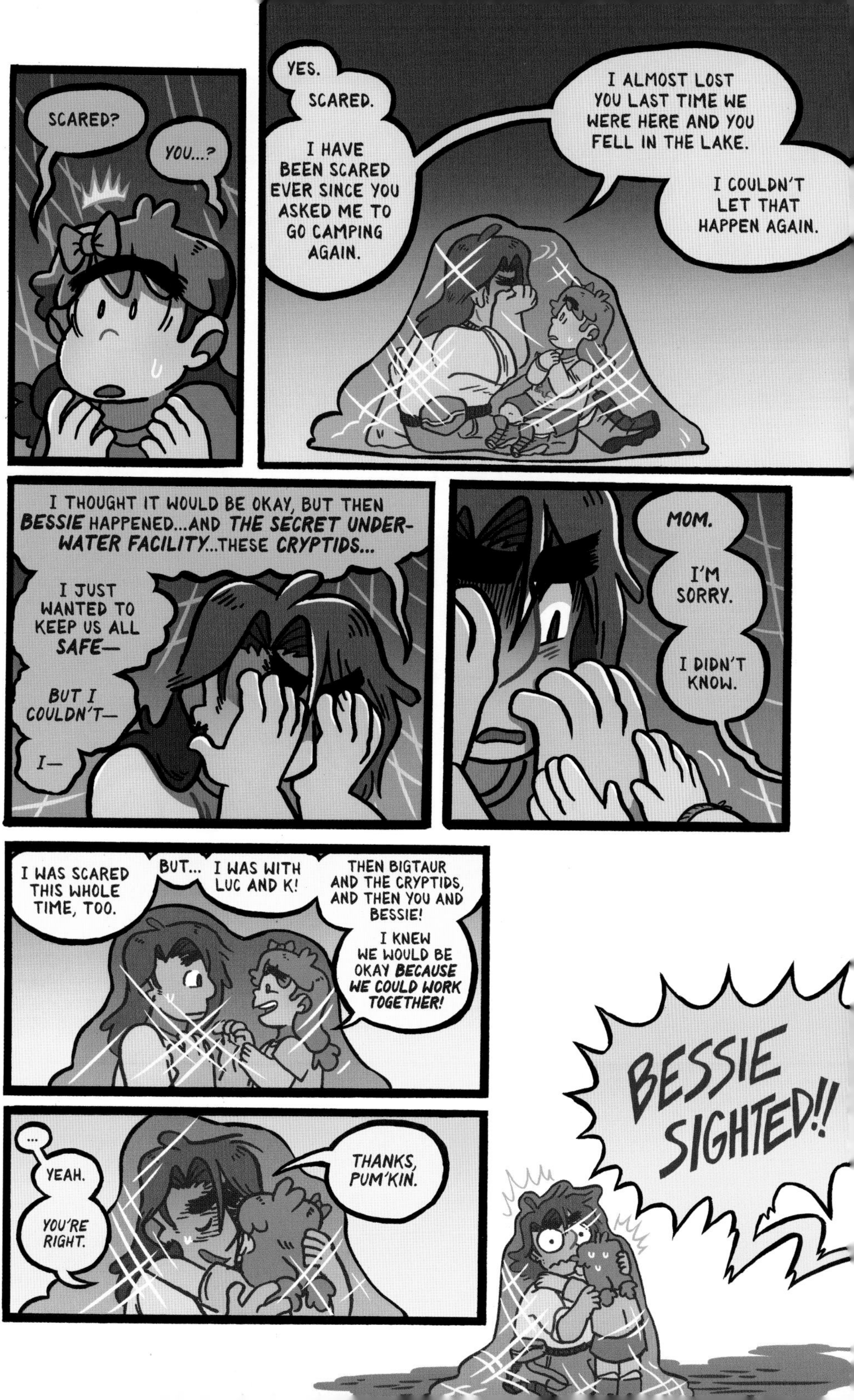
SCARED?
YOU...?
YES.
SCARED.
I HAVE BEEN SCARED EVER SINCE YOU ASKED ME TO GO CAMPING AGAIN.
I ALMOST LOST YOU LAST TIME WE WERE HERE AND YOU FELL IN THE LAKE.
I COULDN'T LET THAT HAPPEN AGAIN.
I THOUGHT IT WOULD BE OKAY, BUT THEN BESSIE HAPPENED...AND THE SECRET UNDERWATER FACILITY...THESE CRYPTIDS...
I JUST WANTED TO KEEP US ALL SAFE—
BUT I COULDN'T—
I—
MOM.
I'M SORRY.
I DIDN'T KNOW.
I WAS SCARED THIS WHOLE TIME, TOO.
BUT...
I WAS WITH LUC AND K!
THEN BIGTAUR AND THE CRYPTIDS, AND THEN YOU AND BESSIE!
I KNEW WE WOULD BE OKAY BECAUSE WE COULD WORK TOGETHER!
...
YEAH.
YOU'RE RIGHT.
THANKS, PUM'KIN.
BESSIE SIGHTED!!

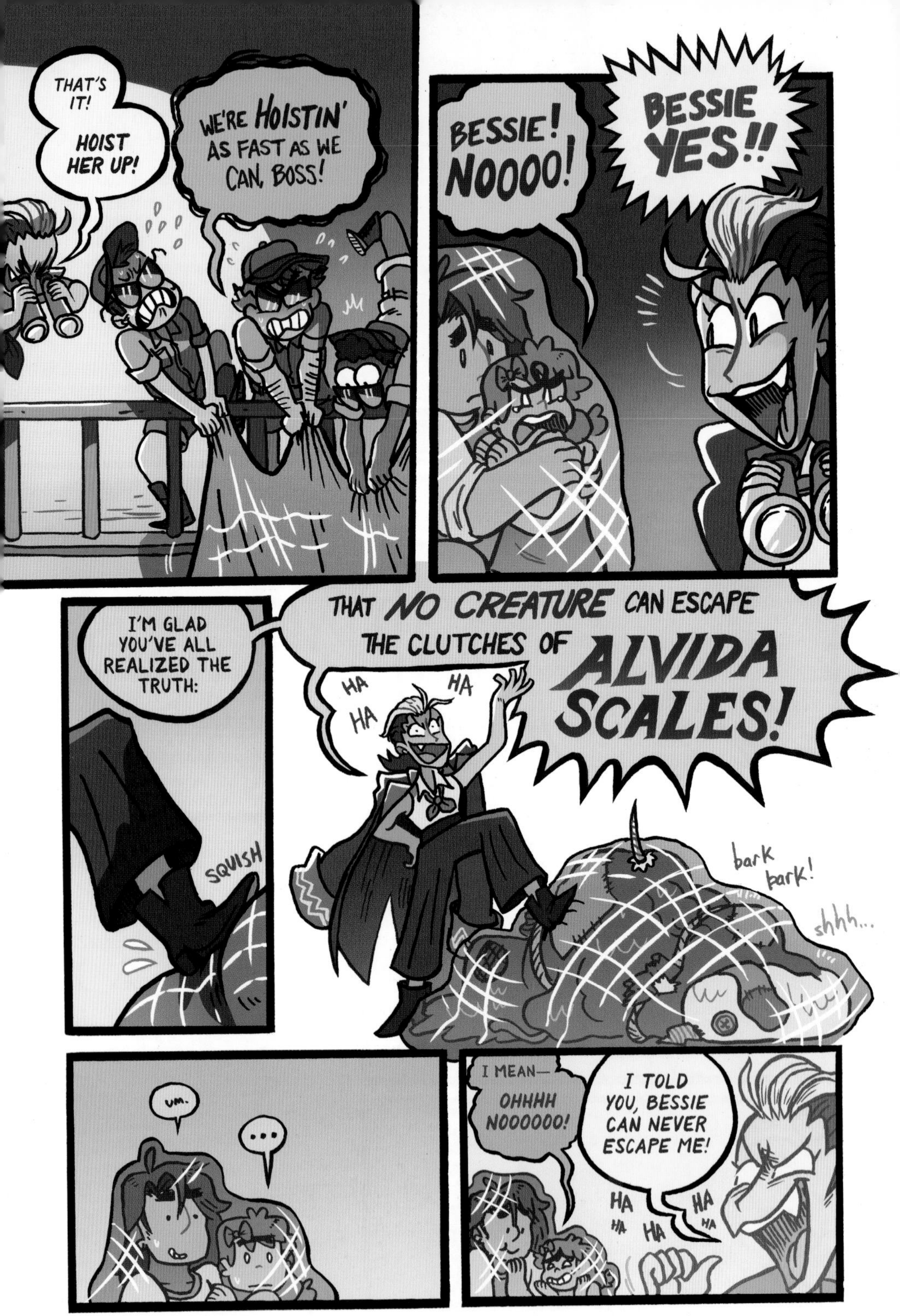
THAT'S IT! HOIST HER UP!
WE'RE HOISTIN' AS FAST AS WE CAN, BOSS!
BESSIE! NOOOO!
BESSIE YES!!
I'M GLAD YOU'VE ALL REALIZED THE TRUTH:
THAT NO CREATURE CAN ESCAPE THE CLUTCHES OF ALVIDA SCALES!
HA HA HA
SQUISH
bark bark!
shhh...
UM.
...
I MEAN— OHHHH NOOOOOO!
I TOLD YOU, BESSIE CAN NEVER ESCAPE ME!
HA HA HA HA HA HA

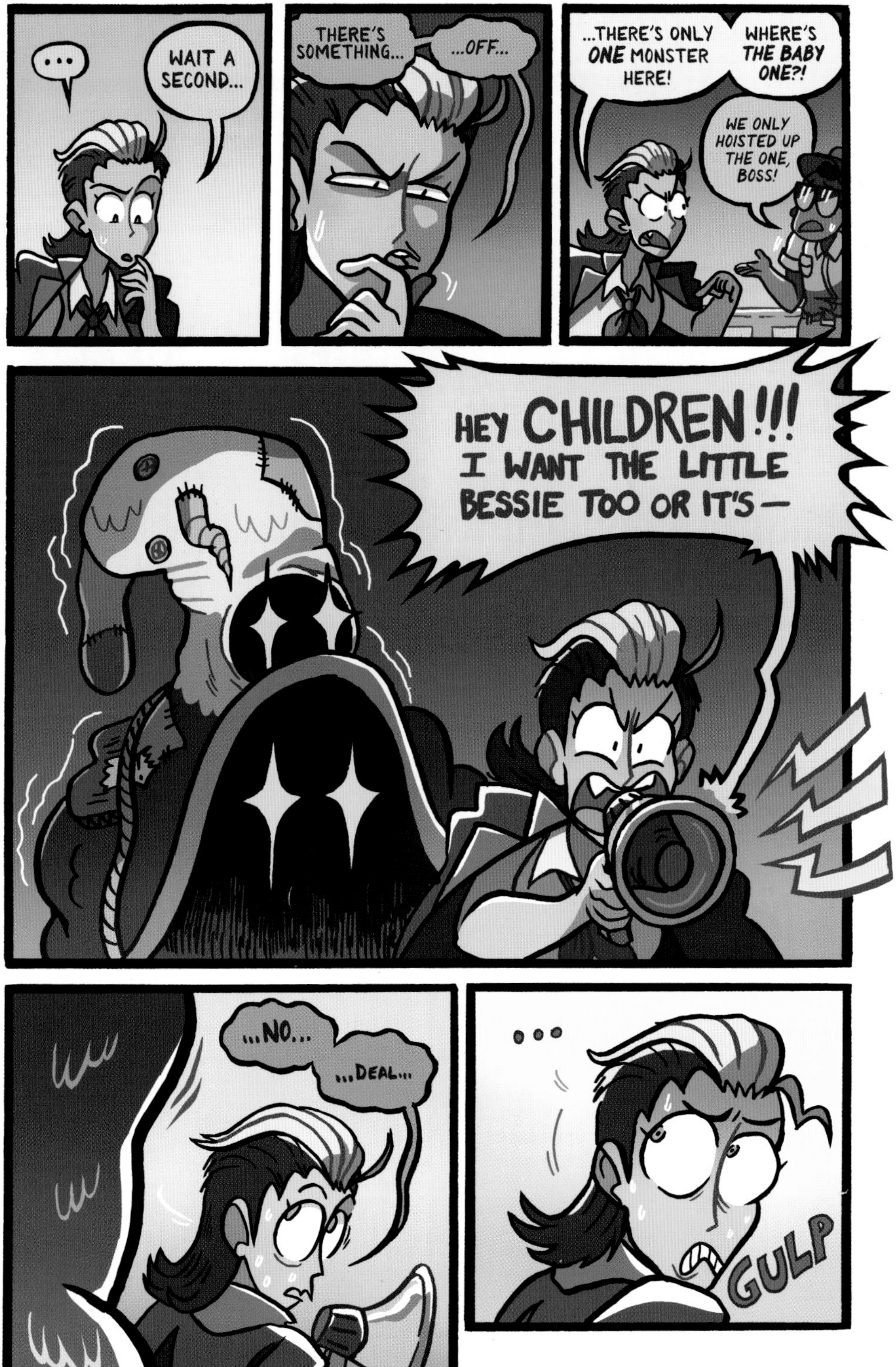

...
WAIT A SECOND...
THERE'S SOMETHING...
...OFF...
...THERE'S ONLY **ONE** MONSTER HERE!
WHERE'S **THE BABY ONE?!**
WE ONLY HOISTED UP THE ONE, BOSS!
HEY CHILDREN!!! I WANT THE LITTLE BESSIE TOO OR IT'S—
...NO...
...DEAL...
...
GULP

Operation: Stop Alvida!!!!

☑ Disguise as Bessie, fool Alvida

CHILDREN?! CRYPTIDS?! AGAIN?!

"AGAIN"? SHE'S JOKING, RIGHT?

THAT COULDN'T POSSIBLY HAVE FOOLED—

THIS IS THE *THIRD TIME* WE'VE DONE THIS.

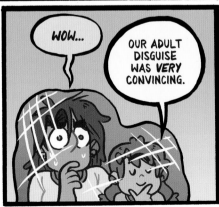

WOW...

OUR ADULT DISGUISE WAS *VERY* CONVINCING.

☑ Fight off Alvida and her lackeys

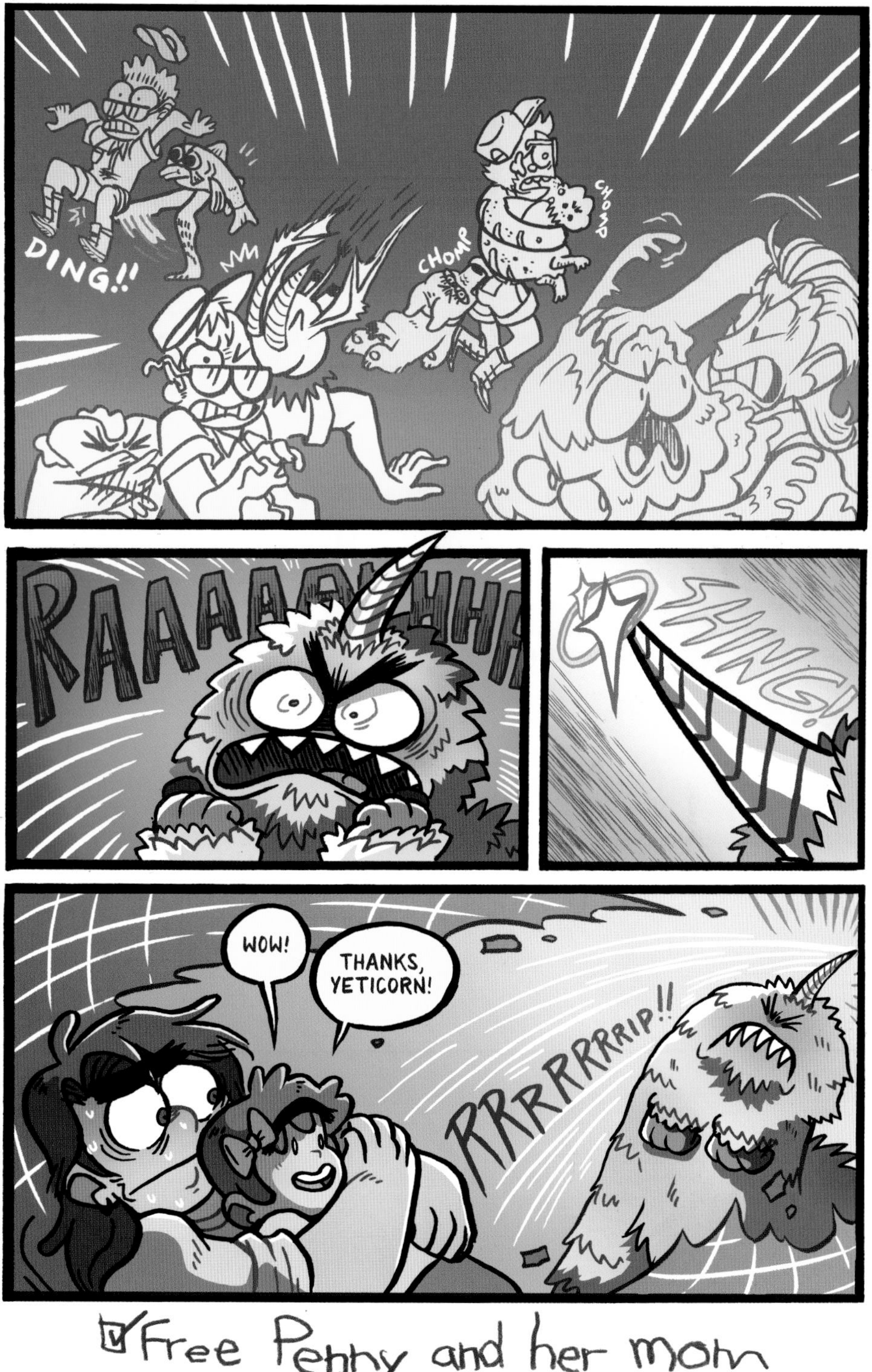
DING!!
CHOMP
CHOMP
RAAAA
SHING!
WOW!
THANKS, YETICORN!
RRRRRRRIP!!

☑ Free Penny and her mom

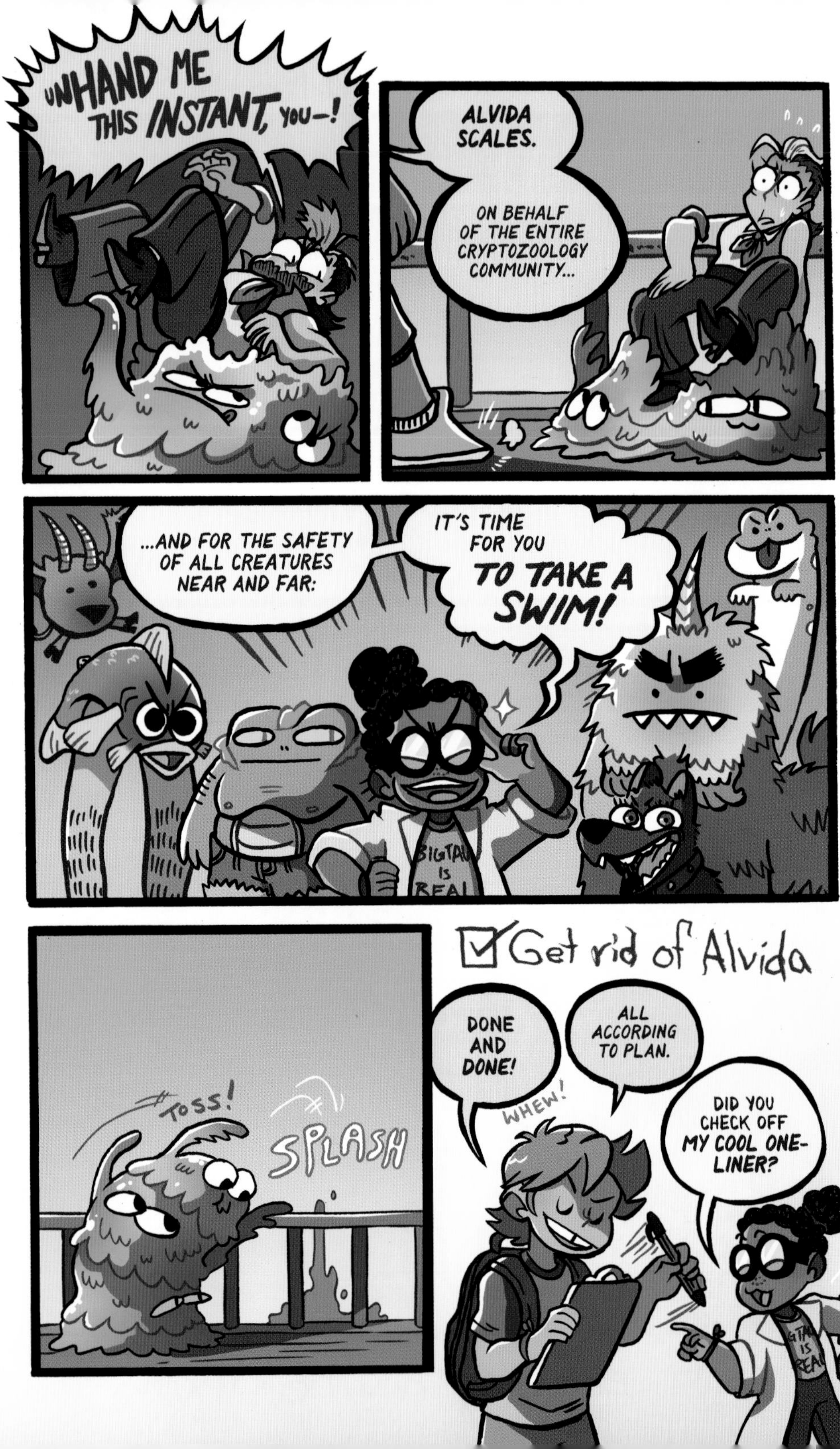

UNHAND ME THIS INSTANT, YOU—!
ALVIDA SCALES.
ON BEHALF OF THE ENTIRE CRYPTOZOOLOGY COMMUNITY...
...AND FOR THE SAFETY OF ALL CREATURES NEAR AND FAR:
IT'S TIME FOR YOU TO TAKE A SWIM!
BIGTAIL IS REAL
TOSS!
SPLASH
Get rid of Alvida
DONE AND DONE!
ALL ACCORDING TO PLAN.
WHEW!
DID YOU CHECK OFF MY COOL ONE-LINER?

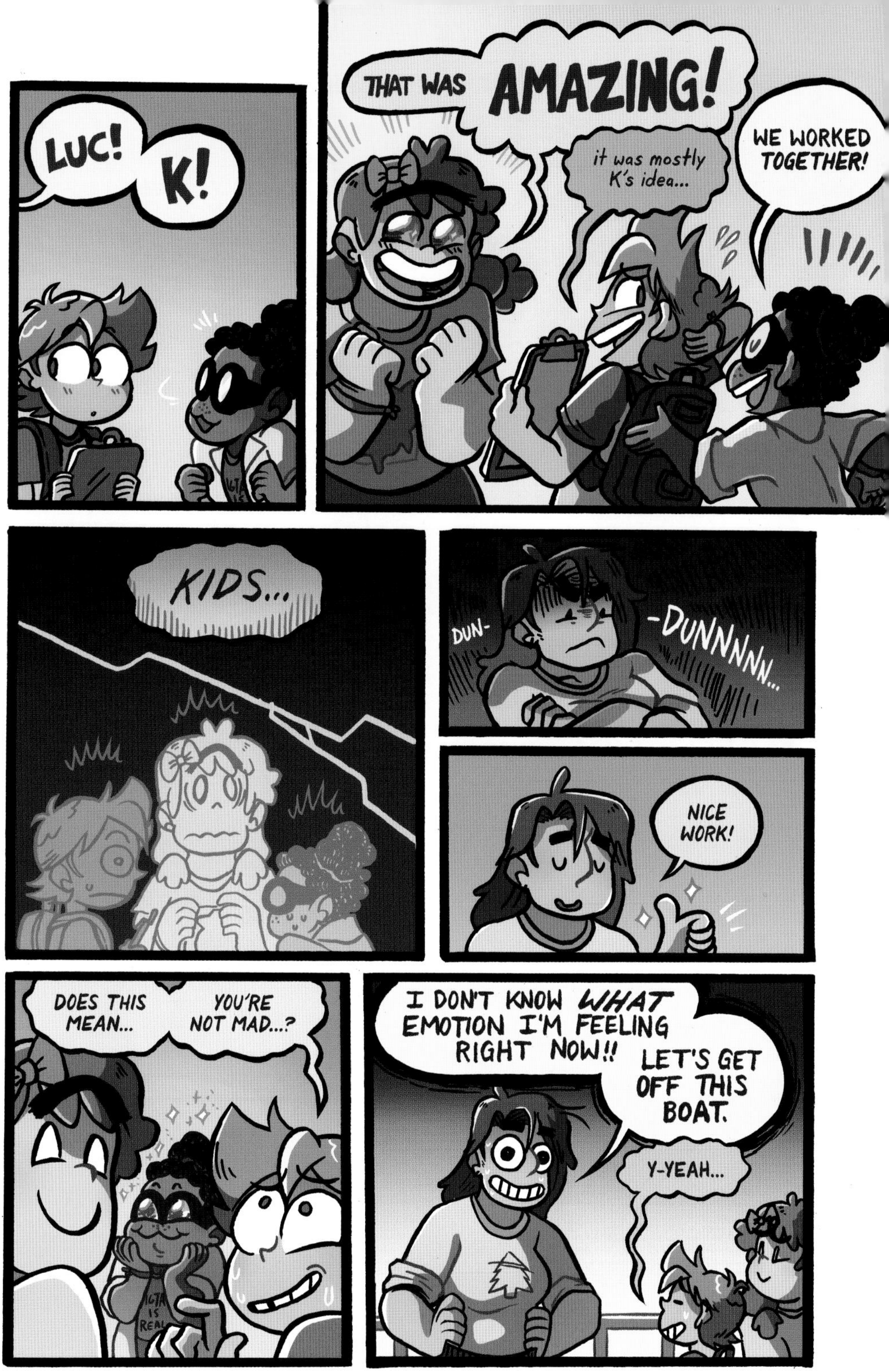
LUC!
K!
THAT WAS AMAZING!
it was mostly K's idea...
WE WORKED TOGETHER!
KIDS...
DUN-
-DUNNNNN...
NICE WORK!
DOES THIS MEAN...
YOU'RE NOT MAD...?
I DON'T KNOW WHAT EMOTION I'M FEELING RIGHT NOW!!
LET'S GET OFF THIS BOAT.
Y-YEAH...

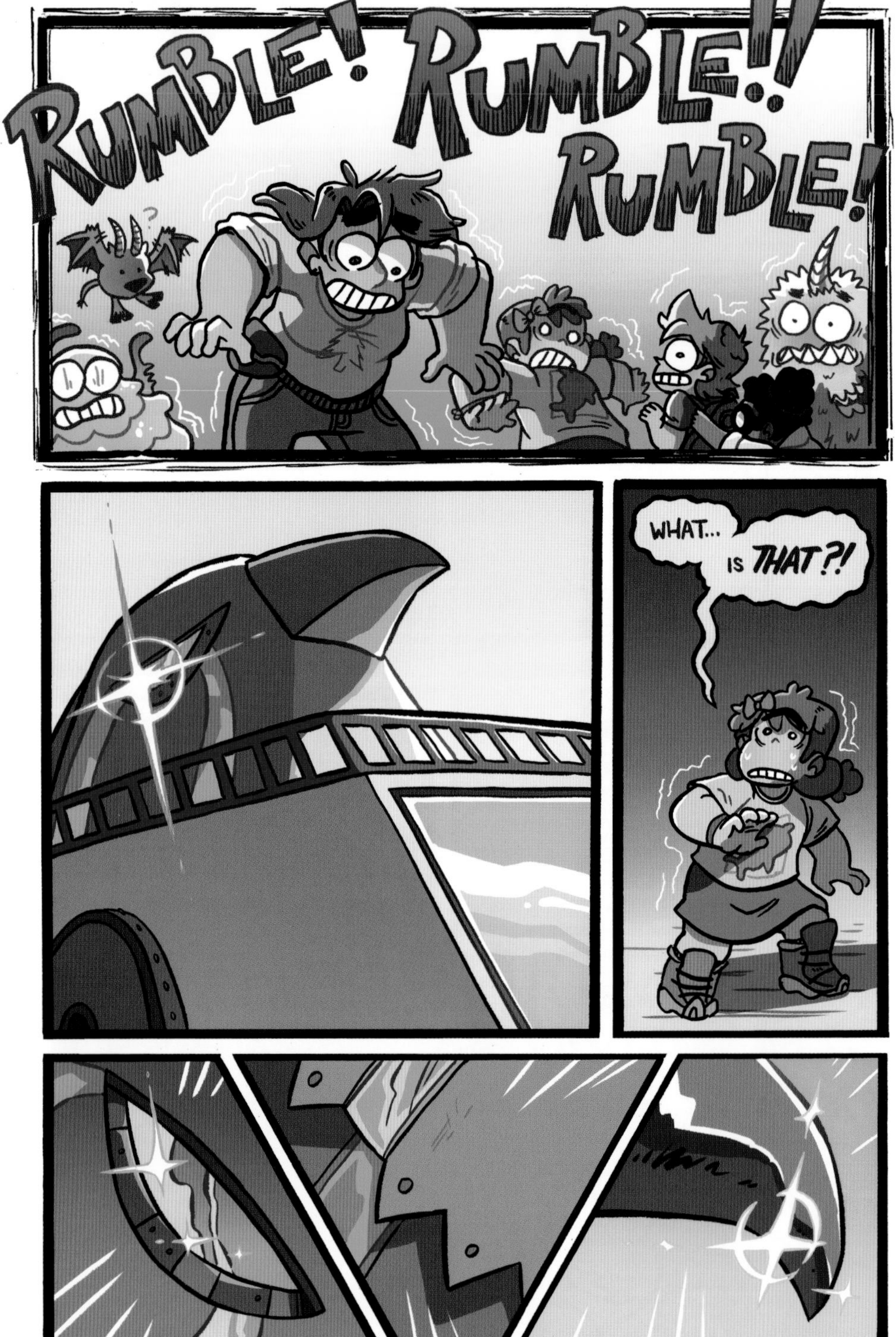
RUMBLE! RUMBLE!! RUMBLE!
WHAT...
IS THAT?!

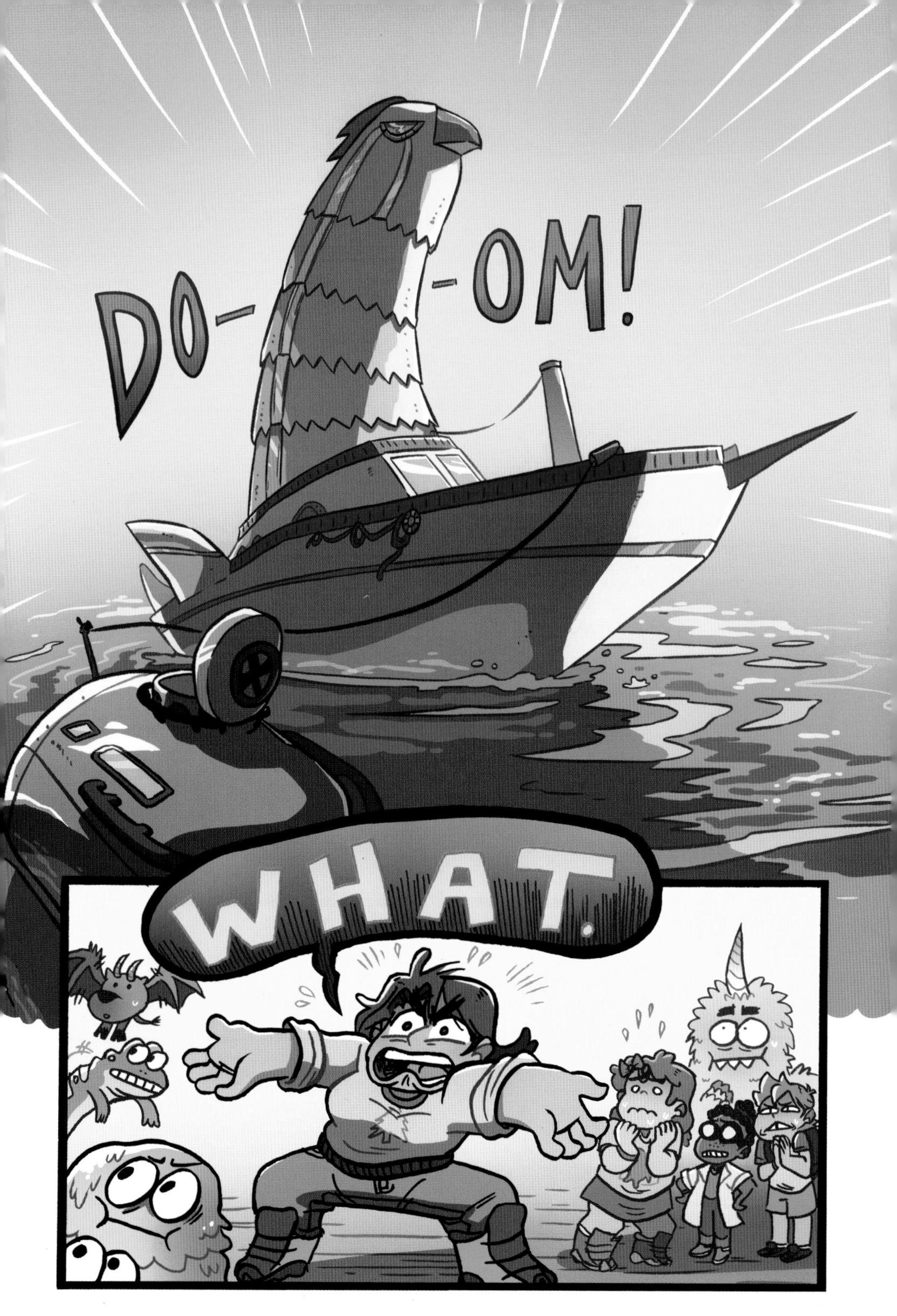
DO—
—OM!
WHAT.

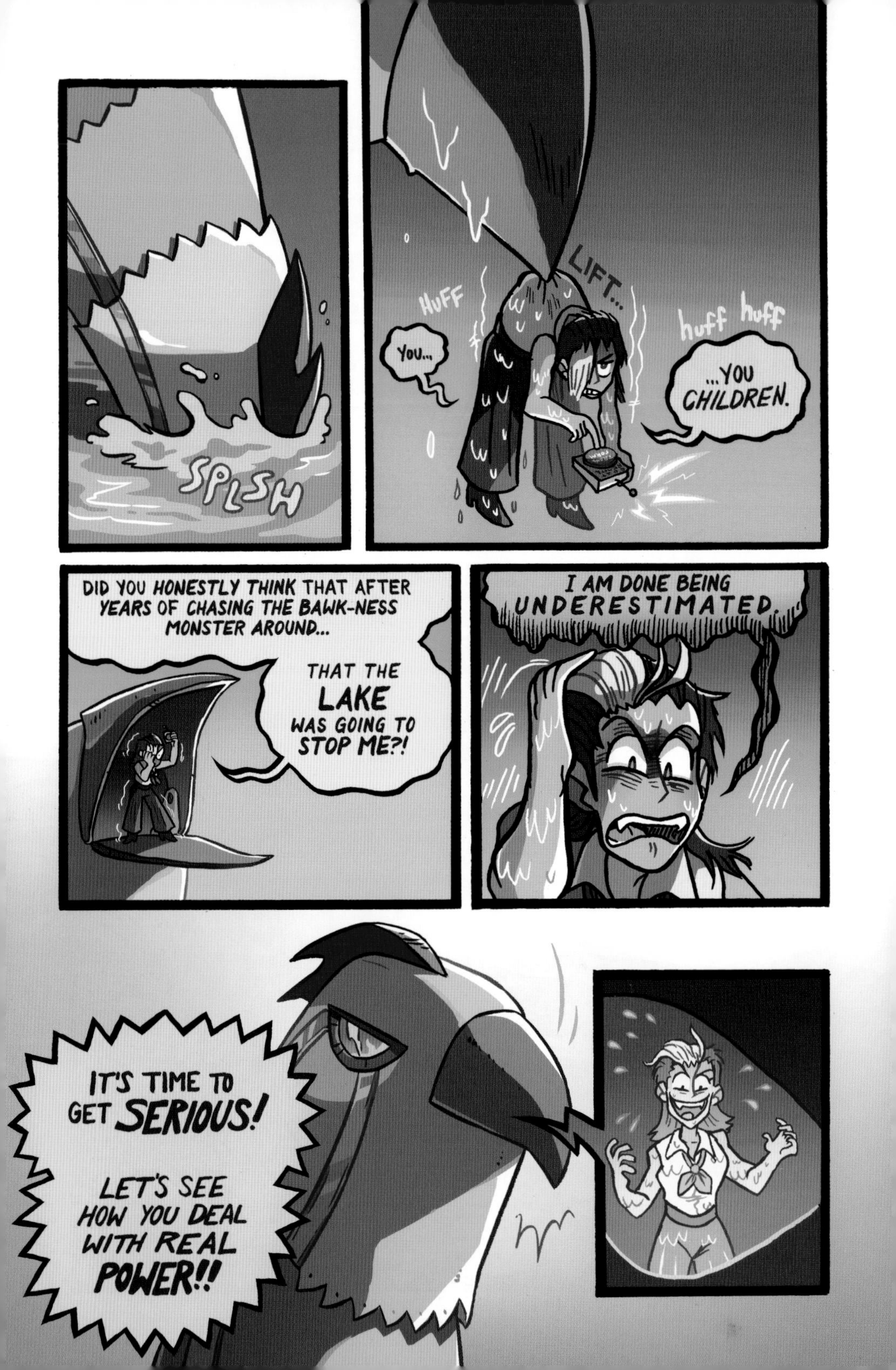
SPLSH
LIFT...
HUFF
YOU...
huff huff
...YOU CHILDREN.
DID YOU HONESTLY THINK THAT AFTER YEARS OF CHASING THE BAWK-NESS MONSTER AROUND...
THAT THE LAKE WAS GOING TO STOP ME?!
I AM DONE BEING UNDERESTIMATED.
IT'S TIME TO GET SERIOUS!
LET'S SEE HOW YOU DEAL WITH REAL POWER!!

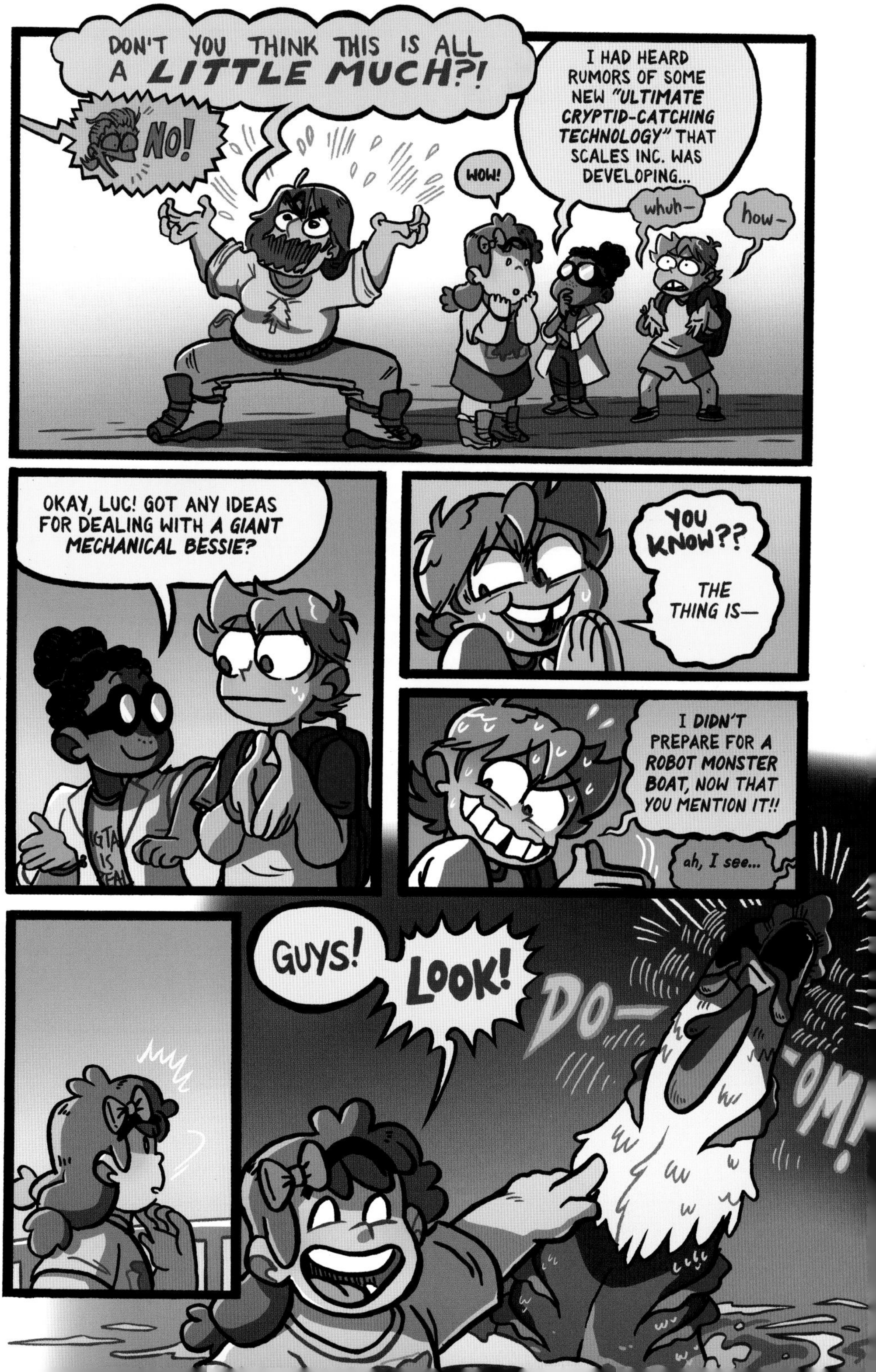

DON'T YOU THINK THIS IS ALL A LITTLE MUCH?!
NO!
WOW!
I HAD HEARD RUMORS OF SOME NEW "ULTIMATE CRYPTID-CATCHING TECHNOLOGY" THAT SCALES INC. WAS DEVELOPING...
whuh-
how-
OKAY, LUC! GOT ANY IDEAS FOR DEALING WITH A GIANT MECHANICAL BESSIE?
YOU KNOW??
THE THING IS—
I DIDN'T PREPARE FOR A ROBOT MONSTER BOAT, NOW THAT YOU MENTION IT!!
ah, I see...
GUYS!
LOOK!
DO-
-OM!

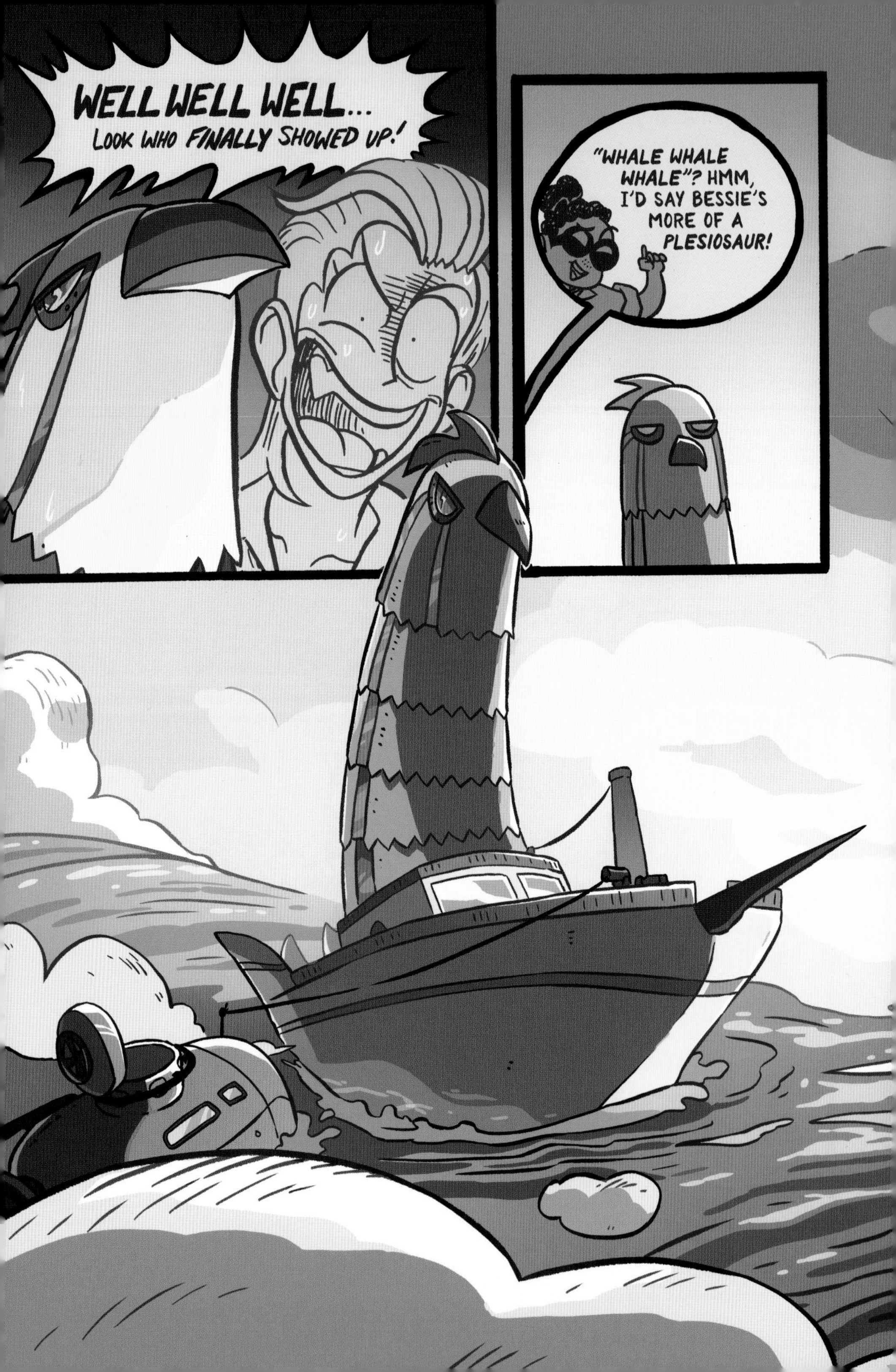
WELL WELL WELL...
LOOK WHO FINALLY SHOWED UP!
"WHALE WHALE WHALE"? HMM, I'D SAY BESSIE'S MORE OF A PLESIOSAUR!

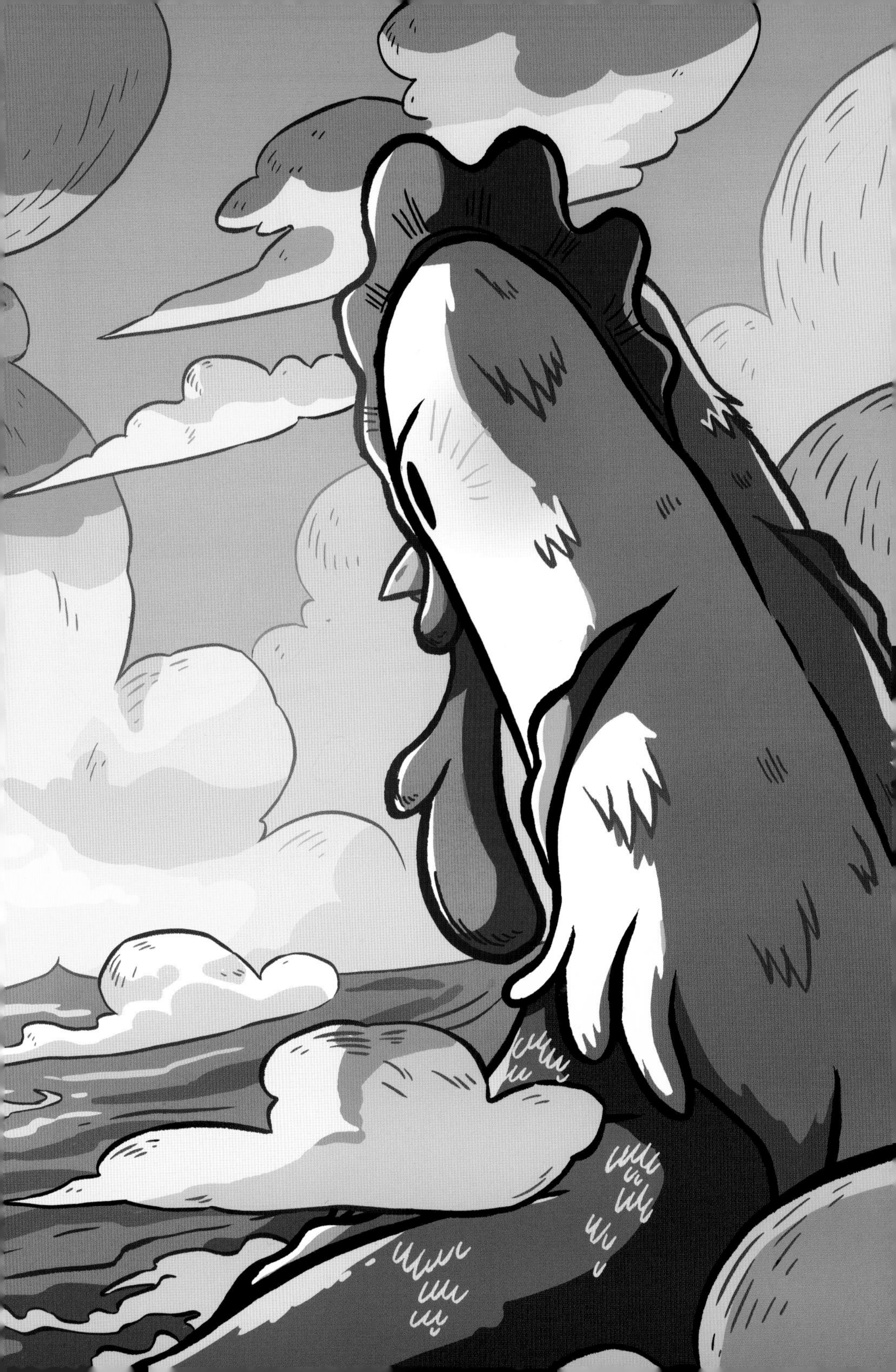

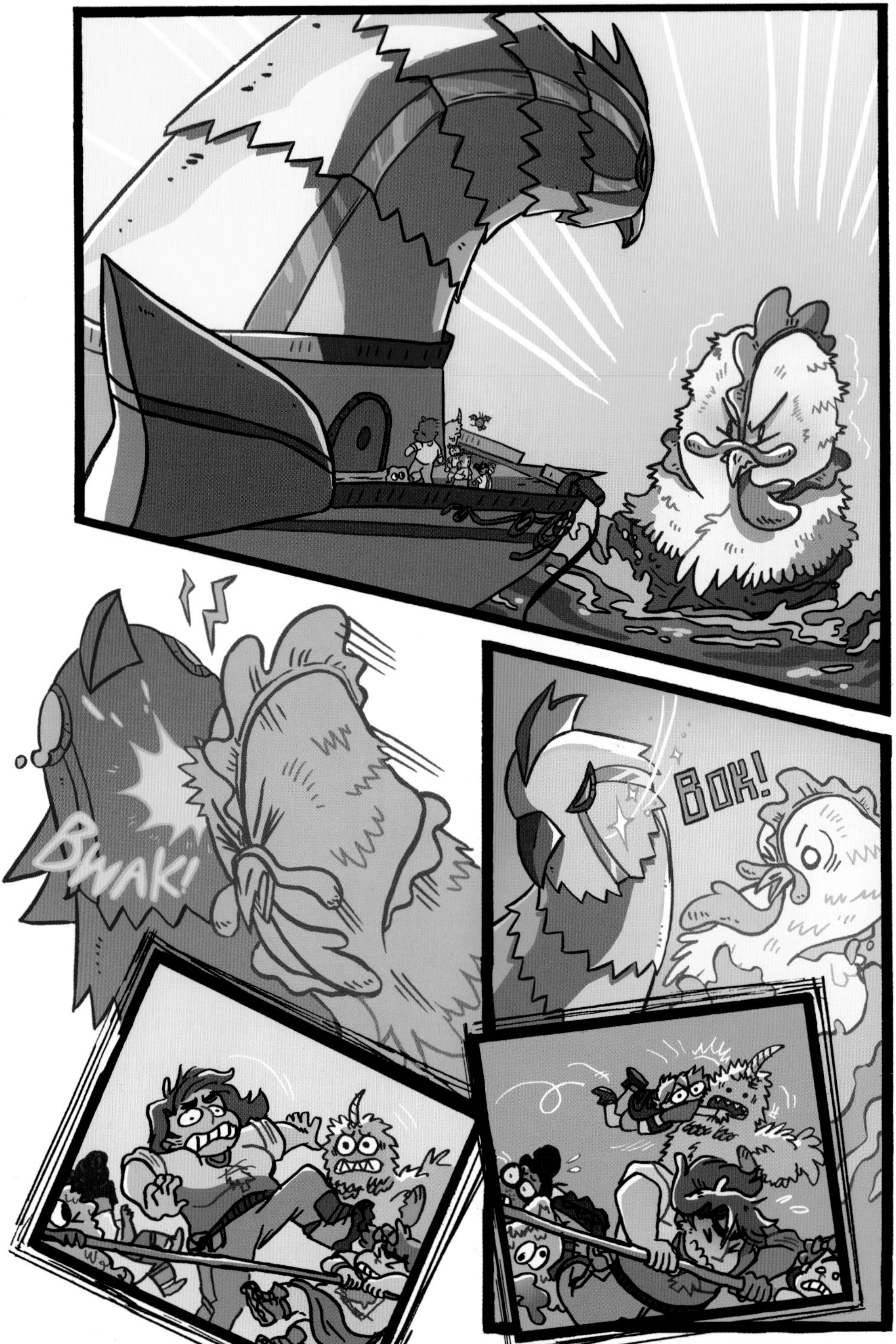
BWAK!
BOK!

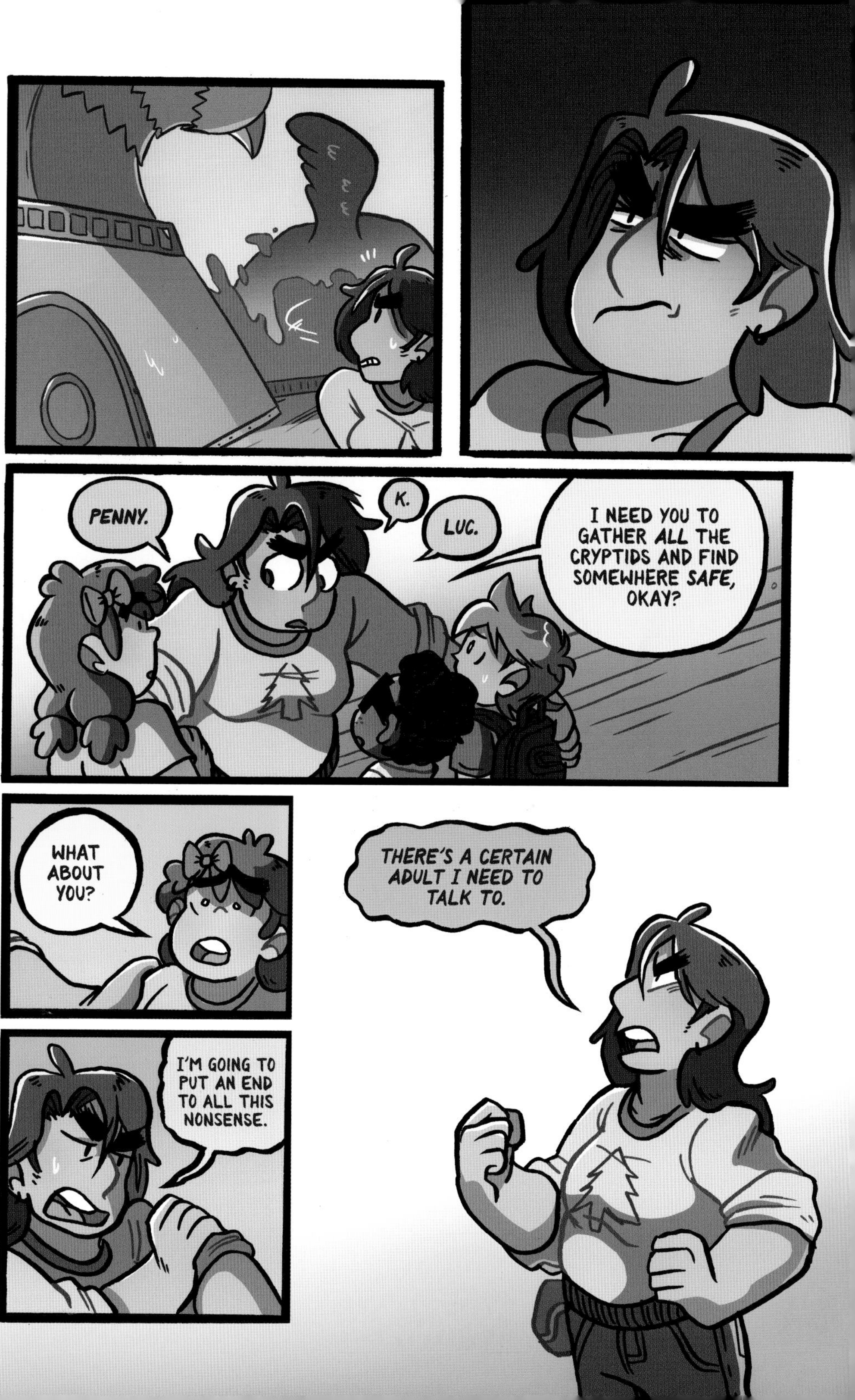
PENNY.
K.
LUC.
I NEED YOU TO GATHER ALL THE CRYPTIDS AND FIND SOMEWHERE SAFE, OKAY?
WHAT ABOUT YOU?
THERE'S A CERTAIN ADULT I NEED TO TALK TO.
I'M GOING TO PUT AN END TO ALL THIS NONSENSE.

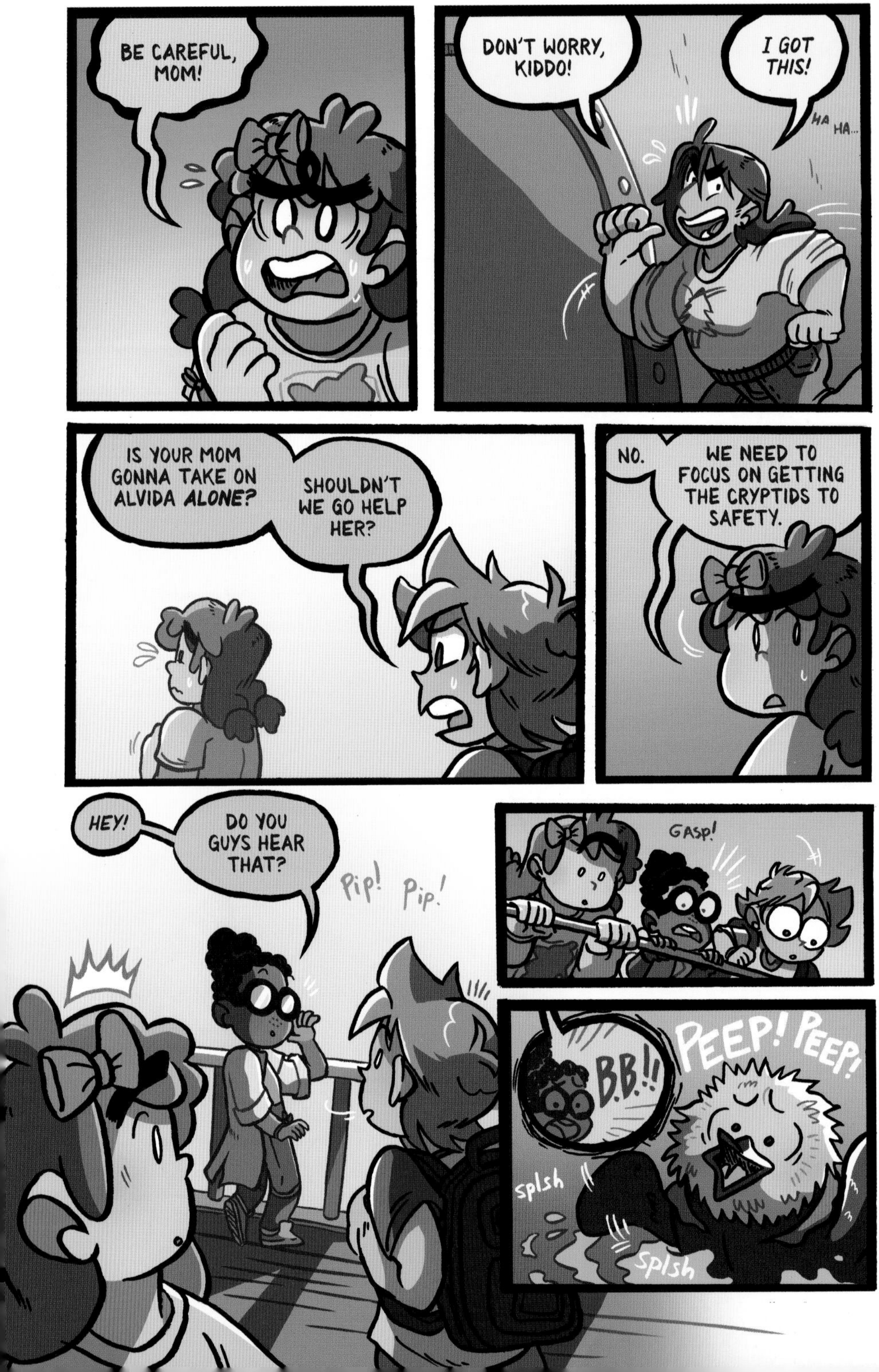
BE CAREFUL, MOM!
DON'T WORRY, KIDDO!
I GOT THIS!
HA HA...
IS YOUR MOM GONNA TAKE ON ALVIDA ALONE?
SHOULDN'T WE GO HELP HER?
NO.
WE NEED TO FOCUS ON GETTING THE CRYPTIDS TO SAFETY.
HEY!
DO YOU GUYS HEAR THAT?
Pip! Pip!
GASP!
B.B.!!
PEEP! PEEP!
splsh
splsh

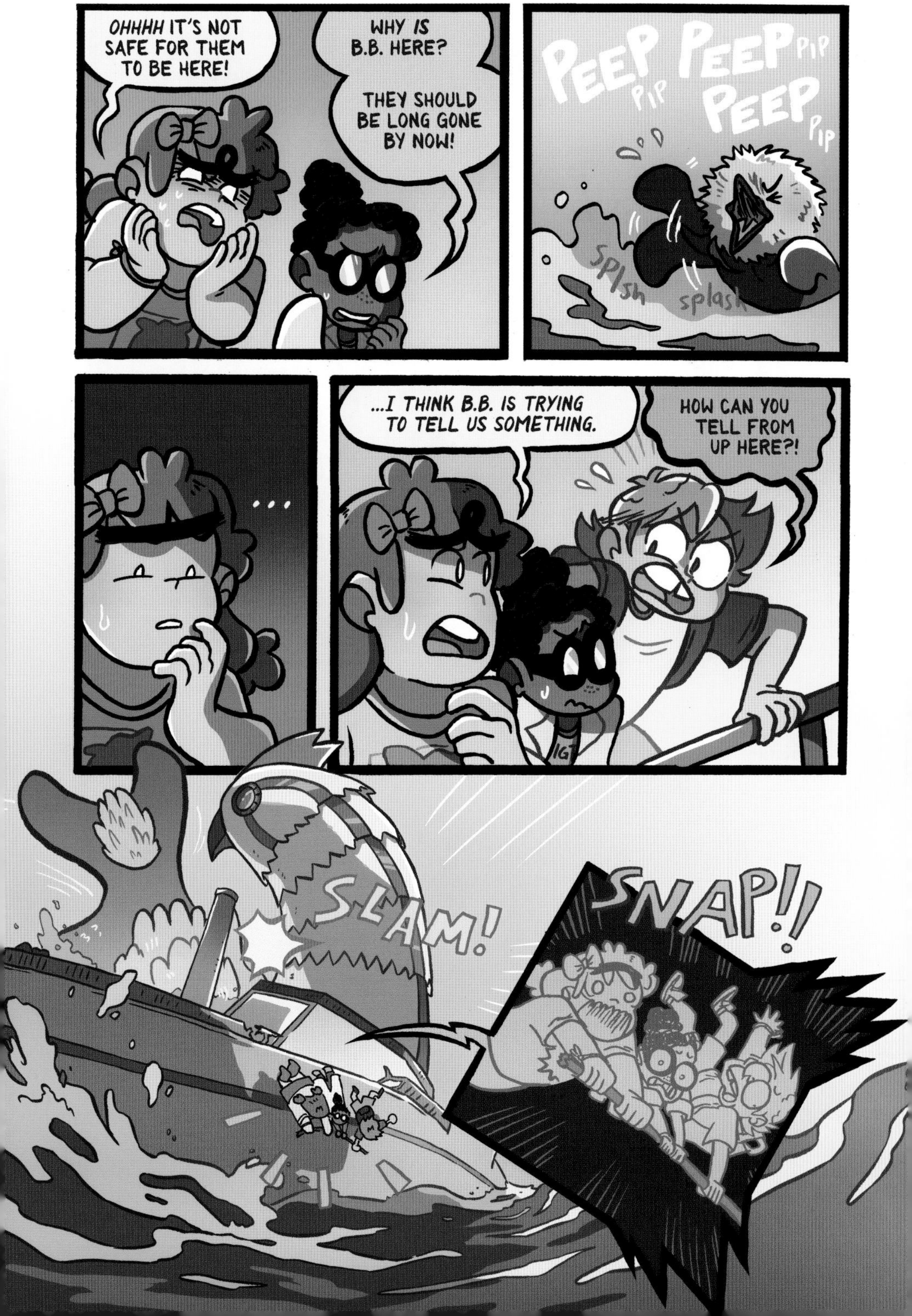
OHHHH IT'S NOT SAFE FOR THEM TO BE HERE!
WHY IS B.B. HERE?
THEY SHOULD BE LONG GONE BY NOW!
PEEP PIP PEEP PIP PEEP PIP PIP
splsh splash
...
...I THINK B.B. IS TRYING TO TELL US SOMETHING.
HOW CAN YOU TELL FROM UP HERE?!
SLAM!
SNAP!!

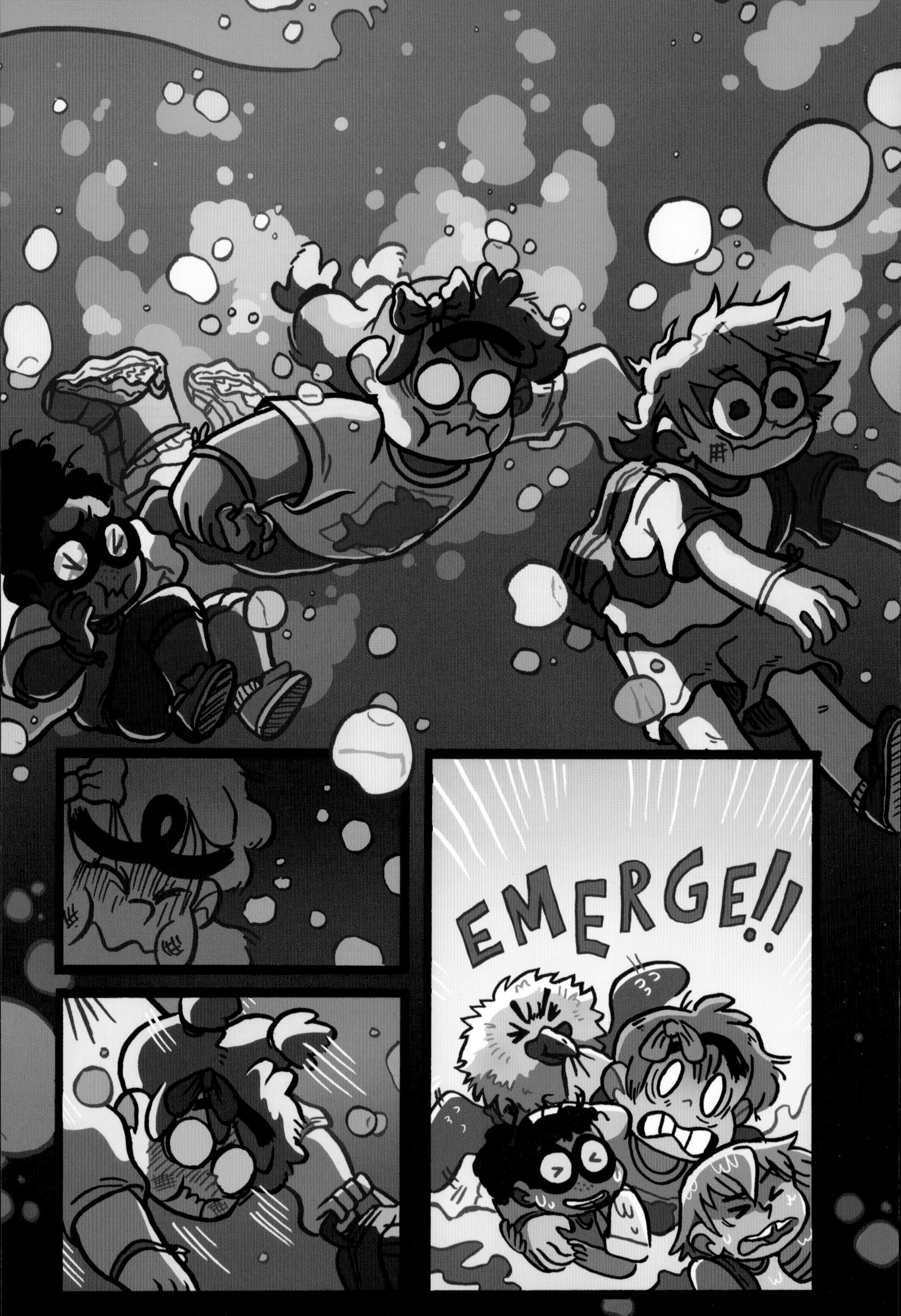
EMERGE!!

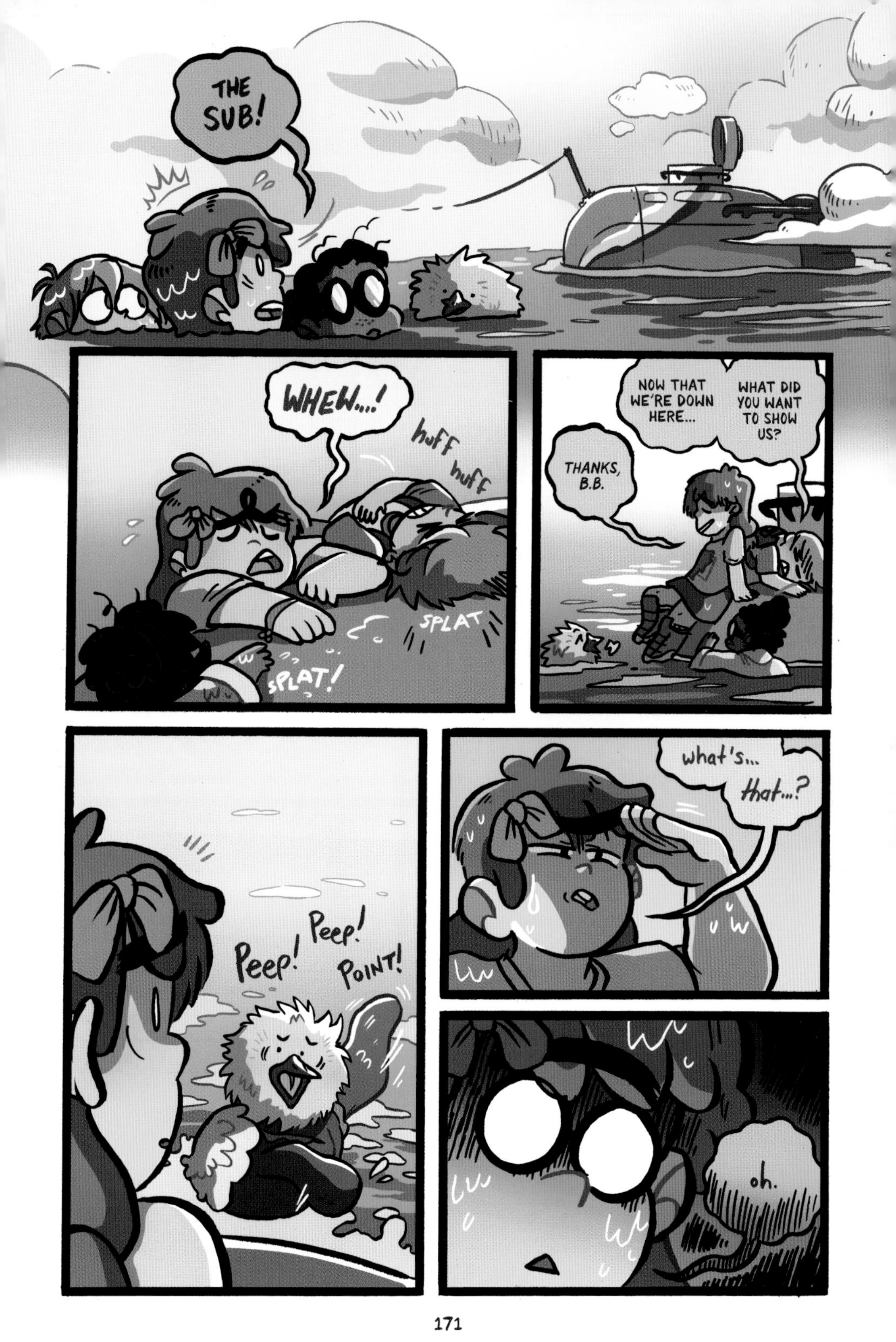
THE SUB!
WHEW...!
huff huff
SPLAT
SPLAT!
THANKS, B.B.
NOW THAT WE'RE DOWN HERE...
WHAT DID YOU WANT TO SHOW US?
Peep!
Peep!
POINT!
what's... that...?
oh.

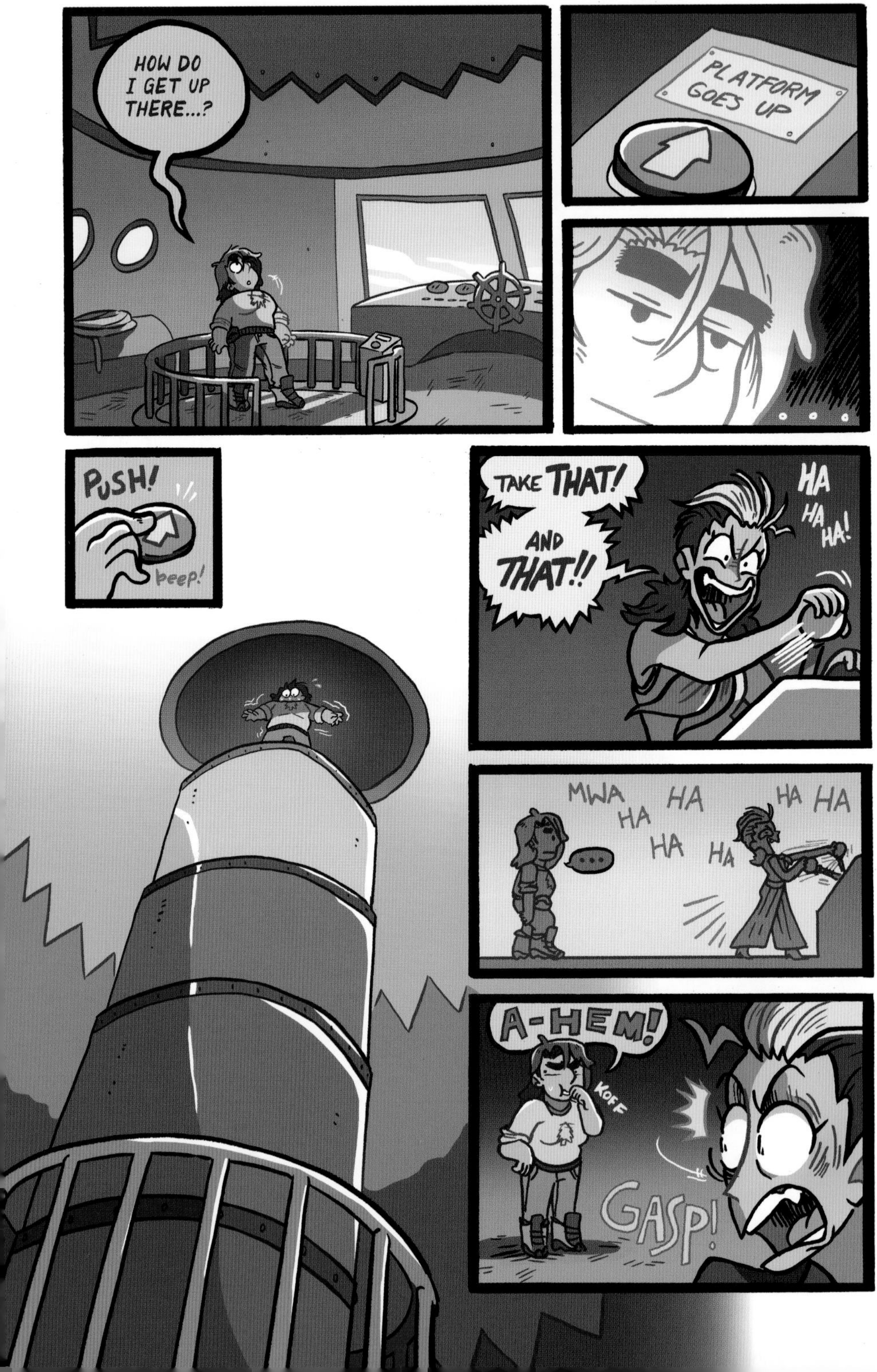
HOW DO I GET UP THERE...?
PLATFORM GOES UP
PUSH!
beep!
TAKE THAT!
AND THAT!!
HA HA HA!
MWA HA HA HA HA HA HA HA
...
A-HEM!
KOFF
GASP!

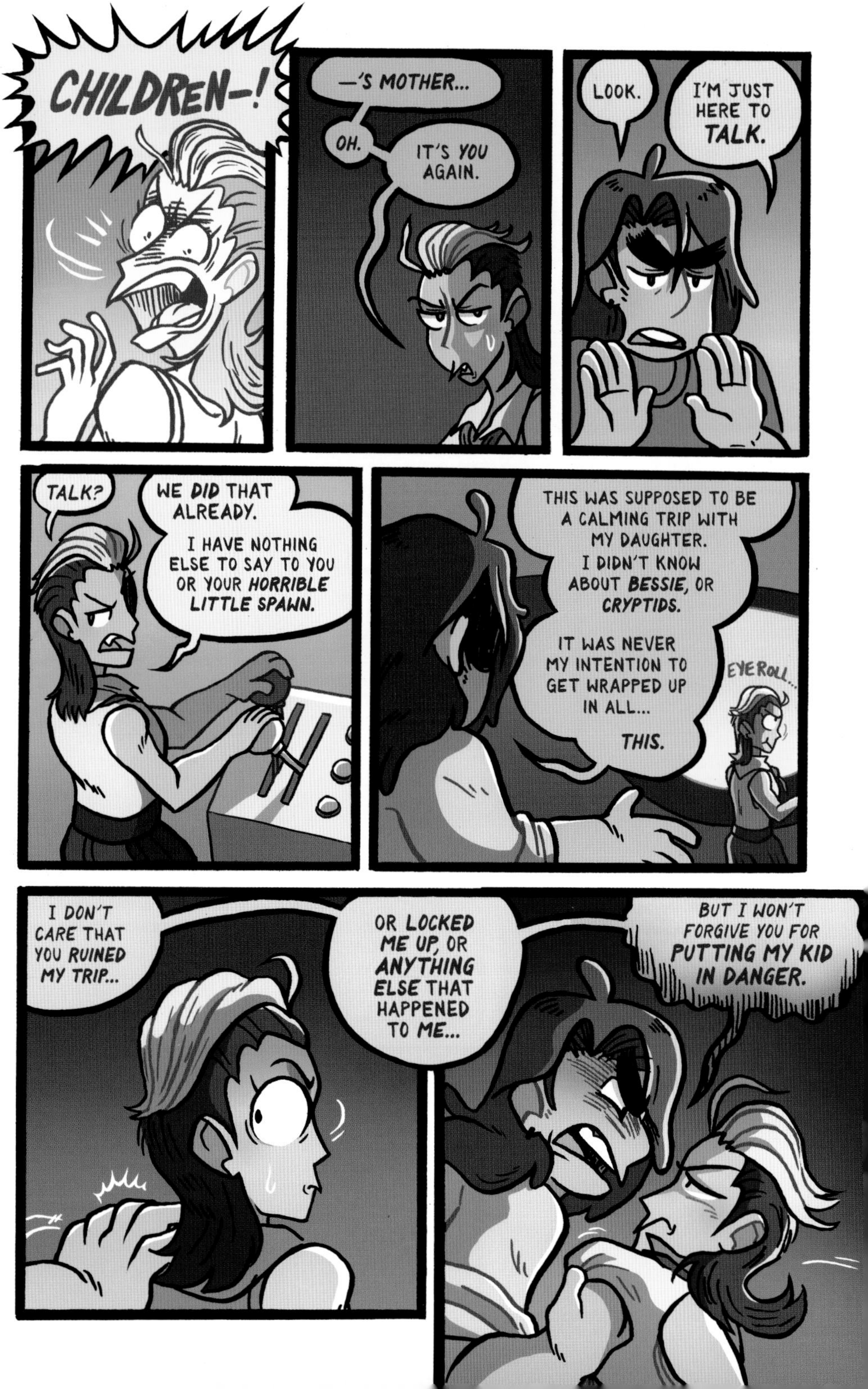
CHILDREN–!
—'S MOTHER...
OH.
IT'S YOU AGAIN.
LOOK.
I'M JUST HERE TO TALK.
TALK?
WE DID THAT ALREADY.
I HAVE NOTHING ELSE TO SAY TO YOU OR YOUR HORRIBLE LITTLE SPAWN.
THIS WAS SUPPOSED TO BE A CALMING TRIP WITH MY DAUGHTER.
I DIDN'T KNOW ABOUT BESSIE, OR CRYPTIDS.
IT WAS NEVER MY INTENTION TO GET WRAPPED UP IN ALL... THIS.
EYE ROLL...
I DON'T CARE THAT YOU RUINED MY TRIP...
OR LOCKED ME UP, OR ANYTHING ELSE THAT HAPPENED TO ME...
BUT I WON'T FORGIVE YOU FOR PUTTING MY KID IN DANGER.

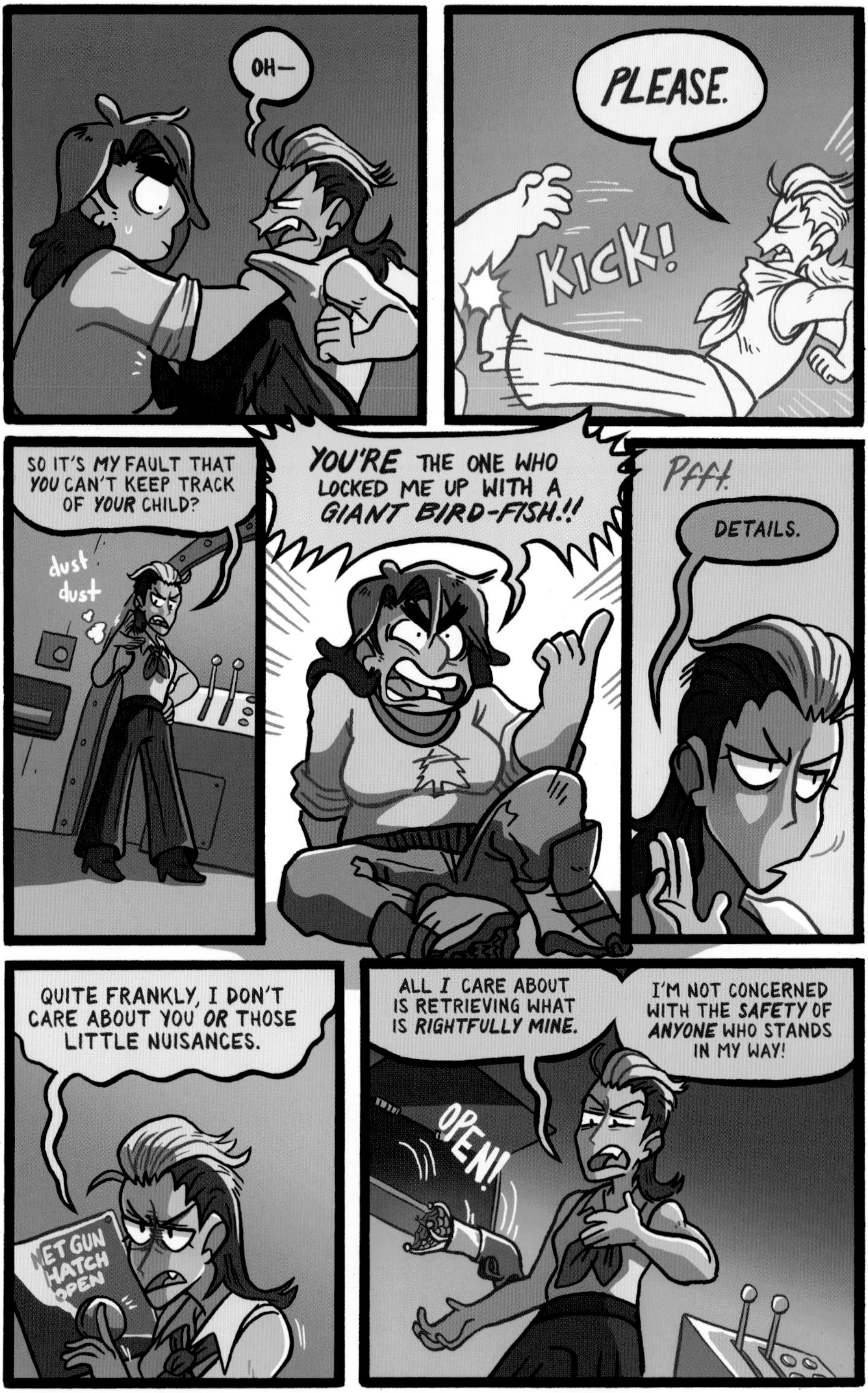
OH—
PLEASE.
KICK!
SO IT'S MY FAULT THAT YOU CAN'T KEEP TRACK OF YOUR CHILD?
dust dust
YOU'RE THE ONE WHO LOCKED ME UP WITH A GIANT BIRD-FISH!!
Pfft.
DETAILS.
QUITE FRANKLY, I DON'T CARE ABOUT YOU OR THOSE LITTLE NUISANCES.
NET GUN HATCH OPEN
ALL I CARE ABOUT IS RETRIEVING WHAT IS RIGHTFULLY MINE.
I'M NOT CONCERNED WITH THE SAFETY OF ANYONE WHO STANDS IN MY WAY!
OPEN!

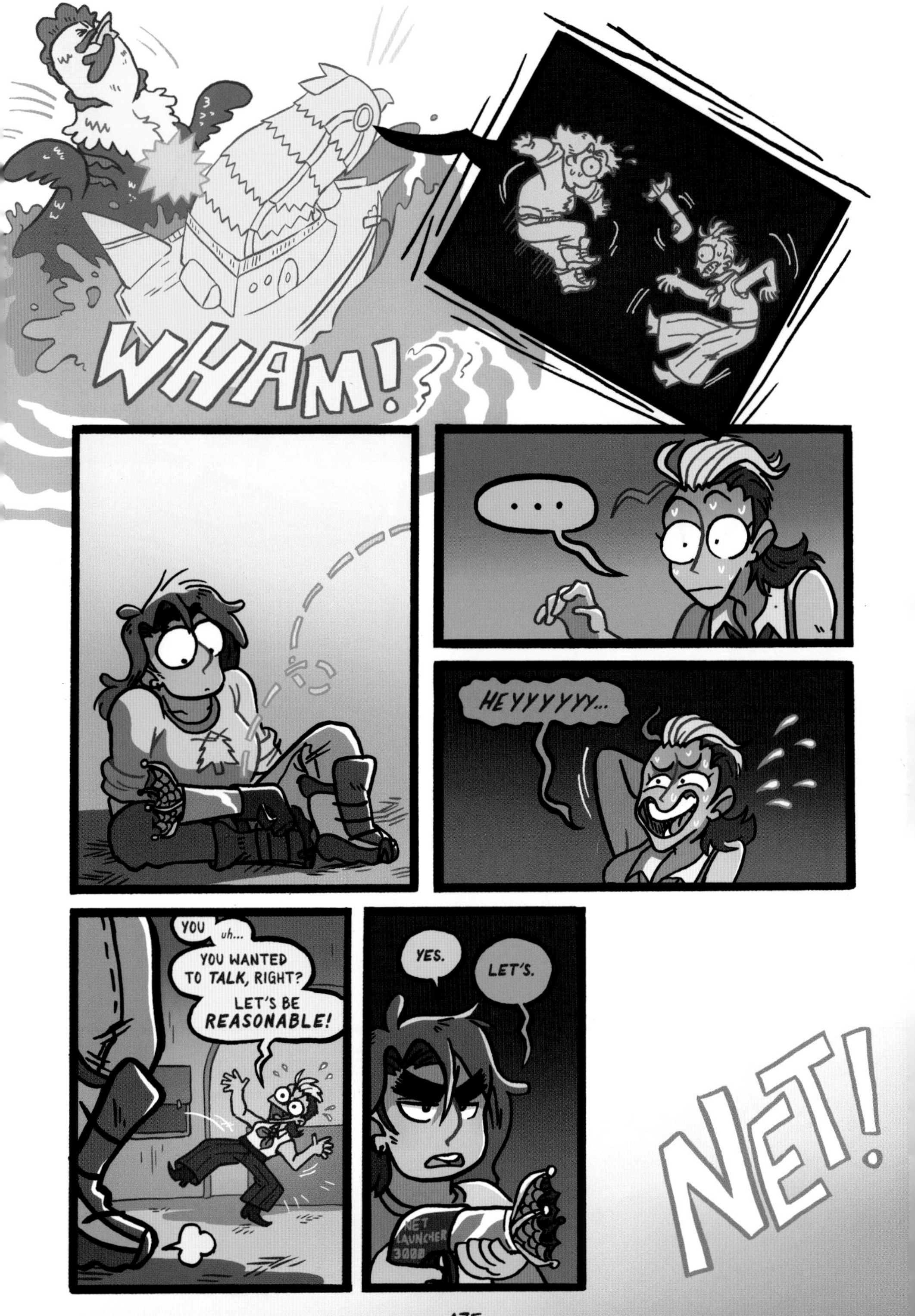
WHAM!
...
HEYYYYYY...
YOU
uh...
YOU WANTED TO TALK, RIGHT?
LET'S BE REASONABLE!
YES.
LET'S.
NET LAUNCHER 3000
NET!

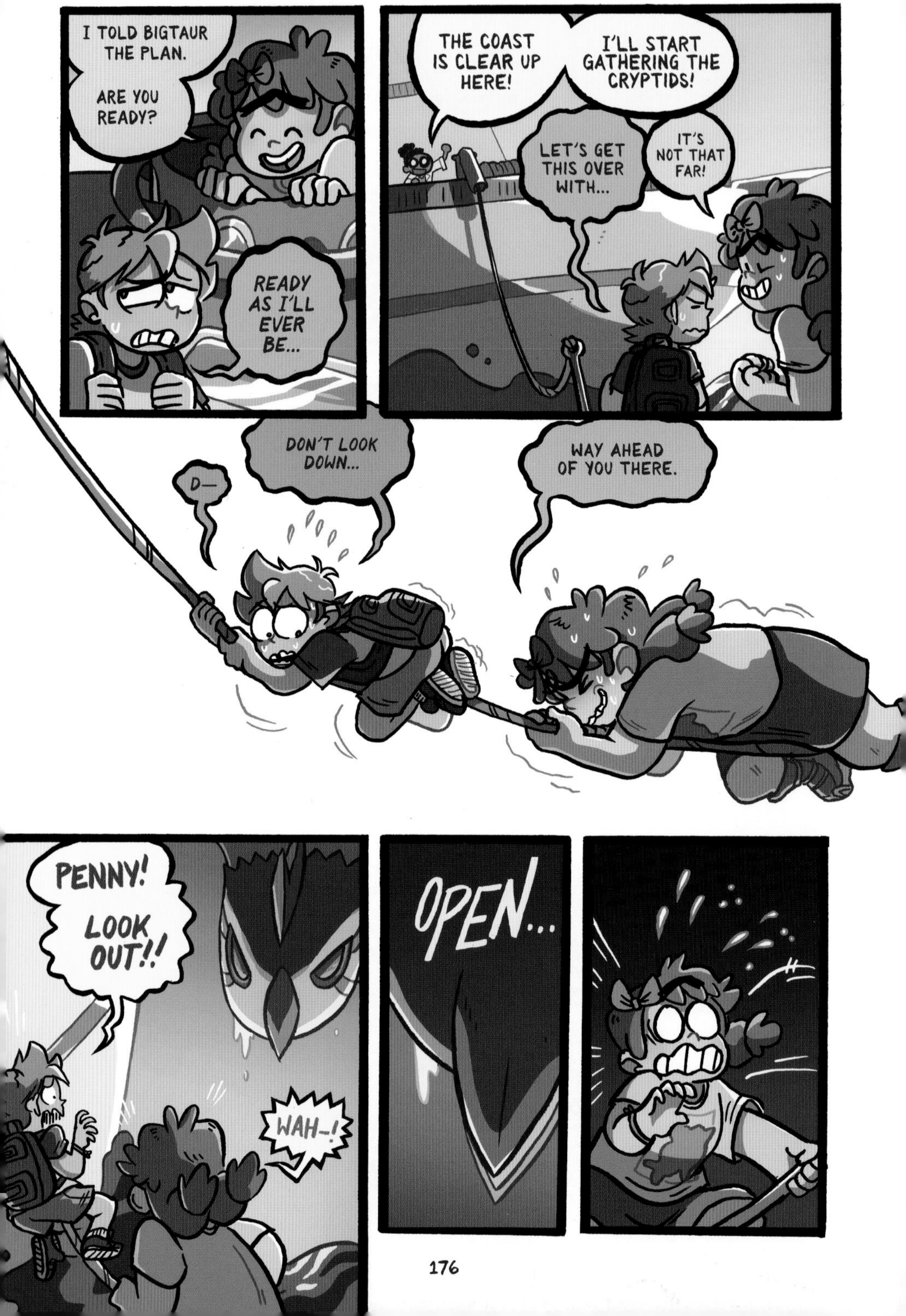
I TOLD BIGTAUR THE PLAN.
ARE YOU READY?
READY AS I'LL EVER BE...
THE COAST IS CLEAR UP HERE!
I'LL START GATHERING THE CRYPTIDS!
LET'S GET THIS OVER WITH...
IT'S NOT THAT FAR!
D—
DON'T LOOK DOWN...
WAY AHEAD OF YOU THERE.
PENNY!
LOOK OUT!!
WAH–!
OPEN...

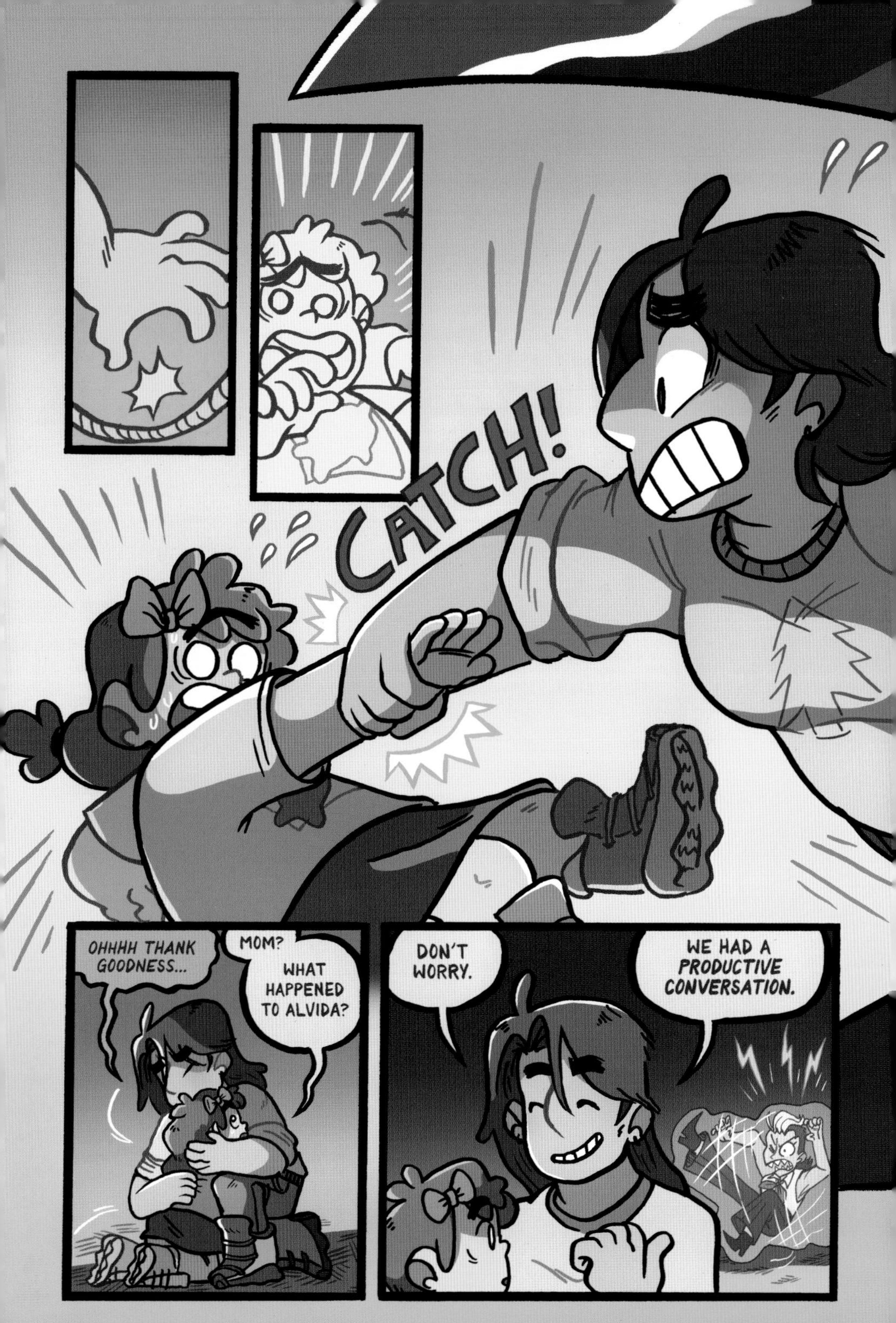
CATCH!
OHHHH THANK GOODNESS...
MOM?
WHAT HAPPENED TO ALVIDA?
DON'T WORRY.
WE HAD A *PRODUCTIVE* CONVERSATION.

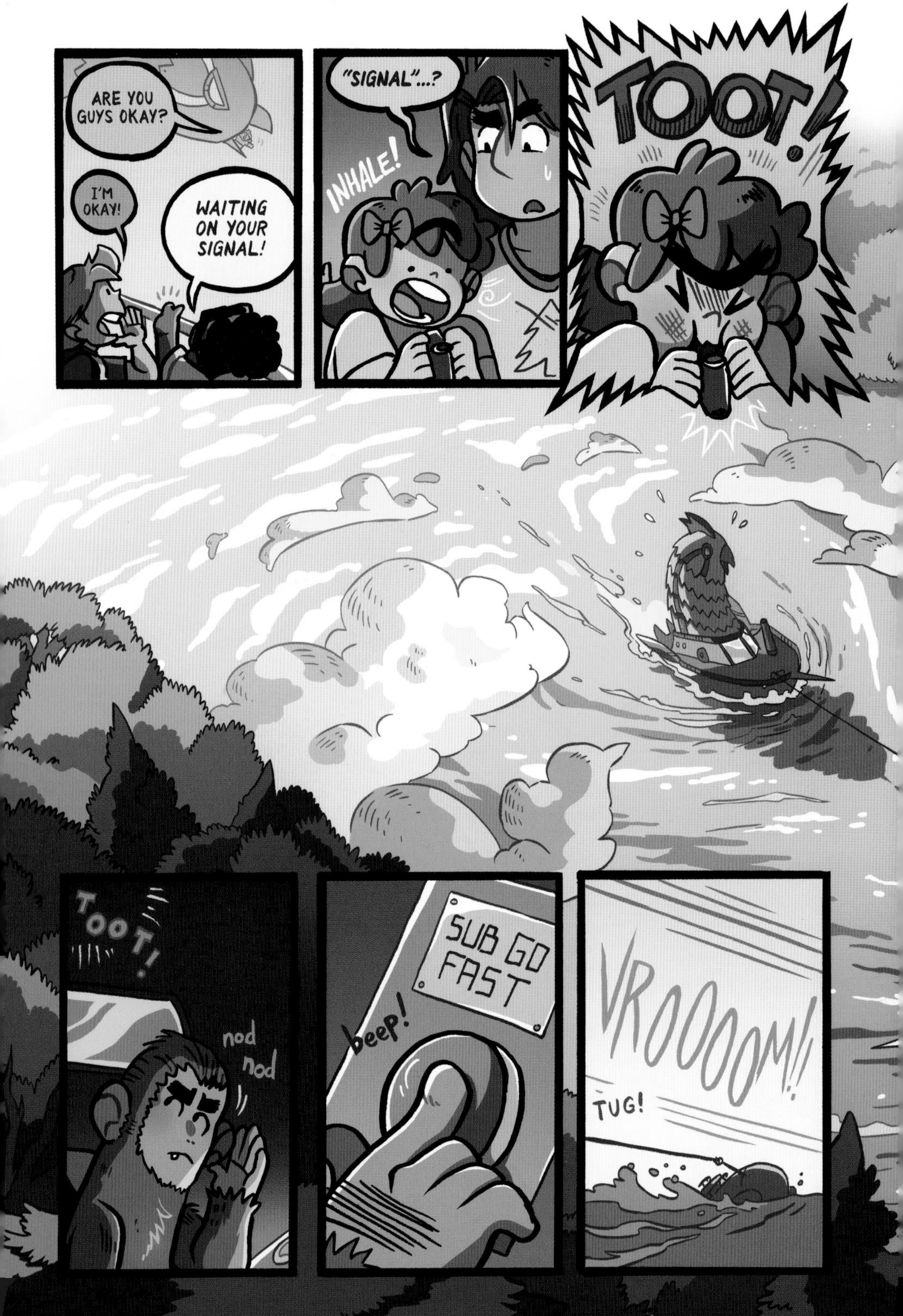
ARE YOU GUYS OKAY?
I'M OKAY!
WAITING ON YOUR SIGNAL!
"SIGNAL"...?
INHALE!
TOOT!
TOOT!
nod nod
SUB GO FAST
beep!
VROOOOM!!
TUG!

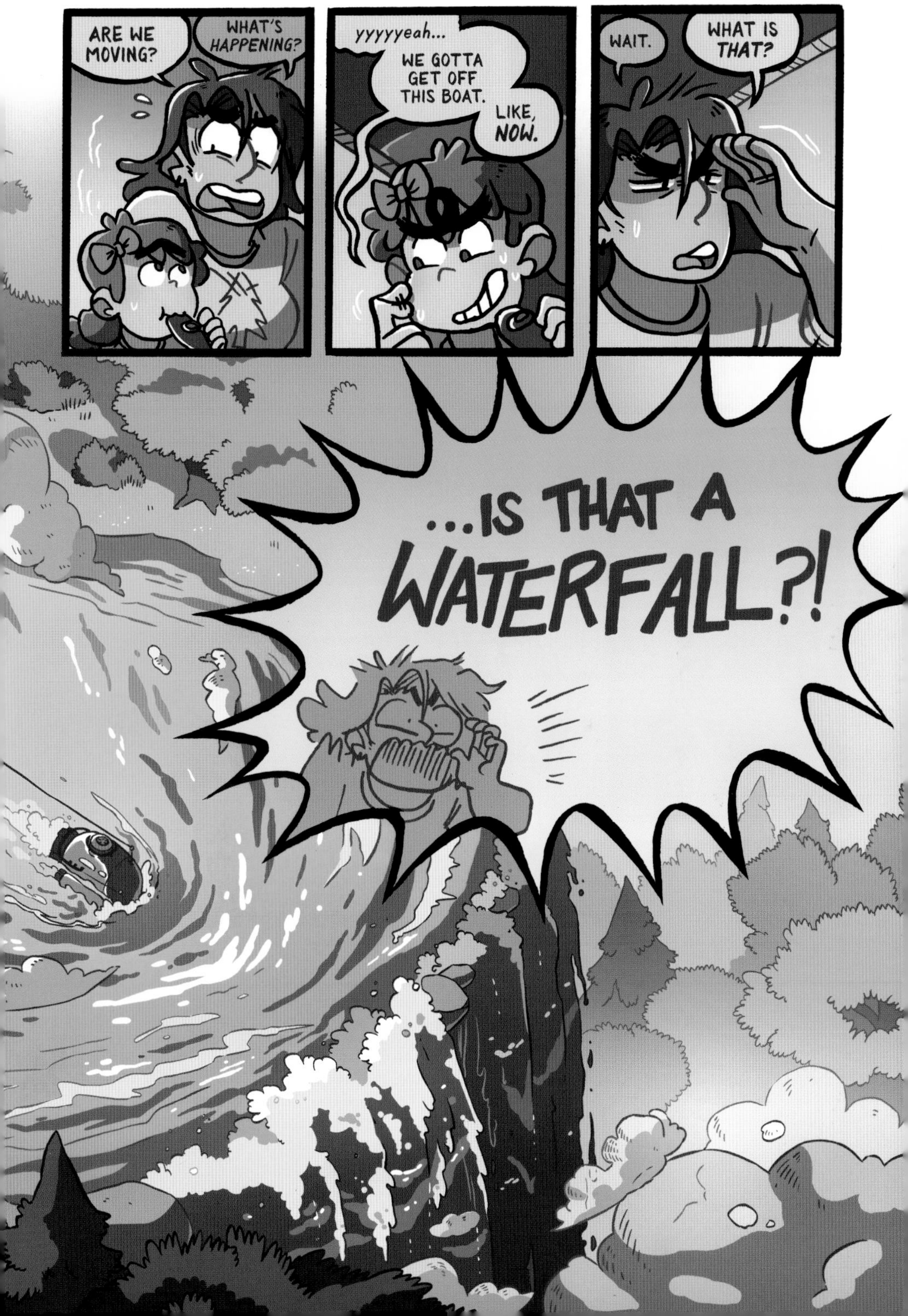
ARE WE MOVING?
WHAT'S HAPPENING?
yyyyyeah...
WE GOTTA GET OFF THIS BOAT.
LIKE, NOW.
WAIT.
WHAT IS THAT?
...IS THAT A WATERFALL?!

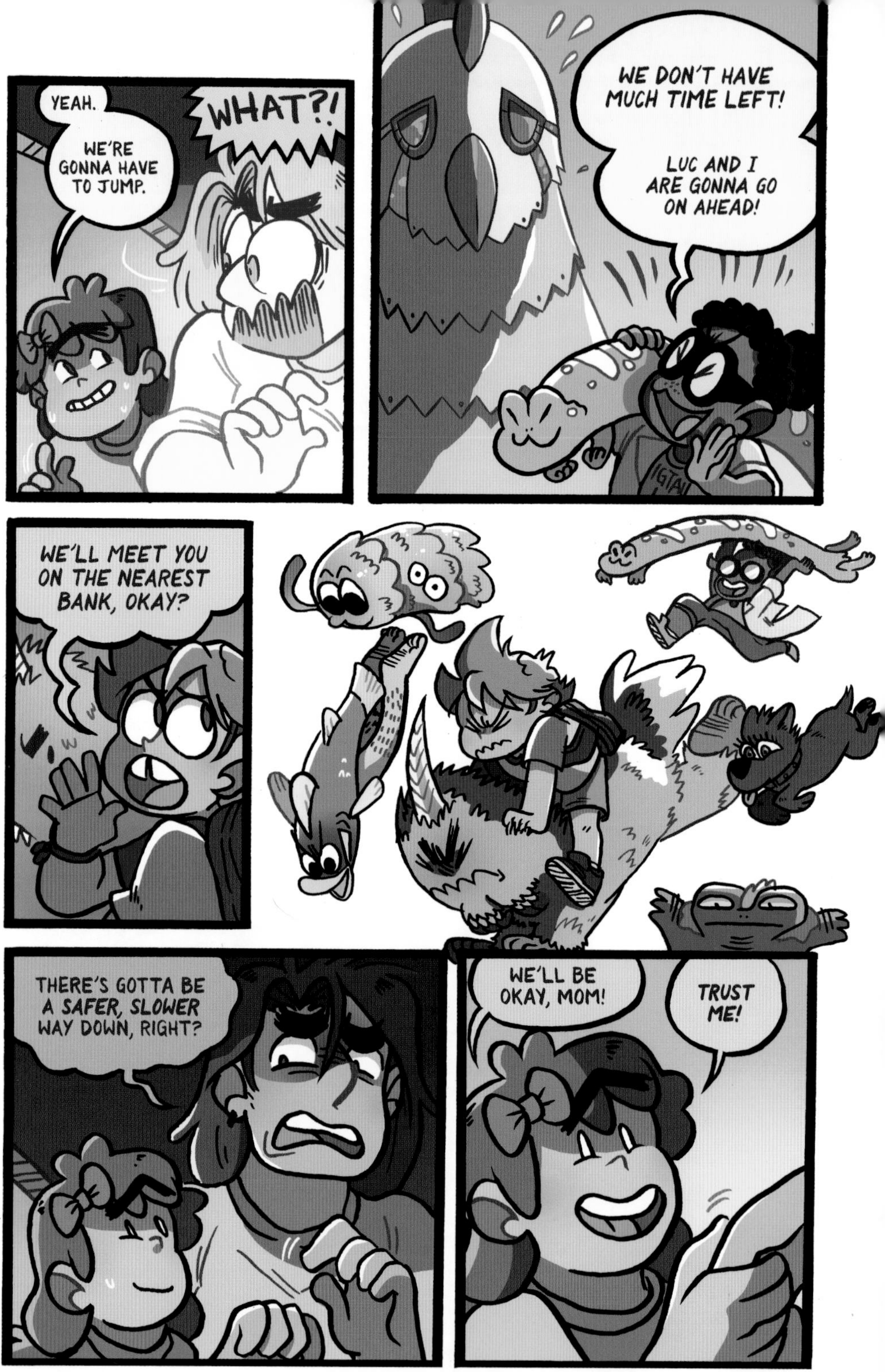
YEAH.
WE'RE GONNA HAVE TO JUMP.
WHAT?!
WE DON'T HAVE MUCH TIME LEFT!
LUC AND I ARE GONNA GO ON AHEAD!
WE'LL MEET YOU ON THE NEAREST BANK, OKAY?
THERE'S GOTTA BE A *SAFER, SLOWER* WAY DOWN, RIGHT?
WE'LL BE OKAY, MOM!
TRUST ME!

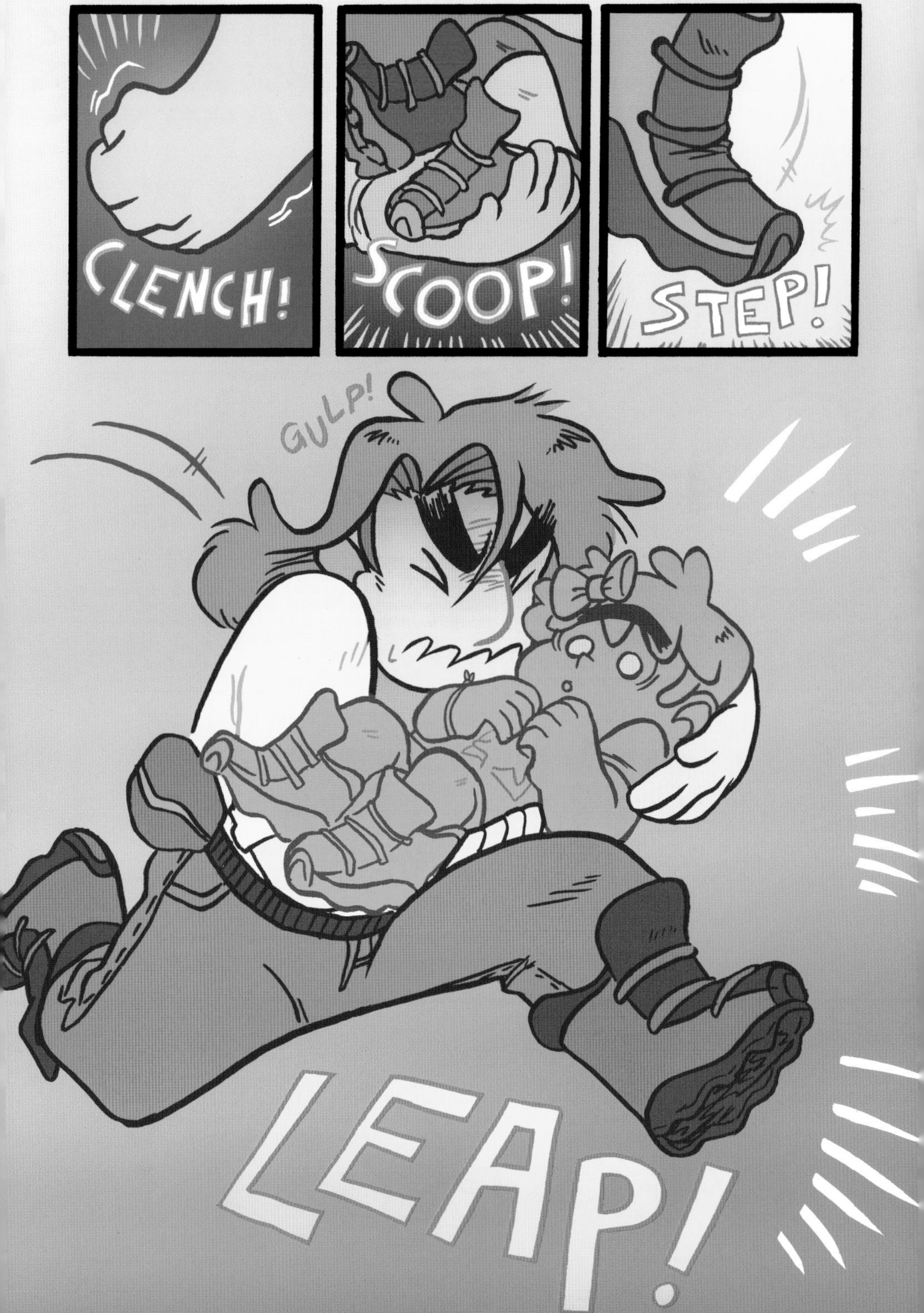
CLENCH!
SCOOP!
STEP!
GULP!
LEAP!

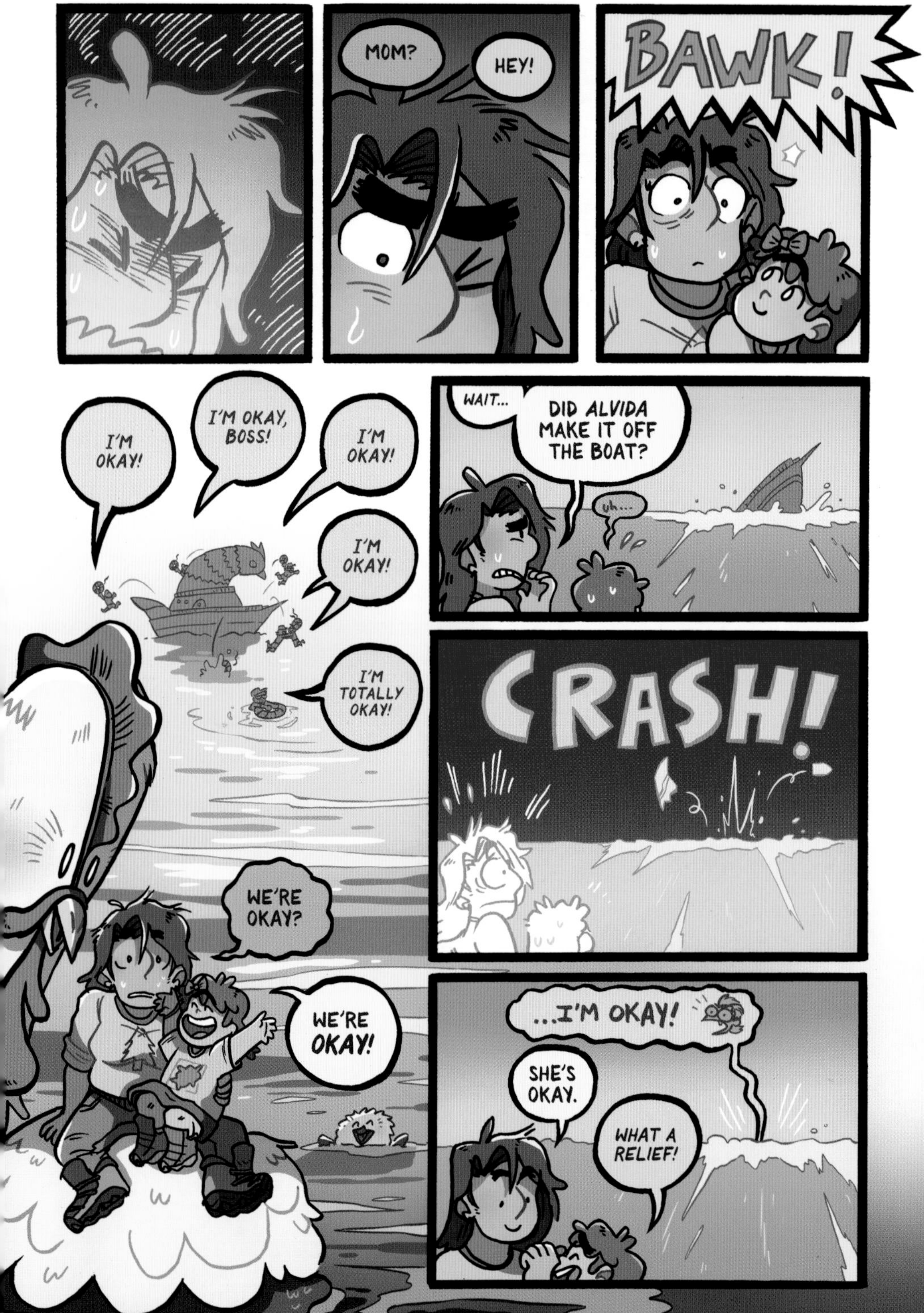
MOM?
HEY!
BAWK!
I'M OKAY!
I'M OKAY, BOSS!
I'M OKAY!
I'M OKAY!
I'M TOTALLY OKAY!
WE'RE OKAY?
WE'RE OKAY!
WAIT...
DID ALVIDA MAKE IT OFF THE BOAT?
uh...
CRASH!
...I'M OKAY!
SHE'S OKAY.
WHAT A RELIEF!

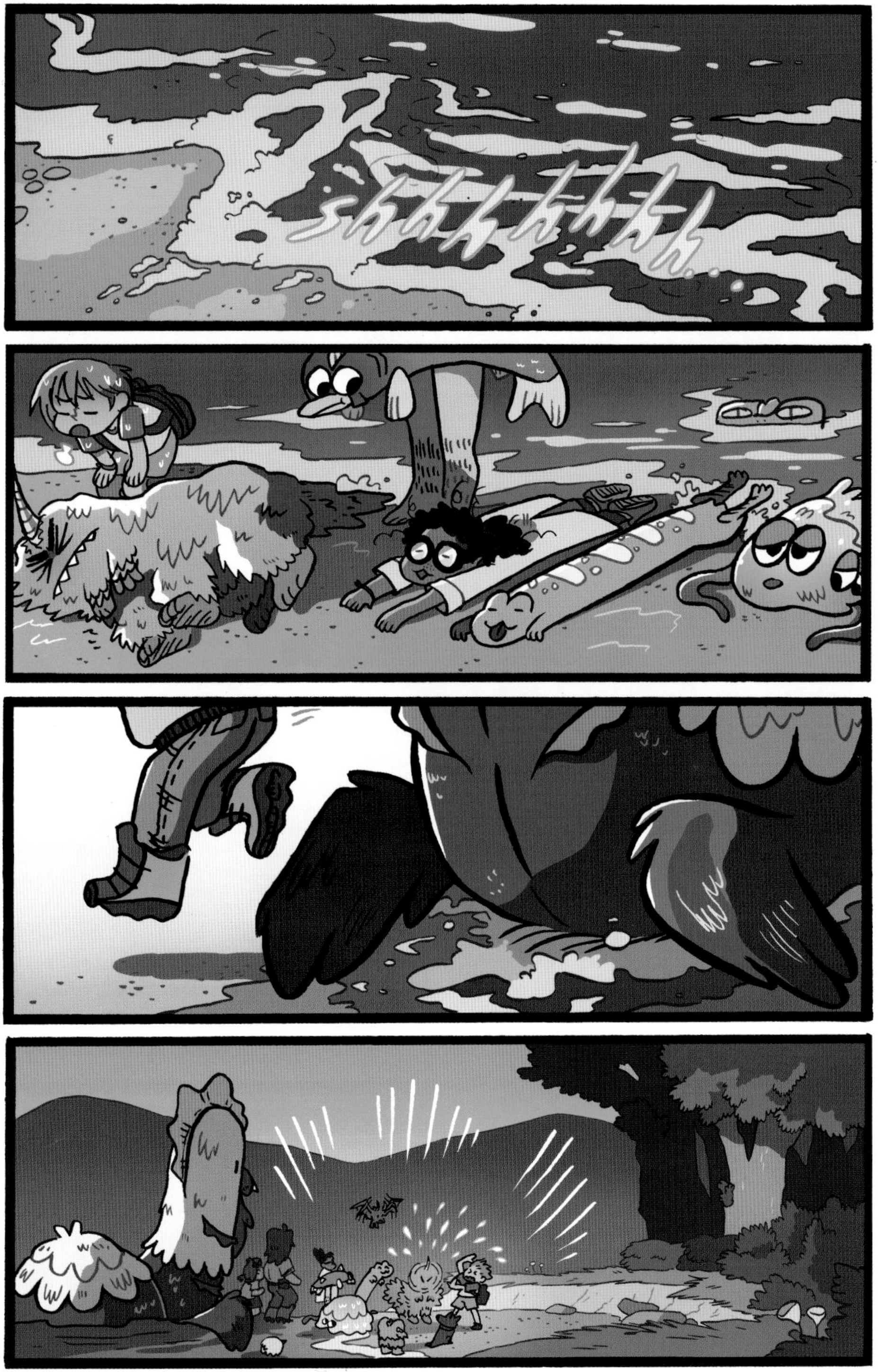
shhhhhhh..

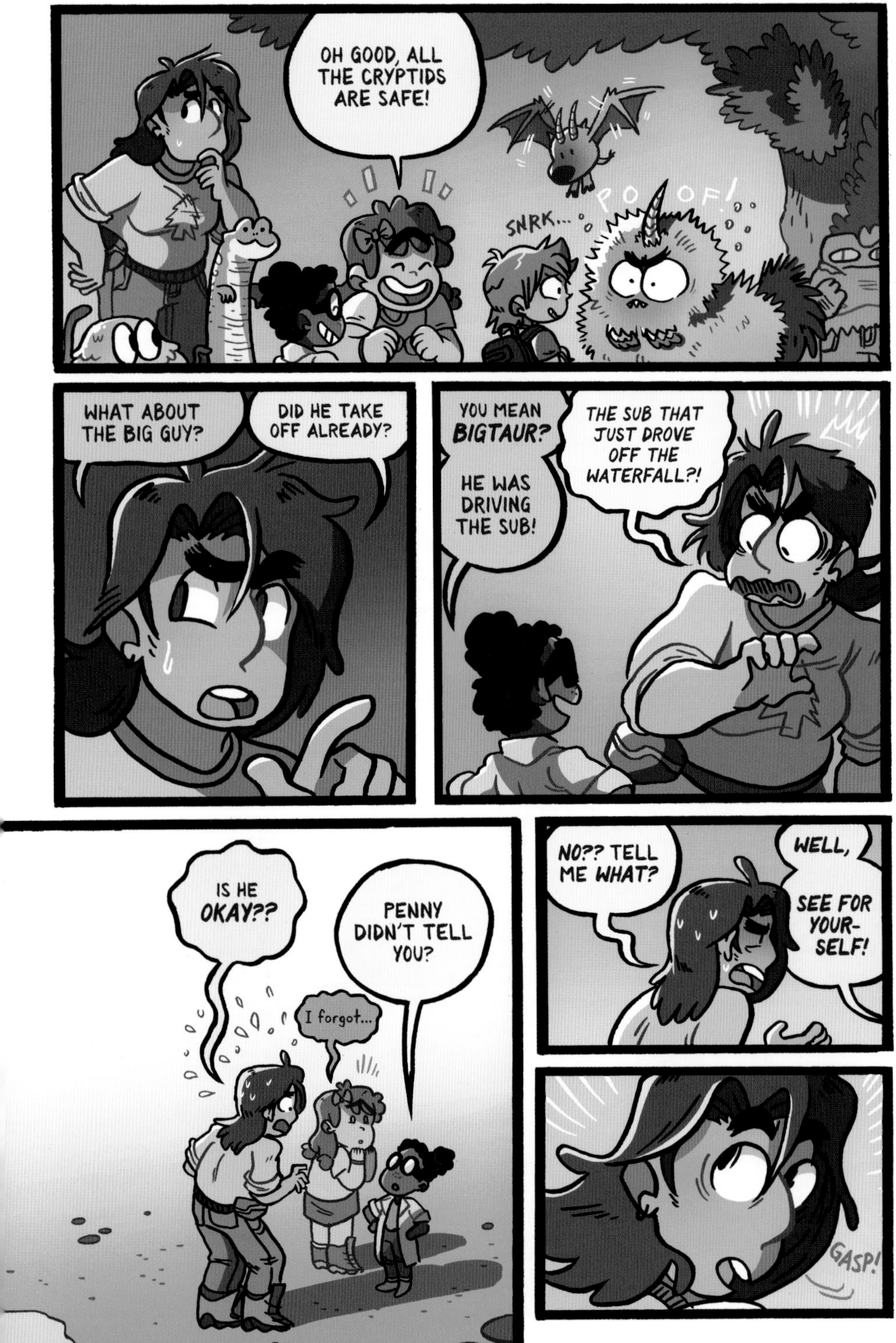
OH GOOD, ALL THE CRYPTIDS ARE SAFE!
SNRK...
POOF!
WHAT ABOUT THE BIG GUY?
DID HE TAKE OFF ALREADY?
YOU MEAN BIGTAUR?
HE WAS DRIVING THE SUB!
THE SUB THAT JUST DROVE OFF THE WATERFALL?!
IS HE OKAY??
PENNY DIDN'T TELL YOU?
I forgot...
NO?? TELL ME WHAT?
WELL,
SEE FOR YOURSELF!
GASP!

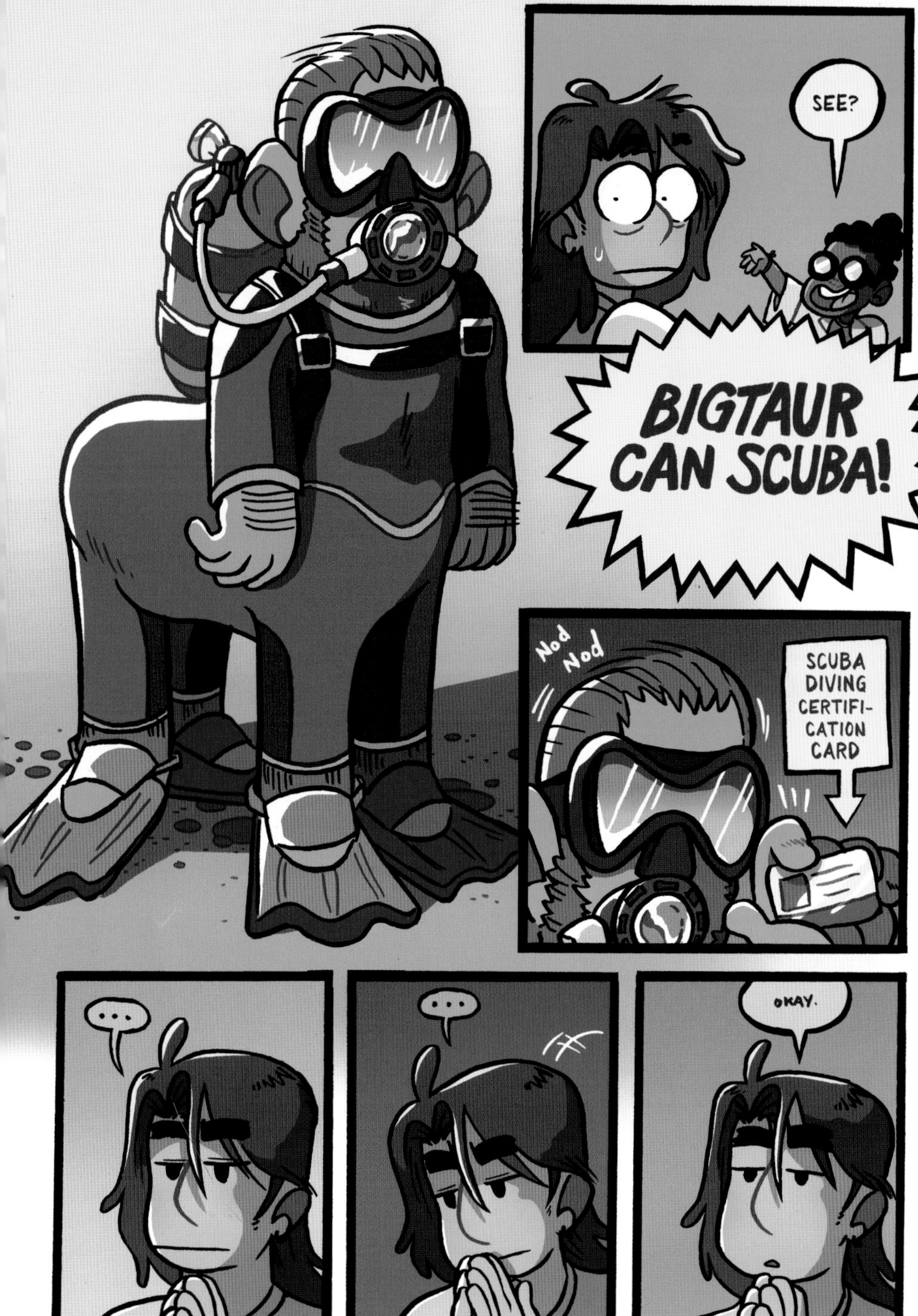
SEE?
BIGTAUR CAN SCUBA!
Nod Nod
SCUBA DIVING CERTIFI-CATION CARD
...
...
OKAY.

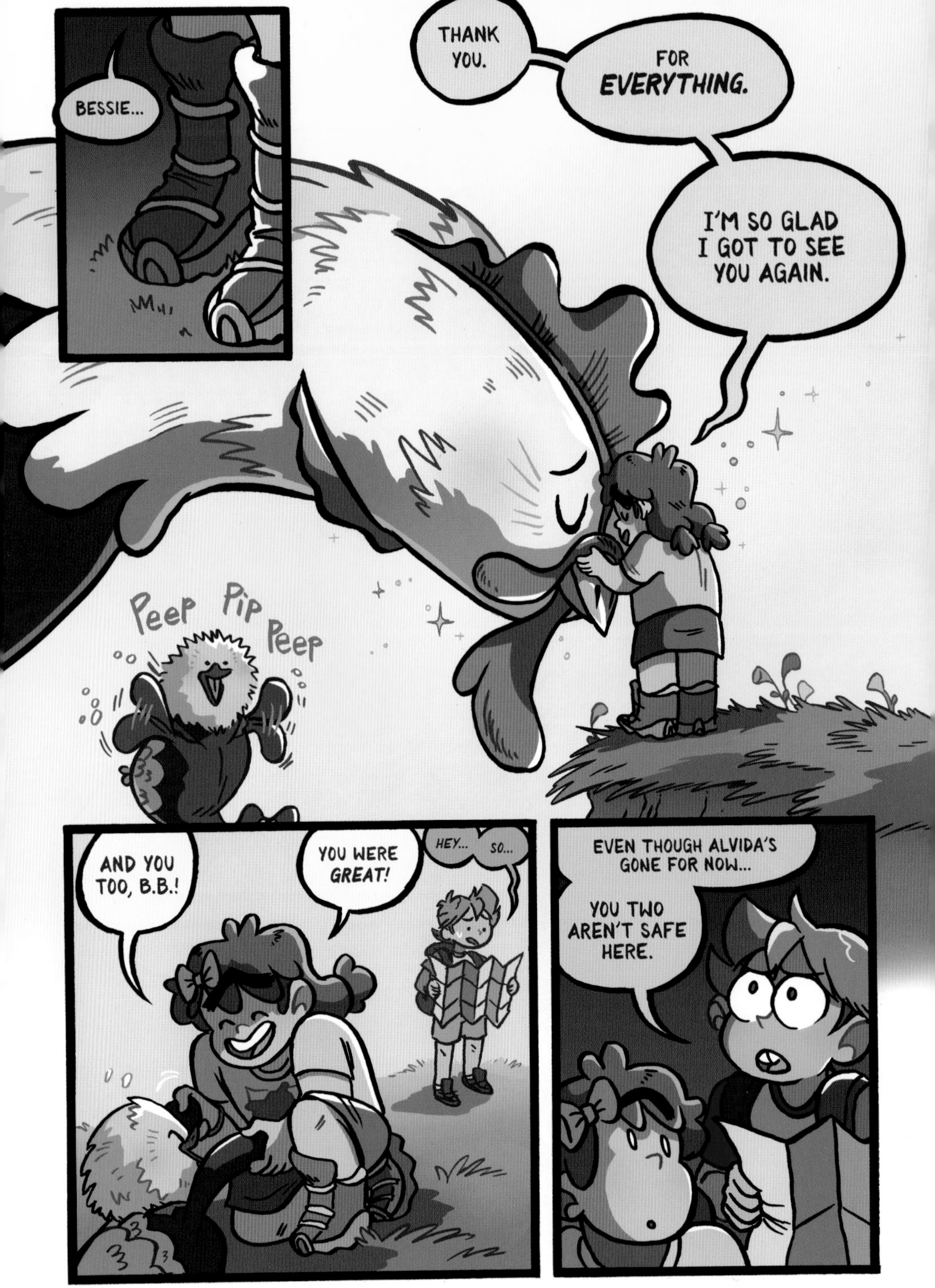
BESSIE...
THANK YOU.
FOR EVERYTHING.
I'M SO GLAD I GOT TO SEE YOU AGAIN.
Peep Pip Peep
AND YOU TOO, B.B.!
YOU WERE GREAT!
HEY...
SO...
EVEN THOUGH ALVIDA'S GONE FOR NOW...
YOU TWO AREN'T SAFE HERE.

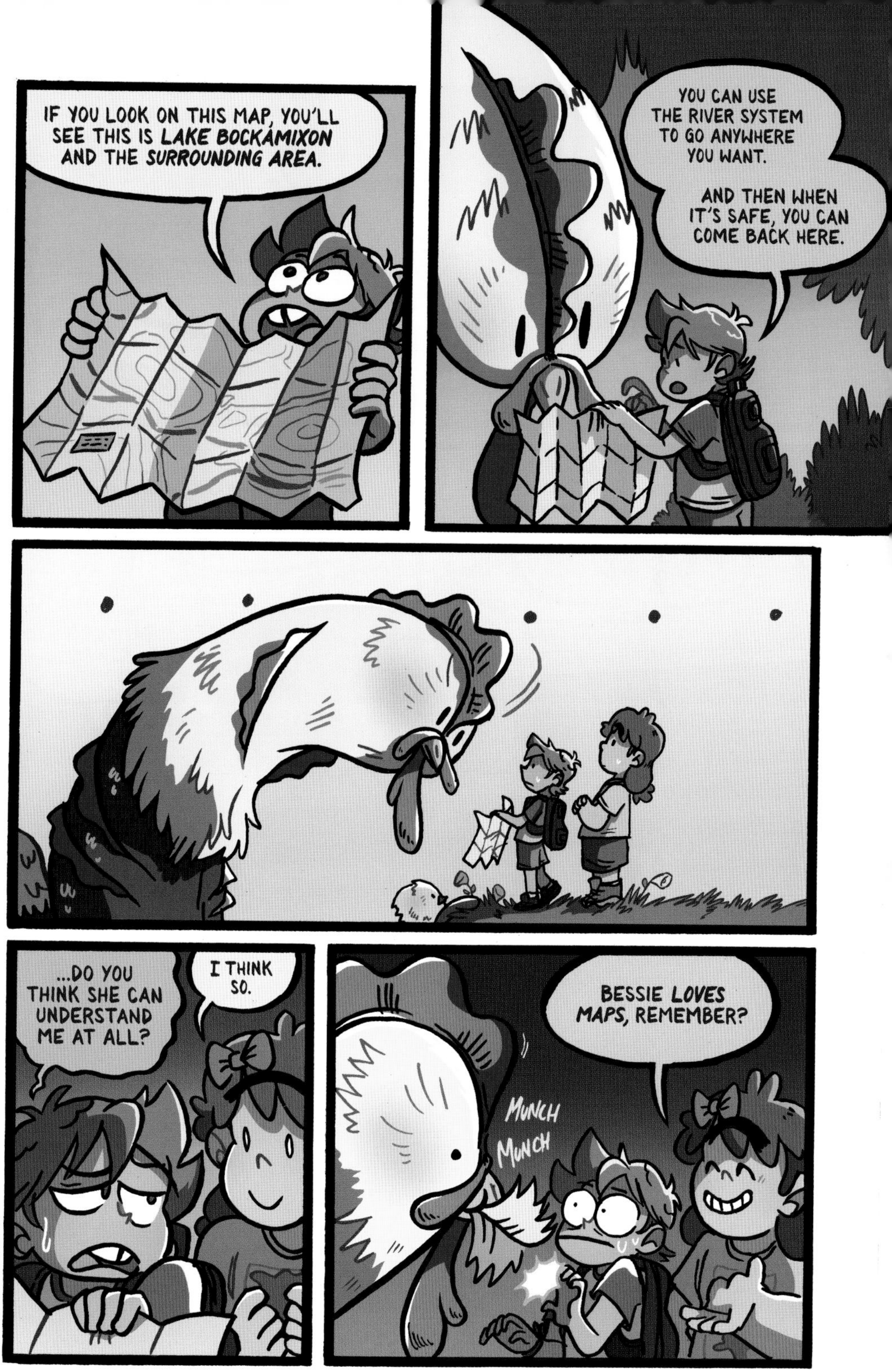
IF YOU LOOK ON THIS MAP, YOU'LL SEE THIS IS LAKE BOCKÁMIXON AND THE SURROUNDING AREA.
YOU CAN USE THE RIVER SYSTEM TO GO ANYWHERE YOU WANT.
AND THEN WHEN IT'S SAFE, YOU CAN COME BACK HERE.
...DO YOU THINK SHE CAN UNDERSTAND ME AT ALL?
I THINK SO.
BESSIE LOVES MAPS, REMEMBER?
MUNCH
MUNCH

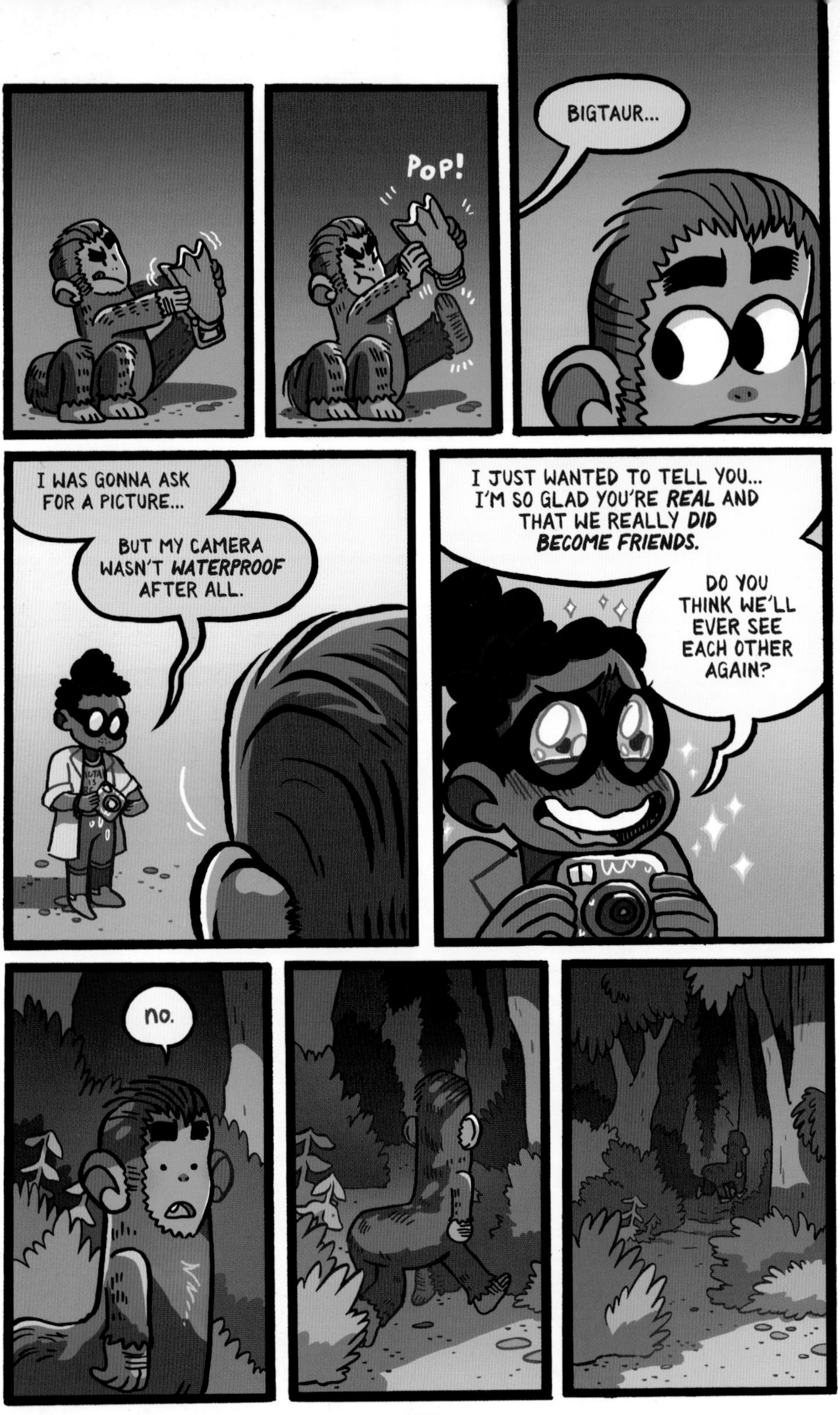
POP!
BIGTAUR...
I WAS GONNA ASK FOR A PICTURE...
BUT MY CAMERA WASN'T WATERPROOF AFTER ALL.
I JUST WANTED TO TELL YOU... I'M SO GLAD YOU'RE REAL AND THAT WE REALLY DID BECOME FRIENDS.
DO YOU THINK WE'LL EVER SEE EACH OTHER AGAIN?
no.

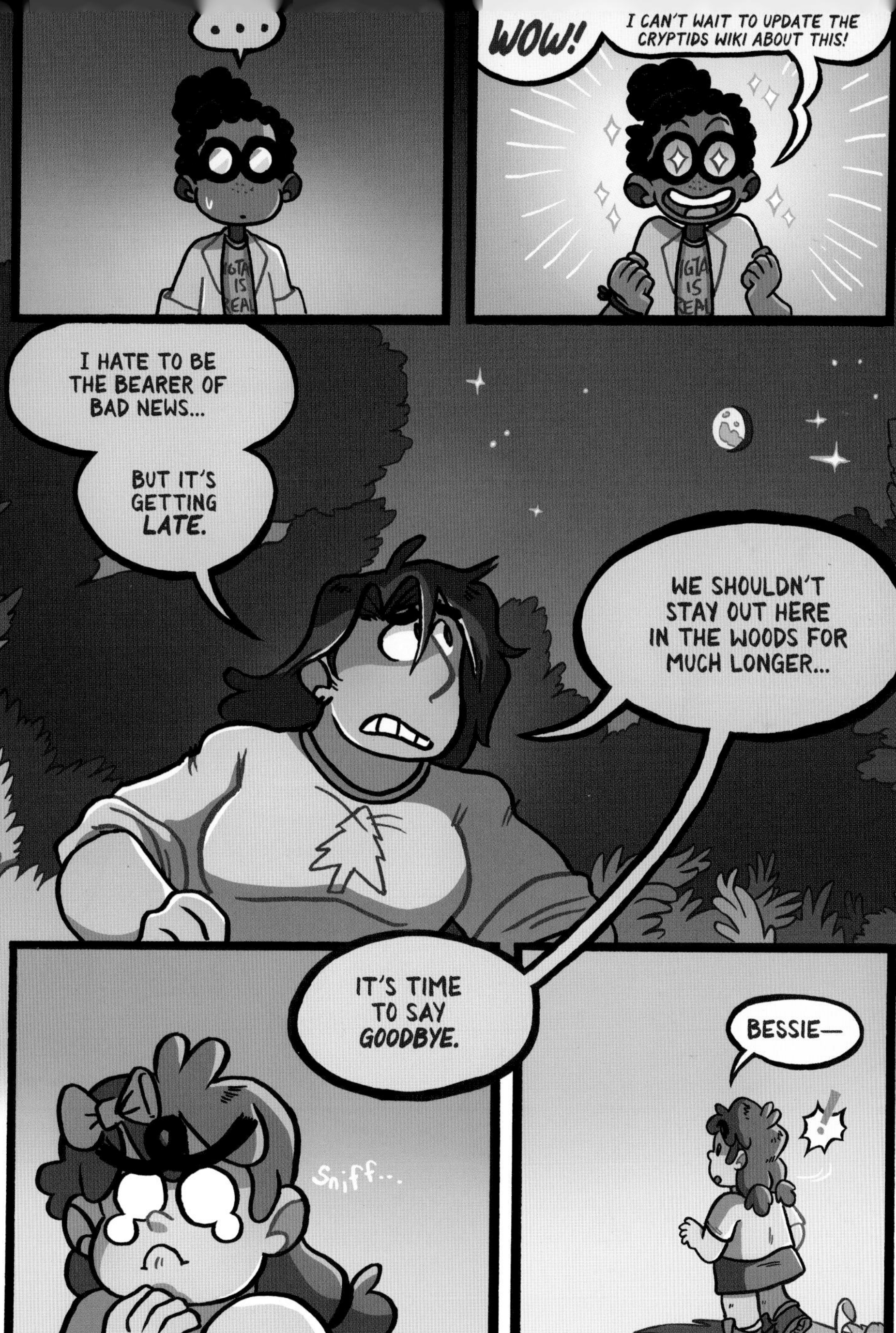
...
WOW!
I CAN'T WAIT TO UPDATE THE CRYPTIDS WIKI ABOUT THIS!
I HATE TO BE THE BEARER OF BAD NEWS...
BUT IT'S GETTING LATE.
WE SHOULDN'T STAY OUT HERE IN THE WOODS FOR MUCH LONGER...
IT'S TIME TO SAY GOODBYE.
Sniff...
BESSIE—

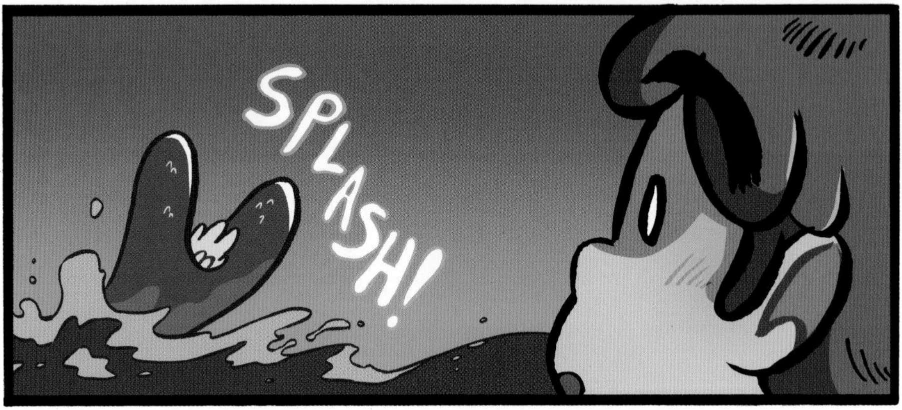
SPLASH!

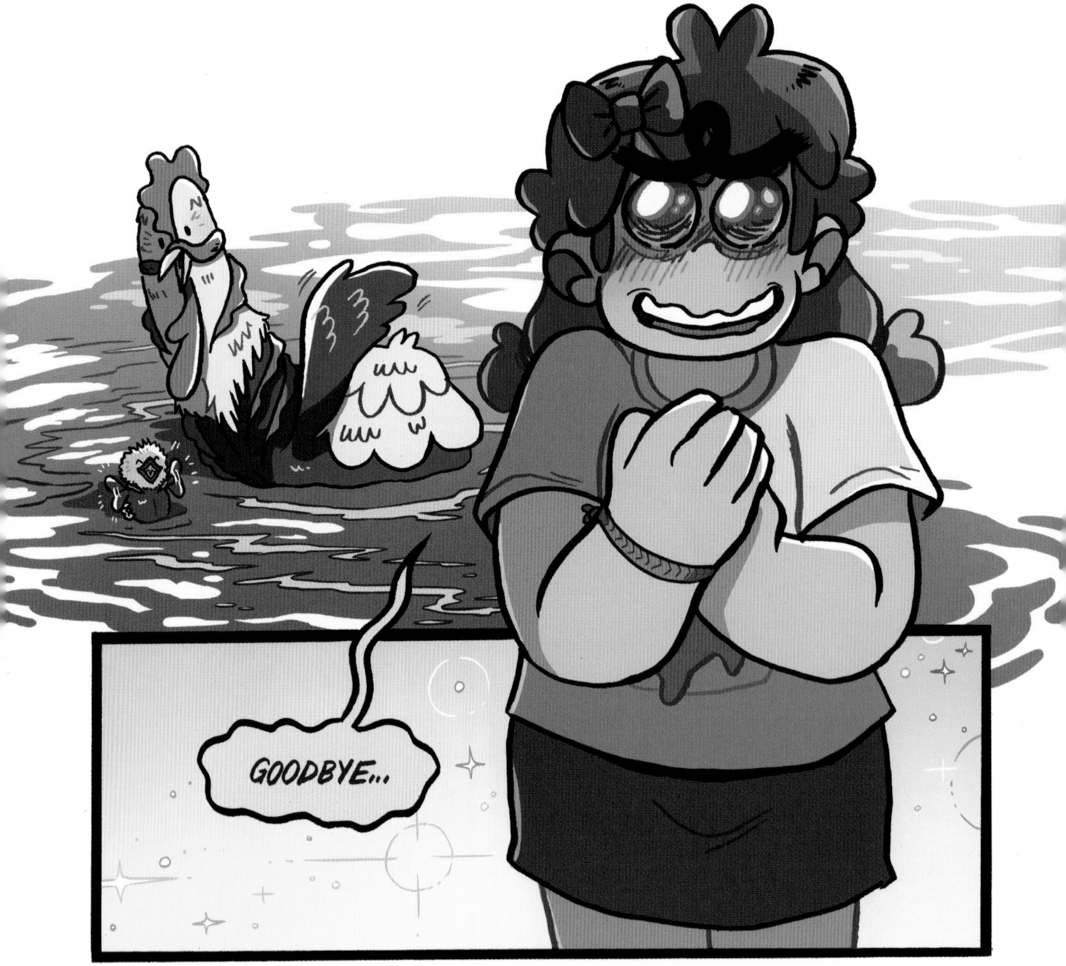
GOODBYE...

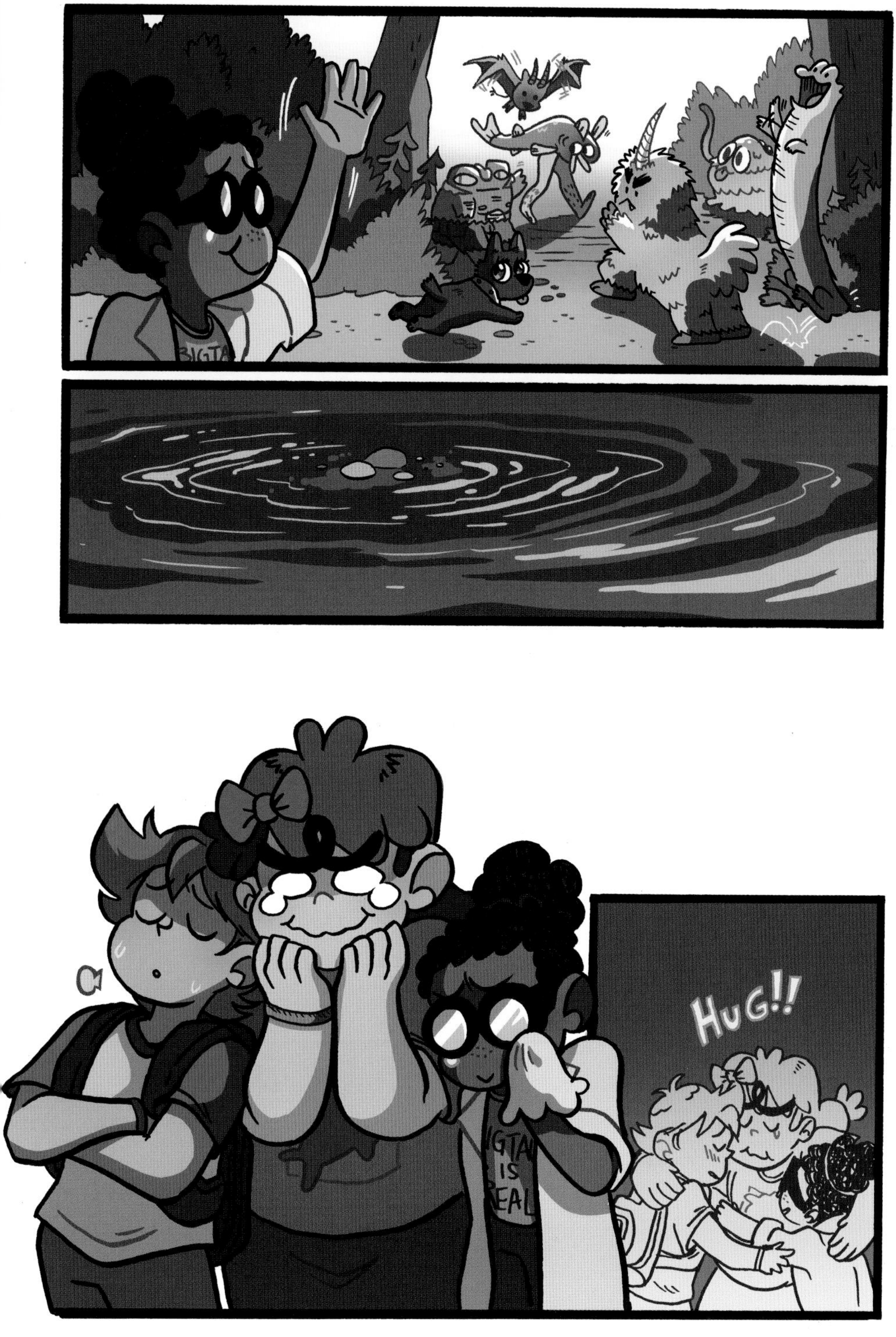
HUG!!

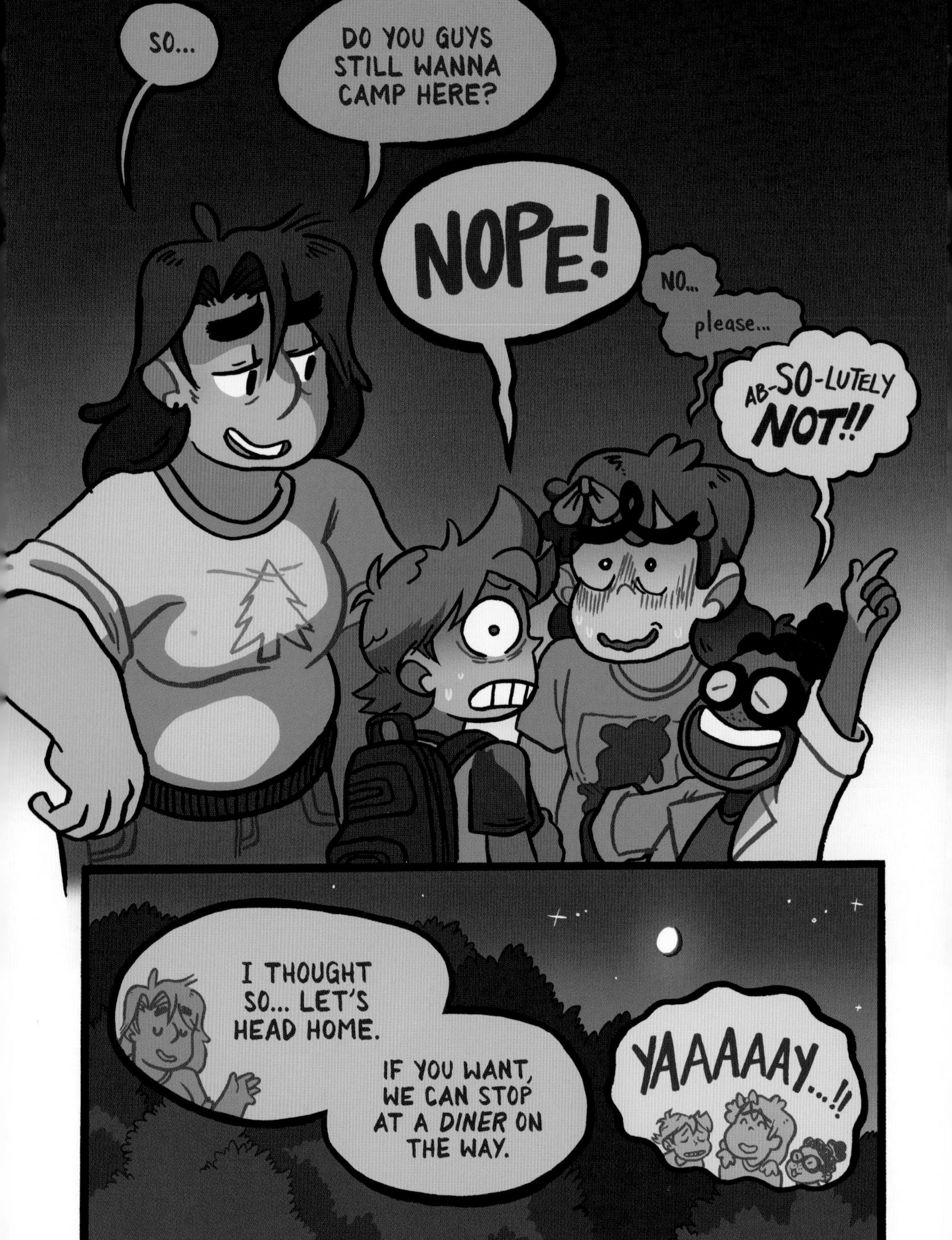
SO...
DO YOU GUYS STILL WANNA CAMP HERE?
NOPE!
NO...
please...
AB-SO-LUTELY NOT!!
I THOUGHT SO... LET'S HEAD HOME.
IF YOU WANT, WE CAN STOP AT A *DINER* ON THE WAY.
YAAAAAY...!!

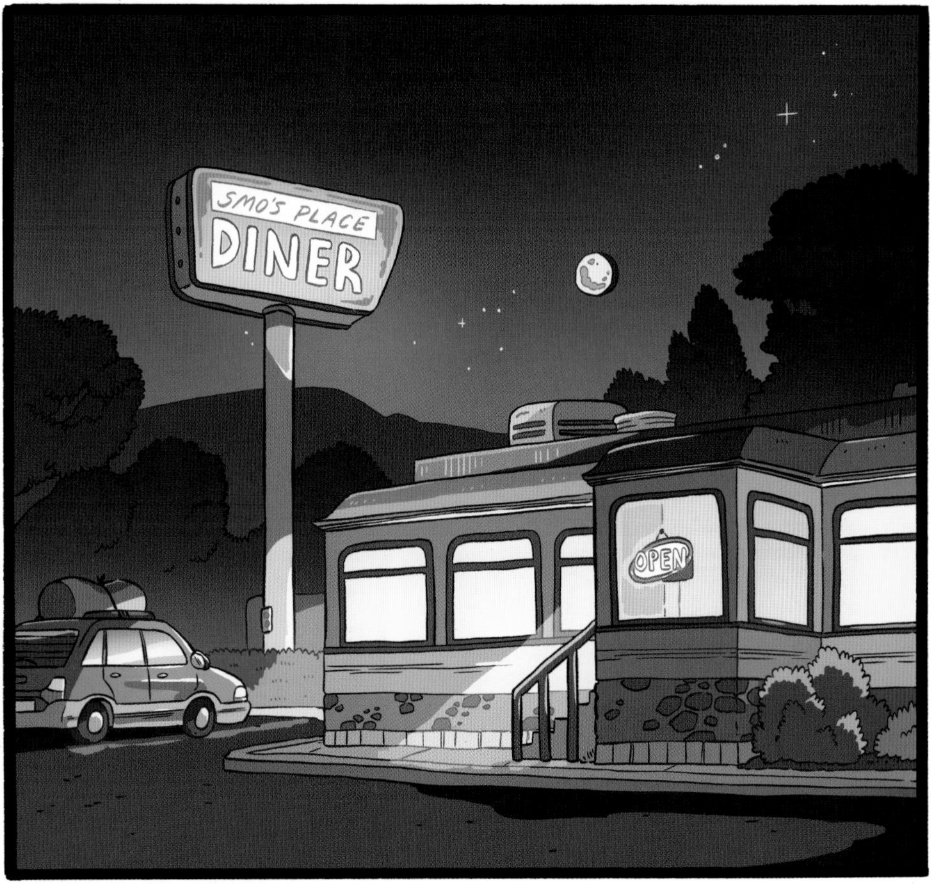
SMO'S PLACE
DINER
OPEN

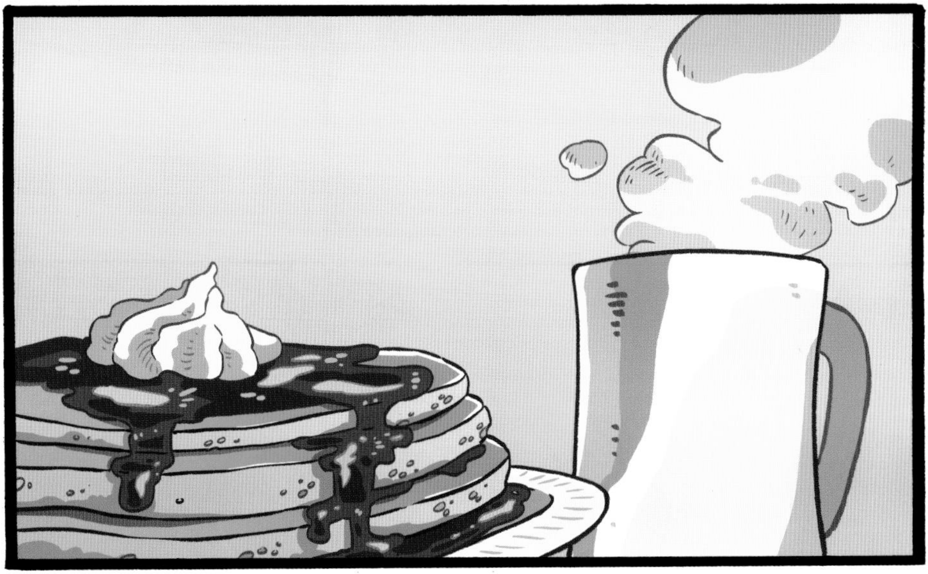

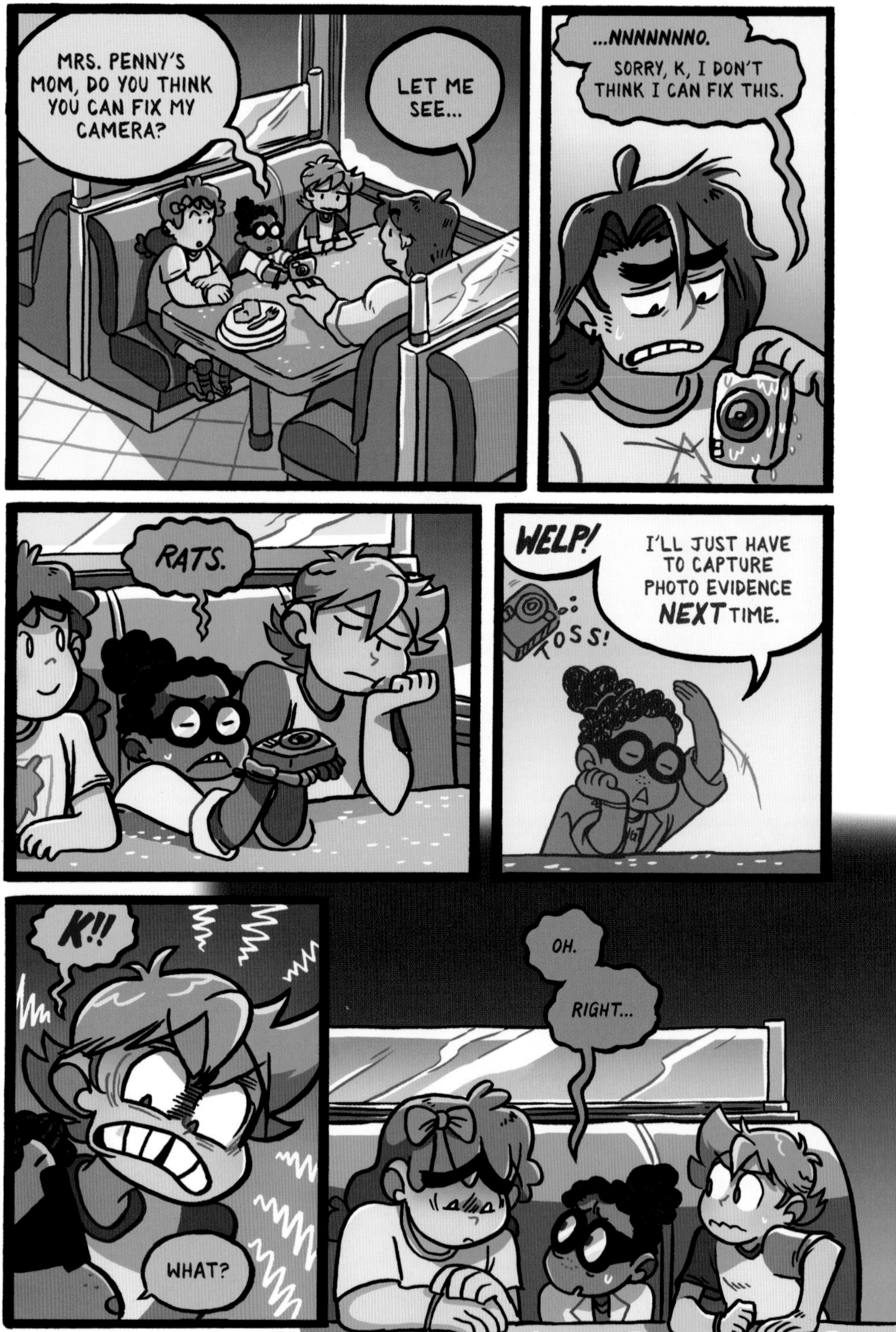
MRS. PENNY'S MOM, DO YOU THINK YOU CAN FIX MY CAMERA?
LET ME SEE...
...NNNNNNNO.
SORRY, K, I DON'T THINK I CAN FIX THIS.
RATS.
WELP!
I'LL JUST HAVE TO CAPTURE PHOTO EVIDENCE NEXT TIME.
TOSS!
K!!
WHAT?
OH.
RIGHT...

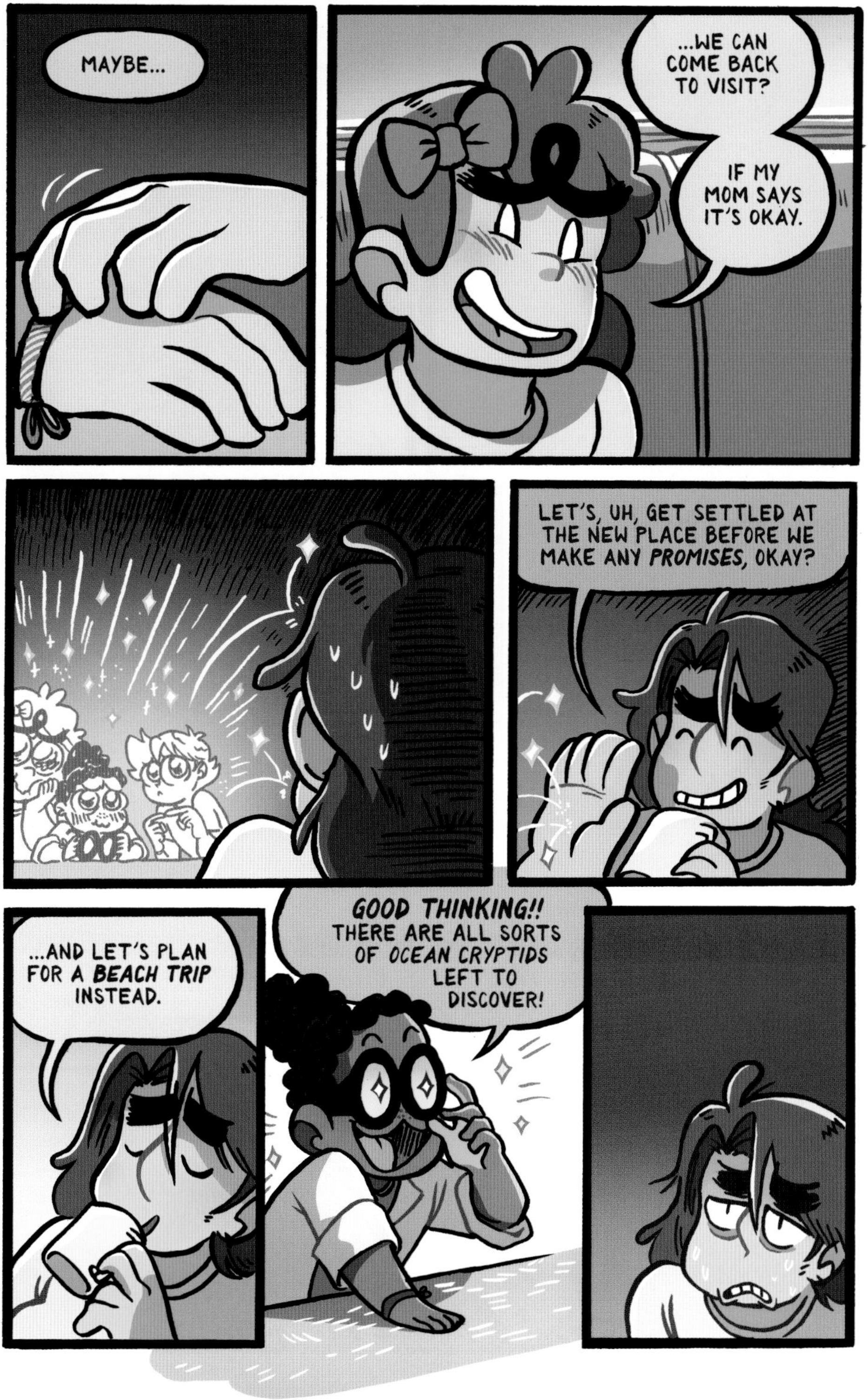
MAYBE...
...WE CAN COME BACK TO VISIT?
IF MY MOM SAYS IT'S OKAY.
LET'S, UH, GET SETTLED AT THE NEW PLACE BEFORE WE MAKE ANY *PROMISES*, OKAY?
...AND LET'S PLAN FOR A *BEACH TRIP* INSTEAD.
GOOD THINKING!! THERE ARE ALL SORTS OF *OCEAN CRYPTIDS* LEFT TO DISCOVER!

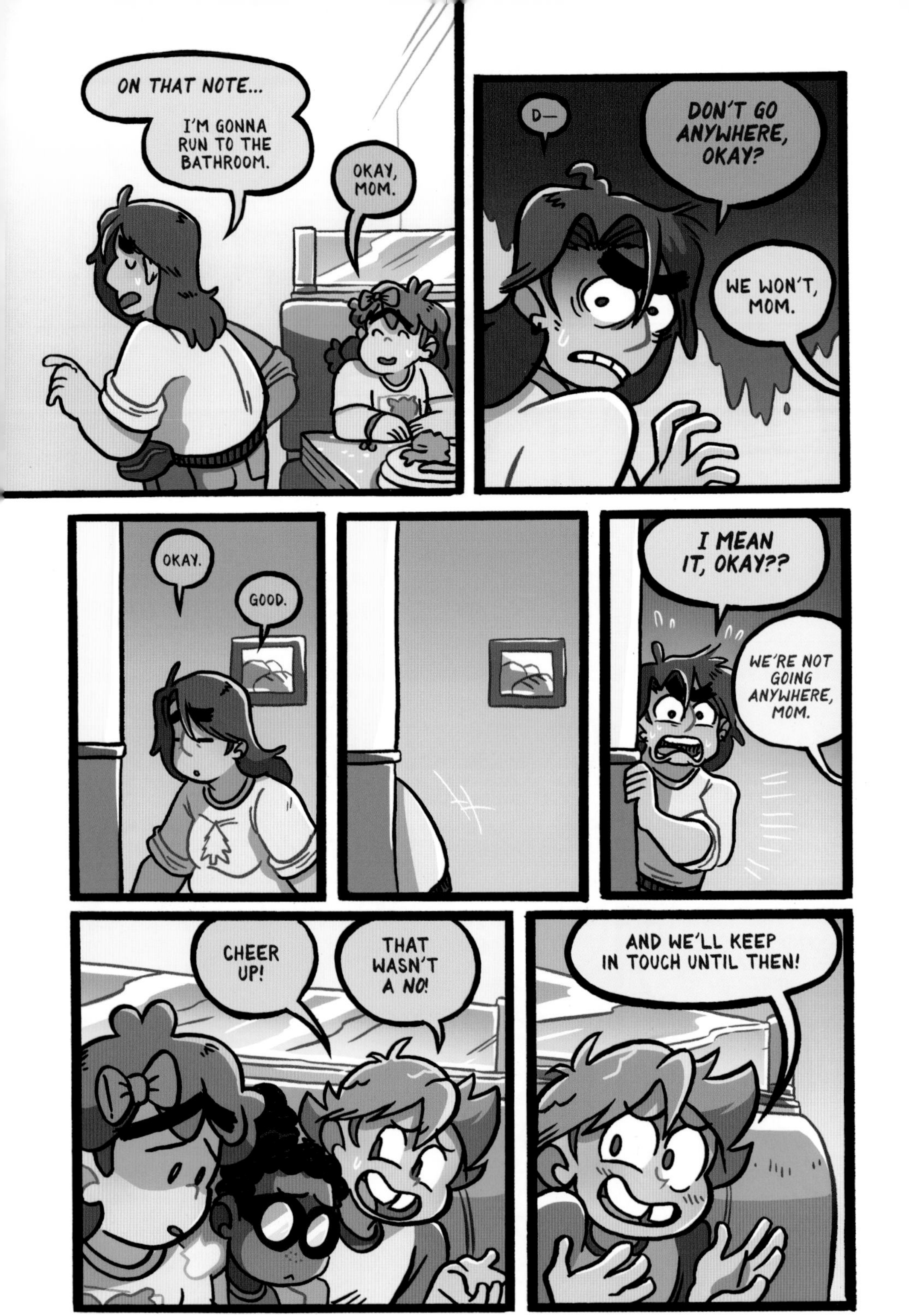
ON THAT NOTE...
I'M GONNA RUN TO THE BATHROOM.
OKAY, MOM.
D—
DON'T GO ANYWHERE, OKAY?
WE WON'T, MOM.
OKAY.
GOOD.
I MEAN IT, OKAY??
WE'RE NOT GOING ANYWHERE, MOM.
CHEER UP!
THAT WASN'T A NO!
AND WE'LL KEEP IN TOUCH UNTIL THEN!

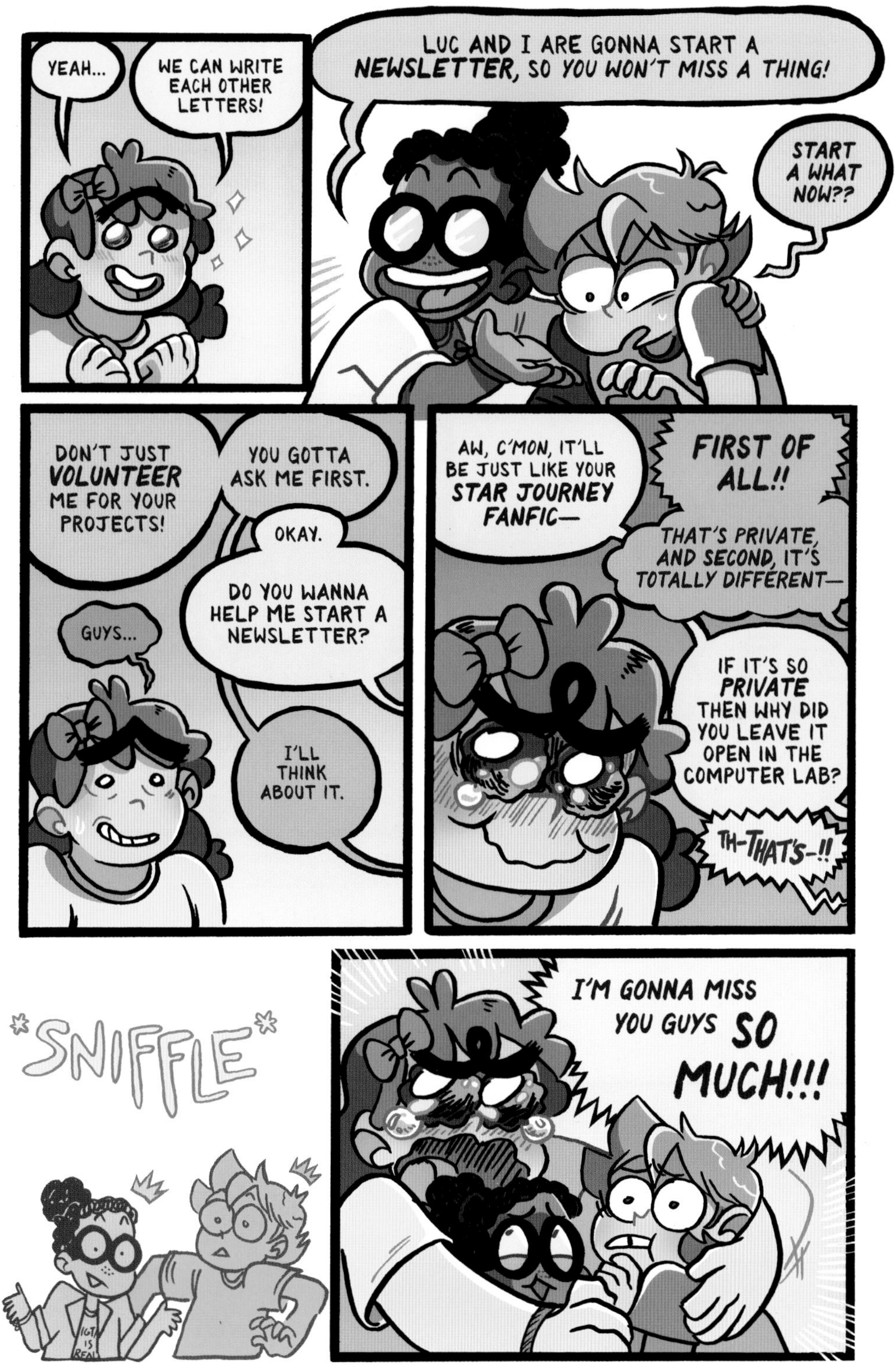

YEAH...
WE CAN WRITE EACH OTHER LETTERS!
LUC AND I ARE GONNA START A NEWSLETTER, SO YOU WON'T MISS A THING!
START A WHAT NOW??
DON'T JUST VOLUNTEER ME FOR YOUR PROJECTS!
YOU GOTTA ASK ME FIRST.
OKAY.
DO YOU WANNA HELP ME START A NEWSLETTER?
GUYS...
I'LL THINK ABOUT IT.
AW, C'MON, IT'LL BE JUST LIKE YOUR STAR JOURNEY FANFIC—
FIRST OF ALL!!
THAT'S PRIVATE, AND SECOND, IT'S TOTALLY DIFFERENT—
IF IT'S SO PRIVATE THEN WHY DID YOU LEAVE IT OPEN IN THE COMPUTER LAB?
TH-THAT'S-!!
SNIFFLE
I'M GONNA MISS YOU GUYS SO MUCH!!!

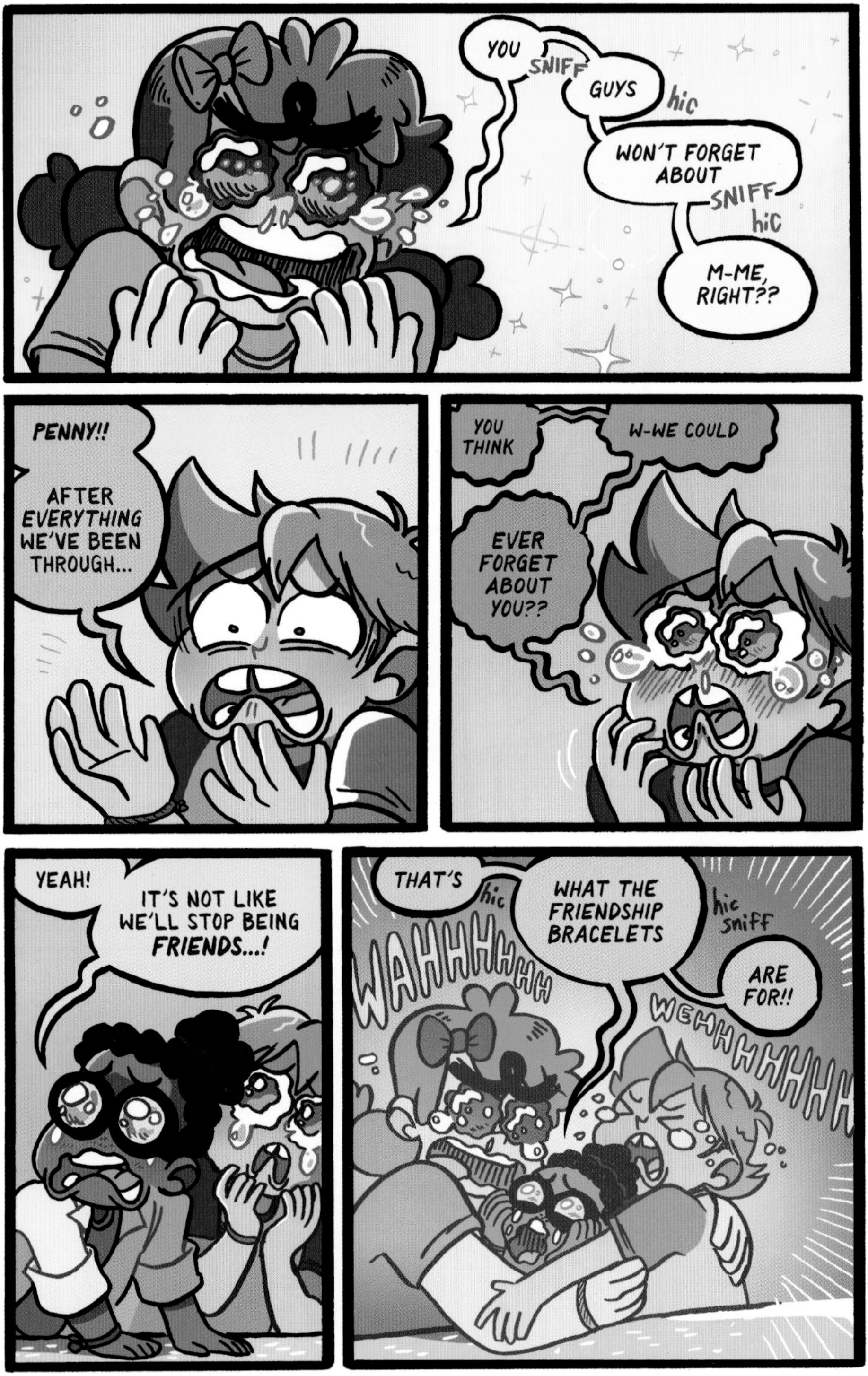
YOU
SNIFF
GUYS
hic
WON'T FORGET ABOUT
SNIFF
hic
M-ME, RIGHT??
PENNY!!
AFTER EVERYTHING WE'VE BEEN THROUGH...
YOU THINK
W-WE COULD
EVER FORGET ABOUT YOU??
YEAH!
IT'S NOT LIKE WE'LL STOP BEING FRIENDS...!
THAT'S
hic
WHAT THE FRIENDSHIP BRACELETS
hic
sniff
ARE FOR!!
WAHHHHHHH
WEHHHHHHHHH

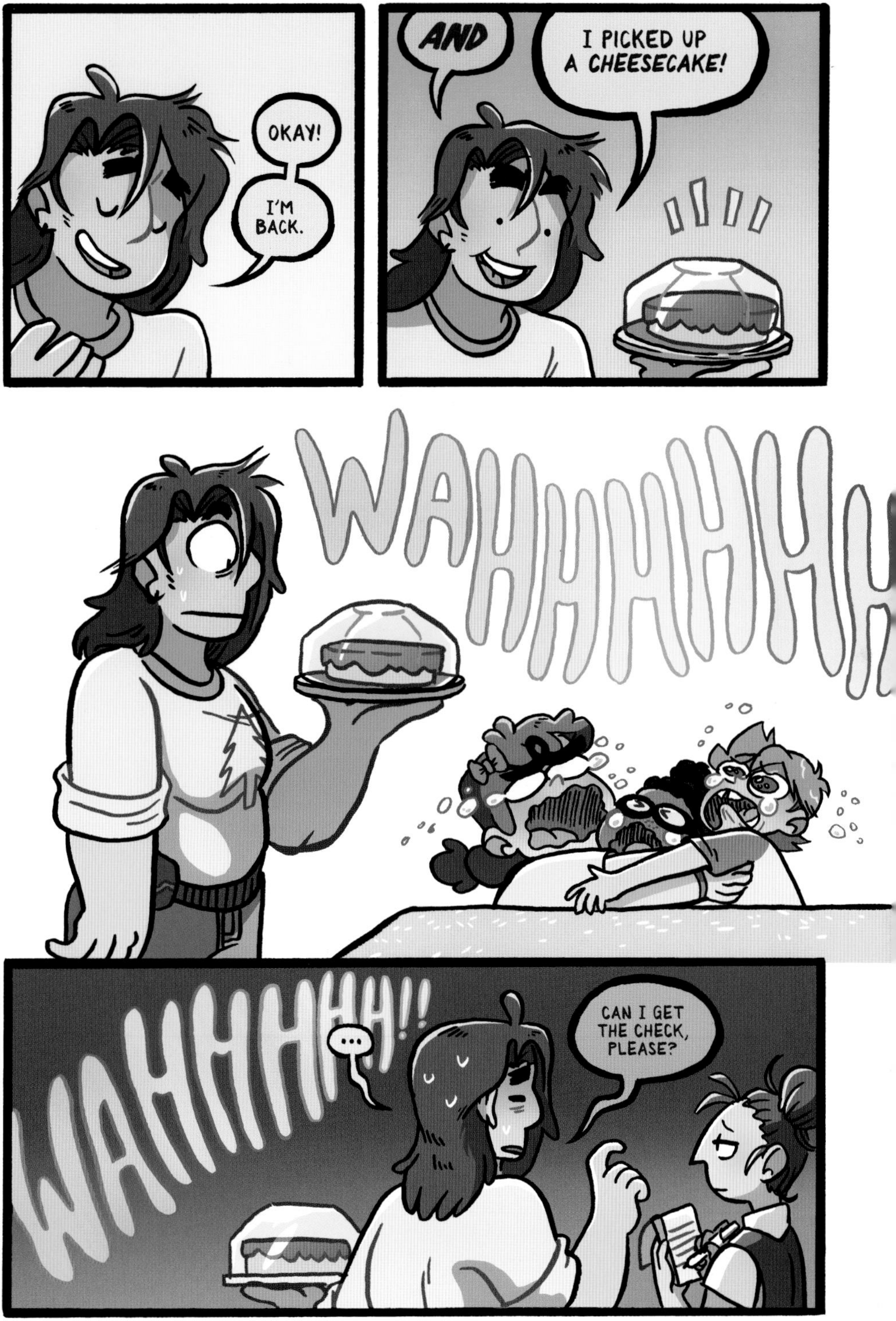
OKAY!
I'M BACK.
AND
I PICKED UP A CHEESECAKE!
WAHHHHHHHH
WAHHHHHH!!
...
CAN I GET THE CHECK, PLEASE?

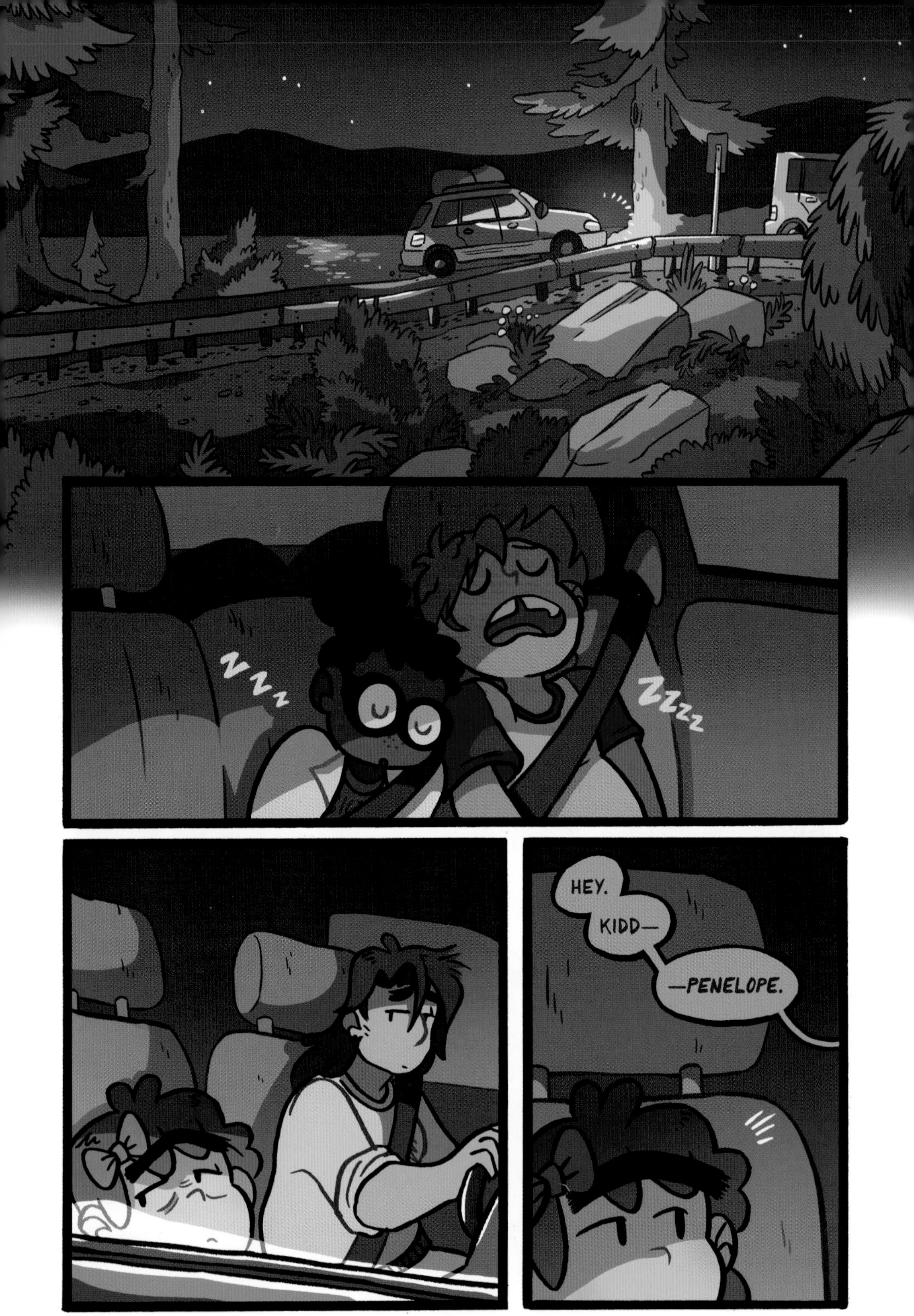
Z Z z
ZZzz
HEY.
KIDD—
—PENELOPE.

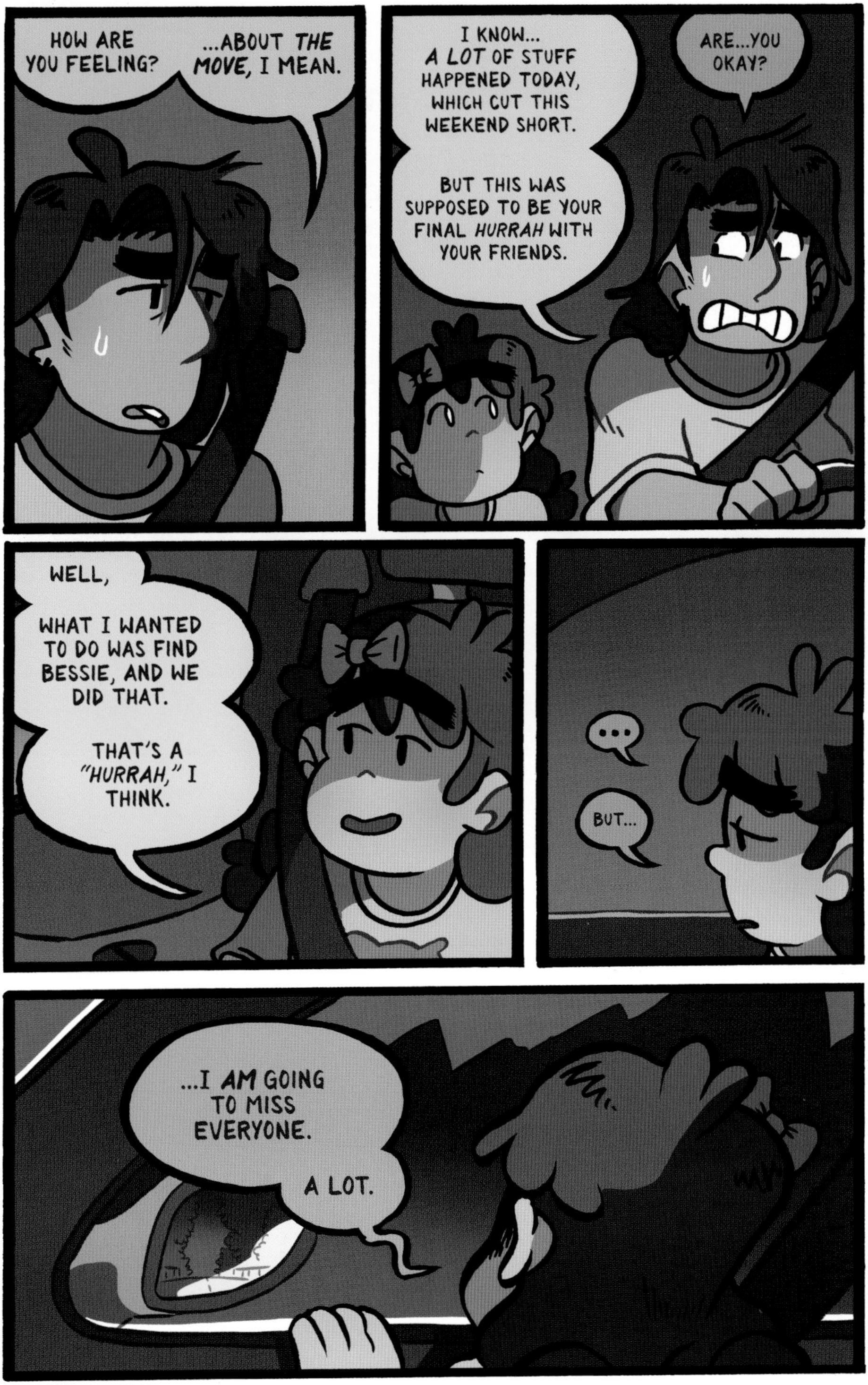
HOW ARE YOU FEELING?
...ABOUT *THE MOVE,* I MEAN.
I KNOW... *A LOT* OF STUFF HAPPENED TODAY, WHICH CUT THIS WEEKEND SHORT.
BUT THIS WAS SUPPOSED TO BE YOUR FINAL *HURRAH* WITH YOUR FRIENDS.
ARE...YOU OKAY?
WELL,
WHAT I WANTED TO DO WAS FIND BESSIE, AND WE DID THAT.
THAT'S A *"HURRAH,"* I THINK.
...
BUT...
...I **AM** GOING TO MISS EVERYONE.
A LOT.

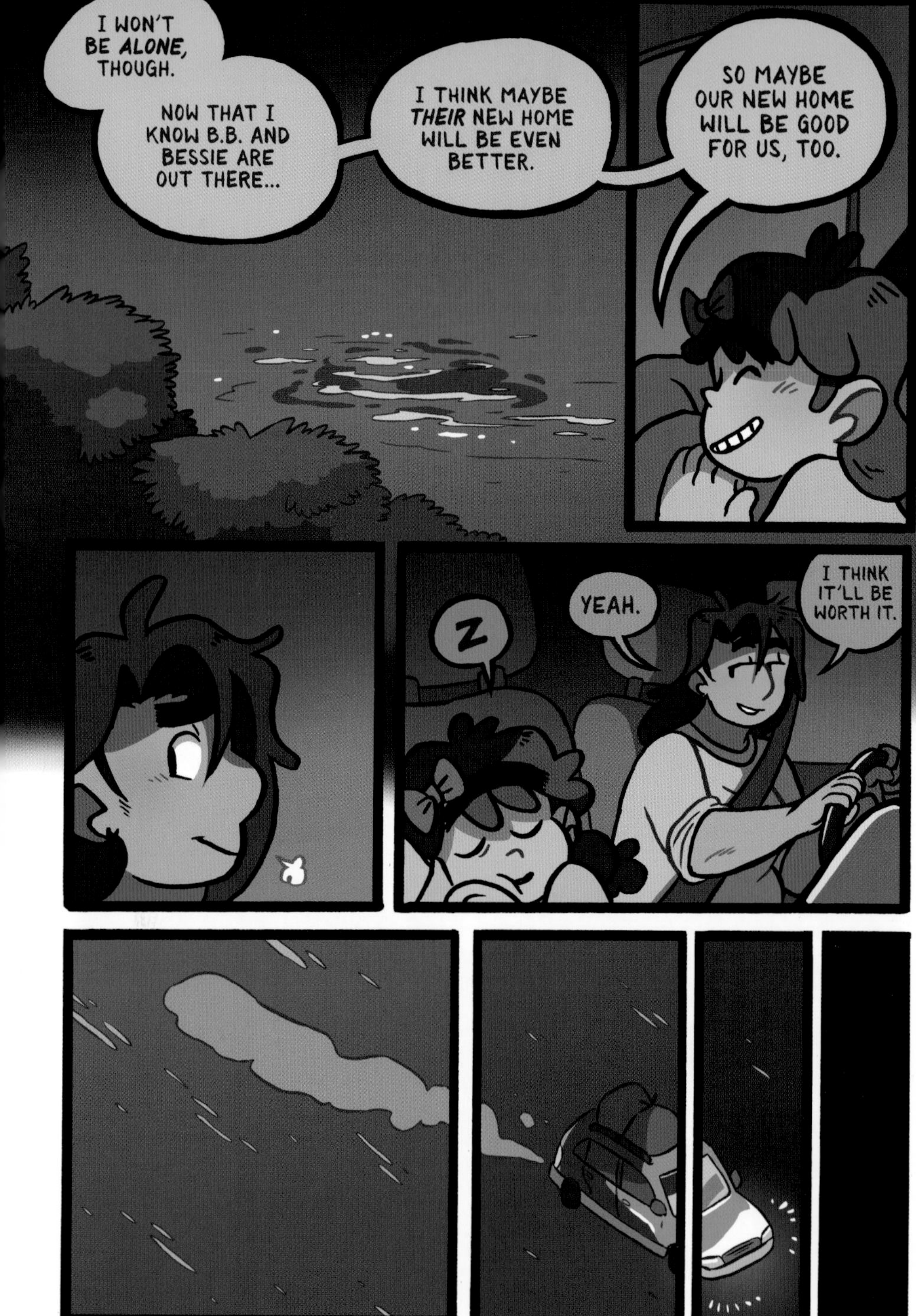
I WON'T BE *ALONE,* THOUGH.
NOW THAT I KNOW B.B. AND BESSIE ARE OUT THERE...
I THINK MAYBE *THEIR* NEW HOME WILL BE EVEN BETTER.
SO MAYBE OUR NEW HOME WILL BE GOOD FOR US, TOO.
Z
YEAH.
I THINK IT'LL BE WORTH IT.

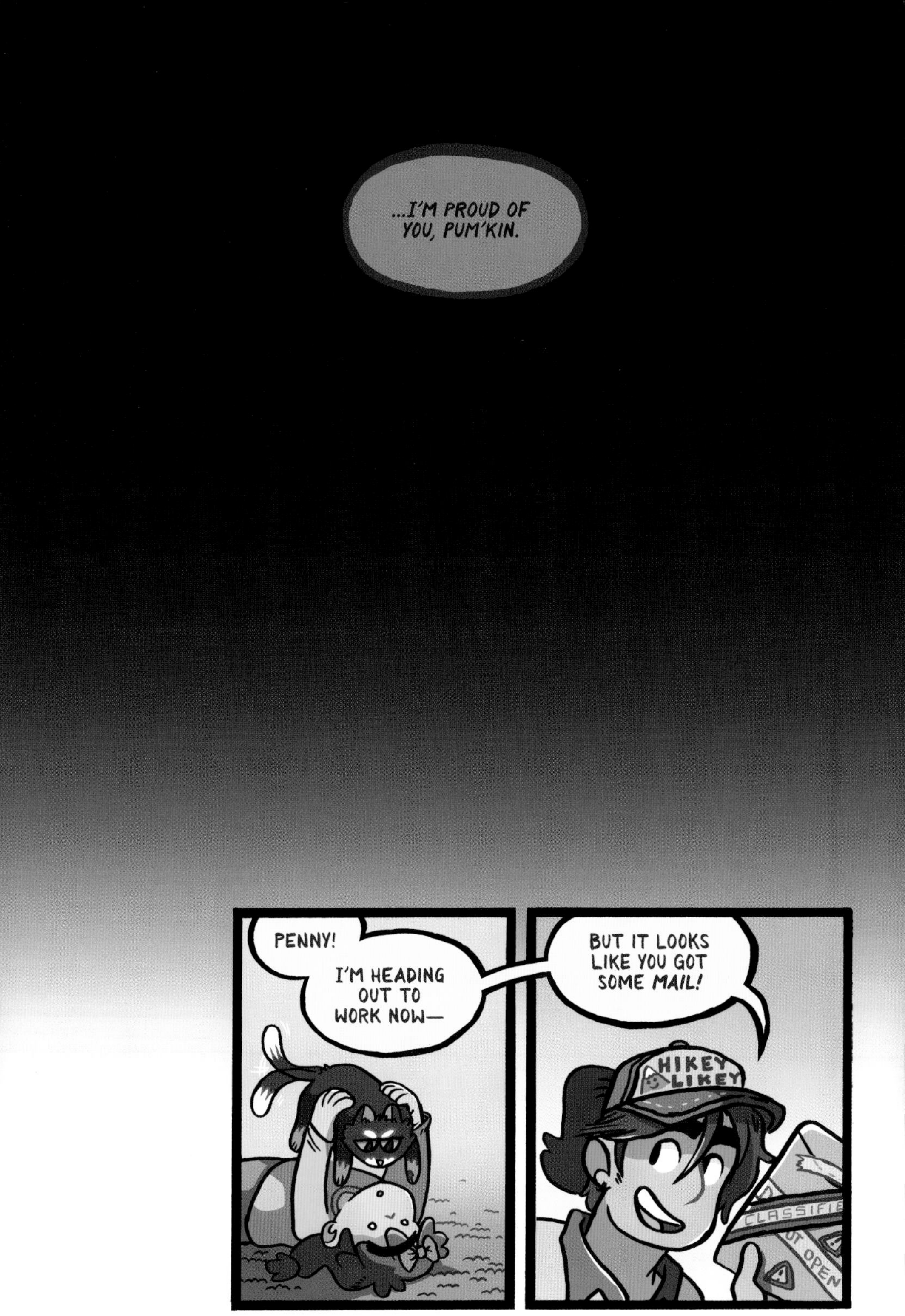
...I'M PROUD OF YOU, PUM'KIN.
PENNY!
I'M HEADING OUT TO WORK NOW—
BUT IT LOOKS LIKE YOU GOT SOME MAIL!
HIKEY LIKEY

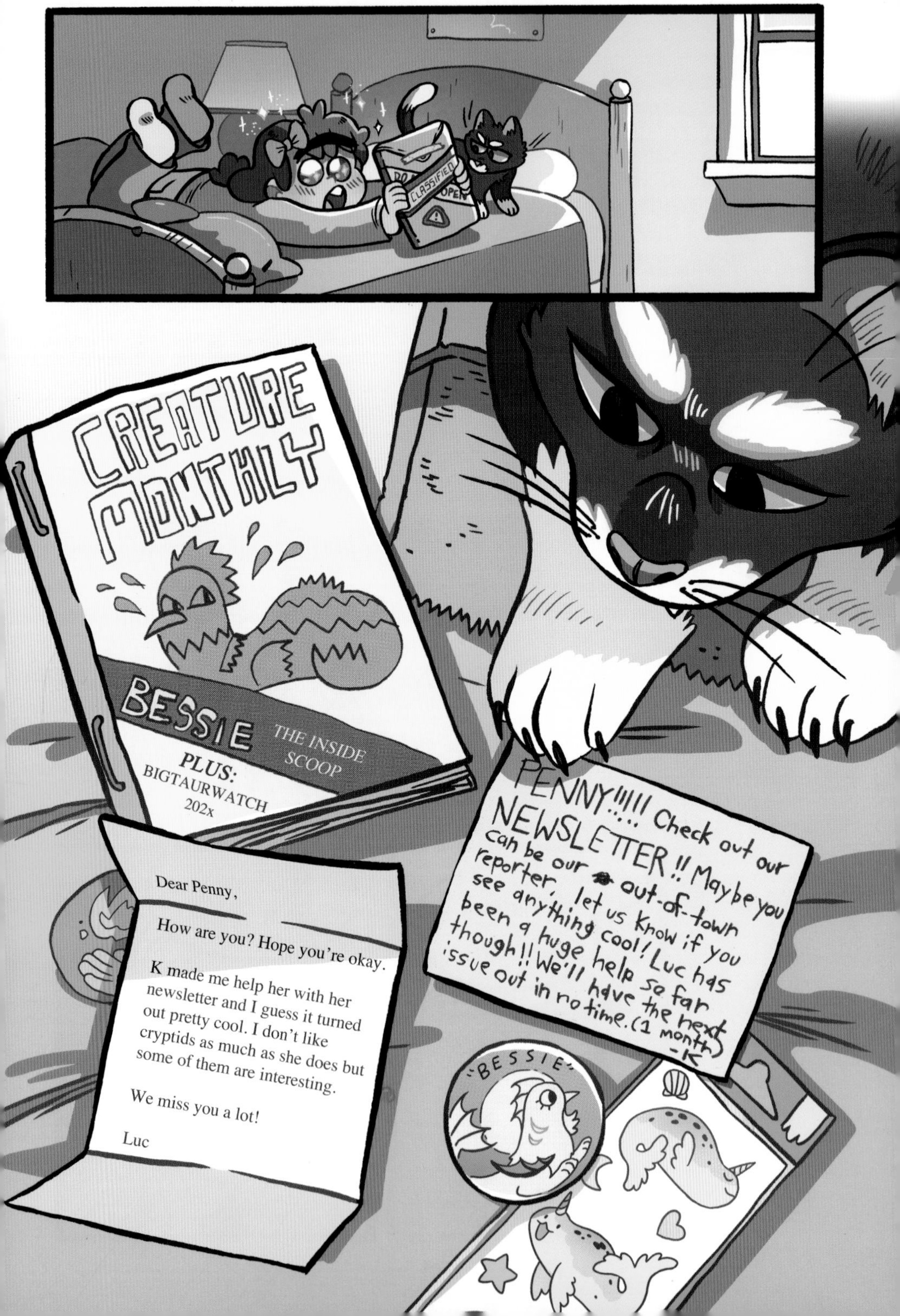

DO
CLASSIFIED
OPEN
CREATURE MONTHLY
BESSIE
THE INSIDE SCOOP
PLUS:
BIGTAURWATCH
202x
PENNY!!!!! Check out our NEWSLETTER!! Maybe you can be our out-of-town reporter, let us know if you see anything cool! Luc has been a huge help so far though!! We'll have the next issue out in no time. (1 month) -K
Dear Penny,
How are you? Hope you're okay.
K made me help her with her newsletter and I guess it turned out pretty cool. I don't like cryptids as much as she does but some of them are interesting.
We miss you a lot!
Luc
BESSIE

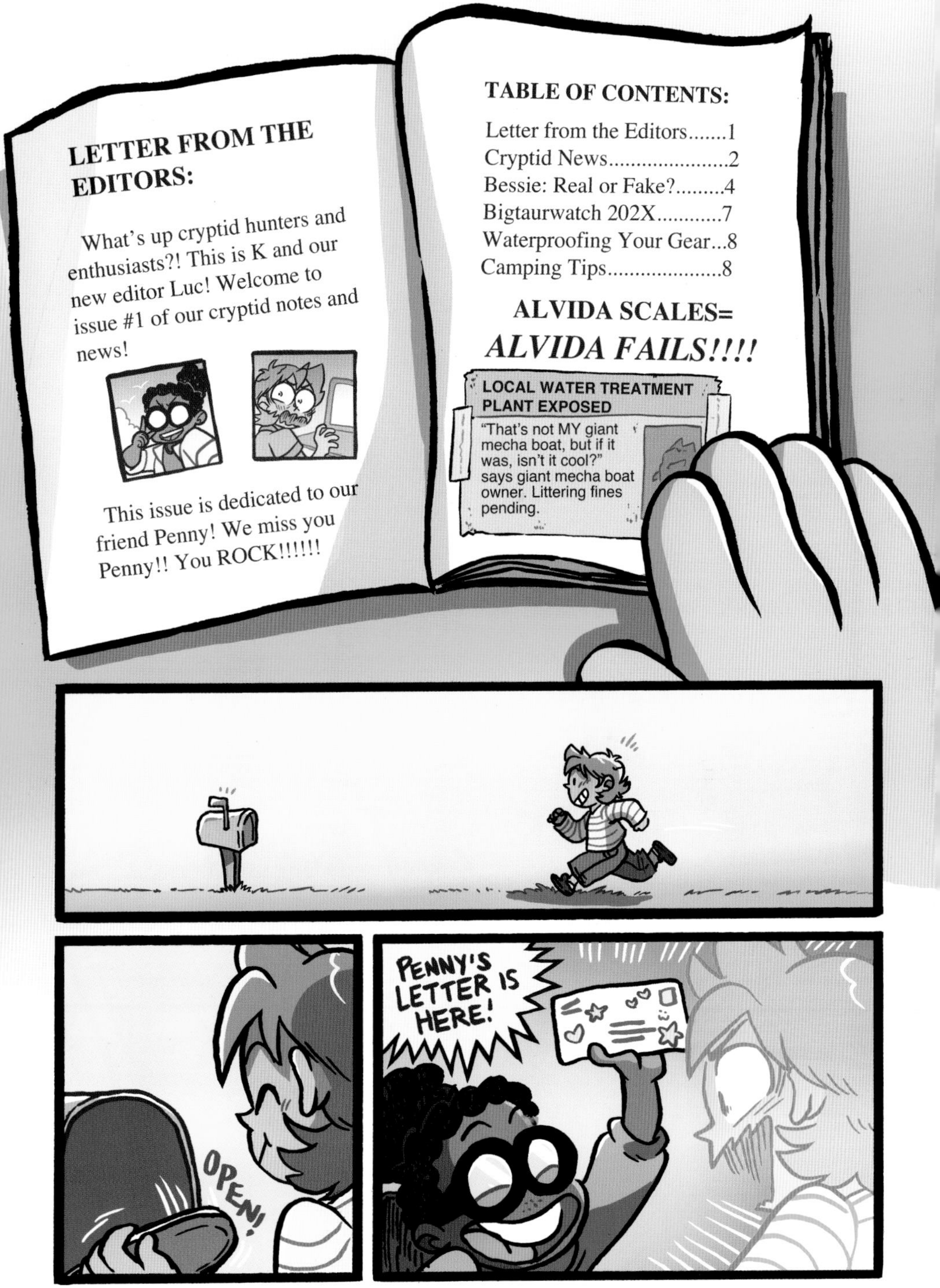

LETTER FROM THE EDITORS:
What's up cryptid hunters and enthusiasts?! This is K and our new editor Luc! Welcome to issue #1 of our cryptid notes and news!
This issue is dedicated to our friend Penny! We miss you Penny!! You ROCK!!!!!!
TABLE OF CONTENTS:
Letter from the Editors.......1
Cryptid News......................2
Bessie: Real or Fake?.........4
Bigtaurwatch 202X............7
Waterproofing Your Gear...8
Camping Tips.....................8
ALVIDA SCALES=
ALVIDA FAILS!!!!
LOCAL WATER TREATMENT PLANT EXPOSED
"That's not MY giant mecha boat, but if it was, isn't it cool?" says giant mecha boat owner. Littering fines pending.
OPEN!
PENNY'S LETTER IS HERE!

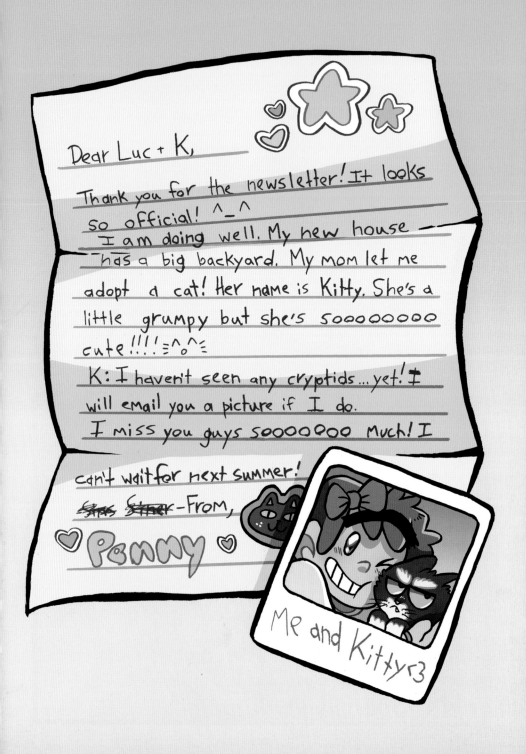

Dear Luc + K,

Thank you for the newsletter! It looks so official! ^_^

I am doing well. My new house has a big backyard. My mom let me adopt a cat! Her name is Kitty. She's a little grumpy but she's soooooooooo cute!!!! =^o^=

K: I haven't seen any cryptids... yet! I will email you a picture if I do.

I miss you guys soooooooooo much! I can't wait for next summer!

~~Sin~~ ~~Sincer~~ -From,

♡ Penny ♡

Me and Kitty ♡3

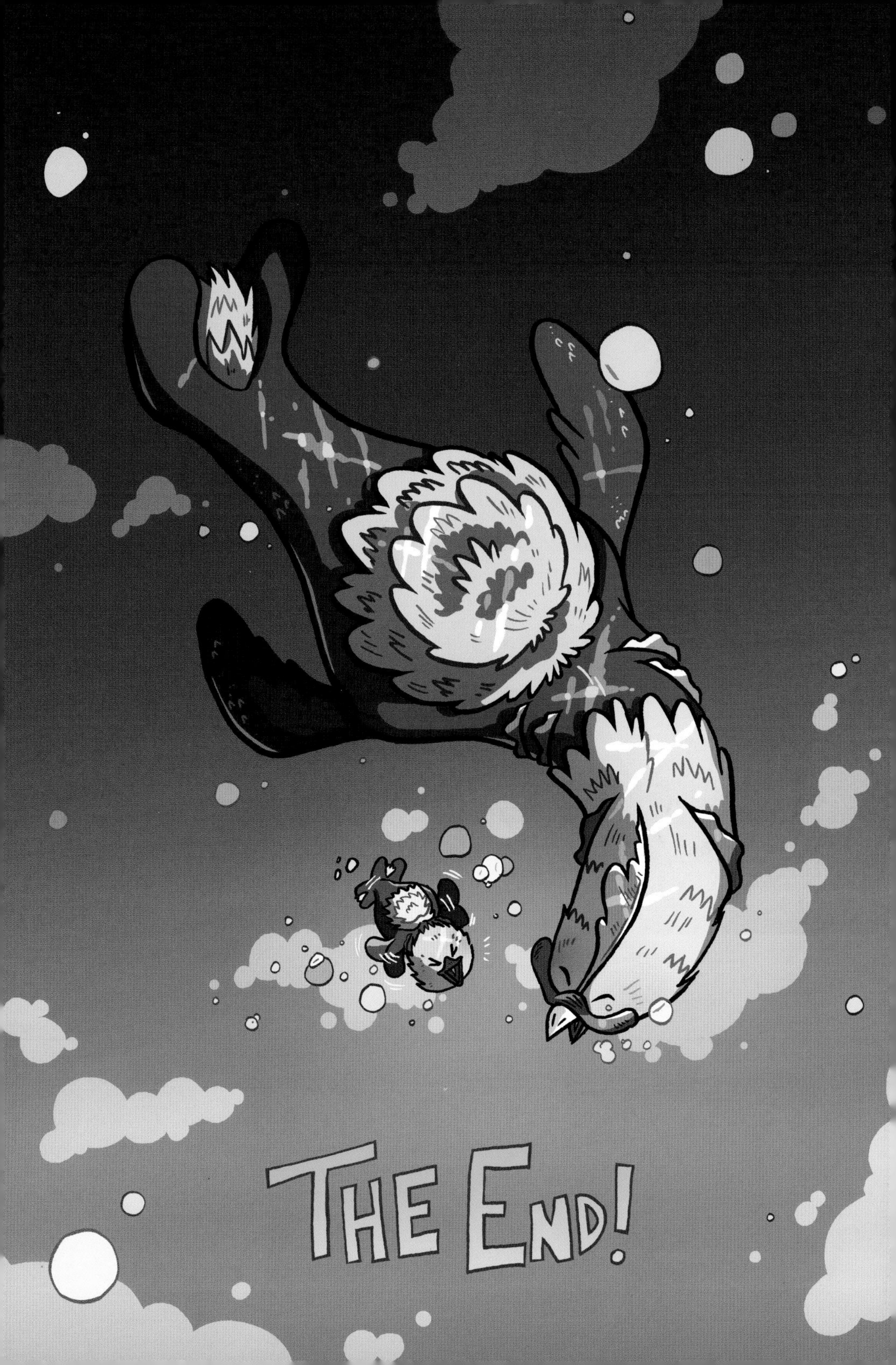
THE END!

CAST BIOS

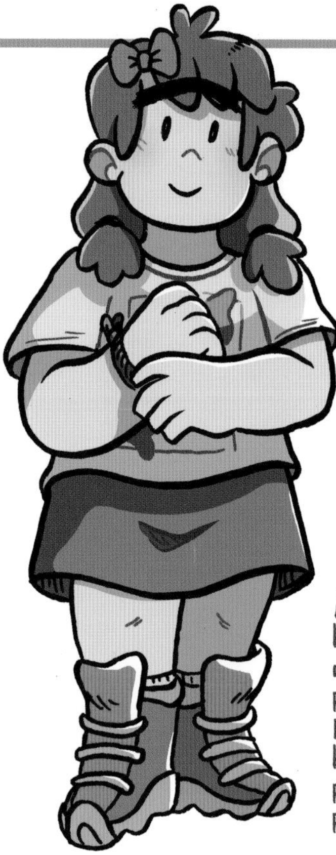

Penny has a big heart, loves animals of all kinds, and always tries to see the best in people. Fell in the lake when she was younger.

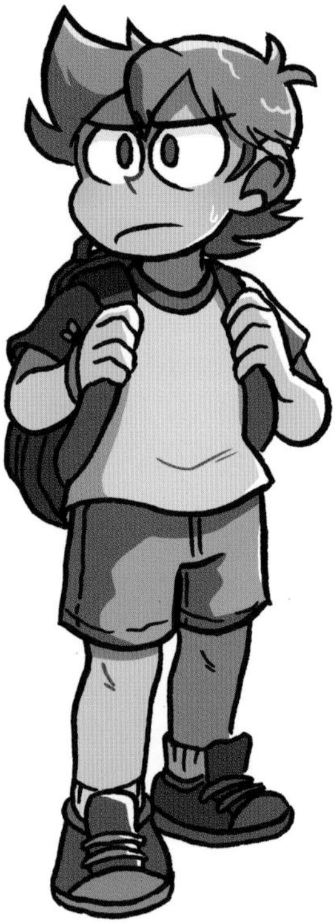

Luc is a reformed bully and ex-Girl Scout who seeks to atone for pushing Penny in the lake years ago by becoming responsible, protective, and prepared.

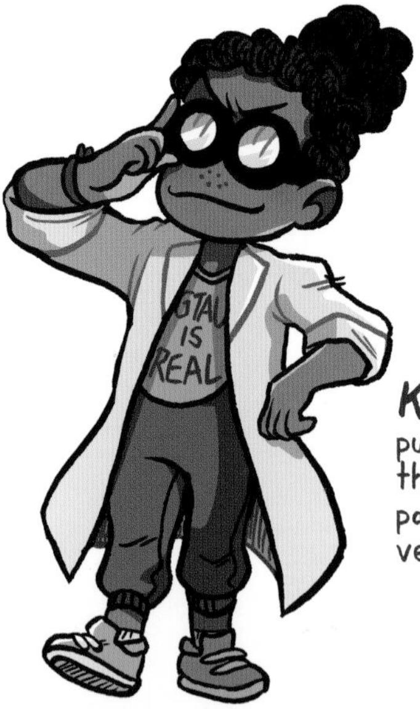

K believes in cryptids, and pursues scientific knowledge about them with seemingly limitless passion. Not outdoorsy, but very optimistic and creative.

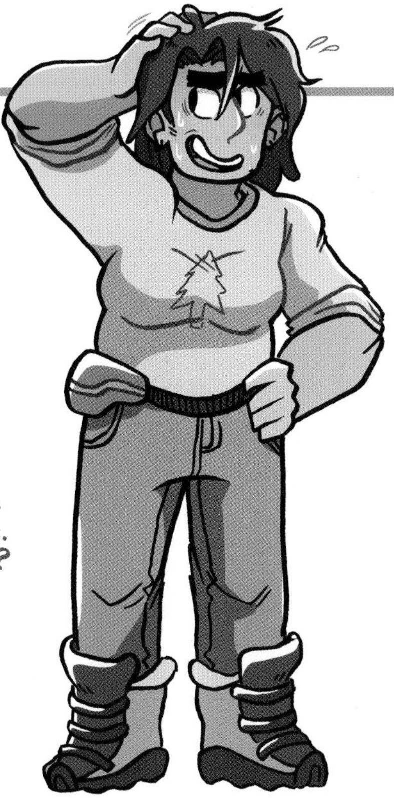

Ronnie is Penny's mom. Practical, friendly, and overprotective of her daughter. Works at the local camping supply store Hikey Likey.

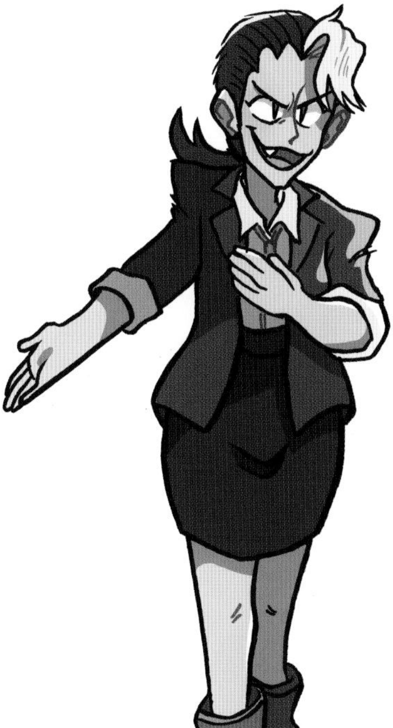

Alvida captures and sells cryptids. What's her deal...?

The titular Bawk-Ness Monster, ***Bessie,*** is a local legendary creature that has the head of a chicken, the body of a prehistoric aquatic creature, and the heart of a friend. Notoriously difficult to catch a glimpse of, let alone capture. She rescued Penny from drowning years ago.

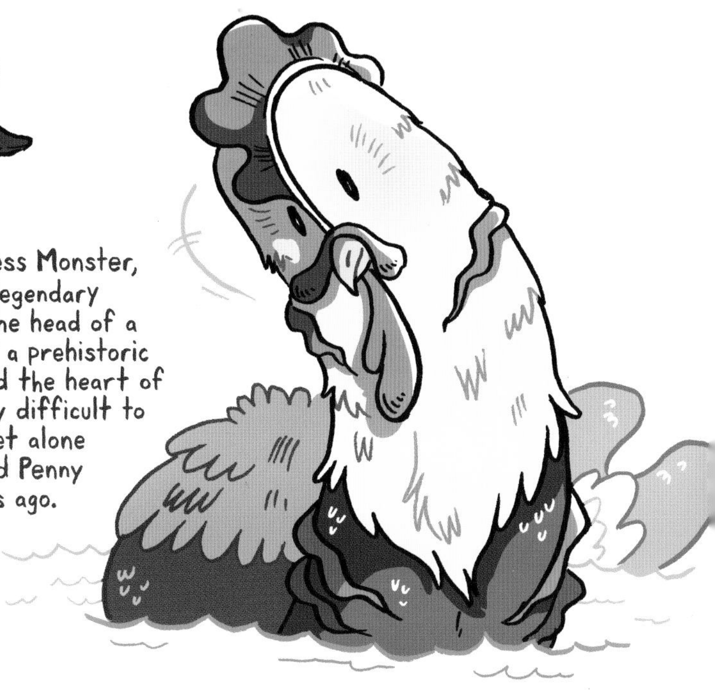

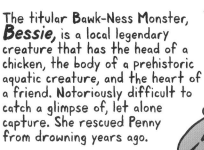

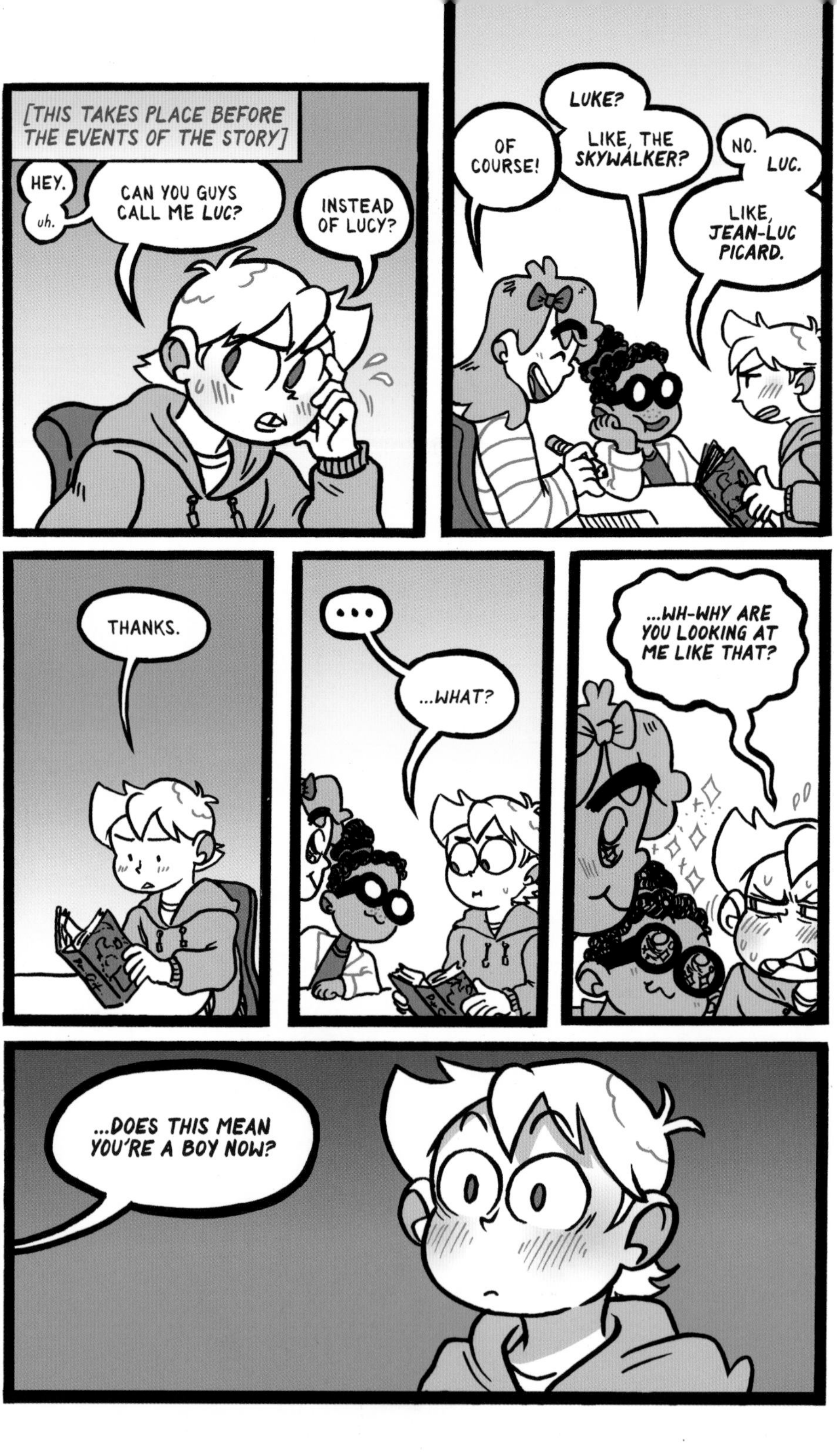
[THIS TAKES PLACE BEFORE THE EVENTS OF THE STORY]
HEY.
uh.
CAN YOU GUYS CALL ME LUC?
INSTEAD OF LUCY?
LUKE?
OF COURSE!
LIKE, THE SKYWALKER?
NO.
LUC.
LIKE, JEAN-LUC PICARD.
THANKS.
...
...WHAT?
...WH-WHY ARE YOU LOOKING AT ME LIKE THAT?
...DOES THIS MEAN YOU'RE A BOY NOW?

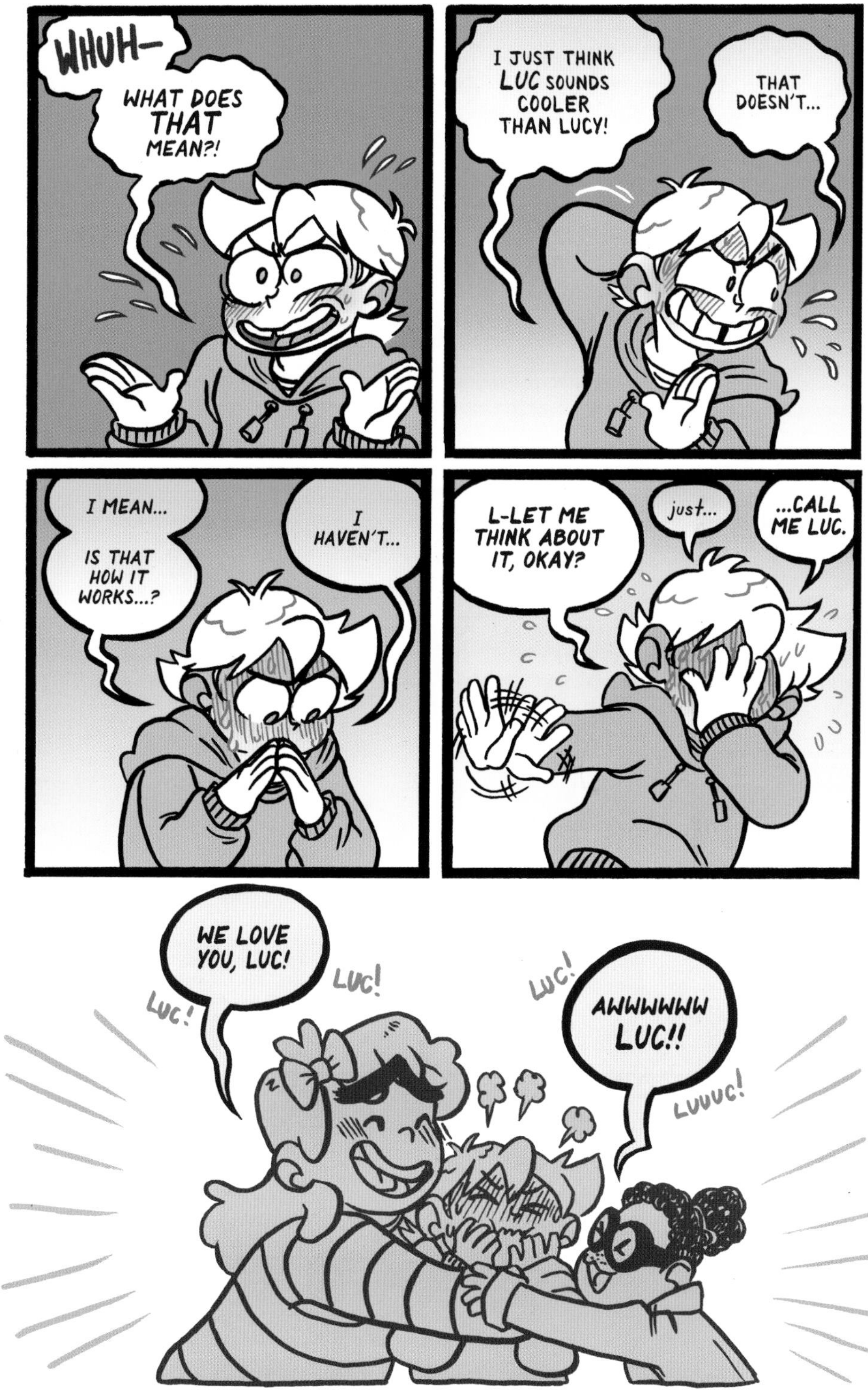
WHUH-
WHAT DOES THAT MEAN?!
I JUST THINK LUC SOUNDS COOLER THAN LUCY!
THAT DOESN'T...
I MEAN...
IS THAT HOW IT WORKS...?
I HAVEN'T...
L-LET ME THINK ABOUT IT, OKAY?
just...
...CALL ME LUC.
WE LOVE YOU, LUC!
LUC!
LUC!
LUC!
AWWWWWW LUC!!
LUUUC!

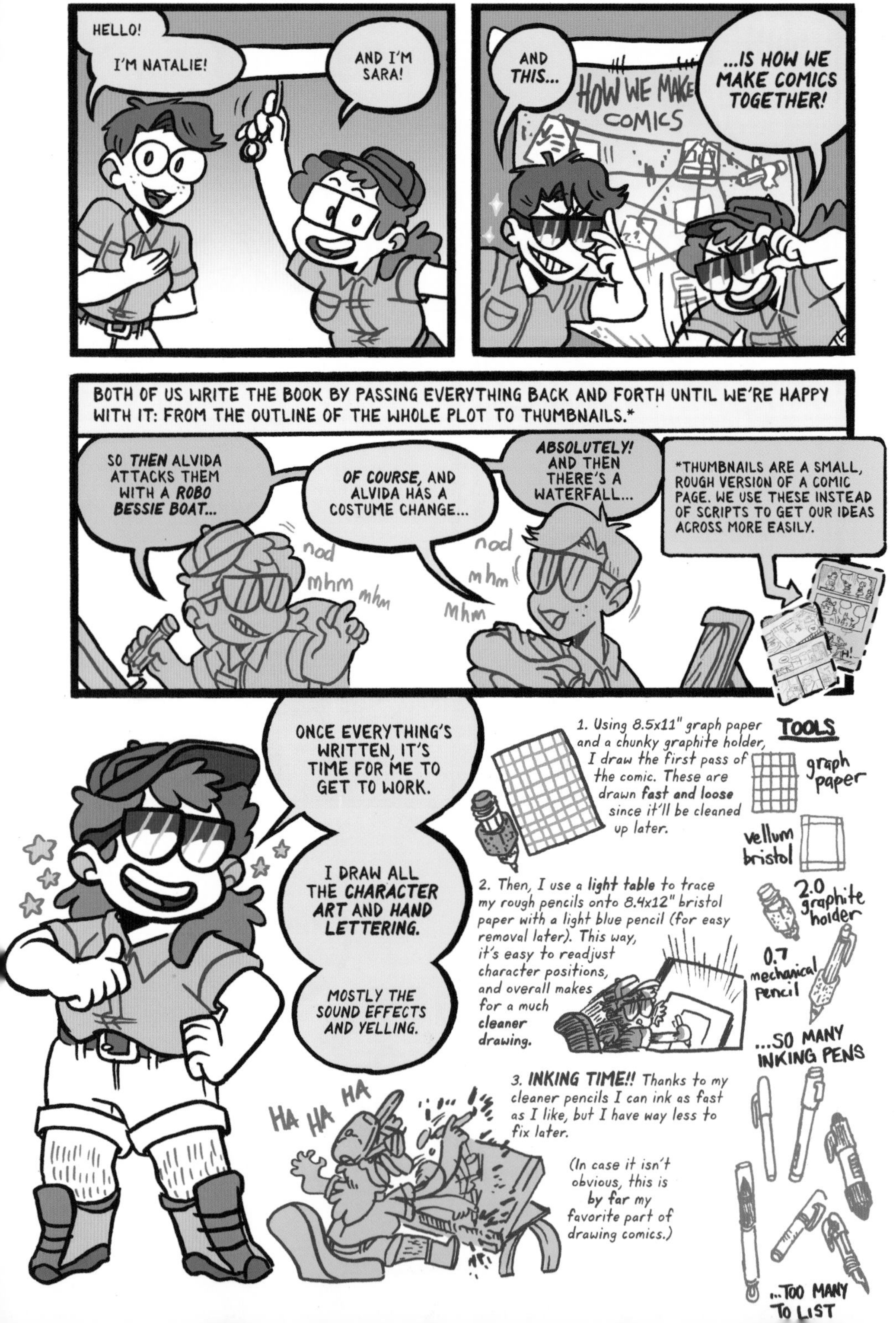
HELLO!
I'M NATALIE!
AND I'M SARA!
AND THIS...
HOW WE MAKE COMICS
...IS HOW WE MAKE COMICS TOGETHER!
BOTH OF US WRITE THE BOOK BY PASSING EVERYTHING BACK AND FORTH UNTIL WE'RE HAPPY WITH IT: FROM THE OUTLINE OF THE WHOLE PLOT TO THUMBNAILS.*
SO *THEN* ALVIDA ATTACKS THEM WITH A *ROBO BESSIE BOAT...*
OF COURSE, AND ALVIDA HAS A COSTUME CHANGE...
ABSOLUTELY! AND THEN THERE'S A WATERFALL...
*THUMBNAILS ARE A SMALL, ROUGH VERSION OF A COMIC PAGE. WE USE THESE INSTEAD OF SCRIPTS TO GET OUR IDEAS ACROSS MORE EASILY.
nod
mhm
mhm
nod
mhm
mhm
ONCE EVERYTHING'S WRITTEN, IT'S TIME FOR ME TO GET TO WORK.
I DRAW ALL THE *CHARACTER ART* AND *HAND LETTERING.*
MOSTLY THE SOUND EFFECTS AND YELLING.
1. Using 8.5x11" graph paper and a chunky graphite holder, I draw the first pass of the comic. These are drawn **fast and loose** since it'll be cleaned up later.
TOOLS
graph paper
vellum bristol
2.0 graphite holder
0.7 mechanical pencil
...SO MANY INKING PENS
...TOO MANY TO LIST
2. Then, I use a **light table** to trace my rough pencils onto 8.4x12" bristol paper with a light blue pencil (for easy removal later). This way, it's easy to readjust character positions, and overall makes for a much **cleaner drawing.**
3. **INKING TIME!!** Thanks to my cleaner pencils I can ink as fast as I like, but I have way less to fix later.
HA HA HA
(In case it isn't obvious, this is **by far** my favorite part of drawing comics.)

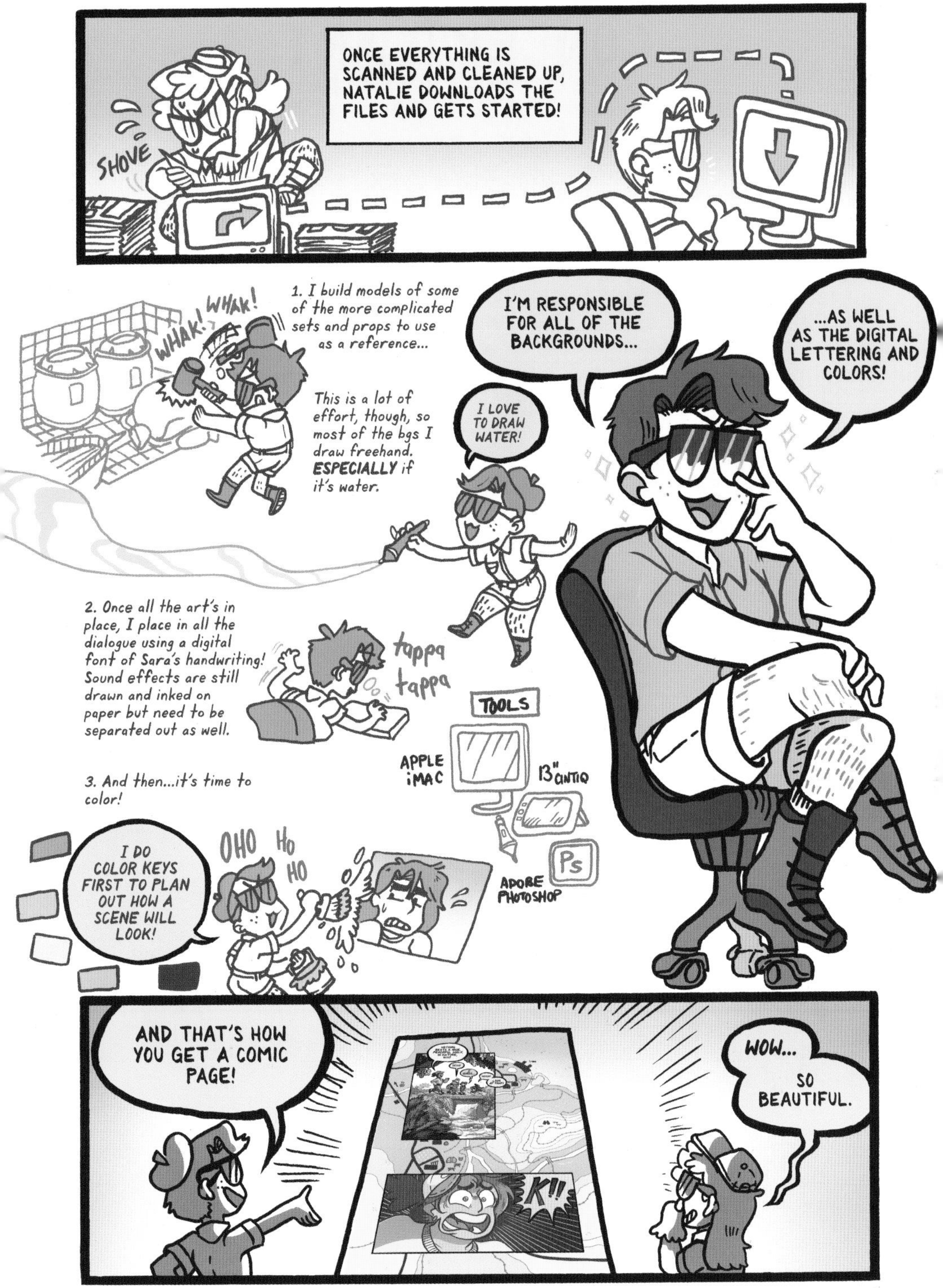
SHOVE
ONCE EVERYTHING IS SCANNED AND CLEANED UP, NATALIE DOWNLOADS THE FILES AND GETS STARTED!
1. I build models of some of the more complicated sets and props to use as a reference...
WHAK! WHAK!
WHAK!
This is a lot of effort, though, so most of the bgs I draw freehand. ESPECIALLY if it's water.
I LOVE TO DRAW WATER!
I'M RESPONSIBLE FOR ALL OF THE BACKGROUNDS...
...AS WELL AS THE DIGITAL LETTERING AND COLORS!
2. Once all the art's in place, I place in all the dialogue using a digital font of Sara's handwriting! Sound effects are still drawn and inked on paper but need to be separated out as well.
tappa tappa
TOOLS
APPLE iMAC
13" CINTIQ
ADOBE PHOTOSHOP
Ps
3. And then...it's time to color!
I DO COLOR KEYS FIRST TO PLAN OUT HOW A SCENE WILL LOOK!
OHO HO HO
AND THAT'S HOW YOU GET A COMIC PAGE!
K!!
WOW... SO BEAUTIFUL.

CONCEPT ART

We initially thought of Bessie as a sea serpent, but eventually ended up making her a softer, more plesiosaur-looking creature. Here are some exploration sketches figuring out how much "chicken" and how much "sea monster" we needed to mix together to get the combo just right.

SKIN OVER MOTH IS FLAT, SKIN UNDER WATER

COMB GOES ALL THE WAY OVER HEAD

FLUFFY...

NECK CAN RECEDE INTO FEATHERS, LIKE A HERON

NECK GILL

MOTTLED BACK SCALES

FUZZY

SHOOP!

Baby Bessie (B.B.) ended up with a very "baby seal" look...I look at them and want to protect them!

FLIPPERS

So graceful...

BESS 101

ALL ABOUT TEXSL-VANIA'S MOST FAMOUS BIRD-FISH

Not all concept art is 2D artwork—Natalie made a little mockup of K and Penny's "Bessie 101" zine during the writing phase to pitch the concept and to use as a reference for drawing it into the book.

BESSIE FACT

· Summer 1997 "Bessiemania" hit! Many of these sightings were later confirmed as hoaxes ...or WERE they!?

DON'T POLLUTE MY LAKE

st sighted in 19XX at Lake kamixon Park, Texslvania

OK-NESS

Bessie is now used as a

Color planning/color scripts...Natalie did some of these digitally and some with watercolor on paper.

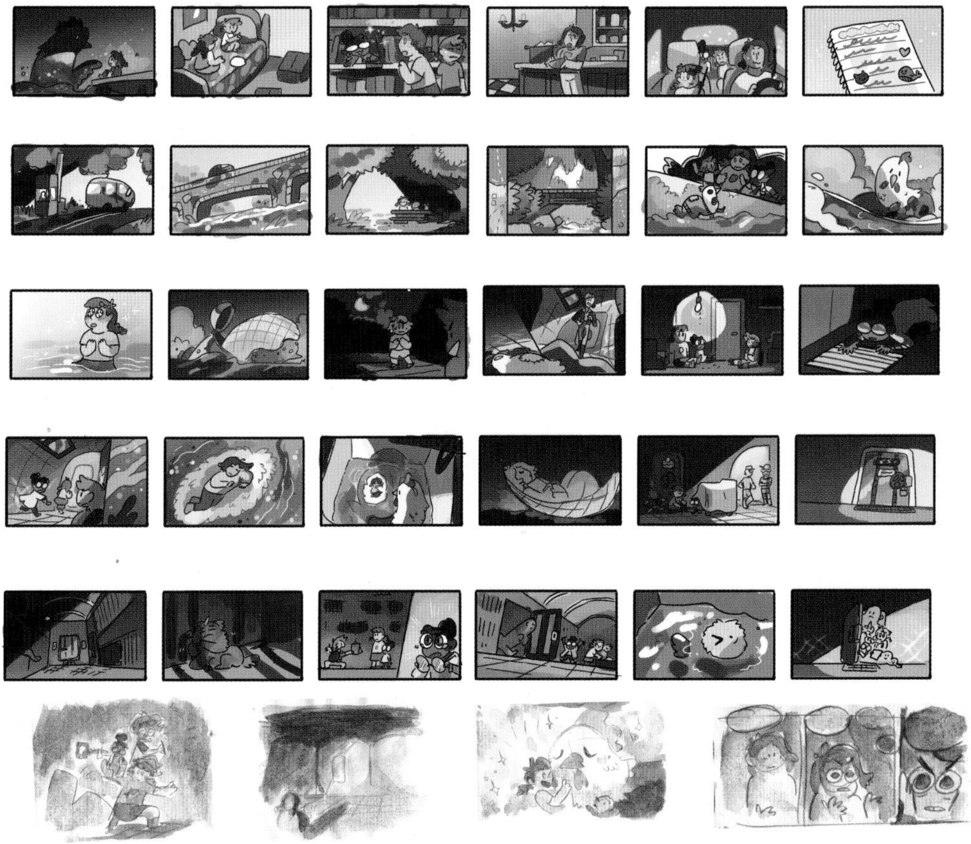

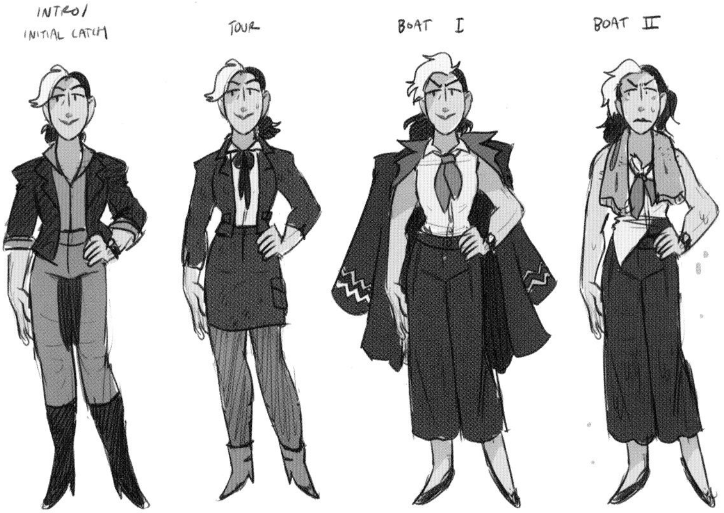
INTRO/
INITIAL CATCH
TOUR
BOAT I
BOAT II

Here is the Alvida costume changes guide. Everyone loves a good dramatic villain entrance, right?

Her "character color" is orangey-red, so all of her outfits have a red accent.

Thankfully, all of the other characters in the book have less complex wardrobes...

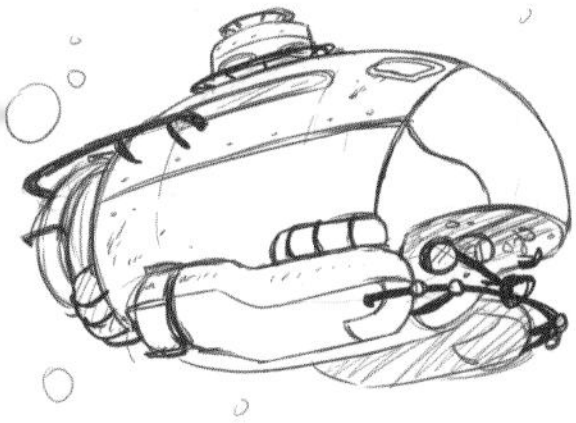

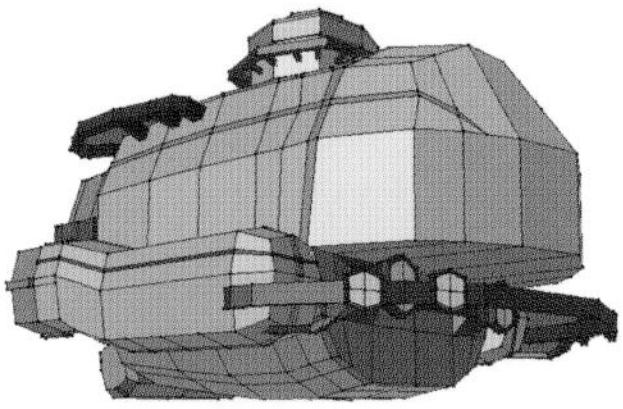

Vehicles are sketched and then rendered as 3D models for extra reference material. These came out so cute!

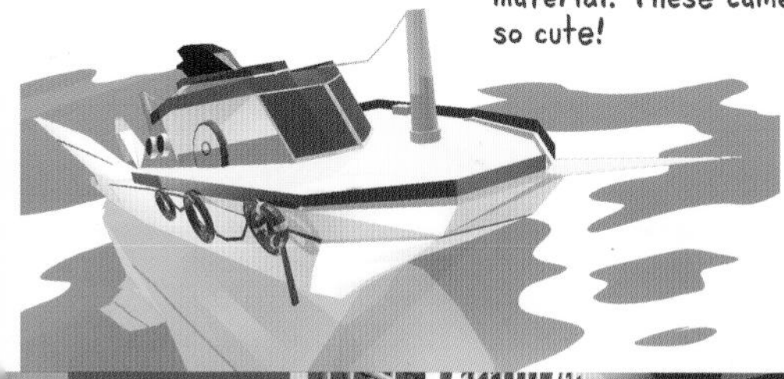

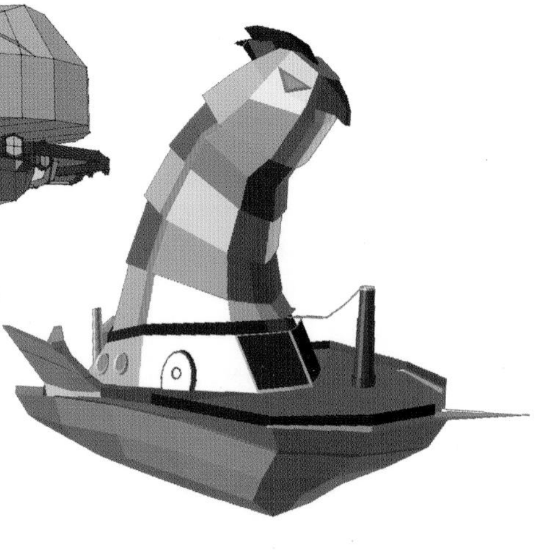

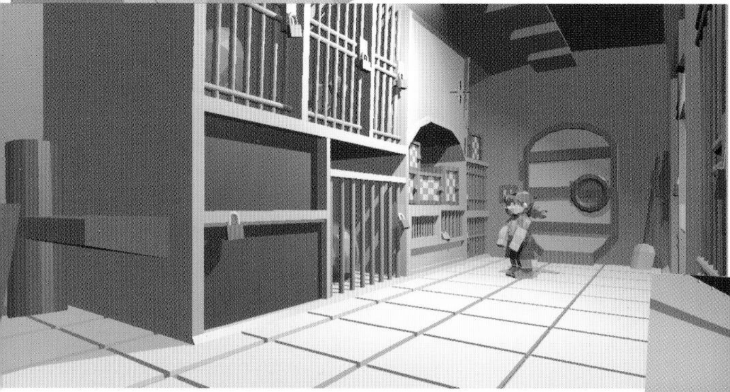

Here are some snapshots from 3D models built for certain location references.

They were built using 3D modeling software called Blender. It took a while to get used to—the Bessie tank chamber was built before the "asset room" and you can really tell...

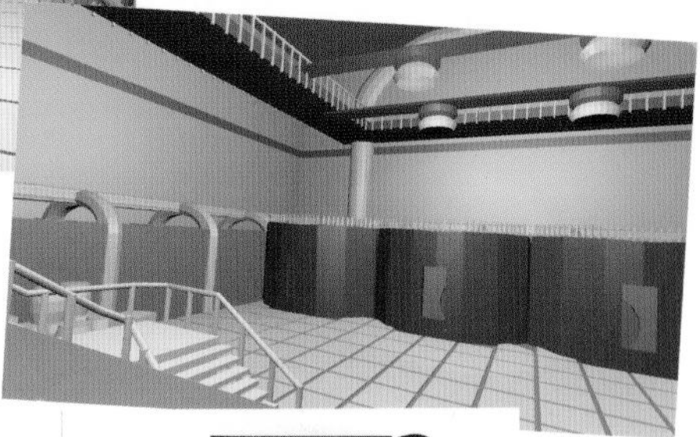

These needed some tweaks in the drawing stage to fit the compositions we wanted, but the nice thing about concept art is it doesn't have to be perfect! It's just for the artists to plan out where they are going.

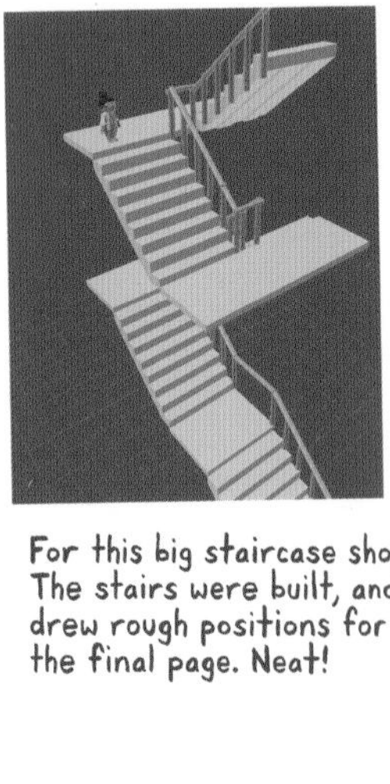

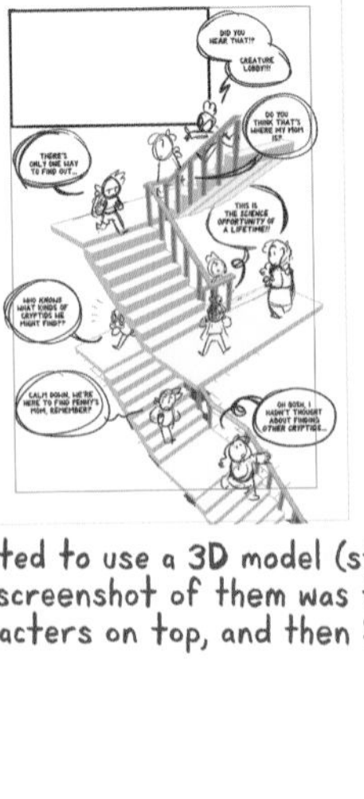
DID YOU HEAR THAT!?
CREATURE LOBBY!!!
DO YOU THINK THAT'S WHERE MY MOM IS?
THERE'S ONLY ONE WAY TO FIND OUT...
THIS IS THE SCIENCE OPPORTUNITY OF A LIFETIME!!
WHO KNOWS WHAT KINDS OF CRYPTIDS WE MIGHT FIND??
CALM DOWN, WE'RE HERE TO FIND PENNY'S MOM, REMEMBER?
OH GOSH, I HADN'T THOUGHT ABOUT FINDING OTHER CRYPTIDS...

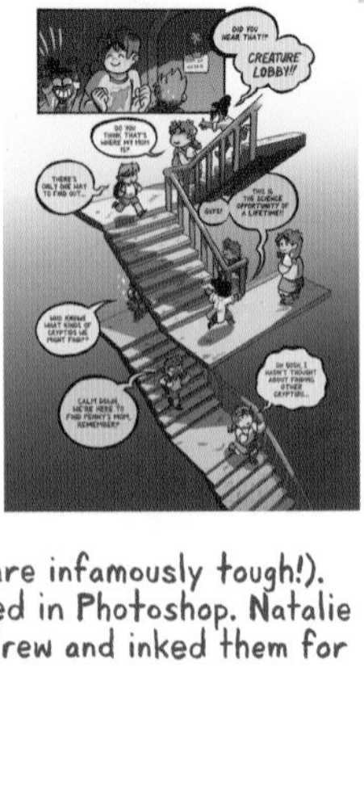
DID YOU HEAR THAT!?
CREATURE LOBBY!!
DO YOU THINK THAT'S WHERE MY MOM IS?
THERE'S ONLY ONE WAY TO FIND OUT...
GUYS!
THIS IS THE SCIENCE OPPORTUNITY OF A LIFETIME!!
WHO KNOWS WHAT KINDS OF CRYPTIDS WE MIGHT FIND??
OH GOSH, I HADN'T THOUGHT ABOUT FINDING OTHER CRYPTIDS...
CALM DOWN, WE'RE HERE TO FIND PENNY'S MOM, REMEMBER?

For this big staircase shot we wanted to use a 3D model (stairs are infamously tough!). The stairs were built, and then a screenshot of them was tweaked in Photoshop. Natalie drew rough positions for the characters on top, and then Sara drew and inked them for the final page. Neat!

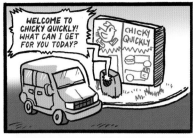

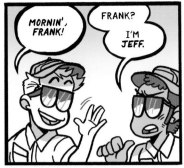

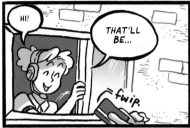

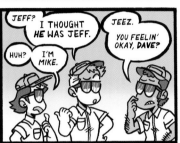

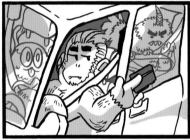

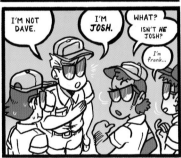

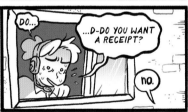

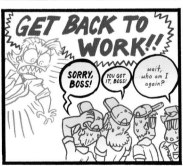

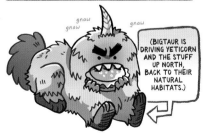

WELCOME TO CHICKY QUICKLY! WHAT CAN I GET FOR YOU TODAY?
CHICKY QUICKLY
HI!
THAT'LL BE...
fwip.
DO...
...D-DO YOU WANT A RECEIPT?
no.

gnaw
gnaw
gnaw
(BIGTAUR IS DRIVING YETICORN AND THE STUFF UP NORTH, BACK TO THEIR NATURAL HABITATS.)

MORNIN', FRANK!
FRANK?
I'M JEFF.
JEFF?
I THOUGHT HE WAS JEFF.
HUH?
I'M MIKE.
JEEZ.
YOU FEELIN' OKAY, DAVE?
I'M NOT DAVE.
I'M JOSH.
WHAT?
ISN'T HE JOSH?
I'm frank...
GET BACK TO WORK!!
SORRY, BOSS!
YOU GOT IT, BOSS!
wait, who am I again?

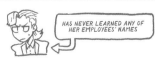

HAS NEVER LEARNED ANY OF HER EMPLOYEES' NAMES

SPECIAL THANKS:

Everyone at our publisher First Second for all their help: *Molly* for their incredible book design work; *John* for the great font of Sara's handwriting that we used for this book; *Ben, Calista,* and *Kiara* for the fantastic editorial; our wonderful early readers; and everyone else whose hands blessed this mess.

Our agent, *Steven,* for helping this book get made in the first place!

As always, *our friends and family:* Without their love, inspiration, and support we couldn't continue to make books. Art cannot be made alone. <3

Everyone reading the comics we make...thank YOU!

Last but not least, our muse: *Tilly.*